D1560319

DATE			

GREGORY

MCDONALD

THE FLETCH CHRONICLE: THREE

FLETCH'S FORTUNE
FLETCH'S MOXIE
FLETCH AND THE MAN WHO

Rediscovery Books
HILL & COMPANY, PUBLISHERS • BOSTON

Library of Congress Cataloging-in-Publication Data

Mcdonald, Gregory, 1937–
    The Fletch chronicle: three

    (Rediscovery books)
    Contents: [1] The Fletch chronicle — Fletch's For-
tune — Fletch's Moxie — Fletch and The Man Who.
    1. Fletch (Fictitious character) — Fiction.
2. Detective and mystery stories, American. I. Title.
II. Series.
PS3563.A278A6 1987   813'.54   87-8742
ISBN 0-940595-10-9 (v. 1)

Designed by Milton Glaser, Inc.
Printed in the United States of America

INTRODUCTION

I f I may paraphrase Matthew Arnold, at least ninety percent of an author's work is self-criticism. Do people who do not write ever realize this? Most of what an author does is not visible. When an author submits a novel he has a solid idea of what it is he is offering. He must then be very silent for a very long time listening to hear if there is any confirmation at all that people are reading the novel he thinks he wrote. Never may he say, *This is what the work is, what it means.* If he needs to say it, then clearly this is not what the work is, or what it means, or people would know it and he would not need say it. Privately, albeit subjectively, he has been through the most intense critical process. Then he must go through the process of public and, one hopes, objective criticism. It's rather like sending a well-known, well-loved child off to school and for years thereafter hearing teachers' comments, some of praise, which strike the parent as wrong, some of complaint, which strike the parent as wrong, some of praise and complaint which strike the parent as correct. One hopes the child is around a long time, grows up, becomes an adult, develops his own definition of who and what he is. The author as parent is intensely interested in what other people say about his book as child, and sometimes learns from these comments. Yet he is always deeply committed to his own view. In the case of the novel, *Running Scared,* at this writing now old enough to vote, the author has heard radically changing comment over the years; yet he knows the novel has not changed. The novel, *Love Among the Mashed Potatoes,* or *Dear M.E.,* seems distinctly an IQ test. *Safekeeping* seems to provide the author with a thermometer to test the reader's emotions. Given a nine-book series such as *The Fletch Chronicle,* this author has discovered over the years that which novel a certain reader prefers and which novel a reader likes least, especially as there is no general agreement, seems as much an insight into this or that reader as this or that book. Criticism in America, I once appalled a New York audience by stating, is usually like telephoning long distance and having someone under the age of five answer. Fulfillment is when a book and an author are around long enough for the author to hear increasing public confirmation of his silent, private view of a work. The genuine payday for an author, that day when ninety percent of his work begins to be perceived, if it ever comes at all, is a long time coming. Until that day, he remains uncomfortable, a foreigner in his own land.

At least at first, the author must realize that the world does not ask him to write a novel. The world does not care if he does not write. The author is made to feel, I guess quite properly, that writing fiction is an act of aggression. When the world resists, rejects, reviles what he does, he must remember that he is the root cause of his own grief. It is the author's best hope that he is identifying, researching, frequently using himself as an experiential instrument, and responding to human need. He is trying to sneak literature across. When the world robs him and exploits him unfairly, he cannot go on strike or quit, because the world will not notice or care. When the world grants his work any perception or attention, including the financial freedom to continue his writing by buying his work, he feels intense gratitude, and, truthfully, a great uneasiness that perhaps he has forced himself, his work upon a world which really did not ask for it.

This author has experienced sixteen years in the discovery of Fletch and his world. Because of the non-sequential way in which the nine novels have been published, in the process he has had the rare, if not unique, experience of simultaneously experiencing the reader's discovery of Fletch and his world. This has brought an unusual element to the work. Listening, I have been able to learn from the reader, and incorporate some interesting aspects into the work which would not have been there otherwise. I repeat that little of this input has come from what stands as contemporary criticism. If objective criticism is the creative person's opposable thumb, every contemporary author is writing with only eight fingers. Much of the success of the Fletch novels has been the result of my unusual partnership with the reader. Comments made to me in personal letters, in cafes, buses, street corners, libraries, book distributor warehouses, barnyards, housing projects, at odd times, always unexpected, in a million odd places around the world, not just the United States, have been to me the most telling and constructive comments. At least in this author's head, a small bell goes off when I hear something I have not heard before, especially if it has the ring of truth. I do not mean to make too much of this point, but a rare aspect of *The Fletch Chronicle* is the unusual cooperative relationship between the writer and the reader that has evolved with this work.

Of all, this author has the most reason to be grateful.

As a single, small example of constructive input, I had written more than one Fletch novel when a woman talking to me casually pointed out that Fletch and Flynn are not victims. We are all victims of circumstances, she said, or appear to be, at least initially. By whatever wit, wisdom, intelligence, energy we possess we try not to end as victims. To this spirit she attributed the popularity of these stories. Yes, that element had been in the stories; no, I had not been conscious of it. Henceforth I was conscious of it and therefore perhaps better and more consistent, possibly more subtle, at implementing this concept.

On the other hand, I remember once warning a team that wanted to translate Fletch to film to ignore speculations regarding Fletch as a symbol or a representative of this, that, or the other, the stories as sociological or psychological reports, the themes as philosophical treatises. At their best, they entertain.

At times, the sixteen years I worked with Fletch seemed long and hard. In retrospect, the time seems brief and joyful. At times, I was convinced I knew precisely what I was doing. Now I have no idea what I have done. At times, desperately, I wanted to get away for good and all from this strange personality of my pen. Now, terribly, I miss mulling the adventures of my old pal.

In this volume are *Fletch's Fortune*, which describes at least conventional journalism; *Fletch's Moxie*, which notes a difference between an illusion and a reality; *Fletch and The Man Who*, in which our hero, as mature as he gets, finds himself, without losing his principles, virtually protecting an establishment figure.

— *Gregory Mcdonald*
Camaldon Farm

FLETCH'S FORTUNE

FOR Susi, Chris, and Doug

ONE

"**C**IA, Mister Fletcher."

"Um. Would you mind spelling that?"

Coming into the cool dark of the living room, blinded by the sun on the beach, Fletch had smelled cigar smoke and slowed at the French doors.

There were two forms, of men, sprawled on his living-room furniture, one in the middle of the divan, the other on a chair.

"The Central Intelligence Agency," one of the forms muttered.

Fletch's bare feet crossed the marble floor to the carpet.

"Sorry, old chaps. You've got the wrong bod. Fletch is away for a spell. Letting me use his digs." Fletch held out his hand to the form on the divan. "Always do feel silly introducing myself whilst adorned in swimming gear, but when on the Riviera, do as the sons of habitués do — isn't that the motto? The name's Arbuthnot," Fletch said. "Freddy Arbuthnot."

The man on the divan had not shaken his hand.

The man in the chair snorted.

"Arbuthnot it's not," said the man in the chair.

"Not?" said Fletch. "Not?"

"Not," said the man.

The patterns of their neckties had become visible to Fletch.

His nose was in a stream of cigar smoke.

There were two cigar butts and a live cigar in the ash tray on the coffee table.

Next to the ash tray, on the surface of the table, was a photograph, of Fletch, in United States Marine Corps uniform, smiling.

Fletch said, "Golly."

"Didn't want to disturb you on the beach with your girl friend," said the man in the chair. "The two of you looked too cute down there. Frisking on the sand."

"Adorable," uttered the man on the divan.

Both men were dressed in full suits, collars undone, ties pulled loose. Both their faces were wet with perspiration.

"Let's see some identification," Fletch said.

This time he held his hand out to the man in the chair, palm up.

The man looked up at Fletch a moment, into his eyes, as if to gauge the exact degree of Fletch's seriousness, then rolled left on his hams and pulled his wallet from his right rear trouser pocket.

On the left flap was the man's photograph. On the right was a card which said: "CENTRAL INTELLIGENCE AGENCY, United States of America," a few dates, a few numbers, and the man's name — Eggers, Gordon.

"You, too." Fletch held out his hand to the man on the divan.

His name was Richard Fabens.

"Eggers and Fabens." Fletch handed back their credentials. "Would you guys mind if I got out of these wet trunks and took a shower?"

"Not at all," said Eggers, standing up. "But let's talk first."

"Coffee?"

"If we wanted coffee," said Fabens, standing up, "we would have made it ourselves."

"Part of the CIA training, I expect," Fletch said, "Trespass and Coffee-Making. A Bloody Mary? Something to raise the spirits on this Sunday noon?"

"Cool it, Fletcher," said Eggers. "You don't need time to think." He put the tip of his index finger against Fletch's chest, and pressed. "You're going to do what you're told. Get it?"

Fletch shouted into his face, "Yes, sir!"

Suddenly Eggers's right hand became a fist and smashed into precisely the right place in Fletch's stomach with incredible force, considering the shortness of the swing.

Fletch was hunched over, in a chair, trying to breathe.

"Enough of your bull, Fletcher."

"I caught a fish like him once." Fabens was relighting his cigar. "In the Gulf Stream. He was still wriggling and fighting even after I had him aboard. I had to beat the shit out of him to convince him he was caught. Even then." He blew a billow of cigar smoke at Fletch. "Mostly I beat him on the head."

"Yuck," said Fletch.

"Shall we beat you on the head, Fletcher?" Eggers asked.

Fletch said, "Anything's better than that cigar's smoke."

Eggers's voice turned gentle. "Are you going to listen to us, Irwin?"

Fletch said, "El Cheap-o."

Turning from the French doors, El Cheap-o in mouth, Fabens asked, "What happened to your girl friend? Where'd she go?"

"Home." Fletch squeezed out breath. "She lives next door." He sucked in breath. "With her husband."

He raised his head in time to see Eggers and Fabens glance at each other.

"Husband?"

"He sleeps late," Fletch breathed. "Sundays."

"Jesus," said Eggers.

"Wriggle, wriggle," said Fabens.

Fletch straightened his back in the chair. He ignored the tears on his cheeks.

"Okay, guys. What's the big deal?"

"No big deal." Eggers rubbed his hands together. "Easy."

"You're just the right man for the job," said Fabens.

"What job?"

"You know the American Journalism Alliance?" Eggers asked.

"Yes."

"They're having a convention," Fabens said.

"So?"

"You're going."

"Hell, I'm not a working journalist anymore. I'm unemployed. I haven't worked as a journalist in over a year."

"What do you mean?" said Eggers. "You had a piece in *Bronson's* just last month."

"That was on the paintings of Cappoletti."

"So? It's journalism."

"Once a shithead, always a shithead," said Fabens.

"May your cigar kill you," said Fletch.

"You're going," said Eggers.

"I'm not even a member of the A.J.A."

"You are," said Eggers.

"I used to be."

"You are."

"I haven't paid my dues in years. In fact, I never paid my dues."

"We paid your dues. You're a member."

"You paid my dues?"

"We paid your dues."

"Very thoughtful of you," Fletch said.

"Think nothing of it," said Fabens. "Anything for a shithead."

Fletch said, "You could have spent the money on a better grade of cigars. Preferably Cuban."

"I'm a government employee." Fabens looked at the tip of his cigar. "What do you expect?"

"Peace?"

"The convention starts tomorrow," Eggers said. "Outside of Washington. In Virginia."

"Tomorrow?"

"We didn't want you to have too long to think about it."

"No way."

"Tomorrow," Fabens said. "You're going to be there."

"I'm having lunch with this guy in Genoa tomorrow. Tuesday, I'm flying down to Rome for an exhibition."

"Tomorrow," said Fabens.

"I don't have a ticket. I haven't packed."

"We have your ticket." Eggers waved his hand. "You can do your own packing."

Fletch sat forward, placing his forearms on his thighs.

"Okay," he said. "What's this about?"

"At the airport in Washington, near the Trans World Airlines' main counters, you will go to a baggage locker." Fabens took a key from his jacket pocket and looked at it. "Locker Number 719. In that locker you will find a reasonably heavy brown suitcase."

"Full of bugging equipment," said Eggers.

Fletch said, "Shit, no!"

Fabens flipped the key onto the coffee table.

"Shit, yes."

"No way!" said Fletch.

"Absolutely," said Fabens. "You will then take another airplane to Hendricks, Virginia, to the old Hendricks Plantation, where the convention is being held, and you will immediately set out planting listening devices in the rooms of all your colleagues, if I may use such a term for you shitheads of the fourth estate."

"It's not going to happen," said Fletch.

"It's going to happen," said Fabens. "In the brown suitcase — and forgive us, we had trouble matching your luggage exactly — there is also a recording machine and plenty of tape. You are going to tape the most private, bedroom conversations of the most important people in American journalism."

"You're crazy."

Eggers shook his head. "Not crazy."

"You are crazy." Fletch stood up. "You've told me more than you should have. Bunglers! You've given me a story." Fletch grabbed the key from the coffee table. "One phone call, and this story is going to be all over the world in thirty-six hours."

Fletch backed off the carpet onto the marble floor.

"Blow smoke in my face. You're not going to get this key from me." Fabens smiled, holding his cigar chest-height.

"We haven't told you too much. We've told you too little."

"What haven't you told me?"

Eggers shook his head, seemingly in embarrassment.

"We've got something on you."

"What have you got on me? I'm not a priest or a politician. There's no way you can spoil my reputation."

"Taxes, Mister Fletcher."

"What?"

Fabens said again, "Taxes."

Fletch blinked. "What about 'em?"

"You haven't paid any."

"Nonsense. Of course I pay taxes."

"Not nonsense, Mister Fletcher." Fabens used the ash tray. "Look at it our way. Your parents lived in the state of Washington, neither of them well-to-do nor from well-to-do families."

"They were nice people."

"I'm sure. Nice, yes. Rich, no. Yet here you are, living in a villa in Cagna, Italy, the Mediterranean sparkling through your windows, driving a Porsche . . . unemployed."

"I retired young."

"In your lifetime, you have paid almost no federal taxes."

"I had expenses."

"You haven't even filed a return. Ever."

"I have a very slow accountant."

"I should think he would be slow," continued Fabens, "seeing you have money in Rio, in the Bahamas, here in Italy, probably in Switzerland. . . ."

"I also have a very big sense of insecurity," Fletch said.

"I should think you would have," Fabens said. "Under the circumstances."

"All right. I haven't paid my taxes. I'll pay my taxes, pay the penalties — but after I phone in the story that you guys are bugging the convention of the American Journalism Alliance."

"It's the not filing the tax reports that's the crime, Mister Fletcher. Punishable by jail sentences."

"So what? Let 'em catch me."

Eggers was sitting in a chair, hands behind his head, staring at Fletch.

"Peek-a-boo," Fabens said. "We have caught you."

"Bull. I can outrun you two tubs anytime."

"Mister Fletcher, do you want to know why you haven't filed any tax returns?"

"Why haven't I filed any tax returns?"

"Because you can't say where the money came from."

"I found it at the foot of my bed one morning."

Eggers laughed, turned his head to Fabens, and said, "Maybe he did."

"You should have reported it," said Fabens.

"I'll report it."

"You have never earned more than a reporter's salary — about the price of that Porsche in your driveway — in any one year . . . legally."

"Who reports gambling earnings?"

"Where did you get the money? Over two million dollars, possibly three, maybe more."

"I went scuba diving off the Bahamas and found a Spanish galleon loaded with trading stamps."

"Crime on top of crime." Fabens put his cigar stub in the ash tray. "Ten, twenty, thirty years in prison."

"Maybe by the time you get out," laughed Eggers, "the girl next door will be divorced."

"Oh, Gordon," Fabens said. "We forgot to tell Mister Irwin Maurice Fletcher that in one of my pockets I have his TWA ticket to Hendricks, Virginia. In my other pocket I have his extradition papers."

Eggers slapped his kidney. "And I, Richard, have a warm pair of Italian handcuffs."

Fletch sat down.

"Gee, guys, these are my friends. You're asking me to bug my friends."

Fabens said, "I thought a good journalist didn't have any friends."

Fletch muttered, "Just other journalists."

Eggers said, "You don't have a choice, Fletcher."

"Damn." Fletch was turning the baggage locker key over in his hands. "I thought you CIA guys stopped all this: domestic spying, bugging journalists. . . ."

"Who's spying?" said Eggers.

"You've got us all wrong," said Fabens. "This is simply a public relations effort. We're permitted to do public relations. All we want are a few friends in the American press."

"You never know," said Eggers. "If we know what some of their personal problems are, we might even be able to help them out."

"All we want is to be friendly," said Fabens. "Especially do we want to be friendly with Walter March. You know him?"

"Publisher. March Newspapers. I used to work for him."

"That's right. A very powerful man. I don't suppose you happen to know what goes on in his bedroom?"

"Christ," said Fletch. "He must be over seventy."

"So what," said Eggers. "I've been reading a book. . . ."

"Walter March," repeated Fabens. "We wish to make good friends with Walter March."

"So I do this thing for you, and what then?" Fletch asked. "Then I go to jail?"

"No, no. Then your tax problems disappear as if by magic. They fall in the Potomac River, never to surface again."

"How?"

"We take care of it," answered Eggers.

"Can I have that in writing?"

"No."

"Can I have anything in writing?"

"No."

Fabens put the Trans World Airlines ticket folder on the coffee table.

"Genoa, London, Washington, Hendricks, Virginia. Your plane leaves at four o'clock."

Fletch looked at his sunburned arm.

"I need a shower."

Eggers laughed. "Putting on a pair of pants wouldn't hurt any, either."

Fabens said, "I take it you choose to go home without handcuffs?"

Fletch said, "Does Pruella the pig pucker her pussy when she poops in the woods?"

T W O

"So you're going to bug the entire American press establishment? Just because someone asked you to?"

Gibbs's voice was barely audible. Fletch had had a better connection when he had called from London.

Across the National Airport waiting room a brass quartet was beginning to play "America."

Fletch pushed the brown suitcase he had taken from Locker Number 719 out of the telephone booth with his foot and slammed the door.

"Fletch?"

"Hello? I was closing the door."

"Are you in Washington now?"

"Yes."

"Did you have a nice flight?"

"No."

"Sorry to hear that. Why not?"

"Sat next to a Methodist minister."

"What's wrong with sitting next to a Methodist minister?"

"Are you kidding? The closer to heaven we got, the smugger he got."

"Jesus, Fletch."

"That's what I say."

"Can you still sing a few bars of the old Northwestern fight song?"

"Never could."

In college, Don Gibbs had believed in the football team (he was a second-string tackle), beer (a case between Saturday night and Monday morning), the Chevrolet car (he had a sedan, painted blue and yellow), the Methodist Church (for women and children), and applied physics (for an eventual guaranteed income from American industry, which he also believed in, but which, upon his graduation, had not returned his faith by offering him a job). He had not believed in poetry, painting, philosophy, people, or any of the other p's treated in the humanities — an attitude generally accepted by American industry, but not when manifested by the candidate for a job so obviously.

He and Fletch had been roommates in their freshman year.

"The only thing I learned in college," Fletch said into the phone, "is that all our less successful classmates went to work for the government."

"Who placed this call?" Gibbs's throat muscles had tightened. "Tell me that, Fletcher. Did you call me, or did I call you? Are you asking me to help you, or am I asking you to help me?"

"Gee whiz, Don. You forgot to take your Insensitive Pill this morning."

"I'm sick to death of you guys knocking us in the press whenever you feel like it, but whenever you have a problem that hurts even a little bit you're crying over the phone at us."

"Bullshit, Don. I've never knocked you in the press. You've never been important enough to knock."

"Oh, yeah?"

They might as well have been seventeen-year-old freshmen arguing at eleven o'clock at night over who got to take a shower first. Fletch always hated to wait twenty minutes while Gibbs went through his shower routine; Gibbs hated the mirrors steamed by the time he got to take his shower.

Fletch said, "Yeah. Furthermore, I'm not asking you a favor. I'm asking you a question."

"What's the question, Irwin Maurice? Do you have the legal right to bug the entire American press establishment? No! Absolutely not." His voice lowered. "But then again, Irwin Maurice Fletcher, I suspect you always have bugged the entire American press establishment."

"Funny, funny." He had to grant that; he had to give him something. "Since when are you a lawyer? I'm not asking for legal advice. I know it's not nice to bug my friends with the intention of blackmail — even if I'm not the guy who's going to be putting the screws to 'em — you shits are. My question is: Do I have to do this?"

There was a long silence from the other end of the phone.

Fletch said, "Hello? Don?"

The line clicked.

"Fletch?"

"Hello."

"I'm trying to answer your question. Would you mind going over all the facts again?"

Don Gibbs's voice had moderated. It had become more mature, reasonable, responsible. It also had lowered half an octave.

"I gave you all the facts when I called you from London, Don."

"Just to make sure I've got everything straight."

"You're just trying to take advantage of a local phone call from an old friend to make you look busy at your desk," Fletch said. "Bastard."

Fletch knew it wasn't a local phone call.

The number he had dialed supposedly was a Pentagon number. But he knew he was talking to Don Gibbs in that curious underground headquarters of American intelligence in the mountains of North Carolina.

"I have a plane to catch."

"Just run it by me again, Fletch."

"Okay. Two of your goons broke into my house in Cagna, Italy, yesterday morning, Sunday —"

"Names?"

"Gordon Eggers and Richard Fabens."

"Eggers, Gordon and Fabens, Richard. Right?"

"You government jerks do everything backwards."

"Did you get their identification numbers off their credentials?"

"No. But they had numbers. Lots of numbers."

"Doesn't matter. When you say they broke into your house, what precisely do you mean?"

"I think they entered through the French windows, doors, whatever you call them. The house was open."

"Did they actually break anything?"

"Amazingly enough — no."

"So they entered your house."

"They entered it uninvited. Unexpected. Unwanted. They tres- passed."

"What are you doing with a house in Italy?"

"I live there."

"Yeah, but why? I mean, are you working for a wire service or something?"

"No. I'm doing some writing on art. I had a piece in *Bronson's* last month. I'm trying to do a biography of Edgar Arthur Tharp, Jun- ior. . . ."

"The cowboys-and-Indian artist?"

"Gee. You know something."

"Wasn't he a friend of Winslow Homer?"

"No."

"Have you given up investigative reporting altogether?"

Fletch dropped a pause into the conversation. "I'm on a sabbatical."

"Fired again, uh? I'm glad I'm not one of the more obvious successes in my class."

"There's no job security," Fletch said, "without complete obscurity."

"So what did these two gentlemen want?"

"They weren't gentlemen."

"Sorry to hear that. We usually send only our finest abroad. I haven't made it yet."

"Not surprised."

"What did they want?"

Across the terminal the band was playing "The eyes of Texas are upon you. . . ."

"They told me to come to the A.J.A. convention, here in Hendricks, Virginia, and bug my ever-loving colleagues — get tape recordings of their bedroom conversations — and turn the tapes over to them, for blackmail purposes. They said there would be a suitcase full of bugging equipment here in a locker in Washington, and it is here." Through the door of the phone booth Fletch noticed how badly the suitcase he had just taken from Locker 719 matched the rest of his luggage. "Are you telling me you don't know all this already, Don?"

Don Gibbs said, "It's not often we get another perspective on one of our operations."

"When I called you from London last night, I asked you to look into all this."

"I have," Don said. "I've checked pretty thoroughly."

"So why am I standing in a phone booth, late for a plane I don't want to take anyway, going over it all with you again?"

"Tell me again why you agreed to do it. I just want to see if it checks out with what I know."

"Oh, for God's sake, Don! I'm being blackmailed."

"I know that, but tell me again how."

"Well . . ."

"It won't hurt to tell me, Fletcher. Don't I already know?"

"Nice guy." The floor of the phone booth was filthy. "Taxes."

"You've never paid any?"

"Just whatever was withheld from my salary." He was pressing the phone against his ear. "Even for those years I never filed a return."

"Uh-uh. And what about the last year or two?"

"I've never filed a return."

"It says here you have money you can't account for. Is that right?"

"Yeah."

"What?"

"Yes."

"So why are you calling me?"

"You're my friend in the American Intelligence community."

"We're not friends."

"Acquaintance. I'm trying to report to someone in the home office — someone responsible — that your guys down the line are blackmailing me to bug the private lives of some of the most important members of the American press — newspapers, radio, and television."

"Don't you think our right hand knows what our left hand is doing?"

"No, I don't. And if you do, you should be ashamed of yourselves."

"I'm not ashamed of myself. Nobody's blackmailing me."

"Come on, Don! Jesus Christ!"

"How do you think we gather intelligence, Fletcher? By reading your lousy newspapers? From network news?"

"Don, this isn't legitimate, and you know it."

"I know lots of things." Gibbs's voice had risen again, slightly. "You said when you called from London that the guys who talked to you were particularly interested in getting information on old Mister March."

"Yes. That's right. Walter March. I used to work for him."

"What does that mean to you?"

"That they single out March?"

"Yes."

"He's an incredibly powerful man. March Newspapers." Fletch's right ear was becoming hot and sore. "Listen, Don, I've only got a few minutes to make that plane, if I'm going to make it. Are you telling me . . . ?"

"No, Mister Fletcher. I'm telling you."

It was a much older, deeper voice.

"Who is this?" Fletch asked.

"Robert Englehardt," the voice said. "Don's department head. I've been listening in."

"Man!" Alone in the phone booth, Fletch grinned. "You guys can't do anything straight."

"I guess you're calling Don to ask if this assignment is something you have to take on."

"You've got it."

"What do you think the answer is?"

"It sounds to me like the answer is yes."

"You have the right impression."

There was another click on the line.

Fletch asked, "Don, are you still there?"

"Yes."

"I know you guys are so wrapped up in your own mysteriousness you can't answer a simple question yes or no, but why the extra degree of mysteriousness about this?"

"What mysteriousness?"

"Come on, Don."

"We've just been trying to make absolutely sure that the A.J.A. convention is still on."

"Still on? Why wouldn't it be?"

"You journalists are always the last with the news, aren't you?"

"What news?"

"Walter March was murdered this morning. At the convention. So long, Fletcher."

THREE

"Hello, hello," Fletch said, as he buckled himself into the seat next to the girl with the honey-colored hair and the brown eyes. "I get along well with everybody."

"You don't even get along with plane schedules," she answered. "They've been holding the plane for you for ten minutes."

It was a twelve-seater.

"I was on the phone," Fletch said. "Talking to an old uncle. He doesn't talk as fast as he used to."

The pilot slammed the passenger door and pulled the handle up.

"I forgive you," the girl said. "Why are you so tan?"

"I just arrived from Italy. This morning."

"That would have been excuse enough."

The pilot had started the engines and turned the plane away from the terminal.

"Ask me if I had a nice flight."

They had to shout. The plane had three propellers, one of them right over their heads.

"Did you have a nice flight?"

"No." Taxiing to the runway, the small plane was very bouncy. "Ask me why I didn't have a nice flight."

"Why didn't you have a nice flight?"

"I sat next to a Methodist minister."

She said, "So what?"

"The closer to heaven we got, the smugger he got."

She shook her head. "Jet lag affects different people in different ways."

Fletch said, "My uncle didn't think it was funny either."

"Not only that," the girl said, "but telling it to your uncle probably took up the whole ten minutes we waited."

"I'm a loyal nephew."

The plane stopped. Each of the three engines was gunned. With the left engine still running high, the brakes were released and the plane swung onto the runway. Gathering speed, it bounced and vibrated down the runway until the bounces got big enough, at which point the plane popped into the air.

The plane rose and banked over Washington and the sound of the engines diminished somewhat.

The girl was looking out her window.

She said, "I love to look at Washington from the air. Such a pretty place."

"Want to buy it?"

She gave him the sardonic grin he deserved. "You say you get along well with everybody?"

"Everybody," Fletch said. "Absolutely everybody. Methodist ministers, uncles, terrific-looking girls sitting next to me on airplanes . . ."

"Am I terrific-looking?" she shouted.

"Smashing."

"You mean smash-mirrors kind of smashing?"

"I dunno. Maybe. How's your husband?"

"Don't have one."

"Why not?"

"Never found anybody good enough to marry me. How's your wife?"

"Which one?"

"You have lots?"

"Have had. Lots and lots. Gross lots. Practically anybody's good enough to marry me."

"Guess that lets me out," she said.

"I ask people to marry me too quickly," Fletch said. "At least that's what the Methodist minister said."

"And they all say yes?"

"Most have. It's a thing with me. I love the old institutions. Like marriage."

"It's a problem?"

"Definitely. Will you help me with it?"

"Of course."

"When I ask you to marry me, please say no."

"Okay."

Fletch looked at his wristwatch and counted off ten seconds under his breath.

"Will you marry me?" he asked.

"Sure."

"What?"

"I said, 'Sure.' "

"Well, you're not much of a help."

"Why should I help you? You get along well with everybody."

"Don't you?"

"No."

"I can see why not. Underneath that terrific exterior, you're weird."

"It's a defense mechanism. I've been working on it."

"Have you ever been in Hendricks, Virginia, before?" Fletch asked.

"No."

"Are you going to the A.J.A. Convention?"

"Yes."

Fletch thought most, if not all, the people on the plane were.

Two seats in front of him was Hy Litwack, anchorman for United Broadcasting Company.

Even the back of Hy Litwack's head was recognizable as Hy Litwack.

"Are you a journalist?" Fletch asked.

"You think I'm a busboy?"

"No." Fletch considered his thumbs in his lap. "I hadn't thought that. You're a newsperson."

"With *Newsworld* magazine."

"Women's stuff? Fashion? Food?"

"Crime," she said, looking straight ahead.

"Women's stuff."

Fletch was smiling behind his hand.

"Newspersons' stuff. I've just come back from covering the Pecuchet trial, in Arizona."

Fletch did not know of the case.

"What was the verdict?" he asked.

She said, "Good story."

"Yee." He slapped himself on the cheek. "Yee."

She looked into his eyes. "I wouldn't expect any other verdict."

"Do you know Walter March was murdered this morning?"

"I heard about it from the taxi radio on the way to the airport. Do you have any of the details?"

"Nary a one."

"Well." She straightened her legs as much as they could be straightened in the cramped airplane. "I have two notebooks. And three pens." Touching her fingers to her lips, she yawned. "And are you a journalist?" she asked. "Or a busboy?"

"I'm not sure," he answered. "I'm on a sabbatical."

"From what company?"

"Practically all of them."

"You're unemployed," she said. "Therefore you're working on a book."

"You've got it."

"On the Vatican?"

"Why the Vatican?"

"You're working on the book in Italy."

"I'm working on a book about Edgar Arthur Tharp, Junior."

"You're working on a book about an American cowboy painter in Italy?"

"It brings a certain perspective to the work. Detachment."

"And, I suspect, about thirty tons of obstacles."

"Do obstacles come by the ton?"

"In your case, I think so. The rest of us measure them in kilograms."

She put her hand on his on the armrest, slipped one of her fingers under two of his, raised them and let them fall.

"I think I detect," she said, "what with all your ex-wives and ex-employers, that your life lacks a certain consistency — a certain glue."

"Rescue me," Fletch said. "Save me from myself."

"What's your name?"

"I. M. Fletcher."

"Fletcher? Never heard of you. Why so pompous about it?"

"Pompous?"

"You announced your name, *I am Fletcher.* As if someone had said you weren't. Why didn't you just say, *Fletcher?*"

She was still playing with his fingers.

"My first initial is *I.* My second initial is *M.*"

"Hummmm," she said. "An affliction since birth. Does the *I* stand for Irving?"

"Worse. Irwin."

"I like the name Irwin."

"No one likes the name Irwin."

"You're just prejudiced," she said.

"I have every reason to be."

"You have nice hands."

"One on the end of each arm."

With her two hands she made a loose fist out of his left hand, brought it a few inches closer to her, and dropped it.

She was still looking at his hand.

"Would you run your hands over my naked body, time and again?"

"Here? Now?"

"Later," she said. "Later."

"I thought you'd never ask. Shall I send them in to you by Room Service, or come myself?"

"Just your hands," she said. "I don't know much about the rest of you — except that you get along well with everybody."

He took her hand in his, and she put her left hand on top of his.

She had pulled her legs into her seat.

"Ms., you have me at a disadvantage."

"I sincerely hope so."

"I don't know your name."

"Arbuthnot," she said.

"Arbuthnot!" He extricated his hand. "Not Arbuthnot!"

"Arbuthnot," she said.

"Arbuthnot?"

"Arbuthnot. Fredericka Arbuthnot."

"Freddie Arbuthnot?"

"You've heard of me? Behind that Italian tan, I detect a sudden whiteness of pallor."

"Heard of you? I made you up!"

The plane was on its landing run into Hendricks Airport.

She truly looked puzzled.

"I don't get it," she said.

"Well, I do."

Fletch unclasped his seat belt.

He said again, "I do."

FOUR

Mrs. Jake Williams — Helena, she insisted people call her — the hostess at the American Journalism Alliance Convention — had a way of greeting people as if they were delighted to see her.

"Fletcher, darling! Aren't you beautiful!"

She extended both hands beyond her bosom.

"Hi, Helena, how are you doing?"

He leaned over her and kissed her.

They were standing near the reception desk in the hotel lobby.

An airport limousine had been waiting for them when their airplane had touched down.

Ignoring his luggage, Fletch had gone directly to the limousine and sat in it.

In a few moments, a quiet Fredericka Arbuthnot opened the car door and slid in next to him.

After the luggage had been stowed on top of the car and most of

19

the other passengers from the airplane had taken seats, they left the airport, went through a small village blighted by a shopping center and straight out a rolling road to the plantation.

Almost immediately outside the village were the plantation's white rail fences, on both sides of the road.

Fletch lowered his head to look through the windshield as the car turned into the plantation driveway.

On both sides of the driveway was a golf course. A brightly dressed foursome was on a green down to the left. The car came to a full stop to let a pale blue golf cart cross the gravel driveway.

The plantation house was a mammoth red-brick structure behind a white, wooden colonnade, with matching red-brick additions at both sides and, Fletch supposed, to the rear. They were motel-type units, but well-designed, perfectly in keeping with the main house, the rolling green, the distant white fences.

On the last curve before the house, Fletch glimpsed through the side window a corner of a sparkling blue swimming pool.

No one had said a word during the ride.

The driver's polite question, aimed at the passengers in general, "Did you all have a nice flight?" when he first got into the car received no answer whatsoever.

It was as if they were going to a funeral, rather than a convention.

Well, they were going to a funeral.

Walter March was dead.

He had been murdered that morning at Hendricks Plantation.

Walter March had been in his seventies. Forever, it seemed, he had been publisher of a large string of powerful newspapers.

Probably everyone in the car, at one point or another in their careers, had had dealings with Walter March.

Probably almost everyone at the convention had.

These were journalists — some of the best in the business.

Smiling to himself, Fletch realized that if any one of them — including himself — had been alone in the car with the driver, the driver would have been pumped for every bit of information, speculation, and rumor regarding the murder at his imagination's command.

Together, they asked no questions.

Unless in an open press conference, where there was no choice, no journalist wants to ask a question whose answer might benefit any other journalist.

Fletch waited until his luggage was handed to him from the top of the car, and then went directly into the lobby.

While Helena Williams was greeting Fletch, Fredericka Arbuthnot, with her luggage, came and stood beside him.

She was continuing to look at him quizzically.

"Hello, Mrs. Fletcher," Helena said, shaking Freddie's hand.

"This isn't Mrs. Fletcher," Fletch said.

"Oh, I'm sorry," Helena said. "We're all so used to greeting anyone with Fletch as Mrs. Fletcher."

"This is Freddie Arbuthnot."

"Freddie? So many of your girls have had boys' names," Helena said. "That girl we met with you in Italy, Andy something or other. . . ."

"Barbara and Linda," Fletch said. "Joan . . ."

"There must be something odd about you I've never detected," she said.

"There is," said Freddie Arbuthnot.

"Furthermore, Helena," Fletch said. "Ms. Arbuthnot and I just met on the plane."

"That's never been a major consideration before," Helena sniffed. "I remember that time we were all having dinner together in New York, and I noticed you were looking at a girl at the next table, and she was looking at you, and next thing we knew, you were both gone! You hadn't even excused yourself. Not a word! I remember you missed the *tarte aux cerises, flambée.*"

"I did not."

"Well, anyway." Helena said to Freddie, "just like everything else Fletch does, he is the most spectacular dues-payer. He's coughed up every dime he's owed the American Journalism Alliance lo these many years. . . ."

"She knows," Fletch said.

"We were all staggered, Fletch darling."

"I was a little surprised myself," Fletch said. "Don't let word get around, okay, Helena? Might ruin my reputation."

"Fletch darling," Helena said, with mock sincerity, hand on his forearm, "nothing could do that."

Fletch said, "I'm sorry about Walter March, Helena."

Helena Williams pushed the mental button for A Distraught Expression.

"The crime of the century," she said. She had been married to Jake Williams, managing editor of a New York daily, for more years than anyone who knew Jake could believe. "The crime of the century, Fletch."

"Hell of a story," Freddie muttered.

"We had a vote this morning, those of us who were here, to decide if we would continue the convention. We decided to open it on time. Well, with all these people coming, what could we do? Everything's arranged. Anyway, the police asked everybody who was here to stay. Having the convention running will help take everybody's mind off this terrible tragedy. Walter March! " She threw her hands in the air. "Who'd believe it?"

"Is Lydia here, Helena?" Fletch asked.

"She found the body! She was in the bath, and she heard gurgling! She thought Walter had left the suite. At first, she said, she thought it was the tub drain. But the gurgling kept up, from the bedroom. She got out of the tub and threw a towel around herself. There was Walter, half-kneeling, fallen on one of the beds, arms thrown out, a scissors sticking up from his back! While she watched, he rolled sideways off the bed, and landed on his back! The scissors must have been driven further in. She said he arched up, and then relaxed. All life had gone out of him."

Helena's expression of shock and grief was no longer the result of mental button-pushing. She was a lady genuinely struggling to comprehend what had happened, and why, and to control herself until she could.

"Poor Lydia!" she said. "She had no idea what to do. She came running down the corridor in her towel and banged on my door. I was just up. This was just before eight o'clock this morning, mind you. There was Lydia at my door, in a towel, at the age of seventy, her mouth open, and her eyes closing! I sat her down on my unmade bed, and she fell over! She fainted! I went running to their suite to get Walter. I was in my dressing gown. There was Walter on the floor, spread-eagled, eyes staring straight up. Naturally, I'd thought he'd had a heart attack or something. I didn't see any blood. Well, I thought I was going to faint. I heard someone shrieking. They tell me it was I who was shrieking." Helena looked away. Her fingers touched her throat. "I'm not so sure."

Fletch said, "Is there anything I can get you, Helena? Anything I can do for you?"

"No," she said. "I had brandy before breakfast. Quite a sizable dose. And then no breakfast. And then the house doctor here, what's-his-name, gave me one of those funny pills. My head feels like there's a yellow balloon in it. I've had tea and toast."

She smiled at them.

"Enough of this," she said. "It won't bring Walter back. Now you must tell me all about yourself, Fletch. Whom are you working for now?"

"The CIA."

He looked openly at Freddie Arbuthnot.

"I'm here to bug everybody."

"You've always had such a delightful sense of humor," Helena said.

"He's bugging me," Freddie muttered.

"I've heard that joke," Fletch snapped.

"Would you children like to share a room?" Helena asked. "We are sort of crowded — "

"Definitely not," Fletch said. "I suspect she snores."

"I do not."

"How do you know?"

"I've been told."

"Well, you're just so beautiful together," Helena said. "What is one supposed to think? Oh, there's Hy Litwack. I didn't see him come in. I must go say hello. Remind him he's giving the after-dinner speech tonight."

Helena episcopally put her hands on Fletch's and Freddie's hands, as if she were confirming them, or ordaining them, or marrying them.

"We must have life," she said, "in the presence of death."

Helena Williams walked away to greet Hy Litwack.

"And death," Fletch said, softly, "in the presence of life."

F I V E

In his room, Fletch, still wet from his shower, sat on the edge of his bed and opened the suitcase he had taken from Locker 719 at Washington's National Airport.

Through the wall he heard Fredericka Arbuthnot's hair drier in the next room.

A porter had led them through a door at the side of the lobby, down a few stairs, around a corner, and along the corridor of one of the plantation house's wings. Fletch carried his own bags.

The porter stopped at Room 77, put down Freddie's luggage, and put the key in the lock.

"Where's my room?" Fletch asked.

"Right next door, sir. Room 79."

"Oh, no."

Over the porter's shoulder, Freddie grinned at him.

"Give me my key," Fletch said.

The porter handed it to him.

"You know," Fletch said to Freddie, "for someone who's a figment of my imagination, you cling real good."

She said, "Your luggage doesn't match."

There were four doors to his room — one from the corridor, locked doors to the rooms each side of his, and one leading outdoors.

Before he took his shower, he had opened the sliding glass doors. Before him was the swimming pool, sparsely populated by women and children. To the left was a bank of six tennis courts, only two of which were being used.

Every square centimeter of the suitcase's interior was being used.

In the center was the tape recorder, with the usual buttons, cigarette-pack-size speakers each side. It was already loaded with fresh tape. In the pocket of the suitcase lid were thirty-five more reels of tape — altogether enough for a total of seventy-two hours of taping.

Across the top of the suitcase, over the tape recorder, were two bands of stations, each having its own numbered button, each row having twelve stations. To the right was a fine tuner; to the left an ON-OFF-VOLUME dial.

In a pocket to the left of the tape recorder was a clear plastic bag of nasty-looking little bugs. Fletch shook them onto his bedspread. There were twenty-four of them, each numbered on its base.

Fletch tested one against his bedside lamp and proved to himself the bug's base was magnetic.

Below the tape recorder was a deep slot, about a centimeter wide, running almost the length of the suitcase. Toward each end were finger holes. Fletch inserted his index fingers, crooked them as much as space allowed, and pulled up — perfectly ordinary rabbit ears, telescopic antennae.

And in a pocket to the right of the tape recorder were a wire and a plug and an extension cord.

Nowhere — not on the tape recorder, nor the tape reels, not even on the suitcase — was a manufacturer's name.

Fletch extended the antennae, plugged the machine into a wall socket, turned it on, chose bug Number 8, put it against the bedside lamp, pressed the button for station Number 8, pushed the RECORD button, and said the following:

"Attention Eggers, Gordon and Fabens, Richard!" The red volume-level needle was jumping at the sound of his voice. The machine was working. Fletch turned the volume dial a little counterclockwise. "This is your friend, Irwin Maurice Fletcher, talking to you from the beautiful Hendricks Plantation, in Hendricks, Virginia, U.S. of A. It's not my practice, of course, to accept press junkets; but, seeing your insistence I take this particular trip was totally irresistible, I want to tell you how grateful I am to you for not sending me anyplace slummy."

Fletch released the RECORD button, pushed the REWIND and PLAY buttons.

His own voice was so loud it made him jump to turn the VOLUME dial for counterclockwise. A very sensitive instrument.

He listened through what he had said so far.

Chuckling to himself, Fletch turned the machine off and padded in his towel to the bathroom for a glass of water before sitting on the edge of his bed and pushing the RECORD button again.

"Obviously," he said to the room at large, "I could fill up seventy-two hours of tape with jokes, stories, songs, and tap dancing but, if I understand correctly, that is not why I am here.

"In the event of my death, or whatever, I want anyone who discovers this formidable machine in my room to understand what it is doing here, and what I am doing here.

"I am being blackmailed by the Central Intelligence Agency — under threat of spending twenty years or more in prison, for failing to file federal income tax returns, illegally exporting money from the United States, plus, not being able to account for the source of the money in the first place — to bug and record the private conversations of my colleagues at the American Journalism Alliance Convention at Hendricks Plantation.

"Who'd ever think having a fortune could be so much trouble?

"My three reasons for going along with this quote assignment un-quote are obvious to any journalist.

"To Eggers, Gordon, Fabens, Richard, Gibbs, Don, Englehardt, Robert, and all you other backwards people whose asses are where your mouths are supposed to be, so far I have the following to tell you.

"First, I suspect you all suck goats' cocks and lay hens.

"Second, the person you are most interested in having me bug, old Walter March, is dead. So there.

"Which, of course, causes me to wonder if the reason for your interest in him and the reason for his murder have anything in common.

"Third, Fredericka Arbuthnot has done a terrific job of clinging to me so far. She is magnificently seductive. However, you guys have to be some kind of special stupid. What you've done is like sending a man into battle with an arrow through his head.

"More jokes and stories later. I'll try to learn all the verses of 'The Wreck of the *Edmund Fitzgerald*' to sing to you at bedtime."

Fletch turned the machine off and sat another moment, hands in lap, looking at it.

Then he put the suitcase on the floor, leaving it open, and slid it under the bed with his toe. Kneeling, he forced the antennae under the box spring.

He lay on his stomach on the floor, unplugged the machine, and shoved all the wire under the bed, so none of it would be visible from anywhere in the room, and replugged it, running the wire between the bed's headboard and the wall.

Wriggling out from under the bed, his left biceps landed on paper — an envelope.

Sitting cross-legged on the floor, he picked up the envelope. He was sure it had not been there before. It must have fallen out of the suitcase. It had not been sealed.

Dear Mister Fletcher:

Our representatives in Italy, in explaining your assignment to you, mentioned only the name of Mister Walter March.

As you have now seen, the equipment we provided you has twenty-four listening devices and stations. We would like to have our public relations effort directed specifically at those on the following list. You may disperse the remainder of the listening devices in the quarters of those younger journalists you feel are most apt to rise to positions of power and influence, in time. We will not consider this assignment completed unless all the devices have been used profitably. . . .

Next to each name on the list was the journalist's network, wire service, newspaper, or magazine affiliation.

They were all so well known there was absolutely no need to list their affiliations.

On the list were Mr. and Mrs. Walter March, Walter March, Junior, Leona Hatch, Robert McConnell, Rolly Wisham, Lewis Graham, Hy Litwack, Sheldon Levi, Mr. and Mrs. Jake Williams, Nettie Horn, Frank Gillis, Tom Lockhart, Richard Baldridge, Stuart Poynton, Eleanor Earles, and Oscar Perlman.

"Sonsabitches," Fletch said. "Sonsabitches."

There was no signature, of course — just the words, in tiny print at the very bottom of the letter, "WE USE RECYCLED PAPER."

S I X

Fletch picked up the ringing telephone and said, "Thank you for calling."

"Is this Ronald Albemarle Blodgett Islington Dimwitty Fletcher?" a woman's voice asked.

"Why, no," Fletch answered. "It isn't."

Who would be calling him *rabid?*

He remembered vaguely an old joke someone had once told about Fletch biting a dog on a slow news night.

Who else?

"Crystal!" he said. "My pal, my ass! How the hell are you?"

Giggling. Per usual. In her throat. Per usual. Sardonically silly old Crystal.

"Are you here?" he asked. "Has the Crystal Palace shivered and shimmied into my very own purview?"

She began to sing the words, "All of me. . . ." He joined in halfway through the first bar.

"Still heavily concerned with your tonnage, eh, old girl? Still down in the chins?"

Crystal Faoni was not pellucid. She, too, had been cursed by her parents when it had come time to delete "Baby Girl Faoni" from the birth register and substitute something more specific.

Crystal was dark, with black hair which could have been straight, or could have been curly, but wasn't either; blessedly, basically heavy, with monumental bones, each demanding its kilogram of flesh; the appetite of a bear just after the first snowfall.

She also had huge, wide-set brown eyes, the world's most gorgeous skin, and a mind so sprightly and entertaining apparently it had never felt the need to cause her body to do anything but the sedentary.

She and Fletch had worked together on a newspaper in Chicago.

"Are you well?" he asked.

"I thought we could meet in the bar before the Welcoming Cocktail Party, and have too much to drink."

"I plan to go sit in the sauna and have a rub." Skimming the hotel's brochure on the bedside table, Fletch had noticed there were an exercise room, a sauna, and a massage room open from ten to seven.

"Oh, Fletch," she said. "Why do you always have to be doing such healthy things?"

"I've been on airplanes and in airports the last twenty-four hours. I'm stiff."

"You've already had too much to drink? You don't sound it."

"Not that way. Are you still working in Chicago?"

"Why," she asked rhetorically, "do people go to conventions?"

"To wear funny hats and blow raspberry noisemakers?"

"No."

"I don't know, Crystal. I've never been to a convention before."

"Why are you here, I. M. Fletcher?"

Lord love a duck, he said to himself. Everyone who knew him would know that convention-going was not his thing.

Neither was dues-paying.

He said, "Ah. . . ."

"Let me guess. You're unemployed, right?"

"Between jobs."

"Right. Let's return to our original question: Why do people go to conventions?"

"To get jobs?"

"About half. Either to get jobs, if they are unemployed, or to get better jobs, if they are employed."

"Yes."

"About a third of the people at conventions are looking for people to hire. A convention, dear Mister Fletcher, as you well know, is one great meat market. And, as I don't need to remind you, I am one great piece of meat."

"If memory serves, you do help fill up a room."

"It is not possible to overlook me."

"What about the other sixteen-point-seven percent?"

"What?"

"You said half the people are here to get jobs and a third are here to give jobs. That leaves sixteen-point-seven percent. Almost. What are they doing here?"

"Oh. Those are the people who will drop anything they are doing, including nothing, at any time, and go anywhere, for any reason, at someone else's expense, preferably, their company's."

"Gotcha."

"Except for poor little Crystal Faoni, who is here — as I expect you are — by the grace of a rapidly dwindling savings account."

"Crystal, how did you know I'm unemployed?"

"Because if you were employed you would be working on a story somewhere, and no one could divert you to attend a convention even under threat of execution. About right?"

"Now, Crystal, you know I always do what I'm told."

"Remember that time they found you asleep under the serving counter in the paper's cafeteria?"

"I had worked late."

"But, Fletch, you weren't alone. One of the all-night telephone operators was with you."

"So what?"

"At least you had your jeans on, all zipped up nicely. That was all you were wearing."

"We had fallen asleep."

"I guess. Jack Saunders was absolutely purple. The cafeteria staff refused to work that day. . . ."

"People get upset over the most trivial things."

"My missing lunch, Fletcher, is not a trivial thing. If you had been working for old man March at that point, you would have been fired before you reached for your shirt."

"You worked on a March newspaper, didn't you?"

"In Denver. And I was fired from it. On moral grounds."

"Moral grounds? You?"

"Me."

"What did you do, overdose on banana splits?"

"You know all about it."

"I do not."

"Everyone knows all about it."

"I don't."

"No, I suppose you don't. I don't suppose anyone would bother to pass on such a juicy piece of moral scandal to you. You're the source of so many such scandals yourself. You'd just say 'Ho hum' and gun your motorcycle."

"Ho hum," Fletch said.

"You know, instead of being on the telephone all this time, we could be curled in a dark corner of the bar, tossing down mint juleps or whatever the poison of the house is."

"Are you going to tell me?"

"I was pregnant."

"How could anyone tell?"

"Pardon me while I chuckle."

"Were you married?"

29

"Of course not."

"So why was that Walter March's business?"

"I didn't act contrite enough. I had told people I intended to have the baby, and keep it. That was back in those days. Remember? We all thought things had changed?"

"Yeah."

"I had gotten pregnant on purpose, of course. An absolutely great guy. Phil Shapiro. Remember him?"

"No."

"An absolutely great guy. Good-looking. Brainy. Happily married."

"So what happened to the kid? The baby?"

"I thought I could handle having a baby without being married. But I sure couldn't handle having a baby without being either married or employed."

"Abortion?"

"Yeah."

"Shit."

"That's what happened to my savings account the last time it got over two thousand dollars."

"Great old Walter March."

"He fired a great many people on moral grounds."

"Oddly enough, he never fired me."

"He never caught you. Or probably he heard so much about you, he never believed any of it. Even I can't believe everything I've heard about you."

"None of it is true."

"I was there that morning they found you under the cafeteria counter. And I hadn't had breakfast."

"Sorry."

"So whoever stuck the scissors into noble old Walter March was inspired."

"Did you?"

"I'd be pleased to be accused."

"You probably will be. You fit into the category of people who had a motive. He took a child away from you. Were you here this morning?"

"Yes."

"You had the opportunity to kill him?"

"I suppose so. Lydia said the door to the suite was open when she found him. Anyone could have walked in and scissored him."

"What else do you know about the murder, Crystal?"

"That it's going to be the best reported crime in history. There are more star reporters at Hendricks Plantation at this moment than have ever been gathered under one roof before. In fact, I suspect more are showing up unexpectedly, simply because of the murder. Do you realize what it would be worth to a person's career to scoop the murder of Walter March — with all this competition around?"

"Yeah."

"It would be worth more than a handful of Pulitzer Prizes."

"Whose scissors was it? Do you know?"

"Someone took it from the hotel desk. The reception desk."

"Oh."

"You thought you had the murder solved already, eh, Fletcher?"

"Well, I was thinking. Not many people carry scissors with them when they travel — at least ones big enough to stab someone — and anyone who would carry scissors that big most likely would be a woman. . . ."

"Fletcher, you must get rid of this chauvinism of yours. I've talked to you before about this."

"It's a moot point now anyway, if the scissors came from the hotel desk, where anybody could palm them."

"Anyway," Crystal said. "It's hilarious. All the reporters are running around, pumping everybody. The switchboard is all jammed up with outgoing calls. I doubt there's a keyhole in the whole hotel without an ear to it."

"Yeah," Fletch said. "Funny."

"You go have your rub, sybarite. Will I see you at the Welcoming Cocktail Party?"

"You bet," Fletch said. "I wouldn't miss it for all the juleps in Virginia."

"You'll be able to recognize me," Crystal said. "I'll be wearing my fat."

S E V E N

"Another one," the masseuse said.

Fletch was lying on his back on the massage table.

She was working on the muscles in his right leg.

He had been told he would have to wait more than an hour for the masseur to be free.

31

The masseuse was a big blond in her fifties. She looked Scandinavian, but her name was Mrs. Leary.

He had waited until she was finished with his right arm before mentioning Walter March.

His question was: "Did Walter March come in for a massage last night?"

The masseuse said, "I'm beginning to understand just how you reporters operate. How you get what you write. What do you call 'em? Sources. Sources for what you write. You're always quoting some big expert or other. 'Sources.' Huh! Now I see you all just rush to some little old lady rubbin' bones in the basement and ask her about everything. I'm no expert, Mister, on anything. And I'm no source."

Fletch looked down the length of himself at the muscles in her arms.

"Experts," he said, "are the sources of opinions. People are the sources of facts."

"Uh." She dug her fingers into his thigh. "Well, I'm no source of either facts or opinions. I'll tell you one thing. I've never been so busy. You're the ninth reporter I've massaged today, every one of 'em wanting me to talk about Mister March. I suppose I should make somethin' up. Satisfy everybody. It's good for business. But I'm near wore out."

Having worked for him, Fletch knew Walter March had massages frequently. Apparently at least eight other reporters knew that too.

"If you want a massage, I'll give you a massage." She took her hands off him, and looked up and down his body. "If you want me to talk, I'll talk. I'll just charge you for the massage. Either way."

Fletch looked into a corner of the ceiling.

He said, "I tip."

"Okay."

Her fingers went into his leg again.

"Your body don't look like the other reporters'."

Fletch said, "Walter March."

"He had a good body. Very good body for an old gentleman. Slim. Good skin tone, you know what I mean?"

"You mean you massaged him?"

"Sure."

"Not the masseur?"

"What's surprising about that? I'm rubbing you."

"Walter March was sort of puritanical."

"What's that got to do with it?"

She was working her way up his left leg.

Fletch said, "Oh, boy."

"That feel good?"

Fletch said, "Life is hard."

"Walter March was a pretty important man?"

"Yes."

"He ran a newspaper or something?"

"He owned a lot of them."

"He was very courteous," she said. "Courtly. Tipped good."

"I've got it about the tip," Fletch said.

She finished his left arm.

Suspending her breasts over his face, she rubbed his stomach and chest muscles vigorously.

"Oh, God," he said.

"What?"

"These are not ideal working conditions."

"I'm the one who's doing the work. Turn over."

Face down, nose in the massage table's nose hole, Fletch said, "Walter March." He couldn't get himself up to asking specific questions in a sequence. He blew the bunched-up sheet away from his mouth. "Tell me what you told the eight other reporters."

"I didn't tell them much. Not much to tell."

She lifted his lower left leg and, with a tight grip, was running her hand up his calf muscle.

"Oi," he said.

"Are you Jewish?"

"Everyone who's being tortured is Jewish."

"Mister March said nice day, he said he loved being in Virginia, he said they'd had nice weather the last few days in Washington, too, he said he wanted a firm rub, like you, with oil. . . ."

"Not so firm," Fletch said. She was doing the same thing to his right calf muscles. "Not so firm."

"He asked if I was Swedish, I said I came from Pittsburgh, he asked how come I had become a masseuse, I said my mother taught me, she came from Newfoundland, he asked me what my husband does for a living, I said he works for the town water department, how many kids I have, how many people I massage a day on the average, weekdays and weekends, he asked me the population of the town of Hendricks and if I knew anything about the original Hendricks family. You know. We just talked."

Fletch was always surprised when publishers performed automatically and instinctively as reporters.

Old Walter March had gotten a hell of a lot of basic information —
background material — out of the "little old lady rubbing bones in
the basement."

And, Fletch knew, March had done it for no particular reason, other
than to orient himself.

Fletch would be doing the same thing, if he could keep his brain
muscles taut while someone was loosening his leg muscles.

She put her fists into his ass cheeks, and rotated them vigorously.
Then she kneaded them with her thumbs.

"Oof, oof," Fletch said.

"You've even got muscle there," she said.

"So I'm discovering."

She began to work on his back.

"You should be rubbed more often," she said. "Keep you loose.
Relaxed."

"I've got better ways of keeping loose."

He found himself breathing more deeply, evenly.

Her thumbs were working up his spinal column.

He gave in to the back rub. He had little choice.

Finally, when she was done, he sat on the edge of the table. His
head swayed.

She was washing the oil off her hands.

"Was Walter March nervous?" he asked. "Did he seem upset, in any
way, afraid of anything? Anxious?"

"No." She was drying her hands on a towel. "But he should have
been."

"Obviously."

"That's not what I mean. I had a reporter in here earlier today. I
think he could have killed Walter March."

"What do you mean?"

"He kept swearing at him. Calling him dirty names. Instead of asking
about Mister March, the way the rest of you did, he kept calling him
that so-and-so. Only he didn't say so-and-so."

"What was his name?"

"I don't know. I suppose I could look up the charge slip. He was a
big man, fortyish, heavy, sideburns and mustache. A Northerner. A
real angry person. You know, one of those people who are always
angry. Big sense of injustice."

"Oh."

"And then there was the man in the parking lot yesterday."

She put her towel neatly on the rack over the wash basin.

"When I drove in yesterday morning, he was walking across the parking lot. He came over to me. He asked if I worked here. I thought he was someone looking for a job, you know? He was dressed that way, blue jeans jacket. Tight, curly gray hair although he wasn't old, skinny body — like the guys who work down at the stables, you know? A horse person. He asked if Walter March had arrived yet. First I'd ever heard of Walter March. His eyes were bloodshot. His jaw muscles were the tightest muscles I'd ever seen."

"What did you do?"

"I got away from him."

Fletch looked at the big, muscular blond woman.

"You mean he frightened you?"

She said, "Yes."

"Did you tell the other reporters about him?"

"No." She said, "I guess it takes nine times being asked the same questions, for me to have remembered him."

EIGHT

AMERICAN JOURNALISM ALLIANCE
Walter March, President

SCHEDULE OF EVENTS
Hendricks Plantation
Hendricks, Virginia

Monday
6:30 P.M. Welcoming Cocktail Party
Amanda Hendricks Room

"Hi," Fletch said cheerfully. He had stuck his head around the corner of the hotel's switchboard.

Behind him, across the lobby, people were gathering in the Amanda Hendricks Room.

The telephone operator nearer him said, "You're not supposed to be in here, sir."

Both operators looked as startled as rabbits caught in a flashlight beam.

"I'm just here to pick up the sheet," he said.

"What sheet?"

He popped his eyes.

"The survey sheet. You're supposed to have it for me."

The further operator had gone back to working the switchboard.

"The sheet for us to take the surveys."

"Helen, do you know anything about a survey sheet?"

The other operator said, "Hendricks Plantation. Good evening."

"You know," Fletch said. "From Information. The sheet that says who's in which room. Names and room numbers. For us to take the surveys."

"Oh," the girl said.

She looked worriedly at the sheet clipped onto the board in front of her.

"Yeah," Fletch squinted at it. "That's the one."

"But that's mine," she said.

"But you're supposed to have one for me," he said.

She said, "Helen, do we have another one of these sheets?"

Helen said, "I'm sorry, sir. That room does not answer."

Fletch said, "She has another one."

"But I need mine," the girl said.

"You can Xerox hers."

"We can't leave the switchboard. It's much too busy."

She connected with a flashing light. "Hendricks Plantation. Good evening."

"Give me yours," Fletch said. Helpfully, he slipped it out of its clip. "I'll Xerox it."

"I think the office is locked," she whispered. "I'll ring, sir."

"All you have to do is move Helen's." He reached over and put Helen's information sheet between them. "And you can both see it."

The operator said, "I'm sorry, sir, but a cocktail reception is going on here, and I don't think many people are in their rooms."

Helen scowled angrily at him, as she said, "The dining room is open for breakfast at seven o'clock, sir."

"Tell me." Fletch was looking at the sheet in his hands. "Lydia March and Walter March, Junior, aren't still in the suite Walter March died in this morning, are they?"

"No," the operator said. "They've been moved to Suite 12."

"Thanks." Fletch waved the telephone information sheet at them. " 'Preciate it."

NINE

8:00 P.M. Dinner
Main Dining Room

Fletch had saw-toothed seven edges of two credit cards letting himself into over twenty rooms and suites at Hendricks Plantation before he got caught.

He had just placed bug Number 22 to the back of the bedside lamp in Room 42 and was recrossing the room when he heard a key scratching on the outside of the lock.

He turned immediately for the bathroom, but then heard the lock click.

An apparent burglar, he stood in the middle of Room 42, pretending to be deeply concerned with the telephone information sheet, wondering how he could use it to give some official explanation for his presence in someone else's room.

Next to each room number and occupant's name was the number of the bug he had planted in the room.

The door handle was turning.

"Ahem," he said to himself. No official frame of mind was occurring to him.

"Ahem."

The door was being pushed open unnaturally slowly.

In the door, swaying, breathing shallowly, thin red hair splaying up from her head, an aquamarine evening gown lopsided on her, was the great White House wire service reporter, Leona Hatch.

Watery, glazed eyes took a moment to focus on him.

Her right shoulder lurched against the door jamb.

"Oh," she said to the apparent burglar. "Thank God you're here."

And she began to fall.

Fletch grabbed her before she hit the floor.

Dead-weight. She was totally unconscious. She reeked of booze.

Gently, he put her head on the floor.

"Zowie."

He turned down her bed before carrying her to it and putting her neatly on it.

He put on the bedside lamp.

She was wearing a tight necklace — a choker he thought might choke her — so he lifted her head and felt around in the seventy-odd-years-old woman's thin hair until he found the clasp. He left the necklace on her bedside table.

He took off her shoes.

Looking at her, he wondered what else he could do to loosen her clothes, and realized she was wearing a corset. His fingers confirmed it.

"Oh, hell."

He rolled her onto her side to get at the zipper in the back of her gown.

"Errrrrrr," Leona Hatch said. "Errrrrrrrr."

"Don't throw up," he answered, with great sincerity.

Pulling her gown off her from the bottom, he had to keep returning to the head of the bed and pulling her up toward the pillows by the shoulders. Or, before the gown was off her, she would have been on the floor.

He tossed the gown over a side chair, and realized he had to repeat the process with a slip.

The corset took great study.

In his travels, Fletch had never come across a corset.

In fact, he had never come across so many clothes on one person before.

"Oh, well," he said. "I suppose you'd do it for me."

"Errrrrrrrr," she protested every time he revolved her to get her corset off. "Errrrrrrrr!"

"How do I know? Maybe you already have."

Finally he left her in what he supposed was the last level of under-clothes, loosened as much as he could manage, and flipped the sheet and blanket over her.

"Good night, sweet Princess." He turned out the bedside lamp. "Dream sweet dreams, and, when you awake, think kindly on the Bumptious Bandit! 'Daughter, did you hear hoofbeats in the night?' " He left a light on across the room, to orient her when she awoke. " 'Father, Father, I thought it were the palpitations of my own heart!' "

Letting himself out, the telephone information sheet firmly in hand, Fletch said, " 'It were, Daughter. Booze does that to you.' "

TEN

9:00 P.M. Welcoming Remarks
TERRORISM AND TELEVISION
Address by Hy Litwack

"I was afraid you'd show up," Bob McConnell said.

Dinner was half over when Fletch arrived to take his assigned seat, at a corner table for six.

McConnell — a big man, fortyish, heavy, with sideburns and a mustache — had been alone at the table with Crystal Faoni and Fredericka Arbuthnot.

"I knew a table for six, empty except for two girls and myself, was too good to last."

"Hi, Bob."

"Hi."

"They put us together," Fredericka Arbuthnot said to Fletch. "Isn't that chummy?"

"Chummy."

Fletch glanced at the considerable distance to the head table.

"I guess none of us is considered too important," he said. "Another few feet to the right, through the wall, and we could stack our dishes in the dishwasher without leaving the table."

Bob said, "Yeah."

A few years before, Robert McConnell had left his job at a newspaper and spent ten months as press aide to a presidential candidate.

It would have been the chance of a lifetime.

Except the candidate lost.

His newspaper had taken him back, of course, but begrudgingly, and at the same old job.

His publisher, Walter March, had considered his mistaken judgment more important than his gained experience.

Walter March's judgment hadn't been wrong.

He had had his newspapers endorse the other candidate — who had won.

And it had taken Robert McConnell the interim years to work himself out of both the emotional and financial depression taking such a chance had caused.

Crystal said, "How was your massage, sybarite?"

Bob said, "You had a massage?"

To a good reporter, everything was significant.

"I was sleepy, afterwards," Fletch said.

"I should take massages," Crystal said. "Maybe it would help me get rid of some of this fat."

"Crystal, darling," Fletch said. "You're a bore."

"Me?"

"All you do is talk about your fat."

Because he was late, the waiter placed in front of Fletch — all at one time — the fruit cup, salad, roast beef, potato, peas, cake with strawberry goo poured over the top, and coffee.

"You want a drink?" the waiter asked.

Fletch said, "I guess not."

"My fat is all anybody ever talks about," Crystal said.

"Only in response to your incessant comments about it." Fletch chewed the pale slices of grapefruit and orange from the fruit cup. "Historic Hendricks Plantation," he said. "Even their fruit cup is antebellum."

"I never, never mention my fat," Crystal said.

Purposely, humorously, she began to fork his salad.

"You never talk about anything else." Fletch pulled his roast beef out of her range. "You're like one of these people with a dog or a horse or a boat or a garden or something who never talk about anything but their damn dog, horse, boat, or, what else did I say?"

"Garden," said Freddie.

"Garden," said Fletch. "Boring, boring, boring."

Crystal was sopping up the salad dressing with a piece of bread. "It must be defensive."

"Stupid," Fletch said. "You have nothing to be defensive about."

"I'm fat."

"You've got beautiful skin."

"Meters and meters of it."

She reached for his dessert.

Fredericka Arbuthnot said to Robert McConnell, "This is I. M. Fletcher. He gets along well with everybody."

"This stupid American idea," Fletch said, "that everybody has to look emaciated."

Crystal's voice was muffled through the strawberry-goo-topped cake. "Look who's talking. You're not fat."

"Inside every slim person," Fletch proclaimed, "is a fat person trying to get out."

"Yeah," muttered Freddie. "But through the mouth?"

"If you'd stop telling people you're fat," Fletch declaimed, "no one would notice!"

Her mouth still full of cake, Crystal looked sideways at Fletch.

She could contain herself no longer.

She and Fletch both began to laugh and choke and laugh and laugh.

With her left hand Crystal was holding her side. With her right, she was holding her napkin to her face.

Not laughing, Fredericka Arbuthnot and Robert McConnell were watching them.

Crystal began to reach for his coffee.

Fletch banged her wrist onto the table.

"Leave the coffee!"

Crystal nearly rolled out of her chair — laughing.

Robert McConnell had signaled the waiter.

"Bring drinks, all around, will you? We need to catch up with these two."

The waiter scanned the dead glasses on the table, and looked inquiringly at Fletch.

Bob said, "Fletch?"

"I don't care."

"Bring him a brandy," Bob said. "He needs a steadier."

"Bring him another dessert," Crystal said. "I need it!"

Fletch sat back from his plate.

"Oh, I can't eat any more. I've laughed too hard." He looked at Crystal. "You want it, Crystal?"

"Sure," she said.

The plate stayed in front of Fletch.

Freddie asked Fletch, "Who were you talking to in your room?"

"Talking to?"

"I couldn't help hearing you through the wall."

"Hearing me through the wall?"

"It sounded like you were practicing a speech."

"Practicing a speech?"

"I couldn't hear any other voice."

"I was talking to Crystal," Fletch said. "On the phone."

"No," Freddie shook her head. "It sounded recorded. At one point, when I first heard you, you blurted out something. As if the playback volume was too high."

"Oh, yeah. I was using a tape recorder. Few notes to myself."

"A few notes on what?" Bob sat up straight so the waiter could set the drink in front of him.

"Ah, ha!" Crystal said. "The great investigative reporter, Irwin Maurice Fletcher, has discovered who killed Walter March!"

"Actually," Fletch said. "I have."

"Who?" Freddie said.

Fletch said, "Robert McConnell."

Across the table, Bob's eyes narrowed.

Freddie looked at Bob. "Motive?"

"For having his newspapers endorse the opposition," Fletch said, "a few years back. It snatched the candy apple right out of Bob's mouth. Didn't it, Bob?" Robert McConnell's face had gone slightly pale. "If March's newspapers hadn't endorsed the opposition, Bob's man probably would have won. Bob would have gone to the White House. Instead, he ended up back at the same old metal desk in the City Room, facing a blank wall, with thousands of dollars of personal bank loans outstanding."

Fletch and Bob were staring at each other across the table, Fletch with a small smile.

Freddie was looking from one to the other.

"A few notes on what?" Bob asked.

Fletch shrugged. "A travel piece. I've been in Italy. By the way, has anyone seen Junior?"

Walter March, Junior, was the sort, at fifty, people continued to call "Junior."

"I hear he's drinking," Crystal said.

"Jake Williams took him and Lydia for a car ride." Bob sat back in his chair, relaxed his shoulders. "He wanted to get them out of here. Get Junior some air."

Freddie said, "You mean the police are making Mrs. March and son stay at this damned convention, where Walter March was murdered? How cruel."

"I suspect they could do something about it," Bob said, "if they want to."

Crystal said, "When you have the power of March Newspapers behind you, you are apt to be very, very conciliatory to petty authority."

"At least, openly," Bob said.

"At least, initially," Fletch said.

"Oh, come on," said the lady who had said she was from *Newsworld* magazine, but didn't appear to know very much. "Newspaper chains aren't very powerful, these days."

The three newspaper reporters looked at each other.

"March Newspapers?" Crystal Faoni said.

"Pretty powerful," Robert McConnell said.

"Yeah," Fletch said. "They even publish other months of the year."

There was the tinkle of spoon against glass from the head table.

"Here it comes," Bob McConnell said. "The afterdinner regurgitation. Duck."

Fletch turned his chair, to face the dais.

"Anybody got a cigar?" Bob asked. "I've always wanted to blow smoke up Hy Litwack's nose."

Helena Williams was standing at the dais.

"Does this thing work?" she asked the microphone.

Her amplified voice bounced off the walls.

"No!" said the audience.

"Of course not!" said the audience.

"Ask it again, Helena!" said the audience.

"Good evening," said Helena, in her best modulated voice.

The audience stopped scraping its chairs and began restraining its smoke-coughs.

"Despite the tragic circumstances of the death of the president of the American Journalism Alliance's president, Walter March" — she stopped, flustered, took a deep breath, and, in the best game-old-girl tradition, continued — "it is a pleasure to see you all, and to welcome you to the Forty-Ninth Annual Meeting of the American Journalism Alliance's Convention.

"Walter March was to make a welcoming speech at this point, but. . . ."

"But," Robert McConnell said, softly, "old Walter's being sent home in a box."

". . . Well," Helena said, "of course there is no one who can stand in his place.

"Instead, let us recognize all that Walter has done, both for the Alliance, and, for each of us, individually as newspeople, over the years. . . ."

"Yeah," said Robert McConnell.

"Yeah," said Crystal Faoni.

". . . and join in a moment of silence."

"Hey, Fletch," Bob said in a stage whisper, "got a deck of cards?"

There was a moment of quiet muttering.

Across the room, Tim Shields was waving at a waiter to bring him a drink.

"I'm sure it has nothing to do with the tragic circumstances," Helena said, "but the after-dinner speech scheduled for Wednesday evening by the President of the United States has been canceled. . . ."

"Oh, shucks." Bob looked at Fletch. "And here I brought two pairs of scissors."

". . . However, the Vice-President has arranged to come."

"The Administration has decided not to ignore us completely," Crystal Faoni said, "just because we've taken to stabbing each other in the back more openly than usual."

"Just one other announcement," Helena said, "before I introduce Hy Litwack. Well, why don't I just introduce Virginia State Police Captain Andrew Neale, who has been placed in charge of poor Walter's . . ."

Helena stepped away from the microphone.

A man with salt and pepper short hair, a proper military bearing in a tweed jacket, stood up from a table near the main door and walked to the dais. Clearly, he had not expected to be called upon.

Bob McConnell said, "I betcha he says, 'Last, but not least.' "

With poise, but blushing slightly, Captain Neale addressed the microphone.

"Good evening," he said, in a soft, deep drawl. "Accept my sympathy for the loss of the president of your association."

"Accepted," Bob muttered. "Easily accepted."

"First," Captain Neale said, "I've asked that your convention not be canceled. I'm sure that the death of Walter March casts a tragic pall over your meetings. . . ."

"An appalling pall," said Bob.

". . . but I trust you all will be able to go about your business with as little interference as possible from me and the people working with me.

"Second, of course we will have to take statements from those of you who were actually here at Hendricks Plantation this morning at the time of the tragic occurrence. Your cooperation in being available to us, and open with us, will be greatly appreciated.

"Third, I realize that I am surrounded here by some of the world's greatest reporters. Frankly, I feel like Daniel in the den of lions. I understand that each of you feels the necessity of reporting the story of Walter March's murder to your newspapers or networks, and I will try to be as fair with you as I can. But please understand that I, too, have to do my job. Many of you have already come to me with questions. If I do nothing but answer your questions, I won't be doing my job, which is to investigate this tragedy, and there won't be any answers. As solid facts are developed, I will see that you get them. It would help if there were no rumor or speculation."

"Here it comes," Bob said.

Captain Neale said, "Last, but not least, if any of you have genuine information which might help in this investigation, of course we will appreciate your reporting that information to me or one of the people working with me.

"Someone at Hendricks Plantation murdered Walter March this morning, with premeditation. No one has been allowed to leave the plantation since this morning. Someone here — most likely in this room — is guilty of first degree murder.

"I will appreciate your cooperation in every way."

Captain Neale started from the microphone, bent back to it, and said, "Thank you."

"Good old boy," said Bob. "Good cop."

"Bright and decent," said Crystal.

Freddie Arbuthnot said, "Ineffectual."

Helena said Hy Litwack needed no introduction, and so she gave him none.

Bob McConnell said, "I bet he says, 'Don't shoot the messenger.' "

Crystal and Fletch shrugged at each other.

Hy Litwack, anchorman for evening network news, was highly respected by everyone except other journalists, most of whom were purely envious of him.

He was handsome, dignified, with a grand voice, solid manner, and had been earning a fabulous annual income for many years. He was staffed like no journalist in history had ever been staffed.

An additional point of envy was that he was also an incredibly good journalist.

Unlike many another television newsman, he kept his showmanship to a minimum.

And, unlike many other journalists of roughly comparable power and prestige, there was minimal evidence of bias in his reporting — even in the questions he asked in live interview situations. He never led his audience, or anyone he was interviewing.

Also enviable was his on-camera stamina, through conventions, elections, and other continuous-coverage stories.

Hy Litwack had been at the top of the heap for years.

Next to him at the head table sat his wife, Carol.

"Good evening." The famous voice cleared his throat. "When I have

45

an opportunity to speak, I try to speak on the topics I find people most frequently ask me about, whether I wish to speak about them or not.

"Recently, people have been asking me most about acts of terrorism, more specifically about television news coverage of acts of terrorism, most specifically whether by covering terrorism, television news is encouraging, or even causing, other terrorists to implement their dreadful, frequently insane fantasies.

"I hate witnessing terrorism. I hate reading about it. I hate reporting it — as I'm sure we all do.

"But television did not create terrorism.

"Terrorism, like many another crime or insanity, is infectious. It perpetuates itself. It causes itself to happen. One incident of terrorism causes two more incidents, which cause more and more and more incidents.

"Never was this social phenomenon, of acts of terrorism stimulating other acts of terrorism, on and on, more apparent than at the beginning of the twentieth century.

"And television, or television news, at that point had not yet even been dreamed of.

"An act of terrorism is an event. It is news.

"And it is our job to bring the news to the people, whether we personally like that news, or not."

Bob McConnell whispered, "Here it comes."

"Blaming television," Hy Litwack continued, "for causing acts of terrorism simply by reporting them is as bad as shooting the messenger simply because the news he brings is bad. . . ."

E L E V E N

In the privacy of their bedroom, Carol Litwack was saying to her husband, ". . . Live to be a hundred, I'll never get over it."

"Over what?"

"You. I don't know."

At a distance there was the sound of gargling.

Before leaving for dinner, Fletch had tuned the receiver to Leona Hatch's room, Room 42, so he could check on her later, make sure she was as comfortable as possible. All he had expected to hear on the tape was snoring and "Errrrrrr's."

But that wasn't the way the marvelous machine worked.

Like all things governmental, it had its own system of priorities.

It took him a while to figure it out.

First he heard Leona Hatch snoring in Room 42, on Station 22, then Station 21 lit and he heard Sheldon Levi's toilet flushing in Room 48, then Station 4 lit and he heard Eleanor Earles saying in Suite 9, ". . . Dressed to hear Hy Litwack's stupid speech. Ugh! But if I don't, I suppose there'll be three pages in *TV Guide* about my snubbing the pan-fried son of a bitch at the American Journalism . . ." and then Station 2 lit and he heard Carol and Hy Litwack talking in Suite 5.

Any noise in any room in which he had placed a lower-numbered bug had precedence over any noise in any room in which he had placed a higher-numbered bug.

Fletch studied his telephone information sheet, and the notes he had made on it regarding which bugs he had put where, and discovered he had placed bugs instinctively more or less in accordance with the machine's priorities.

To keep himself straight at what he was doing, and, in fear of eventually being caught as he let himself into other people's rooms, he had planted the lower-numbered bugs in the rooms of the more important people: Station 1 was Suite 12, Lydia March and Walter March, Junior; Station 2, the Litwacks, in Suite 5; Station 3, Helena and Jake Williams, in Suite 7; Station 4, Eleanor Earles, in Suite 9. In Suite 3, now empty — it being where Walter March had been murdered — he had placed bug Number 5. And, in Room 77, Fred-ericka Arbuthnot's, he had placed bug Number 23.

"My, my," Fletch said of his marvelous machine, "it walks, it talks, cries 'Mama!' and piddles genuine orange juice!"

Hy Litwack spent a long time gargling his famous throat — every bubble and blurp of which Fletch faithfully recorded.

Carol Litwack was saying, "Here you are, the most successful, re-spected journalist in the country, in the whole world, a multimillionaire on top of that, and you still feel you can't say what you want to say, what you think is the truth."

"Like what?" Hy Litwack's voice sounded tired and bored.

"Well, what you just said about terrorism and television downstairs is not what you've said to me about terrorism and television."

Clearly, Hy Litwack was having a bedtime conversation with his wife which did not interest him much. "I mentioned the possibility

47

that the more publicity we give terrorists and murderers the more other kooks are apt to commit acts of terror and murder for the publicity alone. Too many people want to be on television, even with a gun in hand, or in handcuffs, or lying face down in the street with their backs riddled with police bullets . . . how much more of my speech would you like me to repeat to you? I admitted all that. I said I worry about it. But I don't know what to do about it. No one does. News is news, and it's seldom good."

There was a feminine sigh. "That's not what you've said to me at all."

"What have I said different?"

"Hy, you know you have. Time after time you've said to me the networks give maximum exposure to acts of terrorism in progress because it gets the ratings up."

Hy Litwack said, "They make for good drama."

"People tune in, especially, to see if the hostages or whoever have gotten machine-gunned yet. Or had their heads chopped off. You know you've said this."

"Yes," Hy Litwack said. "I've said this. To you."

"You didn't say it tonight. In your speech. An ongoing act of terrorism and the whole network news department comes alive. You rush to the studio, day or night. People switch on their TV sets. Audience ratings go up."

"I said they make for good drama."

"The advertisers' commercials get more exposure," Carol said. "Here some little nut out in Chicago, or Cleveland, is holding twenty people hostage to protest the establishment in some way, and in boardrooms all across the country the establishment is cheering because the poor little nut is helping to sell the establishment's products to all the other nuts and thus make the establishment richer!"

"Everything makes the establishment richer."

"You've said that. To me. Why didn't you say it in your speech tonight? Are you so establishment yourself you can't say what you really think, as a journalist?"

"No," said Hy Litwack. "But I'm a good enough journalist to keep my cynicism to myself."

There was what seemed to Fletch a long silence. He was waiting to hear where the marvelous machine would switch next.

He was about to experiment, to see if he could run the machine manually, when he again heard Carol Litwack's voice. "Oh, Hy. You don't know what I'm talking about."

"I guess not," said the famous voice, now sleepy.

"This afternoon you rushed down here to Virginia early, and immediately taped that phony eulogy on Walter March for the network evening news. 'The great journalist, Walter March of March Newspapers, is dead,' you intoned, 'shockingly murdered at the convention of the American Journalism Alliance, of which March was the elected president.' "

"I never said 'shockingly murdered.' "

"You even put on your tight-throat bit."

"You can check the tape."

"Whatever you said."

"Whatever I said."

"You didn't even know Walter March. Really."

"No man is an island."

"The few times you met him you told me the same thing about him. He was a cold fish."

"Carol? Would you mind if we went to sleep now?"

"You're not listening."

"No. I'm not."

"Just because all you famous newspeople are here, because it's a cheap story, cheap drama, because you're competing with each other between martinis, you're giving Walter March's murder more publicity than World War Two!"

"Carol!"

The famous voice was no longer sleepy. It sounded as if someone had just declared World War Three.

"You still don't know what I'm saying."

"Do I have to sleep in the living room?"

"You don't know what you're doing," Carol said. "You can't."

"Carol . . ."

"Giving March's murder all this publicity — all you're doing is inciting some other kook — maybe hundreds of publicity-hungry kooks — to see if they can stick a knife, or scissors, or whatever, into the back of some other quote great American journalist unquote."

"Carol, for God's sake!"

There was another long silence.

Then Carol Litwack's voice said, "I just hope the next quote great American journalist unquote murdered isn't you."

Fletch switched to Station 22, and heard only one "Errrrrrr" in three minutes of snores.

He discovered that if he depressed a station button, and shoved it up a little, it would catch and remain on that station.

On Station 23 he heard the shower running and Fredericka Arbuthnot singing a little ditty that apparently went, "Hoo, boy, now I wash my left knee; Hoo, boy, now I wash my right knee. . . ."

Fletch said, "Hoo, boy. Nice knees. Treacherous heart."

Fletch scanned the other stations.

There was conversation on Station 8, in syndicated humorist Oscar Perlman's suite.

". . . like this and five dollars and you couldn't even get a good dollar cigar."

"There's a good dollar cigar now?"

"I'm in. Two."

"Three little words. Make 'em nice."

"Nice? One, two, three. Those are nice?"

"You're asking? You dealt 'em."

"I deal without prejudice."

". . . Litwack."

Oscar Perlman had written a play and a few books and had been on television often and his was the only voice Fletch recognized.

Listening, Fletch could not even be sure how many men were in the room.

He presumed they were all Washington newspapermen.

"Fuckin' phony."

"Who's talking about Litwack?"

"You recognized the description? I'm out."

"He's just good-lookin'," said Perlman.

"He's no journalist. He's just an actor."

"All us plug-uglies are jealous of him," said Perlman, " 'cause he's good-lookin'."

"He's no actor, either. Anybody see him jerking himself off over March's death on the evening ersatz news show?"

"Ersatz? Wha's'at, ersatz?"

" 'There's no business, like show business,' that's news. . . ."

"How much of Litwack's income comes from his face, Walter?"

"His face and his voice? Thirty percent."

"Ninety percent, Oscar. Ninety percent."

"He looks like everybody's father. As last seen. Laid out in the coffin."

"Whose deal?"

"Something all you guys are too jealous to recognize," said Oscar Perlman, "is that Hy Litwack is a good journalist."

"A good journalist?"

"Don't bother. I'm folding right now. Your dealing has driven me to drink."

"Shit."

"Oscar, I thought I saw you sitting downstairs listening to Hy Litwack's speech. In fact, I thought I saw you sitting next to me?"

"I was there."

"You heard that speech and still tell us you think Hy Litwack is a good, honest, no-bullshit journalist?"

Someone else said, "That speech was written for some afternoon ladies' society out in Ohio. Not for his colleagues, Oscar."

"That's true. Hit me once, and hit me twice, and hit me once again, it's been a long, long time."

"Fuckin' superior bastard."

"So?" Oscar Perlman said. "He's not the first speaker who misjudged his audience. What are you going to do, wrap a coaxial cable around his neck and turn on the juice?"

"At least he might have asked one of his three thousand staff members to write a new speech for us."

"Another reason you're all jealous of him," said Oscar Perlman, "is because Hy Litwack has a big, six-figure income."

There was a momentary silence.

Someone said, quietly, "So have you, Oscar."

"Yeah. But you bastards have figured out a way of taking it away from me — over the poker table."

There was a laugh.

"Oscar's defending Hy because they're both establishment. The two richest men in journalism."

"That's right," said Oscar. "Only Litwack's smarter than I am. He doesn't play poker."

"You going to do a column on Walter March's death, Oscar?"

"I don't see anything funny about getting a pair of scissors up the ass. Even I can't make anything funny out of that."

"You can't?"

"Pair of deuces. Pair of rockets."

"And the devils are up and away, Five-Card Charlie."

"No," said Oscar Perlman. "I can't."

"How much money has Walter March cost you, Oscar?"

"It's not the money. It's the grief."

"Sizable bill. First, when you were working for him in Washington, for years March refused to syndicate you. He wouldn't even let your column run in other March newspapers."

"He said what was funny in Washington no one would think funny in Dallas. He was wrong about Dallas."

"Then when the syndicate picked you up, he sued you, saying you had developed the column while working on his newspaper, and he had the original copyright."

"No one ever got rich working for Walter March."

"How much did all that cost you, Oscar?"

"Nothing."

"Nothing?"

"You can't sue talent."

"You didn't buy him off?"

"Of course not."

"Legal fees?"

"There were some."

"Grief?"

"A lot. I'll never forgive him. Frankly, I'll never forgive him. Never."

"Then immediately he started nudging, saying if your column was going to run, it had to run in his newspapers. Right?"

"The bastard threatened about every contract I've had with every newspaper in this country."

"This has been going on for years and years. Right, Oscar?"

"What are you doing, playing cards or working on a story?"

"I don't get it," another voice said. "So Walter March has been biting your tail all these years. Why all the grief? Lawyers are for grief. You can't afford lawyers, Oscar?"

"You don't know how Walter March operated?"

"Look at that. Nine, ten, Queen."

"Tell me."

"If you don't know how Walter March operated, you never worked for him."

"Yeah, I only need one."

"A little blackmail. Always a little blackmail."

Someone else said, "That son of a bitch had more private eyes on his payroll than he had reporters. Paid 'em better, too."

"And they didn't have to write."

"A cute man. Real cute."

"Shit. Son of a bitch. I'm out."

"You mean Walter March has been blackmailing you, Oscar?"

"No. Just trying to find a way to. Pair of eyes behind every bush. I'm flying first class — there's always the same son of a bitch flying coach. No matter what city I'm in, there's always someone waiting for me in the hotel lobby to see if I go up in the elevator alone. Nuisance value, you know?"

"Dear old saintly Walter March operated like that?"

"Dear old saintly Walter March. The president of your American Journalism Alliance. You voted for him? Give me one card, so long as it's the King of Clubs."

"I'm very grateful to him," said Oscar Perlman. "Kept me straight all these years. I've never had the opportunity to lie to my wife."

"Oscar, you don't think dear old saintly Walter March getting a scissors up the ass is funny?"

Oscar Perlman said, "Not worth a column."

"I take it we're not sleeping together?"

Fletch said into the phone, "Who is this?"

It was 1:20 A.M. He had been asleep a half-hour.

"Damn you!" said Freddie Arbuthnot. "Damn your eyes, your nose, and, your cock!"

The phone went dead.

It wasn't that Fletch hadn't thought of it.

He knew she'd washed her knees.

T W E L V E

Tuesday
8:30 A.M. Prayer Breakfast
      Conservatory

And in the morning, the phone was ringing as he entered his room.

He took off his sweaty T-shirt before answering.

"Have you seen the papers?" Crystal asked.

"No. I went for a ride."

"Ride? You're unemployed and you rented a car?"

"I'm unemployed and I rented a horse. They use less gas."

"A horse! You mean one of those big things with four legs who eat hay?"

"That's a cow," Fletch said.

"Or a horse."

It took Crystal a moment more of exclamations before accepting the idea that someone would get up before dawn, find the stables in the dark, rent a horse, and ride over the hills eastward watching the sun rise, "without a thought for breakfast."

It had been a pleasant horse and a great sunrise.

And taking the horse from the stables and bringing it back, Fletch had not seen the man in the blue denim jacket, with tight, curly gray hair, who had approached the masseuse, Mrs. Leary, in the parking lot two mornings before and asked her about the arrival of Walter March.

"I want to read you just one 'graf from Bob McConnell's story in March's Washington newspaper regarding the old bastard's murder."

"Pretty extensive coverage?"

"Pages and pages. Two pages just of photographs, going back to and including a shot of the bastard at the baptismal font."

"He deserves every line," said Fletch. "Dear old saintly Walter March."

"Anyway, Bob nailed you."

"Yeah?"

"I'll just read the paragraph. First he names all the big names here at the convention. Then he writes, 'Also attending the convention is Irwin Maurice Fletcher, who, although never indicted, previously has figured prominently in murder trials in the states of California and Massachusetts. Currently unemployed, Fletcher has worked for a March newspaper.' "

Fletch was pulling off his jeans.

He had listened to McConnell phoning in his story the night before.

"A pretty heavy tat for tit, Fletcher. Methinks you'll not jokingly accuse Bob McConnell of first-degree murder again. At least, not in his presence."

"Who was joking?"

"There are some pretty vicious people around here," Crystal said. "You didn't know?"

"Breakfast?"

"Got to shower first."

"Please do."

THIRTEEN

9:30 A.M. IS GOD DEAD, OR JUST DE-PRESSED?
Address by Rt. Rev. James Halford
Conservatory
10:00 A.M. IS ANYONE OUT THERE?
Weekly Newspapers Group Discussion
Bobby-Joe Hendricks Cocktail Lounge

Fletch had breakfast in his room, listening to Virginia State Police Captain Andrew Neale questioning Lydia March and Walter March, Junior, in Suite 12.

There were the preliminary courtesies — Captain Neale saying, "I know this must be terribly difficult for you, Mrs. March"; Lydia saying, "I know it's necessary"; his saying, "Thank you. You have my sympathy. I would avoid disturbing you at this point if it were at all possible" — while Fletch was spooning his half a grapefruit.

Junior had to be fetched from his bedroom.

"Junior's a little slow this morning," Lydia said. "Neither of us is getting any sleep, of course."

"Hello, Mister Neale," Junior said.

His voice was not as clear as Lydia's or Neale's.

"Good morning, Mister March. I've told your mother that you have my sympathy, and I hate to put you both through this. . . ."

"Right," Junior said. "Hate to go through it. Hate to go through the whole shabby thing."

"If you would just go over the circumstances of your husband's . . . You don't mind my using a tape recorder, do you?"

Junior said, "Tape recorder?"

"Of course not, Captain Neale. Do anything you like."

"As an aid to my memory, and hopefully, so I won't have to disturb you again. It's most important that we fix the timing of this . . . incident precisely."

"Incident!" said Junior.

"Sorry," said Neale. "All words are inadequate. . . ."

"Apparently," said Junior.

"We're particularly interested in . . ."

"I'll do my best, Captain," Lydia said. "Only it's so . . ."

55

"Mrs. March, if you can just describe everything, every detail, from the moment you woke up yesterday morning?"

"Yes. Well, we, that is, Walter and I, were scheduled to have breakfast at eight o'clock yesterday morning with Helena and Jake Williams — Helena is the Executive Secretary of the Alliance — to go over everything a final time before the mobs arrived, you know, discuss any problems there might have been. . . ."

"Were there any you knew of?"

"Any what?"

"Any problems."

"No. Not really. There was a small problem about the President."

"The president of what?"

". . . the United States."

"Oh. What was that?"

"What was what?"

"The problem with the President of the United States."

"Oh. Well, you see, he doesn't play golf."

"I know."

"Well, you see, he was scheduled to arrive at three in the afternoon. By helicopter. The problem was what to do with him until dinner. Presidents of the United States have always played golf. Almost always. At these conventions, the President goes out and walks around the golf course with a few members of the press, and it makes good picture opportunities for the working press, and it makes it seem to the public that we're doing something for him, helping him to relax, giving him a break from work, and that the press and the President can be friendly, you know. . . ."

"I see."

"But the President, this President, doesn't play golf. The night before, Jake — that's Mister Williams — over drinks — well, we were talking about this and Jake was making silly suggestions, of what to do with the President of the United States for four hours. He suggested we fill up the swimming pool with catfish and give the President a net and let him wade in and catch them all. I shouldn't be saying this. Oh, Junior, help!"

"What did you decide?"

"I think they were deciding to put up softball teams, the President and Secret Service and all that against some reporters. Only Hendricks Plantation doesn't have a softball field, of course. Who has? And Jake was saying, what would happen if the President of the United States got beaned by the Associated Press?"

"Really, Mister Neale," Junior said.

"Right," Neale said. "Mrs. March . . ."

"At least the Vice-President plays golf," she said.

"At what time did you wake up, Mrs. March?"

"I'm not sure. Seven-fifteen? Seven-twenty? I heard the door to the suite close."

"That was me, Mister Neale," Junior said. "I went down to the lobby to get the newspapers."

"Walter had left his bed. It's always been a thing with him to be up a little earlier than I. A masculine thing. I heard him moving around the bathroom. I lay in bed a little while, a few minutes, really, waiting for him to be done."

"The bathroom door was closed?"

"Yes. In a moment I heard the television here in the living room go on, softly — one of those morning news and features network shows Walter always hated so much — so I got up and went into the bathroom."

"Excuse me. How did your husband get from the bathroom to the living room without coming back through your bedroom?"

"He went through Junior's bedroom, of course. He didn't want to disturb me."

"Mrs. March, are you saying that, in fact, you did not see your husband at all yesterday morning?"

"Oh, Captain Neale."

"I'm sorry. I mean, alive?"

"No. I didn't."

"Then how do you know it was he in the bathroom yesterday morning?"

"Captain, we've been married fifty years. You get used to the different sounds of your family. You know them, even in a hotel suite."

"Okay. You were in the bathroom. The television was playing softly in the living room. . . ."

"I heard the door to the suite close again, so I thought Walter had gone down for coffee."

"Had the television gone off?"

"No."

"So, actually, someone could have come into the suite at that point."

"No. At first, I thought Junior might have come back, but he couldn't have."

"Why not?"

"I didn't hear them talking."

"Would they have been talking? Necessarily?"

"Of course. About the headlines. The newspapers. The bulletins on the television. My husband and son are newspapermen, Captain Neale. Every day there are new developments. . . ."

"Yes. Of course."

"After getting the newspapers," Junior said, "I went into the coffee shop and had breakfast."

"So, Mrs. March, you think you heard the suite door close again, but your husband hadn't left the suite, and you think no one entered the suite because you didn't hear talking?"

"I guess that's right. I could be mistaken, of course. I'm trying to reconstruct."

"Pardon, but where were you physically in the bathroom when you heard the door close the second time?"

"I was getting into the tub. I don't shower in the morning. I discovered years ago that if I take a shower in the morning. I can never get my hair organized again, for the whole day."

"Yes. You had already run the tub?"

"Yes. While I was brushing my teeth. And all that."

"So there must have been a period of time, while the tub was running, that you couldn't have heard anything from the living room — not the front door, not the television, not talking?"

"I suppose not."

"So the second time you heard the door close, when you were getting into the tub, you actually could have been hearing someone leave the suite."

"Oh, my. That's right. Of course."

"It would explain your son's not having returned, your husband's not having left, and your not hearing talking."

"How clever you are."

"Then, what? You were sitting in the tub. . . ."

"I'm not sure. I think I heard the door open again. I believe I did. Because, later, when I went into the living room, when I . . . I . . . the door to the corridor was open."

"All right, Mother."

"I'm sorry, Captain Neale. This is difficult."

"Would you like to take a break? Get some coffee? Something?"

"Would you like an eye-opener, Captain Neale?"

"An eye-opener?"

"I'm making myself a Bloody Mary," Junior said.

"Oh, no, Junior," Lydia March said.

"A little early, for me," Neale said.

"Let's get it over with," Lydia said. "I heard Walter coughing. He never coughs. Not even in the morning. He's never smoked. . . . Then

I heard him choking. It got worse. I called out, 'Walter! Are you all right? Walter!' "

"Take your time, Mrs. March."

"Then the choking stopped, and I thought he was all right. The telephone began ringing. Walter always picked up the phone on the first ring. It rang twice, it rang three times. I became very alarmed. I screamed, 'Walter!' I got out of the tub as fast as I could, grabbed a towel, opened the door to the bedroom. . . ."

"Which bedroom?"

"Ours. Walter's and mine . . . Walter was sort of on the bed, the foot of the bed, his knees sort of on the floor, as if he hadn't quite made it to the bed . . . he had come from the living room . . . the bedroom door was open . . . the scissors . . . I couldn't do a thing . . . he slipped sideways off the bed . . . Walter's a big man . . . I couldn't have caught him even if I had been able to move! He rolled as he slipped. He fell on his back . . . the scissors . . . face so white . . . Captain Neale, a big blood bubble came up between his lips. . . ."

"Mister March, why don't you give your mother some of that?"

"Come on, Mother."

"No, no. I'll be all right. Just give me a moment."

"Just a sip."

"No."

"We can postpone the rest of this, if you like, Mrs. March."

"I don't even remember going through the living room. I went through the open door to the corridor. I was just thinking, Helena, Helena, Jake . . . I knew they were in 7 . . . we had met for drinks there the night before . . . there was the back of a man . . . there was a man in the corridor walking away, lighting a cigar as he walked . . . I didn't know who he was, from behind . . . I ran toward him . . . then I realized who he was . . . I ran to Helena's door and began banging on it with my fist . . . Helena finally opened the door. She was in her bathrobe. Jake wasn't there. . . ."

"Mrs. March, did you go back into that suite?"

"My mother has not been back in that suite since."

"I was on Helena's bed. They left me alone. For a long time. I could hear people talking loudly, everywhere. Eleanor Earles came in. I asked her to find Junior. . . ."

"Did you know, at that point, your husband was dead?"

"I don't know what I knew. I knew he had landed on the scissors. I asked for someone to get Junior."

"And, Mister March?"

"I was in the coffee shop. I heard myself being paged in the lobby. Eleanor Earles was on a house phone. I came right up."

"What did Ms. Earles say to you, Mister March?"

"She said something had happened. My mother wanted me. She was in the Williamses' suite — Number 7."

"She said, 'Something has happened'?"

"She said, 'Something has happened. Come up right away. This is Eleanor Earles. Your mother's in Jake Williams's suite — Number 7.' "

"What did all that mean to you?"

"I couldn't imagine why Eleanor Earles was calling me about any-thing. In the elevator I was thinking, maybe there had been an ac-cident. I don't know what I was thinking."

"Mrs. March, are you all right?"

"Yes."

"Mrs. March. Who was the man in the corridor?"

"Perlman. Oscar Perlman."

"The humorist?"

"If you say so."

"Why didn't you speak to him?"

"Oh."

"I'm sorry? You said you ran toward him, and then you didn't speak to him."

She said, "Oscar Perlman has been very unkind to my husband. For years and years. Very unfair."

"Mother . . . realize what you're saying."

"I'm sorry, Mrs. March. You'll have to explain that."

"Well, years ago, Oscar used to work on one of the March family newspapers, and he thought he could write a humor column. He always was lazy. I've never thought him funny. Anyway, Walter encouraged him. He really developed the column for Oscar. Then, well, as soon as the column was established in one March newspaper, Oscar went off and sold it — and himself — to this syndicate. . . . Very unfair. Walter was terribly hurt. Even last year, when Walter was nominated for the presidency of the Alliance, Oscar was saying bad things about him. Or, so we heard."

"What sort of bad things?"

"Oh, foolish things. Like he tried to pass a bylaw saying only journalists could vote in the Alliance election, no private detectives."

" 'Private detectives'? What was that supposed to mean?"

"Oh, who knows? Oscar Perlman's a fool."

"Mister March, do you know what 'no private detectives' means?"

"It doesn't mean anything," Walter March said. "Oscar Perlman has a coterie of followers — mostly Washington reporters — poker players all — and he keeps them entertained with these sophomoric gags. I don't know. March newspapers is pretty well-known for its investigative reporting. Maybe he was trying to make some gag on that. I really don't know what it means. No one did."

"Utter hateful foolishness," Lydia March said.

"Mrs. March, your husband was a powerful man. He had been all his life. . . ."

"I know what you're about to ask, Captain Neale. I've been lying awake, thinking about it myself. Walter was a powerful man. Sometimes powerful men make enemies. Not Walter. He was loved and respected. Why, look, he was elected President of the American Journalism Alliance. That's quite a tribute to a man — from his colleagues, people he had worked with all his life — now that Walter was, well, about to retire."

"Speaking of that, I'm a little uncertain. Who takes over, who runs March Newspapers, now that your husband . . ."

"Why, Junior, of course. Junior's president of the company. Walter was chairman."

"I see."

"And Walter was retiring as soon as he had served out his term, here at the Alliance."

"I see."

"No one in this world, Captain, had reason to murder my husband. Why, you can see for yourself. In this morning's newspapers. Even on the television. Hy Litwack's nice eulogy last night. The reporters are terribly upset by this. Every one of them, Captain Neale, loved my husband."

FOURTEEN

11:00 A.M. GOD IS IN MY TYPEWRITER, I KNOW IT
Address by Wharton Kruse
Conservatory

BULLDOGGING THE MAJOR MEDIA — OR BIRDDOGGING?
Weekly Newspapers Group Discussion
Bobby-Joe Hendricks Cocktail Lounge

"Mister Fletcher?"

Fletch squinted up from the poolside long chair at the young man in tennis whites, HENDRICKS PLANTATION written on his shirt.

"Yeah?"

"You phoned for a court at eleven o'clock?"

"I did?"

"I. M. Fletcher?"

"One of us is."

"We have you down for a tennis court at eleven o'clock."

"Thanks."

"Will you be needing equipment, sir?"

"I guess so. Also a partner. Playing tennis alone takes too much running back and forth."

"You mean, you want the pro?"

"I guess not. Someone means to provide me with exercise."

"Stop at the pro shop a little before eleven. We'll fix you up with a racket and balls — whatever you need. Have whites?"

"Send them to my room, will you? Room Seventy-nine."

"Sure. Thirty waist?"

"Guess so. Just ask the bellman to leave them inside the room. I have sneakers."

"Okay."

"Thanks," Fletch said.

A chair scraped next to him.

Fletch turned his head and squinted again.

"You're Fisher, aren't you?"

Stuart Poynton was sitting beside him, in expensive leisure clothes, green shirt, maroon slacks, yellow loafers — as pleasant to look at as lettuce, tomato soup, and a lemon.

"Fletcher," Fletch said.

"That's right. Fletcher. Someone told me about you."

"Someone tells you about everyone."

To be polite, one could refer to Stuart Poynton as a syndicated political columnist.

No one was ever polite about Stuart Poynton.

His columns demonstrated very little interest in politics — just politicians, and other power people.

His typical column had four to six hot, tawdry, indicative items (years ago, Senator So-and-so and his family had vacationed at a hunting lodge owned by a corporation his subcommittee is now regulating; Judge So-and-so was seen leaving a party in Georgetown at three in the morning; Congressman So-and-so fudged his fact-finding junket to Iran so he could visit his son in Zurich) — some of which were accurate enough to attract suits.

Always going for the jugular, in his desire to reform others, over the years he had accomplished little — except to harden everyone's jugular.

"You know who I am?" he asked. "Poynton. Stuart Poynton."

"Oh," Fletch responded to this forced humility. "Nice to meetcha."

"Well, I was thinking this." Stuart Poynton was staring at his hands clasped between his knees, in thinking this. "Little hard for me to operate around here. Too much meeting and greeting going on. Well, point is, everyone here knows who I am, and everyone is sort of, you know, watching me." He looked sideways at Fletch. "Got me?"

"Gotcha."

"Makes it hard for me to operate, you know, carry on my own investigation. Find out anything. And this Walch March thing is a hell of a story."

"You mean Walter March?"

"I said Walter March. Point is, I can ask questions and so forth, but these idiotic conventioneers — well, you know, they seem to get a great kick out of giving Stuart Poynton a bum steer. Some of them have tried already. Jeez, you can't believe some of the crazy things they've told me around here — and with a straight face!"

Fletch said, "Gotcha."

"I can't blame 'em, of course. It's a convention after all. Fun and games are part of it."

Fletch had raised his chairback a few notches.

"Point is, I am Stuart Poynton." Again the sideways look. "Got me?"

"You got it right."

"And I am here."

"Gotcha."

"And the whole world knows that I'm here."

"Right."

"And here — here, at Kendricks Plantation — there's an important story."

"Hendricks Plantation."

"What?"

"Hendricks. H, as in waffle."

"I feel I ought to come up with something on the Walch March murder."

"Walter."

"You know, as a decent, self-respecting journalist. Some insight. Something indicative. You know, some little item or items that will mean something, prove to be right through the apprehension, trial, and conviction of the murderer."

"I don't see how you can do that without solving the crime."

"Well, that would help."

"Solving the Walter March murder would make a good item for your column," Fletch said mildly. "Might be worth a 'graf or two."

"Point is," Poynton said, "everyone knows I'm here. Everyone knows there's a big story here. But I'm so well-known here, if you get me, my hands are tied."

"Gotcha."

"Jack Williams tells me you're a hell of an investigative reporter."

"You mean Jake Williams?"

"That's what I said."

"Good old Howard."

"Yeah. Well, I asked him last night who he thought could help me out. You know, shag a few facts for me. You're unemployed?"

"Presently unencumbered by earned income."

"You have no outlet?"

"Only the kind you can flush."

"I mean, if you had a story, it would probably be difficult for you to get it published?"

"There's no front page being held for me."

"I thought not. Maybe we can work something out. What I'm thinking is this." Poynton again went into his staring-at-hands-clasped-between-his-knees propositional pose. "You be my eyes and ears. You know — do legwork. Circulate. Talk to them. Listen to them. If you do any keyhole stuff, I don't want to know about it. Just the facts — all I want. See what you can dig up. Report to me."

Fletch let the next question hang silent in the air.

Poynton sat back in his chair. " 'Pending on what you come up with, of course — when I get back to New York — well, maybe I could use another legman."

" 'Maybe'?"

"The three I have are pretty well-known. Which is why I can't bring them in here. Everyone in the business knows who they are. In fact, they've about served their purpose."

"Hell of an offer," Fletch said.

Poynton glanced at him nervously.

"Legman for Walter Poynton. Wow!"

"Stuart," said Stuart Poynton.

Fletch looked at him, puzzled.

" 'Course, I'd pick up your expenses here at the convention, too," Poynton said, " 'cause you'd be working for me." Poynton turned full-face to Fletch. "What do you say. Will you do it?"

"You bet."

"You will?"

"Sure."

"Shake on it." Poynton held out his hand, and they shook. "Now," he said, reclasping his hands, "what have you got so far?"

"Not much," Fletch said. "I haven't really been working."

"Come on," Poynton said. "Reporter's instincts . . ."

"Just arrived yesterday. . . ."

"Must have heard a few things. . . ."

"Well . . . of course."

"Like what?"

"Well, I heard something funny about the desk clerk."

"The desk clerk here at the hotel?"

"Yeah. Seems Walter March got very angry when he arrived. Desk clerk made some fresh crack at Mrs. March. March took his name and said he was going to report him to the manager in the morning. . . . Someone said the clerk's pretty heavily in debt. You know — the horses."

"That would tie in with the scissors," Poynton said.

"What scissors?"

"The scissors," Poynton said. "The scissors found in Walch March's back. They came from the reception desk in the lobby."

"Wow!" said Fletch.

"Also the timing of the murder."

"What do you mean?"

"The clerk would have to nail March before he left his room in the morning. Before the hotel manager arrived at work. Before March had a chance to report the clerk to the manager."

"Hey," Fletch said. "That's right!"

"Another thing," Poynton said. "There's been the question of how anyone got into the suite to murder March in the first place."

Fletch said, "I don't get you."

"The desk clerk!" Poynton said. "He'd have the key."

"Wow," Fletch said. "Right!"

Again the nervous glance from Poynton.

"Sounds worth investigating," he said. "See what you can dig up."

"Yes, sir."

Three youngsters were throwing something into the pool and then diving after it.

"I heard something else," Poynton said.

"Oh? What?"

"Ronny Wisham."

Fletch said, "You mean Rolly Wisham?"

"That's what I said."

"Must be the noise from the pool."

"Seems Walch March had started an editorial campaign to get this Wisham character fired from the network, and ordered March newspapers coast-to-coast to follow up."

"Really? Why would he do that?"

"Apparently this Wisham is one of these bleeding-heart reporters. An advocate journalist."

"Yeah."

Rolly Wisham did features for one of the networks, and they were usually on Society's downside — prisoners, mental patients, migrant workers, welfare mothers. He always ended his reports saying, "This is Rolly Wisham, with love."

"Son of a bitch," said Fletch.

"March thought he was unprofessional. As President of the A.J.A. he wanted Ronny Wisham drummed out of journalism."

"That would be a motive for murder, all right," Fletch said. "Walter March could have succeeded in a campaign like that — to get rid of someone."

"Jack Williams confirmed last night that these articles were going to run. Then there'd be an incessant campaign against this Ronny Wisham character."

"And these articles are not going to run now?"

"No. Jack Williams feels beatin' up on somebody like Ronny Wisham would result in a sort of bad image for Walch March."

"I see," said Fletch. "Very clear."

Freddie Arbuthnot appeared around the hedge.

She was wearing tennis whites and carrying a racket.

"Williams said he was sure the other managing editors in the chain would feel the same way."

"Sure," said Fletch.

Poynton saw Freddie approaching them, and stood up.

"See what you can dig up," he said.

"Thanks, Mister Poynton."

Fletch got out of the long chair and introduced Fredericka Arbuthnot and Stuart Poynton by saying, "Ms. Blake, I'd like you to meet Mister Gesner."

As they shook hands, Poynton gave Fletch a glance of gratitude and Freddie gave him her usual *You're weird* look.

After Poynton ambled away, Freddie said, "You get along well with everybody."

"Sure," Fletch said. "I'm very amiable."

"That was Stuart Poynton," she said.

"Are you sure?"

"Why did you introduce him as whatever?"

"Are you Ms. Blake?"

"I am not Ms. Blake."

"Are you Freddie Arbuthnot?"

"I am Freddie Arbuthnot."

"Are you sure?"

"I've looked it up."

"You have nice knees. Very clean. Hoo, boy!"

She blushed, slightly, beneath her tan.

"You've been listening through my bathroom wall."

"Whatever do you mean?"

"That was a little song I was taught. As a child." She was blushing more. "The 'Wash Me Up' song."

"Oh!" Fletch said. "There is a difference between boys and girls! I was taught the wash-me-down song!"

She put her fist between his ribs and pushed.

"There's a difference between people and horses," she said. "People and weirdos."

"Playing tennis?" he asked.

"Thought I might."

"You have a partner, of course."

"Actually, I don't."

"Odd," said Fletch. "There seems to be a court reserved in my name. Eleven o'clock."

"And no partner?"

"None I know of."

"That is odd," she said. "One ought to have a partner, to play tennis."

"Indeed."

"Makes the game nicer."

"I suspect so."

"Would you please go get dressed?"

"Why are people always saying that to me?"

"I suspect people aren't always saying that to you."

"Oh, well," said Fletch.

"Ms. Blake is waiting for you," Freddie Arbuthnot said softly. "Patiently."

FIFTEEN

12:00 Cocktails
Bobby-Joe Hendricks Lounge

From TAPE
Station 17
Room 102 (Crystal Faoni)

"Hi, Bob? Is this Robert McConnell?

"This is Crystal Faoni . . . Crystal Faoni. We sat at the same table last night. I was the big one in the flower-print tent. . . . Yeah, isn't she gorgeous? That's Fredericka Arbuthnot. I'm the other one. The one twice the size people spend half the time looking at. . . .

"Say, I really dig you, Bob. I think you're great. I read your stuff all the time. . . .

"Yeah, I read your piece this morning. On the murder of Walter March. You mentioned Fletcher, uh? Fletcher. We used to work together. On a newspaper in Chicago. You really put it to him, didn't you . . . what was it you wrote? Something about Fletch's already having figured prominently in two murder cases but never indicted . . . and he used to work for Walter March . . . ?

"Let me tell you something about Fletch. . . .

"Useful information? Why, sure, honey. . . .

"Just a funny story, really. . . .

"See, there was this guy in Chicago Fletch didn't like much, a real badass named Upsie . . . a pimp running a whole string of girls in Chicago, real young kids, fourteen, fifteen, sixteen-year-olds, pickin' 'em up at the bus station the minute they hit town, pilling them up, then shooting them up, putting them straight on the street sometimes the same damn' night they hit town.

"As soon as the kids got to the point where they couldn't stand up anymore, couldn't even attract fleas — which was usually a few months, at most — like as not they'd be found overdosed in some alley or run over by a car. You know?

"A big, nasty business Upsie was running. This fast turnover in girls meant there was very little live evidence against him, ever. What's more, he could pay off heavy, in all directions, up and down the fuzz ladder. . . .

"This was a very slippery badass.

"Fletch wanted the story. He wanted the details. He wanted the hard evidence.

" 'Course he got no cooperation from the police.

"And the newspaper wasn't cooperating, either. The editors, they said, you know, what's one pimp? It isn't worth the space to run the story. Typical.

"And Fletch wasn't doing this precisely right, either.

"Every time he talked a girl into his confidence and began getting stuff he could use as evidence, he'd realize what he was doing, what he was asking them to do, in turning state's evidence — allow themselves to be dragged through the newspapers and television and courts for months, if not years.

"Upsie had already badly damaged their lives in one way.

"Fletch saw himself badly damaging their lives in another way.

"These kids were so young, Bob. . . .

"Anyway, as soon as Fletch got the story from each girl, instead of using it, he found himself getting her to a social service agency, a hospital, or getting up the scratch to bus her home — whatever he thought would work.

"He did this six, eight times maybe.

"Well, Upsie got upset. He was pretty sure, I guess, Fletch wasn't going to be able to print anything on him, ever, what with no police support, no newspaper support, and while Fletch kept sending his best sources of evidence home on a bus . . . but nevertheless, Fletch was hurting Upsie's business by continually taking these girls away from Upsie before they were ready to be wiped.

"Get the point?

"So Upsie sends a couple of goons out, and they find Fletch, drag him out of his car — a real honey, a dark green Fiat convertible, I loved it — and while they hold him at a distance, arms behind his back, they put a fuse in the gas tank and light it and the car blows all over the block.

"The goons say, 'Upsie's upset. Next time the fuse goes up your ass, and it won't be just gas at the other end.'

"So next night — it was a Sunday night — Fletch finds Upsie getting out of his pimpmobile and goes up to him as smooth as cream cheese, hand out to shake, and says, 'Upsie, I apologize. Let me buy you a drink.' Just like that. Upsie's wary at first, but figures, hell, Fletch is aced, he's aced other people easily enough, maybe it might be nice to have someone on the newspaper he has in his pocket, whatever. . . .

"Fletch takes him into the nearest dive, buys Upsie a drink, tries to explain he was just doing his job, but, what the hell, what did the newspaper care, he could end up dead on the sidewalk for all the newspaper cared.

"He had brought a little pill with him — something one of Upsie's girls had given him — and when Upsie was nice and relaxed and beginning to tell Fletch about his having been a nine-year-old newspaper boy on the South Side, Fletch slips the pill into Upsie's gin.

"In a very few minutes, Upsie's swaying, doesn't know what the hell he's doing, begins to pass out, and Fletch, still as smooth as canned apple sauce, walks him out and puts Upsie in the passenger's seat of the pimpmobile at the curb. See?

"He drives Upsie to this heavy, ornate Episcopal church Fletch knows about — knows how to get into that hour of Saturday night — and helps him into the church and sits him on the floor, where Upsie passes out.

"On the floor, Fletch strips Upsie of all his pimp finery.

"Then he places him spread-eagled on his back in the center aisle, bareass, badass naked, and ties his wrists and ankles to the last few pews — did I say spread-eagled? — in the dark.

"Then he takes a thin wire and ties it up around Upsie's balls — around his penis, you know? — and runs that straight and fairly taut to the huge brass doorknob of the heavy front door of the church. There's a purple velvet drape around the door, and the door is solid oak.

"He ties the wire nice and tight to the doorknob.

"Then Fletch goes up to the altar and drags the bishop's chair over so he can sit in it and see Upsie 'way down the center aisle, but Upsie can't see him.

"By and by, Upsie wakes up and groans, obviously not feeling too well, and tries to roll over and finds he's tied to something, all four points, and wakes up more, and tugs at the ropes, and then raises his head to look down at himself and finds he's tied at his fifth point, too.

"He can't see too well in the dark, probably well enough to see that he's in a church, and he remains reasonably relaxed, still groggy from the liquor and the drug, probably curious about what's happening to him, tied spread-eagled and naked, lying on a church floor.

"It's dawn, and light comes into the church, all red and blue and yellow in streaks through the big stained-glass windows, and the wire begins to pick up the light and gleam, and Upsie has his head up all the time, now, as much as his neck muscles can stand it, trying to see where the wire leads.

"In a while there's enough light in the church to start getting into the draped, recessed doorway, and shortly the big, brass doorknob begins to gleam — even Fletch can see it from the altar — and it's clear even from where he's sitting that the wire leads straight from Upsie's balls to the doorknob of these doors which must weigh a ton.

"Upsie sees it too, of course, and begins to figure it out, begins tugging at his ropes, flexing one arm, and then the other, pulling each leg up against the ropes.

"He realizes there's no way he's going to get free, unless someone helps him.

"But he doesn't get the real point of what's happening to him — or what's going to happen to him — until the church bells begin to ring, all over Chicago. It's then he begins shouting, 'Oh, no! Oh, God! Oh, no!'

"He remembers it's Sunday morning and at some point, sooner or later, those heavy oak doors are going to be swung open by hundreds of joyous Christians, en masse, you might say, strong in their faith.

"It's then that Upsie's body fluids begin leaving him. In sheer terror, he pisses almost to the church door, like a skunk shooting at something he knows is going to destroy him. He's lying in his own shit, just tons of it, pouring out of him.

"He's sweating buckets and shaking and pulling at his ropes.

"He knows that when those heavy oak doors are swung open, he's had it.

"Did I say he was yelling? He's yelling and screaming, first the words, 'Help me! Help me, someone!' in this cavernous church with solid stone walls, and then he's yelling every obscenity in the book, in furious anger, tugging at the ropes so hard his wrists and ankles burn through, bleeding, and then he begins to blubber, 'I don't deserve this, I don't deserve this,' and, crying. He thinks about this awhile,

71

and then begins twisting his head toward the altar, yelling, 'Oh, God, I'm sorry! I'm sorry!'

"Fletch picked the right church.

"This particular church didn't have Sunday service until eleven in the morning.

"But a lot of other churches in town had services before then.

"And every time one of the other churches' bells begins to ring, Upsie pulls harder on his ropes, the ropes tying him. He wears the ropes right down to his wrist and ankle bones.

"He even begins biting his left arm, through the muscle, thinking he would chew his arm off, I guess, until he realizes that would do no good: If he chewed off one arm, he still wouldn't be able to untie the rest of himself. See?

"More and more church bells ring around town, calling their congregations to service, and Upsie is screaming more and more incomprehensibly, very hoarse by now, convulsively tugging at his ropes, ever one more time, hoping something would give way, blood and shit all over himself, eyes bulging from his head.

"At ten-thirty — after hours of this — the church bells of that church begin to go off, and Upsie becomes even more frantic. He knows it's only a few minutes now, at most, before that heavy oak door is swung open.

"He's thrashing around the floor, as much as the ropes will let him, twisting and splashing in his own blood and shit.

"Even Fletch couldn't hear him yelling over the sound of the church bells. He could just see his mouth open, jaws straining, tongue extended. Upsie's eyes are rolling in his head, in terror.

"Then the big brass doorknob begins to turn, slowly, slowly.

"Upsie stiffens his body, tries to reach his hands down to his balls — of course they don't reach — actually tries to pull away from the door. . . .

"Oh, by the way, will I see you at lunch, Bob? The menu said something about chicken Divan or salad of your choice. Knowing me, I expect I'll have both. . . .

"What do you mean, 'What happened'? I told you it's a funny story. Fletch is a funny man. . . .

"You can't figure out what happened?

"Jeez, Bob, you're no better than Upsie.

"The church doors swung inward, Bob. Upsie couldn't see that, because of the drapes. . . .

"Fletcher? Oh, he left through the sacristy door.

"Gee, Bob, I thought you knew Fletcher. . . ."

SIXTEEN

From TAPE
Station 22
Room 42 (Leona Hatch)

"Ready for lunch?"

"Just putting on my hat."

"Why do you need a hat? We're not leaving the building."

"If your hair were as thin as mine, Nettie . . ."

"I'd never leave the house," Nettie Horn said. "You feel you must have a trademark, Leona. As if anybody cared."

"I like wearing a hat."

"With your vanity, I just don't understand how you let yourself get so drunk."

"What do you mean?"

"You didn't make it to dinner last night, Leona."

"You did?"

"I did."

"And what happened to you after dinner, Nettie?"

"I'm not perfectly sure. I seem to remember singing around a piano. . . ."

"Nettie, I put myself to bed in a proper manner last night. I even folded my clothes and removed my corset and got under the covers. In fact, I totally unraveled my corset. That took great concentration and deliberation — although why I felt I had to do it, I don't know. Had a dickens of a time putting it all together again this morning. Where did you sleep last nght?"

"I woke up in a chair in my room."

"Fully dressed?"

"Well . . ."

"I know you, Nettie. Somebody just dumped you there. Probably a bellman. Well, I was in my bed with my corset off. Now, don't give me any more of your nonsense about *my* being drunk in public. . . ."

Fletch switched off the marvelous machine to answer his phone.

"Fletcher, old buddy, old friend!"

"Don?"

"Yes, sir, I'm here."

"If this is Don Gibbs, I thought we established when I called you from Washington that we are not buddies, not friends, but, at the most, useless acquaintances."

"How can you say that? Come on. Didn't we learn the Northwestern fight song together?"

"I never learned beyond the first verse."

"What could be verse?" Don Gibbs said.

"Learning the second verse. Golly, Don, you sound full of bonhomie."

"Does that taste anything like Wild Turkey bourbon?"

"You government guys drink good stuff."

"Seldom do I personally get the opportunity to squeeze the taxpayer's wallet. How goes the convention?"

"If I ask where you are will I get an answer?"

"Try it and see."

"Where are you, Don?"

"Here."

"Terrific. Can you be a little more precise as to where 'here' is, geographically, at the moment?"

"Hendricks Plantation. Hendricks, Virginia, U.S. of A."

"Here?"

"You've got it."

"What are you doing here?"

"Thought we'd come along to see how you're doing."

" 'We'?"

"Bob is with me."

"Who's Bob?"

"Bob Englehardt, my honored and beloved department head."

"What are you doing here?"

"This Walter March murder, Fletch. It sort of worries us."

"Why should it? What's the CIA got to do with it? The murder of a private citizen within the United States is a purely domestic matter."

"March Newspapers has foreign bureaus, hasn't it?"

"Boy, you guys have elastic minds."

"By the way, how much poop have you got on the murder?"

"I've got it solved."

"Really?"

"Yeah."

"Out with it."

"No."

"Wait a minute, Fletch. Bob wants to speak to you. I'll come back on the line."

"Mister Fletcher?" Robert Englehardt was trying to lighten his ponderous tone. "May I call you Fletch?"

"I don't know why you call me at all."

"Well, to answer that question, we need you to cover for us. Don has been calling your room since we arrived, so you wouldn't express surprise at seeing us at the various functions here at the hotel and blurt out our actual employer."

"I was playing tennis with What's-her-name."

"Who? What is her name?"

"Exactly."

"Fletch, we're here as observers from the Canadian press."

"Anyone in Canada know that?"

"No. Our official story is that we're thinking of setting up a similar convention, next year, in Ontario. Naturally, we expect you to allow no one here, now or ever, to know whom we actually represent."

"Why in hell should I cover for you guys?"

"For all of the above reasons."

"Again?"

"Failure to file federal tax returns, evasion of federal taxes, deporting United States currency illegally. . . ."

"I've always heard it's more difficult to keep a fortune than to make one."

"Then we have your complete cooperation?"

"How could you think otherwise?"

Robert Englehardt said, "Good. Here's Don."

After a pause in which the clink of an ice cube against a glass was audible, Don Gibbs said, "Fletch?"

"Gee, Don. Your superior didn't say he was looking forward to meeting me."

"Actually, Fletch," Don said, "he's not."

"Gee, Don."

"How's the taping going? Got much dirt yet?"

"It's a marvelous machine. Very sensitive."

"What do you have so far? Anything good?"

"Mostly toilets flushing, showers running, typewriters clacking, and a lot of journalists talking to themselves in their rooms. I never realized journalists are such lonely people."

"That all?"

"No, I also have a complete tape of the *New World* Symphony from somebody's radio."

"You must have more than that."

"People snoring, coughing, sneezing . . ."

"Okay, Fletch. Expect we'll see you around."

"Never saw you before in my life. By the way, Don, what room are you in?"

"Suite 3. They had to give us the suite in which Walter March was murdered. They didn't have any other place to put us."

"Really living it up, uh?"

"The rule book says we can take a suite if nothing else is available."

"I'm glad I'm not a taxpayer," Fletch said. "Bye."

Fletch switched his marvelous machine to Station 5 — Suite 3.

". . . Turkey in school," Don Gibbs was saying. "Always out doing his own thing."

"More?" Robert Englehardt said.

"No one could ever figure out what it was. Gone night after night. Never came to the parties. Used to make jokes about Fletch. They always began with, 'Where's Fletch?' and then someone would make up something ridiculous, like, 'Sniffing the bicycle seats outside the girls' dorms. . . .' "

"Come on. Finish your drink. Let's go to lunch."

"Hey, Bob. We're supposed to be journalists, aren't we? Journalists live it up. I saw a movie once. . . ."

SEVENTEEN

1:00 P.M. Lunch
Main Dining Room

Arriving late at lunch, Fletch put his hand out to Robert McConnell, who was already looking warily at him from his place at the round table, and said, "Bob, I apologize. Let me buy you a drink."

Robert McConnell's jaw dropped, his eyes bugged out, and he turned white.

Robert McConnell bolted from the table, and from the room.

Crystal Faoni was staring at Fletch.

Fletch said to her, "What's the matter with him? Just trying to apologize for accusing him of murder. . . ."

Freddie Arbuthnot looked clean and fresh after their tennis. Clearly she had sung her "Hoo, boy" song again.

Lewis Graham had taken one of the empty seats at the table, and Fletch shook hands with him, saying, "Slumming, eh?"

The man shook hands as would an eel — if eels were familiar with human social graces.

Lewis Graham was a television network's answer to the newspaper editorial.

A gray man with a long face and narrow chin, who apparently confused looking distinguished and intellectual with looking sad and tired, every night for ninety polysyllabic seconds he machine-gunned his audience with informed, intellectual opinion on some event or situation of the day or the week, permitting the people of America to understand there were facts they didn't have yet and probably wouldn't be able to comprehend if they did have them, without his experience, and understandings they could never have, without his incisive intelligence.

Trouble was, his colleagues read the *New York Times*, the *Washington Post*, the *Atlanta Constitution*, the *Los Angeles Times*, *Time*, *Newsweek*, *Foreign Affairs*, and the Old Testament as well as he and could identify the sources of his facts, insights, and understandings, precisely, night after night.

Other journalists referred to Lewis Graham as "the *Reader's Digest* of the air."

It was questioned whether behind his grayness he had any personality he had not lifted from newsprint.

Lewis Graham said, "I didn't know where to sit. I expect lunch is the same at all the tables."

Crystal Faoni was still staring at Fletch after he sat down.

Freddie said, "A fairly even match, if I may say so. Six-four you; six-four me; seven-five us."

"Me," said Fletch.

"It was just your chauvinist pride."

"Me," said Fletch. "Me."

"Not a clear victory. Your arms and legs are longer than mine."

"The thing about tennis," Lewis Graham said, "is that someone has to win, and someone has to lose."

Crystal turned her stare at Lewis Graham.

They all stared at Lewis Graham.

"Tennis always provides a clear victory," Lewis Graham said.

Fletch asked, "Did you read that somewhere?"

Crystal said to Fletch, "I ordered you both the chicken Divan and the chef's salad."

"Thank you for thinking of me," Fletch said. "I don't want both."

"You want one of them?"

"Yes. I want one of them."

"Then I'll have the other one. Well, why should I embarrass myself by ordering two meals for myself — when I can embarrass you instead? You need a little embarrassing."

"Why should you be embarrassed?"

"Oh, come off it, Fletch," Crystal Faoni said. "Have you ever made love to a really fat girl?"

Graham shifted his elbows uncomfortably on the table.

"I'll weigh the question," Fletch said.

"As fat as I am?"

Fletch said, "It's a heavy question."

Lewis Graham cleared his throat and said, "You appear to be giving light answers."

During the lunch (Fletch ate the salad; Crystal ate two Divans, which caused Lewis Graham to quip that all she needed more to entertain was a fireplace and a coffee table), the topic of Walter March's murder arose, and, after listening awhile to Graham's reporting what he had read in the morning newspapers, complete with two Old Testament references to the transitory nature of life, Crystal raised her large, beautiful head from the trough and said, "You know, I heard Walter March announce his retirement."

"I didn't know he had," said Graham.

"He did."

"So what?" Freddie asked. "He was over seventy."

"It was more than five years ago."

"Men look forward to their retirements with mixed feelings," said Graham. "On the one hand, they desire retirement in their weariness. On the other, they shrink from the loss of power, the vacuum, the . . . uh . . . retirement which is attendant upon uh . . . ," he said, ". . . retirement."

Crystal, Freddie, and Fletch stared at Lewis Graham again.

"Was it a public announcement?" Fletch asked.

"Oh, yes," Crystal answered. "A deliberate, official, public announcement. It was at the opening of the new newspaper plant in San Francisco. I was covering. There was a reception, you see, big names and gowns and things, so of course the darling editors sent a woman to write it all up. There were scads of those little hors d'oeuvres, you know, chicken livers wrapped in bacon, duck and goose pâtés, landing fields of herring in sour cream. . . ."

"Crystal," Fletch said.

"What?"

"Are you hungry?"

"No, thanks. I'm having lunch."

"Get on with the story, please."

"Anyway, Walter March was to make one of those wowee, whiz-bang, look at our new plant, look at us, what an accomplishment speeches, and he did. But he also took the occasion to announce his retirement. He said he was sixty-five and he had instituted and enforced the retirement age of sixty-five throughout the company and although he understood better how people felt reaching sixty-five, being forced to retire, when he felt in the prime of his life, years of experience behind him, years of energy ahead of him, wasted, blah, blah, he was no exception to his own rules, he was retiring himself."

"I guess, ultimately, he considered himself an exception to his own rules," Freddie said.

"He always did," said Lewis Graham.

"He even said he was having his boat brought around to San Diego and was looking forward to sailing the South Pacific with wife of umpty-ump years, Lydia. He painted quite a picture. Sailing off into the sunset, hand in hand with his childhood sweetheart, sitting on his poop or whatever it is yachts have."

"He owned a big catamaran, didn't he?" Freddie asked.

"A trimaran," said Lewis Graham. "Three hulls. I chartered it once."

"You did?" Fletch said.

"A few years ago. The *Lydia*. I used to consider Walter March sort of a friend."

"What happened?" Fletch said. "Boat spring a leak?"

Lewis Graham shrugged.

"I don't see anything unusual in this," Freddie Arbuthnot said. "Lots of people get cold feet when it comes time to retire."

Fletch said, "Did he say when he was going to retire, Crystal? I mean, did he give any definite time?"

"In six months. The new plant was opened in December, and I clearly remember his saying he and Lydia were westward-hoing in June."

"He was definite?"

"Definite. I reported it. We all did. It's in the files. 'WALTER MARCH ANNOUNCES RETIREMENT.' And he said the greatest joy of his life was that he was leaving March Newspapers in good hands."

"Whose?" Freddie asked.

Crystal said, "Guess."

"The little bastard," Lewis Graham said. "Junior."

"I saw him this morning," Crystal said. "In the elevator. Boy, does he look awful. Dead eyes staring out of a white face. You'd think he'd died, instead of his father."

"Understandable," said Fletch.

"Junior looked like he was going somewhere to lie down quietly in a coffin," Crystal said. "Everyone in the elevator was silent."

"So," Fletch said, "why didn't Walter March retire when he said he was going to? Is that the question?"

"Because," Lewis Graham said, "the bastard wanted to be President of the American Journalism Alliance. That's the simple reason. He wanted it badly. I can tell you how badly he wanted it."

Graham saw the three of them staring at him again, realized how forcefully he had spoken, and relaxed in his chair.

He said, "I'm just saying he wanted to cap his career with the presidency of the A.J.A. He spoke to me about it years ago. He was canvassing for support, eight, ten years ago."

"Did you offer him your support?" Fletch asked.

"Of course I did. Then. He had a few years to go before retirement, and I had a whole decade. Then."

The waiter was pouring the coffee.

"Two or three times," Lewis Graham continued, "he got his name placed in nomination. I never did. And he never won." Graham pushed the coffee cup away from him. "Until last year. Both our names were placed in nomination."

"I see," Fletch said.

"Well," Graham said, "I don't have the advantage Walter March had — I don't own my own network." Graham looked a little abashed. "I have to retire the first of this year. There's no way I can hang on."

Crystal said, "And the A.J.A. bylaws say our officers have to be working journalists."

"Right," Graham said with surprising bitterness. "Not retired journalists."

"Is that why you stopped considering Walter March a friend?" asked Freddie. "Because you opposed each other in an election?"

"Oh, no," said Graham. "I'm an old man, now, with much experience. Especially political. There are very few things in the course of elections I haven't seen. I've witnessed some very dirty campaigns, in my time." Graham deferred to the younger people at the table. "I guess we all have. One just never expects to be the victim of such a campaign."

A bellman was having Fletch pointed out to him by the headwaiter.

Graham said, "I guess you all know Walter March kept a whole barnyard full of private detectives?"

Crystal, Freddie, Fletch said nothing.

Graham sat back in his chair.

"End of story," he said.

The bellman was standing next to Fletch's chair.

"Telephone, Mister Fletcher," he said. "Would you come with me?"

Fletch put down his napkin and rose from his seat.

"I wouldn't bother you, sir," the bellman said, "except they said it's the Pentagon calling."

E I G H T E E N

"One moment, sir. Major Lettvin calling."

Fletch had been led to a wall phone down the corridor from the entrance to the dining room.

Leaving the dining room, he had seen (and ignored) Don Gibbs.

Through the plate glass window at the end of the corridor, a couple of meters away, he could see the midday sunlight shimmering on the car tops in the parking lot.

"How do," the Major said. "Do I have the honor of addressing Irwin Maurice Fletcher?"

The drawl was thicker than Mississippi mud.

"Right," said Fletch.

"Veteran of the United States Marine Corps?"

"Yes."

"Serial Number 1893983?"

"It was. I retired it. Anyone can use it now."

"Well, sir, some sharp-eyed old boy here in one of our clerical departments, reading about that murder in the newspaper, you know, what's his name? where you at?"

The drawl was so steeped in courtesy everything sounded like a question.

After a moment, Fletch said, "Walter March."

"Walter March. Say, you're right in the middle of things again, aren't ya?"

Fletch said, "Middle of lunch, actually."

"Anyway, this here sharp-eyed old boy — he's from Tennessee — I suspect he was pretty well-known around home for shooting off hens' teeth at a hundred meters — well, anyway, reading this story in the newspaper about Walter March's murder, he spotted your name?"

Again, it sounded like a question.

Fletch said, "Yes."

"Say, you aren't a suspect or anything in this murder, are ya?"

"No."

"What I mean to say is, you're not implicated in this here murder in any way, are ya?"

"I wasn't even here when it was committed. I was flying over the Atlantic. I was coming from Italy."

"Well, the way this story is written, it makes you wonder. Why do journalists do things like this? Ask me, take all the journalists in the world, put 'em in a pot, and all you've got is fishbait." Major Lettvin paused. "Oops. Sorry. You're a journalist, aren't ya? I forgot that for a moment. Sportswriters I don't mind so much."

"I'm not a sportswriter."

"Well, he recognized your name — how many Irwin Maurice Fletchers can there be?" (Fletch restrained himself from saying, "I don't know.") "And checked against our files here at the P-gon, and, sure enough, there you were. Serial Number 1893983. That you?"

"Major, do you have a point? This is long distance. You never can tell. A taxpayer might be listening in."

"That's right." The Major chuckled. "That's right."

There was a long silence.

"Major?"

"Point is, we've been lookin' for ya, high and low, these many years."

"Why?"

"Says here we owe you a Bronze Star. Did you know that?"

"I heard a rumor."

"Well, if you knew it, how come you've never arranged to get decorated?"

"I . . ."

"Seems to me, if a fella wins a Bronze Star he ought to get it pinned to his chest. These things are important."

"Major, it's nice of you to call. . . ."

"No problem, no problem. Just doin' my duty. We got so many people here at the P-gon, everybody doin' each other's lazying, it's a sheer pleasure to have something to do — you know what I mean? — to separate breakfast from supper."

There was a man ambling across the parking lot, hands in the back pockets of his jeans.

"You going to be there a few days, Mister Fletcher?"

"Where?"

"Wherever you are. Hendricks Plantation, Hendricks, Virginia."

"Yes."

The man in the parking lot wore a blue jeans jacket.

"Well, I figure what I'll do is dig up a general somewhere — believe me, that's not difficult around the P-gon — we've got more generals in one coffee shop than Napoleon had in his whole army — we could decorate the Statue of Liberty with 'em, and you'd never see the paint peel — and move his ass down to Hendricks, Virginia. . . ."

"General? I mean, Major?"

The man in the parking lot also had tight, curly gray hair.

"I figure a presentation ceremony, in front of all those journalists — decorating one of their own, so to speak, with a Bronze Star . . ."

The man who had accosted Mrs. Leary in the parking lot.

"Major? I've got to go."

"The Marine Corps could use some good press, these days, you know. . . ."

"Major. I've got to go. An emergency. My pants are on fire. Call me back."

Fletch hung up, turned around, and headed down the corridor at high speed.

He found a fire door with EXIT written over it, pushed through it, and ran down the stairs.

He entered the parking area slowly, trying not to make it too obvious he was looking for someone.

No one else was in the parking lot.

The man had been walking toward the back of the area.

Fletch went to the white rail fence and walked along it, looking down the slope to his right.

He caught a glimpse of the man crossing behind two stands of rhododendrons.

He sprung over the fence and ran down the slope.

When he ran through the opening in the rhododendrons, and stopped, abruptly, to look around, he saw the man standing under some apple trees, hands in back pockets, looking at him.

Slowly, Fletch began to walk toward him.

The man took his hands out of his pockets, turned, and ran, further down the slope, toward a large stand of pine. Behind the pine trees were the stables.

Fletch noticed he was wearing sneakers.

Fletch ran after him, and when he came to the pine trees, his shoes began to slip on the slope. To brake himself from falling, he grabbed at a scrub pine, got sap on his hands, and fell.

Looking around from the ground, Fletch could neither see nor hear the man.

Fletch picked himself up and walked through the pines to the stable area, trying to scrape the sap off his hands with his thumbnails.

In the midday sun, the stables had the quiet of a long lunch hour typical of a place where people work early and late. No one was there.

For a few minutes Fletch petted the horse he had ridden that morning, asking her if she had seen a man run by (and answering for her, "He went thet-away"), and then walked back to the hotel.

N I N E T E E N

2:00 P.M.

VARIOUS USES OF COMPUTERS IN JOURNALISM
Address by Dr. Hiram Wong
Parlor

From TAPE
Station 1
Suite 12 (Mrs. Walter March and Walter March, Jr.)

"Bandy called from Los Angeles, Junior. Some question he can't deal with. And Masur called asking if he should put that basketball scandal on the wires from New York. . . ."

There was no answer.

"Are you having lunch?" Lydia asked her son.

No answer.

"Oh, for God's sake, Junior. Buck up! Your father's dead, and someone has to make the decisions for the newspapers. They can't run themselves. They never have."

Another silence.

"I'm ordering you lunch," she said. "You can't Bloody Mary yourself to death. . . ."

From TAPE
Station 9
Room 36 (Rolly Wisham)

"If you'll permit me a question first, Captain Neale . . ."

"I don't know. Once you journalists start asking questions, you never stop. I've had enough opportunity to discover that."

"Very simply: Why are you questioning me?"

"We understand you might have had a motive to murder Walter March."

"Oh?"

Rolly Wisham's voice did not have great timbre, for a man nearly thirty, but there was a boy's aggressiveness in it, mixed with an odd kindliness.

Listening to the tape, sitting on his bed, picking at the sap on his hands, Fletch kept expecting Wisham to say, "This is Rolly Wisham, with love" — as if such meant anything to anybody, especially in journalism.

"What motive do you think I would have for murdering the old bastard?"

"I know about the editorial that ran in the March newspapers calling your television feature reporting — have I the term right? — let's see, it called it 'sloppy, sentimental, and stupendously unprofessional.' That's precise. I had the editorial looked up and read to me over the phone this noon."

"That's what it said."

"I also know that this editorial was just the beginning of a coast-to-coast campaign to put you in disgrace and get you fired from the network. Every March newspaper was to follow up with articles punching holes in your every statement, every report, day by day."

"I didn't know that, but I guessed it."

"Walter March had begun a smear campaign against you. Frankly, Mister Wisham, I didn't know such things happen nowadays."

"Call me Rolly."

"I think of that kind of smear campaign as being from back in the old days. Dirty journalism. Yellow journalism. What do you call it?"

"It still happens."

"On this assignment," Captain Neale said, "I'm learning a lot of things I didn't particularly want to know."

"Is the campaign against me going to continue? Are the March newspapers going to continue to smear me now that Walter March is dead?"

"I understand it's been called off. Mister Williams — Jake Williams — has called it off."

"Good."

"Not for your sake. He thinks it might hurt the image of the recently departed. Leave a bad taste in the mouths of people regarding Walter March."

"If that's their reasoning, I wish they'd continue with it. Walter March tasted like piss and vinegar."

"Interesting to see how decisions are made in the media. You people are feeding a thousand facts and ideas into human minds a day and, I see, sometimes for some pretty wrong reasons."

"Very seldom. It's just that in every woodpile there's a Walter March."

"Anyway, Mister Wisham, Walter March had begun a campaign to destroy you; he was murdered; the campaign was called off."

"Captain Neale, who tipped you?"

"I don't get you."

"Who told you about the editorial, and the campaign?"

"I'm not a journalist, Mister Wisham. I don't have to give my sources — except in a court of law."

"I'll have to wait, uh?"

"I intend to bring this case into court, Mister Wisham. And get a conviction."

"Why did you say that?"

"What do you mean?"

"Seems a funny thing for you to say. I mean, of course you intend to bring it into court. There was a murder. You're a cop."

"Well . . ."

"Could it be that you've heard some not-very-nice things about Walter March?"

"I've been on the case only twenty-four hours."

"Twenty-four hours investigating Walter March would be enough to make anyone puke."

"Mrs. March assures me he hadn't an enemy in the world. And there is the fact that Walter March was the elected President of the American Journalism Alliance."

"Yeah. And Attila led the Huns."

"Mister Wisham, any man with that much power . . ."

". . . has to have a few enemies. Right. Everyone loved Walter March except anyone who ever had anything to do with him."

"Mister Wisham . . ."

"I have one more question."

"Mister Wisham, I . . . I'll ask the questions."

"Have you ever seen me on television?"

"Of course."

"Often?"

"Yes, I guess so. My working hours . . . I don't have any regular television-viewing hours."

"What do you think of me? What do you think of my work?"

"Well. I'm not a journalist."

"I don't work for journalists. I work for people. You're a people."

"I'm not a critic."

"I don't work for critics, either."

"I find your work very good."

" 'Very good'?"

"Well, I haven't made a study of it, of course. Somehow or other I never thought I'd be asked by Rolly Wisham what I think of his television reporting. Mostly, of course, I look at the sports. . . ."

"Nevertheless. Tell me what you think of my work."

"I think it's very good. I like it. What you do is different from what the others do. Let me see. I have more of a sense of people from your stories. You don't just sit back in a studio and report something. You're in your shirtsleeves, and you're in the street. Whatever you're talking about, dope addicts, petty criminals, you make us see them as people — with their own problems, and fears. I don't know how to judge it as journalism. . . ."

"I wish you were a critic. You just gave me a good review."

"Well, I have no way to judge such things."

"Next question is . . ."

"No more questions, Mister Wisham."

"If I'm good enough at my job to please you, the network, and a hell of a lot of viewers — how come Walter March was out to screw me?"

"That's a question."

"Got an answer?"

"No. But I've got some questions."

"I'm asking them for you."

"Okay, Mister Wisham. You're more experienced at asking questions than I am. I've got the point."

"That's not the point. I'm not trying to put you down, Captain Neale. I'm trying to tell you something."

"What? What are you trying to tell me?"

"You look at television. There are a lot of television reporters. Most of us have our own style. What's the difference between me and the others? I'm younger than most of them. My hair is a little longer. I don't work in a studio in a jacket and tie. My reports are usually feature stories. They're supposed to be softer than so-called hard news. Most of my stories have to do with people's attitudes, and feelings, more than just hard facts. That's my job, and you just said I do it pretty well."

"Mister Wisham . . ."

"So, why me? Why would Walter March, or anyone else, raise a national campaign to get me off the air?"

"Okay, Mister Wisham. Rolly. You asked the question. You could wear an elephant down to a mouse."

"Because he was afraid of me."

"Walter March? Afraid of you?"

"I was becoming an enormous threat to him."

"Ah . . . Someone told me last night — I think it was that Nettie Horn woman — all you journalists have identity problems. 'Delusions of grandeur,' she said. Rolly, a few minutes of network television time a week — I mean, against Walter March and all those newspapers coast-to-coast, coming out every day, edition after edition. . . ."

"Potentially I was an enormous threat to him."

"Okay, Rolly. I'm supposed to ask 'Why?' now. Is that right?"

"I've been trying to tell you something."

"Okay."

"I have more reason to murder that bastard than anyone you can think of."

"Uh . . ."

"Don't tell me I need a lawyer. I know my rights. I came to this convention because the network forced me to. I came with such hatred for that bastard. . . . Frankly, I was afraid to cross his path, to see him, or even hear him, or be in a room with him — for fear of what I might do to him."

"Wait."

"My Dad owned a newspaper in Denver. I was brought up skiing, horsing around, loving journalism, my Dad, happy to be the son of a newspaper publisher. Once a newspaper starts to decline in popularity, it's almost impossible to reverse the trend. I didn't know it, but when I was about ten, Dad's newspaper began to go into a decline. By the time I was fourteen, he had mortgaged everything, including his desk. Goddamn it, the desk he had inherited from his father, to keep the paper running. These were straight bank loans — but unfortunately Dad had made the mistake of using only one bank. He wasn't the sharpest businessman in the world."

"Neither am I. I . . . ."

"Just when Dad thought he was turning the paper around — it had taken five years — this one bank called all the loans."

"Could they do that? I mean, legally?"

"Sure. Dad never thought they would. They were friends. He went to see them. They wouldn't even speak to him. They called all the loans at once, and that was it."

"I don't get it."

"Neither did Dad. Why would the bank want to take over a newspaper, especially when there was hope for its doing well? They wouldn't know how to run it. Dad lost the newspaper. He gave up as decently as he could. He wandered around the house for weeks, trying to figure out what had happened. I was fifteen. There was a rumor around that the bank had sold the newspaper to Walter March, or March Newspapers."

"Okay, it seems like an ordinary . . . ."

"Not a bit ordinary. These bankers were old friends of my father. Huntin', fishin', cussin' and drinkin' friends."

"He was hurt."

"He was curious. He was also a hell of a journalist. In time, he found out what happened. People always talk. Walter March had bought up Dad's loans, lock, stock, and barrel — to get control of the newspaper."

"Why did the bankers let him? They were friends. . . ."

"Blackmail, Captain Neale. Sheer, unadulterated blackmail. He had blackmailed the bankers, individually, as persons. So far, in your twenty-four hours of investigation, have you heard about Walter March and his flotilla of private detectives?"

"I've heard rumors."

"When I was sixteen, Dad died of a gunshot wound, in the temple, fired at close range."

The recording tape reel revolved three times before Rolly Wisham said, "I never could understand why Dad didn't shoot Walter March instead."

"Mister Wisham, I really think you should have a lawyer present. . . ."

"No lawyer."

Captain Neale sighed audibly. "Where were you at eight o'clock Monday morning?"

"I had driven into Hendricks to get the newspapers and have breakfast in a drugstore, or whatever I could find."

"You have a car here?"

"A rented car."

"You could have had breakfast and gotten your newspapers here at the hotel."

"I wanted to get out of the hotel. Night before, I had seen Walter March with Jake Williams in the elevator. They were laughing. Something about the President and golf . . . catfish. I hadn't slept all night."

"Did you drive into Hendricks alone?"

"Yes."

"Okay, Mister Wisham, I don't see any problem. Your face is famous. We can just ask people down in the village. I'm sure they saw you, and recognized you. Where did you have breakfast?"

"I never got out of the car, Captain Neale."

"What?"

"I did not have breakfast, and did not buy newspapers. At least, not until I got back to the hotel."

"Oh, Lord."

"I changed my mind. I drove through that shopping center and said, to hell with it. It was a beautiful morning and the shopping center looked so sterile. Also, of course, I'm forever making simple little plans like going to a drugstore for breakfast — I like people, you know? I like being with people — and I get right up to it, and I realize everybody will recognize me, and giggle, and shake hands, and ask for autographs. I'm not keen on that part of my life."

"Are you saying that no one saw you Monday morning?"

"I guess I prevented anyone from seeing me. I wore sunglasses. I drove around. Over the hills. Maybe I was trying to talk myself out of murdering Walter March."

"What time did you leave the hotel?"

"About seven-fifteen."

"What time did you get back?"

"About nine. I had breakfast in the coffee shop here. I didn't hear about Walter March's murder until later. Ten-thirty. Eleven."

"Okay, Mister Wisham. You say Walter March was smearing you, trying to destroy you. . . ."

"Not 'trying to,' Captain Neale. He was going to. There is no doubt in my mind he would have succeeded."

". . . because you were becoming a potential threat to him."

"Don't you agree? I could never be as powerful as Walter March.

We lost the only newspaper we had. But I have been becoming an increasingly powerful and respected journalist. I'm only twenty-eight, Captain Neale. I have a lot to say, and a forum for saying it. Even having me at this convention, telling people what I know about Walter March, was a threat to him. You've got to admit, I was more a threat to him as a halfway decent and important journalist than if I had become a skiing instructor in Aspen."

"I guess so. Tell me, Mister Wisham, do you happen to know what suite the March family were in?"

"Suite 3."

"How did you know that?"

"I checked. I wanted to avoid any area in which Walter March might be."

"You checked at the desk?"

"Yup. Which gave me an opportunity to steal the scissors. Right?"

"You're being very open with me, Mister Wisham."

"I'm a very open guy. Anyhow, you strike me as a pretty good cop. There's a lot of pressure on this case. Sooner or later, you'd discover Walter March drove my Dad to suicide. Everyone in Denver knows it, and probably half the people here at the convention do. Concealing evidence against myself would just waste your time, and leave me hung up."

"It's almost as if you were daring me, Mister Wisham."

"I am daring you, Captain Neale. I've worked a lot with cops. I'm daring you to be on my side, and to believe I didn't kill Walter March."

TWENTY

3:30 P.M.

COMPUTERS AND LABOR UNIONS
Seminar
Aunt Sally Hendricks Sewing Room

At three-thirty Wednesday afternoon all the tennis courts were in use, the swimming pool area was full, and on the hills around Hendricks Plantation House people were walking and horseback riding.

The bar (Bobby-Joe Hendricks Lounge) was dark and empty except for some people from the Boston press keeping up their luncheon glow with gin and tonics.

And Walter March, Junior, sitting at the bar.

Fletch sat beside him and ordered a gin and bitter lemon from the bored, slow-moving barman.

At the sound of his voice, Junior's head turned slowly to look at him.

Junior's eyes were red-rimmed and glazed, his cheeks puffy, his mouth slack. A small vein in his temple was throbbing. He looked away, slowly, thought a moment, burped, and looked back at Fletch.

He said, "William Morris Fletcher. I remember you."

"Irwin Maurice Fletcher."

"Tha's right. You used to work for us."

"Practically everybody used to work for you."

"Flesh. There used to be a joke about you. 'And the Word was made Fletch.' "

"Yeah."

"There were lots of jokes about you. You were a joke."

Fletch paid the barman.

Walter March, Junior, said, "You heard my father's dead?"

"I heard something to that effect."

"Someone stabbed him." Junior made a stabbing motion with his right hand, his eyes looking insane as he did it. "With a scissors."

Fletch said, "Tough to take."

"Tough!" Junior snorted. "Tough for him. Tough for March Newspapers. Tough for the whole mother-fuckin' world."

"Tough for you."

"Yeah." Junior blinked slowly. "Tough for me. Tough darts. Isn't that what we used to say in school?"

"I don't know. I wasn't in school with you."

There was a long, slow, blinking pause.

Junior said, "My father hated you."

Fletch said, "Your father hated everybody."

Another three blinks.

"I hated you."

"Anyone who hates me is probably right."

"My Jesus father thought you were night and day."

Fletch sipped his drink. "What does that mean?"

Junior tried to look at Fletch in the proper executive fashion. "You know, he wanted to make a thing with you. He loved your balls." Junior's eyelids drooped. "He wanted to bring you along, you know? Make something of you."

"Gee, and I'm not even in journalism anymore. Just a hanger-on."
"Do you remember his trying to frighten you once?"
"No."
"He tried to scare you."
"I don't remember it."
"Tha's because you weren't frightened, shit. You remember the story about the Governor's secretary?"
"Yeah."
"He sent memos to you. Directly. Telling you to blow the story."
"Sure."
"He came to town. Sent for you in his office."
"Yeah."
"Scared the shit out of you."
"Did he?"
"Told you you'd be fired if you wrote the story."
"Five minutes in an office . . ."
Junior's head swooped up toward Fletch. "You wrote the fuckin' story! And then quit!"
"Yeah."
There was a long pause, and two small burps.
"It wasn't the Governor Dad cared about. Not the Governor's secretary. Not the story." This time Junior put the back of his hand to his burp. "It was you."
"There was a long pause," Irwin Maurice Fletcher said, "while Irwin Maurice Fletcher reacted."
"You don't get the point," Junior said.
"I get the point," Fletch said. "People are always shittin' around, and I'm me. I always get the point."
"Apologize."
"Apologize?"
"Jesus, yes. Apologize."
"For what? For everyone else always shittin' around, or for me being me?"
"Before my Dad did that . . ." — apparently, Junior was considering the prudence of saying what he was about to say — "he had every kind of a fix run on you."
Fletch sat quietly over his drink.
"He wanted you," Junior said.
"I was an employee. I wrote that story. Quit. A common incident, in this business."
"Dad didn't want any of that. He wanted you. He ran every kind of a fix on you. Have I said that?"

"No."

"Before he tried to throw the scare into you, he had you worked over with a fine-toothed . . . pig."

"That I don't understand."

"He wanted you. You were tough. You didn't scare."

"He let me resign."

"That, beaut . . .' — Junior leaned toward him — "was because he hadn't figured you out. He gave up, you see."

"He put detectives on me?"

"He liked your style. In the city room. You were a thousand-dollar job, at first. A mere hand job. He couldn't believe what he found out. More. Ten thousand. Fifteen."

"I would rather have taken it in pay."

"He couldn't believe . . . Who were you married to then?"

"I don't remember."

"He said, 'Either all of it's true, or none of it's true.' "

"None of it's true," Fletch said. "At the age of eleven, if you want the truth . . ."

"Stories," Junior said. "Used to get stories about you. At dinner."

Fletch said, "This is very uncomfortable. What a lousy bar. The barman has dirty elbows. No music. What's that noise? 'Moon River.' That's what I mean. No music. Look at that painting. Disgusting. A horse, of all things. A horse over a bar. Ridiculous. . . ."

Junior was blinking over his drink.

"It was me Dad hated."

"What?"

"All my life . . . I grew up . . ."

"Most of us did."

". . . being Walter March, Junior. Walter March Newspapers, Junior. The inheritor of enormous power."

"That can be a problem."

"What if I wanted to be a violinist, or a painter, or a baseball player?"

"Did you?"

Junior closed his eyes tight over his drink.

"I don't even know."

Someone at the table in the corner said, "Walter marched."

Someone else said, "And about time, to boot!"

Fletch looked over at them.

Junior hadn't heard.

"You know, the first day I was supposed to report for work," Junior said. "September. The year I graduated college. They'd let me have the summer off. I walked to the office. Stood across the street from it, staring at it. Twenty minutes. Maybe a half-hour. Then I walked back to my apartment. I was scared shitless. That night, Jake Williams came over to my apartment and talked to me. For hours. Next morning, he picked me up and we walked into the March Newspapers Building together." Junior went through the motions of drinking from his empty glass. "Good old Jake Williams."

Fletch said nothing.

"Fletcher, will you help me?"

"How?"

"Work with me. The way Dad wanted."

"I don't know anything about the publishing side of this business. The business end."

"It doesn't matter."

"It does to me."

Junior tightened his right fist and let it down slowly on the bar, as if he were banging it in slow motion.

"Help me!"

"Junior, I suspect you missed lunch."

"My father loved you so much."

"Come on, I met the bastard — I mean, your father — I mean, your father the bastard, the big bastard five minutes in his office. . . ."

"I can't esplain. I can't esplain."

Fletch, on his bar stool, was facing Walter March, Junior.

There were tears on Junior's cheeks.

Fletch said, "Nappy time?"

Junior straightened up immediately. Suddenly, no tears. No whining voice. No quivering. Princeton right down the spine. Hand firmly around the empty glass. Not deigning to answer.

"Hey, Walt," Fletch said. "I was thinking of a sauna and a rub. They've got this fantastic lady hidden away in the basement, a Mrs. Leary, she gives a great massage. . . ."

Junior looked at him. He was the President of March Newspapers.

"Good to see you again, Fletcher," he said. He cleared his throat. "I guess I just said I'm sorry you didn't stay aboard." He dipped his head to Fletch. "Can I have a drink sent to your room?"

"No, that's all right." Fletch stood up from the bar stool.

He looked at Junior, closely, through the dark of the bar.

"As a matter of fact, Walt." Fletch put his hands in his trouser pockets. "I would like you to send a drink to my room." He drawled, "I'd appreciate it. Room 79." He spoke slowly, softly, deliberately. "A couple of gin and tonics. Room 79. Okay? I'd appreciate it. Room 79."

Fletch wasn't sure how well Junior was hearing him, if at all.
"Thanks, Walt."

TWENTY-ONE

From TAPE
Station 8
Suite 8 (Oscar Perlman)

". . . Yeah."

"May I say, Mister Perlman, how much my wife enjoys your columns."

"Fuck your wife."

"Sir?" Captain Neale said.

"Fuck your wife. It's always, 'My wife likes your columns.' " Clearly,
Oscar Perlman was talking through a well-chewed cigar. "Everytime
I do anything, a book, a play, it's always, 'My wife likes it.' I go to a
party and try to get the topic of conversation off me and my work,
because I know what to expect already. I say, 'What did you think of
Nureyev last night at the National Theater?' 'My wife liked it.' Always,
'My wife liked it.' You saw the latest Bergman? 'My wife liked it.' What
about Neil Diamond's latest record — isn't it somethin' else? 'My wife
liked it.' You read the new Joe Gores novel? 'My wife . . .' What about
King Lear these days? 'My wife says it's chauvinistic. The father expects
something.' Always, 'My wife liked it, didn't like it.' What are the
American men, a bunch of cultural shits? Always what the wife likes.
The men don't have eyes, ears, and a brain? What'sa matter with you?
You can't say you like my column? It's feminine to like my column?
Will your chest suck up your hair and push it out your asshole if you
say you like something other than hockey, boxing, and other nose-
endangering sports?"

"Mister Perlman, I am just a normal veteran. . . ."

"You do fuck your wife, don't you?"

"I have never met such a bunch of strange, eccentric, maybe sick
people . . ."

"Does she say she likes it?"

"Mister Perlman . . ."

"Do you believe everything your wife says? Who should believe everything his wife says anyway? Why don't you say you enjoy my column? I work just for wives? Fred Waring worked for wives. And look at him. He invented Mixmasters. No, he invented Waring blenders. Maybe there's a man who's pleased to have everybody come up to him saying, 'My wife likes your work.' He sold plenty of Waring blenders. Jesus Christ, why don't you just shut up and sit down.

"I have a terrible feeling I've just blown a column on you," Oscar Perlman said. "So already you owe me seventeen thousand dollars. Relax. You want a cigar? Play cards? A little up and down? I don't drink, but there's plenty stuff around.

"Christ. I just blew a column. How's your wife? I'm supposed to be here enjoying. I'm not. I lost twelve hundred bucks last night. These little shits from Dallas. St. Louis. Oof. Twelve hundred bucks. What? You don't want a drink? These cards are dirty. They took twelve hundred from me."

"Mister Perlman, any time you're ready to answer some questions . . ."

"Shoot. So old Walter March got it up-the. Never was up-the more deserved. Everybody else 'round here is writing about it. To me, it isn't funny yet. Make it funny for me. I'll appreciate."

"Mister Perlman!"

"Don't shout at me, you backwater, egg-sucking cop. You've cost me a column already. You were a veteran?"

"Listen. I know you journalists are in the business of asking questions. I'm in the business of asking questions. I'm going to ask the questions. Is that clear?"

"Jesus. He's getting hysterical. You don't play cards at all? You should. Very relaxing."

"Mister Perlman, you used to work for Walter March?"

"Years ago. I worked on one of his newspapers. Twenty-five years ago. Most of the people here at this convention worked for March, one time or another. Why ask me?"

"I'm asking the questions."

"That's not a question."

"You first wrote your humorous column on his newspaper?"

"You say it's humorous? Thank you."

"You first developed your column on his newspaper."

"That's not a question, either, but the answer is yes."

"Then you took the column you had developed on one of March's newspapers — the one in Washington — and sold it to a national syndicate?"

"International. Wives all over the world like my column."

"Why did you walk out on Walter March and sell your column to another syndicate?"

"I'm supposed to starve because the man didn't have a sense of humor? Even his wife didn't have a sense of humor. He refused to syndicate my column even through his own newspaper chain. I gave him enough time. Two, three years."

"Is it true he helped you develop your column?"

"Is it true trees grow upside down? 'It's true,' the dairy maid said, 'if you're always lying on your back.' He allowed the column to run. Irregularly. Usually cut in half. On the obituary page. From his encouragement, I could have had a free funeral, I was so big with the local undertakers."

"And after you went with the syndicate, he sued you, is that true?"

"He didn't win the suit. You can't sue talent."

"But he did sue you."

"You can't sue talent and win. He was laughed out of court. The judge's wife had a sense of humor."

"And then, what?"

Oscar Perlman repeated, "And then, what?"

"Mrs. March says the antagonism between you two has kept up all these years."

"Old Lydia's fingering me, uh? That lady's got sharp nails."

"Has the antagonism between you kept up all these years?"

"How could it? We've had nothing to do with each other. He's been running his newspapers; I've been writing my column."

"Someone told me March never gave up trying to force you to run your column in his newspapers."

"Who told you that?"

"Well, actually, Stuart Poynton."

"Nice guy. Did he get my name right?"

"I was wondering about that. He kept calling you 'Oscar Worldman.' "

"Sounds about right."

"Did you change your name?"

"No. Poynton did. He changes everybody's name. He's a walking justice of the peace."

"Please answer the question, Mister Perlman."

"Did March continue to want my column to run in his newspapers?

Well, in most areas, as things worked out, my column ran in newspapers competing with his. I attract a few readers. Yes, I guess the
matter would continue to be of some importance to him."

"What was the nature of Walter March's, let's say, effort to get your
column back in the March Newspapers."

"You tell me."

"Mister Perlman . . ."

"No one's pinned anything on me since I was a baby. That's an old
line, I'm ashamed to say."

"Are you aware that Walter March kept a large number of private
detectives on his payroll?"

"Who told you that?"

"You journalists are mighty particular about pinning down the sources
of every statement, aren't you?"

"Who told you?"

"Rolly Wisham, for one."

"Rolly? Nice kid."

"Were you aware of Mister March's private detectives, Mister Perlman?"

"If they were any good as private detectives I wouldn't be aware of
them, would I?"

"Did Walter March ever try to blackmail you?"

"How? There's absolutely nothing in my life I could be blackmailed
about. My life is as clean as a Minnesota kitchen."

There was a pause.

Stretched out on his bed, Fletch had closed his eyes.

Finally, Captain Neale said, "Where were you Monday morning at
eight o'clock?"

"In my bedroom. Sleeping."

"You were in the corridor, outside the March's suite."

"I was not."

"You were seen there."

"I couldn't have been."

"Mister Perlman, Mrs. March has given us a very detailed description
of running through the open door of her suite, seeing you in the
corridor, walking away, lighting a cigar, running toward you for help,
recognizing you, then running past you to bang on the door of the
Williamses' suite."

"She was upset. She could have seen green zebras at that point."

"You don't remember seeing Lydia March at eight o'clock Monday
morning?"

"Not even in my dreams. Captain Neale, we played poker until five-thirty in the morning. I slept until eleven, eleven-thirty."

"Is there anyone here you know of Mrs. March could confuse with you?"

"Robert Redford didn't come to this convention."

"You're willing to swear you were not in the corridor outside the March's suite about eight o'clock Monday morning?"

"Lydia March would be a totally unreliable witness about what or whom she saw at that moment in time."

"Is that what you're relying on, Mister Perlman?"

"You want to know who killed Walter March? I'll tell you who killed Walter March. Stuart Poynton killed Walter March. He was trying to kill Lewis Graham, only he got the names and room numbers mixed up."

TWENTY-TWO

4:30 P.M.
THE BIG I: ADVOCACY JOURNALISM —
RIGHT OR WRONG AND WHO SAYS SO?
Seminar
Conservatory

Fletch was kneeling, shoving his marvelous machine back under the bed, when he heard the glass door to the pool area slide open.

He dropped the edge of the bedspread to the floor.

He hadn't realized the sliding glass door was unlocked.

He heard Crystal's voice. "Now I've got the Fletch story to cap all Fletch stories! Tousle-headed Fletch kneeling by his bed, lisping, 'Now I lay me down with sheep'!"

Crystal was in the doorway, her fat twice banded by a black bikini.

"I met a Methodist minister on the airplane the other day." He stood up. "Twelve thousand meters up he taught me to sing 'Nearer, My God, to Thee.'"

He had never seen so much restrained by so little before.

"I'm cold," she said. "My room's way the other side of the hotel. May I use your shower?"

"Of course."

Her skin was beautiful. All of it.

Walking across the room her fat shook so it looked as if it would plop to the floor in handfuls.

"That idiot, Stuart Poynton," she said. "Had me standing waist-deep in the pool a half-hour, talking, trying to get me to do legwork for him."

"Legwork?"

"On the Walter March murder. Someone told Poynton I'm unemployed."

She left the bathroom door open.

"Did you agree?"

"I told him I'd work for *Pravda* first."

"Why did you listen?"

Nude, she was adjusting the shower curtain. Even reaching up, her belly hung down.

"Find out if he knew anything. He had some big story about the desk clerk being afraid March was going to get him fired for being rude to Mrs. March, so he grabbed the desk scissors, let himself into March's suite with the master key, and ventilated Walter March as he stood."

Fletch said, "Where does Poynton get stupid stories like that?"

Crystal stepped into the tub, behind the shower curtain.

"Oh, well," he said.

Fletch stripped and went into the bathroom.

He held the shower curtain aside and said, "Room for two of us in here? Watch where you step."

Under the shower, Crystal's body created the most remarkable cascade.

"Did you bring a sandwich?" she asked. "Anything to eat?"

"Young lady, if it's the last thing I do — and it may be — I am going to teach you to not make disparaging remarks about yourself."

"Nothing to eat, uh?"

"I didn't say that."

"Oh, I've never gone for these high-protein diets."

"Obviously. Repeat after me. I will never insult myself again."

" 'I will never insult . . .' yipes!"

When they fell sideways out of the tub, the shower curtain and the bar holding it came with them.

On the bathroom floor, they tried to unwrap themselves from the shower curtain. Part of it was under them, on the floor.

"Goddamn it," he said. "You're on my leg. My left leg!"

"I don't feel a thing," she said.

"I do! I do! Get off!"

"I can't. The shower curtain . . ."

"Jesus, will you get off my leg! Christ, I think you broke it."

"What do you mean, I broke it? Men are supposed to take some responsibility for situations like this."

"How can I take responsibility when I'm pinned to the floor?"

"You're no good to me pinned to the floor."

"Will you get off my damned leg?"

"Get the shower curtain off me!"

"How can I get the shower curtain off? I can't move."

The shower curtain was yanked, pulled, lifted off from the top.

Fredericka Arbuthnot stood there in tan culottes and a blouse, shower curtain in hand.

Fletch said, "Oh, hi, Freddie."

"Nice to see you, Fletch. Finally."

"Thanks."

Crystal had rolled off him.

Freddie said, "You make a very noisy neighbor."

She dropped the shower curtain, and left.

Fletch was sitting up, feeling up and down his left leg with his fingers.

Face down on the floor, Crystal said, "Did I break it?"

"You didn't break anything."

"You really turn her on, you know?"

"Who?"

"Freddie."

Fletch said, "A bush in the hand . . ."

TWENTY-THREE

6:00 P.M. Cocktails
Amanda Hendricks Room

"Did you have a nice shower?" Freddie asked.

"Thanks for rescuing us. Quite an impasse."

"Oh, any time. Really, Fletch, you ought to wear a whistle around your neck, for situations of that sort."

In the Amanda Hendricks Room, Fletch stood with a Chivas Regal and a soda in hand, Freddie with a vodka gimlet.

Since he had entered the room, Leona Hatch had been eyeing him curiously.

"And," asked Freddie, "do you always sing at play?"

"Was I singing?"

"Something of doubtful appropriateness. I believe it was 'Nearer, My God, to Thee.' "

"No, no. For Crystal, I was singing, 'Nearer, *my God!* to thee.' "

"Such a happy child."

Leona Hatch swayed over to Fletch and said, "Don't I know you?"

She would make it to dinner tonight, but just barely.

"My name's Fletcher." He put out his hand. "I. M. Fletcher."

Leona took his hand uncertainly. "I don't recognize the name," she said. "But I'm sure I know you from somewhere."

"I've never worked in Washington."

"Maybe on one of the presidential campaigns?"

"I've never covered one."

"Funny," she said. "I have the feeling I know you very well."

"You probably do," muttered Freddie. "You probably do."

Don Gibbs and another man appeared behind Leona Hatch.

Gibbs' face was highly flushed.

"Fletcher, old man!"

Almost knocking Leona Hatch over — in fact, knocking her hat askew — Don Gibbs, drink in hand, made a clumsy effort to embrace Fletch's shoulders.

"Ha, ha!" Fletch said. "Ha, ha!"

They remained standing in a circle while Fletch looked into his glass and remained quiet.

Don Gibbs, his face highly decorated with smiles, finally said, "Well, Fletch, aren't you going to introduce us?"

Still looking into his glass, Fletch shrugged. "Oh, I'm sure you all know each other."

He looked up in time to see an odd flicker in Fredericka Arbuthnot's left eye.

Leona was resettling her hat on her head at a completely wrong angle.

"Well, I don't know who they are. Who the hell are they?"

"Oh, Ms. Hatch, I'm sorry," Fletch said. "This is Donald Gibbs. And this is Robert Englehardt. They work for the Central Intelligence Agency. Ms. Leona Hatch."

Gibbs' smile sank down his face, his neck, and disappeared somewhere beneath his shirt collar.

Englehardt, a large man in a loose brown suit, turned white all over his bald head.

Freddie said, "You have the CIA on the brain."

Fletch shrugged again. "And frankly, Ms. Hatch, I have no idea who this young lady is."

Englehardt stepped forward and grabbed Leona's free hand in his paw.

"Delighted to meet you, Ms. Hatch. Mister Gibbs and I are observers at your convention. We're from the Canadian press. We're planning a convention of our own, next year, in Ontario. . . ."

"You don't sound Canadian," she said.

"Pip," said Gibbs. "Pip, pip, pip."

"Pop," said Fletch. "Pup."

"See what I mean?" asked Leona. "Since when have Canadians said 'pip'?"

Englehardt, the top of his bald head dampish, gave Fletch a killing look.

"And you pronounced the word 'observers' wrong, too." Leona Hatch shook her arm. "Mister, you're hurting my hand."

"Oh, I'm sorry."

Englehardt not only released her hand, but, in doing so, took a step backward, thus tipping Leona Hatch a little forward.

This time, she caught herself.

She said, "A Canadian would have said, 'I *am* sorry,' with the stress on the '*am*.' A Canadian never would have contracted 'I' and '*am*' in that sentence under those circumstances."

Don Gibbs had taken several steps backward. He continued to look as if tons of lava were flowing toward him.

Freddie said, "Ms. Hatch, I'm Fredericka Arbuthnot. I work for *Newsworld* magazine."

"Nonsense," sniffed Leona. "No one works for *Newsworld* magazine."

"Ah, here's the beautiful young couple!" Arms extended to embrace the whole world, Helena Williams entered the group. "Hello, Leona. Everything all right?"

Helena looked at Gibbs and Englehardt curiously.

They took several more steps backward.

"Fletch and uh . . ." She was looking at Freddie. "I forget your name."

"So does she," said Fletch.

"Fredericka Arbuthnot," she said. "For short, you may call me Ms. Blake."

"You know, Leona, I offered these young people the Bridal Suite. But they insist they're not married! What's the world coming to?"

"Great improvement," said Leona Hatch. "Great improvement."

Fletch said, "Helena, I haven't seen Jake around much."

"Well, you know. He's trying to spend as much time with Junior as he can. And with Walter gone . . . Well, someone has to make the decisions. Junior isn't quite up to it yet." She gave the back of her hair a push. "I'm afraid Jake isn't enjoying this convention, much. None of us is, I suppose."

"In case I don't see Jake, be sure and say hello to him for me," Fletch said.

Helena put her arms out again, to flap to another group. "I surely will, Fletch."

There was a hoarse whisper in Fletch's right ear. "What the hell do you think you're doing?"

Fletch turned, to face Don Gibbs and Robert Englehardt.

He said, "Have you ever tried to lie to someone like Leona Hatch?"

"She's crocked," Gibbs said.

"Have you ever tried to lie to someone like Leona Hatch — even when she's crocked?"

Englehardt was looking exceedingly grim.

"She'd pin your wings to a board in one minute flat," Fletch said. "In fact, if you noticed, that's exactly what she did do."

Crystal Faoni came through a crowd to them, casting quite a bow wave.

"Ms. Crystal Faoni," Fletch intoned, "allow me to introduce you to Mister Robert Englehardt and Mister Donald Gibbs, both of the Central Intelligence Agency."

Englehardt's eyes closed and opened slowly.

Gibbs's sweaty upper lip was quivering.

Crystal said, "Hi." She turned to Fletch. "I stayed in my room to watch Lewis Graham on the evening news show. You know what he did?"

"You tell me."

"He did a ninety-second editorial on the theme that people should retire when they say they're going to, regardless of how much they have to give up, using Walter March as an example."

"We wrote that for him at lunch," Fletch said.

"I think we can say we contributed to it."

"Did he use the same biblical quotes?"

"Identical."

"Well," said Fletch, "at least one always knows Lewis Graham's sources. May I escort you to the dining room, Ms. Faoni?"

"Oh, goody! Will we be the first ones there? I so like having a perfect record, at the things I do."

"Ms. Faoni," Fletch said, crossing through the cocktail party, her arm in his. "I've just figured something out."

"Who murdered Walter March?"

"Something much more important than that."

"What could be more important than that?"

"The reverse. Death in the presence of life; life in the presence of death."

Crystal said, "Funny the way riddles have always made me hungry."

"Crystal, darling, this afternoon you were trying to get pregnant."

Immediately, she said, "Think we succeeded?"

"Oh, Lord."

"If you remember, I always was very good at math."

They were in the dining room.

"Crystal, sit down."

"Oh, nice. He's taking care of me already." She sat in the chair he held out for her. "Not to worry, Fletcher."

"I promise."

"There's just no way I can be unemployed nine months from now. Good heavens! I'd starve!"

He was sitting next to her, at the empty, round table. "Crystal, you lost a job before, this way. It's an unfair world. You said yourself nothing has changed."

"Oh, yes, it has," she said. "Walter March is dead."

TWENTY-FOUR

7:30 P.M. Dinner
Main Dining Room

"Frankly, I think you're all being dreadfully unfair." Eleanor Earles put her napkin next to her coffee cup. "I've never heard so many spiteful, vicious remarks about one man in all my life as I've heard about Walter March since coming here to Hendricks Plantation."

Fletch was at the round table for six with three women — Eleanor Earles, Crystal Faoni, and, of course, Freddie Arbuthnot. No Robert McConnell. No Lewis Graham.

"You all act and talk like a bunch of nasty children in a reformatory, gloating because the biggest boy among you got knifed, rather than like responsible, concerned journalists and human beings."

Crystal burped.

"What have we said?" asked Freddie.

In fact, their conversation had been fairly neutral, mostly concerning the arrival of the Vice-President of the United States the next afternoon, discussing who would play golf with him (Tom Lockhart, Richard Baldridge, and Sheldon Levi; Oscar Perlman had invited him to a strip poker party to prove he had nothing to hide) and whether his most attractive wife would accompany him.

Freddie had just mentioned the memorial service for Walter March to be held in Hendricks the next morning.

"Oh, it's not you." Eleanor looked resentfully around the dining room. "It's all these other twerps."

Eleanor Earles was a highly paid network newsperson, attractive enough, but resented by many because she had done commercials while working for another network — which most journalists refused to do — and, despite that, now had one of the best jobs in the industry.

Many felt she would not have been able to overcome her background and be so elevated if she had not been seized upon by the networks as their token woman.

Nevertheless, she was extremely able.

"Walter March," she said, "was an extraordinary journalist, an extraordinary publisher, and an extraordinary human being."

"He was extraordinary all right," Crystal said into her parfait.

"He had a great sense of news, of the human story, of trends, how to handle a story. His editorial sense was almost flawless. And when March Newspapers came out for or against something, it was seldom wrong. I doubt Walter March was ever wrong."

"Oh, come now," Fletch said.

"What about the way he handled people?" Crystal asked. "What about the way he treated his own employees?"

"Let me tell you," Eleanor said. "I would have considered it a privilege to work for Walter March. Any time, any place, under any circumstances."

"You never worked for him," Crystal said.

Eleanor said, "You know about the time I was stuck in Albania —
when I was working for the other network?"

Fletch remembered, vaguely, an incident several years before —
one of those three-day wonder stories — concerning Eleanor Earles
in a foreign land. He was a teenager when it happened. It was the
first he had ever heard of Eleanor Earles.

"It was just one of those terribly frightening things." Eleanor sat
forward, her hands folded slightly below her chin. "I and a producer,
Sarah Pulling, had spent five days in Albania, shooting one of those
in-country, documentary-type features for the network. Needless to
say, we'd had to use an Albanian film crew, and, needless to say, we
could film only what they wanted us to, when they wanted us to, and
how they wanted us to. However, getting any film, any story out of
Albania was considered a coup; it had taken months of diplomatic
back-and-forth. Of course they had to accept me as an on-camera
person, and I figured if I kept my eyes and ears open I'd be able to
add plenty of material and additional comments to the sound track
once we got back to New York.

"Despite their ordering us this way and that and putting us up in
their best hotel, which had the ambience of a chicken coop, I think
they tried to be kind to us. They offered us so much food and drink
so continuously, Sarah said she was sure it was their way of preventing
us from doing any work at all.

"So things went along fairly well, under the circumstances. We
hadn't much control over what we had on film, but we knew we had
something.

"The night we were leaving, we packed up and were driven to the
airport by some of the people who had been assigned to be our hosts
and work with us. It was all very jolly. There were even hugs and
kisses at the airport before they left us to wait for the plane.

"Then we were arrested.

"After we had gone through all the formalities of leaving Albania,
most of which we didn't even understand, and were actually at the
gate, ready to board, two men approached us, took us out of the line,
said nothing until everyone else had passed us boarding the plane,
until all the airlines personnel had gone about other business — all
those eyes carefully averted from the two American women standing
silent and somewhat scared with two Albanian bulldogs.

"After everyone had left, they took us by our elbows, marched us
through the airport, and into a waiting car.

"We were brought back into the city, stripped, searched, dressed in sort of short, loose cotton housedress kinds of things that allowed us to freeze, and put in individual, rank, filthy jail cells. Fed those things that look like whole wheat biscuits in pans of cold water, three a day, for three days. No one official ever saw us. No one spoke to us. We were never questioned. Our protests and efforts to get help, get something official happening, got us nowhere. The people who brought us our biscuits and removed our pails just shrugged and smiled sweetly.

"Three days of this. Have you ever been in such circumstances? It's an unreasonable thing. And you find yourself reasoning if they can do it for a day, they can do it for a month. Two days, why not a year? Three days, why not keep you in jail the rest of your life?

"I was sure the network would be yelling at the State Department, and the State Department doing whatever one does under such circumstances and, yes, all that was happening. It was a big news item in the United States and Europe. The network made plenty of hay out of it. They pulled their hair and gnashed their teeth on camera; they made life miserable for several people at the State Department. However, they didn't do whatever was necessary under the circumstances to get us out of jail.

"The afternoon of the fourth day, two men showed up in the corridor between Sarah's and my cells. One of them was an Albanian national. The other was the chief of the Rome bureau of March Newspapers. You know what he said? He said, 'How're ya doin'?'

"Someone unlocked our cells. The two men walked us out of the building, without a word to anyone, and put us, shivering, filthy, stinking into the backseat of a car.

"At the airport the two men shook hands.

"The March Newspapers bureau chief sat in the seat behind us, on the way to Rome, never saying a word.

"At the airport in Rome, all the other passengers were steered into Customs. An Italian policeman took the three of us through a different door, into a reception area, and there, seated in one chair, working from an open briefcase in another chair, was Walter March.

"I had never met him before.

"He glanced up when we came in, got up slowly, closed his briefcase, took it in one hand, and said, 'All right?'

"He drove us into a hotel in Rome, made sure we were checked in, saw us to a suite, and then left us.

"An hour later, we were overcome by our own network people.

"He must have called them, and told them where we were.

"I didn't see Walter March again for years. I sent him many full messages of gratitude, I can tell you, but I was never sure if any got through to him. I never had a response.

"When I finally did meet him, at a reception in Berlin, you know what he said? He said, 'What? Someone was impersonating me in Rome? That happens.'"

Freddie said, "Nice story."

Crystal said, "It brings a tear to my eye."

"Saintly old Walter March," Fletch said. "I've got to go, if you'll all excuse me."

During dinner he had received a note, delivered by a bellman, written on hotel stationery, with *Mr. I. Fletcher* on the envelope, which read: "Dear Fletch — Didn't realize you were here until I saw your name in McConnell's piece in today's Washington paper. Please come see me as soon after dinner as you can — Suite 12. Lydia March."

He had shown the note to no one. (Crystal had expressed curiosity by saying, "For someone unemployed, you sure get interrupted at meals a lot. No wonder you're slim. When you're working, you must never get to eat.")

Eleanor Earles said, "I take it you've worked for Walter March?"

"I have," said Crystal.

"I have," said Fletch.

Freddie smiled, and said, "No."

"And he was tough on you?" Eleanor asked.

"No," said Crystal. "He was rotten to me."

Fletch said nothing.

Eleanor said, to both of them, "I suspect you deserved it."

TWENTY-FIVE

9:00 P.M.

THERE'S A TIME AND A PLACE FOR HUMOR:
WASHINGTON, NOW
Address by Oscar Perlman

The door to Suite 12 was opened to Fletch by Jake Williams, notebook and pen in hand, looking drawn and harassed.

"Fletcher!"

They shook hands warmly.

Lydia, in a pearl-gray house gown, was standing across the living room, several long pieces of yellow Teletype paper in one hand, reading glasses in the other.

Her pale blue eyes summed up Fletch very quickly and not unkindly.

"Nice to see you again, Fletch," she said.

Fletch was entirely sure they had never met before.

"We'll be through in one minute," she said. "Just some things Jake has to get off tonight." Leaving Fletch standing there, she put her glasses on her nose and began working through the Teletype sheets, talking to Jake. "I don't see any reason why we have to run this San Francisco story from A.P. Can't our own people in San Francisco work up a story for ourselves?"

"It's a matter of time," Jake said, making a note.

"Poo," said Lydia. "The story isn't going to die in six hours."

"Six hours?"

"If our people can't come up with our own story on this within six hours, then we need some new staff in San Francisco, Jake."

"Mrs. March?" Fletch said.

She looked at him over the frame of her glasses.

"May I use your john?"

"Of course." She pointed with her glasses. "You have to go through the bedroom."

"Thank you."

When he came back to the living room she was sitting on the divan, demitasse service on the coffee table in front of her, not a piece of paper, not even her glasses, in sight.

She said, "Sit down, Fletch."

He sat in a chair across the table from her.

"Has Jake left?"

"Yes. He has a lot to do. Would you care for some coffee?"

"I don't use it."

He was wondering if his marvelous machine was picking up their conversation. He supposed it was.

He wondered what Mrs. March would say if he began singing Gordon Lightfoot's "The Wreck of the *Edmund Fitzgerald*," as he had promised the machine he would.

"Fletch, I understand you're not working."

She was pouring herself coffee.

"On a book."

"Oh, yes," she said. "The journalist's pride. Whenever a journalist hasn't got a job, he says he's working on a book. How many times have I heard it? Sometimes, of course, he is. What's keeping the wolf from the door?"

"My ugly disposition."

She smiled, slightly. "I've heard so much about you, from one source or another. You were one of my husband's favorite people. He loved to tell stories about you."

"I understand people like to tell outrageous stories about me. I've heard one only lately. Highly imaginative."

"I think you and my husband were very much alike."

"Mrs. March, I met with your husband for five minutes one day, in his office. It was not a successful meeting, for either of us."

"Of course not. You were too much alike. He had a lot of brashness, you know. Whenever he was presented with alternatives, he always thought up some third course of action no one else had considered. That's about what you do, isn't it?"

Instead of saying "Yes" or "No," Fletch said, "Maybe."

"My point is this, Fletch. Walter is dead."

"I'm sorry I didn't say you have my sympathy."

"Thank you. March Newspapers will need a lot of help. Everything now falls on Junior's shoulders. He's every bit the man his father was, of course, even better, in many ways, but . . ." She fitted her coffee cup to its saucer. ". . . This death, this murder . . ."

"It must be a great shock to Junior."

"He's lived so much in his father's . . . They were great friends."

"Mrs. March, I'm a working stiff. I'm a reporter. I know how to get a story and maybe how to write it. In a pinch I can work on a copydesk. I know a good layout when I see one. I know nothing about the publishing side of this business, how you attract advertising and what it costs per line, how you finance a newspaper, buy machinery. . . ."

"Junior does. He's really very good at the back room mechanics of this business." She poured herself more coffee. "Fletch, this is very much a horse-and-wagon sort of business. The horse has to be in front of the wagon. What a newspaper looks like and how it reads is the horse, and the wagon it pulls is the advertising and whatnot. If a newspaper isn't exciting and important, you can have all the clever people in the world in the back room and it won't work out as a business."

"There's Jake Williams. . . ."

"Oh, Jake." She let her hand flop, in disparagement. "Jake is sort of old, and worn-out."

Jake Williams was a good twenty years younger than Lydia March.

"What I'm asking you, Fletch is: would you help Junior out? He has a terribly tough row to hoe just now. . . ."

"I doubt he'd want me to."

"Why do you say that?"

"I bumped into him in the bar this afternoon, and we had a little chat."

"The bar, the bar!" Her face was annoyed and pained. "Really, Junior's got to pull up his socks, and very soon."

"He seems to have some ambivalent feelings toward me."

"Junior doesn't know what he feels at the moment. He's keeping himself as drunk as he can. To be frank, I suppose a little bit of that is understandable, under the circumstances. But, really, becoming totally inoperable . . ."

"I think he's afraid."

Her eyes opened wide. "Afraid?"

"I never really had a sense of how much your husband was doing — and how he was doing it — until I came to this convention and started hearing the gossip. Your husband's death was pretty ugly."

Lydia fitted her back into the corner of the divan and stared at the floor.

The lady had much to think about.

"Mrs. March, more than five years ago, your husband announced his retirement. Publicly. All the newspapers carried it. Why didn't he retire?"

"Oh, you heard Lewis Graham tonight. On television."

"I heard about it."

"What a pompous ass. You know, he ran against my husband last year for the presidency of the A.J.A. So he takes all the resentment and hatred he has for my husband, and turns it into ninety seconds of philosophical network pablum."

"Why didn't your husband retire when he said he was going to?"

"You don't know?"

"No."

She was sitting up, looking uneasy. "It was because of that stupid union thing Junior did."

Fletch said, "I still don't know."

"Well, a huge union negotiation was coming up, and Junior thought he'd be clever. Our board of directors had been putting pressure on him for some years, you know, saying they thought he had led too sheltered a life, was too naive. They thought all he wanted was to do his day's work and go home at five o'clock to his wife. Of course, that was before she left him. They insisted he travel more, and, of course he did take that trip to the Far East. . . ."

Fletch remembered that Junior had filed a dispatch from Hong Kong which began, "There are a lot of Chinese . . . ," and every March newspaper printed it on the front page, faithfully, just to make the son of the publisher look ridiculous, which he did.

". . . So I guess Junior wanted to show his father and the board of directors that he had some ideas of his own, could operate in what he thought was a manly manner. Even Walter, my husband, thought the negotiations were going too smoothly. Even points brought up by our side as negotiating points were being accepted, almost without discussion. Of course, some of the union members smelled a rat and began nosing around. Don't you know about this? Walter did his best to keep it quiet. I guess he succeeded. It was discovered that Junior had invested in a large bar-restaurant with the president of the labor union. Well, he had advanced the man the down payment and had accepted a first and second mortgage on the place. Obviously, the union president hadn't contributed a damn thing. Junior thought it was all right, because he had done it out of personal money, not company funds. There was hell to pay, of course. The National Labor Relations Board got involved. There was talk of sending both Junior and the union man to jail. We lost one newspaper because of it — the one in Baltimore. There was no question Walter could leave under such circumstances. And, of course, a thing like that takes years to settle down."

Fletch's inner ear heard Lydia say, *He's every bit the man his father was, of course, even better, in many ways. . . .*

"We're all entitled to one mistake," Lydia said. "Junior's was a beaut. You see, Fletch, it was really the fault of the board of directors, for doubting Junior so. He felt he had to prove something. You do understand that, don't you, Fletch? You see, I think Junior needs a special kind of help. . . ."

Again, Lydia was sitting back on the divan, staring at the floor, clearly a very troubled person.

"Mrs. March, I think you and I should talk again, in a day or two. . . ."

"Yes, of course." With dignity, she stood up and put out her hand. "Of course, it is now when Junior most needs the help. . . ."

"Yes," Fletch said.

"And in reference to what you said" — Lydia continued to hold his hand — "Junior and I did speak about you tonight, at dinner. He agrees with me. He would like to see you involved in March Newspapers. I wish you'd talk with him more about it. When you can."

"Okay."

At the door, she said, "Thanks for coming up, Fletch. I'm sure you didn't mind missing Oscar Perlman's afterdinner speech. Think of the people down there in the dining room, laughing at that dreadful man. . . ."

TWENTY-SIX

10:00 P.M.

WOMEN IN JOURNALISM: Face It, Fellas —
Few Stories Take Nine Months to Finish
Group Discussion
Aunt Sally Hendricks Sewing Room

From TAPE
Station 4
Suite 9 (Eleanor Earles)

Eleanor Earles was saying, ". . . Thought I'd go to bed."

"I brought champagne."

"That's nice of you, Rolly, but really, it is late."

"Since when is ten o'clock late?" asked Rolly Wisham. "You're showing your age, Eleanor."

"You know I just got back from Pakistan Sunday."

"No, I didn't know."

"I did."

"How are things in Pakistan?"

"Just dreadful."

"Things are always dreadful in Pakistan."

"Rolly, what do you want?"

"What do you think I want? When a man comes calling at ten o'clock at night, bearing a bottle of champagne . . ."

"A very young man."

"Eleanor, darling, 'This is Rolly Wisham, with love. . . .' "

"Very funny, you phony."

"Eleanor. You're forgetting Vienna."

"I'm not forgetting Vienna, Rolly. That was very nice."

"It was raining."

"Rain somehow turns me on."

"Shall I run the shower?"

"Honestly, Rolly! Look, I'm tired, and I'm upset about Walter. . . ."

"Big, great Walter March. Sprung you for bail once, in Albania. And what have you been doing for him ever since?"

"Knock it off, twerp."

"How come everyone in the world is a twerp? Except one old bastard named Walter March?"

"Okay, Rolly, I know you've got all kinds of resentments against Walter because of what happened to your dad's newspaper, and all."

"Not resentment, Eleanor. He killed my father. Can you understand? Killed him. He didn't make the rest of my mother's life any string symphony, either. Or mine. The word 'resentment' is an insult, Eleanor."

"It all happened a long time ago, in Oklahoma. . . ."

"Colorado."

". . . And you know only your side of the story. . . ."

"I have the facts, Eleanor."

"If you have facts, Rolly, why didn't you ever go to court with them? Why haven't you ever printed the facts?"

"I was a kid, Eleanor."

"You've had plenty of time."

"I'll print the facts. One day. You'd better believe it. Shall I open the champagne?"

"No."

"Oh, come on, Eleanor. The old bastard's dead."

"Did you kill him, Rolly?"

"Did I murder Walter March?"

"That's the question. If you want to be intimate with me, you can answer an intimate question."

"The question you asked was: Did I murder Walter March?"

"That's the question. What's the answer?"

"The answer is: maybe." There was the pop of the champagne bottle cork, and the immediate sound of its being poured.

"Really, Rolly."

"Here's to your continued health, Eleanor, your success, and your love life."

"You don't take a hint very easily."

"Not bad champagne. For domestic."

"What is it you really want, Rolly? We can't duplicate Vienna in the rain in Hendricks, Virginia, with an air conditioner blasting."

"Let's talk about Albania."

"That's even worse. I don't like to talk about Albania."

"But you do. You talk about Albania quite a lot."

"Well, it made me famous, that incident. You know that. The network took damn good care of me after that. And damn well they should have. The twerps."

"I've never believed your story about Albania, Eleanor. Sorry. Journalistic skepticism. I'm a good journalist. Fact, I just got a good review from a people. More champagne? Suddenly you're being strangely unresponsive."

"I haven't anything to say."

"You mean, you haven't anything you've ever said."

"You came here to find out something. Right, Rolly? You came here for a story. Rolly Wisham, with love and a bottle of champagne. Well, there is no story, Rolly."

"Yes, there is, Eleanor. I wish you'd stop denying it. You've told the story so often, attributing what Walter March did for you to Walter March's goodness, you've blinded everybody to the simple, glaring fact that Walter March wasn't any good. He was a prick."

"Even a prick can do one or two good things, Rolly."

"Eleanor, I think you've just admitted something. I suspect I picked a fortunate metaphor."

"Get out of here, Rolly."

"Walter March had to have some reason for springing you out of Albania. He sent his own man in. His Rome bureau chief. You know what it must have cost him. Yet he never took credit for it. He didn't even scoop the story. He let our old network take the credit. Come on, Eleanor."

"Rolly. I'm going to say this once. If you don't get out of here, I'm going to call the police."

"The Hendricks, Virginia, police?"

"House security."

"Come on, Eleanor. Tell old Rolly."

"Jesus, I wish Walter had lived. He would have nailed you to the wall."

"Yes," Rolly Wisham said. "He would have. But he can't now. Can he, Eleanor? There are a lot of things he can't do now. Aren't there, Eleanor?"

A phone was ringing. Lying on his bed, half-asleep, Fletch wasn't sure whether the phone was ringing in Eleanor Earles's room, or his own.

"You're . . ."

"Shall I leave the champagne?"

"You know what to do with it."

"Good night, Eleanor."

It was Fletch's own phone ringing.

TWENTY-SEVEN

"Ye Olde Listening Poste," Fletch said.

He had sat up, on the edge of his bed, and thrown the switch on the marvelous machine before answering the phone.

"Hell, I've been trying to get you all night."

"You succeeded. Are you calling from Boston?"

How many hours, days, weeks, months of his life in total had Fletch had to listen to this man's voice on the phone?

"I've never known a switchboard to be so damned screwed up," Jack Saunders said. "It's easier to get through to the White House during a national emergency."

"There's a convention going on here. And the poor women on the switchboard have to work from only one room information sheet. Are you at the *Star*?"

Jack had been Fletch's city editor for more than a year at a newspaper in Chicago.

More recently, they had met in Boston, where Jack was working as night city editor for the *Star*.

Fletch had even done Jack the minor favor of working a desk for him one night in Boston during an arsonist's binge.

"Of course I'm at the *Star*. Would I be home with my god-awful wife if I could help it?"

"Ah," Fletch said. "The Continuing Romance of Jack and Daphne Saunders. How is the old dear?"

"Fatter, meaner, and uglier than ever."

"Don't knock fat."

"How can you?"

"Got her eyelashes stuck in a freezer's door lately?"

"No, but she plumped into a door the other night. Got the door knob stuck in her belly button. Had to have it surgically removed." Fletch thought Jack remained married to Daphne simply to make up rotten stories about her. "I saw in the Washington newspaper you're at the convention. Working for anyone?"

"Just the CIA."

"Yeah. I bet. If you're at a convention, you must be looking for a job. What's the matter? Blow all that money you ripped off?"

"No, but I'm about to."

"I figure you can give me some background on the Walter March murder."

"You mean the *Star* doesn't have people here at the convention?"

"Two of 'em. But if they weren't perfectly useless, we wouldn't have sent 'em."

"Ah, members of the great sixteen-point-seven percent."

"What?"

"Something a friend said."

"So how about it?"

"How about what?"

"Briefing me."

"Why?"

"How about 'old times' sake' as a reason?"

"So I can win another award and you not even tell me but go accept it yourself and make a nice, humble little speech lauding teamwork?"

Such had actually happened.

Saunders said, "I guess technically that would come under the heading of 'old times' sake' — in this instance."

"If I scoop the story, will you offer me a job?"

"I'll offer you a job anyway."

"That's not what I asked. If you get a scoop on this, will you make with a job?"

"Sure."

"Okay. You want background or gossip at this point?"

"Both."

"Walter March was murdered."

"No foolin'."

"Scissors in the back."

"Next you're going to say he fell down dead."

"You're always rushing ahead, Jack."

"Sorry."

"Take one point at a time."

" 'Walter March was murdered.' I've written it down. "

"He was murdered here at the convention, where everybody knows him, and a great many people hate him."

"He's the elected president."

"You know that Walter March kept a stable of private detectives on his permanent payroll?"

"Of course I do."

"His use of them has irritated many people — apparently given many people reason to murder him. In fact, if you believe what you hear around here, dear old saintly Walter March was blackmailing everybody this side of Tibet."

"Do you know whom he was blackmailing and why?"

"A few. He's been having Oscar Perlman followed and hounded for years and years now."

"Oscar Perlman? The humorist?"

"Used to work for March. His column got picked up by a syndicate, and has been running in March's competing newspapers ever since."

"That was a thousand years ago. "

"Nevertheless, he's been hounding Perlman ever since. "

"So why should Perlman stab March at this point, when he hasn't before?"

"I don't know. Maybe March's goons finally came up with something. "

"Oscar Perlman," Jack Saunders mused. "That would be an amusing trial. It would make great copy."

"Lydia March says she saw Perlman in the corridor outside their suite immediately after the murder. Walking away."

"Good. Let's stick Perlman. Anything for a laugh."

"None of this is printable, Jack."

"I know that. I'm the editor, remember? Daphne and all those ugly kids of mine to feed."

"Rolly Wisham hated Walter March with a passion. He has reason, I guess, but I think his hatred borders on the uncontrollable."

" 'Rolly Wisham, with love'?"

"The same. He says he was so upset at seeing March in the elevator Sunday night, he didn't sleep all night."

"What's his beef?"

"Wisham says that March, again using his p.i.'s, took the family newspaper away from Rolly's dad, and drove him to suicide."

"True?"

"How do I know? If it is true, it happened at a dangerous age for

Rolly — fifteen or sixteen — I forget which. Loves and hatreds run deep in people that age."

"I remember. Did Wisham have the opportunity? You said he was there Sunday night."

"Yeah, and he has no working alibi for Monday morning. He says he was driving around Virginia, in sunglasses, in a rented car. Didn't even stop at a gas station."

"Funny. 'This is Rolly Wisham, with love, and a scissors in Walter March's back.' "

"You know March was planning a coast-to-coast campaign to get Wisham thrown off the air?"

"Oh, yeah. I read that editorial. It was right. Wisham's a fuckin' idiot. The world's greatest practitioner of the sufferin'-Jesus school of journalism."

"Keep your conservative sentiments to yourself, Saunders. You've been off the street too long."

"Two good suspects. We'll start doing background on them both right away. Anyone else?"

"Remember Crystal Faoni?"

"Crystal? Petite Crystal? The sweetheart of every ice cream store? She used to work with us in Chicago."

"She tells me that once when she was pregnant without benefit of ceremony, March fired her on moral grounds. Crystal had no choice but to abort."

"That bastard. That prude. Walter March was the most self-righteous . . ."

"Yes and no," Fletch said.

"Well, I'll tell you, Fletch. Crystal has the intelligence and imagination to do murder, and get away with it."

"I know."

"I'd hate to have her as an enemy."

"Me too."

"I shiver at the thought. I'd rather have a boa constrictor in bed with me. This Captain Andrew Neale, who's running this investigation, what do you think of him?"

"He's no Inspector Francis Xavier Flynn."

"Sometimes I think Inspector Francis Xavier Flynn isn't, either."

Flynn was the only person working for the Boston Police Department with the rank of Inspector.

"I think Neale's all right," Fletch said. "He's working under enormous pressure here — the press all over the place — trying to interview

121

professional interviewers. He's under time pressure. He can keep us here only another twenty-four hours or so."

"Is there anyone else, Fletch, with motive and opportunity?"

"Probably dozens. Robert McConnell is here."

"McConnell. Oh, yeah. He was what's-his-face's press aide. Wanted to go with him to the White House."

"Yeah. And Daddy March endorsed the other candidate, coast-to-coast, which may have made the difference, gave Bob his job back, and sat him in a corner, where he remains to this day."

"Bob could do it."

"Murder?"

"Very sullen kind of guy anyway. Big sense of injustice. Always too quick to shove back, even when nobody's shoved him."

"I noticed."

"We'll do some b.g. on him, too. Who's this guy Stuart Poynton mentions in tomorrow's column?"

"Poynton mentions someone? The desk clerk?"

"I've got the wire copy here. He mentions someone named Joseph Molinaro."

"Never heard of him. I wonder what his name really is."

"I'll read it to you. 'In the investigation of the Walter March murder, local police will issue a national advisory Thursday that they wish to question Joseph Molinaro, twenty-eight, a Caucasian. It is not known that Molinaro was at the scene of the crime at the time the crime was committed. Andrew Neale, in charge of the investigation, would give no reason for the advisory.' Mean anything to you, Fletch?"

"Yeah. It means Poynton conned some poor slob into doing some legwork for him."

"Fletch, sitting back here in the ivory tower of the *Boston Star* . . ."

"If that's an ivory tower, I'm a lollipop."

"I can lick you anytime."

"Ho, ho."

"My vast brain keeps turning to Junior."

"As the murderer?"

"Walter March, Junior."

"I doubt it."

"Living under Daddy's thumb all his life . . ."

"I've talked with him."

"That was a very heavy thumb."

"I don't think Junior's that eager to step into the batter's box, if you get me. Mostly he seems scared."

"Scared he might get caught?"

"He's drinking heavily."

"He's been a self-indulgent drinker for years, now."

"I doubt he could organize himself enough."

"How much organization does it take to put a scissors in your daddy's back?"

Fletch remembered the stabbing motion Junior made, sitting next to him in the bar, and the insane look in his eyes as he did it.

Fletch said, "Maybe. Now, would you like to know who the murderer is?"

Jack Saunders chuckled. "No, thanks."

"No?"

"That night, during the Charlestown fires, you had it figured out the arsonist was a young gas station attendant who worked in a garage at the corner of Breed and Acorn streets and got off work at six o'clock."

"It was a good guess. Well worked-out."

"Only the arsonist was a forty-three-year-old baker deputized by Christ."

"We all goof up once in a while."

"I think I can stand the suspense on this one a little longer."

"Anyway, Christ hadn't told me."

"If you get a story, you'll call me?"

"Sure, Jack, sure. Anything for 'old times' sake.' "

TWENTY-EIGHT

From TAPE
Station 5
Suite 3 (Donald Gibbs and Robert Engelhardt)

"Snow, beautiful snow!"

From his voice, Fletch guessed Don had had plenty of something.

"Who'd ever expect snow in Virginia this time of year?"

Fletch couldn't make out what Engelhardt muttered.

"Who'd ever think my dear old department headie, Bobby Engelhardt, would travel through the South with snow in his attaché case? Good thing it didn't melt!"

Another unintelligible mutter from Engelhardt.

"Well, I've got a surprise for you, too, dear old department headie,"
Gibbs said. " 'What's that?' you ask with one voice. Well! I've got a
surprise for you! 'Member those two sweet little things in Billy-Bobby's
boo-boo-bar lounge? 'Sweet little things,' you say together. Well, sir,
I had the piss-pa-cacity to invite them up! To our glorious journalists'
suite. This very night! This very hour! This very minute! In fact, for
twenty minutes ago."

"You did?"

"I did. Where the hell are they? Got to live like journalists, right?
Wild, wild, wicked women! Live it up!"

"I invited someone, too." Engelhardt's voice sounded surprisingly
cautious.

"You did? We gonna have four broads? Four naked, writhing girls?
All in the same room?"

"The lifeguard," Engelhardt said.

"The lifeguard? Which lifeguard? The boy lifeguard? There weren't
any other type. I looked."

Engelhardt muttered something. There was a silence from Gibbs.

Then Engelhardt said, "What's the matter, Don? Don't you like a
change?"

"Jesus. Two girls and a boy. And us. For a fuck party. An orgy.
Bob . . ."

"Take it calm, Gibbs."

"Where's the bourbon? I want the bourbon. Back of my nose feels
funny."

The doorbell in the suite was ringing.

"And the Lord High Mayor ate pomegranates," Don Gibbs said.
"Surprising fellas, department heads. Lifeguards with snow on. Boy
lifeguards."

". . . Confront new situations," Engelhardt said. "Part of your training. Field training."

"Never saw anything about it in the manual."

Engelhardt said, "You can do it that way, too."

Fletch's own phone was ringing.

"Hello?"

He had turned the volume down on his machine.

It was Freddie Arbuthnot.

"Fletcher, I thought I'd be more subtle. Meet you for a swim? Or
have you about had it for today?"

"Are you in your room?"

"Yes."

"Can't you hear my tape recorder?"

"That's how I knew you were still awake."

"Then you should be able to figure out I'm working very hard. On my travel piece."

"By now, I think, you'd have said everything there is to say about Italy."

"You can never say enough about Italy. A gorgeous country filled with gorgeous people . . ."

"All work and no play . . ."

"Makes jack."

"Why don't you stop working, and come for a swim? We can have the pool all to ourselves."

"What time is it in your room?"

"Midnight. Twelve-thirty-five. What time is it in yours?"

"My dear young lady. Crystal Faoni got very cold in that pool during the mid-afternoon."

"And with all her insulation."

"She was chilled."

"I saw your efforts to warm her up."

"Now, if she got cold in mid-afternoon, what do you think might happen to us at half-past midnight?"

"We might get warmed up."

"You miss the point, Ms. Arbuthnot."

"The point is, Mister Fletcher, you shot your wad."

"The point is, Ms. Arbuthnot . . ."

She said, "And I thought you were healthy," and hung up.

There was a poker party, or the poker party, going on in Oscar Perlman's suite, a whacky tobacky party in Sheldon Levi's, silence in the Litwacks'; Leona Hatch was issuing her "Errrrrr's" regularly; Jake Williams was on the phone to a March newspaper in Seattle, sounding very tired (something about how to handle a story about a fistfight among major-league baseball players in a downtown cocktail lounge); in her room Mary McBain appeared to be all alone, crying; Charlie Stieg was in the last stages of a seduction scene with a slightly drunk unknown; Rolly Wisham and Norm Reid were tuned to the same late-night movie in their rooms; Tom Lockhart's room was silent.

Fletch switched back to Station 5, Suite 3.

"Switch!" Don Gibbs was shouting. "Everybody switch! Swish, swish, swish, I SAID!"

There was a considerable variety of background noises, some of which Fletch had difficulty identifying.

A girl's voice sang, "Snow, beautiful snow . . ."

"Everybody get your snow before it melts," Don Gibbs said.

There was the sound of a hard slap.

Engelhardt's voice, low and serious, said, "When I pay money, I want to get what I pay for."

"Cut that out," Gibbs said. "I said, 'Switch!' Everybody switch!"

A young man's voice said, "You're not paying for that, bastard."

"Switch! I said!"

Fletch listened long enough to make sure a second female voice was recorded by his marvelous machine.

Then Don Gibbs was saying, "Whee! We're living like journalists! Goddamn journalists. Goddamn that Fletch! Live like this alla time. Disgusting!"

Fletch put his marvelous machine on automatic, for Station 5, Suite 3, and took a shower.

TWENTY-NINE

Wednesday

The sun was up enough to have dissipated the dew and, after a long but gentle gallop, make Fletch hot enough to stop and pull off his T-shirt and wrap it around his saddle horn.

When he stopped to do so his eye caught the sun's reflection off a windshield between trees, up the side of a hill, so he rode to a point well behind the vehicle and then up through scrub pine level to it, where he found an old timber road. He rode back along it.

Coming around a curve in the road, he stopped.

A camper was parked in the road.

Behind it, lying on his back, blood coming from his mouth, was the man he had been looking for, the man the masseuse, Mrs. Leary, had mentioned, the man in the blue jeans jacket, the man with the tight, curly gray hair.

He was obviously unconscious.

Over him, on one knee, going through a wallet, now looking up at Fletch apprehensively, was none other than Frank Gillis.

Fletch said, "Good morning."

"Who are you?" Gillis asked.

"Name of Fletcher."

Gillis returned to his investigation of the wallet. "You work here?"

"No."

"What then? Staying at the hotel? Hendricks?"

"Yes."

"You a journalist?" There was a touch of incredulity in Gillis's voice.

"Off and on." Fletch wiped some sweat off his stomach. "You're Frank Gillis."

"You got it first guess."

For years, Frank Gillis had been traveling America finding and reporting those old, usually obscure stories of American history, character, odd incidents, individuals, which spoke of and to the hearts of the American people. During days when America had reason to doubt itself both abroad and at home, Gillis's features were a tonic which made Americans feel better about themselves, even if only for a few minutes, and, probably, during the nation's most trying days, did a lot, in their small way, to hold the nation together.

Fletch said, "And you just mugged somebody."

Gillis stood up and dropped the wallet on the man's chest.

"Yeah, but guess who," he said. "Get down. Come here. Look at him."

Gillis was a man in his fifties, with gentle, smiling eyes and a double chin.

Fletch got off his horse and, holding the reins, walked to where Gillis was standing.

He looked down at the man on the ground.

His was a much younger face than Fletch had expected — much, much younger than indicated by the gray hair.

"My God," Fletch said.

"Right."

"Walter March."

Gillis was looking around at the tops of the trees, fists on his hips, still visibly provoked.

"Why'd you mug him?"

"I have a distinct dislike of people flicking lit cigarettes into my face." He ran his hand over his cheek, left of his nose. "I only hit him once."

"You know him?"

"Don't care to. I stopped to ask for directions." The great explorer of contemporary America smiled sheepishly. "I was lost. This guy was standing here behind the camper, rolling a cigarette. When I saw his face, I was astounded. I said, 'My God, you're the spitting image of . . .' and a real rotten look, real pugnacious, came into his face, so I stopped, and he lit his cigarette, and he said, 'Of who?' and I said, 'Old March, Walter March,' and, flick, the cigarette went into my face and I'd hit him before I knew it." He looked down at the much younger, inert man. "I only hit him once."

"You hit good," Fletch said. "Glad I don't smoke."

"No way to get a story," Gillis said, rubbing his knuckles.

On the ground, the man's head and then his left leg moved.

"What's his name?" Fletch asked.

"Driver's license says Molinaro. Joseph Molinaro. Florida license."

The camper had Florida license plates.

"Golly," said Fletch. "This guy's only twenty-eight years old."

Gillis looked at him sharply, and then said, "Young body. You're probably right."

Suddenly, Molinaro's eyes opened, immediately looking alert and wary, even before shifting to focus on Fletch and Gillis.

"Good morning," Fletch said. "Seems you took a nap before breakfast."

Molinaro sat up on his elbows, and then reacted to pain in his head.

His wallet slipped off his chest onto the dry dirt of the road.

"Take it easy," Fletch said. "You've already missed post time."

Molinaro's eyes glazed and he looked as if he were about to sink to the ground again.

Fletch put his hand behind Molinaro's arm.

"Come on. You'll feel better if you get up. Get the blood going again."

He helped Molinaro stand, waited while he wiped the blood off his lips, examined it on his hand.

Molinaro looked sourly at Gillis.

Throwing off Fletch's hand, Molinaro staggered the few steps to the back of the camper and sat on the sill of the open door.

"You have some bad habits," Gillis said. "And I have a quick temper."

"Your name Joseph Molinaro?" Fletch asked.

The man's eyes moved slowly from Gillis to Fletch without losing any of their bitterness.

He said nothing.

"What relation are you to Walter March?" Gillis asked.

Still the man said nothing.

"Are you his son?" Fletch asked.

The man's eyes lowered to the road, and then off into the scrub pine.

And he snorted.

Fists again on hips, Gillis looked expressionlessly at Fletch.

A mosquito was in the air near Fletch's face. He caught it in his hand.

Gillis went to the side of the road and gathered up his horse's reins and slowly returned to where he had been standing.

He said to Molinaro, "You are Walter March's son. With that face you have to be. Did you murder him?"

Molinaro said, "Why would I murder him?"

"You tell us," Gillis said.

"The son of a bitch is no good to me dead," Molinaro said.

Gillis watched him with narrow eyes, saying nothing.

"What good was he to you alive?" Fletch asked.

Molinaro shrugged. "There was always hope."

There was another silent moment while Molinaro rubbed his temples with the heels of his hands.

Finally, Fletch said, "Come on, Joe. We're not out to get you." He had considered telling Molinaro that Poynton had reported there would be a national advisory issued that morning saying the police wanted to question him. He had also considered advising Captain Andrew Neale of the whereabouts of Joseph Molinaro. "We're not even looking for a story."

Molinaro said, "Just nosy, uh?"

Joseph Molinaro had been in the vicinity of the crime at the time the crime was committed.

He had accosted Mrs. Leary in the parking lot Sunday morning, and Walter March had been murdered Monday morning.

Clearly, Joseph Molinaro was a close relative of Walter March.

Fletch said, "What good was Walter March to you alive?"

"I wrote three or four polite letters when I was fifteen, asking to see him. No answers." Molinaro's fingers were touching his jaw, gently. "When I was nineteen, I took a year's savings, working in a laundry, for Christ's sake, went to New York, lived in a fleabag for as long as I could hold out, just to bug his secretary, asking for an appointment. First I gave my name, then I gave any name I could think of. He was always out of the country, out of the city, in conference." He winced.

"I had even bought a suit and tie so I'd have something to dress in, if he'd see me."

"He was your father?" Gillis asked.

"So I've always heard."

"Who told you? Who said so?" Gillis asked.

"My grandparents. They brought me up. In Florida." Molinaro was looking at Gillis with more interest. "I never even saw your fist," he said.

"You never do," said Gillis. "You never see the knockout punch."

"You used to box? I mean, professionally?"

Gillis said, "I used to play piano."

Molinaro shook his head, as much as his head permitted him. "Fat old fart."

"You want to not see my fist again?"

Molinaro stared at him.

"You're Frank Gillis, the television guy."

"I know that," Frank Gillis said.

"I've seen you on television."

"How come you roll your own?" Gillis asked.

"What's it to you?"

"Just unusual. Ever work in the Southwest?"

"Yeah," Molinaro said. "On a dude ranch, in Colorado. And one day I read Walter March owned a Denver newspaper. So I gave up my job and went to Denver and spent every day, all day, outside that newspaper building. Finally, one night, seven o'clock, he came out. Three men with him. I ran up to him. Two of the men blocked me off, big bruisers, the third opened the car door. And off went Walter March."

"Did he see you?" Fletch asked. "Did he see your face?"

"He looked at me before he got into the car. And he looked at me again through the car window as he was being driven off. Three, four years ago. Son of a bitch."

"You know, Joe," Gillis said. "You're not too good at taking a hint."

"What's so wrong with having an illegitimate son?" Molinaro's voice rose. "Jesus! What was ever wrong with it? Even in the Dark Ages, you could say hello to your illegitimate son!"

Standing in the sunlight on a timber road a few kilometers behind Hendricks Plantation, Fletch found himself thinking of Crystal Faoni. *I didn't act contrite enough. . . . He fired a great many people on moral grounds. . . . I'd be pleased to be accused . . .*

"Your father was sort of screwed up," Fletch said.

Molinaro squinted up at him. "You knew him?"

"I worked for him once. Maybe I spent five minutes in total with him." Fletch said, "Your five minutes, I guess."

Molinaro continued to look at Fletch.

Gillis asked, "You came to Virginia in hopes of seeing him?"

"Yeah."

"How did you know he was here?"

"President of the American Journalism Alliance. The convention. Read about it in the papers. The *Miami Herald*."

"What made you think he'd be any gladder to see you this time than he was last time?"

"Older," Molinaro said. "Mellower. There was always hope."

"Why didn't you register at the hotel?" Gillis asked. "Why hide up here in the woods?"

"You kidding? You recognized me. I planned to stay pretty clear of the hotel. Until I absolutely knew I could get through to him."

"Did you contact him at all?" Fletch asked.

"On the radio, Monday night, I heard he'd been murdered. First I knew he'd actually arrived here. I'd been noseying around. Hadn't been able to find out anything."

"Yeah, yeah, yeah," Gillis said. "So why are you still here?"

There was hatred for Gillis on Molinaro's face. "There's a memorial service. This morning. You bastard."

Gillis said, "I'm not the bastard."

He got on his horse and settled her down.

"Hey, Joe," Gillis said. "I'm sorry I said that." The hatred in Molinaro's face did not diminish. "I mean, I'm really sorry."

Fletch said, "Joe. Who was your mother?"

Molinaro gave Fletch the hatred full-face.

And didn't answer.

Fletch stared into the younger, unlined face of Walter March.

He stared into the unmasked hatred.

Having known, slightly, the smooth, controlled, diplomatic mask of Walter March, Fletch was seeing the face now as it probably really was.

Probably as the murderer of Walter March had seen him.

"Joe." Fletch mounted his horse. "Your father was really screwed up. Morally. He made his own laws, and most of 'em stank. Whatever you wanted from your father, I suspect you're better off without."

Sullenly, bitterly, still sitting on the doorsill of the camper, Joseph Molinaro said, "Is that your eulogy?"

"Yeah," Fletch said. "I guess it is."

THIRTY

8:00–9:30 A.M. Breakfast
Main Dining Room

The pool was empty, and no one was around it except one man — a very thin man — sitting in a long chair, dressed in baggy, knee-length shorts, a vertically striped shirt open at the throat, and polished black loafers.

Next to his chair was a black attaché case.

Fletch had approached the hotel from the rear, still shirtless and sweaty.

While he was fitting his key into the lock of the sliding glass door, the man came and stood beside him.

He seemed peculiarly interested in seeing the key go into the lock.

"Good morning," Fletch said.

"IRS," the man said.

Fletch slid the door open. "How do you spell that?"

"Internal Revenue Service."

Fletch entered the cool, dark room, leaving the door open.

"Let's see, now, you have something to do with taxes?"

"Something."

He sat on a light chair, the attaché case on his knees.

Fletch threw his T-shirt on the bed, his room key on the bureau.

The man opened the attaché case and appeared ready to proceed.

Fletch said, "You haven't asked me to identify myself."

"Don't need to," the man said. "It appeared in a Washington newspaper you were here. I was sent down. The room clerk said you were in Room 79. You just let yourself in with the key to room 79."

Fletch said, "Oh. Well, you haven't identified yourself."

The man shook his head. "IRS," he said. "IRS."

"But what do I call you?" Fletch asked. "I? I.R.? Mister S.?"

"You don't need to call me anything," IRS said. "Just respond."

"Ir."

Fletch went to the phone and dialed Room 102.

"Calling your lawyer?" IRS asked.

"Crystal?" Fletch said into the phone. "I need a couple of things."

She said, "Have you had breakfast?"

Fletch said, "I forget."

"You forget whether you've had breakfast?"

"I'm not talking about breakfast."

"Was it that bad? I had the pancakes and sausages, myself. Maple syrup. I know I shouldn't have had the blueberry muffins, but I did. It was a long night."

"I know. And you may be eating for two now, right?"

"Fletch, will you ever forgive me?"

"We'll see."

"Good. Then let's do it again."

"I had some difficulty explaining to hotel management how the bar for the shower curtain got ripped out."

"What did you tell them?"

"I told them I tried to do a chin-up."

"They believed that?"

"No. But one has to start one's lying somewhere."

"Were they nasty about it?"

"They were perfectly nice about saying they would put it on my bill. Listen, I need a couple of things. And I have a guest."

"Freddie Arbuthnot? No wonder you forgot breakfast."

Fletch looked at IRS. The man was almost entirely Adam's apple.

"Close."

The man's shoulders were little more than outriggers for his ears.

"Anything, Fletcher darling, love of my life. Ask me for anything."

"I need one of those cassette tape recorders. You know, with a tape splicer? I need to splice some tape. Do you have one?"

"Mine doesn't have a splicer. I'm very sure that Bob McConnell has one, though."

"Bob?"

"Would you like me to call him for you?"

"No, thanks. I'll call him myself."

Crystal said, "I think he's disposed to cooperate with you in any way he can."

"Mentioning me in his piece has caused me a little bit of trouble."

IRS was flicking his pen against his thumbnail, impatiently.

"What's the other thing, darling?"

"I finished my travel piece. Want to send it off. Do you have anything like a big envelope, a box, wrapping paper, string?"

"There's a branch post office in the lobby."

"Yeah."

"They sell big mailers these days."

"Oh, yeah."

"Big insulated envelopes, boxes, right up to the legal limit in size."

"Yeah. I forgot."

"Over the door there's a sign saying 'United States Post Office.' "

"Thank you, Crystal."

"If you get lost in the lobby, just ask anyone."

"Crystal? I'm going to say something very, very rotten to you."

"What?"

"The dining room is still open for breakfast."

"Rat."

Fletch hung up but continued standing by the bed. He needed a shower. He thought of jumping in the pool. He wanted to do both.

"If we might get down to the business at hand?" IRS said.

"Oh, yeah. How the hell are ya?"

"Mister Fletcher, our records indicate you've never filed a tax return."

"Gee."

"Are our records accurate?"

"Sure."

"Your various employers over the years — and, I must say, there is an impressive number of them — have withheld tax money from your income, so it's not as if you'd paid no tax at all."

"Good, good."

"However, not filing returns is a crime."

"Shucks."

"As a matter of personal curiosity, may I ask why you have not filed returns?"

"April's always a busy month for me. You know. In the spring a young man's fancy really shouldn't have to turn to the Internal Revenue Service."

"You could always apply for extensions."

"Who has the time to do that?"

"Is there any political thinking behind your not paying taxes?"

"Oh, no. My motives are purely esthetic, if you want to know the truth."

"Esthetic?"

"Yes. I 've seen your tax forms. Visually, they're ugly. In fact, very

offensive. And their use of the English language is highly objection-
able. Perverted."

"Our tax forms are perverted?"

"Ugly and perverted. Just seeing them makes my stomach churn. I
know you wallahs have tried to improve them but, if you don't mind
my saying so, they're still really dreadful."

IRS blinked. His Adam's apple went up and down like a thermometer in New England.

"Esthetics," he muttered.

"Right."

"All right, Mister Fletcher. We haven't heard from you at all in
more than two years. No returns. No applications for extensions."

"Didn't want to bother you."

"Yet our sources indicate you have had an income during this period."

"I'm still alive, thank you. Clearly, I am eating."

"Mister Fletcher, you have money in Brazil, the Bahamas, Switzerland, and Italy."

"You know about Switzerland?"

"Quite a lot of money. Where did you get it?"

"I ripped it off."

" 'Ripped it off'?"

" 'Stole it' seems such a harsh expression."

"You say you stole it?"

"Well, you weren't there at the time."

"I certainly wasn't."

"Maybe you should have been."

"Did you steal the money in this country?"

"Yup."

"How did you get the money out of the country?"

"Flew it out. In a chartered jet."

"My God. That's terribly criminal."

"Why does my not paying taxes and illegally exporting money
bother you more than the fact I stole the money in the first place?"

"Really!"

Fletch said, "Just an observation."

Fletch picked up the phone and dialed Room 82.

"Bob? This is your friend Fletcher."

There was a long pause before Robert McConnell said, "Oh, yeah. Hi."

"Crystal tells me you have a cassette tape recorder with a tape splicer
attachment."

"Uh. Yes."

"Wonder if I might borrow it for a few hours?"

Robert McConnell was envisioning his sensitive parts tied to a cathedral door if he said no. Dear Crystal.

"Uh. Sure."

"That's great, Bob. You going to be in your room?"

"Yes."

"I'll be by in a few minutes." Fletch started to hang up, but then he said into the receiver, "Bob, I appreciate. Let me buy you a drink."

The only response was a click.

IRS said, "Mister Fletcher, I hope you realize what you've admitted here."

"What's that?"

"That you stole money, illegally exported it from the country, failed to report it as income to the Internal Revenue Service, and have never filed a federal tax return in your life."

"Oh, that. Sure."

"Are you insane?"

"Just esthetic. Those tax forms . . ."

"Mister Fletcher, you seem to be signing yourself up for a long stretch in prison."

"Yeah. Okay. Make it somewhere South. I really don't like cold weather. Even if I have to be indoors."

There was a knock on his door.

"Have I answered your questions satisfactorily?" Fletch asked.

"For a start." IRS was returning things to his attaché case. "I can't believe my ears."

Fletch opened the door to a bellman.

"Telegrams, sir. Two of them." He handed them over. "You weren't in your room earlier, sir."

"And sliding them under the door, you would have lost your tip. Right?"

The bellman smiled weakly.

"You've lost your tip anyway."

Fletch closed the door before opening the first telegram:

GENERAL KILENDER ARRIVING HENDRICKS FOR BRONZE STAR PRESEN-
TATION MID-AFTERNOON — LETTVIN.

IRS was standing in his droopy drawers, attaché case firmly in hand, staring at Fletch incredulously.

He came toward the door.
The second telegram said:

BOAC FLIGHT 81 WASHINGTON AIRPORT TO LONDON NINE O'CLOCK
TONIGHT RESERVATION YOUR NAME. WILL BE AT BOAC COUNTER
SEVEN-THIRTY ON TO RECEIVE TAPES — FABENS AND EGGERS.

At the door, IRS said, "Mister Fletcher, I must order you not to
leave Hendricks, not to leave Virginia, and certainly not to leave the
United States."
Fletch opened the door for him.
"Wouldn't think of it."
"You'll be hearing from us shortly."
"Always nice doing business with you."
As IRS walked down the corridor, Fletch waved good-bye at him —
with the telegrams.

THIRTY-ONE

9:30 A.M.
PROBLEMS WITH FOREIGN CORRESPONDENCE:
On Renting a House in Nigeria,
Finding a School For Your Kids in Singapore,
Getting a Typewriter Fixed in Spain,
and Other Problems
Address by Dixon Hodge
Conservatory

10:30 A.M.
WHAT TIME IS IT IN BANGKOK?: An Editor's View
Address by Cyrus Wood
Conservatory

[11:00 A.M. Memorial Service for Walter March]
St. Mary's Church, Hendricks

11:30 A.M.
THE PLACING OF FOREIGN CORRESPONDENTS:
Pago Pago's Cheaper, but the Story's in Tokyo
Address by Horsch Aldrich
Conservatory

Fletch had a shower, swam a few laps in the pool, dressed, and went to the hotel's writing room, next to the billiards room at the back of the lobby.

On a bookshelf near the fireplace was a copy of *Who's Who in America*, which he pulled down and took to a writing table.

Fletch had learned the habit a long time before of researching the people with whom he was dealing, through whatever resources were within reach.

Sometimes the most simple checking of names and dates could be most revealing:

MARCH, WALTER CODINGTON, publisher; b. Newport, R.I., July 17, 1907; s. Charles Harrison and Mary (Codington) M.; B.A., Princeton, 1929; m. Lydia Bowen, Oct., 1928; 1 son, Walter Codington March, Jr. March Newspapers, 1929–: treas., 1935; vice-pres., corp. affs., 1941; mergers & acquisitions, 1953; pres., 1957; chmn., pub. 1963–. Dir. March Forests, March Trust, Wildflower League. Mem. Princeton C. (N.Y.C.), American Journalism Alliance, Reed Golf (Palm Springs, Ca.), Mattawan Yacht (N.Y.C.), Simonee Yacht (San Francisco). Office: March Building, 12 Codington Pl New York City NY 10008

MARCH, WALTER CODINGTON, JR., newspaperman; b. N.Y.C., Mar. 12, 1929; s. Walter Codington and Lydia (Bowen) ATT.: Princeton, 1941. m. Allison Roup, 1956: children — Allison, Lydia, Elizabeth. March Newspapers, 1950–: treas., 1953; vice-pres., corp affs., 1968; pres., 1973–. Dir. March Forests, March Trust, Franklin-Williams Museum, N.Y. Symphonia, Center for Deaf Children (Chicago). Mem. American Journalism Alliance, Princeton C. (N.Y.C.). Office: March Building, 12 Codington Pl New York City NY 10008

EARLES, ELEANOR (MRS. OLIVER HENRY), journalist; b. Cadmus, Fla., Nov. 8, 1931; d. Joseph and Alma Wayne Molinaro; B.A. Barnard, 1952; m. Oliver Henry Earles, 1958 (d. 1959). Researcher, Life, 1952–54; reporter, N.Y. Post, 1954–58; with Nat'l. Radio, 1958–61, Eleanor Earles Interviews; Nat'l. Television Net.: Eleanor Earles Interviews, 1961–65; with U.B.C., 1965–; Midday Dateline Washington, 1965–67; Gen. Ass'n. Evening News, 1967–74; Eleanor Earles Interviews, 1974–. Author: Eleanor Earles Interviews, 1966. Recipient Philpot Award,

1961. Dir. O.H.E. Interests, Inc., 1959–. Mem. American Journalism Alliance, Together (Wash., D.C.). Office: U.B.C., U.N.
Plz New York City NY 10017

Fletch put *Who's Who* back on the shelf and crossed the lobby to
the post office, where he bought a large, insulated envelope.

Then he went to Room 82 to borrow the cassette tape recorder
from the newly laconic Robert McConnell.

Much of the remainder of the morning he spent in his room, splicing
tape.

Finished, he placed all the reels of used tape in the envelope (except
the one spliced reel he left ready to play in his marvelous machine)
and addressed the envelope to Alston Chambers, an attorney he knew
in California. Boldly, he marked the envelope: "HOLD FOR I. M.
FLETCHER."

On the way to lunch, Fletch returned McConnell's tape recorder
and mailed the envelope.

THIRTY-TWO

12:30 P.M. Lunch
Main Dining Room

Captain Andrew Neale was at the luncheon table for six, with Crystal
Faoni and, of course, Fredericka Arbuthnot. No Robert McConnell.
No Lewis Graham. No Eleanor Earles.

"Has anyone noticed," Fletch asked, "that anyone who shares a meal
with the three of us never returns?"

"It's because you get along so well with everybody," Freddie said.

"Whom shall we have for lunch today?" Crystal asked. "Poor Captain
Neale. Our next victim."

Sitting straight in his light, neat jacket, Captain Neale smiled dis-
tantly at what was clearly an in-joke.

"You're not thinking of keeping us all here beyond tomorrow morning, are you?" Crystal asked.

"Tonight, you mean," said Freddie. "I have to leave on the six-forty-
five flight."

"You're not keeping us beyond the end of the convention." Crystal was only passably interested in her fruit salad.

"I don't see how I can," Captain Neale said. "Almost everyone here has made a point of telling me how important he or she is. Such a lot of important people. The seas would rumble and nations would crumble if I kept any of you out of circulation for many more minutes than I had to."

Crystal said to Fletch, "I told you I'd like this guy."

"Have people been beastly to you?" Freddie, grinning, asked Neale.

"I thought reporters were people who report the news," Neale said. "The last couple of days, I've gotten the impression they are the news."

"Right," Crystal said solemnly to her fruit salad. "News does not happen unless a reporter is there to report it."

"For example," said Fletch, "if no one had known World War Two was happening . . ."

"Actually," Crystal said, "Hitler without the use of the radio wouldn't have been Hitler at all."

"And the Civil War," said Freddie. "If it hadn't been for the telegraph . . ."

"The geographic center of the American Revolution," Fletch said, "was identical to the center of the new American printing industry."

"And then there was Caesar," Crystal said. "Was he a military genius with pen in hand, or a literary genius with sword in hand? Did Rome conquer the world in reality, or just its communications systems?"

"Weighty matters we discuss at these conventions," Freddie said.

"Listen," Crystal said. "You know I take such comments personally. If I had two breakfasts, blame Fletch. Did you try those blueberry muffins this morning?"

"I tried only one of them," Freddie said.

Crystal said, "The rest of them were good, too."

Captain Neale was chuckling at their foolishness.

Fletch said to him, "People here have given you a pretty rough time, uh?"

Captain Neale stared at his plate a moment before answering.

"It's been like trying to sing 'Strawberry Fields Forever' while your head's stuck in a beehive."

"Literary fella," Crystal told her salad.

"Musical, too," said Freddie.

"Questioning them, they question me."

"Reporters ain't got no humility," Crystal said.

"When they do answer a question," Neale continued, "they know exactly how to answer it — for their own sakes. They know exactly how to present facts absolutely to their own benefit — what to reveal, and what to conceal."

"I suppose so," said Freddie. "Never thought of it that way."

"I'd rather be questioning the full bench of the Supreme Court."

"There are only nine of them," said Freddie.

Crystal said, "I'd say from reading the press you've given away very little. There have been no newsbreaks — except for Poynton's — since the beginning."

"Poynton's?" Neale asked.

"Stuart Poynton. You didn't read him this morning?"

"No," Neale said. "I didn't."

"He said you want to question a man named Joseph Molinaro regarding the murder of Walter March."

"That was in the newspaper?" asked Neale.

"Who is Joseph Molinaro?" Crystal asked.

Neale smiled. "I suppose you'd like to know."

"Oh, no," Crystal said airily. "I've just been through a list of those attending the convention, a list of all hotel employees, the voting list in the town of Hendricks, the membership list of the American Journalism Alliance, *Who's Who*, and, by telephone, the morgue of *People* magazine. . . ."

"You must be curious," commented Neale.

Freddie said, "Who is Joseph Molinaro?"

Captain Neale said, "This is the perfect day for a fruit salad. Don't you think?"

"In a way," Fletch said, quietly, "everyone here is a bastard of Walter March. Or has been treated like one."

Neale dropped his fork, but caught it before it went into his lap.

Crystal said brightly, as if introducing a new topic, "Say, who is this Joseph Molinaro, anyway?"

Neale, applying himself to his lunch, seemingly unperturbed, said, "There is no way I can keep any of you beyond tomorrow morning, or tonight, or whenever."

"I understand I'm on the six-forty-five flight out of here." Fletch looked at Freddie. "Me and my shadow. I'm catching a nine o'clock from Washington to London."

She did not look at him.

Fletch said to Neale, "I don't see how you could have accomplished very much, in just a couple of days. Under the circumstances."

"We've accomplished more than you think," Neale said.

"What have you accomplished?" Crystal asked like a sledgehammer.

To Neale's silence, Fletch said, "Captain Neale has narrowed it down to two or three people. Or he wouldn't be letting the rest of us go."

Neale was paying more attention to the remainder of his salad than Crystal would do after trekking across a full golf course.

Fletch hitched himself forward in the chair and addressed himself to Crystal, speaking slowly. "The key," he said, "is that Walter March was murdered — stabbed in the back with a pair of scissors — shortly before eight o'clock Monday morning, in the sitting room of his suite."

Crystal stared at him dumbly.

"People lose sight of the simplicities," Fletch said.

Under the table, Freddie kicked him hard, on the shin.

Fletch said, "Ow."

"I just felt like doing that," she said.

"Damnit." He rubbed his shin. "Are you trying to tell me I don't get along well with everybody?"

"Something like that."

"Well, you're wrong," Fletch said. "I do."

The waiter was bringing chocolate cake for dessert.

"Oh, yum!" said Crystal. "Who cares about death and perdition as long as there's chocolate cake?"

"Captain Neale does," said Fletch.

"No," said Neale. "I care about chocolate cake."

"There is evidence," Fletch said, the pain in his shin having abated, "that Walter March was expecting someone — someone he knew. He was expecting someone to call upon him in his suite at eight o'clock or shortly before." Fletch had a forkful of the cake. "Someone to whom he would have opened the door."

Freddie was continuing to look disgusted, but she was listening carefully.

Neale appeared to be paying no attention whatsoever.

Fletch asked him, mildly, "Who was it?"

"Good cake," Neale said.

Fletch said, "Was it Oscar Perlman?"

Neale didn't need to answer.

He looked at Fletch, both alarm and despair in his eyes.

"And who was it who told you Walter March was expecting Oscar Perlman?" Fletch asked. "Junior?"

Neale's throat was dry from the cake. "Junior?"

"Walter March, Junior," Fletch said.

"Jesus!" Neale's eyes went from one to the other of them, desperately.

"Don't you print this. None of you. I didn't say a word. If one of you prints . . ."

"Don't worry." Fletch put his napkin on the table, and stood up. "Crystal and I are unemployed. And Freddie Arbuthnot," he said, "doesn't work for *Newsworld* magazine."

THIRTY-THREE

1:30 P.M.

MY EIGHT TERMS IN THE WHITE HOUSE
Address by Leona Hatch
Main Dining Room

Fletch said, "Mrs. March, I've been trying to understand why you murdered your husband."

Sitting in a chair across the coffee table from him in Suite 12, her expression changed little. Perhaps her eyes grew a little wider.

"And," Fletch said, "I think I do understand."

He had appeared at her door, carrying the marvelous machine.

She had answered the door, still dressed in black, having returned from the memorial service shortly before. Near the door was a luncheon tray waiting to be taken away.

At first, she looked at him in surprise, as it was an unseemly time to call. Then she obviously remembered he had promised they would talk again about his working for March Newspapers. And the suitcase in his hand suggested he was about to leave.

He said nothing.

Sitting on the divan, he placed the marvelous machine flat on the coffee table.

Now he was opening it.

"Statistically, of course," he said, "in the case of a domestic murder — and this is a domestic murder — when a husband or wife is murdered, chances of the spouse being the murderer are something over seventy percent."

Perhaps her eyes widened again when she saw that what was in the suitcase was a tape recorder.

"Which is why," Fletch said, "you chose to murder your husband here at the convention, where you knew your husband would be surrounded by people who had reason to hate him to the point of murder."

Her back was straight. Her hands were folded in her lap.

"Listen to this."

Fletch started the tape recorder.

It was the tape of Lydia March being questioned by Captain Neale, edited:

"At what what time did you wake up, Mrs. March?"

"I'm not sure. Seven-fifteen? Seven-twenty? I heard the door to the suite close."

"That was me, Mister Neale," Junior said. "I went down to the lobby to get the newspapers."

"Walter had left his bed. It's always been a thing with him to be up a little earlier than I. A masculine thing. I heard him moving around the bathroom. I lay in bed a little while, a few minutes, really, waiting for him to be done."

"The bathroom door was closed?"

"Yes. In a moment I heard the television here in the living room go on, softly — one of those morning news and features network shows Walter always hated so much — so I got up and went into the bathroom."

"Excuse me. How did your husband get from the bathroom to the living room without coming back through your bedroom?"

"He went through Junior's bedroom, of course. He didn't want to disturb me. . . ."

". . . Okay. You were in the bathroom. The television was playing softly in the living room. . . ."

"I heard the door to the suite close again, so I thought Walter had gone down for coffee."

"Had the television gone off?"

"No."

"So, actually, someone could have come into the suite at that point."

"No. At first, I thought Junior might have come back, but he couldn't have."

"Why not?"

"I didn't hear them talking."

"Would they have been talking? Necessarily?"

"Of course. . . ."

"So, Mrs. March, you think you heard the suite door close again, but your husband hadn't left the suite, and you think no one entered the suite because you didn't hear talking?"

"I guess that's right. I could be mistaken, of course. I'm trying to reconstruct."

"Pardon, but where were you physically in the bathroom when you heard the door close the second time?"

"I was getting into the tub. . . ."

". . . You had already run the tub?"

"Yes. While I was brushing my teeth. And all that."

"So there must have been a period of time, while the tub was running, that you couldn't have heard anything from the living room — not the front door, not the television, not talking?"

"I suppose not."

"So the second time you heard the door close, when you were getting into the tub, you actually could have been hearing someone leave the suite."

"Oh, my. That's right. Of course."

"It would explain your son's not having returned, you husband's not having left, and your not hearing talking."

"How clever you are. . . ."

Fletch switched off the marvelous machine.

Listening, Lydia March's eyes had gone back and forth from the slowly revolving tape reel to Fletch's face.

Fletch said, "When I first arrived at Hendricks Plantation, and Helena Williams was telling me about the murder, I noticed she particularly mentioned what you had heard from the bathroom. I think she said something about your hearing gurgling and thinking it was the tub drain. Not precisely what you said here. But Helena could have reported what you heard from the bathroom only if you had made a point of telling her."

Fletch rested his back against a divan pillow.

"Captain Neale wasn't a bit clever," he said. "He never went into the bathroom to discover what could be heard from there.

"I did."

"Last night, when I came to visit you, you and Jake Williams were talking here in the living room. I went into the bathroom. The doors of both bedrooms to the living room were open — which gave me a much better chance to hear than you supposedly had. I closed both bathroom doors. I did not run water. I did not flush the toilet. I listened.

"Mrs. March, I could not hear you and Jake talking. You could not have heard the television, especially on low.

"I did not hear Jake leave the suite. You could not have heard the door closing — as you said you did.

"Perhaps your hearing is better than mine, but my hearing is forty years younger than yours.

"As Oscar Perlman might say, I have twenty-twenty hearing.

"Mrs. March, the closets to both bedrooms are between the bathroom and the living room. Architects do this on purpose, so you cannot hear.

"You made too much of an issue of the front door of the suite being open. You gave evidence you couldn't have had. It was important for you to convince everyone that you heard the door close when Junior left the suite, but that it was open when you came into the living room.

"You lied.

"Why?

"Despite everything we know about your husband, how badly he treated people, his private detectives, his sense of security, you had to convince people he had opened the door to someone else, who stabbed him in the back.

"Simplicity. The simple truth is that there were two of you in a suite, with the door to the corridor closed and locked, and one of you was stabbed.

"Who did it?"

He leaned forward again, and again pressed the PLAY button on the tape recorder.

Lydia March's voice came from the speakers:

". . . There was a man in the corridor, walking away, lighting a cigar as he walked . . . I didn't know who he was, from behind . . . I ran toward him . . . then I realized who he was. . . ."

"Mrs. March. Who was the man in the corridor?"

"Perlman. Oscar Perlman."

"The humorist?"

"If you say so. . . ."

Fletch switched off the machine again.

He said, "Mrs. March, you made three mistakes in laying down potential evidence that Oscar Perlman is your husband's murderer.

"The first isn't very serious. Perlman says he was playing poker until five-thirty in the morning and then slept late. That he was playing poker until five-thirty in the morning can be confirmed, and I suppose Neale has done so. He could have gotten up, murdered your husband, and gone back to bed, or whatever, but it doesn't seem likely.

"A much more serious mistake you made is in the timing of it all.

"According to your story, someone stabbed your husband in the living room. Sitting in the bathtub, you heard choking, whatever, called out, got out of the tub, grabbed a towel, went into the bedroom, saw your husband stagger in from the living room, roll off the bed, drive the scissors deeper into his back, arch up, et cetera, and die. Then you ran through the bedroom, the living room, and into the corridor.

"And you try to indicate that the man who might have stabbed your husband is — just at that point — still in the corridor, walking away?

"You lied.

"Why?

"The third mistake you made in saying Oscar Perlman was in the corridor outside the suite is most serious.

"But I'll come back to that."

Again, Fletch settled himself on the divan.

He said, "Unfortunately for you, the people who had the best motives and opportunity to kill your husband are all highly skilled at handling an interview. They're all reporters. Rolly Wisham, for example, did nothing to divert suspicion from himself. Oscar Perlman didn't even pretend he had an alibi. Lewis Graham didn't hesitate to be open — almost indict himself. Even Crystal Faoni was quick to realize she was a possible suspect — and didn't hesitate to admit it. Perhaps it was unconscious on their parts, but I think they all have enough experience to have realized instinctively they had all been set up as clay pigeons.

"By you. By your choice of the time and the place of the murder.

"I always look for the controlling intelligence behind anything and everything. In this case, it was yours."

"Why? Why, why, why?"

Lydia March continued sitting primly in her chair. Her head had raised slightly, and she was looking somewhat down her nose at him.

"In October, 1928, you married Walter March, who was due to graduate from Princeton in June, 1929.

"Odd. Especially in those days. Not to have waited for graduation.

"Not so odd. Junior was born five months later, in March, 1929.

"What was the expression for it in those days? A shotgun marriage?

"Was Walter March the father of your child?

"Or, being the heir to a newspaper fortune, was he just the best catch around?

"Were you sure Walter was the father? Was he?

"You're a wily woman, Mrs. March.

"You remained married to Walter March for fifty years. Never had another child.

"There was an enormous newspaper fortune to be inherited.

"But Walter was an old war-horse. He wouldn't give up. Perfect health. He announced his retirement once, and then, when Junior goofed up, didn't retire.

"And all this time, as Junior was getting to be fifty years old, losing his wife, his family, drinking more and more, you saw him becoming weaker and weaker, wasting away."

Fletch stared a long moment at the floor.

Finally, he said, "There is a time for fathers to move aside, to quit, to die, to leave room for their sons to grow.

"Even if they are just the image of the father, rather than the blood-father.

"Walter wasn't moving aside.

"Did he somehow know, instinctively, Walter, Junior, wasn't his son?"

Fletch jerked the marvelous machine's wire from the wall socket.

"You killed your husband to save your son."

He was wrapping up the wire. "Do you know your husband had another son? His name is Joseph Molinaro. Your husband had him with Eleanor Earles, I guess, while she was a student at Barnard.

"And did you know that Joseph Molinaro is here?

"He came here to see your husband.

"Maybe another son on the horizon — if you knew it — made you even more desperate to protect your own son."

Fletch closed and latched the cover of the suitcase.

"Of course, I'm going to have to talk with Captain Neale — if you don't first.

"By the way," he said. "Thanks for the job offer.

"Same way you Marches do everything. Either buy people off, or blackmail them into a corner.

"After more than half a century of this, you have a most uncanny instinct as to whom to buy off or blackmail."

He stood up and picked up the suitcase.

"Oh," he said. "The third, most terrible mistake you made in saying Oscar Perlman was in the corridor was that you said it in Junior's presence.

"The big idiot has blown the game again.

"He's gone and told Captain Neale that Perlman had an appointment to see your husband at eight o'clock Monday morning."

Lydia was looking up at Fletch from her chair.

Her expression did not change at all.

Fletch said, "You don't understand the significance of that, do you?"

Her expression still didn't change.

"Again, Junior was overdoing the clever bit. Why would he lie to support you, unless he knows you were lying?

"He knows you killed your husband."

Her eyes lowered, slowly.

Her lips tightened, and turned down at their corners.

Her eyes settled on her hands, in her lap.

Slowly, her hands opened, and turned palms up.

"Mrs. March," Fletch said. "You're killing your son."

Fletch was almost back to his room, carrying the marvelous machine, before he realized that during the time he had just spent with her, Lydia March had not said one word.

THIRTY-FOUR

3:00 P.M.
ARRIVAL OF THE PRESIDENT OF THE UNITED STATES
(Cancelled)
ARRIVAL OF THE VICE-PRESIDENT OF THE UNITED STATES

Fletch heard the helicopter banging away overhead as he crossed the lobby to the French doors.

Most of the conventioneers were on the terrace behind Hendricks Plantation House to watch the helicopter land on the lawn. The sunlight brought out the bright colors of their clothes. Mostly they were still chattering about Leona Hatch's insider's report on her eight terms as a White House reporter.

When Fletch came onto the terrace, the helicopter had retreated to the sky over the far ridge of trees.

Leona Hatch pulled herself away from an admiring group of young people, and approached Fletch.

"I'll swear I know you," she said. "With my dying breath, I'll swear."

He put his hand out to her.

"Fletcher," he said. "Irwin Fletcher."

She shook hands, limply, her eyes searching his face, sharply.

"I feel I know you very well," she said.

149

Fletch was looking for Captain Neale.

Junior, sallow and slump-shouldered, was standing with Jake Williams, watching the helicopter.

"I can't get over this feeling, this certainty, that I know you well," Leona Hatch said. "But I can't remember. . . ."

Fletch saw Neale standing with some uniformed Virginia State policemen.

"Excuse me," he said to Leona Hatch.

He touched Neale's elbow.

Neale looked at him.

The slight expression of annoyance in Neale's face was replaced by a gentle, respectful curiosity.

Obviously, Neale was remembering from lunch that Fletch seemed to know more about the murder of Walter March than the others did, and, in addition, could make some very good guesses.

Fletch said, quietly, "I think you should go talk with Lydia March."

Neale looked at Fletch a moment, probably considering questions to ask, but deciding not to ask any.

Captain Neale nodded, and went through the crowd and into the lobby of the hotel.

The helicopter was approaching the lawn below the terrace very slowly.

Fletch had been aware that a group of five men, moving together, had come onto the terrace.

It was not until they were standing at the front of the terrace, next to Junior and Jake Williams, that Fletch looked directly at the men.

Hands in pockets, appearing totally relaxed, watching the helicopter land, was the Vice-President of the United States.

Helena Williams spotted him the same time Fletch did.

She began to rush toward him from the other side of the terrace.

What she was saying was drowned out by the noise of the helicopter.

Junior, remaining oblivious to the presence of the Vice-President of the United States beside him, suddenly rocked back on his heels.

He put his hand up to his face, as if he were about to sneeze.

Fletch saw blood on Junior's neck.

Then a splotch of blood appeared on Junior's white shirt, next to his necktie.

Fletch started toward Junior.

Junior lost his balance and fell against the Vice-President.

Someone screamed.

Jake Williams yelled, "Junior!"

Junior rolled as he fell.

Landing on his back on the flagstones, the two splotches of blood, on his neck and on his shirt, were clearly visible.

Helena was kneeling over him.

Even over the sound of the helicopter, Fletch could hear Jake Williams shout, "Someone is trying to kill the Vice-President!"

One of the four men with the Vice-President spun him around, toward the hotel.

The other three surrounded him closely.

One held his hand out behind the Vice-President's head, as if to shield him from the sun.

They pushed him through the crowd into the hotel.

Crystal Faoni had joined Helena Williams in kneeling over Junior.

Crystal was trying to blow air into Junior's mouth.

The helicopter had settled on the lawn, and its door was opening.

Fletch looked across the lawn, and ran his eyes as closely as he could along the line of trees.

Men in Marine Corps uniform were getting off the helicopter.

At first, Fletch moved very slowly, backing away from the crowd, turning, jumping off the terrace, ambling across the lawn.

He did not break into a full run for the stables until he was well-concealed by the trees.

THIRTY-FIVE

Fletch had no plan.

He could find no one at the stables, so he saddled the horse he had used twice before, fumbling, as he hadn't saddled a horse himself in a long time, alarming the horse with his haste.

Once clear of the paddock area, he laid the whip on her and she poured on speed, but only for a very few moments.

She was a pleasant horse, but not too swift.

Clearly, in all her days on Hendricks Plantation, she had never been asked to be in a sincere hurry.

By the time they had climbed the ridge and were approaching the camper along the timber road she was winded and resentful.

Fletch left her in the deep shade of the woods about twenty meters up the hillside from the camper.

He still had no plan.

The camper was open, but the keys weren't in the ignition.

He looked for the keys under the driver's seat, over the visor, in the map compartment, then, hurrying, moved back into the camper, flipping over the mattress of the unmade bed, glancing in the cabinets, the oven, under the seat cushions of the two chairs.

He went through the pockets of a dark suit hanging from a curtain rod.

On a shelf was an old cigar box. Inside were screws, nails, a few sockets for a wrench, half a pouch of Bull Durham tobacco, and a set of keys, somewhat rusted.

He tried the keys in the ignition.

The third key on the chain fit.

He left it in the ignition.

Standing by the camper, he realized he still didn't have a plan.

From down the road, around the bend, he heard someone cough.

Mentally, Fletch thanked his horse, up in the woods, for being quiet.

Fletch flattened himself against the wall of the camper, next to the rear wheels.

He stuck his head out for a look only once.

Joseph Molinaro was walking toward the camper, ten meters away, a rifle under his right arm.

It had not occurred to Fletch before this that, of course, Joseph Molinaro would be carrying a rifle.

He had not thought to arm himself.

There was no time to go back into the camper.

The few branches and stones in the road at his feet were too small and light to make good weapons.

He had no more time to think.

Fletch had left the camper through the driver's door.

Molinaro was at the back of the camper, heading for the door near the right rear wheels.

Crouching, looking under the camper, Fletch watched Molinaro's feet.

As soon as Molinaro was on the other side of the camper, Fletch moved around to its rear and along its wall.

Just as Molinaro was beginning to climb the three steps into the camper, beginning to bend to go through the door, Fletch hit him on the back of his head, hard, with the side of his hand.

The force of the blow knocked Molinaro's head against the solid door frame.

Instinctively tightening his arm over the rifle, Molinaro fell up the steps, half-in and half-out of the camper.

He rolled over.

His eyes remained open only a second or two.

He appeared to recognize Fletch.

Having already been unconscious once that morning, Molinaro's head settled back on the camper's floor, and he went deeply unconscious.

Fletch took the rifle from under his arm and slid it along the floor of the camper, toward the front.

Picking up Molinaro's legs, Fletch slid his back along the linoleum floor until Molinaro was entirely aboard the camper and the door could be closed.

Fletch climbed the steps to the camper and stepped over Molinaro.

He tore two strips from the bed sheet and tied Molinaro's ankles together.

Then he tied his wrists together, in front of him.

He slammed the back door of the camper, climbed into the driver's seat, and turned the key in the ignition.

The battery was dead.

Incredulous, Fletch senselessly tried the key three or four times.

He groaned.

Molinaro couldn't do anything right.

He had come to Virginia to meet his father.

Never did meet him.

That morning he had gotten up, flicked a cigarette into a stranger's face, and instantly was knocked unconscious.

Then he had let two people know who he was and why he was there.

If the suit hanging from the curtain rod was any indication, Joseph Molinaro actually had gone to Walter March's Memorial Service.

Next, using that rifle on the floor with telescopic sights, he had murdered his half brother.

He had ambled back to his camper, not even having thrown the murder weapon away, never thinking someone who had figured out what he had done might be waiting for him.

And the battery of his getaway vehicle was dead.

Looking at the man, with the tight, curly gray hair, dressed in the blue jeans jacket, unconscious and bound on the floor of the camper, Fletch shook his head.

Then he climbed the hillside and got his horse.

*   *   *

"I see you figured it out just a little faster than I did."

Before leaving the timber road, Fletch met Frank Gillis heading for the camper.

Gillis's horse looked exhausted.

Gillis nodded at Molinaro slung over the saddle of Fletch's horse.

"Is he dead, or just unconscious?"

"Unconscious."

Gillis said, "He seems to spend a lot of time in that condition."

"Poor son of a bitch."

Walking the horse, Fletch held the reins in his right hand, the rifle in his left.

He asked, "Junior dead?"

"Yeah."

Fletch left the road and started through the woods, down the hillside.

Gillis said, "You sure that's the murder weapon?"

"As sure as I can be, without a ballistics test. It's the weapon he was carrying when he returned to the camper."

Remaining on his horse, Gillis followed Fletch through the woods to the pasture and then rode along beside him.

Fletch said, "I wonder if you'd mind putting Molinaro on your horse?"

"Why?"

"I feel silly. I feel like I'm walking into Dodge City."

"So why should I feel silly?"

Frank Gillis chuckled.

"One of us has to feel silly, and you're the one who caught him," Gillis said.

"Thanks."

"Why didn't you use the camper?"

"Dead battery."

Gillis shook his head, just as Fletch had.

"I don't know," Gillis said. "This guy . . . did he murder old man March, or did he think Junior murdered him? Or was he just plain jealous of Junior, now that Molinaro's dream of being recognized by his father was over?"

Fletch walked along quietly a moment, before saying, "You'll have to ask Captain Neale, I guess."

"You know," Gillis said, "everyone thought an attempt was being made on the Vice-President's life."

"Yeah."

"I did, too, at first, until I realize this was another March who was dead. Who'd ever want to kill the Vice-President of the United States? One could have a greater effect upon national policy by killing the White House cook."

"Who was in the helicopter?" Fletch asked.

"Oh, that." Gillis's chins were quivering with mirth. "Some Marine Corps General. He was here for some ceremony or other, a presentation of some kind, pin a medal on someone. And while the General was making this big entrance, landing in a helicopter on the back lawn, the Vice-President of the United States was arriving at the front of the hotel in an economy-size car — completely ignored."

They were both laughing, and Molinaro was still unconscious.

"As soon as everyone realized what had happened, that Junior had been shot, the Secret Service hustled the Vice-President back into his car, and back to Washington, and the General climbed aboard his helicopter and took off. The only thing the Vice-President was heard to say, during his stay at Hendricks Plantation, was, 'My! The military live well!' "

They came onto the back lawns of Hendricks Plantation.

Indeed, the helicopter was gone.

People were playing golf on the rolling greens the other side of the plantation house.

"You want to carry the rifle?" Fletch asked.

"No, no. I wouldn't take from your moment of glory."

Fletch said, "This isn't glory."

Captain Neale saw them from the terrace, and came down to the lawn to meet them.

A couple of uniformed State Policemen followed him.

Neale indicated the man across the saddle of Fletch's horse.

"Who's that?" he asked.

Fletch said, "Joseph Molinaro."

"Can't be," Neale said. "Molinaro's only about thirty. Younger."

Still on his horse, Gillis said, "Look at his face."

Neale lifted Molinaro's head by the hair.

"My, my," Neale said.

Fletch handed his reins to one of the uniformed policemen.

Neale asked Fletch, "Did Molinaro kill young March?"

Fletch handed Neale the rifle. "Easy to prove. This is the weapon he was carrying."

Over Neale's shoulder, Fletch saw Eleanor Earles appear on the terrace.

"Did you speak to Lydia March?" Fletch asked Neale.

"No."

"No?"

Neale said, "She's dead. Overdose. Seconal."

Eleanor Earles was approaching them.

Even at a distance, Fletch could see the set of her face. It seemed frozen.

"She left a note," Neale said. "To Junior. Saying she wouldn't say why, but she had murdered her husband. The key thing is, she said the night they arrived she went back downstairs to the reception desk to order flowers for the suite, and stole the scissors she had seen on the desk when they'd checked in. Now that he's reminded of it, the desk clerk says he was puzzled at the time why she hadn't telephoned the order down. He had also been slightly insulted, because flowers had been put in all the suites, and Mrs. March had said the flowers in Suite 3 were simply inadequate."

Eleanor Earles was standing near them, staring at the man slung over the saddle.

Neale noticed her.

"Hey," he said to the uniformed policemen, "let's get this guy off the horse."

Gillis got off his horse, to help.

Eleanor Earles watched them take Molinaro off the horse and put him on the ground.

In a moment, her face still frozen, she turned and walked back toward the hotel.

From what Fletch had seen, there was no way Eleanor Earles could have known, from that distance, whether her son was dead or alive.

THIRTY-SIX

"Good afternoon. The *Boston Star*."

"Jack Saunders, please."

Fletch had gone directly to Room 102 — Crystal Faoni's room — and banged on the door.

Tired and teary, she opened the door.

Fletch guessed that, badly upset by her experience of trying to breathe life into a dead man — into a dead Walter March, Junior —

Crystal had been napping fully clad on her bed in the dark room.

"Wake up," Fletch said. "Cheer up."

"Really, Fletch, at this moment I'm not sure I can stand your relentless cheer."

He entered her room while she still held onto the doorknob.

He pulled the drapes open.

"Close the door," he said.

She sighed. And closed the door.

"What's the best way to get a job in the newspaper business?" he asked.

She thought a moment. "I suppose have a story no one else has. A real scoop. Is this another game?"

"I've got a story for you," he said. "A real scoop. And, maybe, if we work it right, a job in Boston with Jack Saunders."

"A job for me?"

"Yes. Sit down while I explain."

"Fletch, I don't need a story from you. I can get my own story. Amusing lad though you are, I sort of resent the idea I need to get a story from you or from anyone else."

"You're talking like a woman."

"You noticed."

"Why are you talking like a woman?"

"Because you're talking like a man? You come bounding in here, offering to give me a story, arrange a job for me, as if I were someone who has to be taken care of, as if you, The Big He, are the source of The Power and The Glory Forever and Ever. Ah, men!"

"Golly, you speak well," Fletch said. "You just make that up?"

"Just occasionally, Fletch, you have problems with male chauvinism. I've mentioned it to you."

"Yes, you have."

"I know you try hard to correct yourself and better yourself but, Fletcher, darling, remember there can be no end to the self-improvement bit."

"Thank you. Now may we get on to the matter at hand?"

"No."

"No?"

"No. I'm not accepting a story from you. I'm not accepting a job from you. I wouldn't even accept dinner from you."

"What?"

"Well. Maybe I'd accept dinner."

After his ride into the hills to find Joseph Molinaro and his long

walk back, Fletch was feeling distinctly chilled by Crystal's air conditioner.

"Crystal, do you think this is the way Bob McConnell would respond
to such an offer from me?"

"No."

"Stuart Poynton?"

"Of course not."

"Tim Shields?"

"They're not women."

"They're also not friends."

He popped his eyes at her.

She looked away.

Neither of them had sat down.

He said, "Do you mind if I turn down your air-conditioning?"

"Go ahead."

"Can a man and woman be friends?" he asked.

He found the air conditioner controls. They had been set to HIGH.
He turned them to LOW.

"Are friends people who consider each other?" he asked.

She said, "I can get my own story."

"Do you know Lydia March killed herself?" he asked.

"No."

"Do you know she killed her husband?"

"No."

"Do you know that the shooting this afternoon was not an unsuc-
cessful attempt on the life of the Vice-President, but a successful
attempt on the life of Walter March, Junior?"

"No."

"Do you know who killed Walter March, Junior?"

"No. But I can find out. Why are you telling me all this?"

"You can't find out in time to scoop everyone else and get a job
with Jack Saunders on the Boston *Star*."

"If you know all this, why don't you use it? You haven't got a job
either."

"I'm working on a book, Crystal. In Italy. On Edgar Arthur Tharp,
Junior."

"Oh, yeah." She fiddled around the room, continuing to look unwell.
"You don't have to give me anything."

"Crystal, I have to get on a plane in a couple of hours. I can't afford
to miss it. I can't do the followups on this story. Now will you sit
down?"

"Is all this true?" she asked. "What you just said? Did Lydia March kill herself?"

"Cross my heart and hope to die in a cellarful of Walter March's private detectives. Will you listen, please?"

She sat in a light chair.

At first, clearly, part of her mind was still on the terrace, kneeling over Walter March's son, trying to breathe life into him; clearly, another part of her mind was still wondering why Fletch was insisting on giving her the biggest story of the year, of her career. . . .

"You're not listening," Fletch said. "Please. You've got to be able to phone this story in pretty soon."

Gradually, as her attention focused on what he was saying, her eyes widened, color came back to her cheeks, her back straightened.

Then she began saying, "Fletch, you can't know this."

"I'm giving you much more background than you need, just so you'll believe me."

"But there is no way you could know all this. It's not humanly possible."

"Not all my methods are human," he said.

And she would say, "Fletch, are you sure?"

And she would repeat, "Fletch, how do you know all this?"

"I have a marvelous machine."

Finally, as the pieces fitted together, she became convinced.

"Hell of a story!" she said.

Despite her initial resistance and inattention, Fletch saw there was no reason to repeat any part of the story to Crystal.

She said, "Wow!"

Fletch picked up the telephone and put the call through.

"Who's calling?" a grumpy male voice finally asked.

"I. M. Fletcher."

"Who?"

"Just tell Jack Saunders a guy named Fletcher wants to talk to him."

Immediately, Jack Saunders' voice came on the line.

"I was hoping you'd call," he said.

"How do, Jack. Remember telling me you'd give a job to anyone who scooped the Walter March story?"

"Did I say that?"

"You did."

"Fletch, I said . . ."

"Remember Crystal Faoni? She used to work with us in Chicago."

"I remember she's even fatter than my wife. Hell of a lot brighter, though."

"Jack, she has the story."

"What story?"

"The Walter March story. The whole thing. Tied in a neat, big bundle."

"Last time we talked, you listed her as a suspect in the Walter March murder."

"I just wanted to bring up her name. Jog your memory. Let you know she's here, at the convention."

"Crystal has the Walter March story?"

"Crystal has the job?"

There was only the slightest hesitation.

"Crystal has the job."

Fletch said, "Crystal has the Walter March story."

"Let me talk to her a minute," Jack Saunders said, "before I ask her to dictate into the recorder."

"Sure, Jack, sure."

Crystal came to the phone.

"Hello, Jack? How's Daphne?"

Crystal listened a moment while doubtlessly Jack Saunders said something imaginative and rotten about his wife and she laughed and shook her head at Fletch.

"Say, Jack? You'd better slip me on the payroll pretty quick. My savings are about gone. This has been an expensive convention. Too much to eat around here."

Fletch put the air conditioner dial back on MEDIUM.

Crystal would be on the phone a long time, and it would be hot work.

"Sure, Jack," Crystal said. "I'm ready to dictate. Switch me over to the recorder. I'll see you in Boston Monday."

Fletch opened the door.

"Oh, boy!" Crystal, waiting for the *Star* to straighten out its electronics, cupped her hand over the telephone receiver. "Scoopin' Freddie."

Absently, Fletch said, "What?"

"Scoopin' this story will put me right up there in the big league with Freddie Arbuthnot."

"Who?"

"Freddie Arbuthnot," Crystal said conversationally. "Don't you read her stuff? She's terrific."

"What?"

"Didn't you read her on the Pecuchet trial? In Arizona? Real award-winning stuff. She's the greatest. Oh, yeah. You were in Italy."

"You mean, Freddie . . ."

Crystal, round-eyed, looked at him from the telephone.

Fletch said, "You mean, Freddie is . . ."

"What's the matter, Fletch?"

"You mean, Freddie Arbuthnot is . . ."

"What?"

"You mean, Freddie Arbuthnot is . . . Freddie Arbuthnot?"

"Who did you think she is," Crystal asked, "Paul McCartney?"

"Oh, my God." Verily, Fletch did smite his forehead. "I never looked her up!"

As he began to stagger through the door, Crystal said, "Hey, Fletch."

He looked at her dumbly.

Crystal said, "Thanks. Friend."

THIRTY-SEVEN

"Nice of you to drop by."

Having spent a moment banging on Freddie Arbuthnot's door, Fletch scarcely noticed the door to his own room was open.

Freddie must have left for the airport.

Robert Englehardt and Don Gibbs were in Fletch's room.

Gibbs was looking into Fletch's closet.

Englehardt had opened the marvelous machine on the luggage rack and was examining it.

"I don't have much time to visit," Fletch said. "Got to pack and get to the airport."

"Pretty classy machine," Englehardt said. "Did you use it well?"

"All depends on what you mean by 'well.'"

"Where are the tapes?"

"Oh, they're gone."

Englehardt turned to him.

"Gone?"

"Don, as long as you're in the closet, will you drag my suitcases out?"

"Gone?" Englehardt said.

"Yeah. Gonezo."

Fletch took the two suitcases from Gibbs and opened them on the bed.

"Hand me that suit from the closet, will you, Don?"

Englehardt said, "Mister Fletcher, you're suffering from a misapprehension."

"I'm sure it's nothing aspirin and a good night's sleep can't fix. What about those slacks, Don. Thanks."

"Those men. In Italy. Fabens and Eggers . . ."

"Eggers, Gordon and Fabens, Richard," helped Fletch.

"They aren't ours."

"No?"

"No."

Through his horn-rimmed glasses, Englehardt's eyes were as solemn as a hoot owl's.

Fletch said, "Gee. Not ours."

"They are not members of the Central Intelligence Agency. They don't work for any American agency. They are not citizens of the United States."

"Anything in that laundry bag, Don?"

"Mister Fletcher, you're not listening."

"Eggers, Gordon and Fabens, Richard are baddies," said Fletch. "I'll bet they're from the other side of the Steel Shade."

Englehardt said, "Which is why Mister Gibbs and I came down here to Hendricks. Foreign agents had set you up to provide them with information to blackmail the American press."

Fletch said, "Gee."

Englehardt said, "I don't see how you could think the Central Intelligence Agency could ever be involved in such an operation."

"I checked," said Fletch. "I asked you."

"We never said we were involved," Englehardt said. "I said you had better go along with the operation. And then Gibbs and I came down here to figure it out."

"And did you figure it out?" Fletch asked.

"We've been working very hard," Englehardt said.

Fletch said, "Yeah."

He took off his shirt and stuffed it into the laundry bag.

After riding and walking around the countryside he needed a shower, but he didn't have time.

Englehardt was saying, "I don't see how anyone could think the CIA would be involved in such an operation. . . ."

In the bathroom, Fletch sprayed himself with underarm deodorant.

Don Gibbs said, "Fletch, did you know those guys weren't from the CIA?"

"I had an inkling."

"You did?"

"I inkled."

"How?"

"Fabens's cigar. It really stank. Had to be Rumanian, Albanian, Bulgarian. Phew! It stank. I mentioned it to him. American clothes. American accent. People get really stuck with their smoking habits." Fletch lifted clean shirts from the bureau drawer to his suitcase. "Then, when the Internal Revenue Service wallah paid me a visit, I figured there were either crossed wires, or no wires at all. There was no good reason for putting that kind of pressure on me at that moment."

He was putting on a clean shirt.

Sternly, Englehardt said, "If you knew — or suspected — Eggers and Fabens weren't from the CIA, then why did you give them the tapes?"

"Oh, I didn't," Fletch said.

"You said they're gone."

"The tapes? They are gone."

"You didn't give them to Eggers and Fabens?" Gibbs asked.

"You think I'm crazy?"

"Fletcher," Englehardt said, "we want Eggers and Fabens, and we want those tapes."

"Eggers and Fabens you can have." Fletch took their telegram from the drawer of his bedside table and handed it to Englehardt. "Says here you can pick 'em up tonight at the BOAC counter in Washington, any time between seven-thirty and nine. Very convenient for you."

Fletch grabbed a necktie he had already put in one suitcase. "Also indicates, if you read carefully, that I have not given them the tapes."

Englehardt was holding the telegram, but looking at Fletch.

"Fletcher, where are the tapes?"

"I mailed them. Yesterday."

"To yourself?"

"No."

"To whom did you mail them?"

Fletch checked his suitcases. He had already thrown in his shaving gear.

"I guess that's everything," he said.

"Fletcher," Englehardt said, "you're going to give us those tapes."

"I thought you said the CIA wouldn't be involved in a thing like this."

"As long as the tapes exist . . . ," Gibbs said.

"The tapes are evidence of information gathered by a foreign power," Englehardt announced.

"Bushwa," said Fletch.

He closed his suitcases.

"Fletcher, do I have to remind you how you were forced to do this job in the first place? Exporting money illegally from the United States? Not being able to state the source of that money? Not filing federal tax returns?"

"Are you blackmailing me?"

"It will be my duty," Englehardt said, "to turn this information over to the proper domestic authorities."

"You know," Gibbs giggled, "we didn't know any of that about you — until you told us."

"You're blackmailing me," Fletch said.

Gibbs was standing behind him and Englehardt was standing near the door.

"There's a tape on the machine," Fletch said. "Actually, it's a copy of a tape. The original was mailed out with the others."

Englehardt looked at the tape on the machine.

"Press the PLAY button," Fletch said.

Englehardt hesitated a moment, apparently wondering what pressing the PLAY button might do to him, then bravely stepped to the machine and pressed the button.

The volume was loud.

They heard Gibbs' voice:

"Snow, beautiful snow! Who'd ever expect snow in Virginia this time of year? . . . Who'd ever think my dear old department headie, Bobby Englehardt, would travel through the South with snow in his attaché case? Good thing it didn't melt!

". . . Well, I've got a surprise for you, too, dear old department headie. 'What's that?' you ask with one voice. Well! I've got a surprise for you! 'Member those two sweet little things in Billy-Bobby's boo-boo-bar lounge? 'Sweet little things,' you say together. Well, sir, I had the piss-pa-cacity to invite them up! To our glorious journalists' suite. This very night! This very hour! This very minute! In fact, for twenty minutes ago."

(*Englehardt's voice*): "You did?"

(*Gibbs's voice*): "I did. Where the hell are they? Got to live like journalists, right? Wild, wild, wicked women. Live it up!"

(*Englehardt's voice*): "I invited someone, too."

(*Gibbs's voice*): "You did? We gonna have four broads? Four naked, writhing girls? All in the same room?"

(*Englehardt's voice*): "The lifeguard."

Englehardt turned off the marvelous machine.

"The tape continues," Fletch said. "All through what I'm sure your superiors will provincially refer to as your drunken sex orgy. Lots more references to cocaine. Et cetera. 'Switch!' " he quoted Gibbs, but with a drawl. " 'Switch!' "

Englehardt's shoulders had lowered, like those of a bull about to charge.

His fists were clenched.

The skin around his eyes was a dark red.

" 'Live like journalists,' " Fletch quoted. " 'Disgusting.' "

Gibbs was assimilating more slowly. Or he was in a complete state of shock.

His face had gone perfectly white, his jaw slack. Standing, he was staring at the floor about two meters in front of him.

"Of course, this isn't the original tape," Fletch said. "But the original isn't much better. Same cast of characters, same dialogue. . . ."

Gibbs said, "You bugged our room! Goddamn it, Fletcher, you bugged our room!"

"Of course. You think I'm stupid?"

Englehardt's shoulders had slumped somewhat, his fists loosened.

"What are you going to do?" he asked.

"Blackmail you," Fletch answered. "Of course."

He picked up his two suitcases.

"Six weeks from today, I want to receive official, formal notification that all charges against me have been dropped," Fletch said. "Into the Potomac. If not, the careers of Robert Englehardt and Donald Gibbs will be over."

"We can't do that," said Englehardt.

"That's Abuse of Agency!" said Gibbs.

Fletch said, "You'll find a way."

The airport limousine had gone, so Fletch had had to send for a taxi.

He was waiting in front of the hotel with his suitcases.

Don Gibbs came through the glass door of the hotel, toward him, still looking extremely white.

"Fletcher." His voice was low.

"Yeah?"

The taxi was arriving.

"If you had any suspicion at all Eggers and Fabens weren't from the CIA, why did you go through with this job?"

"Three reasons."

Fletch handed his suitcases to the driver.

"First, I'm nosy."

Fletch opened the door to the backseat.

"Second, I thought there might be a story in it."

He got into the car.

"Third," Fletch said, just before closing the door, "I didn't want to go to jail."

THIRTY-EIGHT

"FREDDIE!"

Her carry-on bag in hand, she was almost at the steps of the twelve-seater airplane.

"FREDDIE!"

His own suitcases banging against his knees, he ran across the airplane parking area.

"FREDDIE!"

Finally, she heard him, and turned to wait for him.

"Listen," he said. Standing before her, he was huffing and puffing.

"Listen," he said. "You're Freddie Arbuthnot."

"No," she said. "I'm Ms. Blake."

"I can explain," he said.

In the late afternoon light, her eyes examined him through narrow slits.

"Uh . . . ," he said.

She waited.

He said, ". . . uh."

And she waited.

"I mean, I can explain," he said. "There is an explanation."

The pilot, in a white short-sleeved shirt and sunglasses, was waiting by the steps for them to board.

"Uh . . . ," Fletch said. "This will take some time."

"We don't have any more time," she said. "Together."

"We do!" he said. "All you have to do is come to Italy with me. Tonight."

"Irwin Fletcher, I have a job to do. I'm employed, you know?"

"A vacation? You could have a nice vacation. Cagna's beautiful this time of year."

"If I had the time, I'd stay here and polish up the Walter March story."

"Polish it up?"

"So far I've only been able to phone in the leaders."

"Leaders? What leaders do you have?"

"Oh, you know. Lydia March's suicide. Her confession note. Junior's murder. Joseph Molinaro . . ."

"Oh," he said. "Ow."

As if thinking aloud, she said, "I'll have to do the polishing in New York, before Saturday morning."

"Then you could come to Italy," he said. "Saturday."

She said, "You know the Jack Burroughs trial starts Monday."

"Jack Burroughs?"

"Fletcher, you know I won the Mulholland Award for my coverage of the Burroughs case last year."

"Oh, yes," he said. "No, actually, I didn't."

"Fletcher, are you a journalist at all?"

"Off and on," he said. "Off and on."

"I'd think you're a busboy," she said quietly, "except busboys have to get along well with everybody."

Five heads aboard the plane were looking at them through the windows.

"I have to be in Italy," he said. "For about six weeks. Or, I should say, I have to be out of this country for six weeks, more or less."

"Have a nice time."

"Freddie . . ."

"Irwin . . ."

"There has to be some way I can explain," he said.

She agreed. "There has to be."

"It's sort of difficult. . . ."

Her eyes were still squinted against the sun.

"In fact, I think it's sort of impossible to explain. . . ."

Freddie Arbuthnot's chin-up smile was nice.

She said, "Buzz off, Fletcher."

There were only two empty seats remaining aboard the plane, one in front (next to Sheldon Levi) which Freddie took, and one in back (next to Leona Hatch) which Fletch got.

Leona Hatch watched him closely while he took off his coat, sat down, and buckled his seat belt.

"I'll swear I've met you before," Leona Hatch said. "Somewhere . . ."

Five rows in front of him, Freddie's golden head was already buried in a copy of *Newsworld* magazine.

Leona Hatch continued to stare at him.

"What's your name?"

"Fletch."

"What's your full name?"

"Fletcher."

"What's your first name?"

"Irwin."

"What?"

"Irwin. Irwin Fletcher. People call me Fletch."

FLETCH'S MOXIE

ONE

"What happened to Steve?" The woman in the canvas chair leaned forward. She had not looked around from the television screen since Fletch entered the pavilion. No one else was there. She was speaking to herself, or to the air. "For God's sake, what's wrong?" she said in a tight, low voice.

Even under the canopy of a sunless day, the screen of the television monitor was blanched by daylight from the beach.

From where Fletch was standing, he could see the pale images flickering on the screen. Across a few meters of beach, between the cameras, standing lights, reflectors, and sound booms, he could see the reality of what was on the screen, the set of *The Dan Buckley Show*, host and guests.

In the middle chair sat Dan Buckley wearing white trousers, loafers, and a light blue Palm Beach shirt. Even at a distance, amiability seemed stuck on his face like a decal. To his left, in a long, white bulky dressing gown sat Moxie Mooney — the gorgeous, perky, healthy, fresh-faced young film star called away from her make-up table to oblige an on-location talk show. To Buckley's right sat Moxie's agent, manager, and executive producer, Steve Peterman in three-piece, pearl-gray suit, black shoes, and cravat.

Only Steve Peterman wasn't sitting properly in his chair. He was slumped sideways. His head was on his right shoulder.

Fletch looked at his watch.

At the back of the talk-show set a heavy, brightly colored, split curtain moved slightly in the breeze. Behind the set, down the beach the Gulf of Mexico was gray-blue in that light. On all sides of the set was the paraphernalia of a much bigger set, the location of the film-in-progress, *Midsummer Night's Madness*, starring Moxie Mooney and

Gerry Littleford. Odd-shaped trailers were parked on the beach, each facing a different direction, as if dropped there. False palm-thatched huts were here and there. Thick black cables ran every which way over the sand. Low wooden platforms, like portable dance floors, were tilted on the beach. Strewn everywhere were the odd-shaped light rigs, reflectors, cameras, and sound cranes. The whole beach looked like a sandbox of toys abandoned by a giant, rich child. Among all these trappings moved the film crew of *Midsummer Night's Madness*, working, apparently oblivious of the taping going on in their midst.

"What happened?" the woman repeated in a hoarse whisper.

Fletch put his glass of orange juice back on the bar table. He stood quietly behind the woman in her canvas chair. She still hadn't looked around at him.

Closer, he could see the monitor more clearly. In a loose headshot, Moxie was alone on screen, laughing. Then she looked to her right, as if seeking confirmation from Steve Peterman, as if turning the conversation over to him. Moxie stopped talking with a short, sharp inhale. Laughter left her face. One eyebrow rose.

The camera pulled back to include Buckley. He looked to his right, to see what had surprised Moxie. His eyes widened. His lips did not move.

The camera pulled back farther. Steve Peterman's eyes stared blankly into the camera. His head was at such an odd angle resting on his shoulder his neck seemed broken. Blood oozed from the lower, right corner of his mouth. It dribbled down his cheek past his ear and onto his cravat.

In the pavilion, the woman in the canvas chair screamed. She stood up. She screamed again. People everywhere on the beach, even on the talk-show set, were looking at her. She clasped her hands over her mouth.

Fletch took her arm. Gently, firmly, he turned her body toward him. Her eyes were affixed to the monitor.

"Come on," he said. "Time for a break."

"What's happening? What happened to Steve?"

"Coffee," he said. "They'll be right back."

He turned her away from the reality of what was happening on the set and away from the unreality of what was happening focused on the television screen.

"Steve!" she called.

He made her walk. She stumbled against the canvas chair. He pushed it out of her way with his bare foot.

"Come on," he said. "Let's see what the canteen has to offer."

"But, Steve . . ." she said.

She put her hands over her face. He put his arm around her shoulder and guided her along.

He walked with her off the pavilion and up the beach to the flat, hard-packed parking lot. There were many trailers parked there.

In a reasonable tone of voice Fletch said, "I don't think there's anything you can do just now."

TWO

"Is Steve Peterman your husband?" Fletch asked. He was careful to use the word *is* rather than *was* although he was sure the latter was appropriate.

In the metal folding chair, her drawn face nodded in the affirmative. "I'm Marge Peterman."

Fletch had found two metal chairs and placed them behind a trailer in the parking lot, out of the way of the traffic he knew would be passing to and from the beach. He sat Marge Peterman in one and went to the canteen. He brought back two cups of coffee, one black, the other with cream and sugar. He offered her both. She chose the black. He put the other coffee on the sand near her feet, and sat quietly in the other chair.

Fletch had arrived at the location of *Midsummer Night's Madness* on Bonita Beach only a half hour before. His credentials from Global Cable News had gained him entry onto location. The security guard told him Moxie was taping *The Dan Buckley Show* and enjoined Fletch to silence. He directed Fletch to the hospitality pavilion where a courtesy bar had been set up to host the television crew and other press after the taping.

There he had found a woman sitting alone on a canvas chair watching her husband on a television monitor.

Now they were sitting together behind a trailer at the edge of a parking lot.

She had sipped her coffee cup dry and then picked the Styrofoam cup to little pieces. Bits of Styrofoam were in her lap and on the sand around her feet like crumbs.

GREGORY MCDONALD

"When are they going to tell me what happened?" she asked.

She could have rebelled from Fletch's ministrations and found out for herself. She didn't. She had understood enough of what she had seen to prefer acute anxiety to dead certainty.

"Breathe deeply," Fletch said.

She took a deep breath and choked off a sob.

The Rescue Squad ambulance was the first to arrive. Blue lights flashing on the gray day, it threaded its way slowly and carefully down onto the beach. A police car arrived next, its siren and lights on, but seemingly in no great hurry. Some local police had already been assigned to the film location. Then two more police cars came screaming, skidding in as if their drivers hoped the cameras were on. Out of the passenger seat of one emerged a middle-aged woman in uniform.

Marge Peterman said, "If they take Steve to the hospital, I want to go with him."

Fletch nodded. The ambulance had not returned from the beach, as it would have if there were any necessity to go to the hospital.

"I mean, I want to go with him in the ambulance."

Fletch nodded again.

Most of the people, the film crew, the television crew, the press, had gone down to the beach like pieces of metal being drawn by a magnet. Now a few were returning. As they returned, they walked with their chins down. Their shoulders seemed higher than normal. And the skin beneath their tans seemed touched by bleach. None was talking.

Fletch could not hear the murmur of the Gulf or even the chatter of the birds among the palm trees.

An airplane taking off from Fort Myers passed overhead.

A young woman in shorts, a halter, and sandals appeared around the corner of the trailer and stopped. She looked back toward the beach, wondering what to do, looking for support. A man with a large stomach extending a dark blue T-shirt, with dark curly hair, a light meter dangling from a string around his neck arrived and stood next to the young woman. He kept looking at Marge Peterman's back. A young policeman joined them. He shoved his hat back off his sweaty forehead and looked toward the road, probably wishing there were traffic to direct. One or two other people came to stand with them.

Dan Buckley came around the corner of the trailer and looked at each of the people standing there. He, too, hesitated. Then he slowly came forward and put his hand on Marge Peterman's shoulder.

She looked up at him.

"Dan . . ."

Fletch gave Buckley his chair and stood aside.

"Mrs. Peterman . . ." Dan Buckley said. "Marge, is it?"

"Yes."

"Marge." He leaned forward in the chair, forearms on his thighs. "It seems your husband . . . It seems Steve is dead. I'm sorry, but . . ."

Buckley's face lost none of its confident amiability in its seriousness, its sadness. Watching him, Fletch wished that if he ever had to take such bad news, it be broken to him by such a professional face as Dan Buckley's. In Buckley's face there was the built-in assurance that no matter how bad the present facts, there would be a world tomorrow, a show tomorrow, a laugh tomorrow.

Marge Peterman stared at Buckley. "What do you mean 'seems to be'?" Her chin quivered. " 'Seems to be dead'?"

Buckley's hands cupped hers. "Is dead. Steve is dead, uh, Marge."

Her face rejected the news, then crumpled in tears. She took her hands from him and put them to her face. "What happened?" she choked. "What happened to Steve?"

Buckley looked up at Fletch. Then he sat back in the chair. His eyes ran along a heavy-duty cable strung over the parking lot.

He said nothing.

The young woman in the halter came forward and put both her hands on Marge Peterman's shoulders. "Come on," she said.

Marge stood up and staggered on the flat ground.

The man in the blue T-shirt took her arm.

Together, the man and the young woman walked Marge Peterman through the trailers to the front of the parking lot.

"What did happen?" Fletch asked Buckley.

Buckley focused on Fletch. "Who are you?" he asked. Fletch was wearing sailcloth shorts, a tennis shirt, and no shoes. "The Ambassador from Bermuda?"

"Sometimes I get coffee for people," Fletch said.

Buckley looked over the bits of Styrofoam on the sand. "He got stabbed." He shook his head. "He got a knife stuck in his back. Right on the set. Right on camera."

"He was quiet about it," Fletch commented.

Buckley was looking at his fingers in his lap as if he had never seen them before. "It could not have happened. It absolutely could not have happened."

"But it did though, huh?"

Buckley looked up. "Get me a cup of coffee, willya, kid? Black, no sugar."

"Black no sugar," Fletch repeated.

Fletch walked toward the canteen, past it, through the security gate, got into his rented car and drove off.

THREE

The first phone call Fletch made was to Global Cable News in Washington, D.C. His call got through to that hour's producer quickly. It was, 'Yes, sir, Mister Fletcher', 'Yes, sir, Mister Fletcher' all the way through the switchboard and production staff.

Recently Fletch had bought a block of stock in Global Cable News. Just ten days before he had toured their offices and studios in Washington.

He had allowed everyone to know he was a journalist and they might be hearing from him from time to time.

"Yes, sir, Mister Fletcher," said that hour's producer.

Fletch looked down at his bare feet on the rotten, sand-studded floorboards of the porch outside the mini-mart. When he was working full time as a journalist, no one in power had ever called him *sir*. They had called him many other things. He had always known, of course, that behind the power of the free press was the power of the buck. He had never felt the sensation of the power of the buck before. He decided he liked the sensation and that he must work to deprive himself, and others, of any such sensation. A *barefoot boy with cheek* should be listened to because he's got a story, not because he was able to buy a few shares in the company.

" 'Sir'?" Fletch said. "To whom am I speaking, please?"

"Jim Fennelli, Mister Fletcher. We met last week when you were here. I'm the bald guy with the big side whiskers."

"Oh, yeah," Fletch said. Jim Fennelli looked like a stepped-on cotton pod. "The gumdrop fetishist."

"That's me," Fennelli chuckled. "A box a day keeps the dentist healthy, wealthy, and sadistic."

"You know *The Dan Buckley Show*?"

"Sure. My mother-in-law fantasizes she's married to the creep."

"They were taping down here on Bonita Beach this afternoon. On location for a movie called *Midsummer Night's Madness*."

"Cute. Prospero's Island in Florida."

Fletch said nothing. No matter how long he lived, he would be amazed at the great mish-mash of information, and misinformation, all journalists carry around in their heads.

"Have I got it right?" Fennelli asked.

"Sure, sure. On the set of the television show were Buckley, Moxie Mooney, and her manager, Steve Peterman."

"So? Mister Fletcher, are you trying to get a publicity shot for somebody? I mean, are you invested in the film, or something? I mean, anything regarding Moxie Mooney will fly, she's gorgeous, but where's Bonita Beach, anyway, north of Naples?"

"Yeah. More south of Fort Myers. Call me Fletch. Makes me feel more like me."

"That's a hike. We'd have to send people over from Miami. You stockholders, you know. Like us to keep our expenses down."

"Send people over from Miami. Steve Peterman was murdered."

"Who?"

"Peterman. Steven Peterman. Not sure if Steven is spelled with a *v* or a *ph*. On television it doesn't matter how his name is spelled anyway, right?"

"Who is he again?"

"Some sort of a manager, a friend, of Moxie Mooney. Some kind of a producer of *Midsummer Night's Madness*."

"Yeah, but so what? Nobody knows who he is."

"You haven't got the point yet."

"My father lives in Naples. It's nice down there."

"He was stabbed to death on the set of *The Dan Buckley Show* while they were taping. While the cameras were running."

There was a pause on the other end of the line. "Yeah, that's good," Fennelli said. "You mean they don't know who did it yet? They will as soon as they look at the tapes. Fast story. A six-hour wonder. I'm not saying it's a bad story."

"Someone was murdered on camera."

"Yeah, but it wasn't a live show. It should be reported, of course."

"Obviously, both Moxie Mooney and Dan Buckley are suspects. They were the only ones within reach."

There was another pause while Fennelli marshalled in his mind his own camera/sound crew, on-camera reporter, his visuals, his story approach, his electronic pick-up.

The mini-mart was off the only road leading into Fort Myers Beach. Several of the cars and vans Fletch had seen in the parking lot of the

Midsummer Night's Madness location had gone by on the road while he was on the telephone. As he was leaving the beach, police loudspeakers had been ordering everyone present to report to the local police station. Because of security on location, police would have the identities of everyone who had been there, of every potential witness. Among these names, they would have to have the identity of the murderer.

"When did this incident occur?" Fennelli asked.

"Three twenty-three P.M."

"Can we go on the air with this right away?"

"I'm sure AP radio news has already run it."

"What do we have they don't have?"

"Beg pardon?"

"You got a new angle to the story? Like, I mean, new news?"

On the road, a white Lincoln Continental went by. Moxie was in the front passenger seat. Fletch couldn't see who was in the back seat.

"Yeah," Fletch said. "One of the prime suspects is about to disappear."

"Yeah? Which one?"

"Moxie Mooney."

The second phone call was to The Five Aces Horse Farm near Ocala, Florida.

"Ted Sills," Fletch said to whoever answered the phone. "This is Fletcher."

Fletch waited a long time. He ran his mind over the rambling ranch house, the swimming pool area, the two guest cottages, the stables, the paddocks, the tack room — all the handsome aspects of Five Aces Farm. At that hour of the day, Ted Sills would be in the tack room talking veterinary medicine and racing strategy over Thai beer with his trainer, whose name really was Frizzlewhit.

There was no breeze on the porch of the mini-mart. It was a gray, sultry day.

"Yes, sir, Fletch," Ted's voice finally boomed into the phone. "You coming by?"

"Just wanted to see if you're using your house in Key West."

"For what?" Ted Sills said. "I'm here at the farm."

"Then may I use your house in Key West?"

"No."

"Oh. Thanks."

"What are you talking about?"

"Want to get away for a few days."

"From what? You're always away. Where are you now?"

"Southwest Florida."

"You want to go to Key West?"

"Yeah."

"There are some nice hotels there."

"Don't want a hotel. Hate to be awakened in the morning by work-eager maids."

"So you don't have to make the bed. Hotels make your breakfast for you, too."

"Need a little p. and q."

"That mean peace and quiet?"

"It do."

"I need the nine thousand dollars you owe me in feed bills."

"That much?"

"The horses you have training here at Five Aces do eat, you know. A race horse cannot train on an empty stomach, you know. A race horse, like the rest of us, is encouraged by gettin' its vittles regular. You know?"

"You'll have it in the morning. Now, may I borrow your house?"

"The house rents for twelve thousand a month."

"Twelve thousand what?"

"Twelve thousand dollars."

"Twelve as in after-eleven-followed-by-thirteen?"

"The very same twelve. You're very good at figures, Fletch, except when it comes to writing them on checks for feed bills."

"You let me stay in The Blue House for free when you were trying to sell me some slow race horses."

"What do you mean, 'slow race horses'? You had a winner last week."

"Really?"

"Speedo Demon won the fourth at Hialeah. You should have been there."

"How much was the purse?"

"Let me see. Uh . . . Your share was two hundred and seventy dollars."

"Some race."

"Well, it was a plug race. And the favorite was scratched."

"Good old Speedo."

"She was faster than five other horses."

"Did the fans stay for the whole race?"

"Fletch, someone's gotta own the losers."

"Why me?"

"I expect they sense that you resent their feed bills. Horses aren't dumb that way. Race horses are like a certain kind of woman, you know. You gotta spoil 'em with a smile on your face."

"Okay. Feed the horses. But, damn it, Ted, make sure their overshoes are buckled before you put 'em in a race, willya?"

"We always buckle their overshoes."

"Now. About The Blue House."

"No."

"I only want it for a few days."

"Twelve thousand dollars. I wouldn't rent it for just a few days. Wouldn't be worth changing the bedsheets."

"You rent it very often at that price?"

"Nope. Never before."

"Uh, Ted . . ."

"I've never rented it before. I don't want to rent it. I put a price on it just because you asked. As a friend."

"Okay. As a friend, I'll take it."

"You will?"

"I will."

"Boy, no other sucker was born the minute you were."

"Make sure the bedsheets are changed."

"That's twenty one thousand dollars you owe me."

"So — some weeks are more expensive than others."

"Will I get the money?"

"In the morning. In nickles and dimes."

"You don't really care about money, do you? I mean, you have no sense of money, Fletch. I've noticed that about you."

"Money's useful when you have to blow your nose."

"Maybe I'll drop by, while you're there. There are a couple of other race horses I'd like to talk to you about."

"Don't expect to stay in your own house, Ted. You'll find the room rent very expensive."

"Naw, I'd stay at a hotel. I'll phone down to the Lopezes. They'll open the house for you. You going down tonight?"

"Yeah."

"I'll tell the Lopezes you tip well."

"Do. And tell good ol' Speedo Demon happy munchin' for me."

Fletch didn't need his credit card for the third phone call he made. It was to the airport in Fort Myers.

The man Fletch spoke to there repeated three times that Fletch was chartering a one-way flight from Fort Myers to Key West, with no stops. Which made it four times he said it altogether. There was something hard, almost threatening in the man's voice when he said *with no stops*.

"There will be no dope aboard the plane," Fletch finally assured him. "Except me."

Fletch pushed open the door to the mini-mart.

The woman behind the counter was Cuban. She looked at his smile and said with an impeccable accent, "How do you do? You need shoes to come in the store."

"Can you direct me to the police station?" Fletch asked.

Immediately, her face expressed genuine concern. "Is there some problem?" She glanced through the windows. "Trouble?"

Fletch grinned more broadly.

"Of course."

FOUR

The lobby of the police station looked like the departure point for a summer camp. The film and television crews sat around in various combinations of shorts, jeans, T-shirts, halters, sandals, boots, sneakers, sunglasses, western hats, warm-up jackets. Plastic and leather sacks bulging with equipment hung from their shoulders and lay at their feet. Fletch had put moccasins on before entering the station.

The local press, two wearing neckties, stood in a clump in the middle of the lobby. There were lightweight sound cameras among them.

Fletch leaned against the frame of the front door.

All these various people engaged in getting various kinds of reality onto various kinds of film eyed each other with friendly distance, like members of different denominations at a religious convention. They were all brothers in the faith but they worshipped at different altars.

A few looked at Fletch curiously, but no group claimed him. He was not proselytized.

Around the room were a few familiar faces he had never seen before in person. Edith Howell, who played older women, mothers, these days; John Hoyt, who played fathers, businessmen, lawyers, sheriffs; John Meade, who played the local yokel in any locale. The young male lead, Gerry Littleford, sat on a bench along the wall in white duck trousers and a skintight black T-shirt. Like a well-designed sports car, even at rest he looked like he was going three hundred kilometers an hour. His lean body seemed molded by the wind. His black skin shone with energy. His dark eyes reflected light as they flashed around the room, seeing everything, watching everybody at once, missing nothing. The girl in the halter who had been kind to Marge Peterman was next to him, leaning against a wall, chewing a thumbnail. Marge Peterman was not there. There was a short, thin, weather-beaten man Fletch had not seen before, even on film, wearing some sort of a campaign hat and longer shorts than others wore. Fletch noticed him now because he was the only person in the room who did not seem a part of any group.

The booking desk was to the left. Across the lobby from it, between two brown doors, was a secretary's desk. One door was labeled CHIEF OF POLICE, the other, INVESTIGATIONS.

The instant the door marked INVESTIGATIONS opened the two mini-cameras were hefted onto shoulders, unnaturally white lights went on, and the two men in neckties, holding up pen-sized microphones like priests about to give blessings, stepped forward. The other reporters followed them.

Her head neither particularly up nor down, her eyes looking directly at no one, Moxie Mooney came through the door and started slowly across the lobby. She was a saddened, concerned person momentarily oblivious to others, despite the light, despite the noise.

Using a Brazilian dance step which hadn't been invented yet and elbows which had had much practice, Fletch shoved forward with the rest of the press. The reporters were murmuring polite questions, *How do you feel? Will shooting continue on* Midsummer Night's Madness?

Fletch's voice was the loudest and sharpest of all: "Ms. Mooney — did you kill Steven Peterman?"

All the reporters jerked their heads to look at him and some of them even gasped.

Moxie Mooney's deep brown eyes settled on him and narrowed.

Fletch repeated: "Did you kill Steve Peterman?"

With a hard stare, she said, "What's your name, buster?"

"Fletcher," he said. Magnanimously, he added, "You can call me Fletch, though. When you call me."

Other reporters t'ched and shook their heads and otherwise expressed embarrassment at their crass colleague.

After staring at him a moment, Moxie said, slowly, clearly into the cameras, "I did not kill Steve Peterman."

The other reporters resumed clucking sympathetic questions. *How long have you known Steve Peterman? Were you close?*

Loudly, Fletch asked: "Ms. Mooney — were you and Steve Peterman lovers?"

When she looked at Fletch this time, there was revulsion in her face.

"No," she said. "Mister Peterman and I were not lovers."

"What were your relations with Peterman?" Fletch asked.

Moxie hesitated, just slightly. "Strictly business. Steve was my manager," she said. "He took care of my business affairs. He helped produce this film." Her eyes closed fully and she took a deep breath. "And he was my friend."

Fletch thought he was doing a sufficiently surreptitious job of fading back through the crowd when he felt a hand on his arm.

He turned.

The short man was squinting at Fletch. He removed his hand.

"Haven't seen you before," he said. "Who are you?"

"I. M. Fletcher. Global Cable News."

"City guy, huh? National news type."

"You got it in one."

Behind the short man, the question rang out: *Do you think the murder of Peterman had anything to do with the earlier hit-and-run incident?*

Fletch couldn't hear Moxie's answer.

"Listen to me, Mister," the short reporter said. "We don't treat people like that around here."

"Like what?"

"That little lady —" The reporter jerked his tape recorder toward the sweat-stained shirt of another reporter: " — just lost her friend to death. Do you understand that? Asking her questions like you just did is just plain uncivil."

"Where you from?" Fletch asked. *"The Girl Scout Monthly?"*

"St. Petersburg."

"Listen, man —"

"Don't you 'listen, man' me." The short man pressed his index finger against Fletch's chest. "You get away from Ms. Mooney and you get away from this story, or you'll find yourself stomped."

Fletch heard a reporter ask: *Ms. Mooney, do you believe there are people trying to stop this film from being made?*

Again, Fletch did not hear her answer.

To the short reporter he said, "That would be uncivil of you."

"Don't you scoff at us, Mister. You work South and you mind your manners — you hear?"

"In this business," Fletch said to the short reporter, "there is no such thing as a wrong question. There are only wrong answers."

As he was leaving the lobby, Fletch heard a reporter ask: *Ms. Mooney, have you yourself received any death threats?*

"Hey," Moxie said.

She got into the front seat of the white Lincoln Continental and closed the door.

"Hey." Fletch was waiting in the back seat. She had taken exactly as long with the press as he thought she would. Without air-conditioning running, the car was hot, even on a gray day.

"Why are you sitting in the front seat?" Fletch asked.

"I'm a democratic star."

A few people were milling around the car, looking in.

"You believe in Equity?"

"And Equity believes in me. I pay my dues."

She sat sideways on the front seat and put her tanned arm along the top of the backrest.

"I may call you Fletch?"

"When you call me."

"That's a funny name. Think of all the things with which it rhymes."

"Yes," he mused. "Cannelloni, for one. Prognathous, lasket, checkerberry, scantling, Pyeshkov, modulas, Gog and Magog."

"You know any other big words?"

"That's it."

"Thanks for what you did for me in there." Moxie smiled. "Pulling the teeth of the other reporters — and all those to come."

"Thought there was a need for one or two clear, simple statements on the incident from you."

"Didn't I do well?"

"You did. Of course."

" 'Steve Peterman was my friend'." Moxie sort-of quoted, with a sort-of choke in her throat. "The bastard. I could have killed him."

"Someone agreed with you, apparently." Outside the window nearest Fletch stood a heavy woman in a gaily printed dress. "Moxie, they have to have this murder solved in a matter of hours."

"Why?" her face was as free of wrinkles as if she had never read a book. Moxie had read books. "Why do you say that?"

"Steve wasn't shot. Like from a distance. He was stabbed. In public."

"Steve was just dying to get on *The Dan Buckley Show*," she drawled.

"There were cameras all over the place. There were cameras working the talk show. Local press were everywhere taking pictures of everything and everybody that had paint on it, whether it moved or not."

"Rather daring of whoever did it."

"And security was so tight on location they have the names and reason for being there of everyone within yodeling distance."

"Good," Moxie said. "Let's consider the damned thing solved."

"Are you sure this isn't one of Peterman's grand publicity schemes gone awry? Like the knife was just supposed to land on the stage, or something?"

"You're kidding. Steve wouldn't risk getting a spot on his slacks if he saw an orphanage on fire."

"Hey," Fletch said.

"What?"

"Stop acting tough."

She read his face. "What am I doing, protecting myself?"

"I would say so," he answered. "It's not every day the guy sitting next to you gets stabbed. A person you know, someone important to you."

"I guess so." She sighed. "I was having real problems with Steve, Fletch. Which is why I asked you to come down. I wanted to talk it out with somebody. I was finding it very difficult to be nice to him."

"Not being nice is not the same as being murderous."

"What?"

"Forget it. You're fighting shock, Moxie. Makin' like a heartless vamp."

"Yeah."

"You know it?"

"I guess so. Sure."

"You and Steve were close at one time."

"Steve was just using me," she said quietly. "Where's Marge? Is she okay?"

Fletch shrugged. "I expect she's being taken care of."

"They questioned her first," Moxie said. "In a car. At the beach."

"I see. Were Steve and Marge close?"

"I wouldn't say Steve was close to anybody but his banker."

"I was thinking of Marge," Fletch said.

"Good," Moxie said. "Steve never thought of her."

Her head was down and she was speaking softly. Beneath her tan, her skin had whitened. The enormity of what had happened was finally sinking into her. "Phew," she said. "I guess I am confused. I'm so used to people dying on stage and on camera with me. You know? Of acting out my reaction."

"I know."

"Steve is really dead?" She had turned her face from him. "Steve is really dead."

He flicked his tongue against the side of her neck. "Hang in there, Moxie." He opened the car door to get out. "I'll pick you up for dinner. Eight o'clock okay?"

"At La Playa," she said.

He had one foot on the pavement.

She cork-screwed around on the front seat. "Fletch?"

"Yeah?" He put his head back inside the car. Her cheeks were wet with tears.

"Find Freddy for me, will you?"

"Freddy? Is he here?"

"Oh, yes."

"Oh, God."

"He's playing the attentive father these days to me, or retired on me, or something."

"Let me guess which."

"He shouldn't be loose in public, with all this goin' on. The murder."

"Is he boozin'?"

"You need to ask?"

There was sand on the rear rug of the Lincoln.

Moxie said, "I suspect all those little squiggles in his brain have finally turned their toes up in the booze. Can't blame 'em. They've been drownin' in booze for years."

Over the car's blue rug, perfect images flashed for Fletch: Frederick Mooney on stage as Willy Loman, Richard III, and Lear. On film as Falstaff, as Disraeli, as Captain Bligh, as a baggy-pants comic, as a decent Montana rancher turned decent politician, as Scanlon on Death Row, as . . .

"He was the best," Fletch said, "even when he was stinko."

"History," Moxie said.

"Where should I look?"

"One of the joints on Bonita Beach. He drove up with us this morning. Freddy never wanders far, when there's a handy bar."

Fletch chuckled. "The thought of Freddy makes poets of us all."

"See you at eight," she said. "Thanks, Fletch."

"Okay."

Walking back toward the police station, Fletch noticed big, blowsy, wet clouds blowing in from the northwest.

F I V E

"Okay," Fletch said to the secretary sitting at the desk between the doors marked INVESTIGATIONS and CHIEF OF POLICE, "I'll see whoever's in charge now."

The woman in the light yellow blouse looked at him as if he had just fallen from the moon. The lobby was still full of people.

"Have you been called?" asked the woman who had been doing the calling.

"No," Fletch said, "but I'm willing to serve."

The Investigations door opened and Dan Buckley came out looking as if he had been tumble-dried. The reporters rose to him like a puff of soot. Even without smiling, there was still amiable assurance on Buckley's face.

The short reporter glared at Fletch and made a point of stepping into the space between him and Buckley.

Are you going to run the tape of this show on television?

"No, no," Buckley answered. "I'm turning every centimeter of tape over to the police. The police will have our complete cooperation. Such a tragedy."

A middle-aged woman with handsomely waved brown hair came through the door marked INVESTIGATIONS. Fletch had never seen a police shirt so well filled. Her badge lay comfortably on her left breast. She had typewritten sheets in her hand. She was about to say something to the secretary.

"I'm next," Fletch informed her.

She, too, looked at Fletch as if he had just arrived from the moon.

"Fletcher," he said.

She looked down her list, turned a page, looked down the list, turned another page, looked down the list. "Honey," she said, "you're last."

Fletch grinned. "I bet you've been wanting to come to the end of that list."

She grinned back at him, waved the typewritten sheets at him, and said, "Come on in."

Going behind her desk, she said, "I'm Chief of Detectives Roz Nachman."

Fletch closed the door behind him.

Sitting down at her desk she peered into the window of her audio-recorder to see how much tape was left.

"Sit down, sit down," she said.

He did.

"Why don't I just give you a statement," he said. "Save time. Save you the bother of asking a lot of questions."

She shrugged. "Go ahead." She pushed the Record button on her tape machine.

"Name's I. M. Fletcher."

Sitting behind her desk, hands folded in her lap, Chief of Detectives Roz Nachman looked at Fletch's moccasins, his legs, his shorts, his tennis shirt, his arms, his neck, his face. Her smile was tolerant: that of someone about to hear a tale about fairies and witches.

"I arrived at the shooting location of the film *Midsummer Night's Madness* on Bonita Beach at about five minutes past three this afternoon. At the security gate, I showed my press credentials from Global Cable News. The security guard told me that the taping would continue until shortly before four. He directed me to the pavilion where a bar had been set up. He said a reception for the television crew and press was planned for after the taping.

"I went directly to the pavilion. Only one other person was present in the pavilion all the time I was there, a woman who later identified herself to me as the wife of the deceased. Marge Peterman. She was watching, on a television monitor, the taping of the show. I could see, at a distance and not clearly, the actual set of *The Dan Buckley Show*. I could also see, but not clearly, the monitor screen. In fact, I was looking at neither. I poured myself a glass of orange juice from the bar. My attention was called to the incident by Marge Peterman's saying, 'What happened to Steve?'.

"I looked across at the set and saw that Peterman was sitting in an odd position. I stood behind Mrs. Peterman to get a better view of the monitor. On the monitor I saw blood dribbling from Peterman's mouth. This was at three twenty-three.

"I helped Mrs. Peterman away from the pavilion, sat her in a chair at the side of the parking lot, got her some coffee, and sat with her alone until three fifty-three when some other people, Dan Buckley among them, came along, broke the news to her, and took charge of her.

"End of statement."

"You are a reporter," Roz Nachman mused. "Concise. To the point. What you could see, what you did see. Exact times by your watch. You didn't mention the ghost you saw pass through the talk-show set and drive a knife into Peterman's back."

"What?"

"Now, Mister Fletcher, despite your very complete and, I'm sure, very accurate statement, will you permit some questions?"

"Sure."

"Good of you. You're sure of the exact time?"

"I'm a reporter. Something happens, I look at my watch."

"Why were you on location of this filming?"

"To see Moxie Mooney."

"On assignment?"

"These days I get to make up my own assignments."

"From your appearance I would have taken you for something less than a managing editor."

"Didn't you know?" Fletch said. "Everyone is something less than a managing editor — star athletes, heads of state, reporters, chiefs of detectives —"

"You said no one else was in the pavilion except you and Mrs. Peterman. Not even a bartender?"

"No. We were alone."

"Did Mrs. Peterman know you were there?"

"I don't think so. I wasn't wearing shoes. I had been told to be quiet during the taping. She was engrossed in watching the monitor . . ."

"If she didn't know you were there, to whom was she speaking when she said, 'What happened to Steve?' or whatever it was she said?"

"She said, 'What happened to Steve?'," Fletch said, firmly.

"Sorry. I'm used to dealing with less, uh, professional witnesses."

"I think Mrs. Peterman was talking to herself. From her tone of voice I would say she was frightened, alarmed. Which is why I moved over behind her, to see what she was seeing."

"Had you ever seen Marjory Peterman before?"

"No."

"During the time you took her away from the pavilion, got her coffee, sat with her, what did she say?"

"Nothing, really. Just little things, like 'What's taking so long?', 'Why doesn't someone come and tell me what happened?' Oh, yeah, she said she wanted to go in the ambulance with Steve."

"So she knew her husband had been wounded, shall we say?"

Fletch hesitated. "She may have known in her heart her husband was dead. He certainly looked dead on the monitor."

"Did she say anything to indicate she knew her husband had been dealt with violently? Murdered?"

Fletch thought. "No. I don't think she said anything more than I've told you."

" 'Don't think'?"

"I know. I know she didn't say anything more." On the foot of the leg crossed over his knee, the moccasin was half off. "Except to identify herself to me as Marge Peterman."

"In response to a question?"

"I had asked her if she was Peterman's wife."

"You saw roughly the same thing Marjory Peterman saw, Mister Fletcher. What did you think had happened to Peterman?"

"I was trying to think what could have happened to him. I guess I was thinking he had suffered some kind of an internal hemorrhage. To account for the blood on his lips."

"You did not consider the possibility of murder?"

"No way. The son of a bitch was on television. I hadn't heard a gunshot. Who'd think of anyone sticking a knife into someone else on an open, daylit stage, with three cameras running?"

"That, Mister Fletcher," said Nachman looking down at her blotter, "is why I've called this meeting. So." She swiveled her chair sideways to the desk. "You had never seen Marjory Peterman before. But you did know Steven Peterman?"

"Ah." Fletch felt color come to his cheeks. "You say that because I called the son of a bitch a son of a bitch."

"Yes," Nachman nodded. "I could characterize that as a clue of your having a previous, personal opinion of the deceased."

"I knew him slightly."

"How's that?" She turned her head and smiled at him. "I think it's time for another one of your concise statements, Mister Reporter."

"About nine months ago, he spent a longish weekend at my home in Italy. Cagna, Italy."

"Italy? Are you Italian?"

"I'm a citizen of the United States. Voting age, too."

"Is Italy where you got those shorts?"

Fletch looked down at his shorts and lifted the hands in his pockets. "They have good pockets. You can carry books in them, notebooks, sandwiches . . ."

"Or a knife," she said simply. "In most of the clothes these film people are wearing you couldn't conceal a vulgar thought. So. Are you going to tell me why Peterman visited you in Italy?"

"Of course."

"Tell me first why you have a house in Italy. I mean, a struggling young reporter, no matter how precise you are . . . Cagna's on the Italian Riviera, isn't it?"

"I have a little extra money."

"Must be nice to be born rich."

"Must be," Fletch said. "I wasn't."

She waited for a further explanation, but Fletch offered none.

"Now, I'd like to know why Peterman visited you at your Italian palace."

"He was travelling with Moxie Mooney. She was on a press tour of Europe. Moxie visited me. At my little villa. He was with her."

Her eyebrows rose. "So? You knew Moxie Mooney before?"

"I've always known Moxie Mooney. We were in school together."

"Some humble reporter," Nachman commented. "Entertains big movie stars and film producers at his Italian estate. Wait until I tell the guys and gals on the local police beat. They can't even afford to go to the movies twice a week. You must spell better than they do."

"Never mind," Fletch said. "They don't like me already."

"So on that weekend at your 'little villa' in Italy, who slept with whom?"

"What a question."

"Yes," Nachman said. "It's a question. Were Moxie Mooney and Steven Peterman intimate?"

"No."

"You're making me ask every question, aren't you?"

"Yes."

"Were you and Ms. Mooney intimate?"

"Sure."

"Why 'sure'? Are you and Ms. Mooney lovers?"

"Off and on."

" 'Off and on'." Chin on hand, elbow on desk blotter, Roz Nachman contemplated what *off and on* could mean. Finally, she shook her head. "I think you should explain."

"Not sure I can."

"Try," she said. "So the hems of Justice will be neat."

"You see." Fletch looked at the ceiling. "Each time Moxie and I meet, here and there, now and then, we pretend we've never met before. We pretend we're just meeting for the first time."

Roz frowned. "No. I don't really see."

"Okay."

"Would you walk that past me again?"

"It's simple." Fletch took another long look at the ceiling. "We've known each other a long time and well. I suppose we love each other. So each time we meet, we pretend we've never met before. Which is true, you see. We never really have met before. Because people today aren't really the same people they were yesterday or the day before. Every day you're a new person; you have new thoughts, new experiences. You should never meet a person and presume she's the same person she was last week. Because she's not. It's just the reality of existence."

"I see," Roz Nachman said, staring at him. "And *then* you jump into bed together?"

"Shucks." Fletch lowered his eyelids.

"If you two have so much fun together, why don't you stay together?"

"Oh, no." Fletch glanced at the tape recorder. "You see, we probably can't stand each other. I mean, in reality."

"Because you're both much too beautiful," Roz Nachman said. "Physically."

"No, no," Fletch said. "Moxie's the most beautiful crittur who's ever eaten a french fry."

"Has she ever eaten a french fry?"

"One or two. When she can get 'em."

"She doesn't look like she's ever eaten a french fry."

"It's more complex than all that. Maybe it's that we both play the same kind of games. We make a poor audience for each other."

" 'Games'." Nachman had picked up a pencil and was running its point loosely back and forth over a piece of paper. "I wonder what that means."

"Why do I feel like I'm sitting in the office of a public school Guidance Counselor?"

"The statement you gave when you first came in here, Mister Fletcher, was factually accurate." Nachman waved her pencil at the tape recorder. "And a complete lie."

"Me? Lie?"

"No wonder you're such a rich reporter you can live on the Italian Riviera."

"I know I flunked Mechanical Drawing, Ms. Frobisher," Fletch said, "but I really want to take Auto Repair a second year."

"You certainly gave the impression you came to Bonita Beach as a reporter to interview Ms. Mooney. You certainly did not volunteer the information that you knew the murder victim, or Ms. Mooney — the latter intimately. Is all this part of some game you're playing?"

"All the information you've elicited from me is irrelevant. I didn't kill anybody."

"I wonder if you'd mind leaving that decision to the authorities?"

"I sure would mind. All I'm saying is that Marge Peterman didn't kill him either. I was with her at the moment Peterman was being murdered."

"The truth, Mister Fletcher, is that no one I've talked with so far on this list testifies to having seen either you or Marge Peterman from shortly after three until shortly before four."

"What are you saying?"

"And I've never known a reporter who can afford a house of any kind on the Italian Riviera."

Fletch said, "I write good."

"Was Ms. Mooney expecting you today?"

"Yes."

"And what kind of a game is she playing?"

"She's not playing any kind of a game. You're turning two-penny psychoanalysis into —"

"Let's go on." Sitting straight at her desk, Nachman referred to some handwritten notes.

"At least I'm answering your questions."

Nachman glared at him. "You know what happens to you if you don't."

"Yeah," said Fletch. "I don't get to take Auto Repair next semester."

"What was your impression of Steven Peterman when he spent the weekend at your house in Italy?"

"You're asking for an opinion."

"Something tells me you have one."

"I do."

"What is it?"

"He was a son of a bitch."

"Why do you say that?"

"Because you asked me."

"Why do you characterize Steven Peterman as 'a son of a bitch'?"

"He was a nuisance. Look," Fletch said, "the house there is on the beach. Above the beach. It's a beach house."

"You're losing your conciseness."

"People hang around in swim suits. Pasta and fish for supper on the patio. A little wine. Music."

"You're saying Peterman didn't fit in."

"Always in a three-piece suit. He wore a cravat. Wouldn't go on the beach because he didn't want sand against his Gucci loafers."

"Intolerable behavior."

"Always on the telephone. Calling Rome, Geneva, Paris, London, New York, Los Angeles, Buenos Aires. I know. I got the phone bill. It would have been cheaper to have had the entire French government for the weekend."

"All right. He was an inconsiderate houseguest."

"Every night he insisted everybody get dressed up and plod through the most expensive cafes, restaurants, night clubs, casinos on the Riviera."

"And you paid?"

"Every time a bill came, he was on the telephone somewhere."

"Okay."

"Worse. Every time he saw Moxie, he bothered her with some clause of some contract, or some detail of her schedule, ran over the names of people she was to meet in Berlin two weeks from then, Brussels, who, what, where, when, why. He never left her alone. She was there to relax."

"And play games with you. You two avoided him?"

"As much as we could. It's hard to ignore a government-in-residence."

"You played hide-and-seek with him."

"Yeah."

"Marjory Peterman was not with you that weekend. Right?"

"Right."

"Where was she?"

Fletch shrugged. "Home milking her minks, for all I know."

"I repeat the question: you have never seen or spoken with Marjory Peterman before today?"

"Right. No. Never."

"You knew the victim, Steven Peterman, and admit not liking him."

"I would never murder anyone over a phone bill. Instead, I just wouldn't pay it. I'd move to Spain."

"And you have this complicated love-slash-hate relationship with Moxie Mooney."

Fletch looked at her from under lowered eyelids. "Don't make too much of that."

She looked evenly back at him. "Frankly, Mister Fletcher, I think you and Ms. Mooney are capable of anything . . . together." She glanced at the tape recorder, at Fletch, and at the typewritten list on her desk. "Okay, Mister Fletcher. I guess I don't need to tell you not to leave the Fort Myers area.

"You don't need to tell me."

Roz Nachman turned off the tape recorder.

S I X

S oaking wet from running through the heavy rain, Fletch slowed at the top of the outside, sheltered stairs when he recognized Frederick Mooney's famous profile.

His back to the white, churning Gulf of Mexico, Mooney was sitting alone at a long table on the second floor verandah of a drinks-and-eat place on Bonita Beach. On the table in front of him was a half empty litre bottle. In his hand was a half empty glass.

Fletch ambled to the bar. "Beer," he said.

"Don't care which kind?" The bartender had the tight, permanently harassed look of the retired military.

"Yeah," Fletch said. "Cold."

The bartender put a can of cold beer on the bar. "Some rain," he said.

"Enough." Fletch popped the lid on the beer can. "Mister Mooney been here long?"

No one else was on the verandah.

"You come to collect him?"

"Yeah."

"Couple of hours."

"Has he had much to drink?"

"I don't know."

Fletch swallowed some beer. "You don't know?"

"Drinks out of his own bottle. Carries it with him. Five Star Fundador Cognac. I don't keep such stuff."

At Frederick Mooney's feet was an airlines travel bag.

"You allow that?"

"No. But he tips well. As long as he pays a big rent for the glass, I don't care. After all, he is Frederick Mooney."

There was a roll of thunder from the northwest. Rain was blowing into the verandah.

"Does he come here every day?"

"No. I think he hits all the places on the beach."

"In what kind of shape was he when you rented him the glass?"

"He'd been drinkin' somewhere else before. Took him ten minutes to get up the stairs. Heard him comin'. Had to help him sit down and then bring his bag over to him."

The rain spray was passing over Mooney.

"Think of a famous, talented man like that . . ." The bartender popped a can of beer for himself. "You an actor, too?"

"Yeah," said Fletch. "At this moment."

"I mean, you've come from the film crew, and all, to pick him up. What films you ever been in?"

"*Song of The South*," Fletch said. "You ever see it?"

"That the one with Elizabeth Taylor?"

"No," said Fletch. "Maud Adams."

"Oh, yeah. I remember."

"He ever talk to anybody?" Fletch asked, nodding to Mooney.

Oh, yeah, he's friendly. He talks to everybody. Usually the old ladies are six deep around him. Young people, too. Mostly he recites lines. Sometimes he gets loud."

"Good for business though, huh?"

"Sure."

"A traveling tourist attraction."

"You'd think he'd be livin' on the Riviera, or something. Superstar like that. He's a lonely man."

"All the wrong people live on the Riviera."

Fletch walked over and stood at the edge of Mooney's table.

Mooney did not look up.

Lightning flashed in the north sky.

"Your daughter sent me for you, Mister Mooney."

Mooney still did not look up. He was breathing rapidly, shallowly. Spray was lightly in his hair and on his shirt.

Suddenly, the great voice came out of this hunched over man, not loud, but with the compelling vibrato of an awfully good cello played by an awfully good musician.

"*No, no, no, no.*" He looked up at Fletch. He spoke companionably. "*Come, let's away to prison. We two alone will sing like birds i' the cage. When thou dost ask me blessing, I'll kneel down, and ask of thee forgiveness.*"

Fletch sat across from him at the empty table.

"*So we'll live, and pray, and sing, and tell old tales, and laugh at gilded butterflies, and hear poor rogues talk of court news; and we'll talk with them, too: who loses and who wins, who's in, who's out; and take upon's the mystery of things, as if we were God's spies; and we'll wear out, in a wall'd prison, packs and sects of great ones that ebb and flow by the moon.*"

Mooney, palm outward, passed his hand between the stormy sky and his face, turning his head as he did so, finally fixing Fletch with a mad stare. Mooney looked utterly insane.

"Jeez."

Terror, horror had skittered up Fletch's spine. He gulped beer and took a breath.

"Actually . . ." Fletch cleared his throat. To his own ears his voice sounded like a flute played in a tin box. "I saw you in *King Lear* once. As an undergraduate. In Chicago. Not so long ago."

Mooney's face turned puckish. "Only once?" he asked.

"Only once. I had to sell my portable radio to afford that once."

"Lear," said Mooney. "The role Charles Lamb said could not be acted."

Fletch raised his beer can. "Nuts to Charles Lamb."

The hand that reached for the glass of cognac shook badly. "Nuts to Charles Lamb."

They drank.

"Do you act?" Mooney asked.

"No."

"What?" Mooney asked. "Not even badly?"

"There's been some trouble," Fletch said slowly, carefully. "On location. Someone's been stabbed."

Mooney's eyes were half-closed. Again his breath was coming in short, shallow strokes.

"There's been a murder," Fletch said.

Mooney sat back. He looked around, at the bar, at the verandah's roof, at the storm outside. His eyes were huge, with huge pupils, dark brown and wide set. Together they were the tragi-comic masks, each capable of holding a different expression simultaneously, one sombre, sad, emotional, the other, objective, thinking. Looking at him closely,

Fletch wondered if one eye might actually be lower in the man's head than the other. He wondered if it was an actor's trick or an accident of birth. He wondered if it was an expression of the man's personality.

Mooney said, *"Do not abuse me."*

"Did you hear me? There's been a murder."

"I gather Marilyn is all right."

"Marilyn? Yes. She's okay. But she was sitting next to the victim when he was stabbed."

"And who was the victim?"

"Steven Peterman."

Mooney frowned. He scratched his gray, grizzly hair.

"Your daughter's manager, producer, whatever."

Mooney nodded.

"They were taping *The Dan Buckley Show*. In the middle of *Midsummer Night's Madness* location."

"Not a play within a play," commented Mooney, "but a stage within a stage."

"Within a stage," added Fletch. "Because the press was there, too, taking videotapes and still photographs."

"And no live audience."

"Not much of a one."

"How removed our art has become. No longer do we perform for the groundlings. For human beings we must distract from playing blackjacks in the dirt. No longer for the Dress Circle or The Balcony. But for banks and banks of cameras." Mooney leaned forward, picked up his glass and chuckled. "For the banks. Peterkin?"

"Peterman. Steven Peterman."

"Peterman was *in camera*." Mooney drained his glass. His eyes glazed. They crossed, slightly. He reached for the bottle with a very shaky hand. "Do you know the expression?"

"The thing is, Moxie's waiting for us."

"We'll just have a drink together, you and I. Talk of who's in and who's out. Get yourself a drink."

"I have one."

Mooney's eyes narrowed to find Fletch's beer can. "So you have."

He had poured himself a good three ounces.

"So who was this Peterperson. Much of a loss to the world, do you think?"

Fletch shrugged. "Moxie's manager. A producer of the film."

"And how did he die?"

"He got stabbed in the back."

Mooney laughed. "Typical of the business. The *hindustry*, as it's now called."

"I'm afraid your daughter is one of the prime suspects."

"Marilyn?"

"Yes."

"I wouldn't put it past her." Mooney looked speculatively over the railing through the storm, not seeing it.

Fletch hesitated. For such a genius, how drunk was drunk; was he seeing lucidity or Lear; was the subject Regan or Moxie? "You wouldn't put what past whom?"

"Murder." Mooney's eyes came back to Fletch. "Past Marilyn."

A worse shiver went down Fletch's spine, and up again where it hit the back of his head like a fistful of feathers.

Mooney lowered his eyes to the scarred table. "She's done it before."

"Done what?" Fletch blurted.

Mooney dug into a scar on the table with his thumb nail. "Murder," he said.

The surf pounded three times on the beach before Fletch had enough easy breath to say, "What are you talking about?"

"That incident at the school," Mooney said. "When Marilyn was thirteen, fourteen. The year her benign Daddy — yours truly — decided to transfer her to a school in England at mid-term. November, I think it was. No one is supposed to know what precipitated the sudden transfer, of course. I said I wanted her near me. I was scarcely in England at all that year."

Fletch said, "I knew she spent a year or two in school in England."

"But you don't know why." Mooney then used the tired voice of someone reciting sad, ancient history. "At the private boarding school she was attending in California, her drama coach . . . maybe I could remember his name . . ." He gulped some of his drink. ". . . Can't. No matter. Little creep. Was found drowned at the edge of the school pond, his feet sticking out. Someone had bopped him on the head with a rock. Knocked unconscious. School authorities investigated. There were only three girls anywhere near the pond that afternoon. Marilyn was the closest. Marilyn was the only one of the three who knew the creep, was a student of his. Marilyn was the pitcher on the school's ball team, entirely capable of forcefully beaning someone with a rock." Mooney hiccoughed. Then he sighed. "She did not like that drama coach. She had written me so — in flaming red pose. I mean, prose."

"The man could have slipped . . ."

"He was face down in the water. He had been hit on the back of the head. Murder most foul . . . and deliberate. Couldn't prove for a certainty who did it . . . that Marilyn did it. She was questioned. Good actress even then. Had her old man's blood, you know. Born with it. Veins are stuffed with it."

"So you hustled her to a school in England."

"Yes," Mooney said slowly. "She was being questioned, questioned, questioned. Don't object to questions, mind you. One or two of the answers might have been . . ." Mooney's voice went up the long trail.

"But if she was guilty of murder —"

Mooney jerked to attention. "She'd still be my daughter, damn it. Brilliant future. All that blood in her veins. Talent shouldn't be wasted." His shoulders eased into a more relaxed posture. "I think of the incident as nothing more than Ulysses bashing in his teacher's head with a lyre. There comes a time when one must do away with one's teacher, one way or another. Granted, Ulysses and Marilyn took a more dramatic approach than others . . ."

Fletch said, "She was having some trouble with Peterman. Which is why she asked me to come down to see her."

"What?" Mooney asked crisply. "You mean you're not in the hindustry at all?"

"No. I'm a reporter."

"Oops. Must mind my manners. Am I being interviewed?"

"No. You're not."

"I'm offended. Why not?"

"Because, sir, you're drunk."

"In your opinion . . ." Mooney paused. He blinked slowly. ". . . I'm drunk?"

"No offense."

"I'm always drunk," Mooney said. "No offense. It's my way of life. My being drunk has never stopped my giving a good interview. Or performance."

"I once read that you'd said you've made as many as thirty films dead drunk and don't remember anything about any of them. Is that true?"

Mooney's head seemed loose. Then he nodded sharply. "Tha's true."

"How can such a thing be true?"

"I love to see movies I know nothing about. Especially when I'm in them."

"I don't get it. How can you get yourself up for a scene, appear not drunk on the screen, when you're drunk?"

"Unreality," Mooney said. "Reality. The distortion of reality. You see?" he asked.

"No."

"I made a whole film, once, in Ankara. A year later, I told a reporter I'd never been in Turkey. Widely quoted. The studio said I'd been misquoted. That I'd said I had never been in a turkey." Mooney laughed. "I've been in turkeys. I guess I've also been in Turkey. Nice place, Turkey. I live in a nice place, in my mind. Filming's easy. It only takes a few minutes a day. I can always get myself up for it."

"Always?"

The pupils of Mooney's eyes were shaking, or glimmering with challenge. "Want to see me get myself up right now?"

Fletch said, "I think I just saw you do it. You were just Lear, in front of my eyes."

"I was? I did? I'll do it again." Mooney composed his face. He took a slow, deep breath. Behind his face something was pulling him to sleep. "I don't feel like it," he said.

He took a drink.

"Sorry, sir," Fletch said. "Don't mean to badger you. Just stupid curiosity, on my part."

" 'S all right," Mooney said cheerily. "I'm used to being an object of ururosity. Cure-urosity."

"You're a great man."

"Like any other," said Mooney.

"Shall we go to the car? It's not raining so hard now."

"The car!" exclaimed Mooney. He looked around himself, then out at the beach. "What, have they stopped shooting for the day. Lose their light?"

"We've been sitting through a hell of a storm. Pouring rain. Thunder. Lightning."

Mooney looked confused, curious. He said, "I thought that was in *King Lear*."

"Come on." Fletch stood up. "Your daughter's waiting."

"Involved in a murder . . ."

"Something like that."

"I wonder . . . if she has a black veil in her wardrobe."

"I don't know," Fletch said. "Time to go."

"That bottle . . ." Mooney pointed at it. ". . . goes in that bag." He pointed at the wrong spot on the floor, to his right rather than his left, to where the airlines bag wasn't.

Fletch capped the bottle and put it in the bag.

There were three other full bottles in the bag, one empty, and some bulky odd rags.

Mooney swallowed the rest of his drink, stood up and lurched.

Fletch grabbed his arm.

"Going now?" the bartender asked.

"Thank you, Innkeeper," Mooney said, "for your superb horse."

" 'Night, Mister Mooney."

"Horsepitality."

Fletch said, *"Will't please your highness walk?"*

Bent over, clutching Fletch's arm, Mooney grinned up at him. *"You must bear with me. Pray you now, forget and forgive. I am old and foolish."*

Getting him down the stairs was a chore. It took almost ten minutes.

When Mooney stepped out from under the roof he looked at the day, at the Gulf, at the rain as if he'd never seen it all before.

"Wet day," he said. "Think I'll go back to the hotel and slip into a dry martini."

"Think I'll go back to the hotel," Fletch said, "and slip into your daughter."

Mooney did not look at Fletch or turn his head but the skin just forward of his ear turned red.

Fletch put him in the back seat of the rented car.

On the drive to Vanderbilt Beach, Frederick Mooney took two swigs from his bottle and fell asleep. He snored loudly enough to awake anyone dozing in any balcony, anywhere.

SEVEN

"May I help you, sir?"

Through the glass of the front door of Hotel La Playa, the red jacketed bellman had seen Fletch drive up, get out of the car, and hesitate. It was after dark and Fletch was shoeless, in wet shorts and shirt.

"Yeah. Will you please tell Ms. Mooney her father and driver are waiting for her?"

"Certainly, sir."

Fletch leaned against the wet car. Even with doors and windows closed he could hear Frederick Mooney snoring in the back seat.

Within five minutes Moxie came through the door and down the steps. She was wearing a simple, short, black dress. And a black veil.

Fletch held the passenger seat's door open for her and got in the driver's side.

In the back seat Frederick Mooney turned quiet.

"My God," Moxie expostulated. "What's the world coming to? Think of a man like Steve Peterman being stabbed to death right before my very eyes!"

"Was it?"

"Beg pardon, young man?"

Fletch headed the car back to Route 41. "Was it before your very eyes?"

"No. Really, I didn't see a thing. I don't see how such a thing could have happened."

"Were you close?"

"Like brother and sister. Steve's been with me years. Helping me. Through thick and thin. Through good times and bad times. Ups and downs."

"Coming and going."

"Coming and going."

"Arrivals and departures."

"Arrivals and departures."

From the back seat, Frederick Mooney said, "Very good, girlie."

Moxie pulled off her hat and veil and threw them on the back seat next to her father. She was grinning. "Thought you'd like it, O. L."

"I understand if you don't carry off this performance very well indeed, darling daughter, your next engagement might be a long one in the cooler."

"He's doing the role of Scanlon," Moxie explained to Fletch.

"Oh."

"The Saint on Murderers' Row."

"I see."

"Was it you what busted the creep's plumbing, daughter?"

"I didn't mean to, honest, I didn't. See I was parin' my nails with this shiv when he come along real careless like and backed into me." Moxie shook her head. "Real careless."

"From what Peterman tells me," Mooney said, "this is a serious matter."

In the front seat, Fletch and Moxie looked at each other in sincere wonderment.

"Peterman?" Moxie asked.

Through the rear view mirror Fletch saw Mooney indicate he meant Fletch.

"Peterman," Mooney said.

"O. L." Moxie exhaled. "This man's name is Fletcher. Peterman is the name of the man what got punctured."

Mooney muttered, "I thought he said his name was Peterman."

"Dear O. L.," Moxie commented. "Always very up on my affairs. Makes a point of knowing everyone in my life. A friend to all my friends. All in all, a doting father."

"So which one got stabbed?" Mooney asked.

Fletch said, "The other one."

"Then you're Peterman," Mooney asserted.

"No," said Fletch. "I'm Fletcher. I'm the one who told you about Peterman."

"It doesn't make any difference," concluded Mooney after a pull on his bottle. "It's a very serious matter."

After a moment, seeing Mooney's head nod in the rearview mirror, Fletch asked Moxie, "You call your father O. L.?"

"Only to his face."

"I never heard that. You've always called him Freddy."

"Originally it was O. L. O. Short for Oh, Luminous One. My mother started calling him that when they were first married, young, starting out. Still does. When her poor confused mind churns out anything at all. I visited her last month. At the home. Poor mama. Anyway, over the years it got shortened to O. L."

"They call me Oh, Hell," Mooney announced from the back seat, his voice resonating in the closed car. "For short, they call me Oh, Heck." He tipped the bottle up to his mouth.

Moxie looked through the rain-spotted window. They had turned north on Route 41. "Where we going?"

"Dinner."

"And what do we do with the superstar in the back seat?"

"Take him with us."

"You've never seen Freddy in a restaurant."

"No."

"People gasp and fall off their chairs. They send over drinks, competitively. They line up to shake his hand and have a few words with him, so he never gets anything to eat. They never seem to realize how drunk he already is. I call it the Public Campaign To Kill Frederick Mooney."

"He's still alive."

"Used to find it damned embarrassing, when I was small. Public Drunkenness Being Praised."

Mooney said, *"I should e'en die with pity to see another thus."*

"Oh, God," Moxie said. "Lear. What got him on Lear? Did I say something Regan-like?"

"I think it started when I first found him in the bar," Fletch said. "The first thing I said to him was something like *'your daughter sent me to fetch you'.*"

"Yes," Moxie said. "That would be enough of a cue to get him going on Lear. And did he recite to you?"

"Yes," Fletch said. "It was marvelous. In thunder and lightning and pelting rain."

Moxie reached back and patted Mooney on the knee. "That's O. K., O. L., I never missed a meal."

"Damned right you didn't," Mooney said.

"You put me in school and mama in the hospital but nobody ever missed a meal."

Mooney shook his head in agreement. "It's a damned serious matter. I told Fletcher that."

Moxie shook her head and turned around again just as they were passing a sign saying 41. "Damned Route 41. Came here to make a movie and it seems I've spent my whole time so far on Route 41. Going back and forth. Vanderbilt Beach to Bonita Beach. Bonita Beach to Vanderbilt Beach. Life's damned hard on a working girl."

"What's this about a hit-and-run accident?" Fletch asked.

"You know about that?"

"Heard a reporter ask you something about it."

"I don't think it's related," Moxie said. "I mean, to Steve's death. It was Geoffrey McKensie's wife."

"Why does that name seem familiar? Geoffrey McKensie?"

"Australian director." Moxie yawned. "A very good Australian director. Maybe the best director in the whole world. He's done three quiet pictures. Don't think any of them have been seen much outside Australia. I've screened all three. They're magnificent. He brings up character beautifully. Very sensitive. You know, he takes the time, the fraction of a second it takes, to permit a character to do something really revealing, maybe contradictory, uh . . . you know what I mean?"

"No."

"Oh. Well. I was really hoping he'd direct this *Midsummer Night's Madness.* I thought he was going to direct it. He came here to direct it."

"And he's not directing it."

"Sy Koller is directing. Who is a nice man, and good enough."

"You mean the man, this McKensie, came all the way from Australia thinking he had a job and didn't have one?"

"With wife."

"How can that happen?"

"Such things happen all the time in the industry. There's a magic hex word in this industry — the word *bankable.*"

"You mean investible?"

"Digestible. In this business when the noncreative people have to make a decision and don't know how to make a decision based on creativity and talent they make the decision based on this word *bankable.* They argue that they can get bankers, investors interested in one property, or person, but not another. What it really comes down to is, *my property and friends are bankable, and your property and friends are not bankable.* You see?"

"And this Godfrey McKensie was declared not bankable?"

"Geoffrey McKensie. Yes."

"After he got here?"

"After he got here Sy Koller became available. Another film he was working on fell through."

"And Sy Koller is bankable?"

"Sy Koller's last five films have all been failures. Financially and critically. Disasters."

"And that makes him bankable?"

"Sure. Steve felt Sy was due to make a good picture."

"And this poor Aussie who's made three good pictures and has flown half way around the world to make a film is not bankable?"

"Right. Because nobody knows his name. Yet. Nobody here has seen his films. Everybody knows Sy Koller's name."

"They know him as a failed director. Pardon me for not believing a word of this."

"It is incredible. Which is why a person like me has a person like Steve Peterman to deal with all this. Who can understand it? Who wants to understand it!"

"Doesn't this man, McKensie, have any rights?"

"Sure. He has the right to sue. He probably is suing. But I don't think a film has been made since *Birth Of A Nation* without people suing. And people should have sued over that, if they didn't. Anyway, about ten days ago Geoffrey McKensie's wife got run over. On Old Route 41. She had stopped at a fruit and flower stand, bought some flowers and was recrossing the road to her car when she got hit. The driver didn't stop."

"Killed?"

"Died three hours later in the hospital."

"No witnesses?"

"Just the woman at the flower stand. She said the car that hit Mrs McKensie was going very fast. Was either blue or green. Driven by either a man or a woman. We're going rather far for dinner, aren't we? All the way into Fort Myers?"

"And McKensie is still around?"

"Sure."

"The funeral . . . I should think he'd want to go home . . . "

"First he had to bury his wife. Then I suppose he had to get lawyers. I hope he's suing. Maybe he has to be on location to make his suit good. I don't know. I like him. This is all terrible."

At a red light Fletch turned right.

"This is the airport," Moxie said.

"Yes, it is."

"We're eating at an airport?"

"More or less."

"We've gone out of our way to eat at an airport?"

Fletch didn't answer.

"Irwin Maurice Fletcher, I have spent enough of my life confronted with the utterly indifferent, unappetizing food served at airports."

"Call me Oh, Wondrous One for short. Or, O-l-l."

"I'll never call you for dinner."

"Be fair. You've never had a good meal at an airport?"

"Never."

"Never ever?"

"Once."

"Where? Which airport?"

"Why should I tell you? Look what you're doing to me. Taking me to dinner at an airport!"

Fletch craned his head lower and looked up through the windshield. "Above an airport, actually."

"Great. Dinner in a Control Tower. Very relaxing."

"Weather's clearing, you see. Thought it might be nice to go up in an airplane, have a leisurely snack while we watch the moon rise."

"Serious?"

"Should time out just about right."

He pulled into a parking space.

She was staring across the front seat at him. "You've hired an airplane for dinner?"

He turned off the motor. "Where else can you two superstars go tonight? One of you has been drinking all day —"

"— all life —"

"— and the other one's as jittery as a talking doll in the hands of a small boy."

"Fletcher, you're something else."

"I know that. *What* else is the question."

He got out and opened the car's trunk. She followed him behind the car.

"What's that?" she asked.

"A picnic basket. Had it made up while I was looking for Freddy. Lots of goodies. Chopped ham and pickle. Shrimp. Champagne."

He took the hamper out and slammed the trunk's lid.

He opened a back door of the car. "Mister Mooney?"

He shook Mooney's arm. The bottle in Mooney's lap was almost empty.

"We're at the airport, sir." Mooney blinked at him. "Thought we'd get high for dinner, sir."

"Very thoughtful of you." Mooney began to climb out of the car. "Very thoughtful indeed, Mister Peterman."

EIGHT

"I don't see the moon," Moxie said.

"Complaints! Have to be patient." Fletch was pouring champagne into long-stemmed glasses. "A little bubbly, Mister Mooney?"

"Never touch the stuff," Mooney said. "Upsets my cognac."

They were sitting in large leather swivel chairs. Each had a safety belt strapped across the lap. The passenger section of the airplane was furnished and decorated partly as a living room, partly as an office.

At first, the pilot who had escorted them across the dark runway had watched worriedly Frederick Mooney's stumbling gait. It did not make him less worried that Frederick Mooney was singing, very loudly and very badly, *If I had the wings of an angel . . .* As they were passing under a light, the pilot's face did a double-look and expressed shock at recognizing Moxie Mooney. He looked sharply and recognized Frederick Mooney. Solicitously, he helped Frederick Mooney up the steps and strapped him into the seat himself.

The plane took off immediately.

"I presume we're to fly in circles," Moxie said.

"How on earth can you fly any other way?" Fletch asked.

Seated, Fletch was setting the pull-out table within easy reach of their chairs with things from the picnic basket. He removed the protective cellophane from the plates of cut, assorted sandwiches. Opened the containers of iced shrimp, lobster tails, their sauces, salads. Dealt plates and cutlery and napkins around the table. Last out of the basket was a little white vase and a long-stemmed red rose. He poured champagne into the vase, put the rose in it, and set the rose in the middle of the table.

Watching him, Moxie said, "You would make an interesting husband, after all."

"I did," Fletch said. "Twice."

"As the lady said," intoned Frederick Mooney, with a cold look at his daughter, "just as they were leading her away, 'I was cursed by marriage to an interesting man'."

Fletch looked from one to another, then said, "Anyone for eats?"

Both Mooneys wordlessly heaped their plates with every food in sight. "Enough for the vanity of film stars," Fletch muttered, helping himself from the remainders. "Good thing I bought for six."

Plate in lap, Mooney swiveled his chair to look out the window while he ate.

"Now," Fletch said to Moxie, after she had downed six quarter-sandwiches, four lobster tails and half her shrimp, "want to tell me why you asked me to come down here? Or have you had enough for today? Or maybe it isn't relevant any more . . . ?"

"You're hard enough to find," grumbled Moxie. "It took me the better part of a week to trace you down."

"I was in Washington," Fletch said, "trying to find the Bureau of Indian Affairs."

"Did you find it?" She was chewing a lobster tail.

"I narrowed it down to one of three telephone booths."

She wiped her hands on a napkin. "I seem to be in real financial trouble."

"How is that possible?"

"You tell me."

"Some nights you're on two television channels simultaneously. You're on the cables so much I should think you'd twang. Your films play the theaters. Last Christmas you did the first one hundred days of *A Broadway Hit* —"

"And I'm drowning in debt. Explain that to me."

"I'd like to understand it myself. You're smudging the American dream. The rich-and-famous dream."

There were tears in her eyes. She ducked her head to her plate. "I work hard. I have to. So many people are counting on me. My work contributes to the income of literally thousands of people now. We've got my mother in this fabulously expensive sanatorium in Kansas. I've taken over some of the cost from Freddy." She lowered her voice. "And I don't have to be much of a fortune teller to say that pretty soon I'm going to have to take it all over. And everyone knows this is just a crazy business I'm in!" she said more loudly. "No security. Bankable today, a bum tomorrow. A person like me can't get so much out of herself if she thinks that next week, next month, next year sometime she's going to be on the sidewalk!"

"Have some shrimp."

"I have some shrimp."

"Have some more shrimp."

"I don't want any more shrimp," she said with annoyance. Then she looked at him. "Was that your Sympathetic Routine Number 12?"

"Number 9, actually. I wish you wouldn't see through me so quickly. It makes me blush."

"You've never blushed in your life."

"Why don't you try to tell me in some sort of narrative form, some sequence —"

"Can't."

"I'm just a simple journalist, temporarily out of work —"

"The whole thing landed on me like a big bomb just a couple of weeks ago. Just before I was due on location for *Midsummer Night's Madness*. Hell of a way to start a picture. Looking drawn and haggard."

"You've never looked drawn and haggard in your life." He looked at the lights in her tanned, blond skin, the lights in her blond hair. "Ashes and honey don't mix."

"Okay," she said. "The story. A couple of weeks ago, I get a call from a man at the Internal Revenue Service who says he's very sorry to bother me *but* . . ."

"With them it's the but that counts."

"Right away I told him to call Steve Peterman, that Steve Peterman takes care of all my business affairs, taxes, etcetera, etcetera. And he said that was why he was calling me personally because maybe Mister Peterman hadn't told me that if I didn't do something within a matter of days, I was going to jail. Me going to jail — not Steve Peterman."

"Oh, Moxie, the Internal Revenue Service always talks tough. I once had a very funny experience —"

"Right now, Fletch, I'm not interested in the comic side of the Internal Revenue Service. I asked the man what he was talking about. He said I had gone way beyond my last extension, and a lot of other things I didn't understand. I asked him to slow down and speak in a language I could understand."

"That's asking a bit too much of any government."

"Well, he did. He was really very kind. I sort of understood him, after a while. Instead of paying my taxes over the last years, Steve has been asking for extensions. So I'm years behind. I asked the man how much I owe. He said they don't know. They think it's a considerable whack of money. But then he said something or other about all the money I've had going in and out of the country makes things rather confusing."

"What money have you had going in and out of the country?"

"I have no idea."

"*Into* the country I understand, maybe. Being in the film business you probably have some foreign income. *Out of* the country I don't understand. Do you have any investments abroad?"

"Not that I know of. Why should I?"

"Well, it's possible Steve had you invested in French perfumery or something."

"He never mentioned it. You haven't heard the worst. I was greatly upset. I called Steve, and that made me more upset. He was distinctly dodgy, Fletch. On the telephone. He said, *Not to worry, Not to worry,* I was about to start principal photography on a film and I should keep my mind on that, he'd take care of everything else. I was so upset I screened *Being There* three times and *Why Shoot the Teacher?* twice."

"Say, you were upset."

"I called Steve back and told him I was taking the next plane to New York. He squawked and gobbled. By the time I got to the apartment in New York and called him, he'd been called away to Atlanta, Georgia. On business."

"While we're speaking of that, Moxie . . ."

Her eyes widened at the interruption.

" . . . You do live pretty well," Fletch said. "You have that big place in Malibu, on the beach, with a pool and screening room. You have that real nice apartment in New York —"

"Look who's talking!" she exclaimed. "A two-bit reporter with a gorgeous place on the Italian Riviera —"

"Oh. That again."

"— who's spent years on a book about some artist —"

"Edgar Arthur Tharp."

She grinned wickedly. "How's the book coming, Fletch?"

"Slowly."

"Slowly! Have you started Chapter Two yet?"

"There have been a lot of distractions."

"I need the house in California, Fletch, for my work. I live there. I need the apartment in New York. For my work. I live there. Neither place is a sun-and-sport *palacia* in Italy!"

"Well, I've had my troubles with the Internal Revenue Service, too."

"No more of your sympathy, thank you. I do believe the Internal Revenue Service, in this case, is right. In New York, I go over to Steve's office, even though I've been told he's not there. Everybody recognizes me, of course. They've been dealing with my stuff for years. I request a quiet office and all the books, all the figures which relate to me and my affairs."

"They had to give them to you."

"They did."

"But why did you ask?"

"Why not? I had to."

"Moxie, there is no way you can understand such books and figures, as you call them, without training. You needed a professional accountant."

"I could understand enough."

"You could understand nothing."

"For years Steve has been telling me I must borrow money, I must borrow money, being in debt was good for me, paying interest greatly improved my tax situation. I hated the whole thought of being in debt. He explained to me it was just paper debt. So every time he shoved papers in front of me, I signed them. Fletch, I discovered that he had borrowed millions of dollars in my name."

"Entirely possible. Probably right . . . I think. I don't know either."

"Fletch, what's a tax shelter?"

"It's a little stick house where you go to live once the Internal Revenue Service is done with you."

"He had borrowed money in my name from foreign banks. Geneva, Paris, Mexico City."

"That seems odd. I really don't know."

"He bought stock with my money, all of which seemed to diminish rapidly in value."

"Bad luck."

"Real estate in Atlantic City. A horse farm somewhere, film companies . . ."

"Moxie, the figures mean nothing to you. They wouldn't mean anything to me either. The way these business types do up their figures is meant to baffle all normal human beings."

"Fletch," she said like a scared child. "I am millions of dollars in debt. To the banks. To the Internal Revenue Service."

She turned her chair and looked out the window.

Fletch gave her the moment of silence.

Frederick Mooney had opened another bottle from his flight bag and had poured into a champagne glass.

"Oh, look," Moxie said finally. "The moon is rising."

"It is?" Fletch said.

"Perfect timing."

He leaned forward to look through the window. The moon really was rising. "How very romantic of me."

"Right in the right spot in my window, too," she said. "Mister Fletcher, are you trying to seduce me?"

"No. You're too drawn and haggard."

She shrugged. "It's always the ones I'm attracted to who won't have me."

After a while, Fletch asked, "What did Steve Peterman say when you confronted him with all this?"

"Just what you said. That I didn't know what I was talking about, everything was too complicated for me to understand, that after principal photography of the film was over he'd go over the books with me and explain everything."

"And the Internal Revenue Service?"

"He said he'd take care of that."

"And you left everything that way?"

"I spent a week trying to find you. I asked you to come down."

"I'm not an accountant. I wish I were. I see three figures together and suffer vertigo."

"I needed a shoulder to cry on."

"I've got two of them."

"Also, Fletch, I hate to speak well of you to your face but you did have one or two successes as an investigative reporter."

"Only recognized as such in retrospect, I fear."

"You've told me a few things you've done."

"Anything to while away the time."

"I thought maybe I'd get your opinion of Steve Peterman."

"He was an annoying son of a bitch."

Frederick Mooney swiveled around in his chair, to face them. "How could I have been seeing Broadway?" he asked.

"That's a good question," Fletch answered.

"We've been flying over Broadway," Frederick Mooney told his daughter. "The Great White Way. The Star Spangled Street. The Magnificent Road Of Light In An Ocean Of Darkness."

"Oh," Fletch said. "We've been flying over the Florida Keys."

"Well, young man." Frederick Mooney burped. "I suspect we're about to land on Herald Square."

NINE

"Fletch! What have you done?"

"What do you mean, what have I done?"

In the dark, Moxie was squinting at the airport where they had landed. "Where are we?"

"Here."

"We're not in Fort Myers."

"We aren't?" He was trying to hustle Moxie and Frederick Mooney from the airplane to the taxi stand. Unfortunately there were signs in all the appropriate places saying KEY WEST.

"We're in Key West!" Moxie said.

"We are?" Fletch took Mooney's clanging flight bag from him. "Darned pilot. Must have landed us in the wrong place."

"Union Square?" enquired Mooney.

"What are we doing in Key West?"

Fletch was walking them around the terminal rather than through it. "You said you were tired of Route 41."

"So?"

"All roads end in Key West. Usually in a pileup."

There were two taxis at the stand.

"Fletch," Moxie said seriously. "That woman. The Chief of Detectives. She told us not to leave the Fort Myers area. At least she told me not to leave the Fort Myers area."

"She mentioned something of the same to me, too."

Moxie faced Fletch on the sidewalk. "Then what are we doing in Key West?"

"Escaping."

"We were told —"

"That has no force in law, you know."

"It hasn't?"

"No. It hasn't. We're not out on bail, or on parole. We haven't been charged with anything."

Frederick Mooney was climbing into the backseat of a taxi.

"Are we fugitives from justice?" she asked.

"Ah, that we may be. It's just that if you run away under such circumstances people are more apt to think you're guilty."

"And we've run away. Great."

"Well, hell, Moxie, aren't you guilty?" Her eyes went from him to the patient taxi driver to Mooney's dark bulk in the back seat. "Not too many people had the opportunity, given the unique circumstances which then prevailed, of sticking ol' Steve. Up there —" Fletch pointed to the sky, "— you gave heavy enough reasons for killing him to bring the airplane down anywhere. Opportunity," Fletch said. "Motive," Fletch said.

"You mean I shouldn't have told you all that?"

"Justification," Fletch said. "Sounded a millimeter away from a confession, to me."

For a moment under the arc lights, Moxie Mooney almost looked drawn and haggard.

"Come on," Fletch said. "Let's go with Freddy. Otherwise, he might not know where he's going."

Moxie sat between them in the back seat of the taxi.

"The Blue House," Fletch said to the driver. "On Duval Street."

The taxi started off.

To Moxie, Fletch said, "I've borrowed a house. From a friend."

Mooney took a drink.

"Listen," Fletch said to Moxie. "A few days of peace and quiet . . ."

Moxie got out of the taxi while Fletch was paying the driver through the side window. She looked up at the lit house.

"Irwin," she said. "This Blue House is not blue."

"It isn't?"

"Am I going crazy? Even in this light I can tell this Blue House is not blue."

Fletch helped Frederick Mooney out of the taxi.

"Key West is an eccentric town," Fletch said. "Doubt you'll be here long enough to get used to it."

Moxie hesitated on the sidewalk. She raised her head and spoke to the sky. "What am I supposed to do?"

"Be nice," Fletch answered, helping Mooney up the three steps.

"Mister Peterson," Mooney said at the top of the stairs. "You are a nice young man, but if you don't stop helping me, I will brain you."

"Sorry." Fletch let go of him.

Mooney swayed on the verandah. "You're upsetting my balance."

Moxie followed them through the doorway. "Why is this Blue House white?"

"Jeez," Fletch said. "You couldn't call it The White House. Wouldn't be respectful."

The Lopezes, who took care of The Blue House, were not in the house. Fletch knew they lived in their own house behind the garden wall. The front door had been left unlocked, the lights on. In the dining room a tray of cut sandwiches had been set out along with a fancy ice bucket full of cans of beer. Lights were on even at the back of the house, in the billiard room.

Fletch zipped around the house turning out the lights. "I'll show you to your rooms."

Moxie said, "It's not even nine o'clock."

"Time means nothing in Key West." He started up the stairs. "Never believe a clock in Key West."

Mooney attacked the stairs. "Charge!" he said.

Plodding after him, Moxie said, "Dear O. L. Your allusion to *Arsenic and Old Lace* under these circumstances is decidedly in poor taste."

Fletch pointed to the first door on the right. "This is your room, Ms. Mooney. I think you'll find everything in order. Towels in the bathroom."

She looked into the room and then across the wide corridor at him. "Do I give you a tip?"

"If you have trouble with the air conditioner, just call downstairs."

Fletch pushed open another door. "This room is yours, Mister Mooney. See? Nice big double bed."

"Very good." Frederick Mooney staggered through the door to his room. "What time do I go on?"

"Not to worry," Fletch said. "We'll call you in plenty of time."

"Just did Lear," Fletch heard Mooney muttering through the door. "Must be *Richard III* tonight."

Moxie was standing in the doorway. Even in her black dress, even standing still, her chin tilted slightly up, the light behind her made her presence, her being, exciting.

"Good night, Ms. Mooney. Sleep well."

"Good night," she said. "Thanks for bringing my luggage."

Fletch said, "I didn't, did I."

In his own room, Fletch walked out of his moccasins, dropped his shirt and his shorts and his undershorts in a heap on the floor, walked through a warm shower in no time at all, and then walked into bed, fell down, and pulled the sheet over him.

Then he laughed.

TEN

"I can hardly wait to get old." On the bed, Moxie ran her legs down his and stretched. "Wrinkled and baggy."

"That's what we all want for you," Fletch said.

"I don't mean old," Moxie said. "Just old enough to have an excuse to get fat and ugly."

"Can hardly wait for the day."

She rolled onto her side and faced him, as he was on his side, and their naked bodies were together all the way up and down except for their stomachs. "I can hardly wait to get some roles with some real character in them."

"Belly rolls, uh?"

"Married women, mothers, nuns, grandmothers, business executives. You know what I mean — women who've lived a little, have some dimension to them and it shows in their faces."

The long door-windows were open to the second-floor balcony and the breeze coming in was slightly humid over their slightly sweaty bodies.

Being Moxie, she had come into his room naked and walked around the room slowly, turning on every light. Her body was totally tanned, as it had to be for her role in *Midsummer Night's Madness*. She had jumped onto his bed, reached down and torn the sheet off him, and then fell on him, flat, jumping to as great a height as she could manage to do so.

Which is why Fletch had turned on his side and they had come to embrace in that position.

"Not like this damned role in *Midsummer Night's Madness*. You know how the scriptwriter wrote in the character for my role? I quote: Beautiful blond female, American build, in twenties, dash Moxie Mooney question mark unquote."

"You sound a natural for the role."

"You call that writing character?"

"Well, you're beautiful, and you're blond, all the way up and down, and you're female, all the way up and down. What's an American build?"

"Guess you're lookin' at it, baby."

"I'm not seeing anything but your eyes, forehead, nose, and cheekbones."

"You're feelin' it, aren't you?"

"Oh, yes. I'm feeling it."

"Feel it some more," she said. "Arr."

"Wait a minute."

"No. Let's not."

Then he was on his back and the breeze seemed cooler to him.

"There are good roles for young people," he said. "There must be."

"Not in *Midsummer Night's Madness*. In *Midsummer Night's Madness* I am body, pure and simple, wide-eyed, innocent, staring, and stupid. All I do is say O! and look alarmed. There are more O's in that script than in ten kilos of Swiss cheese."

"Must be tough bein' just another beautiful face. Body."

Each was spread-eagled on the huge bed, cooling off. Only the tips of their fingers touched.

"Knock it off, Fletcher. I was brought up, trained to do more than stand there and say O! Freddy and I saw to that. I'm not giving you talk-show interview motif number one."

"Sounds it."

For a long moment, she looked at the ceiling. Then she said, "I guess I am. Oh, dear."

"First time you've ever called me dear."

"I didn't call you dear. I called the ceiling dear."

"Watch those expressions of affection, Moxie. Remember, I'm going to have to write to you in the slammer, and our mail will be censored."

"What I'm saying is all this trouble over this film, and the film stinks.

Wooden scenes, turgid dialogue, stereotyped characters. All it really is about is people chasing each other along a moonlit beach at night and whumpin' each other."

"Should be a hit."

"Starring Moxie Mooney."

"And Gerry Littleford."

"And Gerry Littleford. Not up to his talents either."

"If this film is so bad, Moxie dear, why are you doing it?"

"Steve said I had to. Fulfill some contract or other."

"Fulfill some contract you signed?"

"I signed. Or he signed."

"Seems to me you handed over a large slice of your life to Steve Peterman."

"Fletch, a person in my shoes has to trust somebody."

"You're not wearing shoes. I noticed."

"One cannot be one hundred percent creative sharp and one hundred percent business sharp at the same time. It is mentally and physically impossible. Some people pick wonderful business managers in the talent garden, and live happily ever after. I picked a bad apple."

"And if the District Attorney don't get you, the IRS will."

"You make everything sound so cheery."

"Everything is cheery. It's all in the point of view."

"Want me to tell you about this dumb movie?"

"Yeah. Tell me a story."

"Girl. Got it so far?"

"Yeah. American build. I can see her now."

"Small town."

"Anywhere, U.S.A."

"Anywhere. Gets raped by son of chief of police."

"Opening scene?"

"Opening scene."

"Beats the aerial view of the Empire State Building."

"Of course she doesn't tell."

"Why not?"

"Girls frequently don't tell when they've been raped, Mister Fletcher."

"Why not?"

"It embarrasses them," Moxie said uncomfortably. "It's the psychology of the whole thing. For some crazy reason they think it lowers them in the esteem of others."

"Does it?"

"You tell me. Does it?"

"I hate the whole thought."

"Have you been raped?" she asked.

"Sure."

"Have you told?"

"No."

"Why not?"

"It comes up in conversation so seldom," he said.

"You're not letting me get to the point of the movie."

"Get to the point."

"Girl is pregnant. Girl is truly in love with young black male."

"American build?"

"You've seen Gerry Littleford."

"Handsome man. Looks like a Greyhound. Racing dog, I mean. Not the bus."

"White girl and black man get engaged to be married."

"Does he know she's pregnant by another man?"

"Sure. These people really love each other."

"And what happens?"

"Town finds out they intend to get married. Town not pleased. Give black man a hard time. Town discovers girl is pregnant already. And then on midsummer's night town goes crazy and pursues black man through countryside, swamp, woods until he comes to the edge of the ocean where they catch him and beat him to death. Needless to say, rapist-son-of-police-chief deals the killing blow, right into the black man's head while the black man's head is against a rock."

"Yuck."

"*Midsummer Night's Madness.*"

"It plays upon people's worst emotions, Moxie. It really does."

"Oh, come on, Fletch. People don't think that way anymore. Gerry Littleford's wife is white."

"Yeah. In recent years, miscegenation has been made legal. Most places."

"You mean it's still illegal some places?"

"Yes."

"Come on, Fletch. I've read there is no such thing as an American black person without some white blood."

"We're talking about rape again. Aren't we." Fletch sat up on the bed and put his back against the tall, carved wooden backboard.

"I wasn't even thinking of those things." Moxie rolled over and put her chin in her elbow. "I just think as a movie it stinks. It's badly written. I think the whole thing was written between drinks in the Polo Lounge. By people who don't know anything about boys and girls, men and women, human beings, the South, the North, or America. The World. Scene for scene, it just doesn't reflect how people regard each other."

"Moxie?"

"I'm still here. In case you hadn't noticed."

"I'm just thinking. The hit-and-run. Peterman. A question some reporter asked, at the police station. Is it possible someone, or some group is trying to stop this film from being made?"

Her one visible eye looked up and down the wrinkled sheet between them. "No."

"Why not?"

"Commit murder to stop a film?"

"I suppose it's possible."

"People are more sophisticated than that." She curved her back and leaned on her elbows. "It's a bad film, Fletch. It will never be released. No one will ever see it."

"Yeah, but no one knows that, yet."

"I'll tell them, if they ask me."

"You will like hell. In fact, let me ask you this: if filming resumes on this turkey film, will you go back on location and continue starring in it?"

"I have to, Fletch. I have no choice."

"Thanks to dear old Steve Peterman."

"Thanks to dear old Steve Peterman," she repeated quietly.

Somewhere in the house a door slammed. A heavy door.

"What was that?" she asked.

"Oh, no," Fletch said.

He jumped off the bed. "Oh, no."

He ran down the stairs and opened the front door of the house and stepped out onto the porch. He looked down toward the center of Key West.

There was no one in the street except two men walking directly in front of the house.

"Come on all the way out, beautiful!" called one man.

"You're gorgeous!" screamed the other one.

The first one belted the second one, hard. Fletch heard a bottle drop.

He realized he was naked. "Sorry," he said.

He went back in the house and closed the door. Looked in the kitchen. Upstairs, he looked in Frederick Mooney's room.

Returning to his own bedroom, he said, "I guess your father went out for a walk."

"He went out for a drink and some conviviality," Moxie said. " 'Conviviality', he calls it."

"Damn."

"What time is it?"

"Stop asking that question in Key West."

"Is it possible to get a drink in Key West at this hour?"

"Are you kidding?"

"I guess it's early yet anyway. I thought you were putting Freddy to bed a little early."

"Damn, damn," Fletch said. "Damn, damn, damn."

"Nice line," Moxie said. "Up there with O, O, O, O. What's the matter with Freddy going out for a drink? Can't keep him in anyway."

"In case it hadn't dawned on you, O, Luminous Two, I was trying to keep your presence in Key West a deep, dark secret."

"Oh," she said.

"The minute Freddy's famous face hits the light of any bar, up goes the telephone receiver to the press."

"Of course," she said.

"Freddy here: Moxie here. Simple equation."

From the bed, she said, "Nice try, sport. Best laid plans, and all that."

"Damn."

"Damn," she said, looking at him as he stood in the middle of the room. "I think you have an American build."

"Yeah," he said. "I was made in the U.S.A."

ELEVEN

"So how come," Moxie asked very early in the morning in the bright kitchen, "you get to borrow such a nice big house in Key West at a moment's notice?"

Frederick Mooney was asleep in his room. Fletch had checked.

"It belongs to someone I do business with." Carefully, Fletch was trying to make individual omelettes. "A little business. Well, what it comes down to is that I give him money which he feeds to race horses."

"Sounds like a great business."

"The horses like it, I guess."

"Get any manure in return?"

"Nothing but."

"Even in daylight The Blue House is white. First thing I did this morning was run out and check." Moxie was not wearing the only dress she had brought with her. The large backyard of The Blue House was completely walled. "Are you ever going to tell me why it's called The Blue House?"

"Probably."

"But not now, right?"

"Got to be a little mystery in our relationship."

She was squeezing orange juice. "Seems we have quite a big enough mystery to deal with already."

The omelette was sticking to the pan. Fletch turned down the heat. "So who owns The Blue House?"

"Man named Sills. Ted Sills."

"Sounds vaguely familiar."

"Come to think of it, I met him at a party at your apartment."

"You did?"

"Tall guy. Beer belly. Hair plastered down."

"Right. Sounds like everybody who comes to my parties."

"Trouble is, I found myself having a drink with him later, talking about investing in his race horses. Then, later, spent a week with him at his horse farm, and the weekend here in Key West, where I actually signed some papers."

"How come you're rich?" Moxie asked.

The phone rang.

Automatically, Moxie picked it up. "The Blue House," she said. "Mister Blue isn't here." Then she said, "Hi, Gerry! How did you know I was here?" She looked across the kitchen at Fletch. "It's on the news this morning? . . . They even say The Blue House, Key West? Rats . . . " She listened and then said to Fletch, "Gerry Littleford says it was on Global Cable News at six o'clock last night that I had disappeared." She said into the phone, "That's impossible, Gerry. I didn't disappear until eight o'clock." She shook her head at Fletch. "These reporters," she said. "Aren't they awful? . . . Yeah, I know. Freddy was out on the town in Key West and spilled all. He's a very convivial man, Freddy is . . . " She turned her back to Fletch. " . . . Sure, Gerry . . . sure . . . Sure you're not just being paranoid, Gerry? Coke does that to you, you know . . . Sure . . . Okay, that would be great." She turned to Fletch. "What street are we on?"

"Duval."

"Duval," Moxie said into the receiver. "Oh, by the way, Gerry, will you bring a script of *Midsummer Night's Madness?* I didn't bring one, and

I'd like Fletch to read it. . . . What's a Fletch?" With dancing eyes she looked up and down Fletch's naked body. "A Fletch is a short order cook. He burns eggs in short order. See you."

She hung up and went back to squeezing orange juice. "That was Gerry Littleford. Wants to come down. Says the police and press are hounding him. I said okay. Lots of orange juice."

In the pan, the omelette had gone limp. Fletch turned the heat up again.

They had breakfast at the table on the cistern in the backyard.

"After Key West wakes up a little," Fletch said, "I'll go down and buy you some clothes. Make a list of what you need."

She nodded. "These eggs are interesting," she said. "Cooked in layers. Overcooked, undercooked, overcooked, undercooked, all at once. Never had eggs like these before."

"Hope the Lopezes will rescue us, sooner or later."

While Moxie was in the shower, the phone rang again. Fletch answered it.

" 'Allo?"

"Ms. Moxie Mooney, please. This is Sergeant Frankel, Bonita Police."

"Ms. Oxie Hooney? No one here that name. Good bye."

"Where did Ernest Hemingway live?"

"On the street parallel to this. Whitehead Street," Fletch answered. "Great writer. No sense of humor."

Moxie chalked her cue-tip. "What handicap will you give me?"

Fletch triangled the billiard balls. "Have you been playing very much?"

"None at all."

"You play very well. Ten point in a hundred?"

"You flatter me."

"Fifteen?"

"That would be fine but you will beat me."

"Should we play for a stake? You always wished to play for a stake."

"I think we'd better."

"All right. I will give you eighteen points and we will play for a dollar a point."

Moxie commenced to clear the billiard table. "What have you been reading?"

"Nothing," Fletch said. "I'm afraid I am very dull."

"No. But you should read."

"What is there?"

"There is *The Green Hills of Africa*. There is *A Farewell to Arms*."

"No, he didn't."

"What?"

"He didn't say a farewell to arms."

"Then you have been reading?"

"Yes, but nothing recent."

"I thought *The Old Man and The Sea* a very good story of acquisitiveness."

"I don't know about acquisitiveness."

"Poor boy. We none of us know about the soul. Are you *Croyant*?"

"At night."

It became her turn again and she pocketed three balls. "I had expected to become more devout as I grow older but somehow I haven't," she said. "It's a great pity."

"Would you like to live after death?"

"It would depend on the life. This life is very pleasant. I would like to live forever."

"I hope you will live forever."

"Thank you."

Moxie pocketed the last ball. She had won. "You were very kind to play, *Tenente*."

"It was a great pleasure."

"We will walk out together."

She was putting the telephone receiver back on the cradle when he came back into the bedroom.

"That was Geoff McKensie," she said. "He's driving down. He called from Key Largo. Guess he was feeling woebegone."

She was wearing the black dress. She looked hot. He had put on his shorts.

They had heard the Lopezes come into the house.

"I'll go get you some clothes," he said.

In the foyer of The Blue House, the Lopezes greeted Fletch.

"Mister Fletcher," said Mrs Lopez. "Good to have you here again."

Mister Lopez smiled and shook hands and said nothing.

"Thank you for having everything so nicely arranged when we arrived last night."

Mrs. Lopez took his head in her hands and kissed him. "But you ate nothing. You left the sandwiches and drank none of the beer."

"We had something on the plane."

"And this morning I did not make breakfast. Someone else did."

"We tried to clean up our mess."

"I can tell."

"Upstairs is a young woman and her father. And I guess one or two more will be coming for lunch. We can use the sandwiches you made."

"I'll make something fresh."

"I'm going down to the stores," Fletch said.

"Do you want me to go with you?" Lopez asked.

"No," Fletch said. "Just picking up a few things. Until later."

"Until later," said Mrs. Lopez.

T W E L V E

When he returned, walking slowly down Duval Street in the sunlight and warm wind, his arms laden with packages, there were two cars with their trunks open in front of The Blue House. It had taken Fletch much longer to shop for Moxie than he had expected. Originally, there was confusion in the salesman's mind. Clearly he wanted to think Fletch was buying this feminine clothing for himself, and clearly he wanted to play with Fletch in the process.

The short, weather-beaten man Fletch had seen in the police station was unloading a small yellow car. Apparently he had travelled alone. A large blue sedan was disgorging Edith Howell, the actress who could and did look like everybody's mother, and John Meade, who could not stop looking like a hayseed even when he wasn't being paid to do so. They had much luggage. Fletch had not been told to expect Edith Howell and John Meade.

Across the street a small group of tourists, cameras around some necks, stood in a loose group, to watch and chat with each other over what they were and were not seeing. A tourist road-train was crawling by in the street. The tour guide was saying through his amplifier: . . . *Blue House. In residence now in The Blue House is the actress, Moxie Mooney, and her father, the legendary Frederick Mooney. Now The Blue House is being used as a hideout for these celebrities who just yesterday were present when someone literally, really, troo-ooly got murdered on* The Dan Buckley Show. *Arrived late last night in time for old Frederick to grab a few quick ones in the local bistros. Maybe I shouldn't point out their hideout to you, but the fact that they're there is in all the morning newspapers. Coming up on your left . . .*

The front door of The Blue House was wide open.

Moxie was in the dining room stacking a tall pile of napkins. "Thank God," she said, seeing the packages in Fletch's arms. "I'm broiled and baked."

"You have more guests arriving," Fletch said. "Edith Howell. John Meade."

"Yeah. They called from Key Marathon."

"Geoff McKensie. I think."

"You knew he was coming." She was tearing through the packages on the dining room table. "More in the backyard. Gerry Littleford and his wife. Sy Koller flew down with them."

"Sy Koller? We have two directors in the house? Isn't that like having two ladies wearing the same expensive dress?"

Moxie was holding the bottom of a yellow bikini against her black dress. "I think it will fit."

"I just ordered for the American build. Where is everyone going to sleep?"

"There are couches, hammocks, swings on all the balconies."

"Where's Oh, Luminous One?"

"Gone out for some conviviality."

"This house lacks conviviality? It's about to burst with conviviality. Moxie, my idea of getting you away for a few days —"

"I am away. I don't need to hide out." Vexed, she was pincering all the packages from the table against her breasts. "I didn't murder anybody, you know."

"Then we'd better find another suspect," said Fletch. "Damned quick. And it's not going to be easy to find a better suspect than you are."

"I'll go change." She dashed out of the dining room and headed for the stairs. "You go meet the people."

Fletch carried a glass of orange juice into the backyard.

Gerry Littleford was the first to see him. "You're a Fletch," he said.

"Right."

"I'm Gerry." He stood up to shake hands. "This is my wife, Stella."

Stella was the young woman who the day before had taken Marge Peterman in hand.

"You know Sy Koller?"

The heavy man in the stressed T-shirt had also been kind to Marge Peterman the day before. Today's stressed T-shirt was green. He did not rise for Fletch or offer his hand. "I'm sorry," he said to Fletch.

"You're a cook?" Gerry sat down again.

"Moxie only said that before she tried my omelette."

"Not afterwards?"

"No. Not afterwards."

Everyone in the group had a Bloody Mary.

"I really am sorry," Koller said again. His eyes said he was sorry.

"Sorry for what?" Fletch sat in one of the white, wrought-iron, cushioned love seats. It was cooler in the walled garden, without the warm Gulf wind.

"For turning you down for that part."

"You never did."

Koller looked relieved and grinned. "I was sure I had. By my age, son, a director has turned down almost everybody. What have you done?"

"Done?"

"What films have you been in?"

"I'm not an actor."

"But I've seen your work."

"You saw me yesterday. On Bonita Beach. I was with Marge Peterman."

Koller continued to stare at him.

"Illusion and reality," Gerry Littleford said. "It's an occupational hazard. Confusion between what we see and do on the screen and what we see and do in real life. What is real and what is on film?"

"It's a sickness of the whole society," Stella said. "There is no reality for people now unless they do see it on film."

Gerry said, "It's our job to make what happens on film appear more real than reality."

"And sometimes," Sy Koller said, "we succeed."

"Was yesterday real?" Stella asked. "Or just a segment on *The Dan Buckley Show*?"

"I don't know," Sy Koller laughed. "I haven't seen it on television yet. I'll tell you after I do."

Gerry Littleford ran his eyes over the banyan tree. "Is today real?" His arm rested on the back of the love seat, behind his wife's head.

"Any day I'm not working, creating unreality," Sy Koller said quietly, "is not real."

"Yesterday . . . " Gerry said.

228

Through the back door of the house came Edith Howell, Geoff McKensie, and John Meade. Each was carrying a Bloody Mary. The Lopezes were being kept busy.

Koller jumped up. "Geoff!" He tripped on the edge of the cistern greeting McKensie. "This is great! I've been hoping we'd get some time together."

"You mean before I shove off?"

"You were pushed off," said Koller. "Something similar's happened to me. More than once. Come on into the shade."

Everyone greeted everyone else with kisses, except McKensie, who kissed no one. Gerry Littleford introduced Fletch.

Edith Howell acknowledged the introduction by saying, "I didn't know what to do with my bags, dear."

Fletch looked doubtfully at her breasts and she sat down on a wicker chair.

John Meade said, "Good afternoon. Are you our host?"

"I guess so."

"Thank you for having us."

Geoffrey McKensie said nothing. He did not shake hands. But looking at Fletch his eyes clicked like the shutter of a camera's lens.

"The light you got in *The Crow* — fantastic!" Koller walked McKensie to two chairs at the back of the group. "Particularly in that last scene, the final scene with the old woman and the boy. How did you do it?" He laughed. "Do I have to go to Australia to get light like that?"

"What a dreadful drive," Edith Howell said. "On that seven mile bridge I thought my heart would plop into the water."

"Is that why you never stopped talkin'?" Meade asked with a grin.

"As long as one is talking," Edith Howell said, "one must be alive. Is Freddy here?" she asked Fletch.

"He's here somewhere. Guess he went for a walk."

"My, how that man wanders," said Edith.

In the fan-backed wicker chair instinctively Edith Howell seemed to take over the foreground. Gangly in a light iron chair, John Meade seemed to fill up the background. In his eager manners, in his absorbing everything around him, Gerry Littleford always looked ready to go on. The other nonprofessional among them, Stella Littleford, had a cute face but was small and white to the point of sallowness. The way she slumped in her chair put her very much offstage.

"What a magnificent house," Edith Howell said. "Looks so cool and airy. You must tell us all about Key West," she said to Fletch. "How long have you lived here?"

"About eighteen hours."

"Oh." She wrinkled her nose at the back of the house. "It's called The Blue House . . . Maybe the front of it's blue. I didn't notice."

"It isn't," said Fletch.

John Meade laughed. "You sure are a good ol' boy, aren't you?"

Moxie popped out the back door wearing the new yellow bikini. There were more hugs and kisses. She kissed both Sy Koller and Geoffrey McKensie.

She sipped Fletch's orange juice. "There's no vodka in it."

"There isn't?"

"How can you make a Screw Driver without vodka?" she asked.

"You can't," he said.

John Meade laughed.

Moxie sat in the love seat beside Fletch. "Don't tell me. You're all talking shop."

"Stella and I were talking about fishing," Fletch said.

"Now that you bring it up," John Meade drawled. "Sy? Are we going to finish the film?"

Sy looked at Moxie. "I wish I knew."

And Moxie said: "That depends on the banks, doesn't it? If the bankers say we finish, we finish. If the bankers say we don't finish, we don't finish. Jumping Cow Productions."

"Yeah," said Koller. "That's the reality of this business. The only reality."

Littleford said, "We needed a break from filming anyway." He rubbed his left forearm. "I was gettin' weary of gettin' beat up. Give my bruises a chance to heal."

The Lopezes appeared and began handing around trays of sandwiches.

Edith Howell put her hand on Moxie's knee and said, quietly, "I hope it was all right for us to come, dear. I suppose we were all thinking the same thing . . . " Moxie's eyes widened. " . . . At a time like this, you need people around you. Friends."

Moxie stared at her, open-mouthed.

"Have a sandwich," Fletch said. Lopez had placed the fancy beer-ice cooler in the shade. "Have a beer. Want me to get you a beer?"

Moxie didn't answer.

Everyone but Moxie had a sandwich and drink in hand. The Lopezes had returned to the house.

Moxie stood up. She said, slowly, distinctly, "Dear friends. I did not kill Steve Peterman. Anyone who isn't sure of that fact is free to leave."

In the heavy silence, Moxie walked back to the house. She let the back door slam behind her.

Stella Littleford muttered, "That would leave an empty house."

"Shut up," her husband said. He looked apologies at Fletch, and at Sy Koller.

Fletch cleared his throat. "Someone bumped the son of a bitch off."

Stella said, "He probably deserved it. The bastard."

"I have my own theory." Sy Koller waited for everyone's attention. "Dan Buckley."

"That's a good theory," said Fletch.

"He was as close to him as Moxie was."

You're just saying that," Gerry said to Sy, "because he was the only one present not . . . " He waved his sandwich at the group under the banyan tree. ". . . not one of us. Not working with us."

"No." Sy Koller was munching his sandwich. "I know they knew each other. Before. How else do you think Steve Peterman got Buckley to tape his show on location? Buckley doesn't cart himself around to every film location, you know."

Fletch asked, "What else do you know?"

"Well, I know Peterman was to have dinner with Buckley. To discuss business. I'm pretty sure they had done business together. Buckley kept referring to some aluminum mine in Canada, throwing significant looks at Peterman, and Peterman kept smiling and changing the topic of conversation."

"That would be nice." Fletch looked at each of them. "If it were Dan Buckley."

"Sure," Sy Koller said. "Tell me this: who else could have rigged his own set? I speak as a director." He looked at Geoffrey McKensie for confirmation. "A director is responsible for everything that happens on a set. He's the only one who really understands everything on a set, what everything is for, how everything works. As a director I say — take a simple, open set like the one for *The Dan Buckley Show* and get a knife to fall accurately enough and with enough force to get into somebody's back and kill him — that's not easy. You can't rig that in two minutes flat. It had to be Dan Buckley."

"Or someone on his crew," said Meade.

"Did the knife fall?" asked Fletch.

Koller said, "I don't know. Obviously it came from somewhere with force. I was thinking about this all night. I'm sure I could rig that set to put a knife in somebody's back." Generously, he turned to McKensie. "I'm sure Geoff here could, too. But I couldn't figure the best way to do it after thinking about it all night." Summarily, he said: "I think Buckley's the only one who could have had that set primed and working for him yesterday. To kill Peterman."

In the digestive silence, the amplified voice of a tour guide wafted over the back wall. *". . . Mooneys, famous father and famous daughter, being questioned by police regarding the murder yesterday of somebody on the set of* The Dan Buckley Show. *The old man doesn't seem too upset. Hour ago I saw him downtown crossin' the street from Sloppy Joe's to Captain Tony's . . ."*

"Aw, turn it off," McKensie said. "Makes me sick."

Edith Howell again was pointing her nose at the back of The Blue House. "At least," she said, "it's nice to get away from hotel living for a few days."

THIRTEEN

Fletch pushed open the door with his foot and carried the tray into his mid-day darkened bedroom. On the tray were a few cut sandwiches, a pitcher of orange juice and a glass. He placed the tray on the bedside table.

Moxie was an *X* on the bed. She had removed her bikini top.

"I didn't kill Steve," she said.

"We have to find who did, Moxie. You're seriously implicated. Or, you're going to be. Once the facts come out. I mean, about your funny financial dealings with Peterman."

" 'Financial dealings'. I didn't even understand them. I trusted the bastard, Fletch." She groaned. "Millions of dollars in debt."

"I know you didn't understand them. I understand you had to trust someone. Either you had to be a creative person, or a business person. You had an opportunity to throw yourself one hundred percent into your creative life, and it was good for everybody that you did."

"Don't judges and people like the IRS understand that sort of thing? It's not hard to understand."

"Not in this country, anyway. In this country, everything is a business. Being creative is a business. Except you don't have any executive staff, board of directors, business training or experience to fall back on. That's all your fault, you see, because being creative here is really being nothing. In America, a creative person is only as good as his income. When you sign something, it signifies you understand what you're signing. And you're solely responsible for what you've signed."

"But Goddamn it, it happens all the time. You read about it —"

"So you have to protect yourself."

"So Steve Peterman was supposed to protect me."

"So maybe he screwed you."

"And that's what happens all the time. Jeez, Fletch."

"Ignorance is no defense in the law, they say. More to the point, it's almost impossible to prove you didn't know what you didn't know. Playing dumb is a courtroom cliche."

"Courtroom! O-oh. You had to use that word, didn't you?"

"Sorry." He sat on the bed. "Trouble is, you see, you did understand something. You arrived in Steve Peterman's office, during his absence, and went through his books. Two weeks later, sitting next to you, he gets stabbed to death."

There was a long silence in the darkened room. Her eyes roamed the ceiling. She sighed. "Looks bad."

"Moxie, I have a friend in New York, a good friend, who is both a lawyer and a Certified Public Accountant. I believe in this person. He'll need your written permission, but I'd like him to review your books in Steve Peterman's office. So we'll know how much financial trouble you're really in."

"What does it matter? They're going to try me for murder."

"There's a chance — a small chance — you read the books all wrong. That Steve represented you well. That you have no complaints. That you had no motive to murder him."

"Fat chance."

"It's worth a shot. And if the news is bad, it's proven you did have a motive to murder him —"

"Don't tell me. Just lead me to the execution chamber."

"— then at least we'll know that. We have to move fast on this. I expect the authorities will want a look at those books, too. We want to beat them to it."

"What do you want me to do?"

"Sign this piece of paper." He took a paper from the pocket of his shorts and unfolded it. "Giving my friend, Marty Satterlee, permission to review your financial accounts." He took a pen from another pocket.

"Okay." She sat up and signed the paper on his knee.

"I'll call him immediately and send a messenger up to New York with your written permission."

"Send a messenger to New York?"

"There must be someone in Key West who wouldn't mind a free ride to the big city and back."

"Wow. Sounds like you're in the movie business."

"No," Fletch said. "This is serious business."

She lay back on the bed. The back of her hand was on her brow. "Bunch of savages downstairs," she said.

"You seemed glad enough to see them."

"I never thought — until Edith gave me those pastoral eyes — they'd all think I murdered Steve. If they think I murdered someone, why are they so eager to come stay in the same house with me?"

"I don't know," Fletch said. "Maybe because they're friends." Moxie snorted. "Well, their being here is a gesture of support."

"When I want support," Moxie said, "I'll buy a girdle."

"No need for that yet, old thing." His hand passed over her breasts and stomach and hips. "But you might work on it." He picked up the plate of sandwiches. "Cream cheese and olive?"

"No. I just want a nap."

He put down the plate. "Orange juice?"

"No."

"Want company?"

"Just want to sleep. Stop thinkin'. Stop painin'."

"Okay. Hey, Moxie, that Roz Nachman — remember who she is?"

"Yeah. The Chief of Detectives."

"She's one smart, tough woman, I think. I expect we can have some faith in her."

"Okay," Moxie said. "If you say so."

Before Fletch opened the door, Moxie said, "Fletch?"

"Yeah?"

"What do I do about the funeral? I should go to Steve's funeral."

"I don't know."

"I can't stand the thought of it."

"Send flowers. Poison ivy. That will look good in court."

"I'm thinking of Marge."

"Moxie, darlin', in case you haven't got the point of all my fancy-dancin' the last twenty-four hours, right now you have to think about yourself."

There was a moment's silence from the bed. Then she said. "Just now I'd like to stop thinkin'."

"Oh, and Moxie, hate to hit you when you're down, but, one more thing . . . " There was complete silence from the bed. " . . . You just signed a piece of paper in a dark room. You didn't even try to read it." The silence from the bed continued. "You ought to stop doing things like that, Marilyn. Sleep well."

FOURTEEN

"Marty? Fletch. I'm in Key West with Moxie Mooney."

Marty Satterlee said nothing. The conversational was not Marty's style. He received information. He waited until the information he had seemed complete. Then he processed the information. Then he acted upon it. Then he dispensed information.

"In a few hours," Fletch continued, "the actor, John Meade, will be in your office with a piece of paper signed by Moxie giving you authority to examine her financial records in Steve Peterman's office." Fletch explained the rest: that Steve Peterman had been stabbed to death while sitting next to Moxie, and that Moxie worried that her financial affairs, which Peterman had been managing, might be in such disarray as to provide her, in the eyes of the law, with a motive for murdering him. "Will you do it, Marty? As you can see, it's a matter of death or a life's sentence, to coin a phrase." Fletch paused, wondering if he had provided enough information for Marty to go seek more. "Oh, yeah," Fletch added. "There's an element of haste here. John Meade very kindly has offered to fly up to New York with the paper giving you authority to act. He's leaving presently. I expect the police will want a look at these same records. They're probably in court getting permission now."

There was another pause. Fletch believed the information he had given was up to the instant. "How long does it take to discover someone's been playing fast and loose with financial records, Marty?"

"Sometimes hours. Sometimes months."

"Never minutes?"

"Never minutes."

Fletch looked through the door into the billiard room. "Will you do this, Marty? Please?"

Marty Satterlee said, "I'll get some people to help me."

"Thank you, Marty. Please call the instant you have anything."

Fletch gave Marty the telephone number of The Blue House.

*   *   *

Fletch was just standing up from the desk in the small library of The Blue House when the telephone rang.

"*Buena,*" he said into the phone. "*Casa Azul.*"

"Fletch!"

"*No 'sta 'qui.*"

"I know it's you, you bastard. You hang up and I'll twist your head off."

"Ted?" Fletch said. "Ted Sills? Nice of you to call home."

"I want —"

"I know. Like the good landlord you are, you want to know if we found everything in the house to our satisfaction — towels in the bathrooms, clean sheets on the beds, coffee in the cupboards —"

"Screw that."

"The Lopezes are marvelous people. We couldn't have felt more welcome."

"I want you —"

"I bet you want to tell me another of my expensive four-legged sacks of glue won another important horse race."

"Fletcher!"

"How much did I win this time? Two dollars and thirty-five cents?"

"Fletcher, I want you out of that house and I mean right now."

"Ted, you sound serious."

"I am serious! I want you out within the hour!"

"Gee, did I do something wrong, Ted? Use too much hot water? Didn't know you had a problem."

"None of your bull, Fletcher. I saw on TBS you're running a circus in The Blue House. In my house! Frizzlewhit said he heard something about it on the morning news. I couldn't believe it. You said you wanted to get away for a few days."

"I am away. Trying to relax from the strain of being a race horse owner."

"Moxie Mooney! Jeez!"

"Sleeping in your bed at the moment. Doesn't that just make your old loins jump though?"

"Frederick Mooney!"

"You'll need a new placard for the front door: *Mooneys, pere et —*"

"Get them out of my house!"

"Why, Ted, their staying here increases the resale value of your property by at least, I'd say, another twelve thousand dollars."

"Fletcher." Sills spoke with the deliberation of a poker player playing his ace. "You've drawn a murder investigation to my house."

"Oh, that."

"That."

"That will all come out in the wash."

"What? What did you say?"

"Really, you should be here, Ted, if only you could afford the room rent. Edith Howell is here. John Meade is in and out. Gerry Littleford. Sy Koller. Geoff McKensie."

"You're running a hotel for murder suspects! Fugitives from justice!"

"Ted, why take it so personally? They've got to be somewhere."

"Not in my house, damn it. I want you and that whole gang of murder celebrities out of The Blue House and I mean now. Within the hour."

"No."

"No? What do you mean 'no'?"

"You're forgetting something, Ted."

"I'll never forget this."

"You're forgetting I didn't borrow your house. I'm paying rent for it. If you had been kind, and let me borrow your house, of course I'd have no choice but to accede to your wishes. But as a rent payer, I have certain rights — "

"You're not a rent payer, you bastard. I never got the check."

"No? The check is in the mail."

"The deal isn't complete. I never got the check. You don't have anything to prove you sent the check."

"But Ted, I'm in the house. That means something."

"It means you're a guest. And I'm throwing you out."

"Hell of a way to treat a guest."

"I never got the check for the feed bills, either."

"That's coming in dimes and quarters. Look for the truck."

"Fletcher, just hear me out. I let you have The Blue House —"

"At an outrageous rent."

"I didn't want you to have it at all. You never told me you were going to fill the house up with fugitives from a murder investigation."

"Actually, that wasn't my intention."

"It's my house. My home. I don't want pictures of it all over the world on the front pages of police gazettes and scandal magazines."

"Never knew you were so sensitive."

"Get out. Get out. Get those people out of there. Get everybody out of that house. Instantly."

The phone went dead.

Fletch looked into the phone's mouthpiece. "Great instrument of communication," he muttered to himself. "Designed for those who insist upon having the last word."

Mrs. Lopez was in the door of the study. "Anything you want, Mister Fletcher?"

"No, thanks, Mrs. Lopez."

"Coffee? Cold drink?"

Fletch picked up the script of *Midsummer Night's Madness* from the desk. "Maybe I'll pick up a cold drink as I go through the kitchen."

She smiled. "Everyone is napping now."

"Everyone except Mister Meade. He's about to run an errand."

"Me, too," she said. "Shopping. It's nice having so many people in the house. So many people I've only seen in the movies." The woman fluttered her hand in a girlish gesture. "That Mister Mooney! What a man. What a gentleman!"

"You know about the murder?"

She shrugged. "Last night there was another murder. Up the block. Behind the house." Her hand indicated southwest. "A man was stabbed. So it goes. The tour trains are not announcing that murder."

"Why was he stabbed?"

Again Mrs. Lopez shrugged. "He said something. Or he said nothing. He did something. Or he did nothing. He had something. Or he had nothing. Why are people murdered?"

"Or because he was something."

"*Tambien.* Any special foods you like me to get?"

"Good fruit," Fletch said. "Fish. Some cheese?"

"Of course. For how many days should I buy?"

"For a few days," Fletch said. "For a few days at least."

FIFTEEN

While Fletch was reading page 81 of the *Midsummer Night's Madness* filmscript, a woman screamed.

Sitting in the back garden of The Blue House he looked up at the second storey.

It had been Edith Howell who screamed. Now she was shouting. Despite the theatrical timber of her voice, Fletch could not make out what she was saying.

He turned to page 82.

It was a drowsy afternoon.

When Fletch was on page 89, Frederick Mooney stumbled around the corner of the house. He stood in a patch of ground cover.

"There is what says she is a lady in my bed," Frederick Mooney announced.

"Is that a complaint?" Fletch asked.

"I'd rather a woman," admitted Mooney.

"It's Edith Howell," said Fletch.

"Is that who it was? I thought I recognized her from some similar scene . . . let's see, was it *The Clock Struck One?*"

"And down fell the other one?"

"Neither a lady nor a woman: Edith Howell." Mooney's feet tangled in the ground cover as he stepped forward. "Umbrage in feminine flesh."

"She asked for you the minute she arrived."

Mooney lowered himself into a shaded wrought-iron chair. "I think we did a play together once. Can't think what. At least, I remember seeing her night after night for an extended period. You know, like a hotel bathtub."

"You did *Time, Gentlemen, Time* together. On Broadway."

"Oh, yes — that damned musical. How did I ever come to do that damned musical? I was miserable in it for months . . . although the audience seemed to like it. Bad advice, I guess. Are you a theater buff?"

"No more than anyone else."

"Always amazing to me how much more other people know about theater and films than I do."

Fletch smiled. "You are theater and films, Mister Mooney."

"I've done my job," Mooney said. "Like anyone else. If I remember correctly, Mister Peterkin, you said you have nothing to do with the entertainment *hindustry.*"

"Right. I don't."

Mooney tried to read the title of the filmscript on Fletch's lap. *"Midsummer Night's Dream,"* he said. *"Call you me fair?"* he said in a sad, light voice. *"I am as ugly as a bear.* Marvelous the annual income Sweet Will still produces. He should be around to enjoy it."

"Midsummer Night's Madness," Fletch said. "The film Moxie is now doing."

"Oh, yes. Shakespeare in modern togs, I suppose. With this year's psychiatric understandings thrown in."

"No." Fletch bounced the script on his knee. "There seems no relation between the two midsummer nights."

"Just cribbing the title, eh? Wonder someone hasn't written a play called *Piglet,* 'bout a chap who sees the ghost of last night's supper. Alas, poor supper, I ate you well . . ."

"Moxie hasn't talked to you about this script?"

"Moxie does not talk to me." Mooney hiccoughed behind his hand. "Moxie does not seek my advice. I am her drunken father. 'Tis well and just, I say. There were many years when I was caused to ignore her."

"What caused that?"

Mooney's eyes approached Fletch from both sides of his head, and consumed him. "Talent is the primary obligation," said he. "Many men can love a woman and produce children; few can love the world and produce miracles."

Fletch nodded. "Mind if I seek your advice?"

Mooney said neither yes nor no. He searched the ground around his chair. He had not brought his bag of bottles. He had been convivial in the bars of Key West since before lunch, though.

"Why would anyone make a bad movie?" Fletch asked.

"It's like any other business," Mooney said. "People make mistakes. No. Allow me to amend that. No other *hindustry* operates with such a stupifyingly high mistake factor. Could you run your business, Mister Peterkin, with a ninety percent error factor?"

"How could that be?"

"Making a good film means bringing together exactly the right talents with exactly the right material. Not an easy job."

"I still don't get it. No business can keep running if ninety percent of everything it does is wrong."

"And then I can point out to you — as a bitter, burned out old man, mind you — that any business of glamour and big bucks attracts to it more than its share of incompetents and charlatans."

Fletch tried to wrap his eyes around Mooney. "Why should you be bitter?"

"Because I have had more than my share of incompetents and charlatans ruining my sleep and my waking, damaging my work, advising me ill, treating me badly, robbing me —"

"Ho down," said Fletch. "Didn't mean to heat your blood. Too hot a day for that."

Mooney inhaled deeply through his nose. He turned his profile to Fletch and exhaled slowly. Fletch wondered if such was an actor's exercise.

"I don't see how any business — or *hindustry*, as you call it — can run with such a high failure ratio."

Mooney's smile was sardonic. "There are many ways this business operates. The simple answer to your question is that just often enough the right materials come together with the right talents. The miracle of art happens. Even people like you put down your barbells and rush out, money in hand, crazed to see what mammon has wrought. And its payday for the *hindustry*. A single flash of light in the night makes safe the dark."

"I'm just reading this filmscript," Fletch jiggled his knee under it. "I don't know, of course. Never read a filmscript before. It strikes me as pretty terrible. The characters all seem to be like people you meet at a cocktail party — all fronts and no backs. They don't talk the way people really talk. I do a little writing myself — on days when there are hurricanes. It seems to me, in this filmscript much time and space are wasted while the author is floundering around trying to arrive at an idea. All that should be cut away. Don't you think writing should begin after the idea is achieved?" Mooney was looking at him like a bull bored with the pasture. "It treats controversial old issues in an insulting, offensive way. Instead of trying to create any sort of un-derstanding, my reading of it is that it is trying to provoke hatred — deliberately." Again Mooney was surveying the ground around his chair for the bottle bag. "Not a critic of filmscripts, of course," Fletch said. "But I think anyone would have to be crazy to invest a dime in this rubbish."

"Ah, Peterkin," said Mooney, obviously sitting on his own restless-ness. "You just said the magic word: *dime.* Like any other business, the film *hindustry* is about money. Lots of it. Consider this: never does so much money come together over the creation of an illusion." Mooney moved to get out of his chair but did not make it. "Think about that, if you will. Count your illusions, Mister Peterkin." Finally, Mooney succeeded in standing up. "The time for a nap has passed," he an-nounced to the banyan tree, which never napped. "I need a drink to smooth the wrinkles of my day. May I bring you one, Peterson?"

Slowly, he hoped in a theatrical manner, Fletch squinted all around him before asking, "Who's Peterson?"

"Why, you're Peterson, aren't you? Oh, I'm sorry. Peterkin. You're Peterkin. You just said that, I believe. You should have seen an early film of mine, *Seven Flags.*"

"I have."

"Cast of thousands," said Mooney. "And I kept every one of them straight."

SIXTEEN

Lopez called from the back door. "Telephone, Mister Fletcher."
Fletch hesitated. The phone had been ringing all day. Fletch
had told the Lopezes to try not to answer it. He dropped the
filmscript of *Midsummer Night's Madness* onto the cistern and trudged
to the back door.

"Sorry." Lopez's eyes sought sympathy, understanding. "It is the
police. The woman insists you come to the phone. She threatened
me."

A babble of voices was coming from inside the house.

"Okay."

Stella Littleford passed Fletch on her way out the back door. "Watch
out," she whispered.

In the corridor, Edith Howell asked, "Where's Freddy?"

"Don't know. Here somewhere."

"Where's John Meade?"

"Gone on an errand. He'll be back."

In the front hall, dressed only in bikini underpants, Gerry Littleford
stood with his back against the wall. "I don't know." He shook his
head sadly. "I don't know."

Through the open front door, Fletch saw the waiting, staring crowd
across the street had grown.

Frederick Mooney was coming down the stairs. He held a bottle
by its neck.

Behind Fletch, Edith Howell exclaimed, "Freddy! Why, I do declare!
As I live and breathe!"

Halfway down the stairs, Mooney focused on her. He pointed at
her. *"This old moon wanes . . ."*

"Come make me a drink, lover. I'm parched." She took his arm as
he came off the stairs. "A gin and tonic would be nice." She walked
him into the living room. "I found some supplies in here. Sorry I spoke
so harshly to you, when you burst into my bedroom, but, Freddy, it's
been so many years since you did such a thing . . ."

As they passed him, Gerry Littleford said to the floor, "I don't
know."

"Madame," Mooney's voice rang regally from the living room. "I do
not burst. I enter."

In the billiard room, Moxie was turning in circles. "Fletch! I've got to get out of this house!"

"You can't."

"I can't stand it!"

"You'd be mobbed. It wouldn't be safe."

She emphasized every word. "I have to get out of this house!"

Fletch went into the study and picked up the telephone receiver. "Hello?"

"Irwin Fletcher?"

Fletch sighed. "This is Fletcher."

"One moment, please."

From overhead came Sy Koller's heavy voice. He was saying something about the Gulf Stream.

"Mister Fletcher," a voice stated through the telephone.

"Yes."

"This is Chief Nachman. How are you today?"

"Fine. Thank you. Yourself?"

"Fine. Hard work always makes one feel better, don't you think?"

"Glad to hear you're working hard."

"Are you?"

"You bet."

"My hard work may result in some conclusions you're not going to like."

"No way."

"Which is why you flew Ms. Mooney to the ends of the earth last night."

"We're not that far away."

"You're in a place where it is very simple for you to skip the country."

"You noticed that."

"Yes and no. Don't push me too far, Irwin."

"You don't need to call me Irwin."

"You don't like the name Irwin?"

"Kids in school used to call me earwig."

"All right, I'll call you earwig."

"That's not what I meant."

"If, for example, you and Ms. Mooney were to leave the state of Florida, or worse, much worse, continental U.S.A. —"

"Wouldn't think of it."

"— you would find out what a little ol' Chief of Detectives can do. Your disappearing to Key West with a good many of my suspects in this murder case is an inconvenience for me — only that. Understandable, considering the people involved."

"You're being reasonable."

"Furthermore, I think you may have done the right thing."

"I have?"

"Yes. Maybe. I have a funny feeling you've done exactly the right thing. Now, if you'll be good enough to tell me exactly who is with you down there in — what's it called — The Blue House?"

"Moxie."

"Did you know The Blue House is the name of the Korean presidential residence?"

"Frederick Mooney."

"I'd love to see it someday."

"Gerry Littleford. His wife, Stella. Sy Koller. Edith Howell. The Australian director, Geoffrey McKensie."

"John Meade?"

"He's in and out. He'll be back tonight."

"Didn't you just love him in *Easy River?*"

"Don't think I ever saw it."

"Anyone else?"

"Me."

"I wouldn't forget you, earwig."

"Seeing you're being so reasonable, Chief, would you mind telling me a few things?"

"If I can. Will I see it on Global Cable News?"

"Not if you don't want."

"Your loyalties have their priorities, right, Fletcher?"

"What has shown up, so far, on the tapes and films of the murder?"

"Nothing."

"Nothing?"

"Absolutely nothing. We've been up looking at them all night, over and over. Absolutely nothing."

"That's impossible."

"The murder might as well have taken place in an alley in the dark of night, for all the good all those cameras have done us so far. We're having experts come in to look at the films. Did you know there were experts to look at film? I didn't."

"And probably experts at choosing those experts."

"That's true."

"Wouldn't Sy Koller and Geoff McKensie be able to help? They must be expert at looking at film."

"Great. Two of our prime suspects you want called in as experts. Peterman fired McKensie, you know."

"And Koller?"

"Three years ago Sy Koller and Steve Peterman had a fist fight outside a Los Angeles restaurant. Koller had Peterman on the sidewalk and was strangling him when the police arrived. Peterman did not press charges."

"Everybody loved Peterman. For sure. What were they fighting about?"

"A woman, they said."

"By the way, Koller says Peterman and Dan Buckley knew each other. That there was some tension between them."

"You see? You have the makings of a good earwig. Buckley was losing money in some investment Peterman had gotten him into."

"A lot of money?"

"How do I know what's a lot of money to these people? I live in a yellow bungalow six miles from the beach."

"Okay. Point two. This morning Sy Koller said the set for *The Dan Buckley Show* could have been rigged. That is, the knife could have been made to fall from somewhere, could have been propelled from somewhere, mechanically. You know what I mean?"

"We've thought of it."

"I mean, isn't that the way stages work? The stage set itself creates the illusion. Anything can be built into it. Anything can be made to happen."

"We've looked."

"The fact that nothing shows up on the tapes and films so far sort of substantiates his theory, doesn't it? I mean, this thing would have to be rigged by someone who knew where the cameras would be."

"It's a good theory."

"And Koller points out really the only person who would have the time, the expert knowledge, enough control over the set to rig such a thing would be Dan Buckley himself."

"You notice something?"

"What?"

"Koller seems very anxious to pin Dan Buckley."

"Maybe so. But maybe he's right."

"Last night and again this morning we went over that set millimeter by millimeter."

"Come on, Chief. What does your average cop know about stage sets? Your average citizen can be fooled by an eight-year-old magician wearing French cuffs."

"Which is why we have three set designers flying down from New York."

"Experts."

"More experts. This case is going to wreck our budget for this year, and next. Of course, having to call Key West long distance doesn't help the budget any, either."

"You have film experts coming in and stage set experts."

"We have."

"You know what this means . . ."

"It means property taxes will have to go up in this district. Because a bunch of rich film people visited us, and one of them got murdered."

"If you need theater experts to solve this crime, then it means this crime must have been committed by a theater expert."

"Very good, earwig. Especially seeing you're the only person involved who has nothing to do with theater."

People were shouting in the front hall of The Blue House.

"I didn't kill Peterman," Fletch said. "You should have asked."

"We're hiring experts by the planeload, Mister Fletcher," Chief Roz Nachman said. "And I intend to listen to them. I also intend to keep my mind open to the simple explanation."

"Which is?"

"I wish I knew. Someone put a knife in Steven Peterman's back. Granted, it happened under most unusual and complicated circumstances. But it is still a simple crime of violence."

"Anything I can do to help?"

"Yeah. Next time I call answer the phone."

There was another shout from the front hall. It sounded like Sy Koller.

"I'll answer the phone."

"Nice talking with you," Roz Nachman said. "Maybe sometime I'll come down."

"You might as well," Fletch said. "Everyone else has."

"I'll kill you!"

Fletch hurried through the billiard room and along the corridor to the front hall.

Sy Koller stood halfway down the stairs, facing downward.

Gerry Littleford stood just below him on the stairs, facing upward. He was naked. In his right hand was a carving knife.

Gerry was sexually aroused. Every muscle in his lean body was taut. His skin shone with sweat. He was moving like a panther about to pounce.

He was beautiful.

Koller took a step backward, up the stairs.

"What are you all doing to me?" Gerry asked, softly.

"Gerry, you've been working hard," Koller said. "There's been strain."

At the top of the stairs, leaning on the bannister, Geoff McKensie watched. Something in his eyes was turning over like a reel of film.

On the floor of the front hall were Gerry's red bikini underpants.

"No, no," said Gerry. "It's not that. I know it's not that. I'm black. You all think I'm black."

Koller laughed nervously. "Gerry, you are black."

Gerry plunged the knife at Koller's fat, white legs. Koller jumped up another step. His face was wet with sweat, too.

Mrs. Lopez was in the dining room door. "He's got my knife," she said to Fletch.

"Say *man*, Sy. Go ahead. Say *man*. Say *boy*."

"I never called you *boy* in my life. I never would."

Gerry lunged again. Koller stepped sideways on the stair.

"You're insulting me," said Koller.

"I'm a twenty-seven-year-old professional actor!" Gerry screamed.

"Good one, too," Koller said mildly.

"I'm a *man!*"

"Gerry, that's obvious. If you'd just put down the knife. Give it to Fletcher . . ."

"Gerry," Fletch said quietly. "This is not a good day for you to be threatening someone with a knife. It doesn't look good. You know what I mean?"

Gerry pivoted on the stair to look down at Fletch fully.

"Don't call me *boy*."

"Who called you *boy?*"

Mrs. Lopez said, "That's my good knife."

Sy Koller laughed. "Come on, Gerry. You can't expect to be asked to play *Robin Hood of Sherwood Forest.*"

"Everyone's always beatin' up on me," Gerry said.

"That's in the movies, Gerry," Sy Koller said. "You're a well-paid professional actor. At home you drive a Porsche. No one beats you up."

"Goddamn it!" He slashed at Sy Koller's legs.

Koller jumped back, up another stair. His green T-shirt flapped.

Fletch heard Moxie walk along the upper corridor. She, or something like her, appeared at the top of the stairs. They were her legs between white shorts and white sneakers. The torso was hers, in a light blue sport shirt. The head was wrapped in a red kerchief. The face was matted with rouge and powder. Bright red lipstick enlarged her mouth ridiculously. The eyes were covered by giant sunglasses in white plastic frames.

Koller said, as if threatening, "Gerry, I'm not going to jump another stair."

"Oh, for goodness' sake." Moxie started down the stairs.

"Be careful," Fletch said.

She passed Koller and stood on the stair with Gerry. She ignored the knife. She took his erect penis in her hand and shook it as if she were shaking hands. "You need something else to think about, boy."

"You called him *boy*," Koller said. "She called him *boy*."

"I should call him girl?" asked Moxie. "With his prick in my hand?"

Mrs. Lopez climbed the steps, reached around Gerry, and took the knife from his hand. "My good knife," she said. She started back to the kitchen.

"Get Mrs. Littleford, will you?" Fletch asked Mrs. Lopez.

"They're all against me." Gerry confided to Moxie. "You should see what they're doin' to me."

Moxie put her hands on his wet, shining shoulders. "It's just the coke, honey. No one's doing anything to you. Everything's fine. You're fine. It's a nice day."

"It's not the coke. It's what they're doin' to me."

"It's that little white powder you keep puttin' up your nose, sweetheart," Moxie said. "Drugs do funny things to your mind. Have you heard that?"

Gerry was studying Sy Koller's legs. They were unscratched.

Stella came into the front hall. She had a bath towel in her hands.

"Gerry needs an airing," Fletch said to her. "Why don't you walk him any direction from here until you come to water. And throw him in. He needs a swim." Her eyes had heavy lids. "You need a swim, too."

"I'm the one who needs the airing," Moxie said to Fletch. "Get me out of here."

"Dressed like that? You'll attract flies."

"No one will look at me," Moxie said.

"You're kidding."

On the stairs Stella was wiping down Gerry's whole body with the towel.

Looking at them, Fletch said, "Maybe a swim isn't a good idea."

"Who cares?" Moxie took Fletch by the hand.

"Don't swim out too far," Fletch said to Stella and Gerry.

He pulled Moxie sideways a moment and looked into the living room.

Edith Howell and Frederick Mooney were together on a Victorian loveseat. She had a gin and tonic in hand. His drink was in a short brandy glass.

"Revivals," Mooney was opining, "are anti-progress. Been far too many of 'em, lately. We must get ourselves out of the way, and let the young people create anew."

"But, Freddy," Edith said, "*Time, Gentleman, Time* was a great musical. It still is."

"Come on." Fletch tugged Moxie's hand. "We'll go see the sunset. Out the back way. Through the Lopezes' yard."

S E V E N T E E N

"So," Fletch said. They were walking along Whitehead Street. Moxie's beautified head made Fletch feel he was walking along with a gift-wrapped package on a stick. "Gerry Littleford's mind runs to stabbing people with knives."

"That was nothing," Moxie said. "Forget about it."

"Your usual domestic incident? I thought things were getting rather serious there."

"You should never believe an actor," Moxie said. "It's not what's said that counts. It's the delivery."

"Including what you just said."

"I am lying, the liar said," Moxie said. "I wish he wouldn't use that stuff all the time."

"You mean you wish he would use it some of the time?"

"Sure. When he has an angry scene to play. He can become really frightening on the stuff."

"I saw that. But that's not acting, is it? I mean, it's just reacting to a drug."

"Acting is a drug, Fletcher. All art is. A distortion of perspective. A heightening of concentration. But when Gerry's just doing an ordinary hard scene the stuff works against him. Sets his timing off. Makes him overact."

"Do you use that stuff, Moxie? Like, for an 'angry scene'?"

" 'Course not. I'm a better actor than Gerry." She looked across the street, at the big sign on the brick wall. "Wish I could go in there," she said. "I'd love to see Hemingway's bedroom. Also the room where he wrote. That was cute, what we did when we were playing pool. You have a good enough memory to be an actor."

"Moxie, do you think there are different rules for creative people?"

"Sure. There have to be special rules for being that alone."

"Something your father said this afternoon. Something about the obligations of talent being primary. We were talking about his relationship with you, and your mother, I guess. He said: 'Many men can love a woman and have a child; only a few can love the world and create miracles'."

"Dear O.L. Always the pretty turn of phrase." She walked in silence a moment. "I guess he's right."

"How can there be different rules for different people?"

"You just said it yourself, Fletch. I just said it. At the house you just said I couldn't go out — it wouldn't be safe. I just said I wished I could tour Hemingway's house. I wish I would be one hundred percent efficient as a creative person and one hundred percent efficient as a business person. I wish I didn't have to have a Steve Peterman living many of the normal aspects of my life for me." She turned him sideways on the sidewalk. "Look at me."

"I can't." He put his free hand over his eyes to shield himself from the sight of the kilograms of rouge, powder, lipstick, those foolish huge sunglasses on her face. "It's too 'orrible."

"I'm standing on a street in Key West," she said. "A marvelous live and let-live town. But, if you observe closely, I have to stand here observing different rules."

"There's been a murder."

He walked forward again.

"Sure." She walked with him. "If Jane Jones were involved in a murder, she could walk down the street without disguising herself as Miss Piggy. I can't." Crossing a sidestreet, the sun was warm on his face. "It's a question of energies, really," Moxie said. "Where do creative energies come from? If one has them, how does one best use them? When they wear down, how does one refurbish them? It's a joyous problem. It's also a responsibility, you see, all by itself. An extra responsibility. I guess, as Freddy says, a primary responsibility. And one just can't be totally responsible for everything. Few chefs take out the garbage. The day just isn't that long. No one's energies are that great."

Hand in hand, they walked through the long shadows of the palm trees on Whitehead Street.

After a while she dropped her hand.

"I know what your question is," she said in a low voice. "Your question is: do different rules for creative people give them the right to commit murder?"

"Don't cry," Fletch said. "It will make gulleys in your face powder."

"I did not murder Steve Peterman," Moxie said. "It's important that you believe me, Fletch."

Fletch said, "I know."

"Wow!" Moxie said. "What's all this about?"

"Sunset."

There were hundreds of people on the dock. Spaced to keep out of each other's sounds, there was a rock band, a country band, a string ensemble. There was a juggler juggling oranges and an acrobatic team bouncing each other into the air. There was a man dressed as Charlie Chaplin doing the funny walk through the crowd. There was an earnest young man preaching The Word of The Lord and a more earnest young man in a brown shirt and swastika armband preaching racial discrimination, and a most earnest young man satirizing them both, exhorting the people to believe in canned peas. Each had an audience of listeners, watchers, cheerers, and jeerers.

Across the water, the big red sun was dropping slowly to the Gulf of Mexico.

The people milling around on the dock, ambling from group to group, looking at each other, listening to each other, taking pictures of each other, were of every sort extant. One hundred miles of Florida Keys hang from continental U.S.A., like an udder, and to the southernmost point drip the cream and the milk and the scum of the whole continent. There are the artists, the writers, the musicians, young and old, the arrived, the arriving, and the never-to-arrive. There are numbers of single people of all ages, sometimes in groups, the searchers who sometimes find. There are the American families, with children and without, the professional and the working class, the retired and the honeymooners. There are the drug victims and the drug smugglers, the filthy, mind-blown, and the gold-bedecked, corrupt, corrupting despoilers of the human being.

"Wow," said Moxie. "What a fashion show."

The people there were dressed in tatters and tailor-made, suits and strings, rags and royal gems.

"You should talk," Fletch said, grinning into her huge plastic glasses.

"So many people for a sunset."

"Happens every night. Even cloudy nights."

"What an event. Someone should sell tickets. Really. Think what you have to do to get this many people into a theater."

After touring the crowd, listening to the music, watching the performers, Fletch and Moxie found an empty place on the edge of the dock and sat down. Their legs dangled over the water.

"What an outer reality," Moxie said.

"Which reminds me," Fletch said. "Simple enough question: who is the producer of *Midsummer Night's Madness?*"

"Steve Peterman."

"I thought you said he was executive producer, or something."

"He is. Sort of. There is another producer, Talcott Cross. I never met him. His job is finished, for now. He worked at setting things up. Casting. Most of the location work. You know, hiring people."

"Where is he?"

"Los Angeles, I suppose. I think he lives in Hollywood Hills. Steve intended to be the line-producer on this film. That is, stay with it during shooting, and all that."

"So which of them hired Geoff McKensie and which hired Sy Koller?"

"Cross hired McKensie. Peterman fired him."

"And Peterman hired Koller."

"Right."

"So Peterman is more powerful than Cross? I mean, one of the co-producers is more equal than the other?"

"Sure. Cross is more of an employee. Hired to do the production stuff Steve didn't want to do, or didn't have time to do."

"Does Cross get a share of the profits?"

"I suppose so. But probably not as big a share as Steve . . . would have gotten."

Down the dock, also sitting on the edge, a girl in cut-off jeans was staring at Moxie.

"What makes Steve Peterman as a producer more powerful than his co-producer, what's-his-name Cross?"

"Talcott Cross. Everything in this business, Fletch, comes down to one word: the bank. Where the money comes from."

"Okay. That's my question. I thought a producer was someone who raises money for a film."

"A producer does an awful lot more than that."

The girl in cut-off blue jeans nudged the boy sitting next to her. She said something to him.

"But it was Steve Peterman who raised the money for this film."

"Yes. From Jumping Cow Productions, Inc."

"What's that?"

"An independent film company. A company set up to invest in films. The world's full of 'em."

"Forgive me for never having heard of it. Has it made many films?"

"I don't think so. I think it has some others in pre-production. Most likely it has. I don't know, Fletch. It could be a bunch of dentists who have pooled their money to invest in movies. Jumping Cow Productions could be a subsidiary of International Telephone and Telegraph, for all I know."

Half the big red sun had sizzled into the Gulf. A black, ancient-rigged sloop was sailing up the harbor toward them.

"Don't you care who's producing your film?" Up the dock-edge Moxie was causing widening interest among the group of young people. "I mean, if the source of the money is so all-fired important . . ."

Moxie sighed. "Steve Peterman was producing this film."

The top of the sun bubbled on the horizon and was extinguished. In the harbor, in front of the dock, the Sloop *Providence* fired her cannon and ran down the stars and stripes prettily.

And the people on the dock cheered.

Evening in Key West had been declared.

Fletch swung his feet onto the dock and stood up. "Let's go home."

"But, Fletch, after the sunset is better than before. That's when the clouds pick up their colors."

"There aren't any clouds."

She looked at the sky. "You're right."

The young people down the dock had stood up, too.

"Come on," Fletch said. "We can walk slowly. Look back." Moxie got to her feet. "You see the sun set in the ocean all the time anyway," he said.

The girl in cut-offs was facing Moxie. "I know what you're trying to do," the girl said.

Her friends were all around her.

Moxie said nothing. She stepped closer to Fletch and took his arm.

"You're trying to look like Moxie Mooney," the girl laughed.

Moxie said, "Actually, I'm not."

The young people around the girl laughed. One said, "Oh yeah."

The girl said, "Moxie doesn't wear all that crap on her face."

"She doesn't?" Moxie asked.

"She's natural," the girl said. "She don't wear no make-up at all."

"You've seen her?"

"Naw. But she's stayin' somewhere here in Key West."

"She's over on Stock Island," said the boy. "In seclusion."

"Yeah," said another boy. "She murdered somebody."

Moxie's arm flexed against Fletch.

"You really think Moxie Mooney killed somebody?" she asked.

"Why not?" shrugged a boy.

"What are you — a look-alike contest?" asked another girl.

"I want to see her," the girl in cut-offs said. "I'm gonna see her."

"Well," Fletch said. He tugged Moxie's arm. "Good luck."

The girl in cut-offs called after Moxie. "You look sorta like her."

"Thanks," Moxie called back. Miserably, she said, "I guess."

They were walking back on Whitehead Street. There was some color in the sky.

"Anyway," Fletch said in a cheery tone, "I enjoyed talking with your father this afternoon."

"You like him, don't you."

"I admire him," Fletch said. "Enormously."

"I guess he's a brilliant man," Moxie admitted.

"He's funny."

"After all these decades of acting," Moxie said, "he speaks as if every line were written for him. He says *Good Morning* and you have to believe it's a good morning — as if nobody had ever said it before."

"How come he's all-of-a-sudden so attentive to you?"

"He's not. He just landed on me. Can't find work, I guess. Nobody else wants him."

"Did he call you, did he write you, did he arrange to stay with you?"

" 'Course not. He had taken up residence in my apartment in New York. I didn't even know it. When I went there a few weeks ago — you know, to talk to Steve Peterman — there he was at home in my apartment. His clothes and his bottles all over the place. He was nearly unconscious. Looking at cartoons on the television. I had to put him to bed."

"Jesus," Fletch said. "Frederick Mooney looking at cartoons on television. All the bad satires of himself."

"I was pretty upset anyway. Yelling into the phone, trying to find Steve."

"Had you given him a key to the apartment?"

"No. He had never been there before."

"How did he get in?"

"The doorman gave him a key. He is Frederick Mooney, after all."

"I heard someone else say that."

"I mean, everyone knows he's my father. I had never told the doormen to keep him out. What else could they do — have a legendary genius raving in their lobby?"

"Different rules," said Fletch. "This may seem strange to you, Moxie, put me down with those kids on the dock, but I'm proud and pleased to know your father. I find him damned interesting. I mean, for me to really see him and talk with him and know him. Even though he keeps confusing me with a corpse."

"You're not a corpse, Fletcher." Moxie stroked his arm. "Not yet, anyway. Of course, if you get me to sign any more papers in the dark . . ."

"Think of all he's done."

"I had to bring him down here with me. What else could I do with him? Couldn't leave him sitting there in New York."

"So you packed him up and poured him onto the plane."

"He entertained everybody in the first-class section. He had a few drinks, of course. There was a little girl, about twelve years old, sitting across the aisle from him. He started telling her the story of *Pygmalion*. He got everybody's attention by making all Eliza Doolittle's mouth noises. Began playing all the parts at once. Henry Higgins, the father. Then he began singing all the songs from *My Fair Lady*. People were standing in aisles. *Get me to the church, get me to the church, get me to the church on time . . .*" Moxie sawed out flat and guttural. "People crowded up from the coach section."

"Marvelous," Fletch said.

"It's nuts!" she exclaimed.

"Yeah, nuts. But the little girl will never forget it. No one aboard will. Frederick Mooney doing Shaw at thirty thousand feet."

"Nuts!" she said. "Nuts! Nuts! Nuts!"

"I think it's nice."

"Against safety regulations," Moxie said. "Have that many people in the aisles. Utterly nuts."

"The obligations of talent," Fletch said. "Different rules."

"He's a drunk," Moxie said easily. "He's a mad, raving drunk."

"But you love him."

"Hell," she said. "I love him about as much as I love Los Angeles. He's just very big on my landscape."

EIGHTEEN

Dinner at The Blue House was conch chowder, red snapper and Key lime pie. Mrs. Lopez provided the best Key West dining.

Before dinner, Lopez told Fletch Global Cable News had called several times and would like him to return the call. Fletch thanked him and did not return the call.

During dinner Frederick Mooney said to Moxie, *"But yet thou art my flesh, my blood, my daughter — or rather a disease that is in my flesh, which I must needs call mine."*

"Oh, no," Moxie said. "More Lear."

Edith Howell said, "Freddy's a *learing* old man."

"And you, Madame," said Frederick Mooney, "are a bag of wind."

And during dinner, Sy Koller said, "I knew something was going on between Dan Buckley and Steve Peterman. Buckley was not happy with Peterman . . ." He ran through his theory of the murder again, adding the idea this time that maybe Peterman had gotten Buckley into something illegal . . .

Moxie said nothing.

Stella Littleford, looking even smaller and more bedraggled than usual, said, "Marge Peterman." As she spoke, she kept giving sad glances at her husband, who, after his swim, was still acting a little jumpy and at first kept his smiles perfunctory and his conversation to the mannerly minimum. "Wives can get to the point," Stella said, "where divorce isn't adequate. How long had the Petermans been married — ten years? And this was the first time I've ever seen Marge Peterman with her husband. I didn't even know there was a Marge Peterman. And all this time Peterman's been runnin' all over the world, going to bed with people, doin' what he wanted . . ."

"I don't know," Fletch said. "Did Peterman jump in and out of bed with people, Moxie?"

"Steve was interested in only one thing," Moxie said, performing fine surgery on her fish. "Money. And talk, talk, talk, talk, talk. About money."

"A wife gets tired of gettin' shoved aside," Stella Littleford insisted. "Of everybody tellin' her she's not important. Of bein' told to do this, do that, do the other thing, and otherwise shut up and stay in the background. That could drive anybody to murder."

"Stella killed Peterman," giggled Gerry Littleford. "Out of respect for his wife."

Stella colored. "Okay," she said. "Why was Marge Peterman there? She'd never shown up before. There was no weekend planned, or anything. Our work schedule gave Peterman no more time off than it gave us. We had weeks to go before a break."

"Is what you're saying, Stella," Fletch asked. "Is that Marge Peterman showed up on location with the intention of killing her husband?"

"Sure."

"Does anybody know if she was expected?" Fletch looked around at the faces at his table.

"I don't think she was," Sy Koller said. "When you're on location, directors — at least some of us — prefer not to have wives around . . ." He looked quickly at Geoffrey McKensie and then away. "Extraneous people." He looked at Frederick Mooney who was blinking drunkenly over his plate. His eyes settled on Stella Littleford. "Apt to be damned distracting. It's tough enough, you know, dealing with the emotions, the feelings, of the people working on a film. When those people have wives around, and husbands around to back them up, echo everything they say: lovers, retainers, and the odd relative . . ." Again Koller glanced at Mooney. "All telling them they're right, they're wrong, they're this, they're that, they *look tired this morning —*" Koller's voice went to a bitchy falsetto, "*— and is that a pimple coming under your nose? And tell that Sy Koller that scene will never be right until he gives you a stronger exit line . . .* Makes it damned tough for the director." Sy Koller laughed at himself. "Didn't mean to take advantage of a simple question and climb on my hobby horse. No," he said to Fletch. "I don't think Marge Peterman was expected. I think Peterman and I were of one mind on this topic. I bribed my own wife off with a trip to Belgium. I think if Steve knew his wife was coming he could have asked her not to."

"And she would have stayed home in her closet," Stella said with disgust.

"Stroking her chinchilla," put in Edith Howell.

"Well, this time Marge Peterman didn't stay home," insisted Stella Littleford. "She showed up on location and stabbed the bastard."

Gerry snickered.

"Well, where was she during the taping of *The Dan Buckley Show?*" Stella asked.

"With me," Fletch answered.

"And who the hell are you?"

"Nobody."

"He's our host," said Edith Howell. "Would somebody please pass the wine?"

"And later," said Stella, "where was she? We found her over there behind those trailers."

"With me," Fletch said.

"Looked to me like she was hiding," said Stella.

"It's decided." Gerry Littleford put down his knife and fork. "Stella killed Steve Peterman and thus struck another blow for the equality of women."

Mooney's eyes kept closing and his head kept bobbing and he kept eating. He was napping during dinner.

"Investors," said Geoff McKensie.

"Yeah," mocked Moxie. "Let's hear it from the investors."

McKensie wrinkled his eyebrows at her. Apparently, like most taciturn men, when McKensie spoke, he expected to be heard. He waited for attention and then spoke in a tone far friendlier than what he had to say to the people present: "I've been thinking it out. Who had the most reason to kill Steve Peterman? He was really muckin' this film up, he was. Here the company had hired a first class director — me. I only took on the job with the understandin' I could have a free hand with the script. I spent months goin' over that script. My wife and I flew halfway 'round this spinnin' earth. I spent a week in California, thrashing the new script out with Talcott Cross. He approved everything I wanted to do. 'Course, he's a professional, he is. I come out here to this American boot camp for heaven —"

"I think he means Florida," Fletch whispered to Moxie.

"— and here's this Peterman bloke rollin' 'round on his back like a pig turnin' everything on the menu into garbage."

Sy Koller's color was deepening. "You mean, he fired you."

"Right he did," said McKensie. "And he hires a second-rate, has-been director —" McKensie jerked his thumb at his directorial table mate. "— who proceeds to film the original lousy script as if it was half-good. As if it was any good."

"Excuse me for living," said Sy Koller. He was a deep crimson.

"Come on, Geoff," said Edith Howell. "Be fair. You were the victim of a terrible, terrible tragedy. Your wife was killed. You couldn't expect to carry on . . ."

"I'm not used to Yankee-land," said McKensie. "With a little luck,

I never will be, I now think. But where I come from — Down Under — when something like that happens a decent interval takes place. A chap's allowed to take the blow and recover."

"Come on, McKensie," Gerry Littleford said. "You were in no shape to direct after your wife's death. You still aren't. How could you be?"

McKensie's eyes attacked Littleford. "I'll tell you, sonny, your best chance was to film my script. With me directing." He made another disparaging gesture toward Koller. "You haven't got a lawyer's chance in heaven doin' things the way you're doin' 'em."

Fletch was looking at Moxie. His eyes were repeating. *Having two directors in the house is like having two ladies wearing the same expensive dress.*

"What happened here?" McKensie asked rhetorically, dropping his *h*'s onto his plate. "The day after my wife was killed there was no filming — of course. That same damn day this failed director —" Again, he jerked his thumb at Koller. "— is flown in by Steven Peterman. Named the director of *Midsummer Night's Madness*. My script is thrown into the hopper and the day after that, you all start film-ing the original pile of garbage. He didn't even wait until after the funeral."

"I know, Geoff," Moxie said. "I spoke to Steve about that. I thought it was rotten. I tried to get him to hold off filming for a few days —"

"It wasn't respectful, for one thing," said McKensie. "My wife was a lady who deserved a little respect, you know."

"I'm sure she was," Edith Howell said quickly. "I wish we had all known her."

"But Steve said," continued Moxie. "Oh, you know what he said. He said, how many thousands of dollars filming costs a day. How many thousands of dollars it cost to have the whole crew idle."

" 'Idle'," scoffed McKensie. "Respect for the dead, I'd call it. A little respect for the bereaved."

"Steve read me the figures," Moxie said. "Said the investors would have every reason to raise hell if we closed down for a few days."

"Exactly," McKensie said. "Investors. Maybe your investors have got more sense than Peterman gave 'em credit for. Maybe in the old days in Hollywood you could pull the line *investors don't want the movie good — they want it Thursday*. But films cost a bit too much for that, these days. From my experience with investors, they'd rather have a piece of somethin' that has a chance of makin' a profit than a piece of somethin' that stinks so bad it'll have to be buried at sea."

Koller's face was going through the whole color spectrum. "Tell me, McKensie," he said. "If you think *Midsummer Night's Madness* is basically such a lousy script, how come you agreed to direct it in the first place?"

"You don't expect me to be honest about that, do you?" McKensie said.

Koller raised and dropped his hands in despair. "Right now, I don't know what to expect."

"It was my chance to direct in America," Geoffrey McKensie said. "I thought I could make a silk slipper out of a dog's paw. I could have, too." He sat back on his chair. Lopez was clearing the table. "If I were an investor in *Midsummer Night's Madness,* and I knew what was going on on location, I would have murdered Steve Peterman ruddy fast. The bastard deserved it."

"But there was no one on location, Geoff," Gerry Littleford said, "except those of us actively making the film. The location had been secured."

"Bullsdroppings," said McKensie. "At that moment, there were several alleged members of the press on location. You can't tell me one of them couldn't have been a kill artist."

"Me again," said Fletch.

"You," said McKensie. "You're a member of the press? I haven't been able to find a typewriter anywhere in this house. I spent the afternoon lookin'. In your own room, there isn't a pad of paper, or a pencil, a camera . . ."

"Good point," said Fletch.

"What the hell were you doin' on location then?" McKensie asked.

"I admit," said Fletch, "getting on location wasn't that difficult. I expect anybody who really wanted to, could have. But . . . they'd have to show some identification."

Finally, Koller's cholera caroomed. "McKensie," he said, "you're full of down-under dung. So far you've made three small — very small — films, somewhere in the Outback, a million miles from nowhere, no pressure on you, with all the time in the world. Artsy-smartsy films. For God's sake, they haven't even really been released outside Australia. Your world-wide audience would fit into a mini-bus. And everyone in the back seat would only pretend to understand what you're tryin' to do. And suddenly you're God Almighty. The *Grand Auteur.* Listen to me, babe — I've made more films than you've ever seen. You know how many films I've made? Thirty-eight! Okay, so the last five didn't do so well. Three is all you've made, buster! Hell, my wife knows more about directing than you'll ever know, just from listenin' to me talk. And I've made better films than you'll ever make. Damn it all, at least when I film night scenes like in *Midsummer Night's Madness,* I give the audience enough light to see what's goin' on. You make that film and the last third of the picture would be so dark, the audience wouldn't even be able to find their way out of their seats to go home." Koller took a deep breath. "Just because some of us are courteous to you, kid, don't think you're such a hotshot."

McKensie didn't seem too disturbed by this laceration. He was eating his lime pie.

"Well," Edith Howell said into the thick silence, "where did John Meade go? Fletch, you said he was just doing an errand."

"He is. Just ran up to New York for a minute."

"New York?" exclaimed Edith. "For a minute? We're two thousand miles from New York, aren't we?"

"Just for a minute," Fletch said. "Doing an errand for Moxie. He'll be back tonight. John said he'd do anything in the world for Moxie."

"Mister McKensie," boomed Mooney in what doubtlessly was meant to be taken as a proper manner. "Mister Peterkin tells me you are about to commence principal photography on a film of William Shakespeare's *Midsummer Night's Dream.*"

Everyone at table looked at everyone else.

"O. L.," Moxie said gently.

"If so," continued Mooney, now obviously addressing Sy Koller, "I should very much like to be considered for a part, however small . . ."

Gerry Littleford giggled.

"Not Oberon, of course," conceded Mooney, "bit too thick in the leg for that these days. But you might consider me for Theseus, you know. I've played it before, and I've always thought Philostrate a smashing role."

"Really, O. L. Stop it."

"Well, daughter, no one else seems to want to have me, these days. Of course, my managers rather ran up the price of my talents these last few years. I wouldn't pay myself what people have had to pay me. I'm sure all that salary-fee business can be adjusted, for a small role. Mister McKensie —" Frederick Mooney smiled at Sy Koller. "— you're in luck, as you've caught me between engagements, as it were."

"Goddamn it!" Moxie exploded. "Why don't you consider yourself retired?" She pushed her chair back from the table. "Superannuated? Shelved? Out to pasture?"

"Moxie?" Fletch said.

She stood up, nearly knocking her chair over. "Why don't you think of joining mother in the asylum? You put her there. You've put yourself there. Why don't you go?"

Moxie left the dining room.

"Her exits are getting better as the day goes on," Stella commented. "I can hardly wait to see how dramatically she goes to bed."

"She didn't even slam a door that time," Gerry said.

"That was good." Sy Koller looked at where she had been sitting. "She created all the effect of a slammed door without slamming a door. All the effect of knocking over her chair without knocking it over."

"What are you guys talking about?" asked Fletch. "There is no door."

"There's always a door," said Sy Koller, "in your mind."

"I have embarrassed my daughter," uttered Frederick Mooney remorsefully. "She resists thinking of me as a bit player. She forgets, or she never knew, all the small things I have had to do . . . in this business, to keep afloat."

"Coffee, anyone?" Fletch asked. Lopez had appeared with a pot.

"Global Cable News called again," Lopez said while pouring out Fletch's coffee. "A Mister Fennelli. I said I'd give you the message."

"Thank you." Fletch smiled at those remaining at table. "At the moment, I don't think I have anything to report."

NINETEEN

After dinner, Fletch found Geoffrey McKensie in the billiard room playing alone.

Fletch chose a cue stick and McKensie triangled the balls. They played almost through a game without saying anything.

Finally, McKensie said, "Sorry. 'Fraid I behaved pretty badly at dinner. I ran on like a young lady not invited to the garden party."

"Not to worry," Fletch said. "You had some things that needed saying and you said 'em."

Continuing in the tone of one vexed with himself, McKensie clucked, "What will you Yanks think of us Aussies."

"Us Yanks will think of you Aussies as lovingly as we always have." At Fletch's stroke, the cue ball neatly avoided every other ball on the table.

McKensie sank two and took his third shot.

"Good at sports, too," Fletch said. "Damn it." He bounced the cue ball off several, leaving McKensie with a wonderful lay. "Tell me, though — those things you said — were you saying them because you really believe someone in Jumping Cow Productions might really have been gunning for Peterman — or were you just saying them to dump on Koller?"

McKensie took a careful shot and sank two at once.

Fletch hung up his stick.

"I don't know," McKensie said. "It's true — Koller was a good director — back before he sank his integrity in the briny. Nowadays, it doesn't bother him to shoot a bad script — as long as he gets paid for it. What hurts is that he knows better. It's also true that Peterman was mucking things up royally. He deserved the cold steel between his ribs."

Seeing Fletch had quit, McKensie resumed playing by himself and cleaned off the table.

Fletch asked, "Do you think Peterman could have been sabotaging this film on purpose?"

"I can't think of a reason. Nobody likes to lose money." McKensie hung up his own cue. "But I'll tell you, Peterman couldn't have done more to torpedo that film if he were doin' it deliberate."

"Drink?" Fletch asked. "There's some bad American beer."

"Brought some scripts with me from home," McKensie said. "Think I'll go do some work on 'em. Somethin' tells me Koller won't want to continue talkin' shop with me this night."

TWENTY

Outside in the dark, Edith Howell and Sy Koller were sitting in the comfortable chairs on the cistern sipping large Scotches.

"Do you know," Edith Howell said to Fletch as he sat down with them, "that Freddy has escaped the premises again?"

"Key West is a good place to go out."

"He's like a cat. When you think he's in he's out and out in."

"Gone out for conviviality," Fletch said. "Do you worry about him?"

"Freddy? Good God, no. He has millions."

Fletch swallowed what to him was a *non sequitur*. "Of dollars?"

"Tens of millions. I know that for a fact."

Fletch shook his head. "Somehow, I thought he was broke. I think Moxie thinks he's broke."

"Tens of millions," repeated Edith Howell. "I know of what I speak. I have friends whose friends are friends of Freddy, if you know what I mean. He has millions all over the world, just lying around."

"Pity you can't get your grubby fingers on it all, Edith," Sy Koller said.

"I'm tryin', darlin', I'm tryin'. Did you hear him in there asking the world for a bit part in a movie that's not even being made? The poor dear. He needs looking after."

"He's as crazy as a mosquito in the dressing room of a chorus line," said Sy Koller. "Gonezo."

"It's interesting to know him," Fletch said.

"That's because you don't," said Edith Howell. "Knowing Freddy is like having a rare disease: shortly the interest pales and what's left is pain."

Sy Koller laughed. "Apparently you're willing to put up with the pain, Edith. For all those millions."

"For a short while, darling. After all, Freddy's liver can hardly be made of molybdenum."

TWENTY-ONE

"Well, darlings," Edith Howell picked up her drink and stood up. "If you're not chatting you might as well be dead, I always say. Or asleep." Sitting out in the night, she and Sy Koller and Fletch had been silent for two minutes. "So I might as well go to bed."

After she closed the door to the house behind her, Sy Koller lifted his drink to Fletch and said, "I like my drink, too, you see."

"You've had a hard day," Fletch said. "Attacked with a knife by one of your actors. Orally attacked by one of your colleagues."

"Ah, the perils of being a director." Sy Koller chuckled. "Being a director is like being the father of a large family of berserk children who keep slipping in and out of reality. We get paid for hazardous duty, but not enough."

"I thought I should tell you," Fletch said slowly, "that the police know that you and Peterman had a fist fight outside a Los Angeles restaurant three years ago."

"They do? How do you know that?"

"Talked to Chief of Detectives Roz Nachman this afternoon. She called. She accused me of having hijacked all her prime suspects."

"I'm a prime suspect?" Koller ran his palm over his stubbly chin and cheeks. "I shouldn't be."

"No?"

"Why should I put myself out of a job? Now that Peterman's dead the future of *Midsummer Night's Madness* is dubious."

"You mean you won't even finish filming it?"

"Well," Koller snorted. "Peterman was the only one who seemed to believe in the property."

"Didn't you believe in it?"

"Not really. Peterman gave me the script and said he wanted it shot exactly as written."

"You never even saw McKensie's script?"

"No. Peterman said it was a pile of dung."

"Do you think it would have been?"

"Probably not. But it was clear to me that McKensie had every reason in the world to sue Peterman, so how could I ask to use his script? It would confuse matters. You don't know this business, do you?"

"No."

"Think of having a career where you have to find a whole new job every six months."

"Finding a job is the hardest job there is."

"That's the director's life. And the actor's life. And the set designer's. It brings a certain element of the frantic to this business. And a great deal of hot air."

"But don't you get rich and famous after a while? Able to pick and choose?"

"Seldom. You make a pile of money, and you spend a pile and a half. Because you're so frantic. You blow it on hot air, keeping up the image. The more money you make the more frantic you become, the more you blow it on hot air and the deeper into debt you go, which makes you more frantic."

In the trees night birds were gossiping.

"Anyway, the police say you were fighting over a woman."

"Is that what they say? I guess it's what we said at the time."

"That you had Peterman down on the sidewalk and were strangling him when you were pulled off."

"Yeah," Koller sighed. "It felt good."

Fletch said: "She must have been one fantastical woman."

"I wish I'd ever known a woman worth strangling someone over."
Koller lit a cigarette. "Methinks, mine host, you enquire as to why I
was strangling Steve Peterman."

"Just curious," said Fletch. "Did he stick you with one of his telephone bills?"

Koller took a drink. "Happy to tell you. Because my strangling Steve
Peterman three years ago is the best evidence I've got that I didn't
stab him yesterday."

Fletch waited. The tip of Koller's cigarette glowed brightly.

"I caught him out in a fraud," Koller said. "I resented it. I hated it.
Peterman wasn't the first to work this scam, and he wasn't the last.
But, Fletcher, this business can be so dirty . . . sometimes it gets to
you. What he was doing was raising money for a film which didn't
exist, and never would. He had gotten ahold of something which
looked like a filmscript, a story about some South American *patron* and
his daughter and a priest and a revolutionary — a complete mess.
Anybody who knew anything about the business would know it wasn't
a filmscript. It was just a hundred pages of people saying hello and
goodbye and making speeches at each other. He had been out peddling
this to people who didn't know better across this broad land — you
know, the doctors and the shoemakers, the widows and the orphans,
all who dream of making a financial killing on a big movie while having
their lives touched with glamor. They'd be invited to the opening in
New York. Also the Academy Award ceremony of course. He told
the suckers he just wanted start-up money, to be paid back when and
if he got the film capitalized."

"But not to be paid back if he did not get the film capitalized?"

"Of course not. Told them it was going to be filmed in El Salvador.
Even had an El Salvadorean S. A. Had no intention of trying to
capitalize it. You never heard of this scam?"

"No."

"I figure he'd raised about a half million dollars, all of which had
disappeared down this El Salvadorean hole." Koller stubbed out his
cigarette. "I hated this for two reasons. It's bad for the business. The
next guy who goes out and tries to raise start-up money for a film
might be honest. The more of these little cheats there are running
around, the harder it is for the honest guy." Koller drank. "The second
reason, of course, was that he was using my name. He had told these
people maybe he could get Sy Koller to direct. That we'd had conversations. That we were in negotiations."

"Not true?"

"I'd never met the son of a bitch. First I'd heard about it was when Sonny Fields told me he'd heard it was going on." Koller lit another cigarette, his lighter flaring in the dark garden. "So, one night after more to drink than was good for me, I met Peterman in a Los Angeles bar, pulled him out to the sidewalk by his coat collar, proceeded to hit him upside the head. He fell to the sidewalk. I sat on top of him and proceeded to throttle him. It felt real good. His neck was soft. No muscle at all. Wonder I didn't kill him before nosey people interfered."

"Why didn't Peterman press charges?"

"Why didn't I have him arrested for fraud?"

"I don't know."

"We came to an amicable settlement. Peterman said he was just using this scam to raise money for a real film, somewhere down the road. My career wasn't looking too good. Aforementioned frantic need to gain employment. So . . ."

"So . . . ?"

"I agreed that if he ever had a real film to direct, I would direct it. We laid the fight off on a woman."

"You blackmailed him."

"We blackmailed each other. It's the way much of this business works, old son."

"And what happened to the half a million dollars?"

"It went into Peterman's pockets. And then into his shoes and his wife's furs."

"So *Midsummer Night's Madness* came along, starring Moxie Mooney, whom Peterman by then controlled, and Gerry Littleford —"

"And Talcott Cross hires Geoffrey McKensie to direct. I called Steve Peterman."

"Had you seen the script?"

"No. But I had a pretty good idea it wasn't much good."

"Why would you want to direct a loser?"

"Well . . . . In the three intervening years my career had sunk so low I was getting the bends. You understand?"

"How would directing a stinker help your career?"

"It would prove I could get employed. It would also provide me with some much needed money. You know about money?"

"I'm learning."

"End of story," said Koller. "As long as Peterman was producing, Koller was directing. Peterman dead: Koller dead. *Ergo* the one person absolutely guaranteed not to kill Steven Peterman is yours truly. Maybe it's a shameful story," Koller concluded, "but it's a hell of an alibi."

"Fletch?" Moxie's voice came from the upper balcony of The Blue House. "Are you out there?"

"Yo." He stepped under the balcony.

She said, "If you give me any of that Romeo crap, I'll spit on your head."

"If only your fans could hear you now."

"Go find Freddy for me, will you? I was sort of rough on him."

"Yes, you were."

"If I want criticism," she said irritably, "I'll ask for it."

"You're asking for it."

TWENTY-TWO

After a long silence, while Fletch waited, the man's voice drawled over the phone, "Sorry. Chief Nachman says she can't come to the phone now."

"Please," said Fletch, with as much dignity as he could enlist. "Tell her it's her earwig calling."

"Earwig? You mean that little no-see-'um bug?"

"Right." Alone in the study at the back of The Blue House Fletch smiled. "Earwig."

There was another long silence before Chief of Detectives Roz Nachman picked up. "Yes, Fletcher?"

"Thank you for answering, Chief. You're working late."

"Has one of your house guests become overwhelmed with remorse and confessed to murder?"

"It's a classier crime than that."

"I know it is."

"I have a line of investigation for you, though. Just a suggestion, really."

"Suggest away."

"Steve Peterman must have had some kind of a car. A rented car or something. Everyone was up and down that Route 41 so much, between the two beaches."

"I suppose so."

"I suggest you check Peterman's car to see if it's been in an accident. A hit-and-run accident."

Nachman did not pause long. "You talking about McKensie's wife?"

"Just a thought. Wouldn't take much to check it out."

"I see."

"For what it's worth," Fletch said.

"All right."

"Is there still nothing showing up on all that film?"

"Nothing."

"And the experts aren't discovering anything funny about the set?"

"Nothing."

"That's a real significant fact in itself."

"Good night, Irwin. I'm busy."

TWENTY-THREE

The inside, the bar area of Durty Harry's, was virtually empty, but there was a huge crowd sitting and standing on the patio, all facing into the same corner.

Fletch got a beer from the bar and went out to the patio. Quite a diverse collection of people had gathered. There were the tourists in the best light-colored clothing one can really only buy in a big city but never really wear in one. Their faces and arms and legs were red and stiff with sunburn. There were the genuine denizens of Key West, the Conchs, who prefer to keep themselves as pale as Scandinavians in deep Scandinavian winters. They think of the sun as enemy, and run through it from building to car and car to house. There were some art-folk of all ages, their faces and bodies looking as if they'd lived plenty, their bright, quick eyes showing they wanted to live plenty more. There were the cocaine cowboys in their stringy leather and denim; the girls in their full skirts and full blouses and dead hair. And there were the drunks, with the weird blue in their skin which results from mixing too much constant alcohol with too much constant sun.

And sitting in the corner, the object of everyone's attention, sat and spoke Frederick Mooney. With his gray hair, stubble of beard, broad face and big eyes, he easily could have been the reincarnation of the person whom the people in Key West would most like to see reincarnated — Ernest Hemingway. Mooney was Papa, all right, and these were his children gathered around him.

Sipping his beer, Fletch leaned against the door-jamb and listened.

". . . not glorious, not glamorous at all," Mooney was saying. "Anyone who thinks so knows nothing. Anyone who thinks acting is simply a matter of popping the eyes in surprise . . ." Mooney popped his eyes in surprise at the crowd; there was a titter of admiration. ". . . of doing a double-take . . ." Mooney did a doubletake; the people laughed. ". . . quivering the chin . . ." Mooney's chin quivered apparently uncontrollably; the people laughed harder. ". . . to weep . . ." Tears swelled in Mooney's eyes and dribbled down his cheeks; the people applauded. ". . . don't know what acting is." The virtuoso wiped his instrument dry and thrust it forward at his audience. "An actor must learn his craft. And his skill is not just in learning to control every muscle of his face. Not just in learning how to set his shoulders expressively. Not just in learning that how he places his feet — even when they are out of sight, off-camera — invariably is more important than anything he does with his face, because how you place your feet, how you balance yourself, how you posture yourself says more about who you are, your attitudes than anything else."

Sitting back in his chair in the attitude of a grandfather at the end of a full meal, Mooney reached for the bottle of cognac on the table, brought it to his lips, and took a good-sized swallow. "Thirsty work, this." He anticipated a burp, worked it up from his innards, gave full sound to it. He blinked and smiled in happy relief at his audience, and they applauded.

"The craft, the skills," Mooney said. "Barrymore once said, he'd rather have straight legs than know how to act. Of course, Barrymore had straight legs." He paused to allow his audience to laugh, and they did. "An actor must learn how to move in his clothes. You know that a man moves differently in a toga than he does in blue jeans . . . than he does in medieval hose . . . than he does in black tie. But do you know an actor must learn these skills? Even if an actor does not smoke those dirty weeds . . ." Disdainfully, Frederick Mooney waved his hand at a woman smoking a cigarette, ". . . he must learn to handle a cigarette as if he were addicted. One handles a cigarette differently than one handles a cigar. Few actors are, in themselves, violent people. No acting schools I've heard of have pistol firing ranges. Yet when an actor handles a gun, he must have learned to do so . . . so naturally that the gun seems an extension of his hand — not something strange and foreign to him, but something so much a part of his being, so necessary to his mental attitudes that the audience knows he can use it and will use it. My training was such, having been dragged up through the music halls of England and the carnivals of America as well, I not only learned the rhythms of Shakespeare, but how to handle a sword and fence with it as if my life depended upon it. I learned to ride a horse both like a Guardsman and an American Indian. John Wayne once said that he didn't know much about method acting, but he sure knew how to stop a horse on the mark. Of course, John Wayne could stop a horse on the mark." Again his audience chuckled. Looking at his audience, tying them all together by his gaze, Mooney saw Fletch. In his eyes there was only the barest flicker of recognition. He continued his lecture. "It may not seem it to you — oh, you who watch an actor act and think you can judge him, but who haven't the slightest knowledge or appreciation of the skills he employs to entertain you — but an actor must learn to ride a horse and a motorcycle, to use a rope, a lariat, to drink from a wine flagon, and open a bottle of champagne, to hold a violin, and to perform a right uppercut to the jaw — perfectly."

Mooney stopped talking. He moved his eyes over the surface of the small table before him like a farmer looking for first signs of a crop. He seemed to find no growth, and his look was sad.

Finally, sensing his lecture was over, the people began asking him questions.

Mister Mooney, how did you enjoy playing opposite Elizabeth Taylor?

What's the greatest role you've ever played?

Is it true you actually took heroin to play the jazz pianist in Keyboard?

Mooney folded his arms over the table and dropped his head. "Nothing's true," he muttered. "Nothing's true. It's all a lie."

Fletch worked forward through the crowd. He stepped over some people sitting on the floor.

What's your next picture going to be?

"Nothing's true."

You think you could ride a horse now, the state you're in?

Fletch picked up Mooney's flight bag. Mooney raised his head slowly and looked Fletch in the eye a long moment.

"Ah, Mister Paterson."

"Came to carry your bag," Fletch said.

"Kind of you." Widely, he pointed at the bottle on the table and at the bag. "That bottle goes in that bag," he said.

Fletch put the cork in the bottle and the bottle in the flight bag.
Did you really get malaria making Jungle Queen?
"Yes," Mooney answered, standing up, "and I've still got it."
You've just got the shakes, Mooney. The sweats.
Mooney stumbled a few times picking his way through the crowd
but never actually fell. Fletch did not hold onto him. At that moment,
Mooney was far from being the graceful, competent person he was
just describing, with all the skills of an actor.
The people who were most kind in getting out of his way, letting
him pass, were those most apt to reach out to him, touch him, touch
his clothes as he passed.
"I want to say good night to the dog," Mooney said to Fletch.
"Dog?"
"The black dog."
Again, when they were in the less congested bar area, Mooney said,
"I really would like to say good night to that dog."
"I don't see a dog, Mister Mooney."
"Big, black dog," Mooney said. "Name of Emperor."
Fletch looked around. "I don't see any dog, Mister Mooney."
"He's on the other side of the bar," Mooney said.
"Why don't we go this way? It's quicker."
"All right." He smiled wonderfully at Fletch. "I've given that lecture
ten thousand times," he said. "Know it as well as the ravings of *Richard
III.* It's all nonsense, of course."
At the entrance to the alley, Mooney looked back into the bar. "A
clean, well-lighted place," he said.

TWENTY-FOUR

The phone rang and Fletch was off the bed and across the
room answering it before he really knew what he was doing.
"Hello?"
"Fletch?" It was Martin Satterlee ready to dispense infor-
mation.
"Good morning, Martin." Fletch sat in the chair next to the tele-
phone table. "What time is it in New York?"
Through the windows to the balcony first light was in the sky.
"Five-fifteen A.M."

"Then it must be here, too." Moxie was not in his bed. She had chosen to spend the night in a hammock on the balcony. "Find anything?"

"Not as much as we could have found if we hadn't been interrupted. An hour ago, the authorities swooped into Peterman's office, where we were working, and laid claim to all Ms. Mooney's financial records. Asked us politely but firmly to leave."

"They were quick. Did you show them Moxie's authorization?"

"Of course. It was not my scheme to be thought a burglar in the night. They had papers from a higher authority."

"Their piece of paper beat your piece of paper, huh?"

"Their piece of paper was signed by a judge. My piece of paper was signed by a movie star."

"So you're going to tell me everything is all right, and Moxie was just having a bad dream about all this . . ."

"Does *Yellow Orchid* mean anything to you, as a film title?"

"No."

"*In Ramon's Bed?*"

"No."

"*Twenty Minutes to Twelve?*"

"No, don't think so."

"*Midsummer Night's Madness?*"

"Of course. That's the film Moxie is making now."

"Are they actually making it?"

"I'm not sure. They have been."

"*Sculpture Garden?*"

"No."

"These are all films supposedly being made — I should say, financed — by Jumping Cow Productions."

"Yes. All right."

"The sole proprietor of Jumping Cow Productions is Ms. Marilyn Mooney."

"Holy Cow."

"Chief Executive Officer and Treasurer is, or was, Steven Peterman."

"Wave that in front of me again, Marty. Moxie owns Jumping Cow Productions?"

"One hundred percent."

"I know she doesn't know that. She keeps referring to Jumping Cow as 'them' and 'they.' In fact, I think she's been waiting word from someone at Jumping Cow as to whether filming on *Midsummer Night's Madness* is to continue."

"She's waiting to hear from herself."

"Wow."

"You can say she didn't know about it, Fletch, but her signature is in all the appropriate places. The Delaware incorporation papers, loan agreements —"

"Talk to me about the loan agreements, Marty."

"I wish I could tell you everything. I can't. Cops *interruptus*. We were able to discover there are huge sums of money floating around for no reason we were able to discover. Millions of dollars. Some of the monies seem to have been raised to produce these films — but we can't find any evidence that any of these films exist in any form whatsoever, except *Midsummer Night's Madness* which, by the way, seems to have a remarkably low budget. There are loans from Swiss banks and Colombian banks and Bolivian banks. Some of these loans seem to have been used to repay loans to banks in Honduras, Mexico, the Bahamas. Thoroughly confusing. On some loans, we couldn't find schedules of repayment, or that anything at all had been repaid. On other loans, which were being repaid, we couldn't find the pieces of paper which said the loans had actually been taken out in the first place."

Fletch had drawn his knees up and put his feet in the chair. He was warmer that way. "All this under the banner of Jumping Cow Productions?"

"No. A huge, huge amount of this activity is under her own name, personally."

"That's bad."

"I think so."

"Marty, how would you say she stands in general, financially, ahead or behind?"

"Haven't you been listening? Tons of money which exist on paper under her name, and under Jumping Cow Productions, Inc., don't seem to be anywhere."

"Stolen."

"Disappeared."

"Then, financially, she is behind."

"I'd say so. If you were looking for a motive for murder, you found one. A big one."

"I wasn't, actually."

"I can't see how she can ever get out of trouble. No matter how young she is. Millions are missing. Of course, maybe if we had another three weeks with the books, we could find some of it."

"Can't she claim bankruptcy?"

"It's not just money I'm talking about, Fletch. A lot of baffling financial activity has been happening under her name. Again, I wasn't able to spend enough time with her financial records to use the word fraud advisedly —"

"Ow."

"And her tax filings have been negligent. I mean negligible. Negligent and negligible. Minimum filings, maximum extensions. There were IRS pieces of paper among her records but no real reportings of income, outgo, profit, loss."

"Jail."

"Well. For next year she shouldn't plan too big a New Year's Eve party."

"But she wasn't doing all that bad stuff. She didn't even know about it."

"It was going on under her name, and she signed things."

"Marty. What about her personal assets?"

"Well, she owns a cooperative apartment in New York — mortgaged to the maximum. Also a very expensive property in Malibu, California, also mortgaged to the maximum. Her ownership of common stock follows a very distinct pattern. She would purchase at fifty and sixty dollars a share and sell at twelve and sixteen dollars a share."

"Always?"

"Few exceptions."

"Tax losses? Do you think Peterman was trying to create tax losses?"

"He was creating losses, all right. Huge losses. No preferred stock, no bonds. And the companies in which she was invested were foreign companies no one ever heard of. I mean, like a chain of bakeries in Guatemala."

"Must be dough in that."

"A Mexican trucking company. A restaurant in Caracas, Venezuela."

"Caramba!"

"An unrelieved tale of woe, Fletch. The only other thing she seems to own in this country is half interest in a horse farm in Ocala, Florida."

"Oh."

"That mean something to you? Five Aces Farm."

"Oh." Fletch counted his toes. "The alleged owner of that farm, Ted Sills, was a friend of Peterman's. I guess. That is, I met Sills at a party at Moxie's apartment once in New York. Peterman introduced us."

"Well, your friend Moxie has paid for the shipment of an awful lot of race horses between here and Venezuela."

"Oh. But, Martin, Moxie didn't even recognize Ted Sills's name when I mentioned him yesterday. We're even staying in Ted Sills's house. Right now."

"Small world."

"Even I've invested in some of the son of a bitch's race horses."

"Maybe I should go through your papers, too."

"Maybe you should. Hell's bells, Marty, what does all this add up to?"

"I don't know. Wasn't able to spend that long with her papers. On the face of things, it looks like your Moxie Mooney had an excellent motive for killing Steven Peterman. The best. Not once, but several times."

"That's what the police will say, isn't it?"

"I expect so. Of course, they could always find a factor which makes everything come out all right. But I doubt it. Experience has taught me, Fletch, that honest people do not bury their honesty in dishonest-seeming records."

"Martin, is there any way all this shifting of money about, taking loans, losing money could be thought to benefit Moxie?"

"I don't know."

"I mean, isn't it pretty clear from the papers she's the victim here?"

Martin Satterlee thought a short moment. "The presumption is, Fletch, that when a person goes in for sharp practices, he is doing so with some idea of personal benefit in mind."

"But, Marty, everything's such a mess!"

"People who go in for sharp practices usually make a mess. They usually lose. Losing, Fletch, is no evidence of virtue."

"Oh."

"I must also point out to you — seeing you sought my advice — the very real possibility that your friend, Moxie Mooney, is lying to you from start to finish."

"She'd have to be a pretty good liar."

"Isn't that what an actor is — a pretty good liar?"

"Come on, Marty."

"Consider it as a very real possibility, Fletch. I'm not sitting in judgment of your friend. Sooner or later someone will, I expect. Consider the possibility that she was in this financial razzle-dazzle with Steve Peterman, and that she murdered him only when she discovered she was being swindled, too. My early judgment would be — if I were making a judgment — that your friend, Moxie Mooney, is either awfully guilty or awfully stupid."

"She's just in trouble."

"And she knew it, right?"

"Why do you say that?"

"Why else would you have asked me to go look at Peterman's books?"

"Moxie-the-murderess is a concept I'm having difficulty wrapping my mind around."

Martin Satterlee said: "I'm pretty sure most people who commit murder have a friend somewhere."

TWENTY-FIVE

"You don't look like you slept well," Moxie said. She was looking up at him from a hammock on the second storey of The Blue House.

"Up to a point, I did." Fletch had gone back to bed at a quarter to six, but he had not slept. He listened to the quiet house. He got out of bed again at eight-thirty only because he heard the Lopezes come into the house. He also heard the grinding gears and squeaking brakes of trucks and buses.

In the hammock, Moxie stretched and yawned.

"Thought we'd go sailing today," Fletch said. "We can rent a catamaran on one of the beaches."

"That would be nice."

Somewhere in the house, a window smashed. In the street in front of the house, someone was yelling.

"Stay here," Fletch said.

On the balcony, he walked around the corner to the front of the house. Gerry and Stella Littleford were already there. They were looking out onto the street. As Fletch approached, they looked at him. On their faces were shock, confusion, anger, hurt, amazement. They said nothing.

In the street in front of The Blue House were two old, rickety yellow school buses, three trucks big enough to carry cattle, a few vans, and some old cars. On the sides of the yellow schoolbuses in big black letters was written SAVE AMERICA.

People from these vehicles were milling in the street. And some of these people wore white hooded robes with eye and nose holes cut in their faces. And others wore brown shirts and brown riding britches and black jackboots and black neckties and black arm bands with red swastikas on them. And some of these people were women in cheap house dresses. And some were children.

"Look at the children," Stella said.

Some men were passing demonstration signs down from the trucks. The signs were passed along from hand to hand. The signs said KEEP AMERICA WHITE, HOLLYWOOD SELLS U.S. SOUL, NO RACIAL MIX. One sign, carefully handprinted, read NO MONGURILIZATION! And these signs came to be held by the men in white hooded robes, and by the women, and by the children.

"I guess they mean me," Gerry Littleford said.

"No," Stella Littleford said. "They mean me."

To the left, the thirty Neo-Nazis were trying to appear military. A man with a red band around his hat was yelling at them as they were lining up. They all had beer bellies they were sucking in while tucking their chins in to show they all had dewlaps.

Moxie was standing beside Fletch and she put her hand on his on the railing.

"These people must have driven all night," Fletch said.

"These aren't people," Moxie said.

In the street someone said, *There's Moxie Mooney,* and *Cunt!, Whore!* were shouted in both men's and women's voices and a voice said, *Isn't that ol' Gerry Littleford up there?* and a rock bounced off the wall of the house behind where they were standing and fell to the floor near their feet.

From one of the trucks, *My country 'tis of thee* began to blare.

Fletch said to Moxie, "You don't think people care about such things anymore? You think there came a moment in history when everyone wised up and love and understanding pervaded the world? Well, it hasn't happened yet, babe. Maybe on television, but not in real life."

Moxie said, "The sick, the stupid, and the scared."

With two rows of uniformed plodgies standing behind him, the man distinguished by a red band around his hat began to shout a speech over the sound of music: *"We all know what this is about! We all know what is happening! We all know what is happening to the world! Who runs Hollywood which makes the movies? The Jews! Who runs the newspapers which sell the movies? The Jews! Who owns the movie theaters which show the movies? The Jews! Who owns the television networks which push the movies into our homes, spoiling the minds of our children? The Jews! And who pays the Jews? The Communists! The Jewish people do not mix. Oh, no — they do not marry outside*

their race! They marry outside their race and their families say they're dead! The
Russians do not marry outside their race! Oh, no — they send the Jews out of
their country . . .

Moxie giggled. "This is getting confusing."

Along Duval Street, from the houses, guest houses, and coffee
shops, and from the side streets ordinary citizens began to appear.
They stood apart from these others, their eyes wide, their mouths
open. They spoke to each other in disbelief. A large number of them
were gathering. A woman shrieked: *Be Nice!* The fishermen began to
appear in the crowd, the real fishermen and the sport fishermen and
even the other kind of fishermen who always came back to Key West
with a full cargo of shrimp they had bought with their other, more
valuable cargo. Fletch recognized two or three people who had been
at Durty Harry's the night before, listening to Frederick Mooney.

A Cuban-American boy, a Conch, about eight or ten years old, sat
cross-legged on the ground behind a man in a white robe. Fletch
watched the boy take a cigarette lighter from the pocket of his shorts.
It took him five or six tries to get flame from the lighter. Then he set
fire to the hem of the man's robe.

. . . land of liberty . . .

The man jumped, beat his burning robe with his arm, and kicked
the kid, hard, rolling him over in the gutter. He kicked the kid again,
in the head. By then, the robe was burning well. A woman was trying
to grab the robe off him. He kept kicking the kid.

The crowd rushed the people who had driven all night. Rocks went
through the air in all directions. Sticks appeared from nowhere. Here
and there, on bare skin and on the white robes red blood began to
appear. Women were screaming, in Cuban and English. The man
distinguished by the red band around his hat ordered his uniformed
plodgies to drive a wedge through all these screaming, hitting, kicking,
yelling people and the uniformed plodgies went into the fray. They
were beaten nicely.

From the center of Key West finally there came the sounds of sirens.

Fletch took Moxie's elbow. "Let's go."

"Where we going?"

"Sailing," Fletch said. "It's a nice day for sailing."

Edith Howell in her dressing gown was carrying a cup of coffee up
the main stairs of The Blue House. "Something I've never understood,"
she said to Moxie and Fletch, "is how one can be a Jew and a Com-
munist at the same time. A tree and a stone cannot be the same thing.
Either one is one thing, or one is another . . ."

"Sick people," Moxie answered.

Lopez was waiting in the front hall. He wore a clean white jacket. He said, "Mister Fletcher, Mister Sills is on the phone. He says if I don't put you on the phone, he fires me."

Sy Koller came out of the dining room with his cup of coffee. He said to Moxie, "We're a part of an international conspiracy?"

"Throw 'em a script, Sy," Moxie answered. "Let 'em see how bad it is."

Koller said, "I'd suspect Peterman's hand behind this foolishness — you know, for publicity — if he weren't dead."

Fletch said to Lopez, "Did you tell Sills what's going on outside?"

Outside were the sounds of sirens and hysterical screaming.

"No," said Lopez.

Fletch went down the corridor and through the billiard room to the study.

He lifted the telephone receiver from the desk.

"Good morning, Ted," Fletch said into the phone. "Nice day. We're just going sailing."

"Why am I hearing sirens?"

"Sirens?"

Ted Sills said, "I'm hearing sirens over the phone. While I've been waiting. Was someone singing *My country 'tis of thee* . . . ?"

"I wasn't. Not this morning."

"I heard people screaming. I'm still hearing people screaming."

"Must be a bad connection."

"What's going on there, Fletch?"

"Just settling down for breakfast. Maybe you heard Edith Howell practicing on the scales."

Somewhere in the house another pane of glass smashed.

"What was that?" Ted Sills asked over the phone.

"What was what?"

"Sharp noise. Sounded like glass breaking."

"Must have been at your end, Ted."

"Sounds like a riot's going on."

"Must be your telephone cord, Ted. Give it a tug and see if it clears up."

"Fletcher, I have told you and your little playmates to get out of that house."

"Yes, you did, Ted."

"You're still there."

"Having a few days of peace and quiet."

"I heard on the morning news you're still there. In The Blue House."

"That reminds me, Ted. When does the rubbish get picked up? Want to make sure Lopez puts it out."

"I want you to get out of the goddamned house!" Ted Sills shouted.

"Now, now, Ted. No wonder your phone is broken."

"All right, Fletcher, I'm coming down there. With a shotgun. And if you're not out of that house by the time I get there —"

"You'll hardly be noticed. By the way, Ted, you never told me Moxie Mooney is half-owner of Five Aces Farm."

There was silence from Ted Sills's end of the line. From Fletch's there were three sounds which could have been light-caliber gunshots.

"I happened to find out just this morning," Fletch said. "I didn't know you two knew each other."

Ted Sills said, "Ms. Mooney has a financial interest in this farm. What's that to you?"

"Nothing. Just think it odd that here you have two such nice financial partners, Moxie and me, staying in your resort house, and you want us out."

"Fletcher . . ." Ted Sills sighed. "You don't know what you're doing. You've turned that house into a circus."

"Not me, Ted."

Moxie appeared in the doorway of the study. Her eyes were huge. "Stella Littleford's been hurt," she said.

"Sorry, Ted," Fletch said into the phone. "Gotta go."

"What did I just hear?" Sills shouted. "Who's been hurt?"

"The three-minute eggs," said Fletch. "Their feelings are hurt. I'm not there eating 'em."

He hung up and followed Moxie into the front of the house.

Stella Littleford was sitting like a dropped doll on the floor of the front hall. Her hands were over her forehead. Blood was seeping through her fingers.

Sy Koller was kneeling beside her. "Definite need for stitches," he said to Fletch.

The front door was open.

A low haze of riot gas drifted over the street. Police had set up sawhorse barricades in a U in the street at the front of The Blue House. Two were knocked over. There were a few discarded white robes on the road. There was also one of the uniformed plodgies sitting on the road in a position nearly identical to Stella Littleford's, another dropped doll, also holding his head.

To the right, down Duval Street, away from the riot gas, hand-to-hand fighting and mouth-to-mouth shouting was continuing.

Directly across the street, a sinewy armed fisherman was puncturing the tires of the school buses and trucks with his fishing knife.

Gerry Littleford ran into the yard followed by two young men with a stretcher. His eyes were red and runny from the gas.

"Shit forever," he said to Fletch. He pointed to a broken rum bottle on the front porch. "Someone pegged Stella with that. Cut her head."

Clearly there had still been rum in the bottle when it broke. The shattered glass was in a puddle.

An ambulance was backing down the street, over one of the fallen sawhorses, to the front door of The Blue House.

In the front hall, Mrs. Lopez was handing wet cloths to Moxie who was handing them to Sy Koller who was applying them to Stella Littleford's forehead. The young men who brought the stretcher stopped all that. They put a pile of dry gauze against the cut and taped it lightly.

They helped Stella onto the stretcher.

"Want me to go to the hospital with you?" Fletch asked Gerry.

"I do not."

"Want Sy to go?"

Gerry said, "I do not."

"Okay," Fletch said. "I'll see you later."

Gerry followed the stretcher-bearers through the front door.

Fletch stood on the front porch watching them put Stella into the back of the ambulance.

When Moxie joined him, he said. "Watch your feet. Broken glass."

The riot gas was dissipating. A swinging, kicking crowd came back down Duval Street from the right, knocking over another barricade. Fletch supposed the demonstrators were trying to get back to their buses and trucks. Their signs were broken and trampled around the trucks as were the record player and the amplifiers. The trucks, the buses, and some of the cars had flat tires. But by then there were too many personal angers and personal scores to settle and the pushing and the punching continued.

From above their heads, from the upper front balcony of The Blue House boomed the world's best trained, most voluminous voice: *"Four score and seven years ago . . ."*

"Oh, God," said Moxie.

In fact, the people in the street did look up. That's Frederick Mooney! And they did stop fighting.

"... *our forefathers brought forth on this continent* ..."

"Good ol' Freddy," said Fletch. "Let's go sailing."

"... *a new nation* ..."

Fletch and Moxie walked through the house to the back. Even in the backyard they could hear Mooney's *Gettysburg Address*. All other noises had ceased.

"Think of that volume of sound," Moxie said, "coming out of a head that must hurt as much as his does!"

TWENTY-SIX

After they sailed awhile, Moxie said, "I suppose I should ask you, seeing it wasn't so long ago you put me on an airplane ostensibly for dinner and landed me far enough away from the scene of the crime to make me a fugitive from justice, if now you have me in a sailboat, do you mean to flee the country with me?"

"Damn," said Fletch at the tiller. "You caught me. You penetrated my purposeful plot."

Moxie's eyes were full of the sunlight reflected from the sea. "I've always heard Cuba is a gorgeous country."

Up to that point, they had said little to each other.

They had walked to a Cuban-American restaurant and had a quiet breakfast. Some of the people there had recognized Moxie and smiled at her in a friendly way and kept their dignity by otherwise leaving her alone. During breakfast, Moxie wondered aloud if Stella Littleford would have a scar on her forehead forever and Fletch said he thought Stella had suffered a concussion as well because there had been quite a lot of rum in the bottle that had hit her. The *señora* of that restaurant made a picnic lunch for them and put it in a cardboard box. Fletch also bought a six-pack of cold soft drinks.

They walked the long way around, along the water, until they came to a beach where Fletch rented a catamaran. He put the food and the drinks aboard. Boys on the beach helped them push the catamaran into the surf. Fletch boosted Moxie aboard and then climbed aboard himself.

The process of launching put enough water in the bottom of the boat to soak the cardboard picnic box. Moxie showed Fletch the soggy box as he was finding the wind and beginning to sail on it and they laughed. She rescued the sandwiches and the fruit and rolled the box into a ball and dropped it into the bottom of the boat.

Moxie was wearing her bikini and she removed the top but she kept herself more or less in the shade of the sail. She said, "Talk to me."

"About what?"

"Something nice, please."

"Edith Howell says if you're not talking you're dead, or something."

"If Edith Howell ever stopped talking everyone else would die. Of shock."

"She has her eyes on your father's millions."

Moxie snorted. "Millions of empty cognac bottles. She's welcome to 'em." She put herself on her side and trailed her fingers in the water. "Talk to me about something nice. Like how come you're so rich."

"You're asking me if I'm rich?"

"Well, you're not working. You have that nice place in Italy."

"That's sort of a rude question, from a girl I just met."

"I know. Answer me anyway."

"It's a long story."

"I've got all day."

"It's sort of an impossible story to tell. In detail."

"Did you do something wrong, Fletch? Are you a crook?"

"Who, me? No. I don't think so."

"What happened?"

"Not much. One night I found myself alone in a room with a lot of cash. The cash was there because I had been hired to do a bad thing. I had not done the bad thing. But the bad thing had happened anyway. Coincidentally."

"Boy, why don't you spare me a few details?"

"I told you it's a long story."

"So you took the money . . ."

"I had to. Leaving it there would have embarrassed people. It would have raised questions."

"Robbery as an act of kindness?"

"I thought so at the time."

"What did you do with the money?"

"I didn't know what to do with it. I had never been very good with money."

"No foolin'. I remember the time . . ."

"What time?"

"Forget it. I'm still mad."

"There should never be money between friends."

"That's it," said Moxie. "There wasn't any. Unfortunately, you had invited me to one of Los Angeles' most posh eateries."

"Oh. That time."

"That time."

"Yes."

"I wouldn't mind getting my watch back sometime. The one the restaurant took."

"A Piaget, wasn't it?"

"With little diamonds."

Fletch asked, "What time is it?"

She put herself on her stomach. "Who cares?"

Fletch said: "Exactly."

Moxie inhaled slowly and exhaled with a great sigh. "Oh, Fletch. Oh, Fletch — you never change."

He smiled at her, showing her all his front teeth. "I just get better."

"Worse. So what did you do with all this money you stole?"

"I didn't steal it."

"It just fell into your lap."

"Something like that. Long story. The money was on its way to South America, see, so I went with it. I'm very big on seeing actions completed. Essential to my psyche."

"Then how come you haven't finished writing the biography of Edgar Arthur Tharp?"

"I'm working on it. I was in South America. I didn't know what to do with the money. Maybe I felt a little badly about having it. Maybe I was trying to get rid of it. So I bought gold with it."

"Oh, no."

"I did."

"And the price of gold shot up?"

"Someone mentioned that to me. In a bar. So I felt worse. I got rid of the gold. Quick. Yuck. I hated the oil companies, thought they were givin' the world a royal screwin', they were bound to get their comeuppance —"

"So you put your money into oil companies?"

"Yes. I did."

"And their value shot up?"

"So I heard. That made me feel worse."

"I can believe."

"I got rid of that yucky stuff as quick as I could. I've done terribly."

"And where's the money now?"

"Well, I decided my investment policy wasn't very sound. Very responsible. You know what I mean? I had been buying things I didn't like."

"So you decided to buy things you did like?"

"I decided to use the money to help out, instead of hinder. I heard General Motors was having such a tough time nobody was buying its stock."

"So you bought General Motors?"

"So I bought General Motors. And the cable-electronics companies looked risky, so I put some money into them."

"Good Lord, Fletch. God! You're so incompetent!"

"Well, I never said I was any good with money."

"You should have taken a course. *How To Invest.*"

"Yes," Fletch said. "I suppose I should have."

"You just never cared about money!"

"No," said Fletch. "I don't."

When they got to the Gulf Stream she went overboard and he lowered the sails and, except for the light lines to the boat he tied to his ankles, he got naked, too, and went overboard and they played and made love in the water, only the light, drifting boat kept pulling him away from her by the ankles and he kept getting too much water up his nose and they both laughed so hard they ran out of breath and nearly drowned but they did succeed, but they were slow to leave the water and climb back into the boat anyway.

"As long as we're talking about money," he said.

"Is this still nice talk?"

"Jumping Cow Productions, Incorporated," he said.

They had sailed back to an empty beach and run the catamaran up onto the fine sand. They took their food and drinks ashore and had a picnic. The drinks were very warm but they drank them anyway, for the sake of putting fluid into their bodies. The sandwiches had dried out. Mostly they ate the fruit.

After eating, they lay in the sand. It was late enough in the afternoon and there were enough passing clouds so the sun would not burn their tanned skin. Fletch waited a long while. Finally she put herself on her side and she put her hand on his hip and he put himself on his side as well and put his head on his hand. Her face told him he had her attention, but she did not expect to talk about money at this time.

"Tell me, Moxie," he said. "What does the cow jump over?"

"The moon," she answered easily. Then her face changed. She looked at him as if he had struck her. Then she rolled over onto her back. She covered her eyes with one hand. "Mooney," she groaned.

"Right. Moxie Mooney." She continued to lie flat on her back beside him on the sand, her hand covering her eyes from the sun. "You are sole proprietor of Jumping Cow Productions, Incorporated. Martin Satterlee called me this morning."

"Good." She rolled onto her stomach. "I'll close that goddamned movie down faster than anything you ever saw."

"*Midsummer Night's Madness?*"

"*Fini* to *Midsummer Night's Madness.* To Edith Howell, Sy Koller, Geoff McKensie, Gerry Littleford, Talcott Cross, the whole damned bunch of 'em. Goodbye to that stupid script. Goodbye to Route 41."

"I take it you did not know you are sole proprietor of Jumping Cow Productions?"

"I did not. I certainly did not."

"Moxie, when you went into Peterman's office — a couple of weeks ago — what did you actually learn? What did you actually find out that upset you so, you know, enough to cause you to ask me to meet you here?"

"I couldn't find any real tax reports. I kept asking the staff for the tax files. They kept bringing me folder after folder with all this crazy stuff in them, loan agreements with banks in Honduras and Switzerland and Mexico. I didn't know what it all meant, but I got madder and madder." Her voice dropped. "Or more and more scared."

Fletch lay back on the sand, folding his hands behind his head. "Marty couldn't do a very thorough job of looking at your financial records. Four o'clock this morning the police came in and took them all."

"Oh, God! The police have my financial records?"

"You knew they —"

"I didn't know anything, Fletch!" Moxie snapped. She pounded her fist on the sand. "Damn!"

She got up and walked at an angle down the beach to the water's edge and then kept walking along the water.

After a long while, when she didn't come back he took their garbage

back to the boat and turned it around in the light surf and otherwise
prepared for departure.

Then he sat on one of the hulls and waited while Moxie walked
back down the beach.

They launched the boat together.

"Moxie?" Again they were sailing, the low sun at their stern. She
sat, the picture of dejection, chin on hand, elbow on knee. "You know
the guy who owns The Blue House?"

"No. How could I?"

"His name is Ted Sills. You said yesterday you don't know him."

"I don't."

"Apparently you are a co-owner with Ted Sills of a Florida horse farm."

She wrinkled her face at him. There was salt on her skin and a small
dab of sand on one cheekbone. "We're partners in something?"

"Five Aces Farm. Ocala, Florida."

She shrugged. "News to me."

"I guess he was a friend of Steve Peterman's."

"Listen, Fletch." She sounded tired and angry and tired of being
angry. "Why don't you just give it to me in simple?"

"Wish I could. As I told you, Marty didn't get very far into your
records when the cops arrived. He seems to agree with your two main
fears: that you are in tax trouble; that you do owe huge and unlikely
sums of money to banks all over the world."

Moxie Mooney looked all over the horizon. "Which way did you
say Cuba is?"

He pointed. "That way."

"You want to come with me, or should I start swimming?"

"An awful lot of inexplicable financial activity has been going on
under your name."

"Inexplicable . . . and you expect me to explain?"

"Marty couldn't explain it. He couldn't understand it."

"Is it your friend Marty's opinion that something crooked has been
going on?"

"He was trying not to have an opinion."

"But he had to try hard, right?"

"Right." Fletch hitched in the main sheet. "He seemed to feel all
that much activity couldn't have been going on without your knowing
about it."

The red light from the setting sun full in her face, Moxie just stared
at Fletch.

Fletch said, quietly: "In other words, Moxie, chances are pretty good your average judge is going to believe you're lying."

"Lying," she said.

"About everything."

She looked at the paper sandwich wrappers and empty soda cans on the deck of the cockpit. "The way you were lying this morning? About all your money?"

Fletch chuckled. "Yeah."

"Come on, Fletch. Games are games. This isn't fun."

She studied the junk in the bottom of the boat a long time.

Then she put her hand on his knee. "Hey, Fletch. Thanks for the nice day."

"Nice to make your acquaintance," he said.

He was sailing for the right beach. Leaving that morning he had lined the beach up with the martello towers.

"In other words," Moxie said, "going through my financial records, the cops are going to find I had tons of reasons for killing Steve Peterman."

"It looks that way."

The centerboard was up. Near the beach, Fletch was looking for the heads of late swimmers on the water.

"Fletch." Moxie shivered. "Please find someone else to pin this murder on."

"I'm tryin', babe," Fletch said. "I'm tryin'."

It was dark and walking through the side streets in her loose beach wrap, her head down, Moxie attracted no attention.

Fletch said, "There's one other small matter . . ."

"Boy, you're really giving it to me today. I thought we were just going to talk about happy things."

"I got you out of the house just so we could talk."

"You took me sailing so you could beat up on me."

"Your father told me about your going to school in England . . ."

Quietly, Moxie said, "You knew I went to school in England. Almost two years."

"I never knew why."

"Freddy was being paternal that year. Wanted me near him."

"But he wasn't in England that year."

"He was supposed to be. His schedule got changed."

"Moxie . . ." Fletch took her hand. "Hey," he said. "Your father said something about your drama coach at school getting murdered."

Her hand went limp in his. "I was only fourteen."

"God! What does that mean?"

She pulled her hand from his. "It means Freddy didn't think I needed all that pressure on me at the age of fourteen!"

" 'Pressure'! 'Pressure'?"

She veered on the rough sidewalk. They were then on a dark, empty sidestreet. She was walking a meter away from him. "Do you think I murdered Mister Hodes?"

" 'Think', I don't think anything. I didn't even know the guy's name."

"He was a little shit," Moxie muttered.

"I think you were gotten out of town damned fast. Way out. Out of the country. And you went."

"I was fourteen, for God's sake." They had stopped walking. "I didn't mind going to school in England. It sounded cool."

"I ask you if you murdered somebody and all you say is you were fourteen!"

"Is that what you think? You think I murdered the birdy drama coach?"

"I don't know what to think. I hate what I think. Why don't you answer me?"

Across the sidewalk her eyes glowered.

"Think what you want, Fletcher."

She began to walk. She walked with her fists clenched at her sides.

She walked ahead of him all the way to the house.

They approached The Blue House from the rear.

Moxie, well ahead of him, head down, zipped through the back gate into the garden.

When Fletch got to the back gate Lopez was coming through with a rubbish barrel.

"Ah," Fletch said. "Tomorrow's the day the rubbish gets picked up."

Lopez grinned at him. "A lot of broken glass, Mister Fletcher. They threw a lot of stones."

"I know. Any real damage?"

"No. It's all cleaned up. Tomorrow I will start replacing the windows which were broken."

On top of the barrel that Lopez had just set down were three empty apple juice bottles.

"Sorry about this morning," Fletch said. "All the noise. Damage. Mess. Guess I'm not a very good tenant."

Lopez's grin grew even broader. "It's fun," he said. "This house is empty so much. The excitement is good. Don't think about it."

TWENTY-SEVEN

"How many stitches?" Fletch asked.

In the hospital bed Stella Littleford didn't look any more sallow than usual. The surgical dressing on her forehead was not as big as Fletch expected.

"Six." She did not smile.

Gerry Littleford sat in a side chair, his feet propped up on the bed. On top of his shorts he was wearing a hospital johnny. He had left The Blue House that morning without a shirt. Apparently he had not been back to the house since. He also wore paper slippers on his feet.

"They're keeping her overnight," Gerry said. "Concussion."

"I brought you some flowers," Fletch said. "Nurse ate them." He crossed the room and leaned his back against the window sill. "What happened this morning anyway? I didn't see . . . I was on the phone."

"There was a riot," Gerry Littleford said drily.

"I went out into the front yard and shook my fists at those dirty bastards and called them dirty bastards," Stella said. "Dirty bastards."

"Does it hurt to talk?"

"It does now." She tried not to laugh. "It didn't this morning."

"She got bonked," Gerry said. "Someone threw a rum bottle at her."

"Someone must have really cared," Fletch said. "There was still rum in the bottle."

"Good." Stella again tried not to laugh.

"I've never seen you laugh before," Fletch said to her.

"She does everything she's not supposed to do," Gerry said, "when she's not supposed to do it. Like marrying me."

Stella's eyes moved slowly to Gerry's face. Fletch could not read the expression in them.

"Question," Fletch said. "Have either of you heard before from these groups? Threatening letters, phone calls, anything?"

Neither answered him.

"I'm just wondering," Fletch said, "how much these groups wanted that film stopped."

Still, neither answered him.

"Hey," Fletch said. "There's been a murder. Maybe two. Stella's in bed with a concussion. Stitches in her forehead. This morning we saw demonstrations demanding the film be stopped. It's a reasonable question."

Gerry asked, "Has the film been stopped?"

And Fletch didn't answer. "Have you heard from any of these groups before?"

Gerry put his feet flat on the floor and sat straight in his chair as if about to give testimony in court. "To be honest — yes."

"Letters?"

"With pamphlets enclosed. Keep-the-white-race-pure pamphlets. You know? So you honkies can go a few more centuries without soul."

"There have been phone calls, too, Gerry," Stella said.

"Phone calls," Gerry said.

"Threats?"

"My black ass will get burned, if I make the film. I'll get a shot in the head." Gerry's eyes roamed over Fletch's face. "It's hard for a black man to tell a real threat from normal white man's conversation."

"Did you tell anybody about these threats?"

"Like who?"

"Anybody in authority. Steve Peterman. Talcott what's-his-name. Sy Koller. The cops."

"You think I'm crazy? Making this film is my employment. I'm not lookin' to get unemployed."

"Do you still have any of these letters, pamphlets?"

" 'Course not. Throw 'em away. Gotta throw 'em away."

"Do you remember any of the names, groups that sent you these letters?"

"They all have these long, phony names. You know: My Land But Not Your Land Committee Incorporated; Society To Keep 'em Pickin' Cotton."

"You got a call from a black group, too, Gerry."

"Yes, I did." Gerry smiled. "Some of the brothers want to keep soul to ourselves a few more centuries."

"Gerry," Fletch asked, "sincerely — do you think the production of *Midsummer Night's Madness* seriously was being threatened by any of these groups? Like to the point of murder?"

"I don't know. They're madmen. How can you tell when madmen are serious?" More quietly, he said, "Yeah. I think there were murderers in that group this morning that attacked the house. People capable of

murder. Plenty of 'em. That rum bottle coulda killed Stella. I just
doubt they're up to organizing anything as clever as the murder of
Steve Peterman. Whoever got Steve was no dope."

"I guess you're right."

The nurse brought in a vase of roses. There were no other flowers
in the room.

"Ah!" Fletch got off the window sill. "You didn't eat 'em."

"I had supper at home," the nurse said. "Daffodils."

Fletch was at the door. "Coming back to the house, Gerry?"

"Sure," he said. "Later."

TWENTY-EIGHT

In the cool night, Fletch walked around Key West for awhile. He
found himself in the center of the old commercial district so he
went down the alley to Durty Harry's. Frederick Mooney was not
there. Few were. There was no band playing either.

He sat at the bar and ordered a beer. A clock he had seen said ten
minutes past eleven but clocks in Key West are not expected to tell
the real time. Clocks in Key West are only meant to substantiate
unreality.

A dog, a black dog, a large black dog walked through the bar at
the heels of a man who came through a door on the second storey
and down a spiral staircase.

"What's that dog's name?" Fletch asked the young woman behind
the bar.

"That's Emperor. Isn't he a nice dog?"

"Nice dog." Fletch sipped his beer. He did not want the beer. The
early morning phone call from Satterlee, the demonstrations, the day
of sailing and swimming in the wind and sun made him glad to sit
quietly a moment. He thought about Global Cable News and how
quickly his phone call had been answered and he was allowed to speak
to that hour's producer because he was a stockholder. It should be the
story that counts, not who is calling it in. Anything can be checked
out. Your average stockholder is not any more honest or accurate than
your average citizen. Fletch decided if he ever had a big story again
he'd call it into Global Cable News under a phony name. It would be

an interesting experiment — for a stockholder. He wanted to sleep. He left the rest of his beer on the bar. "Nice dog," he said.

TWENTY-NINE

Something woke him up. It was dawn. Fletch remained in bed a minute listening to the purposeful quiet. It was too purposeful.

He got out of bed and went out onto the balcony.

There were two policemen in the sideyard. They looked back up at him.

In the dawn he could see the flashing blue lights of police cars at the front of the house.

"Shit," Fletch said.

He ran along the balcony against the wall to the back of the house and around the corner. Gerry Littleford was curled up asleep in a hammock.

Fletch shook his shoulder. "Gerry. Wake up. It may be a bust."

Gerry opened one eye to him. "What? A what?"

Were the police there to arrest someone for murder? No, there were too many of them. There were now three cops in the backyard. Were they there because they had been tipped off there would be another demonstration? No, they were in the yard. Some judge had given them a warrant to be on and in the property.

"It sure looks like a bust to me," Fletch said quietly.

"A bust?"

"Shut up. Get up. Get rid of whatever shit you have." Fletch pulled up on one side of the hammock and Gerry fell out the other side landing like a panther on braced fingers and toes. "Down the toilet, Gerry. *Pronto.*"

In the bedroom Fletch put on his shorts and shirt.

"What's happening?" Moxie said into her pillow.

"You might get dressed. The cops are here."

Instantly she sat up. Instantly there was no sign of sleep in her face. Instead there was the look of someone cornered, frightened but who would fight.

"I know," Fletch said. "You didn't kill Steve Peterman. Ho-hum."

And three policemen were standing on the front porch. When Fletch opened the front door to them they seemed surprised. They had not rung the bell or knocked.

"Good morning," Fletch said. "Welcome to the home of the stars. Donations are tax-deductible."

The policemen seemed shy. There were five police cars in the street. The roof lights of three were flashing. Despite the demonstration the day before, the street was clean.

Fletch held his hand out to them, palm up. A policeman put a folded paper into Fletch's palm. Nevertheless, he said, "May we come in?"

Fletch held their own paper up to them. "Guess this says you may."

In the front hall one of the policemen said, "I'm Sergeant Henning."

Fletch shook hands with him. "Fletcher. Tenant of this domicile."

"We have to search this domicile."

"Sure," Fletch said. "Coffee?"

The sergeant looked around at all the other policemen coming into the house, through the front and back and verandah doors, and said, "Sure."

In the kitchen Fletch put a pan of water on the stove and got out two mugs. "Thanks for your help yesterday."

"Actual fact, we weren't much help. Got here late. Things had gone too far. Things like that don't happen here in Key West anyway."

"Not on your daily agenda, huh?"

"Actual fact, sort of hard to know what to do. Those bimbos are citizens, too. Sort of got the right to demonstrate."

"Were there any actual arrests?" Fletch spooned instant coffee into the mugs. From upstairs he could hear people moving around. Furniture being moved. Then he could hear Edith Howell's voice pitched high in indignation.

"Nine. They'll be released this morning."

"No one threw that rum bottle at Mrs. Littleford, huh?" The water in the pan was bubbling.

"None of the people we arrested did." The sergeant smiled ruefully. "We asked every one of 'em, we did. Politely, too."

Fletch poured the water into the mugs and handed one to the police sergeant.

"Any sugar?" the sergeant asked. Fletch nodded to the bowl on the counter. "I need my sugar." The sergeant helped himself. "Coffee and sugar. It's what keeps me bad-tempered."

Two other policemen came into the kitchen and began searching through it.

"Appreciate it if you wouldn't make too much of a mess," Fletch said. "Know Mrs. Lopez?"

"Sure," a cop said.

"She'll have to clean up."

He went out onto the back porch with his coffee. The sergeant followed him.

"Can you tell me why you're searching the house?" Fletch asked.

The sergeant shrugged. "Illegal substances."

"Yeah, but why? What's the evidence you had to get a warrant?"

"It was good enough for the judge. That sure is a nice banyan tree. I haven't been in this house in years." He grinned at Fletch. "You in the movies, too?"

"No."

"Just one of those cats who likes to associate with movie people, huh?"

"Yeah. A hanger-on."

"It must be sort of disappointin', seein' these people up close. I mean, when no one's writin' their lines for 'em, no one's directin' how they act. I'd rather leave 'em on the screen."

"I'm sure they'd rather be left on the screen."

"That Mister Mooney sure is one big drunk. Seen him downtown. He needs a keeper."

"He's a great man."

"One of our patrolmen drove him home the other night. First night you were here."

"Thank you."

"Chuck said Mooney recited all the way home." The sergeant chuckled. "Something about Jessie James being due in town. Better watch out for him." The sergeant drank some coffee. Upstairs Edith Howell was exclaiming, proclaiming, declaiming. "This whole country's drunk. Stoned on something."

"Whole world."

"The people have discovered drugs. Not enough to do any more. Machines do the hard work. Recreational drugs, we're callin' 'em now. Baseball is recreation . . . fishin'. Too much time."

"Not everyone can go fishin'. Not everyone can go to baseball."

"The whole damned world's stoned on one thing or another."

Saying nothing, a policeman held the back door open. His eyes were bloodshot.

The sergeant left his coffee mug on the kitchen counter. The kitchen was really very clean.

John Meade was standing in the front hall. A policeman was standing beside him. John Meade was wearing gray slacks and brown loafers and a blue button-down shirt and handcuffs.

He smiled at Fletch. "Ludes."

"Sorry, John," said Fletch. "I never thought of you."

"Brought 'em back from New York."

The sergeant took a tin container from the policeman. "Quaaludes," the sergeant said. "A controlled substance. You have a prescription, Mister Meade?"

"My doctor died," John Meade said. "Eleven years ago."

"Sorry to hear that. I sure liked you in *Easy River.*"

"So did I," said John Meade.

The sergeant was examining the tin box. "You sure didn't get this from any legitimate source, Mister Meade. You're supportin' the bad guys, actual fact."

Other police were coming into the front hall.

"Hey, Sergeant," Fletch said. "Does this have to happen? Do you have to take Mister Meade in?"

"Yeah," Sergeant Henning said. "Too many witnesses. Too many cops around."

THIRTY

Fletch retreated to the small study at the back of The Blue House. On the front stairs Edith Howell was screaming her rage that the police had taken John Meade away in handcuffs. She was screaming at Frederick Mooney to go do something about it. There had not been a sound from Frederick Mooney. Fletch wasn't even sure he was in the house. Edith Howell was dressed in blue silk pajamas, blue silk slippers, and a blue silk robe. Her hair was in pin curls and her face clotted with cream. Sy Koller's head had appeared over the second-floor bannister looking painfully hung over. Lopez and Gerry Littleford were in the backyard throwing a tennis ball back and forth. Mrs. Lopez was in the kitchen making real coffee, starting breakfast. Neither Geoffrey McKensie nor Moxie had come down.

Fletch did not mind telephoning Five Aces Farm that early in the morning. Horse people are always up early.

The phone rang so long without being answered Fletch sat at the desk.

Finally a man's voice answered.

"This is Fletcher. May I speak with Mister Sills, please?"

"Not here, Mister Fletcher. This is Max Frizzlewhit."

"Mornin', Max. Ted must have been off pretty early. Is there a race somewhere?"

"Yeah, there's a race. But he's not at it. I'm just about to go with the trailer. 'Cept the phone kept ringin' and ringin' down here at the stables. One of your horses, too, Mister Fletcher," Frizzlewhit sped along in his English accent. "Scarlet Pimple-Nickel. Call to wish her luck?"

"Does she have a chance?"

"No. If she had half a chance we would have moved her to the track yesterday. She's not worth stable fees."

"Then why are you running her?"

"She needs the exercise."

"Oh, good."

"She needs the experience."

"Will she ever be any good, Max?"

"No."

"Then why do I own her?"

"Beats me. She may have looked good that week you were here."

"Never again?"

"And never before, I think."

"Maybe I brought something out in her."

"Maybe. You ought to come by more often, Mister Fletcher."

"To buy more horses?"

"You ought to go to the track."

"It's too embarrassing, Max."

"Maybe if you went to the track ol' Scarlet Pimple-Nickel would perform for you, keep her eye on the finish instead of on a bunch of horses' asses." If only the horses he trained ran as fast as Frizzlewhit talked . . .

"This horse has an anal fixation, is that it?"

"I'm not sure she's an actual pervert, Mister Fletcher. It just may be that she'd never seen anything but other horses' asses."

"Very understanding of you, Frizzlewhit."

"Hey, you have to be, in this business. Horses are just like people."

"No," Fletch said. "They're smarter. They don't invest in people and make 'em run around a track."

"That's true. They are smarter that way."

"So where did Mister Sills go?"

"He left the country."

"Ah. Was this a sudden trip, would you say?"

"He packed and left last night. He was plannin' to go to the race today."

"A sudden trip. Did he mention which country he's favoring?"

"France. He mentioned France."

"And which way was he going?"

"By airplane, Mister Fletcher."

"I mean, through Miami? New York?"

"Atlanta, I think."

"Then he's gone. Left the country."

"Can't be sure. Cousin Heath, from Piddle — you know I had a cousin lives in Piddle? — came to see me and got into that Atlanta airport and wasn't heard from Tuesday noon till Saturday teatime. Said he kept expectin' somethin' to happen, and nothin' did."

"I'm going to tell people to keep their eye on you, Frizzlewhit."

"Wish you would. Sometimes it gets lonely down here with the horses."

"Even you can outrun 'em, huh?"

"Some of 'em are no improvement over stayin' still."

"Will Mister Sills call you?"

"Prolly."

"You might tell him The Blue House was busted this morning. For drugs."

"Yeah? You had a rave-up down there just yesterday, didn't you? Nasties and the bedsheet bunch. Saw it on television, I did. What's going to happen tomorrow?"

"That's always the question, isn't it?"

"That's what makes a horse race."

"Damn," said Fletch. "I didn't think you knew what makes a horse race."

And Fletch did not mind telephoning Chief of Detectives Roz Nachman at that early hour. Police stations are supposed to be open for twenty-four-hour-a-day service. If she wasn't there yet he should be able to leave a message.

But she was there.

"Aren't you getting any sleep at all, Chief?"

"Thank you for your concern, Mister Fletcher."

"Thank you."

"For what?"

"Staging that drug bust this morning. Here at The Blue House. I'm sure I'll figure out why in a minute. Trying to discover who's sleeping with whom? You could have asked. You did before."

"How's the weather in Key West?"

"Nice."

"It's nice here, too."

"Having John Meade busted in Key West for a few Quaaludes is not nice of you."

"John Meade?"

"He could end up with a jail sentence, you know. He's a big name. Make good headlines for the authorities in Key West."

"Was he in illegal possession of a controlled substance?"

"That's why he's being held."

"I'm sorry. Loved him in *Easy River*."

"So did he. He won't be able to use his talents to give you much more pleasure if he's in the hoosegow."

"So I'll see *Easy River* again. It's on the TV all the time. Now — regarding that question you asked? Regarding Steven Peterman's car?"

"Yes?"

"We had it checked out. The car was in the parking lot on Bonita Beach. A blue Cadillac."

"A rented car?"

"Yes. No damage. Not a scrape. So that's the end of that great line of investigation."

"What date did he rent the car?"

There was a long silence from Chief of Detectives Roz Nachman. "That's a good point. Are you trying to get ahead of me, Mister Fletcher?"

"Would you expect him to keep a damaged car? A damaged rented car?"

"I wonder what date he actually arrived in Florida."

"I don't know. I should think you'd know by now."

"I would, too. Okay . . ."

"So that line of investigation is still open?"

"We'll check further."

"Another thing. You must know that yesterday we had sort of a riot here. A demonstration. Some violence."

"It was in all the papers. On TV. Everybody's name mentioned but yours. Who are you, Mister Fletcher?"

"Chief, one of these groups might really have been trying to stop this film. I mean, to the point of murder. Gerry Littleford said last night that he had received threatening letters and phone calls —"

"Does he have any of the letters?"

"No. But the riot yesterday — Stella Littleford did get hurt. Some of these people can be vicious. Insanely vicious.

"Vicious but not smart. I don't think your average bigoted tub-of-lard is up to getting on location and then making a knife magically appear between the ribs of somebody sitting on a well-lit stage in daylight surrounded by cameras. . . . Do you, earwig?"

"No."

"Keep trying, earwig. Things are looking worse and worse for your Ms. Moxie Mooney. I need a devil's advocate."

"What do you mean?"

"Well, all those film experts we hired — they're coming down pretty heavily on her. That dance she did."

"What dance?"

"Didn't you see her? Thought you were there."

"What dance?"

"Just before the, you know, murder. Moxie Mooney got up from her chair and did a little dance. She was showing Dan Buckley some little dance step she did in *A Broadway Hit*."

"In her bathrobe?"

"Make-up robe, dressing gown, whatever you want to call it. It's terrycloth. We have it. I should think it would be too big for her."

"So she couldn't have done it."

"So she could have. After she did her little dance step, she went back to her own chair, crossing behind where Peterman and Buckley were sitting."

"She crossed behind them."

"Yes. Behind. It's in all the videotapes. In fact, it looks a little unnatural. From where she finished her dance, she could have walked directly back to her chair, or behind Peterman and Buckley. She chose to walk behind them."

"Oh, God."

"The experts have drawn lines all over the stage floor. They talk in cubes. Do you understand that?"

"No."

"Neither do I. Upshot of it is they said it would have been more direct, and more natural for her to walk in front of the men. It looks a little unnatural to me. But, keep tryin', earwig. Believe me, I'd rather find some group of crazies guilty of murder than Moxie Mooney. This is not the way I want to become a famous detective."

"Are there any other leads you're following?"

"Sure. But let me keep a few secrets, will you? Again I warn you, Fletcher: don't you and Ms. Mooney leave Key West, except to come back here."

"I hear you."

"Some people were a little nervous when you went sailing yesterday."

"You know about that?"

"The Coast Guard did a helicopter over you."

"Oh, no."

"Oh, yes. They said you were real cute together. Said it was just like watching a movie."

THIRTY-ONE

"Cats will bark before I ever accept an invitation to stay in your house again, Mister What's-your-name Fletcher," Edith Howell stated at breakfast.

"What Katz?" asked Sy Koller. "Sam Katz or Jock Katz?"

They were crowded at the white iron-framed glass table on the cistern in the backyard of The Blue House. Moxie had not yet come down to breakfast.

"A riot out of control one morning. People throwing rocks at the house. Bopping poor Stella with a bottle. Why didn't you call the police?"

"Jock Katz always barked," Sy Koller said. "He barked all the time."

"A police raid this morning, at dawn. They came right into my bedroom while I was sleeping! I threw my aspirin bottle at the damned cop. Hit him, too, right on the cheek."

"Sam Katz never barked. Sam was a pussy cat."

"And they yank John off and charge him with being in possession of medicine, or something . . ."

"Are you saying we were raided by the police this morning?" Frederick Mooney asked.

"We were, Freddy." Edith put her hand on his. "Isn't it terrible?"

Mooney extricated his hand to deal with the grapefruit. "Never heard a thing."

"They swarmed all over the house, Freddy," Edith said.

"Like roaches," grinned Gerry Littleford.

"You mean they entered and searched my bedroom while I slept?" Freddy asked.

"Yes, dear," commiserated Edith.

"How forward of them," said Freddy. "I trust I was sleeping well."

"I'm sure you were sleeping handsomely, dear."

Lopez poured orange juice into Fletch's glass. "Global Cable News is on the phone."

"Tell them I'll call them back, please."

"Fletcher," Edith Howell asked, "do you realize one of your house-guests is in the hospital and another is in prison?"

"We're dropping like flies," Koller said through a mouthful of scrambled eggs.

"Roaches," said Gerry Littleford.

"You Yanks don't see the comic side of anything," Geoff McKensie said.

Sy Koller stopped chewing and stared at him.

Moxie appeared in her bikini with a light, white open linen top.

"Good morning, sweets," Edith gushed.

Gerry Littleford squeezed against Sy Koller to make room for her.

Fletch hitched his chair sideways. One leg stuck in a crack. Looking down, he jumped the chair leg out of the crack. On top of the cistern was a half-meter cut square. East and west on the square were hinged lift-rings.

"Did you sleep?" Mooney asked his daughter. "I hear there was a disturbance."

Lopez was back with a fresh pot and poured Moxie's coffee.

"Anybody know how these old cisterns work?" asked Fletch.

"Might as well get it over," Moxie said. She sipped her black coffee. "I've heard from the producers." She gave Fletch a long, solemn look, warning him not to correct her. "The production is cancelled."

Thus was almost everybody at breakfast fired. Geoffrey McKensie had already been fired.

Mooney did not permit the silence to last too long. "Is that the production of *Midsummer Night's Dream,* daughter?"

"O. L.!" she said in exasperation.

"That's too bad." Mooney's eyes ran up the banyan tree. "I was rather hoping to be offered a part."

"But why?" Edith had caught her breath. "Everything was going so well." Moxie snorted. "Well, at least I think so, and I'm sure John would back me up, if he weren't in jail for medicine. My part was the best I've had in a long time. I was doing so well at it. With the help of dear Sy, of course."

"Who did you speak to?" Gerry Littleford asked.

"Didn't quite catch the name," Moxie answered. "It was a legitimate phone call."

Sy Koller asked: "Why did they call you?"

"I just happened to answer the phone." Moxie Mooney was lying well. "We're all relieved of our contracts as of today."

"Fired," Gerry Littleford said.

"Ah, the vicissitudes of this business," consoled Mooney.

"But it's not fair!" said Edith. "I sublet my apartment in New York. I gave up a perfectly good legitimate theater offer. Where will I go, what will I do? Freddy!"

"Yes?" Mooney answered formally, stiff-arming being called upon.

"Well, McKensie," Sy Koller looked the man straight in the eyes. "Looks like your suit against Jumping Cow Productions won't be much good to you now."

"Damned fools." McKensie had reddened beneath his tan. "Too cheap to take a few days' proper mourning for the director's wife yet when a few congenital idiots wrap themselves in bedsheets and throw a few rocks at a house, they collapse and cancel the production, losing everything they've invested in it!"

"Are such things insured?" Fletch asked.

"You've got to look on the comic side of things, McKensie," Sy Koller said. Koller was not laughing, or smiling, or looking at all pleased.

"It's the bad publicity that killed it," Moxie said. "The man said."

"There's no such thing as bad publicity," said Edith Howell. "Especially these days. Any publicity is good. The more the better. Murder, riots, raids. Why we've been top of the news three days running! And the film isn't even made yet. Freddy, tell them there's no such thing as bad publicity."

"It's not only the bad publicity," Moxie said. "The press has begun to refer to *Midsummer Night's Madness* as a badly-written, cheaply-produced exploitation picture. The film will never live down its reputation now."

"Even if you use my script," McKensie said. "Even if I direct. I don't want anything to do with it."

Koller smiled. "And thus dies a lawsuit. We all heard you say that, McKensie. We're all witnesses."

Gerry Littleford asked, quietly, "Are they saying this picture exploits the race issue?"

Moxie took a deep breath. "Yes. Of course. Somebody must have gotten ahold of a script. Gratuitous violence, in black and white and color."

"Everyone can do with a bit of a rest, I'm sure," said Mooney. "It's been a trying time."

"Freddy! Not me!" squeaked Edith. "You have no idea of my income the last year or two! I don't have your money, Freddy!"

"Indeed not," agreed Mooney.

No one was eating. Moxie had eaten nothing. Koller, McKensie and Littleford had stopped eating, and food was left on their plates. Mooney, however, had cleaned his plate twice.

Mooney blinked his eyes brightly at the group. "Anyone for a drink?"

"Hair of the dog," Koller said to his plate.

"Eye opener," said McKensie.

"Anything," said Edith Howell. "Damn all cows, jumping or otherwise, and their milk!"

"Trying times," said Mooney.

Gerry Littleford said: "Well . . . whoever was trying to stop this production . . . succeeded."

THIRTY-TWO

"If John Meade turns State's Evidence," Fletch asked carefully, "will you drop whatever charges there are outstanding against him?"

He did not know where the police station in Key West was, so he had taken a taxi. He also wanted to be there before too many papers had been filled in regarding Meade, and before too many newspapers had been filled in regarding Meade.

Sergeant Henning had appeared as soon as Fletch asked the desk man if he could see him.

Apparently the sergeant did not rate an office, maybe not even a desk.

They were sitting on a bench at the side of the police station lobby.

"What evidence?" Sergeant Henning asked.

"He doesn't have it yet," Fletch answered. "Because I haven't given it to him yet."

"Evidence about what?"

"Look, Sergeant, you didn't raid The Blue House this morning just to bust a beloved movie actor for a few Quaaludes."

"That's right," the sergeant said. "I didn't." He stood up. "You want some coffee?"

"No thanks."

The sergeant wandered behind the counter and into the back room. When he returned he had a half-empty Styrofoam cup of coffee in his hand.

"You're saying you think you know something you can use to get Meade off the hook?"

"No," Fletch said. "Sorry. I don't *know* it. I have an idea."

"Why didn't you tell me before? When I was at the house this morning?"

"Because I didn't have the idea this morning. I hadn't noticed something. And I hadn't noticed it because I wasn't suspicious before you showed up."

"You're being mighty foxy."

"No. I'm offering you cooperation."

"For a price."

"John Meade doesn't belong in your jail, and you know it. Every time you cops bust an admired person for drugs, you're making drug-taking seem more admirable, more acceptable, and you know it. You're doing the same thing an advertising agency would be doing hiring John Meade to advertise soft drinks or chewing tobacco."

"So people who are famous shouldn't be arrested?"

"That's not what I'm saying. There are no special rules. I guess. Maybe there are. I don't know. If you've got a real case, you have to do something about it. Otherwise, you've got to look at the end result of what you're doing. Just like everybody else. It's called prudence."

"Busting John Meade is imprudent?"

"It's stupid. It sells drugs. Is it the object of the police to sell drugs?"

"Never heard this argument before."

"Maybe I've been a movie star hanger-on too long. All of three days."

Sergeant Henning sat down. "What do you want to say?"

"I want to see John Meade."

"Let me see if I've got this right: you want to tell John Meade

omething he can use to turn State's Evidence, as you call it, to get
imself off?"

"Right."

"Technically, not correct."

"Sorry."

"In other words, you're saying if we let John Meade go, you'll tell
s something that might be useful?"

"Let him go and destroy all papers relating to his ever having been
n this police station."

"Why don't you just tell me directly?"

"Why don't you make the damn deal?"

"Oh!" Sergeant Henning smiled. "Okay."

"Okay?"

"Okay. I swear to it on my grandmother's grave."

"Was your grandmother a nice lady?"

"The best."

"The owner of The Blue House is Ted Sills."

"I know that."

"Ted distinctly did not want to rent The Blue House to me. I forced
im. I needed to get Moxie somewhere, not too far away from Fort
Myers, where she could recuperate . . ."

"From Peterman's murder."

"Yeah. Peace and quiet."

"You've had a lot of that."

"Not much. Finally Sills suggested an exorbitant rent. I surprised
im by agreeing to it."

"How much?"

"You wouldn't believe. Anyway, as soon as he sees on the television
hat Frederick and Moxie Mooney are staying in The Blue House and
rowds and news cameras are collecting outside, he calls up and starts
creaming. He sounds like a puppy with a bone suddenly surrounded
y the neighborhood mongrels."

"Can't blame him."

"Sergeant, he doesn't want attention attracted to that house — any
ind of attention. He calls time and again, each time getting more
hrill, more threatening. Last time he called, he said he was coming
fter me with a shotgun."

"And yet you stayed."

"I had a choice? How do you move someone like Edith Howell?
Getting old Mooney out of a bar requires the tact and logistical brains
f an Eisenhower."

"Chuck told me. Threatened him with Jessie James."

"This morning you raided The Blue House."

"And found nothing."

"Glad to hear you say that. After you left, I called Ted Sills. T⋯ report to him his house had been raided. Well, sir, he left the countr⋯ suddenly last night. When he was supposed to be at a horse rac⋯ today."

"Yeah, Fletcher, you've got the point: we think Sills is a big-volum⋯ drug runner. So when are you going to get to the news?"

"It hits me that Ted Sills doesn't want attention drawn to The Blu⋯ House because there are drugs in it. This morning you guys searche⋯ the place. No drugs."

"No drugs at all."

"Glad to hear you say that." Fletch focused his eyes across the roo⋯ and blinked. "John Meade going to be released?"

"On my grandmother's grave."

"All reports regarding him destroyed?"

"I'll eat them for lunch. With mayonnaise. Where's the heroin?" Fletch looked at the sergeant. "I don't really know."

"Great. Why am I sitting here talking to a . . ."

"A what?"

"I don't know what!"

"During breakfast, I noticed that on the surface of the cistern in th⋯ backyard of The Blue House is what looks to me like a trapdoor⋯ Because of the salt in the air, whatnot, I can't tell if the trapdoor i⋯ newer than the cistern, you know? The lift-rings are rusted. I als⋯ don't know how cisterns work."

"They have to be cleaned."

"I do know the Lopezes tell me The Blue House hasn't used cister⋯ water since the water treatment plant was built over on Stock Island.⋯

"Did you lift the hatch and look in the cistern?"

"No."

"Why not?"

"I'm not a cop. Besides," Fletch said, "if I found there weren't an⋯ drugs in the cistern, I wouldn't have anything to talk with you about.⋯

"Jeez. No wonder you get along with those flakey movie stars."

"I don't, really. Edith Howell says she'll never visit me again. I'⋯ all broken up about it."

"I bet. She threw an aspirin bottle at Officer Owen King. Raised ⋯ welt on his cheek. Would have brought her in for assaulting an officer⋯ but the lady happened to be in bed when she threw the bottle. Actua⋯ fact, the incident might have caused titterin' in the courtroom."

308

"Must maintain the dignity of the fuzz."

"You said it."

"Do I have a good idea?"

"Worth checking out." Sergeant Henning stood up and started to amble toward the back room again.

"Are you bringing Mister Meade out?"

"Sure," Sergeant Henning said, "soon as he finishes autographin' everybody's gunbelts."

THIRTY·THREE

Fletch stood on the second floor back balcony of The Blue House, his hands on the railing. He was watching the policemen in the backyard. Sergeant Henning was directing the removal of furniture from the top of the cistern.

Downstairs, in the living room, a morning cocktail party was in progress. Edith Howell, Sy Koller and Frederick Mooney stood in a close triangle, drinks in their hands, drinks in their heads, outshouting reminiscences at each other. *It wasn't Olivier who said that. I was there at the time* . . . Geoffrey McKensie sat alone at the side of the room, sipping from a glass of dark whiskey. John Meade had gone to the kitchen for a late breakfast or an early lunch. Mrs. Lopez said Gerry Littleford had gone to the hospital to collect Stella. Lopez had gone to the hardware store to buy window glass. Moxie was sitting in the bedroom staring at a game show on television.

In the backyard, two policemen lifted the hatch easily. Sergeant Henning looked down and then knelt down and reached into the cistern. He pulled up one plastic bag. Then another.

He looked up at Fletch on the balcony and gave the thumbs-up sign.

Fletch waved back.

"The fog is beginning to clear." In the bedroom, Fletch flicked off the television. Sitting with her legs in the double-width chair, Moxie simply looked at him. "The cops just found a lot of heroin — I guess it is — in the cistern in the backyard."

Her expression remained blank. "Did you help them find it?"

"Sure."

"Why?"

"I don't like heroin. I don't like people who import heroin illegally. I don't like people who sell heroin to other people."

"I don't see how it helps me." Then she shook her head with distaste at what she had just said. "You said I have to think of myself now."

"You do. But things are beginning to become clearer. Listen, Moxie, this is my best guess at the moment." He remained standing in the bedroom. "Steve Peterman and Ted Sills were friends. We knew that. They were also in business together. We didn't know that."

"Smuggling shit."

"Yeah. I would say Sills was on the smuggling end of it; Peterman the financial end. Sills used The Blue House as a stash. Which is why he owns it. Which is why the Lopezes have been so lonely. The house isn't really used for anything else. Except maybe —" Fletch grinned ruefully at himself, "— to entertain damned fools who can be talked into investing in slow race horses. Peterman was moving an awful lot of money around, in and out of the country, from banks in Honduras, Colombia, to banks in Switzerland, France, under the name of Jumping Cow Productions, and, most regrettably, under your own name. Moxie, you were being used like a laundry. An awful lot of money was being washed — at least loosened up, freed, moved — under your name."

"Did they think they could get away with it forever?"

"Moxie, they didn't give one damn about you."

"That's nice."

"I would say that in order to make Jumping Cow Productions continue looking like a viable film company, Peterman ultimately knew he had to make a film. Or appear to be making a film. But a successful film would only draw attention to Jumping Cow Productions."

"So he was purposely making a bad film."

"Purposely."

She sighed. "A film so bad it couldn't even be released."

"It must have blown his mind when Talcott Cross actually hired a good director, Geoff McKensie, who then showed up with a good script."

Moxie almost laughed. "Dear Steve."

"That put him in quite a pickle. He had to get rid of McKensie and bring in a washed-out director who would film a bad script exactly as it was written — badly."

"Okay, okay. Are you saying Sills murdered Peterman?"

"I don't think so."

"Sills wasn't even on location. He couldn't have been."

"He could have had someone get on location and kill Peterman. But why would Sills want to kill Peterman?"

"Trouble between them."

"Clearly, Sills isn't better off with Peterman dead. He hightailed it to France last night. At least the way things have worked out, he isn't better off."

Moxie was distinctly looking tired. "What are you telling me. Fletch?"

"I don't know. Moxie, why the hell did you go along with acting in a bad, offensive movie? You're too good for that."

"I understood there was another script. A good one. McKensie's, I guess. When I arrived in Naples, I understood McKensie was directing. Then things happened awfully fast. McKensie's wife was dead. Koller was directing. We were shooting the original script. The whole film company, the crew were on location. My mind was taken up with where Freddy was, when was *he* going to get run over? What was I supposed to do, walk out? On my own friend-agent-manager-producer?"

"Still —"

"Fletch. Remember the time I had a broken wrist in London?"

"I never knew you had a broken wrist in London."

"I did. I was in the middle of filming *The Face of Things*. I broke my wrist. I was really blue. Steven flew in from somewhere within a matter of hours. Moved me into an even more expensive, more comfortable suite at the Montcalm. Surrounded me with flowers. Smoothed out all the contract nonsense. Got a special, removable cast rigged for my wrist. Showed them all how we could continue filming even if I did have a broken wrist."

"You filmed *The Face of Things* with a broken wrist?"

"About half of it. See it sometime. In about half the film, I don't use my left hand at all."

"And you're saying Peterman's doing all that was some kind of a favor?"

"Seemed so at the time."

"How's your left wrist?"

She wriggled it. "I have almost full use of it."

"Some favor."

"I needed the money. A lot of people were able to keep working."

"Yeah, you're really well off now. Peterman saw to that, all right. Terrific guy."

"Oh, Fletch!"

"Don't get angry with me."

"Well, what's all this supposed to come down to? I'm a fool, I'm a murderer, and now I'm some kind of big gangster? Now I'm responsible for scrambling the brains of half the people in the country?"

"Not half."

"Any people?" Tears rolled down Moxie's cheeks. "What good does all this do me? Next to me, Eva Braun looks like Madame Curie!"

The phone rang twice. They ignored it.

"Take it easy, Moxie. I'm just reporting that we're coming to some sort of an understanding of what happened. We know more than we did."

"You're just getting me in worse trouble! I'm an innocent person! I didn't kill anybody! I don't know anything about this business! I don't know anything about drugs!"

Quietly, Fletch said, "I think if Peterman were alive, I'd kill the son of a bitch."

"Terrific! So I did, right?"

"You had plenty reason to."

"Well, I didn't." Leaning forward, she dried her tears on her linen jacket. "Here I am, sitting in this stupid house, crying my eyes out, people throwing rocks —"

"Sy Koller knows all about this funny money movie business. I've talked to him. I wonder to what extent he was in on all this. He knew Peterman and Buckley were in some sort of a deal together."

"Go get Sy Koller arrested. He can direct his own execution. That way it will never come off."

There was a knock on the door.

Lopez was in the corridor. "Chief . . ."

"Nachman?"

"The police. On the phone. She says she must speak to you."

"Okay. I'll take the call downstairs."

In the bedroom, Moxie had gotten up from her chair and clicked on the television set. Noon weather was being reported. The report was that it was a nice day.

Koller had just climbed the stairs. He was a little out of breath. His black T-shirt was more than usually strained.

In the corridor, Fletch said to him, "Sy, that story you told me the other night. Was it last night? About that fight you and Peterman had."

Koller was looking with big eyes at Fletch from close-up. Fletch could smell the liquor on his breath.

"You said Peterman was putting up phony movies and pocketing the money he raised. But you knew he was actually concealing the movement of drug money around the world. Right?"

Koller raised his hand as if to grab something at eye level. "That's how I had him by the short hairs."

Koller lumbered down the corridor toward his room.

"Sy? You knew *Midsummer Night's Madness* was never going to be released . . ."

At his door, Koller turned around. "Anything for a job, boy. Anything for a week's pay."

He closed the door behind him.

THIRTY-FOUR

"And how's the weather on Bonita Beach now?" Fletch said into the phone. "Still photogenic?"

"I'm not in Fort Myers," Chief of Detectives Roz Nachman said. "I'm at the airport in Key West. And I've put my last coin into the phone box waiting for you to pick up the phone."

"Sorry. Catching the noon weather report on television."

"I'm waiting to be picked up by the local force."

"They've had a busy morning. Up early, rousting the citizens —"

"I called you earlier, before I left the office but someone insisted you weren't there."

"I was helping the police on an underground matter. You have news?"

"Just keep everybody at the house until I arrive, please."

"What's your news?"

"If everybody isn't there when I arrive, I'll hold you responsible, Mister Fletcher."

"Did Steve Peterman rent a car before he rented the car you examined?"

Nachman paused. "Yes. An identical blue Cadillac. From another company. The day of the accident, he turned one car in at the airport, leaving it in the parking lot, and rented another one."

"And was the first car damaged?"

"Yes."

"Had it been in a hit-and-run accident?"

"Yes. Blood, bits of cloth beneath the front fender. The fender itself had been washed off."

"The blood match?"

"We're presuming it does. We'll know soon. There's a police car. I'd better go outside so they'll see me. Don't let anybody leave, Fletcher."

"We'll be glad to see you, Chief. At least I will."

THIRTY-FIVE

Upstairs, Fletch went back into the bedroom and closed the door. The television was still running, softly. On a women's talk show, herpes was being discussed.

Fletch sat in the double-width chair with Moxie. He took her hand.

"Nachman is on her way over from the airport," Fletch said. "To arrest Geoffrey McKensie for the murder of Steven Peterman."

The television was telling women not to feel badly about having herpes.

"Peterman killed McKensie's wife," Fletch said. "Ran her down with a rented blue Cadillac."

Again tears were rolling down Moxie's cheeks.

"You see," Fletch said, "Koller was right: McKensie did know how to rig a set."

Moxie freed her hand. She stood up. She walked to the bed and sat on its edge.

She sobbed.

Fletch grabbed a tissue from the bedside table and handed it to her. "I'd think you'd be relieved."

"Poor Geoff." She blew her nose. "Poor damn Geoff. Why did they have to find out?"

She began to choke. She went into the bathroom. She closed the door.

Fletch listened to her sobbing and blowing her nose and sobbing some more.

"I'll be downstairs," he said to the closed door.

THIRTY-SIX

Mrs. Lopez opened the front door of The Blue House when the police arrived. Fletch was in the living room, within sight of the front door. He had walked around the house seeing where everyone was.

Chief of Detectives Roz Nachman entered. Sergeant Henning was behind her.

Fletch shook hands with them. "McKensie is in the small library at the back of the house. Trying to arrange a flight to Sydney."

Nachman said: "Good."

"Having a busy day, Sergeant."

"Busier than some."

Moxie came down the stairs. She had put on the white linen trousers and the sandals Fletch had bought her. Obviously she had washed her face with cold water, but her eyes still showed she had been crying.

"Hello, Chief," she said.

Chief Nachman said to her: "You have the right to remain silent —"

"What!" Fletch yelled.

"Will you please allow me to finish reciting this lady her rights?"

"You're arresting Moxie?"

"If you'd stop making so much noise."

"But you can't!"

"I can. I should. I must. I am arresting Ms. Moxie Mooney for the murder of Steven Peterman."

Frederick Mooney stood in the living room door. His eyes were hollow, empty.

"Geoff McKensie killed Peterman!" Fletch exclaimed. He looked around. McKensie was standing down the corridor outside the billiard room door. "Peterman killed McKensie's wife!"

"Sorry, Mister McKensie," Nachman said. "You didn't know that before, did you?"

In the shadow of the deep corridor, McKensie's ruddy complexion paled.

"Of course he knew it!" insisted Fletch.

"He wasn't even on location that day, Mister Fletcher. Not in the afternoon. He was in Miami, seeing lawyers."

"I saw him at the police station."

"He was at the police station, yes. He heard the news on the car radio and came directly to the police station. He was not on location."

"He rigged the set."

"The set was not rigged," said Nachman. "So say the experts."

"God," said Fletch.

Nachman fully recited Moxie Mooney her rights. To Fletch, it sounded like the mumblings over a grave. Staring at Nachman, Moxie's eyes were glazed. Mrs. Lopez's face was long. In the living room doorway Mooney swayed stupidly. Down the corridor, McKensie was leaning against a table.

"What evidence?" Fletch asked lamely.

"Cut it out, Fletcher," Nachman said, as if admonishing a child. "All the evidence in the world. Motive: we've had a report on her financial records. Whatever swindles Moxie and Peterman were pulling, it had certainly gone sour for Moxie. Opportunity: she was on the stage with him; she was wearing a bulky bathrobe in which a knife could be easily concealed; she crossed behind him just as he was stabbed. Dan Buckley was also on the stage, but there was no way he could have concealed that knife in his clothes, and he never left his chair. Motive and opportunity make the case."

Silently, looking as if he were going someplace to be sick, Frederick Mooney crossed the front hall to the stairs. His fingers just barely touched Moxie's sleeve.

Her eyes watched him climb the stairs.

Sergeant Henning released handcuffs from his belt. He said to Fletch: "Okay if I arrest her? She's talented and famous."

"It's not okay!" Fletch shouted. "No handcuffs!"

"Sorry, Miss," Henning said to Moxie. "Police department rules."

"Don't I get to get my toothbrush?" Moxie asked.

"We supply toothbrushes now," Nachman said. "Especially for capital offenses."

Moxie held out her wrists. Moxie Mooney was looking drawn and haggard.

She smiled at Fletch. "What's your line about bravery?"

Fletch answered numbly, "Bravery is something you have to think you have to have it."

"Yeah," Moxie said. "I'll think on that."

"I'm going with you," Fletch said.

Roz Nachman said, "Sorry, earwig, you're not. Not enough room in the helicopter."

Sergeant Henning was guiding Moxie through the front door, gently, by her elbow.

Moxie was looking back at Fletch. "Hey, Fletch?" she asked. "You've never told me. Here's your chance. Why is this house called The Blue House?"

Nachman put her nose up at the corners of the ceilings. "Used to be a whore house," she said.

"Really?" Fletch said. "I never knew that."

In the front hall, Fletch turned in a complete circle.

McKensie approached. Bitterly he said to Fletch, "Thanks, mate."

Then he went up the stairs.

From the front porch of The Blue House Fletch watched them put Moxie in the police car. Chief of Detectives Roz Nachman got in the back seat with her.

He watched the car drive off.

He stared at where the car had been. *Moxie . . . fun and games . . . so many images of Moxie . . . on this beach and that beach . . . in the street . . . in the classroom . . . in little theaters . . . in this room and that . . . getting into the back of a police car in handcuffs.*

Behind him, Mrs. Lopez said, "Can I get you something, Mister Fletcher? Maybe a drink . . . ?"

He said: "Apple juice."

She said, "We don't have apple juice."

"You don't?" He turned to her.

"We never have apple juice. Why have apple juice in the land of orange juice?"

Fletch stared at her.

"I can make you a nice rum drink with orange juice."

"Excuse me."

Fletch went by her and up the stairs.

THIRTY-SEVEN

Fletch knocked on Frederick Mooney's bedroom door and entered without waiting to be invited.

Mooney was sitting in a Morris chair, his hands in his lap. Silently, he watched Fletch.

"How long you been sober?" Fletch asked.

"Over three years."

The airlines flight bag was on the floor beside the bed. Fletch hunkered down next to it. He lifted one of the bottles from it. He uncapped the bottle and sniffed the contents.

"You can't get apple juice in most bars," Mooney said.

Fletch left the bottle on the bureau. "You're one hell of an actor."

"I thought you knew that." Mooney shifted in his chair. "Of course I had the advantage. Once people think of you as a drunk, they see you as a drunk."

"Moxie said you were drunk when she arrived at her apartment in New York."

"I had set the stage, knowing she'd show up sometime. Empty bottles around, dirty smelly glasses . . ."

"But why?"

"I wanted to see her, as it were, without being seen. She would have shut off the reformed Frederick Mooney. I had shut her off too many years. Her behavior would have been cool and proper in front of the great man, her father. I decided the best way to see her, to really see her, get to know her, was as a dependent. In front of a helpless old man, blind drunk, Marilyn was herself. I've really gotten to know her, the last few weeks. She's really quite marvelous."

"But she hasn't gotten to know you."

"It doesn't matter," said Frederick Mooney. "It's all on film."

"So at the apartment in New York you heard everything. Everything about Peterman —"

"Of course. I even read *Midsummer Night's Madness* one afternoon while she was out. I knew the fiddle was on. You see, Fletch . . ." Fletch, in continued shock, glanced at the man. He could not get his mind around the dimensions of this man's acting genius. All that Peterman-Peterkin-Peterson-Paterson routine had been consciously created. ". . . in my twenties, I was virtually ruined by one of these charlatan friend-managers, the word *friend* italicised. I was dragged through courts for five years. Someone I had trusted. It virtually ruined my work, my sleep, my health. One is made to feel so vulnerable, so weak. And doing creative work while being made to feel weak and vulnerable is immensely hard. Mind breaking. Creative people should receive some protection by law. There really aren't that many of us, and our time is short, our energies limited. Our energies should not be drained by lawyers playing at their paper games. Something similar happened to me again in my late thirties. If I had known then what I know now —

that energies do not last forever — I would have killed anyone who so assaulted me."

"Instead you killed Steve Peterman."

"I haven't been able to do much for Moxie, as a father. I didn't want her to be dragged through the courts for years, humiliated, made a fool, her life and work laid out in little boxes, her every privacy invaded. Preventing all that was something I could do for her."

"How did you do it?"

"I'm an actor. A well-trained actor."

"You know how to ride a horse like a Guardsman and an Indian, how to handle a gun as if it were a natural extension of your hand . . ."

"You heard that little sermon I gave at Durty Harry's." Mooney's eyes wandered over the palm trees outside the windows. "Always used to go over well at colleges."

"Downstairs just now," Fletch said, "when they were carting Moxie away, I remembered her telling me, years ago, that as a kid in the carnivals, whatever, small-town travelling shows, you were even a part of a knife-throwing act. That was just after I realized I had seen three empty apple juice bottles in the rubbish."

"You'd be surprised how your youthful physical skills come back to you after you've become absolutely teetotal." Mooney smiled. "I was never the drinker I was made out to be, anyway. I cultivated the image. I could heighten the audience's suspense by making them wonder if I was too drunk to go on, too drunk to finish the play. I believe Kean used the same trick. *There's old Mooney, drunk again. It can't be him who's acting so beautifully, but some god acting through him.* You see, everyone had seen *Hamlet* before, knew the story. They had to be made unsure as to whether Mooney could play *Hamlet.* Again. And again and again. Believe me, friend and lover of my daughter, no one could do what I've done as drunk as I'm supposed to have been. Of course I didn't make twenty or thirty pictures without knowing what I was doing. People will believe anything . . ."

"Mister Mooney, how did you actually commit the murder? There were cameras everywhere."

"I made myself into a rubbish man. A few rags, more hair, more beard, a discouraged way of standing, walking, wandering around location picking up the odd candy wrapper, cigarette pack." He chuckled. "Edith Howell asked me to move a trash barrel away from her trailer. Didn't ask. Demanded. Called me a lazy old lout, when I moved slowly on my supposedly sore feet. Not a very nice lady, Edith Howell."

"She has her eyes on your millions."

"She was always looking the wrong direction onstage, too. She'd look a meter more upstage than she was supposed to be looking, a meter more downstage. That woman drove me nuts all during *Time, Gentlemen, Time.*"

"And have you millions of dollars?"

"Sure."

"Many millions?"

"Why not? I've practiced a rewarding profession. Worked hard all my life, and been well paid for it. Never had expensive tastes. One hotel room is very much like another."

"Oh. Moxie thinks you're broke."

"It's been good for her soul to think so."

Fletch sighed.

"So," Mooney continued, "as an old, tolerated member of the custodial staff, I even watched them build the set for *The Dan Buckley Show.* You think I don't know how to work out camera angles? I approached the slit curtain at the back of the set from all the way down the beach, from the water's edge. I had to walk in a very carefully worked-out Z. I never showed up on film. And thankfully there wasn't much breeze. The curtain stayed more or less still."

"Why did you throw the knife into Peterman's back just after Moxie walked behind him?"

"Did I? I didn't know that. I wasn't watching, you see, I couldn't without being seen. I threw the knife at exactly that moment the breeze split the curtain."

"And then walked in a Z back to the water's edge."

"Yes. And by the time you found me in that bar I had been doing my drunk act for a good two hours or more. And I had convinced the bartender that I was drunk when I arrived."

"And no one thought you capable of such a thing."

"Not even you."

"And how did you get on and off location so easily?"

"After all," said Frederick Mooney, "I am Frederick Mooney."

"Yeah. I've heard."

"Making me stop and identify myself, sign in, sign out — really. Not all the rules have to apply to me, you know."

Fletch shook his head and chuckled. "There is a big black dog named Emperor who goes in and out of Durty Harry's. I went back the next night. I had thought it was something you had seen instead of a pink elephant."

"Fletch . . . it is all right if I call you Fletch, isn't it?"

"I don't know. I was getting sort of used to Peterkin."

"Would you mind having a drink with me?"

"Are you serious?"

"In that flight bag there's another bottle. The real stuff. There are two glasses in the bathroom."

"Sure."

When he was done pouring the drinks Fletch left that bottle on the bureau, too. He handed one glass to Mooney.

"Here's to you, Mister Mooney. It's real interesting knowing you."

"Here's to you, Mister Fletcher. You tried your best, I think."

After the cognac cleared in Fletch's throat, he asked, "Did you mean to get away with it?"

"No." Mooney seemed quite certain on that point. "Of course I expected to be found out."

"Then why did you commit such a clever crime?"

"I like doing things well. Furthermore, puzzling everyone has given me a little more time with Marilyn. Not much."

"What did you expect to do once you were found out?"

"Fade into the background, Fletch, fade into the background. Disguise myself as a pink-kneed, short-pants tourist, or an aged beach bum, or a bewhiskered priest, and slither into the common human pool. I rather fancied retirement for myself in some out-of-the-way place within walking distance of a good, warm, friendly pub, where people care not for theater or films."

"You can't do that now. They've arrested Moxie."

"I couldn't do that anyway, now, you bastard." Mooney grinned ruefully. "You ruined that. You put me on an airplane and landed me on a spit of sand at the end of the world. There's no way off Key West for Frederick Mooney. Frederick Mooney couldn't charter a boat or a plane out of Key West disguised as a bedbug. Such people look too closely at you. The first night I was here I went out to investigate. And found there was no way off this damn place for me. I walked so much, I got so tired, I went into a bar and did my drunk act. Had the cops drive me home. One road out of here, and Edith Howell has told me about all those bridges between here and the mainland." Affection was in Mooney's look and his chuckle. "You bastard."

"Sorry. Do you know Peterman killed McKensie's wife? Ran her down with a car."

"Doesn't surprise me. He was wrecking a lot of people, and would wreck many more. What was this all about? A drug scam?"

"Yeah."

"Well," said Mooney, "when the corner candy and newspaper store isn't selling candy and newspapers, you know it must be in some other business."

Fletch put his empty glass on the bureau. "Guess you and I have to fly back to Fort Myers together."

Mooney said, "We don't want to keep Marilyn under duress too long."

"By the way," Fletch asked. "Why didn't you come clean downstairs — before they took her away?"

"Would you believe I was stunned? I had heard so many murder theories floating around, I thought we had plenty more time to be together. I didn't know that Moxie had crossed behind Peterman. Truly stunned. I couldn't think how to handle it downstairs. Here I had successfully passed myself off as a sick old man. What was I supposed to say — *I'm sober and I did it?* Moxie would have said, *Oh, hell!*"

"O. L."

"It will take them a moment to believe this one. The curtains will have to close and the lights will have to come up. Young man, I know my audience."

Fletch said, "I'll go phone around to charter a plane."

Mooney's empty glass was on the arm rest of his chair. His fingers were folded in his lap.

At the door, Fletch said, "One more question, Mister Mooney. When you and I first met, in that bar on the beach, you told me that Moxie — Marilyn — might have murdered someone, a teacher, a drama coach, when she was fourteen."

Mooney nodded.

"Why did you tell me that — if you knew she hadn't killed Peterman?"

"To keep suspicion — particularly your suspicion — away from me. I knew Marilyn had sent for you. I knew who you are — an old friend and lover of Marilyn's. I knew it would be most difficult for you to believe Marilyn guilty of murder. I made it easier for you. I planted a doubt in your mind."

"You blinded me," Fletch said, "I haven't thought straight since." Fletch's hand was on the door knob. "What was true about the story — anything?"

"Did you ask Marilyn about it?"

"Yes."

"And did she assure you she did not kill Mister Hodes?"

"No. She didn't."

"Ah, that Marilyn." Smiling, Mooney shook his head. "She sure knows how to keep an audience."

THIRTY-EIGHT

It took Fletch longer than he expected to charter a plane to Fort Myers. He finally found a charter service in Miami willing to fly down to Key West to pick them up. It would be a while before the plane arrived.

Going back into the front hall, Fletch saw through the open front door that Geoffrey McKensie was in the street putting his luggage into the small yellow car.

A dozen or so people were watching the house from across the street.

Fletch went out to the sidewalk. He stood quietly a moment. Then he said to McKensie: "I'm sorry everything has worked out so rotten for you."

A garbage truck went by. Painted on its side was WE CATER WEDDINGS.

His head in the trunk, McKensie said, "Every time us Aussies leave Australia we get used as cannon fodder."

"History doesn't say so."

McKensie slammed the trunk. "You won't see this lad on these shores again."

"Sorry you feel that way. You ran up against one cheap crook, a murderer —"

"That's not all, brother." McKensie got into the car, closed the door, rolled down the window, started the engine. "I've had my experience with the American film industry. My first and my last."

He drove off.

In the front hall, Edith Howell said, "I'm so sorry, Fletcher. Geoff told us all about the police dragging Moxie away. Not that I blame her for doing in that Steve Peterman. Awful man! I always said so, didn't I, John?" John Meade had carried luggage down the stairs. Stella and Gerry Littleford were coming down the stairs with luggage, as was Sy Koller. Everyone was carrying luggage except Edith Howell. "We were just hoping she'd have a little more time before she was incarcerated. She's been working so hard."

In the street a rubber-neck wagon was going by . . . *arrested this afternoon the actress, Moxie Mooney, for first-degree murder. Another tale of Key West . . .*

Fletch decided not to trouble anyone with the facts. Let these people go. Getting Frederick Mooney out of the house and to the airport would be much easier without his being encircled by the shock and clucking of these people.

"Where's Freddy?" Edith asked. "Getting as drunk as he can as fast as he can, I expect."

"Maybe."

"Oh, I know my Freddy," said Edith. "I wouldn't have that man for all his millions. Scrambled eggs for brains."

"You'd get employed faster, Edith, as Mrs. Frederick Mooney." Sy Koller said.

All the people carrying luggage were trying to get around the person not carrying luggage. Edith Howell centered herself nicely in the front hall.

"I don't think Freddy's the great actor people make him out to be, either," said Edith. "In *Time, Gentlemen, Time,* he jumped on my every line. Most annoying. 'Course I knew how much he wanted to get back to his dressing room for a drink."

Fletch watched them go through the process of leaving. It was as if they were leaving a hotel. Edith Howell jabbered to John Meade about getting to Miami, *over those bridges,* before dark. The Littlefords said they had to go back to Vanderbilt Beach where they had left luggage. Sy Koller was grumbling that he supposed he had to go back to Bonita Beach to oversee the shutting down of the *Midsummer Night's Madness* location. "If I don't at least go through the motions," Sy said, "I suppose I'll never get employed again." Stella Littleford carried her bandaged head stiffly and said nothing. Only John Meade shook hands and said good-bye and said thank you.

Before getting into the car Gerry Littleford said, "Oh, yeah. Fletch. Someone called. With an English accent. Didn't catch the name. Talked fast. I didn't know where you were. He said to tell you Scarlet something-or-other, Pumpernickel? won a twenty-five-thousand-dollar purse."

"No foolin'."

"Didn't know you were into horse racing."

"Didn't know Scarlet Pimple-Nickel was either."

If he were a doorman, they might have tipped him. As it was, they all drove off in two cars, discouraged for the moment, Fletch believed, but only for the moment, nevertheless sure that on some tomorrow the right material and the right people would come together and they would create an unreality more credible than reality, and be paid, and be applauded.

THIRTY-NINE

This time after knocking on Frederick Mooney's bedroom door, Fletch waited to be invited in. There was no response. He knocked again.

He opened the door.

Frederick Mooney was on his back on the bed. On the bedside table were a drinking glass and one of the bottles, three-quarters full.

Fletch closed the door and went to the bedside. "Mister Mooney?" He shook the man's arm. "Oh, come on. I don't need a final act."

He sniffed the bottle on the bedside table. Cognac.

"Come on," said Fletch. "I'm sure you can also hold your breath and play dead longer than anyone else who's ever been on the stage."

On the bed the other side of Mooney was an empty tablet bottle. The cap was off. Fletch reached over Mooney and picked up the bottle. The label was for prescription sleeping tablets.

"Mister Mooney!" Fletch said. "You set the stage nicely. Now let's go."

He shook him again. "Jeez," Fletch said. "Do I believe it?"

He felt for the pulse in Mooney's wrist. There was none. Frederick Mooney was not breathing at all.

"O.L.!" Fletch dropped Mooney's hand. "Goddamn it, now you're not acting at all!"

A curtain of wetness slipped down over Fletch's eyes. The afternoon light from the windows was bright.

On the desk were two envelopes and an open note. Fletch went to the desk. The two envelopes were sealed. One said, *Ms. Marilyn Mooney;* the other, *The Authorities.*

The open note was to him.

Fletcher,

"If I may ask you to do us one more favor? Please deliver these notes as addressed.

The letter to the authorities describes how and why I killed Steven Peterman in such detail that they will have no choice but to believe me. My doctor will testify that I have been teetotal since I developed a heart problem more than three years ago, and I have provided the authorities with his name.

The letter to Marilyn cannot explain all. Perhaps you can help her to understand. It says I have enjoyed spending these weeks with her, watching her, applauding her, loving her from behind the curtain, as it were. I am also telling her that I am leaving her enough money so that she certainly should be able to pay off all these financial charges against her, however great, and maybe have enough left over for a quiet, non-working weekend sometime in her life.

I am reminded now of all the thousands of nights I have left some theater somewhere, tired to the bones, and walked alone to some hotel, only perchance to sleep, wondering as I walked why such talents, such expertise, such energy is spent creating an illusion for a handful of people, for a few hours. What for? One can suspend reality, but never conquer it.

Thanks for having me.

Frederick Mooney

FORTY

I n the quiet house, Fletch went back downstairs, along the corridor, through the billiard room and into the small library at the back of the house.

He sat at the desk.

He called Chief of Detectives Roz Nachman's telephone number and left the message asking her to return the call immediately upon her arrival.

He called Miami and enquired about the airplane he had chartered. It had already left. He asked the dispatcher to radio the pilot that now Fletch would need the airplane for a return flight to Fort Myers.

Then, for the first time, Fletch remembered that days before he had abandoned a rented car at Fort Myers airport. His luggage was still in the car.

Then he called Washington, D.C. Now was the time to see if Global Cable News would listen to just any *barefoot boy with cheek* who happened to have a story.

A woman answered, saying, "Good afternoon. Global News. May I help you?"

"Hello," Fletch said. "My name is Armistad . . ."

ONE

"**F**letch, my man! Good! You got here!"

"Where?"

Shirtless and shoeless, Fletch was standing in a midtown motel room in a middle-sized town in a middle-sized state in Middle America. He had turned on the shower just before the phone rang.

"I want you to go to Dad's suite," Walsh Wheeler said. "Immediately. 748."

"Why don't you say 'Hello,' Walsh?"

"Hello." The sounds behind Walsh were of several people talking, men and women, the clink of glasses, and, at a distance, heavy beat music — bar noises.

"Why don't you ask me if I had a nice flight?"

"Stuff it. Isn't time for all that."

"Are we enjoying a crisis already?"

"There's always a crisis on a political campaign, Fletch. On a presidential campaign, all the crises are biggies. You've only got a few minutes to learn that." Despite the background noises, Walsh was speaking quietly into the phone. "Wait a minute," he said. At the other end of the phone someone was speaking to Walsh. Fletch could not make out what the other person was saying. His mouth away from the phone, Walsh said, "Any idea who she is?" There was more conversation wrapped in cotton. "Is she dead?" Walsh asked.

Steam was coming through the door of Fletch's bathroom.

"Who's dead?" Fletch asked.

"That's what we're trying to find out," Walsh said. "Your plane was late? You're late."

"Landed unexpectedly in Little Rock. Guess the pilot had to drop off some laundry."

"You were supposed to be here at six o'clock."

"Your dad's very popular in Little Rock. Took a survey of an airport security cop. He said, 'If Wheeler doesn't become our next President, guess I'll have to run for office myself.' What a threat!"

Speaking away from the phone again, Walsh Wheeler said, "Whoever she is, she has nothing to do with us. Nothing to do with the campaign."

Fletch said, "I wish I knew the topic of this conversation."

"I'm downstairs in the lounge, Fletch," Walsh said. "I'll handle things here, but you get yourself to Dad's suite *tout*."

"It's ten-thirty at night, isn't it?"

"About that. So what?"

"I've never met the candidate. Your esteemed pa. The governor."

"Just knock on the door. He doesn't bite."

"And then what do I say to the next President of These United States? 'Wanna buy a new broom?' "

"Never known you to be at a loss for words. Say, 'Hello, I'm your new genius press representative.' "

"Barging in on The Man Who at ten-thirty at night without even a glass of warm milk —"

"He won't be in bed, yet. Doctor Thom's still down here in the bar."

"Now, look, Lieutenant, a little clarification of orders would make the troops a little more lighthearted in their marching."

"This could be damned serious, Fletch. Someone just said the girl is dead."

"Death is one of the more serious things that happen to people. Now, tell me, Walsh, what girl? Who's dead?"

Walsh coughed. "Don't know."

"Walsh —"

"A girl jumped off the motel's roof. Five minutes ago, ten minutes ago."

"And she's dead?"

"So they say."

"Terrible! But what's that got to do with your father? With you? With me?"

"Nothing," Walsh said firmly. "That's the point."

"Oh. Then why don't I take a nice shower, climb into my footy pajamas, and meet your dad at a respectable hour in the morning? Like between coffees number one and two?"

"Because," said Walsh.

"Oh, that's why! Walsh, a death in the motel where the candidate is staying shouldn't even be commented on by the candidate. People die in motels more often than they get warm soup from room service. I'm not saying one thing has to do with another —"

"I agree with you."

"I mean, you don't want to make a story by overreacting, by having me rush to your dad's suite in the middle of the night when I don't even know the man."

Walsh coughed again. His voice lowered. "Apparently she jumped, Fletch. They're saying from the roof right over Dad's suite. Over his balcony. Photographs have already been taken of the building. Arrows will be drawn."

"Oh."

"Arrows that swoop downward."

"Oh."

"The bored press, Fletch. Starving for any new story. Any new angle."

"Yeah. Implication being the young lady might have used the balcony of the candidate's room as a diving board to oblivion. Certain newspapers would make something of that. *Newsbill*."

"I knew you had something other than pretzels between the ears."

"Potato chips."

"Go to Dad's suite. Answer the phone if it rings. Say you're new on the job and don't know what anybody's talking about."

"Easy enough. True, too."

"I'll try to have his phone turned off at the switchboard. But not all switchboards are incorruptible."

"I seem to remember having corrupted one or two myself. Suite number what?"

"748. I'll be right up. As soon as I ace the switchboard and do my casual act in the bar. Convince the press we're not reacting to the girl's death."

"Walsh? Give it to me straight. Does the girl have anything to do with us? I mean, the campaign? The presidential candidate?"

Walsh's voice dropped even lower. "It's your job, Fletch, to make damned sure she didn't."

T W O

S he was alone in the elevator when the door opened.

In the corridor, Fletch was pulling on his jacket. For a moment, he thought his eyes were playing a joke on him: the girl with the honey-colored hair and the brown eyes.

"Freddie!" he exclaimed. "As I live and breathe! The one and only Freddie Arbuthnot."

"Fletch," she said. "It is true."

"Going my way?" he asked.

"No," she answered. "I'm on my way up."

He scooted through the closing doors. In the elevator, the button had been pushed for the eighth floor.

"I'm glad to see you," he said.

"You never have been before."

"Listen, Freddie, about that time in Virginia. What can I say? I was wrong. That journalism convention — you know, where we met? — was full of spooks, and I had every reason to think you were one of them."

"I'm an honest journalist, Mr. Fletcher." Freddie tightened her nostrils. "Unlike some people I don't care to know."

"Honest," he agreed. "As honest as fried chicken."

"Well known, too."

"Famous!" he said. "Everybody knows the superb work Fredericka Arbuthnot turns in."

"Then, why didn't you know who I was in Virginia?"

"Everybody knew except me. I was just stupid. I had been out of the country."

"You don't read *Newsworld?*"

"My dentist doesn't subscribe."

"You don't read the *Newsworld Syndicate?*"

"Not on crime. Gross stuff, crime. Reports on what the coroner found in the victim's lower intestine. I don't even want to know what's in my own lower intestine."

"I make my living writing crime for *Newsworld.*"

"You're the best. Everyone says so. The scourge of defense attorneys everywhere."

"Is it true Governor Wheeler is making you his press representative?"

"Haven't met the old wheez yet."

The elevator door opened.

"One look at you," she said, "and he'll send you back to playschool."

He followed her off the elevator onto the eighth floor. "What are you doing in whatever town we're in, Freddie? Interesting trial going on?"

Walking down the corridor, she said, "I've joined the campaign."

"Oh? Given up journalism? Become a volunteer?"

"Not likely," she said. "I'm still a member of the honest, working press."

"I don't quite get that, Freddie," Fletch said a little louder than he meant to. "You're a crime reporter. This is a political campaign."

She took her room key from the pocket of her skirt. "Isn't a political campaign somewhat like a trial by jury?"

"Only somewhat. When you lose a political campaign in this country, you don't usually go to the slammer."

She turned the key in the lock. "Do I make you nervous, Fletcher?"

"You always have."

"You're going to tell me you don't know anything about the girl who was murdered in this motel tonight."

"*Murdered?*"

"You don't know anything about it?"

"No."

"She was naked and beaten. Brutally beaten. Don't need a coroner to tell me that. I saw that much with my own eyes. I would guess also raped. And further, I would guess she was either thrown off a balcony of this motel, or, virtually the same, driven to jump."

Fletch's eyes were round. "That only happened a half hour ago, Freddie. You couldn't have gotten here that fast from New York or Los Angeles or — or from wherever you hang your suspicions."

"Oh, you do know something about it."

"I know a girl fell to her death from the roof of this motel about a half hour ago."

"Dear Fletch. Always the last with the story."

"Not always. Just when there's Freddie Arbuthnot around."

"I'd invite you into my room," Freddie said, "but times I've tried that in the past I've been wickedly rebuffed."

"What else do you know about this girl?"

"Not as much as I will know."

"For sure."

"Good night, Fletcher darling."

Fletch stood foursquare to the door which was about to close in his face.

"Freddie! What is a crime reporter doing covering a presidential primary campaign?"

Door in hand, she stood on one tiptoed foot and kissed him on the nose.

"What's a newspaper delivery boy doing passing himself off as a presidential candidate's press secretary?"

THREE

"Who is it?" The voice through the door to Suite 748 was politely curious. Fletch was used to hearing that voice making somber pronouncements about supersonic bombers and the national budget.

"I. M. Fletcher. Walsh told me to come knock on your door."

The door opened.

Keeping his hand on the doorknob, his arm extended either to embrace or restrain, Governor Caxton Wheeler grinned at Fletch while his eyes worked Fletch over like a football coach measuring a player for the line. Fletch fingered his collar and regretted having put back on the shirt he had been wearing all day.

Governor Caxton Wheeler's face was huge, a map of all America, his forehead as wide as the plains states, his jaw as massive as all the South, his eyes as large and set apart as New York and Los Angeles, his nose as assertive as the skyscrapers of Chicago and Houston.

"Hello," Fletch said. "I'm your new genius press representative."

Smile growing stiff on his face, the presidential candidate stared at Fletch.

Fletch said: "Wanna buy a broom?"

"Well," the governor said, "I want a clean sweep."

"And I'll bet you want to sweep clean," Fletch said.

"Were you ever one of them?" the governor asked.

Fletch looked around him in the motel corridor. "One of who?"

"The Press."

"The Press is The People, sir."

"Funny," said The Man Who. "I thought the government is. Come in."

The governor took his hand off the doorknob and wandered in stockinged feet into the living room of the suite.

Fletch closed the door behind him.

The living room was decorated in Super Motel. There was a bad painting on the wall, oil on canvas, of a schooner under full sail. (In Fletch's room there was a cardboard print of the same ship under full sail.) The four corners of the coffee table surface and the hands of the chair arms had chipped gold paint on them.

There were several liquor bottles on a side table.

The governor nodded to them. "Want a drink?"

"No, thanks."

"I was afraid you'd say that."

"May I get you one?"

"No." The governor sat on the divan. "My wife doesn't approve. She says I have to get all my energy and all my relaxation from The People. I doubt if the sweet thing knows it, but what she is describing is a megalomaniac."

The Man Who wore an open, washed-out, worn, sagging brown bathrobe. Over the breast pocket, in green, was CW. The robe draped his big, bare, white belly.

Fletch's eyes moved back and forth from the deep tan of the governor's face and the lily whiteness of the governor's belly.

"You look like you just got home from summer camp," the governor said. "Will the press accept you?" Fletch said nothing. The governor had not asked him to sit down. "A campaign is tough, and it's exciting, and it's boring. Not to worry." On the coffee table in front of the governor, papers had spilled out of a brief case. "By the end of this campaign — if we win this primary, that is — you'll look as dissipated as a schoolchild in March."

The other side of the room, beyond the governor, was a sliding glass door onto the balcony. The drapes were open.

Slowly, as if wandering aimlessly, Fletch crossed the room to the balcony doors. Trying to make the question sound conversational, he asked, "If you lose this primary, is the campaign over?"

"You win votes in a primary; you win contributions. You lose, and the contributions dry up. Motels and gas stations expect even presidential candidates to pay their bills. It's the American way."

Fletch snapped on the balcony light outside the glass doors. "Does the press know you're short of funds?"

The governor did not turn around in the sofa to look at Fletch. "We don't issue a financial report every day. But we have to get the message out through the press that we need money. If they ever thought our campaign was broke, they'd desert us faster than kittens leave a gully in the January thaw."

On the balcony, the snow and ice, the slush, had been stirred up, walked on. A section of the railing had been scraped clean of snow.

"Have you been out on the balcony tonight?" Fletch asked.

Finally the governor turned around in his seat. "No. Why? At least, I don't think so."

"Somebody has been."

"Some of the press were in earlier. For drinks. Some of the staff. Lots of cigarette smoke. I might have stepped out for some fresh air. I do things like that. Or a quiet word with someone. Must be slushy out there."

Fletch turned off the balcony light and pulled the drapes closed. "Would there be people in your suite if you weren't here? I mean, other than motel staff?"

"Sure." The governor turned around to face the coffee table again. "For traffic, my suite is second only to O'Hare International Airport. In fact, where is everyone now? Why isn't the phone ringing?"

"Walsh had it turned off at the switchboard." Fletch went through the living room and down the little corridor to the front door of the suite.

"Why did he do that?"

Fletch opened the door and tried the outside knob. "Your door is unlocked."

"Sure. People come in and out all the time. What are you, a press agent or a security man?"

Fletch closed the door and came back into the living room. "Looks like you need a good security agent."

"Flash is all I need for now. He doesn't bother anybody. So," the governor said, "you and Walsh knew each other in the service. I remember hearing about you."

"Yes, sir. He was my lieutenant."

"Was he any good that way?"

"You mean your son? As a lieutenant?"

"Yeah. What kind of a lieutenant was he?"

"Pretty good. He'd show up once in a while."

The governor chuckled. "But not too much, eh?"

"He was okay. Let us do our jobs. Didn't care about much else."

"That's my boy. Run a hands-off administration. Walsh thinks you'd be just right for this job." The governor wrinkled his eyebrows. "Insisted you be flown in immediately. Wants me to announce first thing in the morning that you're my new press secretary."

Fletch shrugged. "I was available."

"Which means you were unemployed."

"Working on a book," Fletch said.

"On politics?"

"On an American western artist. You know: Edgar Arthur Tharp, Junior."

"Oh, yeah. Great stuff. But what's that got to do with politics?"

"Not much."

"You used to work for newspapers?"

"A lot of them." Fletch grinned. "One after another."

"Are you saying you weren't successful as a journalist?"

"Sometimes too successful. Depends on how you look at it."

The governor sat back and sighed. "A kid who looks like he belongs on a tennis court with an interest in cowboy art: as a politician's press agent, you're not a dream."

"Isn't American politics a crusade of amateurs?"

"Who said that?"

"I did. I think."

"You're wrong. But it has a nice ring to it." Leaning over, the governor made a note on one of the papers on the coffee table. "See? You're working already. Displaying talent as a phrasemaker." He sat back and smiled. "That line might be worth thousands of dollars in contributions. You sure no one said it?"

"No."

"I'll say it. Then it will have been said."

"I thought you said the statement is wrong."

"I don't qualify as an amateur. Elected to Congress twice, the governorship three times. But every new campaign is a starting over." The governor flipped the pen onto the table. "Anyway, Walsh says you're smart, resourceful, and willing to work cheap. Workin' cheap doesn't sound so smart to me."

"Then make me smarter," Fletch said. "Pay me more. If it would make you happier. I don't mind."

The governor chuckled. "Guess it's time Walsh had a real pal somewhere in this campaign. All the pressure has been comin' down on him. Hasn't had a day off, an hour off, since I don't know when. He's got a much harder job than the one I've got. He does all the logistics:

who goes where, when, why, says what to whom. My firing James last night didn't make it any easier for him. Or me. You heard about all that, I suppose?"

"Walsh told me something about it last night when he phoned. Read the press reports at the airport."

The governor's face looked truly sad. "I knew James for twenty years. No: twenty-two, to be exact. Political reporter for the down-home newspaper. The newspaper that endorsed me for both Congress and the governorship. James was a personal advisor, a good one, totally honest. Even had Washington experience. I thought if I ever ran for President, he sure would be with me. To the end. Then he screwed up. Brother, did he ever screw up."

"The newspapers said he resigned over a policy dispute with you. Something about South Africa."

"The press was kind to us on that one. The policy dispute was not about South Africa. It was about Mrs. Wheeler." The governor took a deep breath. "The first incident wasn't so important. I was able to get people to laugh it off. He mentioned to some reporters in the bar that Mrs. Wheeler spends two and a half hours each and every morning getting up and putting on her face."

"Does she?"

"No. She spends time making herself beautiful, of course. Every woman does. It's damned hard on a woman, living out of suitcases, going from motel to motel, making public appearances all day, damned near all night. She always looks nice. Anyway, the newspapers reported it."

"It was reported with a vengeance."

"Made her look like a very superficial, self-indulgent woman. I turned it into a joke, saying that's why we had to have two bathrooms on the second floor of the governor's mansion. I said that on the road I'm apt to spend two hours every morning just trying to find my razor."

"Yeah, that was good."

"It was just this week that James really screwed up. It was in the newspapers yesterday. He told the press Mrs. Wheeler canceled — at the last minute, mind you — a visit to the Children's Burn Center so she could play indoor tennis with three rich old lady friends."

"True?"

"Look — what does Walsh call you, Fletch? — she made time to play tennis with some friends she hadn't seen in years, wives of some influential fat cats around this state, who would never have forgiven her if she didn't make time for them. She raised some badly needed money for this campaign."

"Schedule conflicts must happen all the time."

"You bet. And it's the press representative's job to shag a foul ball like that, not pitch it to the press. I'm convinced James went out of his way to make sure the press got the wrong slant on that story."

"Yeah, but why would he do that?"

"God knows. He's not the world's greatest admirer of my wife. They've had a few disagreements over the years. But liking people has nothing to do with politics. In this life, if you stay with only people you *like*, the normal person would have to move every ten days. Politics is advantageous loyalty, son. Loyalty is what you buy, with every word out of your mouth; loyalty is what you sell, with every choice you make. And when you sell loyalty, you'd better make sure your choice is to your own advantage. James sold out twenty-two years of loyalty to me for the dubious twelve-hour pleasure of embarrassing my wife in public."

Listening, Fletch had wandered to every part of the living room. The governor's shoes were not anywhere in the room.

"If Mrs. Wheeler had to cancel an appointment, she had to cancel an appointment, and that's all there is to it. If you don't know what our daily schedule looks like, feels like yet, you will within a few days." The governor lowered his voice. "If you stay with us, that is."

"I understand."

"What do you understand?"

"I understand the job of press secretary is to keep paintin' the picket fence around the main house. Just keep paintin' it. Whatever's goin' on inside, the outside is to look pretty."

The governor smiled. "The question is, Mr. I. M. Fletcher . . ." The governor took a cigar stub from the pocket of his robe and lit it. "By the way, what does I. M. stand for?"

"Irwin Maurice."

"No wonder you choose to be called Fletch. The question is, Mr. Irwin Maurice 'Fletch' Fletcher — have I got it all right?"

"Tough on the tongue, isn't it?"

"The question is" — the governor brushed tobacco off a lower tooth — "what do you believe in?"

"You," Fletch said with alacrity. "And your wife. And your campaign. Is that the answer you want?"

"Not bad." The governor squinted at him over the cigar smoke. "For a start. Why do you want to work on this campaign?"

"Because Walsh asked me. He said you need me."

"And you were between jobs . . ."

"Working on a book."

"You got the money to take time off and work on a book?"

"Enough."

"Where'd you get the money?"

"You can save a lot of money by not smoking."

"What do you think of my domestic policy?"

"Needs refining."

"What do you think of my foreign policy?"

"Needs a few good ideas."

The governor's grin was like seeing a chasm open in the earth. "I'll be damned," he said. "You're an idealist. You mean to be a good influence on me."

"Maybe."

The governor looked at him sharply and seemed to be serious when he asked: "And do you have any good ideas?"

"Just one, for now."

"And what would that be?"

"To be loyal to you." Fletch grinned. "Until I get a better offer. Isn't that what you just said politics is all about?"

Scraping the ash off his cigar onto a tray, the governor said, "You learn fast enough. . . ."

FOUR

"Where's Dr. Thom?"

"Coming right up."

"I want to go to sleep."

Walsh Wheeler had entered his father's suite without knocking. Fletch saw that Walsh knew the door was unlocked.

In the living room, Walsh handed his father a piece of paper from the top of the sheaf he was carrying. "Here's your schedule for tomorrow."

The governor dropped the paper on the table without looking at it.

Walsh handed Fletch two sheets of paper, one from the top of the pile, one from the bottom. "Here's Dad's schedule for tomorrow . . . and Mother's schedule for tomorrow. Have these copied and under the door of every member of the press by six in the morning. All the press are on the eighth floor of this motel."

"Is there no one on the eighth floor but members of the press?"

"I don't know. I guess so. No reason why you shouldn't deliver to every door on the eighth floor. We're not trying to keep Dad's whereabouts a secret. Leave some downstairs on the reception desk, too. And have some on you to hand out to the local press." Walsh poured out two Scotches with soda and handed one to Fletch. "Oh, yeah. At the back of the campaign bus there's a copying machine. For your use and your use alone." Walsh smiled at his father. "James's first major press announcement was that if any member of the press touched his copying machine, James would disarm him or her — literally." Walsh sipped his drink. "Maybe you should make the same announcement."

"Don't tell Fletch to do anything the way ol' James did it. One thing might lead to another."

"A copying machine and a quick wit," Walsh said. "That's all you need to be a press representative, right?"

"He's got a quick wit," the governor said. "He makes me laugh."

"Oh, yeah." Walsh sat next to the best reading lamp. He made himself look comfortable, legs crossed, drink in hand, papers in lap. "How do you guys like each other so far?"

The governor looked at Fletch and Fletch looked at the governor.

"Don't know how the press will accept him," the governor said. "Fletch looks like breakfast to someone with a hangover."

Smiling, Walsh looked up at Fletch. "What do you think, Fletch?"

"Well," Fletch drawled, "I think Governor Caxton Wheeler can get this country moving again."

"I believe it!" Walsh laughed.

"I'll say one thing," the governor chuckled. "There's been so much cow dung on the floor since he came into the room, I had to take off my store-bought shoes!"

Fletch looked from one to the other. "Where *are* your shoes?" he asked.

Father and son continued their moment of easy, genuine admiration, love for each other, enjoyment in each other.

Fletch sat down.

"Okay, Dad, let's go over your schedule for tomorrow, just quickly. We've only got a few days before the primary in this state. We've got a real chance to win, but we haven't won yet. Without killing you, we've got to make the best use of your time."

Slowly, the governor sat up and took the schedule in his hands. He yawned. His cigar stub was burned out in the ashtray.

"Seven forty-five," Walsh said, "you'll be at the main gate at the tire factory. These guys are worried about two things: foreign import of tires, of course; and they're afraid their union bosses will call a strike sometime in April."

"Union boss name?" the governor asked.

"Wohlman. By the way, Wohlman's wife has just left him, and some of the membership say this is making him act meaner and tougher toward management than they want."

Dully, the governor said: "Oh."

"At eight-thirty, you've having coffee with Wohlman, first name Bruce, and . . ."

Only glancing at the items on the governor's schedule for next day, Fletch listened. Walsh seemed the perfect aide. He had the answers to most questions the governor asked. *"Where's breakfast?" "There will be a breakfast box on the bus."* He made notes to get the answers he did not know. *"How far does a farm family have to go to get to a medical facility 'round there?" "I'll find out."* Walsh did not balk at taking anything on himself. And he was not insistent, but gently urging when the governor began to balk. *"Why am I at Conroy School at ten o'clock? I keep telling you, Walsh, ten-year-olds don't vote. Isn't there some better use of my time this close to the primary?" "Their parents do, Dad, and so do the teachers, and all their relatives. And they're all more interested in the future generation and education than they are in bank failures in Zaire. That's what they're living and working for." "I'll be late for the downtown rally in Winslow. Then I'll have to do more I-couldn't-find-my-toothbrush jokes." "We'll have a band playing until you get there."* Sitting on the divan, the governor seemed to get more old, fat, and tired as the session went on.

Walsh, on the other hand, seemed to have attained some level of nirvana. His tone of voice did not alter. His speech pace, even with the governor's interruptions, was consistent. His concentration was as steady as an athlete's in midgame.

Walsh had changed since his days in uniform, of course. He was heavier by twenty pounds; his hair was thinner. His skin was gray. There was something in Walsh's eyes that had not been there before. Instead of being just ordinary human eyes, looking around casually, seeing and not seeing things, Walsh's eyes now seemed overfocused, too bright, rather as if whatever he was looking at was getting his full concentration. Fletch wondered whether in fact Walsh was seeing anything.

"If all goes well," Walsh concluded, "we'll have you at the hotel in Farmingdale by six. The mayor of Farmingdale is throwing a dinner for you. Well, he's throwing a dinner for himself, a fund-raiser, but you're the main attraction."

"What do I have to do the next morning?"

"Thought you might like to catch up with the newspapers. Bed rest."

"Put a hospital visit in there," the governor said. "Farmingdale must have a hospital. Special attention on any kids with burns."

"Yes, sir." Walsh made a note.

The governor rubbed his eyes. "Okay, Walsh. Anything else I'm supposed to know?"

Walsh glanced at Fletch. "There's something you're not supposed to know."

The governor looked at each of them. "What am I not supposed to know?"

"A girl jumped off the roof of this motel about an hour and a half ago."

"Dead?"

"Yeah."

"How old?"

"Twenties. They say."

"Damned shame."

"Apparently she jumped from the roof right over your windows."

The governor looked at Fletch. "So that's why you showed up at my door tonight? Checked the balcony. The door." He looked at Walsh. "Turned off the phone. You guys are working together already."

"People had been on your balcony," Fletch said quietly. "Your front door was unlocked."

"You don't know anything about it," Walsh said.

"In fact, I do," the governor said. "I heard the sirens. Saw the ambulance lights flashing. How can I pretend it didn't happen?"

"I guess she actually jumped just as you were coming into the hotel."

"No one said she jumped," Fletch said. "Someone told me the girl was naked and had been beaten before she hit the sidewalk."

"Anyone we know?" the governor asked.

Walsh shrugged. "A political groupie, best I can find out."

"No."

"A political *groupie?*" asked Fletch.

"Yeah," Walsh said. "There are people who think political campaigns are fun. They follow the campaign — literally. They travel from town to town with the candidate's party, try to get into the same hotels — generally just hang around. Women mostly, girls; but men too. Sometimes they turn into useful volunteers."

"Was this girl a volunteer?" the governor asked.

"No. Dr. Thom saw the body. Said he thinks she's been with us less than a week. Never saw her doing anything for the campaign."

"Name?"

"Don't want you to know her name, Dad. When reporters ask you about her, I don't want the expression on your face that you'd ever heard her name before."

"Okay. Can we do something nice? Send flowers — ?"

"Nothing, please. She was just someone who happened to be in the motel. Fletch has the job, as of right now, of denying this girl had anything to do with the campaign. And without making an issue of it."

Fletch said, "You said the woman had been trailing the campaign for almost a week."

Walsh said: "That's the problem."

A thin man in an oversized sport coat, carrying a little black bag, entered the suite. He too did not knock.

The governor said to him, "Want to go to sleep, Dr. Thom."

"Go to sleep you will," said the doctor. "You're not getting eight hours every night."

"I will tomorrow night," the governor said. "If all goes well."

"Come on," Walsh said to Fletch. "We've got one or more things to do."

As Walsh and Fletch were leaving the suite, Dr. Thom was saying, "You've got to get eight hours every night, Governor. Every night. If Walsh can't work it out for you, we'll have to get someone else to run your campaign."

"Listen, Bob. I got real tired around four o'clock today. Couldn't think. Started repeating myself."

"Okay," Dr. Thom said. "Okay. I'll give you something after lunch tomorrow. . . ."

FIVE

"Got to leave Mother's schedule in her suite for her," Walsh said as they walked down the corridor. His jaw was particularly tight.

"Does this Dr. Thom travel with the campaign?" Fletch asked.

"Shut up."

The door to Suite 758 was unlocked. Walsh seemed to know it would be.

They entered a suite identical to the one they had just left. The chips on the gold paint seemed identical. The painting of the ship was oil on canvas. Even the bottles on the bar seemed identical, with identical quantities missing.

The lights in the room were low.

Walsh dropped a schedule on the coffee table. "Close the door," he said to Fletch. "Let's sit down a minute."

Fletch closed the door.

Walsh did not brighten the lights. He sat in an armchair identical to the one he had just left in his father's suite, at the side of the room next to a reading lamp turned low. "Mother isn't due in on the plane from Cleveland until after one. We can talk a little."

"Didn't know your parents were separated," joked Fletch. He sat in the same chair he had just been in. At least it looked and felt the same.

Carrying on at his regular pace, Walsh said: "Yes. Dr. Thom travels with the campaign. He is available to the candidate and his wife, the staff, members of the press, volunteers, bus drivers, pilots, whoever else. Have ringing in the ears? See Dr. Thom. Intestinal problems? Line forms at the rear."

"That's not what the question meant, Walsh."

"No. That wasn't what your question meant." Walsh took a deep breath. "My parents are not separated. On the campaign trail mostly they stay in separate suites because their schedules are different. Their sleep is important. They have different staffs, for the most part."

"Have you lost your sense of humor?" Fletch asked.

"I don't like stupid questions in the corridor of a public motel."

"There was no one in the corridor, Walsh. It's past midnight."

"Don't care. Someone could have heard you."

Fletch noticed that across the dark living room, the door to the bedroom was closed.

"You either understand what I'm saying, Fletch, or you can go back to Ocala, Florida, and play the horses, or whatever you were doing."

"So what are you saying, Lieutenant? Give it to me in small words, simple sentences."

"Loyalty, Fletch. Absolute loyalty. We're on a campaign to get my father, Governor Caxton Wheeler, elected President of the United States. I want you to be the campaign's main press representative. As

347

such, you will see things and know things you will question. When this happens, you are to ask me, but you are to ask me in private. You just saw Dr. Thom carry his little black bag into Dad's room after midnight. And you were going to ask me about it in the corridor of a public motel."

"That's a no-no," Fletch said.

"That's a no-no. Maybe you're going to see and hear things that surprise you, things you don't like. You don't have to be very old in this world to lose your idealism. Nothing and no one is perfect. When that happens, you shut up about it."

"You mean like when your mother cancels a visit to a children's burn center to play indoor tennis with some old cronies —"

"You sure don't point it out to the press. And if the press happens to pick it up, you put the best face on it possible."

"Walsh, I hate to break your cadence, but I think I know all this. I even accept most of it."

"And you watch the jokes you make. America wants to go to bed at night thinking of the candidate and his wife doing the same things they're doing: vying with each other for the bathroom sink to brush their teeth, sharing a reading lamp in bed, saying little good-night words to each other. Their actually staying in separate suites is logistically necessary, but the public doesn't want to know that. It disturbs the image. It gives certain sick minds the thought that having separate suites gives Dad the opportunity to have other ladies in his room, and therefore they leap to the conclusion that he does."

"I made that joke to you. Privately."

"You see, Fletch, there's always the difference between the image and the reality."

"Really?"

"We put out this image that the governor and his wife are campaigning for the presidency, and that they can take everything in stride, be everywhere at once, make speeches, give interviews, pat children on the head, travel constantly, stand up for hours at a time — yet live, eat, and sleep like normal people. Of course they don't. Of course they can't."

"Dr. Thom is controlling your dad with pills. Or shots. Or something."

"Dr. Thom puts my father to sleep at night, wakes him up in the morning, gives him one or two energy boosters during the day. This is a fact of a modern campaign. It's being done with medical knowledge and medical control."

"And it doesn't affect him?"

"Sure it does. It keeps him going. It permits him to get more out of himself, over longer periods of time, than is humanly possible."

"The world's on a chemical binge."

"Take your eighteenth-century man. Fly him through the air at nearly the speed of sound. Walk him through crowds of screaming, grabbing people, any one of whom might have a gun and the intent to use it. Have sirens going constantly in the ears. Put him in front of a television camera and have him talk to a quarter of a million people at the same time, his every word, his every facial expression being weighed, judged, criticized. Do this for weeks, months at a time. See what happens to him. The basic constitution of the human being hasn't changed that much, you know."

"What about you, Walsh?"

"What do you mean?"

"Your dad indicates to me you're under even more stress than he is."

"I'm a little younger than he is."

"Is Dr. Thom helping you out, too?"

"No." Walsh looked into his lap. "I just keep going. What else can't you accept?"

"That young woman, Walsh."

"What about her?"

"It's entirely possible she was thrown from the balcony of your dad's suite. The snow on the balcony had been messed up. Including on the railing. Apparently these principal suites — your parents' — are not locked."

"What of it?"

"A death? A murder?"

"Do you know how many people in this world die every day because of bad governments?"

"I would say hundreds."

"A conservative guess. Let's not keep a potentially great president out of office because some insignificant woman hits a sidewalk too hard."

"What about the local police? Aren't they going to investigate?"

"I've already handled that. The mayor found me downstairs in the bar. He said he hoped this unfortunate incident was not disturbing to the candidate or his party. Asked me to let him know if any of his police pestered us about it."

"You're serious?"

"Told him if anybody had any questions, they should be referred to Barry Hines."

Fletch rolled his eyes. "Things sure are different on a presidential campaign."

"Frankly, I think His Honor, the Mayor, was chiefly worried," Walsh said with mock solemnity, "that with all the national press crawling around, a murder in his fair city might get national attention. Spoil his image of Homeland, America, if the once-his-city gets national attention it's for murder."

"These political reporters wouldn't know how to report a murder anyway," Fletch said. "They're specialists. They have no more interest in murder than they do a boxing match. Beneath them."

"I suppose so."

"Even if there were a murder on the press bus, they'd have to call in police reporters. They have no more ability to report a murder than your average citizen on the street. Which is why I'm so curious as to why we do, in fact, have one crime writer with us."

"Do we?" Walsh asked absently.

"Fredericka Arbuthnot. *Newsworld.*"

Walsh said, "Tomorrow at dawn, this campaign rolls out of this town, probably never to come back. Good luck to the local police. I hope they solve their problems. But I don't want any investigation of this death to touch the campaign. It's just a public relations problem — one you've got to manage." Walsh relaxed more in his chair. "Enough of this. Not important. In general, all I'm saying is, if you're going to be with us, you're going to be with us all the way."

"Why do you want me with you?"

"You've had a lot of experience with the press, Fletch."

"I've worked for a lot of newspapers."

"You ought to know how the press works."

"Very hard."

"How they think."

"Slowly but tenaciously."

"Hill 1918, Fletch."

"Nineteen when?"

Walsh's eyes focused on the dark carpet. Despite the slight smile on his lips, his hairline seemed to pull back and his face turned even more white. "Twelve of us left. Surrounded by the enemy. Who knew we'd had it and were coming in to wipe us out."

"Are you about to tell me a war story?"

"Hundreds of 'em. Either we dug in and got killed. Or tried to blast our way out and got killed."

"War stories . . ."

"You, dogface Fletcher, didn't let your lieutenant choose either obvious alternative. You argued with me. Until I got the point."

"Never could handle authority very well."

"You had us move out of the obvious position, climb the trees, and tie ourselves to the branches. We disappeared. Three days we hung in those goddamned trees."

"Must've gotten hungry."

"It was better than being dead with our parts in our mouths."

"You were big enough to take the suggestion, Walsh."

"I was scared shitless. I couldn't think. The enemy rummaged around below us. They even shot each other. Carried off their dead. They never thought Americans would do such a thing."

"I was saving my own life, *hombre.*"

"Your buddy — what's his name? Chambers? You ever see him anymore?"

"Alston Chambers. Yeah. We talk frequently. He's a prosecutor in California."

"You know how to make the best of a bad situation, Fletch. And a presidential campaign is one bad situation after another."

Fletch glanced at his watch. "It's getting late."

"I've got lots of files to give you tonight. Anyway, what would you be doing if you were home now?"

"Listening to Sergio Juevos, probably."

"Oh, yeah. The Cuban drummer."

"A harpist, actually. From Paraguay."

"A Paraguayan harpist?"

"You've never heard him?"

"You mean, he plays the harmonica?"

"He plays the harp."

"I don't think I've ever heard anyone play the harp."

Across the dark living room, the door to the bedroom opened.

"You haven't lived," Fletch said.

Walsh sighed. "Jut like the old days, Fletch."

"What old days? I thought all days are twenty-four hours. Do some get to be older?"

"Bending my brain," Walsh said.

She came across the room like a specter. She was in a long, gray robe. Her blond hair hung to her shoulders.

Doris Wheeler was much bigger than Fletch expected. Her true size had not come across to him on television or still pictures, maybe because she was usually seen standing next to the governor, who was also a big person. She was tall with extraordinarily big shoulders for a woman.

Fletch stood up.

"Walsh? What are you doing at this hour of the night?"

"Dropping off your schedule for tomorrow." Walsh shot his thumb toward the piece of paper on the coffee table. "Why are you back from Cleveland so early?"

"Had Sully make me an earlier plane reservation. Left the symphony benefit at intermission. I've heard Schönberg." Walsh had not stood up. Doris Wheeler's eyes fastened on Fletch's shirt collar. "Who's this?"

"Fletcher," Walsh said. "Here to help handle the press. Just making sure he's housebroken."

"Why are you up talking so late?"

"War stories," Walsh answered. "Haven't seen each other since the Texas-Oklahoma game. That right, Fletch?"

Doris leaned over her son. She kissed him on the mouth.

"Walsh, you've been drinking." She stood up only partway.

"Had to spend some time in the bar, Mother. Something happened. This girl —"

Doris Wheeler slapped her son, hard. Her hand going down to his face looked as big and as solid as a shovel.

"I don't care about any girl, Walsh. I care about you walking around with liquor on your breath." Walsh did not move. He did not look up at her. "I care about getting your father elected President of the United States."

Fully, stiffly erect, she walked back across the living room. "Now, go to bed," she said.

The door to the bedroom closed.

Fletch stood there quietly.

Walsh's face was two kinds of red. It was dark red where his mother had hit him. It was bright red everywhere else.

Walsh kept his eyes on the papers in his lap.

"Well," Walsh finally said, "I'm glad I gave you my lecture on loyalty before you saw that."

S I X

"Good morning, ladies and gentlemen of the press," Governor Caxton Wheeler said heartily.

From the back of the bus, a man's voice snarled: "*Men* and *women* of the press."

"Women and men," corrected the woman sitting next to Freddie Arbuthnot.

"Persons of the press . . . ?" offered the governor.

Fletch was standing next to the governor at the front of the bus. At six-thirty in the morning the governor apparently was slim, tanned, bright-eyed, and fully rested. He did not use, or need to use, the tour bus's microphone. Also, he did not leave much room for the person standing beside him at the front of the bus.

As a politician will, he filled whatever space was available to him.

"Don't forget the photographers," wire service reporter Roy Filby said. "They don't quite make it as persons."

"Dearly beloved," said the governor.

"Now you're leaving out Arbuthnot!" said Joe Hall.

"All creatures great and small?" asked the governor.

"Why's that man up there calling us a bunch of animals?" Stella Kirchner asked Bill Dieckmann loudly. "Trying to get elected game warden or something?"

"It gives me great pleasure," the governor said, "to introduce one of your own colleagues to you —"

"Hardly," said Freddie Arbuthnot.

"— I. M. Fletcher —"

"Politicians will say anything," said Ira Lapin.

"— whom we've employed to hand out press releases to you —"

"He spelled Spiersville wrong already this morning!" shouted Fenella Baker. "It's *ie*, everybody, not *ee*!"

"— do your research for you, free of charge, dig out an answer to your every question, however obtuse and trivial, and generally, to say things about me I'd blush to have to say myself."

"He's a complete crook," said the man wearing the *Daily Gospel* badge.

"Now, I know some of you miss ol' James," continued the governor.

"I do too . . . more than you'll ever know." The governor pulled his touch-of-sentiment face. To Fletch, seeing the expression in profile, it seemed the governor was too obviously clocking the seconds he held the expression. "But, as you know, ol' James decided he wanted to go somewhere more agreeable."

"Yeah," Lansing Sayer said. "When anyone goes to play tennis, James wants to go play tennis."

"So," said the governor, coloring slightly behind the ear, "I'll leave ol' Fletch in your hands." Walsh had told Fletch to ride the press bus that morning. "Try not to chew him up and spit him out this morning. Can't promise you that lunch is going to be that good."

"Hey, Governor," shouted Joe Hall. "Any response yet to the President's statement on South Africa last night?"

Waving, the governor left the bus.

Fletch picked up the microphone. The bus driver turned on the speaker system for him.

"Good morning," Fletch said. "As the governor's press representative, I make you the solemn promise that I will never lie to you. Today, on this bus, we will be passing through Miami, New Orleans, Dallas, New York, and Keokuk, Iowa. Per usual, at midday you will be flown to San Francisco for lunch. Today's menu is clam chowder, pheasant under glass, roast Chilean lamb, and a strawberry mousse from Maine. Everything the governor says today will be significant, relevant, wise, to the point, and as fresh as the lilies in the field."

"In fact," Fenella Baker said, trying to look through the steamy window, "it's snowing out."

The other side of the motel's front door, Doris Wheeler was climbing into the back of a small, black sedan. Today the campaign would head southwest in the state; the candidate's wife would go north. The governor would ride the campaign bus, in front of the press bus.

"Any questions you have for me," Fletch continued, "write backwards and offer to your editors as think-pieces. Just ask your editors to label such fanciful essays as 'Analysis.' "

"Fletch, is it true you're a crook?" Roy Filby asked.

"No," said Fletch, "but if any of you run short of cash, just ask me and I'll put you in contact with people who will supply you with all you want at a modest charge of twenty-percent interest daily."

"Oh, you work for a credit card company, too?"

"Is it true you saved Walsh Wheeler's life overseas?" Fenella Baker asked.

"That's another thing," Fletch said. "I will never evade any of your questions."

He turned the microphone off and hung it up.

SEVEN

"How does it feel to be an adversary of the press?" From her seat on the bus, Freddie Arbuthnot grinned up at Fletch.

"Some people," announced Fletch, "think I always have been."

"This is Betsy Ginsberg," Freddie said about her seatmate, a slightly overweight, bright-eyed, nice-looking young woman.

"Terrific stuff you write," Fletch said to her. "I've never read a word of it, but I've decided to say things like that on this trip."

Betsy laughed. The diesel engine straining to move the bus out of the motel's horseshoe driveway was making as much noise as a jet airplane taking off.

Freddie pressed her elbow into Betsy's ribs. "Move," she said. "Let me be the first to sink teeth into this new press representative."

"You're just saying that," Betsy said, moving out of her seat, "because he's good-lookin'."

"Is he?" said Freddie. "I never noticed."

Fletch slumped into the seat vacated by Betsy. "I don't know," he said to Freddie. "I don't think I'm gonna make it as a member of the establishment. It's all too new to me."

After doing his copying and delivering chores the night before, Fletch finally had taken his shower and climbed into bed with all the folders Walsh Wheeler had given him. There was a folder stating the candidate's position on each campaign issue, as well as on issues that had not arisen and probably would not arise. Some of the positions were crisp, concise, to the point. Others were longer, not as well focused, and had to be read two or three times before Fletch could discover exactly where the candidate was hedging his position. There were personnel folders, with pictures and full biographies, of each member of the candidate's staff. And there were other folders, not as well organized, on most of the members of the press traveling with the campaign. Some of these too had photographs, personal items regarding their families, political leanings, a few significant clippings. Fletch may have been asleep when the phone rang to wake him up. He wasn't sure.

"So far," he said to Freddie, as the press bus rolled along the highway, "I've received two lectures on absolute loyalty."

"What do you expect?" she asked.

Fletch thought a moment. "I don't believe in absolutes."

"You're in a position, all right," she agreed, nodding. "Between the fire and the bottom of the skillet. As a reporter, you're trained to find things out and report 'em. As a press representative, you've got to prevent other reporters from finding certain things out. Adversary of the press. Against your own instincts. Poor Fletch."

"You're a help."

"You'll never make it."

"I know it."

"That's all right." She patted him on the arm. "I'll destroy you as painlessly as possible."

"Great. I'd appreciate that. Are you sure you're up to it?"

"Up to what?"

"Destroying me."

"It will be easy," she said. "Because of all those conflicts in yourself. You've never tried to be a member of the establishment before, Fletch. I mean, let's face it: you're a born-and-bred rebel."

"I bought a necktie for this job."

She studied his solid red tie. "Nice one, too. Looks like you're already bleeding from the neck."

"Got it in the airport in Little Rock."

"Limited selection?"

"No. They had five or six to choose from."

"That was the best?"

"I thought so."

"You only bought one, though, right?"

"Didn't know how long this job would last."

"Glad you didn't make too big an investment in your future as a member of the establishment. Are you going to tell me about last night?"

"What about last night? I saw you to your room and got the door closed in my face."

"Last night a woman landed dead on the pavement outside your candidate's seventh-floor motel room window. Don't you read the papers?"

"I read the papers. Today's big story is about a hockey riot —"

"To hell with today's big story," Freddie said. "I'm interested in tomorrow's big story."

"Tomorrow's big story will be about how badly the police behaved at the hockey riot."

Freddie talked to herself in the bus window. "This here press representative thinks he can get away with not talking about the young woman who got thrown to her death through the governor's bedroom window last night."

"Come off it. I don't know anything."

"You ought to."

"I noticed none of you hotshots asked the governor about it this morning."

"Questions at this point would be ridiculous."

"Of course."

"At least, questions directed at him."

"But I'm fair game?"

"The definition of a press representative. You are game as fair as any seasoned, roasted, carved, and chewed."

"Freddie, I only know what I heard on television this morning. Her name was Alice Elizabeth Fields —"

"Shields."

"In her late twenties."

"Twenty-eight."

"From Chicago."

"You got that part right."

"She was naked when she landed on the sidewalk. Apparently, she had been brutally beaten beforehand."

"She wasn't raped," Freddie said. "Don't you find that odd?"

"I find the whole thing terrible. Sickening."

The two big buses hurried down the highway through the swirling snow. Behind them were a few cars filled with more staff, volunteer workers, one or two television vans.

"And, Fletch, it is possible her point of departure was the balcony outside the governor's suite."

Slowly, he said, "Yes. The governor had had press and other people in for drinks earlier in the evening. I happen to know the front door to the suite was left unlocked."

"I see. Thanks for being frank with me."

"I know you don't print speculation."

"And" — Freddie sighed — "she had been traveling with the campaign all week."

"Not traveling with the campaign. Just following it. She was some sort of a political groupie. She had no position with the campaign."

"As far as we know. I recognized her when I saw her picture in this morning's *Courier*."

"Had you ever spoken to her?"

"Two or three days ago. In whatever town we were in. I was using the motel's indoor pool. So was she. I said, 'Hi'; she said, 'Hi'; I dove in, did my laps, when I got out, she was gone, I think."

"How would you characterize her?"

"A wallflower. I think she wanted to be with the campaign, but didn't know how to be assertive enough to become a volunteer or something."

"Any chance of her being a real camp follower? A prostitute?"

"Definitely not. But you'd have to ask the men."

"I will." Suddenly Fletch wanted a cup of coffee. "A local matter," Fletch said. "To be investigated by local police. Someone said she hit the pavement just after the governor came into the hotel. While he was still in the lobby, or in the elevator or something."

"May I quote that?"

"No."

"Why not?"

"Because I don't know what I'm talking about."

"Truer words you never spoke."

"Seeing I'm being so frank with you, how about telling me why Fredericka Arbuthnot, investigative reporter for *Newsworld*, specialist in crime, especially murder and other forms of mayhem, is assigned to the presidential campaign of Governor Caxton Wheeler?"

"Having any luck in finding out?"

"I'm asking the only person I know. You."

"You've gone to the source."

"The horse's mouth, as it were."

"Going to wear me down with relentless questioning?"

"Going to give it a try."

"The answer's simple: there's been a murder."

"That was after you arrived, Ms. Arbuthnot. Not even you, I think, awesome reporter that you are, can predict where and when a murder is going to happen a week before the event."

"Oh, dear," she said. "You don't know." She leaned over and began rummaging in the yellow and blue sports bag at her feet. "I didn't think you did." She sat up with a damaged notebook in her hand. And out of it she took a newspaper clipping. She handed it to him. "Almost a week ago," she said. "Another murder. Very similar."

He read the item from *The Chicago Sun-Times*:

Chicago — The body of a woman was found by hotel employees this morning in a service closet off a reception room at the Hotel Harris. Police say the woman was brutally beaten about the face and upper body before being strangled to death.

The night before discovery of the body, the reception room had been used by the press covering the presidential campaign of Governor Caxton Wheeler.

Chicago police report the woman, about thirty, wearing a green cocktail dress and high-heeled shoes, was carrying no identification.

Fletch's desire for a cup of coffee was becoming acute.

He handed the clipping back to her. "The press," he said. "How did you pick up an item like that?"

"You don't know about *Newsworld*'s fancy new electronic systems." She was putting the clipping back into the falling-apart notebook, and the notebook back into the sports bag.

Fletch was having the sensation of thinking without thought. "Up-to-date?"

"So fantastic they take out each other's plugs and then say good night to each other."

"That's up-to-date."

Still leaning over, Freddie appeared to be reorganizing her sports bag. "Be kind to your office computer," Freddie said. "It may be related to someone high up in the National Federation of Labor."

"We're being overcome by machines."

Freddie sat up again. "They'll have their day. Or so they predict. And they're always right. Right?"

"No. Freddie, how far have the Chicago police got with this other murder?"

"Talked with my friend Sam Buck this morning. They still haven't identified the woman."

"Fingerprints on the neck?"

"She was strangled with a cord."

"Oh. Have the Chicago police assigned anyone to this campaign?"

"They can't. Different jurisdictions. They have to treat it as strictly a local matter. They're concentrating on hotel staff."

Fletch looked at what he could see of the other people on the press bus, their heads tipped to read, a man's leg extended into the aisle. "It's a pretty safe bet the murderer isn't a member of the Hotel Harris staff."

"I'd take that bet," Freddie said. "I reported the details of the murder last night to Detective Buck in Chicago this morning."

"Will they assign someone to the campaign now?"

"He said the ways in which the women were murdered are not similar enough."

"Two women beaten and then murdered? I see a similarity."

"One was fully clad, the other naked. One was strangled, the other pushed to her death. Stranglers seldom use any other method of doing people in."

"Was the woman in Chicago raped?"

"No."

Across the aisle, one row ahead of them, sat a heavy man in a bulky overcoat. He was staring straight ahead, expressionless. His eyes bulged. He looked like a frog on a pod.

"Freddie, most likely we have a murderer traveling with us."

"It's that possibility, old man, that has me here. Any reporting I do on the campaign itself, I will consider just routine."

Fletch nodded toward the frog-on-the-pod across the aisle. "Is that the Russian?"

"Solov," said Freddie. "Correspondent from *Pravda*. Here to report on the campaign, get a line on The Man Who for the Kremlin. Wonderful free country, we have here."

"Does he always stare that way?"

"I don't know if he always has," Freddie laughed. "He does now. He's fixated."

"On what?"

"He discovered certain channels on American cable television. The pornographic ones. He's up all night, every night, watching it. Don't ever get the hotel room next to him. Electronic slap-and-tickle all night long. They say he's been catatonic since he arrived."

"I wonder if he builds up enough of a head of steam to beat women to death."

"Oh, not Boris. I understand he's written several articles on the moral degeneracy of America. He thinks we all look at that stuff."

"Would you say he's sexually aberrant?"

"Yes, he's sexually abhorrent."

"I said aberrant."

"Who cares?"

Roy Filby came down the aisle and stopped by Fletch's chair. "Hey, Fletcher. Going to give us the real lowdown on the Moony murder?"

A huge factory was looming on the flat, snowy horizon.

Fletch said, "Great stuff you're writing these days, Roy."

Roy laughed and banged Fletch on the shoulder. "Great house parties you give, Fletch. Someday invite me to one."

"I've given my last house party in Key West," Fletch said.

Roy continued down the aisle. There was a rest room in the back of the bus.

"I suppose these murders could be coincidences," Fletch said.

"Could be," said Freddie. "Not likely."

"I hope so," said Fletch.

Studying his face whimsically, Freddie asked, "So how do you like your new job now?"

"Not much. Freddie, let's you and I agree not to be adversaries on this matter. Tell me what you know as you find out."

"Okay," she said. "If you tell me what you know."

"I will. At least I think I will."

"And you know downright well, Fletch, that the moment's going to come when I have to print what I know."

"Sure. But I know you won't go off half-cocked. I'm not too keen on people who beat up women."

The bus was beginning to slow. There was an enormous metal tire standing on the roof of the factory.

"What are you thinking now?" she asked.

"It's your job to report. It's my job to protect the candidate and his campaign as much as I can. If the murderer is a member of the press, then it's no problem for the candidate. The press is assigned to the campaign. If the murderer is a volunteer" — Fletch waggled his hands just above his lap — "then it's not so bad. The candidate didn't necessarily have anything to do with his selection. If the murderer is a member of his immediate staff, then it's very, very bad. It would mean his judgment of people isn't too reliable. People would say, 'If he put such a person on his staff, think whom he might name Secretary of Defense.'"

Still studying him, Freddie asked, "And if the murderer is the candidate himself?"

Fletch was looking at his still hands in his lap. "Then you'd have one helluva story," he said quietly.

EIGHT

By the time he got off the bus, Fletch could see the governor's nose was already red with cold. Snow was blowing from the northwest and there was a fresh inch or two on the ground. Lights were on in the old red-brick factory. Not a bit dwarfed

by the big factory, the governor stood in the main gate, shaking hands
with most of the factory workers as they arrived. He was wearing a
red-and-black checked, wool hunting jacket over his suit vest, and
thick-soled black workers' boots. To the workers who shook his hand
as they passed by, the governor said such things as *"Mornin', everything
okay with you? Gimme a chance to be your President, will ya?"* and the workers
answered such things as *"Mornin', Governor, like your stand on the waterway."*
*"Got to make more jobs, you know? My brother hasn't found a job in over two
years." "With ya all the way; my aunt's runnin' your campaign over in Shreve,
ya know?" "Hey, tell Wohlman we don't want a strike, okay?"* Some of those
who did not shake hands waved as they passed by and said such things
as *"How're doin', Caxton? Good luck! You'll never make it!"* Others were too
shy to shake the governor's hand, or say anything. And others scowled
at him or at their boots as they went through the gate.

Ten meters away, close enough to see everything and hear almost
everything, the press stood shivering in a herd, their noses aimed into
the wind like sheep hunkered in a stormy pasture, in case The Man
Who got shot, or seized by his heart, or overtaken by some indis-
cretion.

Standing in the factory gate, the governor looked peculiarly alone.
No one was standing near him — not his wife, not Walsh, not his
speechwriters, volunteers. . . .

The campaign staff were all on the warm, well-lit bus.

"Where do we pick up the congressman?" Lee Allen Parke yelled.
He was standing in the front of the bus with two women volunteers,
one about thirty, the other about sixty.

"At the school," Walsh said. In his shirt sleeves, he stood in the
middle of the bus, revolving slowly, like a teacher during students'
workbook time.

From the folders he had studied, Fletch could match names to faces.

At a little table, speechwriters Phil Nolting and Paul Dobson were
in heavy, quiet discussion. They were both drawing lines on a single
piece of paper on the table. They looked like architects roughly de-
signing the structure of a building.

Barry Hines, the campaign's communication chief, sat in a reclining
chair talking on the telephone.

Along the side of the bus, three women sat at pull-out tables,
typing.

That morning's newspapers littered the bus's floor.

Dr. Thom was not in the forward section of the bus.

As Fletch moved down through the noise and confusion of the bus, Walsh shouted, "You all know Fletch!"

None of them did. In response to the shout, they all looked at Fletch and returned to what they were doing. Now they knew him.

"Hey, Walsh!" Barry Hines yelled from the telephone. "Vic Robbins! Upton's advance man?"

"What about him?" Walsh asked.

"His car just went off a bridge in Pennsylvania. Into the Susquehanna River."

"Dead?"

"Unless he was wearing a scuba tank."

"Confirm that, please," Fletch said to Barry. "Pennsylvania State Police."

Barry Hines pushed a button on the telephone in his lap and dialed 0.

Walsh pointed to the last typist in the row. Instantly she pulled the paper she was working on out of her typewriter and inserted a fresh piece.

Walsh dictated: "Upon hearing of the tragic death of Victor Robbins, Governor Caxton Wheeler said, 'There was no one who had better technical understanding of American politics than Victor Robbins. The heartfelt sympathy of Mrs. Wheeler and myself go out to Vic's family, and to his friends, who were legion. I and my staff will do anything to help Senator Upton and his staff in response to their great loss.' "

"Yeah," Barry Hines said, pushing another phone button. "He's dead."

Walsh took the typed statement from the woman and handed it to Fletch. "Why am I doing your work for you?" He smiled. "Immediate release to the press, please."

Paul Dobson asked, "Should Caxton mention Robbins's death in the Winslow speech, Walsh?"

"Naw." Hand rubbing the back of his neck, Walsh turned in a small circle in the middle of the bus. "Just wish Upton weren't going to get all that free press in Pennsylvania, of all places. Why the hell couldn't Robbins have driven himself off a bridge in a smaller state? South Dakota?"

Phil Nolting said, "Some advance men will do anything to make a headline."

"Yeah," said Dobson. "Let's send a suggestion to Willy in California. California's a big state, too. Must have some bridges."

"More active press, too," Nolting said. "The weather's nicer."

Fletch was standing at the copying machine, running off the Victor Robbins press release.

The factory whistle blew. Through the steamy window, Fletch saw the governor turn and go through the factory gates by himself.

"Where's he going?"

The press herd had turned their noses from the wind and were looking toward the campaign bus.

"In to have coffee with the union leader," Walsh answered, not even looking. "What's his name — Wohlman. He'll also have coffee with management."

"Coffee, coffee," said a huge-chested man in a black suit who had stepped through the stateroom door at the back of the bus. "Coffee is bad for him."

"You know Flash Grasselli?" Walsh asked. "This is Fletcher, Flash." Fletch got his hand crushed in the big man's fist. "Flash is Dad's driver, etc."

"And friend," Flash said.

"Couldn't do without Flash," Walsh said, and the big-chested man nodded as if to say, *Damn right.*

"Glad to meet you," Fletch said.

At the front of the bus, while Fletch was trying to get by, Lee Allen Parke was saying quietly to the two volunteers, "Now, you make sure the congressman is made right comfortable, you hear? No matter what time of the morning he comes aboard, you have an eye-opener mixed and ready for him. If he doesn't want it, he won't drink it. . . ."

The press was gathered around the foot of the steps of the campaign bus.

"Where's the statement?" Fenella Baker demanded. Her lips were blue with cold.

"What statement?" Fletch asked.

"The governor's statement regarding Vic Robbins's death." Fenella was staring at the papers in Fletch's hands. "Idiot."

"How do you know about Robbins's death?" Fletch asked. "We got the news only three minutes ago."

"Give us the damned statement!" Bill Dieckmann shouted. "I've got the first phone!"

"You know the governor couldn't possibly have made a statement," Fletch said. "He's in the factory!"

"Are you playing with us?" Ira Lapin yelled.

"No," Fletch said. "Here are the statements." He tried to hand them out, but they were grabbed from him.

Bill Dieckmann said to Betsy Ginsberg, "You I can outrun."

"With a strong tail wind," Betsy said.

"You must have wires screwed into your heads," Fletch muttered.

Andrew Esty scanned the statement, then looked up at Fletch. There was rage in his face. "There's no religious consolation in it! In the statement!" Esty wore a *Daily Gospel* button even in the lapel of his overcoat.

"God," Fletch said.

At varying speeds, the members of the press slid through the snow and wind to the telephones inside the factory's main gates.

Except Freddie Arbuthnot. She stood in the snow, grinning up at Fletch.

"Not interested?" Fletch asked.

"Already phoned it in," Freddie said. "Such a statement has three parts. Compliment the deceased's professional expertise. Consolation for family and friends. Offer of help to opposing campaign. Did I miss anything?"

Fletch watched as a dirty, old taxi pulled up at the factory's main gate. The factory was an expensive taxi ride from anywhere.

"Amazing bunch of savages. Screaming for the governor's statement on a matter they knew the governor couldn't even know about yet."

"Ah, Fletch," Freddie said. "You're turning establishment already."

A man had lifted a battered suitcase out of the taxi. Money in hand, he was arguing with the driver.

"Who's that?" Fletch asked.

Freddie turned around. "That," she said definitely, "is bad news. Mr. Bad News, himself." Turning back to Fletch, she said, "Mr. Michael J. Hanrahan, scourge of respectable journalists everywhere, lead dirt-writer for that chain of daily lies and mischief, the scandal sheet going under the generic name *Newsbill*."

Carrying his suitcase in one hand, a portable typewriter in the other, overcoat hems flapping in the wind, the man was lumbering toward the campaign bus. The taxi driver was shouting something at him, which could not be heard in the wind.

"That's Hanrahan? I hoped never to meet him."

Hanrahan turned his head and spat toward the taxi driver.

"I thought Mary Rice was covering us for *Newsbill*."

"Mary's a mouse," Freddie said. "Hanrahan's a rat."

" 'lo, Arbuthnot." With either a smile or a grimace, Michael J. Hanrahan tipped his profile toward her, looking at her out of the corner of his eye. "Made it with any goats lately?"

"Always a pleasure to witness your physical and mental degeneracy, Hanrahan," Freddie answered. "How many more hours to live do the doctors give you?"

Hanrahan didn't put down either his suitcase or his typewriter case. He shivered in his overcoat.

The skin of his face was puffy, flushed, and scabrous. Between the gaps in his mouth were black and yellow teeth. His clothes looked as stale as last month's bread.

"Never, never use a toilet seat," Freddie advised Fletch, "after Hanrahan has used it."

Hanrahan laughed. "Where's this jackass Fletcher?" he asked ner.

"I'm the jackass," Fletch said.

Hanrahan closed his mouth, tried unsuccessfully to breathe through his nose, then opened his mouth again. "Oh, joy," he muttered. "This kid doesn't even go to the bathroom, I bet. Probably been taught not to. It isn't nice." He put his chin up at Fletch, who was still on the stairs of the campaign bus, and tried to give Fletch a penetrating look with bloodshot eyes, each in its own pool of poison. "Boy, are you in trouble."

"Why's that?" Fletch asked.

" 'Cause you've never dealt with Hanrahan before."

"Dreadful stuff you write," Fletch said.

"All you've had to deal with so far are these milksop pussycats mewing for your handouts."

"Meow," said Freddie.

"You're gonna work for me," Hanrahan said. "You're gonna work your shavvy-tailed ass off."

"What do you want, Hanrahan?"

"I want to sit down with your candidate. And I mean now."

"Not now."

"Today. Within a few hours. I need to ask him some questions."

"About what?"

"About dead broads," Hanrahan snapped. "That broad in Chicago. That broad last night. The brutally slain debutante your candidate leaves behind him everywhere he goes."

"*Newsbill's* electronics must be as good as *Newsworld's*," Fletch said to Freddie.

"*Newsworld's* doesn't use such colorful words," Freddie said. "Archaic though they may be."

"Hell, Hanrahan," Fletch said, "that matter's already wrapped up."

Hanrahan squinted. "It is?"

"Yeah. They took Mary Rice into custody an hour ago. Your own reporter. From *Newsbill*."

"Bullshit."

"He's right, Hanrahan. We all know how far you *Newsbill* writers will go to make a story. Mary just got caught this time."

"The police knew the murderer was Mary because she left someone else's notes at the scene of the crime," Fletch added.

Even Hanrahan's neck was turning red. "You know how many readers I got?" he shouted.

"Yeah," Freddie said. "Everyone in the country who can't read, reads *Newsbill*. Big deal."

"They all vote," Hanrahan insisted to her.

"More's the pity," Freddie said to the ground.

"I want to get together with your candidate now," Hanrahan said. "And no more juvenile crap from you!"

"Doubt the candidate will have all that much time for you, Hanrahan."

"What's the matter?" Hanrahan took a step forward. "Doesn't little boyums like the smell of big bad man's breath?"

"Highly indicative, I'm sure," Fletch said.

"You put me together with your candidate, let me work him over with my bare knuckles, or tomorrow *Newsbill*'s readers are going to be told Governor Caxton Wheeler refuses to answer questions about two recent murders on his campaign trail."

"You just do that, Hanrahan." Fletch turned to climb the bus steps. "It will be the first time you've ever written the truth."

NINE

"Listen to this." Dr. Thom was stretched out on the bed in the candidate's stateroom at the back of the bus. He was reading a book entitled *The Darwinian Theory as Fossil*. " 'For thousands of years, we have been told perfection is not attainable, but a worthy aspiration. In this post-Freudian era, we are told normalcy is not possible, but a worthy aspiration. In one scheme, we might achieve excellence; in the other, mediocrity. In one scheme, we fear despair; in the other, depression.' " The doctor put down the open book on his chest. "What can I do for you?"

"Need to ask you a couple of questions." Fletch had knocked, entered the stateroom at Dr. Thom's drawled "Enter if you must," and sat in one of the two comfortable swivel chairs at the stateroom's desk.

Dr. Thom spoke with extraordinary slowness. "Anyone trying to handle the press can have anything he wants from me: poisoned gas, flamethrowers, machine guns, hand grenades. If I don't have such medical and surgical tools on hand, I shall secure them for you at greatly reduced rates."

"At the moment, I'm inclined to place an order," Fletch said. "I just met Michael J. Hanrahan, of *Newsbill.*"

"The press ought to be an extinct species," Dr. Thom drawled. "They never evolved to a very high level. You can tell by the way they go along the ground, sniffing it. I might suggest to the candidate that the press be handed over to the Department of the Interior. That way their extinction will be guaranteed."

"Got to have the free press," said Fletch.

"Do you really think so? Neither the substance of America's favorite sport, politics, nor the substance of America's favorite food, the hot dog, can bear too much analysis. If the innards of either American politics or the American hot dog were too fully revealed, the American would have to disavow and disgorge himself."

"You against motherhood too?"

Dr. Thom clicked the nail of his index finger against the cover of the book on his chest. "On the evolutionary scale, Woman and The Bird, or course, are superior." He cleared his throat. "Which is why, of course, Man invented the telephone wire."

"I understand you were one of the first people to get to the body of Alice Elizabeth Shields last night."

"I was."

"Will you tell me about it?"

"Have you a morbid curiosity?"

"Fredericka Arbuthnot and Michael J. Hanrahan are not on the press bus to count the votes in congressional districts. They're crime writers."

"You mean the death of Ms. Shields might affect the campaign in some way?"

"They tell me two young women have been murdered on the fringes of this campaign just this last week."

"Oh, dear. And the perpetrator might be one of us?"

"There's a good possibility of it."

"And you'd like to get the facts before they do, so you can put the right spin on them."

"And do so very quietly. Without appearing to do so."

Dr. Thom studied the roof a moment. "Don't the police have any-thing to do with this? Or have they read their own statistical success-rates at solving murders and given up on them? Plan to limit their activities henceforth to placing parking tickets on stationary, nonar-gumentative cars, at which function they are very good?"

"The murders are too spread out. Different jurisdictions. We are blessed in this country by not having a national police force."

"Ah, yes. Guaranteeing that only the smaller, narrower-visioned criminal gets caught."

"Tell me what happened last night."

"I was in the bar. A bellman came in — or the doorman, whatever he was. I'm not sure whether he was looking for a responsible person, a motel manager, a doctor, or for a drink. He said, sort of choking, so that his voice stood out in the tired, somber crowd anyway, 'Some-one jumped off the roof. She's naked.' "

"Exact words?"

"I may not remember everything said in the bar last night, about Senator Upton, Senator Graves, the Middle East, and *The Washington Post*, but I do remember those words exactly. It took a moment for them to sink in."

"Who was with you in the bar at that point?"

"I had been talking with Fenella Baker and Betsy Ginsberg. I had been talking with Bill Dieckmann earlier, but I think he'd left some time before. The usual faces in a motel bar. A few morose businessmen drinking themselves to sleep. A few long-haul, tongue-tied drivers desperate to talk with anybody about anything."

"That all?"

"All I can remember. After the event, of course, after the ambulance had come and gone, the press were in the bar in force. Some had just thrown on coats over their pajamas."

"Tell me about going out to the girl. Examining her."

"Due to the high incidence of malpractice suits these days, you know doctors do not rush in where even fools fear to tread. Of course, if I ever come across a lawyer lying on the sidewalk, I'll tread on his face."

"You don't like lawyers either?"

"Even lawyers' mothers don't like lawyers. If you do a survey, I think you'll find that lawyers' mothers are the strongest advocates of legal abortions in the land."

Fletch fought the mesmerizing quality of the doctor's manner of speech. "Going through the lobby, did you see Governor Wheeler coming in?"

"No. No, I did not. I didn't see the governor at all last night until I went to his suite."

"To put him to sleep."

"To put him to sleep. A middle-aged couple, nicely dressed, was standing over the girl. The man was taking off his overcoat to cover the body. I asked him not to do that. I wanted to examine her."

"Was she still alive at that point?"

"No. I would say death was nearly instantaneous the moment she hit the pavement."

"Not before?"

"I don't think so. My guess is that she landed on the back of her head, breaking her neck, then crashed on her back."

"What eveidence did you see that the girl had been beaten before she fell or was pushed?"

"Her face was badly bruised. Banged eye — her left, I think — blood from her nose, blood from lips, two broken front teeth, two or three badly fractured ribs on her left side. Compound fractures, I mean."

"The coroner announced this morning she had not been raped."

"So what motive? Robbery? Who'd want to steal her clothes? Certainly a beaten, naked female suggests rape."

"Would you say she was a good-looking woman?"

Again Dr. Thom studied the ceiling. "Not beautified, in any way. Not much makeup, if any. A slim build, well-proportioned body, good muscle tone. A plain woman, I'd say."

"While you were examining the girl, a crowd collected?"

"A small crowd. Mostly the press."

"Do you remember who was in the crowd?"

"I did glance through the crowd, to make sure no small children were there. That Arbuthnot woman was there. Now, there's a handsome woman. Fenella Baker had followed me out from the bar. I will not comment on her beauty, or lack thereof. One or two others, I'm not sure who. A truck driver from the bar was the only one who really tried to be helpful."

"I understand you had seen the Shields woman before."

"Yes. I had noticed her the last few days — in the motel elevators, lobbies."

"Why did you notice her?"

"I noticed her because she was one place one day and the next place the next day. She didn't appear to have anything to do with the campaign. Although I did see her breakfasting with Betsy Ginsberg one morning."

"Did you ever see her with any men?"

"Not that I remember. I think she drove herself in a little two-door Volkswagen."

"Why do you think a woman like that would traipse after a political campaign the way she did?"

"It's a candidate's job to be attractive, isn't it? That's why they wear those glue-on tans. Power attracts. They attract all sorts of creatures. Even you and me."

The engine of the bus roared. Immediately the bus began to move.

"Hey!" Fletch stood up. "I'm supposed to be on the other bus."

With his finger holding his reading place, Dr. Thom closed his book. "Guess I should let the patient use the bed." He sat up on the bunk, swinging his legs over the side.

Fletch was rubbing the steam off the window.

Taking off his red-and-black checked hunting jacket, Governor Wheeler opened the stateroom door.

"How do," he said to the two men using his stateroom.

"How many cups of coffee did you have, Caxton?" Dr. Thom asked.

"Just two. But they were black." The candidate smiled as if he had gotten away with something.

"Don't blame me if you jitter."

"What am I supposed to do, ask for skim milk everywhere I go? Caffeine's important to these guys."

In the door behind the governor, Walsh said, "Vic Robbins drove himself off a bridge this morning in Pennsylvania. Dead."

"Yeah?" The governor was putting his hunting jacket on a hanger, and the hanger back in the closet. "He was a real weasel. Have I made a statement?"

"Yup."

"Sent a wreath?"

"Will as soon as we know where to send it. You'd better hit something big and hard in Winslow, or you'll get zilch on the nightly news. The accident will make good, easy television film."

"Yeah. Like what?"

"Phil and Paul are trying to come up with something."

"What have they got so far?"

"Pentagon spending."

"Hell, anything anybody says about that has smelled of hypocrisy since Eisenhower. And he saved his complaints for his farewell address. Get something with a little pizzazz."

Dr. Thom said. "You want anything, Caxton?"

"Yeah. A brain transplant. Go away. Don't come back until you can do one."

Fletch tried to follow Dr. Thom through the stateroom door.

"Hang on, Fletch," The Man Who said. "I think it's time you and I got to know each other a little better."

TEN

"Sounds like gangland, doesn't it?" chuckled Governor Wheeler after the door was closed. "A member of the opposition gets knocked off and we've got a wreath ordered before we know where to send it." He sat in the chair Fletch had just vacated and indicated Fletch should sit on the bed. "American politics is a bit of everything: sports, showmanship, camp meeting, and business negotiation." He bent over and began taking off his boots. "Ask me some questions."

"Ask anything?"

"Anything your heart desires. You know a man more from his questions than from his answers. Who said that?"

"You just did."

"Let's not make a note of it."

"I've got a simple question."

"Shoot."

"Why do you want to be President of the United States?"

"I don't, particularly." The Man Who was changing his socks. "Mrs. Wheeler wants to be Mrs. President of the United States." Smiling, he looked up at Fletch. "Why do you look so surprised? Most men try to do what their wives want them to, don't they? I mean, after ten, fifteen years in the same business, most men would quit and go fishin' if it weren't for their wives driving them to the top. Don't you think so?"

"I don't know."

"Never married?"

"Once or twice."

"I see." The governor, socks changed, shoes on, laces tied, sat back in the swivel chair. "Well, Mrs. Wheeler worked hard during the two congressional campaigns, and the three campaigns for the statehouse, and she worked hard in Washington and in the state capital. It's her career, you see, as much as mine. For my part, I began to see, five or six years ago, that I might have a crack at the presidency, so I deliberately started sidling toward it, positioning myself for it. I'm a politician, and the top job in my career is the presidency. Why not go for it?"

"You mean, you have no deep convictions . . ."

The governor was smiling. "The American people don't want anyone with deep convictions as President of the United States. People with deep convictions are dangerous. They're incapable of the art of governing a democracy because they're incapable of compromise. People with deep convictions put everyone who disagrees with them in prison. Then they blow the world up. You don't want that, do you?"

"Maybe I don't mean convictions that deep."

"How deep?"

"Ideas . . ."

"Listen, Fletch, at best government is a well-run bureaucracy. The presidency is just a doorknob. The bureaucracy is the door. The doorknob is used to open or close the door, to position the door this way or that. But the door is still a door."

"All this stuff about 'highest office in the land' . . ."

"Hell, the highest office in the land is behind a schoolteacher's desk. Schoolteachers are the only people who get to make any real difference."

"So why aren't you a schoolteacher?"

"Didactic but not dogmatic is the rule for a good politician. Who said that?"

"No one yet. I'm still thinking about it."

"The President of the United States should be a good administrator. I'm a good administrator. So are the other gentlemen running for the office, I expect."

"And you don't care who wins?"

"Not really. Mrs. Wheeler cares." The Man Who laughed. "Your eyes keep popping when I say that."

"I'm a little surprised."

"You really wouldn't want an ambitious person to be President, would you?"

"Depends on what one is ambitious for."

"Naw. I'm just one of the boys. Got a job people expect me to do, and I'm doin' it."

"I think you're pulling my leg."

Again The Man Who laughed. "Maybe. Now is it my turn?"

"Sure. For what?"

"For asking a question."

"Do I have any answers?"

"We established last night you've taken this job on the campaign to feed some ideas into it. Last night, going to sleep, I was wondering what ideas you have."

"Really sticking it to me, aren't you?"

"Sometimes you know a man by his answers."

"Governor, I don't think you want to hear Political Theory According to Irwin Maurice Fletcher, scribbler and poltroon."

"I sure do. I want to hear everybody's political theory. Sooner or later we might come across one that works."

"Okay. Here goes." Fletch took a deep breath.

Then said nothing.

The governor laughed. "Called your bluff, did I?"

"No, sir."

"Talk to me. Don't be so impressed. I'm just the one who happens to be running for office."

"Okay." Fletch hesitated.

"Okay?"

"Okay." Then Fletch said in a rush, "Ideology will never equalize the world. Technology is doing so."

"Jeez."

Fletch said nothing.

In the small stateroom in the back of the presidential campaign bus, The Man Who looked at Fletch as if from far away. "Technology is equalizing the world?"

Still Fletch said nothing.

"You believe in technology?" the governor asked.

"I believe in what is."

"Well, well." The governor gazed at the steamy window. "Always nice to hear from the younger generation."

"It's not a political theory," Fletch said. "Just an observation."

Gazing at the window, the governor said. "There are many parts to that observation."

"It's a report," Fletch said. "I'm a reporter."

Only dim light came through the steamed-over, dirt-streaked bus window. No scenery was visible through it. After a moment, the governor brushed his knuckles against the window. Still no scenery was visible.

"Run for the presidency," The Man Who mused, "and see America."

The stateroom door opened. Flash Grasselli stuck his head around the door. "Anything you want, Governor?"

"Yeah. Coffee. Black."

"No more coffee today," Flash said. "Fresh out."

He withdraw his head and closed the door.

The Man Who and Fletch smiled at each other.

"Someday . . ." the candidate said.

"Why is he called Flash?"

"Because he's so slow. He walks slow. He talks slow. He drives slow. Best of all, he's very slow to jump on people." The governor frowned. "He's very loyal." He then swiveled his chair to face Fletch more fully. "How are things on the press bus?"

"Could be better. You've got a couple of double threats there, that I know of."

"Oh?"

"Fredericka Arbuthnot and Michael J. Hanrahan. Freddie's a crime writer for *Newsworld* and Hanrahan for *Newsbill*."

"Crime writers?"

"Freddie is very sharp, very professional, probably the best in the business. Hanrahan is utterly sleazy. I would deny him credentials, if I thought I could get away with it."

"Try it."

"*Newsbill* has a bigger readership than the *New York Times* and the *Los Angeles Times* put together."

"Yeah, but *Newsbill*'s readers are too ashamed to identify themselves to each other."

"So has the *Daily Gospel* a huge readership, for that matter."

"How did we attract a couple of crime writers? Did somebody pinch Fenella Baker's uppers?"

"The murder last night, of Alice Elizabeth Shields, was the second murder in a week that happened on the fringes of this campaign."

" 'On the fringes,' " the governor repeated.

"They may not be connected. Apparently, Chicago police don't think so. There's a strong possibility they are connected. Strong enough, at least, to attract the attention of Freddie Arbuthnot and Michael J."

" 'Connected.' To the campaign?"

"Don't know."

"Who was murdered in Chicago?"

"A young woman, unidentified, strangled and found in a closet next to the press reception area at the Hotel Harris."

"And the woman at the motel last night was murdered?"

"Clearly."

"You're saying I should get myself ready to answer some questions about all this."

"At least."

"So get me ready."

"All right. Tell me about your arriving back at the motel last night."

The governor swiveled his chair forward again. "Okay. Willy drove me back to the motel after the Chamber of Commerce speech."

"Willy Finn, your advance man?"

"Yeah. He flew in as soon as he heard James was out on his ear. We had a chance to talk in the car. After he left me last night, he flew on to California."

"Any idea what time you got to the hotel?"

"None at all. I think Willy was to be on an eleven-o'clock flight."

"You entered the hotel alone?"

"Sure. Presidential candidates aren't so special. There are a lot of us around. At this point."

"Go straight to the elevator?"

"Of course. Shook a few hands on the way. When I got to the suite and opened the door, I saw flashing blue lights in the air outside. Through the living room window. I turned on the lights and changed into my robe. I looked through things people had stuffed into that briefcase."

"You weren't interested in what caused the flashing blue lights, the sirens?"

"My life is full of flashing blue lights and sirens. I'm a walking police emergency."

"Are you sure?"

"What do you mean?"

"You didn't go out onto the balcony, lean over the rail and look down?"

"No."

"Why weren't you wearing your shoes when I got there?"

The governor grinned puckishly. "I always take my shoes off before I go to bed. Don't you?"

"It wasn't because they were wet from your being out on the balcony?"

"I wasn't out on the balcony."

"Someone was. The snow out there was all messed up."

"As I said, a great many people were in that room earlier. I might have even gone out on the balcony myself earlier. That I don't remember."

"You didn't stop at any point on your way to your suite? On another floor, to see someone? Anything?"

"Nope. What's the problem?"

"It doesn't work out, Governor."

"Why not?"

"Time-wise. Either you passed a mob on the sidewalk gathered around a dead girl . . ."

"Possible, I suppose."

"But not likely."

"No. Not likely."

"Or, while you were in the lobby, people — including Dr. Thom — rushed out of the bar to the sidewalk to see what had happened."

"I didn't see either thing."

"One thing or the other had to be true, for you to see the flashing police and ambulance lights from your suite when you got there."

The governor shrugged. "I bored the Chamber of Commerce people to death, but I don't think I killed anybody after that."

"How come Flash wasn't with you last night? Isn't he sort of your valet-bodyguard?"

"I don't like having Flash around all the time. Sometimes I like to sneak a cigar. Also, he doesn't get along too well with Bob."

"Dr. Thom."

"Yes. Bob calls Flash a cretin."

Fletch sat more forward on the edge of the bed. "Hate to sound like a prosecutor, Governor, but did you have personal knowledge of Alice Elizabeth Shields?"

The governor looked Fletch in the eye. "No."

"Do you know anything at all about her murder?"

Again the steady look. "No." In an easier tone, he said, "You seem awfully worried. What should I do? Do you think I should make a statement?"

"Not if it looks like this."

"What should I do? You say we've got these two crime writers attached to us. They're going to write something sometime . . ."

Fletch said, "I think it would look politically good for you to make a special request; ask the Federal Bureau of Investigation to come in and investigate."

"God, no." The governor pressed back in his chair and then forward.

He bounced. "FBI crawling all around us with tape recorders and magnifying glasses? No way! Nothing else would get reported. Nothing I say or do. The story of this campaign would become the story of a crime investigation. It would overwhelm everything I'm doing."

"I'm sure a discreet enquiry —"

"Discreet, my eye. Just one of those gumshoes comes near this campaign . . . The press would sniff him out before he got off the plane."

"At some point in the campaign, you get to have Secret Service protection —"

"I'm not going to call for it before anybody else does. I'm in no more danger than any of the other candidates. What would be my excuse? I saw a man at the Chamber of Commerce dinner last night carrying a gun?"

"Did you?"

"Yes."

"There's a man named Flynn, used to this upper-level sort of thing, I think —"

"No, no, no. Aren't my reasons for not doing so clear?"

"Two women have been murdered —"

" 'On the fringes of the campaign' — your own words."

"It might happen again."

"You run a big campaign like this through the country, and everything happens. Advance men fall off bridges into icy rivers —"

Flash stuck his head around the stateroom's door again. "Coming up to that school, Governor."

"Okay."

Flash came in, closing the door behind him.

"You straight-arm this, Fletch. I'm sorry about the whole thing. I do not take it lightly. But we cannot let this campaign get sidetracked by something that is utterly irrelevant to it. Is that understood?"

"Yes, sir."

The governor stood up. Flash had taken the governor's suitcoat off a hanger on the back of the door, brushed it, and was holding it out for him. "Interesting talking to you," the governor muttered.

"My privilege," Fletch said quietly.

The governor had his hands in the pockets of his suit coat. "Got any money?" he asked.

"Sir?"

"I mean coins. Quarters. Nickels. Dimes. Thought I'd try something out at the school. Got any coins, Flash?"

"Sure." Fletch gave the governor all the coins he had, except for one quarter. Flash gave the governor all his coins.

"And, Fletch, keep those two crime writers away from me."

"Yes, sir."

"Arbuthnot and Hanrahan." The governor was smoothing his jacket. "Sounds like a manufacturer of pneumatic drills."

ELEVEN

"Yeah, that made pictures," Walsh was to say to his father at the end of the Conroy School visit. "Good for local consumption. Nothing compared to Robbins's dumping himself in the Susquehanna River, though. That will lead the national news. In Winslow you've got to come up with something new, Dad. Say something new. You've got to."

Clearly, The Man Who enjoyed his stop at Conroy Regional Primary School.

All the little kids were agog, but not, at first, at The Man Who might be the next President of the United States.

At first they were dazzled by the big buses with fancy antennas and cars and station wagons in the campaign caravan, *all these people from Washington.*

About Stella Kirchner: *Look at that lady's boots! They got red lines in them! That lady's boots got veins all on their own!*

About Fenella Baker: *Ever see so much face powder? Why don't she itch? 'Spose she's dead?*

About Bill Dieckmann, Roy Filby, etc.: *Bet not one of those dudes could dribble a basketball a half a whole minute.*

About the photographers, wearing more than one camera around their necks: *What they need so many cameras for? They only got two eyes!*

In the school auditorium, while Walsh kept glancing at his watch, the school band played "America" six times, the last no better than the first. The school principal made a speech of introduction, asking the students if they all knew where Washington is. "On the news programs!" The little girl with the gold star on her collar, officially called upon, answered, "There's one in the upper left by Seattle, and one in the middle right by the District of Columbia."

379

And the principal asked how long one can be President of the United States.

"Forever!"

"Six years!"

"No, four years!"

"Until you get shot!"

Governor Caxton Wheeler made a little speech, goal-orienting the children. He said the country needs good people who believe they can make a difference for the good of the world.

The Man Who was slow to leave the school. He stood among the children. He played magic with coins he took from his pocket. First he made a coin disappear somewhere between his hands. Then he found the coin in a child's shirt pocket, her ear, his mouth. He leaned down and found a vanished coin in the sneaker of a brightly beaming black boy. Instantly the boy searched his other sneaker. To each child he fooled he gave the coin that mysteriously had disappeared from his hands and just as mysteriously reappeared in some unlikely place, such as up the child's own sleeve.

The children quickly forgot about the cameras and the lights and the "city dudes." They stood on chairs and piled on top of each other, tumbled over each other, begged to be the next fooled by the presidential candidate. The governor laughed as hard as the children. His eyes were as bright as theirs.

They pressed against him. "Don't go, sir. You're better than gym!" He hugged them to him.

The members of the press straggled every which way.

"Hey, Fletch," Roy Filby stage-whispered. "Want to go to the boys' room and pull on a joint?"

Fenella Baker was debating the abortion issue in a loud voice with the dry-mouthed school principal.

Andrew Esty was insisting to someone who could have been a math teacher that *Deuteronomy* be tried as a teaching method.

Mary Rice told Fletch that Michael J. Hanrahan was asleep on the press bus.

A photographer terrified little girls by bringing his camera close to their faces and setting off flash bulbs rapidly. "Look at that skin! Awesome! What kind of crèmes do you use, honey?"

Outside the school's main office, some of the reporters bent over the low wall phones, jabbering rapidly in low voices. Other reporters waited.

What's the story? Fletch wondered. Today presidential candidate Caxton Wheeler urged children to continue growing up?

Outside it had stopped snowing. But the sky was still gray and heavy.

"That was nice," Fletch said to Walsh on the driveway in front of the school.

"Yeah. Dad used to play those tricks on me. It was how he gave me my allowance every week."

"Does he still?"

Walsh grinned. "I still think money should come out of my own nose." As his father approached, he said, "Yeah, that made pictures. . . ."

Two of the television station wagons already were leaving the school's parking lot. The rear end of one wagon slid sideways entering the road.

In the driveway, the governor was waving good-bye to the children through the school windows. "I've got an idea for the Winslow speech, Walsh," he said. "Let me work on it."

"The congressman is supposed to be here." Walsh turned around to face the campaign bus. Then he said, "My God."

At the steps of the campaign bus, between the two women volunteers who were to be the reception committee for the congressman, stood a petite, grandmotherly woman.

The governor turned around.

On the steps of the bus, volunteer coordinator Lee Allen Parke raised his hands in futility.

"The congressman," observed the governor, "appears to be a congressperson. You gave me the name Congressman Jack Snive."

"That isn't Jack Snive," admitted Walsh. "Somebody goofed."

"What is her name?" the governor asked.

"No idea. What district are we in?" Walsh's eyes scanned the face of the school building. "Are we at the right school?"

"Oh, yes," the governor said. "They couldn't have played 'America' that badly without practicing it." He sighed. "Guess I'll have to call her 'Member.' Strikes me as slightly indecent, but that's politics."

Putting his hand out to the congressperson, the candidate trudged through the slush. "Hi ya," he said happily. "I was looking for you. How are you feeling? Great job you're doing for your district."

He helped her aboard the bus. Smiling at his son, he said to her, "I want to hear what your plans are for the next four years."

T W E L V E

"Ooooo," said Betsy Ginsberg when Fletch stopped at her aisle seat on the bus. "Is it now I get your attention?"

The bus went over a speed bump in the school driveway. Fletch grabbed on to the backs of the seats on either side of the aisle.

"Just wanted to ask you if you want a typewritten copy of the candidate's profound remarks at Conroy Regional School."

"Sure." She smiled puckishly. "You got 'em?"

"No."

"Pity. Deathless remarks gone with the wind."

"What kind of a story did some of you find to phone in? I saw you at the phone."

"You don't know?"

"No idea."

"Some press rep you are. You ever been on a campaign before?"

"No."

"You're cute, Fletcher. But I don't think you should be on this one, either."

"What happened?"

"Tell me what happened between you and Freddie in Virginia."

"Nothing. That's the trouble."

"Something must have happened. She's mentioned it."

"Just a case of mistaken identity. At the American Journalism Alliance Convention a year or two ago."

"That the one where Walter March got killed?"

"Yeah."

"So what happened, besides the old bastard's getting killed?"

"I told you. Mistaken identity. Freddie thought she was Fredericka Arbuthnot, and I didn't."

"But she is Fredericka Arbuthnot."

"So I was mistaken."

Andrew Esty rose from his seat at the back of the bus and came forward in a procession of one. He stood next to Fletch. "Mr. Fletcher, that stop at the school raises several issues I'd like to talk to the candidate about."

"Nice stuff you're writing these days, Mr. Esty," Fletch said. "Circulation of the *Daily Gospel* testifies to it."

"Thank you," Andrew Esty said sincerely. "About praying in the public schools."

"I used to pray in school," Roy Filby said from the seat behind Betsy. "Before every exam. Swear like hell afterward."

"What about it?" Fletch asked Esty.

"Is the candidate against children being allowed to pray in school?"

"The candidate isn't against anyone praying anytime anywhere."

"You know what I mean: the teacher setting the example."

"My teacher was a Satanist," Filby said. "She corrected our papers with blood."

Esty glared at him. "The issue of people praying together on federal property —"

"The governor has a position paper on this issue." Standing on the bus swaying down the highway, Fletch's legs and back muscles were beginning to remind him he hadn't really slept in thirty hours.

"I'd like to point out to you, and to the candidate," Esty said unctuously, "that prayer is led in federal prisons."

"Jesus!" exclaimed Filby. "Esty's got a whole new issue. Go for it, Esty! Go, man, go!"

"Officially sanctioned prayer," Esty said precisely.

"Right," said Betsy. "What have prisoners got to pray for?"

"Obviously," Esty continued, "that's a similar so-called violation of the principle of the separation of Church and State."

"Right on," said Betsy. "The last person seen by the condemned man was the Sanitation Department's Joe Schmo. Looking at the sanitation worker's green uniform, the condemned man's final words were, 'Please wrap my mortal remains in the *Daily Gospel*. Sunday edition, if possible.' "

"It's a matter of public prayer on government property," Esty said. "Either you can or you can't."

"Would you like an exclusive interview with the candidate?" Fletch asked.

"Yes. There are one or two things of this nature I'd like to ask him about."

"Me too," chirped Filby. "I want to ask him if he'll permit Schubert's 'Ave Maria' to be sung at the White House!"

"I'll see what I can do," Fletch said to Esty.

Down a few seats, seated at a window, Solov stared bugeyed, blankly. Behind him, Fenella Baker was beckoning at Fletch.

To Betsy, Fletch said, "I have a question for you, okay?"

"The answer is yes," she said. "Anytime. You don't even have to bring a bottle of wine."

Andrew Esty, fingering his *Daily Gospel* button, was glaring at Betsy Ginsberg. He had given up glaring at Roy Filby.

"Later," Fletch said to Betsy.

Roy Filby said to Fletch, "Marvelous, the issues the press dreams up for itself, isn't it?"

Fletch stepped around Esty and went down the aisle to Fenella Baker.

"Two or three questions," she said busily. "First is, did you save the life of Walsh Wheeler while you were in the service together?"

"No, ma'am."

"What is your relationship with Walsh Wheeler?"

"We were in the service together. He was my lieutenant."

"People do make up stories," she said.

"Don't they just?"

"Have you been close friends ever since?"

"No, ma'am. Last time I saw Walsh was at a football game more than a year ago."

"Were you surprised when you were asked to take on the job of press rep on this campaign?"

"It's only temporary," Fletch decided. "Until they can find someone with more experience. I'm not worth writing about."

"I agree," she said. "I do hope they find someone who can spell."

Fletch too wondered why Fenella Baker's face didn't itch. Surely some of that powder had been on it since the days of Jimmy Carter.

"Now about this Shields woman —"

"Who?"

"The girl who was murdered last night."

"Was her name Shields?"

"You know perfectly well what I mean."

"I saw your report on it in the newspaper this morning. Great piece."

"I didn't write on it this morning, mister."

"Oh yeah. You did a think-piece on the hockey riot."

"Are you crazy?"

"I must be. I'm here."

"I wouldn't have written on the Shields murder this morning. It isn't a story yet."

"It isn't?"

"It's not a national story until some connection is made between the girl and the campaign."

"Oh. I see."

"What is the connection between the girl and the campaign?"

On a seat at the rear of the bus, Michael J. Hanrahan appeared to be asleep. His head lolled back on a cushion. His jaw was slack. While Fletch watched, Hanrahan lifted a whiskey pint to his lips and poured down two swallows. He did so without opening his eyes or changing the position of his head.

"What girl?" Fletch asked.

"Next you're going to ask me, 'What campaign?' Are you stupid as well as crazy?"

"I'm trying to follow you, Miss Baker, Apples and bananas —"

"Add up to fruit."

"— make mush."

"Someone said she had been traveling with someone on the campaign. Now, who was it?"

"News to me."

Lansing Sayer, standing in the aisle, touched Fletch on the waist.

Fletch stood straight and turned around. "Are you rescuing me?"

Sayer too turned his back to Fenella Baker. "Fenella," he said, working his mustache histrionically, "is the original eighty-pound bully."

"Great stuff you're writing, Mr. Sayer," Fletch said.

"Want to warn you, ol' boy. Your man is going to be attacked on the so-called welfare shambles in his state. Incidents of people committing welfare fraud."

"When?"

"As soon as he gets back up over thirty percent in the national polls."

"Thank you."

In his seat forward in the bus, Bill Dieckmann was doubled over in pain. Eyes squeezed closed, he held his head in both hands. His white skin glistened with sweat.

Going forward in the aisle, Fletch leaned over and whispered to Freddie, "Do you know what's wrong with Bill Dieckmann?"

Freddie craned her neck to see him. "He does that."

"Does what?"

"Suffers terrible pain. He even whimpers. I think he blacks out sometimes. I mean, I think there are times he doesn't know what he's doing."

Fletch watched him from where he stood. "Isn't there anything we can do for him?"

"Guess not."

Fletch looked forward and aft. "This bus is full of loonies."

"Pressures of the campaign," Freddie said. She continued reading Jay Daly's *Walls*.

Fletch put his hand on Dieckmann's shoulder. "You going to be all right, Bill?" Dieckmann looked up at him with wet eyes. "Want me to stop the bus? Get Dr. Thom?"

With both hands, Dieckmann squeezed his head tighter. "No."

"I will, if you want. What's the matter?"

Eyes squeezed closed again, rocking forward and back in his seat, Dieckmann said in a hoarse whisper, "Leave me alone."

"You sure?"

Dieckmann didn't answer. He suffered.

"Okay," Fletch said. "If you say so."

He went back up the aisle to where Betsy was sitting. She was reading Justin Kaplan's *Walt Whitman*.

He bent over her and spoke quietly. "Someone said he saw you having breakfast a few days ago with the girl who was murdered last night."

"That's right. I did. The breakfast room was filled. People were waiting. The hostess seated us together. Two single women."

"Did you talk?"

"Sure. Civilities over toast."

"You're a reporter, Betsy. I suspect you found out one or two things about her."

"Not really."

"Like not-really what?"

"She was an ordinary, nice person. She'd been working as a sales clerk in a store in Chicago. Mason's, I think, mostly in the bookshop."

"Is that all?"

"She liked to read, said she read three or four books a week. Asked me if I'd read certain people, such as Antonia White, William Maxwell, Jean Rhys, Juan Alonzo. She said Saul Bellow once came up to her counter and asked her for something, some book they didn't have, and he was very courteous about it. She recommended Antonia White's *Frost in May* in particular because, she said, she had gone through parochial schools in Chicago. A Catholic high school, I think she said Saint Mary Margaret's."

"That was the extent of your conversation?"

"No." Betsy was dredging her memory. "Her father had been killed in an accident when she was nine years old. He worked for the Chicago

Waterworks or something. When he was in a ditch, a pipe landed on his head. So she could never think of going to college, you see."

"Oh. Anything else?"

"Her mother never recovered from her father's death, got stranger and stranger, and finally five years ago committed herself to a state home."

"Nothing else?"

"Well, she lived alone in a studio apartment. Married sister, living in Toronto, four children. Her husband owns a gun shop. Sally — that is, Alice Elizabeth Shields; she called herself Sally — had been engaged a couple of times, once to a Chicago policeman who got another girl pregnant and decided he'd better go marry her. Sally never married."

"Is that all you've got?"

"She had something like thirty-seven hundred dollars in a savings account. So she quit her job, sublet her apartment, packed up her Volkswagen, and came a-wandering."

"You didn't get much out of her."

"Just civilities over toast."

"What was her Social Security number?"

"You think I'm nosy?"

"You are a reporter, after all."

"I wasn't interviewing her."

"Why was she following the campaign?"

"Didn't know she was, at that point."

"While you were having breakfast with her, did she mention anyone who is traveling with the campaign by name?"

Betsy thought. "No. But she did seem to know I'm a reporter."

"I wonder if it was something you said."

The bus, at high speed, was climbing a left-curved hill. Fletch had to push off the seat backs not to land on Betsy.

"I mean, she didn't ask me anything about myself."

"You think she had a chance?"

"We were just talking."

"While you were at breakfast with her, did anyone from the campaign say hello to her, nod to her as he went by, wave from across the breakfast room?"

"Not that I remember. She seemed a lonely person."

"Eager to talk."

"As long as she didn't have to be assertive about it."

"You were in the motel bar last night."

"Yes. Drinking rum toffs."

"What's a rum toff?"

"Yummy."

"At any time did you see this girl — Sally, you called her — in the bar with anybody, or leave the bar with anybody, anything?"

"I'm not aware of ever having seen her again since I had breakfast with her in Springfield."

"But you saw her Volkswagen trailing the caravan."

"No. I don't know a Volkswagen from an aircraft carrier."

"They're different."

"I expect so."

"Sea gulls seldom follow a Volkswagen."

"Oh. Well, at least I know the connection between the Shields woman and the campaign."

"What?"

"There isn't one. At least, as far as you can find out. So I won't worry about it. As a story. Yet. Will you tell me if you discover there is a connection?"

"Probably not."

"After all I just told you?"

"Not much. You said so yourself."

"Now I have a question for you."

"You just asked one."

"Walsh has never married, has he?"

"Yes, he likes girls."

"Oh, I can see that. Why don't you introduce me to him? You're his friend."

"You don't know him?"

"Not really. I mean, I've never been introduced as a woman to a man. As a reporter I know him."

"I see."

"He looks like he might go for the homebody type."

"You're a homebody?"

"I could be. If the home had a nice address on Pennsylvania Avenue."

"Sixteen-hundred block."

"Right."

"Lots of rooms to clean."

"You've never seen me with a mop."

"No, I haven't."

"Pink lightning. Flushed with excitement. Ecstasy. You ought to introduce us."

"I will."

"Somebody in a presidential family ought to marry a Ginsberg. We do nice table settings."

"Agreed."

"Tell him you and I worked together in Atlanta."

The bus slowed. The bus driver was looking through the rearview mirror at Fletch.

"I never worked in Atlanta."

"I did."

"Oh. Okay."

"Irwin!" the bus driver shouted.

"Irwin!" Roy Filby echoed. "I'd rather see one than be one!"

"Telephone!" the bus driver shouted. In fact, a black wire led from the dashboard onto his lap.

Fletch said, "We have a telephone?"

"Not for the use of reporters," Betsy said. "Staff only. Want to hear what James said about the duplicating machine?"

"I've heard."

Fletch went forward. The bus driver handed him the phone from his lap.

"Hello?" Fletch said. "Nice of you to call."

Barry Hines said, "You'd better come forward, Fletcher."

"I've always been forward."

"I mean into this bus. Watch the noon news with us."

"Sure. Why?"

"Just heard from a friendly at UBC New York that something unsavory is coming across the airwaves at us."

"What?"

The phone went dead.

Brake lights went on at the rear of the campaign bus. It headed for the soft shoulder of the highway.

Fletch looked for a place to hang up the phone.

"Guess we're stopping for a second. Got to go to the other bus."

The press bus was following the campaign bus onto the soft shoulder.

"Just put the phone back in my lap," the driver said. "I'm not expecting any calls at the moment."

Fletch put the phone in the bus driver's lap.

"How did you know my name is Irwin?" Fletch asked.

The bus driver said: "Just guessed."

THIRTEEN

"We're almost late for the rally in Winslow," The Man Who commented.

"A band will be playing, Dad."

Again the governor tried to see the world through the steamy bus window. "But it's cold out there."

The buses pulled back onto the highway and were gathering speed.

On the campaign bus a small-screened television set had been swung out behind the driver, high up. It faced the back of the bus. A commercial was running for feminine sanitary devices.

"My apologies, ma'am," the presidential candidate said to the congressperson, "for the bad taste displayed by my television set. Not a thing I can do about it." They were sitting next to each other on an upholstered bench at the side of the bus. "Not a damned thing."

Fletch stepped over the governor's feet. He stood near Walsh. "What is it?" He hung on to a luggage rack.

The television newsperson came on and mentioned the news leads: "Coming up: Senator Upton's advance man killed in automobile accident in Pennsylvania; aftermath of a hockey riot, numbers injured and arrested; presidential candidate Caxton Wheeler hands out money to schoolchildren on the campaign trail."

"Jeez!" Fletch turned toward the back of the bus. Arms akimbo, Flash Grasselli stood against the stateroom's closed door. "Would you believe this?"

"Sure," Walsh said. "It's true."

"At least I'm not the number-one news lead," the governor said. "Guess they don't think too badly of bribing schoolchildren."

" 'Bribing schoolchildren.' " echoed Fletch.

Phil Nolting said, "That's what they're gonna make out of it."

A commercial was running for "Sweet Wheat, the breakfast cereal that makes kiddies yell for more."

"Yell with the toothache," Paul Dobson said. "They're yelling because it makes their teeth hurt!"

"Make 'em hypertensive with sugar at breakfast," Phil Nolting intoned, as if quoting, "then slap 'em down at school."

Except for Barry Hines, who was talking quietly on the telephone, those aboard the campaign bus suffered silently as a few more details were given of Victor Robbins's death, film was run; of the hockey riot, film was run. Then: "This morning at Conroy Regional School Governor Caxton Wheeler, while on his campaign for the presidency, handed out coins to the primary school students." Film was run. The Man Who, surrounded by excited children, was doing some trickery with his hands. Then the camera was zoomed in to show in close-up the governor's hand pressing a coin into the hand of a child. "Some received dimes, others quarters, others half dollars. And some got none at all. . . ."

"Did one run all the way home?" Phil Nolting asked.

"Must have," Paul Dobson said. "Somebody must have told on us."

On screen the newsperson was sitting with an extremely thin, hawk-nosed, nervous-looking woman. "Here in our studio with us is the distinguished pediatric psychiatrist, Dr. Dorothea Dolkart, author of *Stop Resenting Your Child* and *Face Up to Bed-wetting.*"

"Jeez," said Paul Dobson. "How can these experts get to the television studios so fast? It's only been an hour. Don't they have other jobs?"

"Doctor Dolkart, you've just seen here on our studio monitor presidential candidate Caxton Wheeler handing out coins to some of the pupils at Conroy School. Can you assess for us the effect this would have upon the pupils?"

"Extremely damaging. Traumatic. First, there is the point that here we have an adult who is making himself popular, or trying to, by the device of handing out money."

"Setting somewhat the wrong standard, you think?"

"An absolutely materialistic standard."

"In fact, he's teaching the children you can buy friendships."

"And this happened in a school setting, where children are used to learning things. With authority, if you understand me."

"Yes. The effect upon the children who didn't receive any money . . . ?"

"Disastrous. Very few people in this country have greater prestige in the eyes of children — in the eyes of any of us — than a presidential candidate. Maybe the President himself, a few football players, what have you. Meeting, even seeing, a man who might become the most powerful leader on earth, is one of the most memorable experiences of our lives. For those who did not receive any coin at all from Governor Wheeler, the implied rejection is severe. These children this morning were scarred for life and, I might add, totally unnecessarily."

On the campaign bus The Man Who said, "Oh, my God."

"And the children who did receive the coins? Do they feel better about things?"

"No. If anything, they feel worse. Because completely arbitrarily they were singled out for this special attention, this gift, from a grown-up of the greatest prestige. It would have been one thing if the candidate had handed out coins to children who had won the honor through some sort of an academic or athletic contest. As it is, the children who actually got the coins from the governor have been burdened with terrible guilt feelings because they received something which they know they didn't deserve, while their schoolmates got nothing at all. . . ."

"I guess James would have stopped me from doing that." The Man Who hung his head in his hands. "He would have known how it would look to the press. What they could make of it. Handing out money to kids. Gee. I guess ol' James is laughing up his sleeve at this moment, wherever he is."

Fletch said to Walsh, "I'm beginning to suspect I have a short career as a press representative."

"It's an impossible job," Walsh said.

The television was offering the usual variety of weather reports.

"Well." The governor put his hand on the hand of the grandmotherly congressperson. "Guess I just wrecked the life of every schoolchild in your district." He smiled at her. "Do you agree?"

She lifted her hand from under his on the divan. "Yes, Caxton. It was totally irresponsible of you. Damned insensitive."

He looked at her a moment to see if she was serious. She was. He stood up and wandered to the back of the bus where Walsh and Fletch were standing.

"Sorry," Fletch said to him. "I thought it looked nice. Was nice."

"Got to be aware of how things look to the press," Walsh said. "Every damned little thing. What they can make of it."

"How do we pick up from here?" Fletch asked the governor. "Make a statement . . . ?"

The governor smiled. "Naw. Let them hang themselves on their own silliness. Psychiatrists be damned. I don't think the American people are apt to consider an older man handing out coins to little kids as Beelzebub." He beckoned Flash forward with his finger and called Barry Hines. When they came, he said, "Listen, guys. In Winslow I don't want that old bitch on the platform with me."

"The congressperson?" Barry asked in surprise.

They were speaking softly.

"Body-block her. Trip her. Hide her purse. Slow her down. I don't care what you do. Just keep her off the platform."

"This is her district, Dad."

"I don't care. She's lookin' to speak against me, anyway. Let's not give what she has to say against me the prestige of pictures of her standin' with me."

"Okay," Flash said.

"We'll show the old bitch exactly how sensitive I am."

The governor opened the door to the stateroom. "Come here, Fletch."

"Yes, sir?"

"Close the door."

Fletch did so. "Again, I'm sorry about that. I never dreamed the press —"

"I'm not about to chew you out."

"You're not?"

" 'Course not. Who was the first one to say 'If you can't stand the heat get out of the kitchen'?"

"Uh — Fred Fenton?"

"Who was he?"

"Cooked for Henry the Eighth." The governor gave him a weird look. "Buried under the chapel at the Tower of London. Forgot to take the poultry lacers out of roast falcons."

The governor chuckled. "You're making that up."

"Sure I am."

"Got anything for me?"

"Anything . . . ?"

"You've been on the press bus most of the morning."

"Oh. Yeah. Lansing Sayer says Upton's team is going to hit you with some evidence of welfare fraud in your state. As soon as you climb back over thirty percent in the popularity polls."

"That so? Good for them. That's smart. There's welfare fraud in every state. Also housebreaking and vandalism. I'll get Barry on that. Have his people put together my record on stopping welfare abuse. Also, let's see: the amount of welfare fraud in other states. I'll make an issue of it myself as soon as I get near thirty percent in the polls."

"Amazing how things become campaign issues."

"Anything else?"

"Andrew Esty wants an exclusive interview with you."

"The *Daily Gospel* guy?"

"Yeah. He's trying to develop something. If people are allowed to pray together in federal prisons, why not in public schools?"

"Wow. 'Take Prayers out of Prisons.' "

"I think he means 'Put Prayer back in Schools.' "

"No foolin'."

The bus was going slowly, obviously in traffic. It was stopping and starting, probably at red lights.

"What do we do for him?" Fletch asked.

"Pray for him," the governor said. "Anything else?"

"Found out more about the woman murdered last night. An intelligent, apparently unattached, lonely woman."

"How do you know she was intelligent?"

"She was a reader. From her reading."

"Political reading?"

"No."

The bus was inching forward. A band could be heard playing.

"Very quickly I'm going to get tired of that topic." The governor leaned over and looked through the steamy window. Instinctively he waved at the crowd outside with the flat of his hand. Fletch was sure no one outside could see the candidate thorough the windows. "Someday I'd love to have a Klezmer band playing for me." the governor said. "I love Klezmer bands."

The bus stopped.

"Walk out with me." The governor took Fletch's arm in his fist. "Stay between me and that congressbitch. Paddle her backward. Got me? Give it to her in the ribs, if you have to."

"Gotcha."

"And tell Lansing Sayer he can have an exclusive interview with me anytime he wants it."

"Yes, sir."

When Fletch opened the stateroom door, their ears were assaulted by the band's playing "Camptown Races."

" 'Jacob, make the horse go faster and faster,' " the candidate said. " 'If it ever stops, we won't be able to sell it.' "

FOURTEEN

"It's nice of you all to come out and give me a chance to talk to you, on such a cold, raw day," The Man Who said. The noontime crowd was crammed into the smallest intersection in Winslow. Advance man Willy Finn had planned the rally for the smallest outdoor space in Winslow deliberately. A small crowd looks bigger in a small space; a larger crowd looks huge. The presidential candidate had attracted a goodsized crowd. "You know, a presidential campaign is just a crusade of amateurs. I can tell you, my friends in Winslow, this campaign to let me serve you the next four years in the White House needs your help."

Standing in slush at the edge of the crowd, Fletch said to himself, "Wow."

At his elbow, Freddie Arbuthnot said, "He said something new."

The mayor, the city council, the chief of police, the superintendent of schools, a judge, the city's oldest citizen (standing up at ninety-eight, bundled well against the cold), probably two dogcatchers and the fence-viewer were the reception committee awaiting the candidate as he got off the bus. A band was playing "The Battle Hymn of the Republic." Not moving from the bottom of the bus steps, Governor Wheeler shook hands with each member of the committee, said a few words to each. The mayor then led him through the crowd to the platform set up on the corner of Corn Street and Wicklow Lane, gestured to the band for quiet, and did his Man-Who speech, peppered with many references to his own efforts to gain control of the city budget.

Fletch watched Barry Hines and Flash Grasselli escort the short congressperson in entirely the wrong direction, right into the middle of the crowd, where she got bogged down shaking hands and listening to her constituents' griefs.

Fletch introduced himself to the local press. He handed out position papers on the crop subsidy programs. He and the local press and only some of the national press stood in a roped-off area to the right of the platform.

Some members of the national press, Roy Filby, Stella Kirchner, Betsy Ginsberg, Bill Dieckmann — who seemed completely re-covered — had spotted a bar-cafe half a block up and decided to go there for drinks during The Speech. "Tell us if he gets shot, or hands out money to the crowd or something, Fletch."

Three television cameras were atop vans and station wagons. News photographers stood near the platform.

Hanging from the second-floor windows of the First National Bank of Winslow at the corner of Corn and Wicklow was a huge American flag. It had forty-eight stars.

Now The Man Who was saying, "The world has changed, my friends. You know it and I know it, but the present incumbent in the

White House doesn't seem to know it. His brilliant advisors don't seem to know it. None of the other candidates, Republican or Democrat, who want to see themselves in the White House the next four years seems to know it. . . ."

"This isn't his usual speech," Freddie said. "This isn't The Speech."

". . . It used to be that what happened in New York and Washington was important in Paramaribo, in Durban, in Kampuchea. Nothing was more important. Well, things have changed. Now we know that what happens in Santiago, in Tehran, in Peking is terribly important in New York and Washington. Nothing is more important."

Fletch said: "Wow."

". . . The Third World, as it's called, is no longer something out there — separate from us, inconsequential to us. Whether we like it or not, the world is becoming more sensitive. The world is becoming covered with a network of fine nerves — an electronic nervous system not unlike that which integrates our own bodies. Our finger hurts, our toe hurts and we feel it as much as if our head aches or our heart aches. Instantly now do we feel the pain in Montevideo, in Juddah, in Bandung. And yes, my friends in Winslow, we feel the pain from our own, internal third world — from Harlem, from Watts, from our reservations of Native Americans . . ."

Fletch said: "Wow."

Freddie was giving him sideways looks.

". . . There is no First World, or Second World, or Third World. This planet earth is becoming integrated before our very eyes!"

"He's not going to . . ."

"He's not going to what?" she asked.

". . . You and I know there is no theology, no ideology causing this new, sudden, total integration of the world. Christianity has had two thousand years to tie this world together . . . and it has not done so. Islam has had six hundred years to tie this world together . . . and it has not done so. American democracy has had two hundred years to tie this world together . . . and it has not done so. Communism has had nearly one hundred years to tie this world together . . . and it has not done so."

"He's doing it."

"He's doing something all right," she said.

Fletch's eyes studied the faces in the crowd. He was seeing faces blue with cold, noses red. He was seeing eyes fixated on The Man Who might become the most powerful person on earth, have some control over their taxes and their spending, their health care, their education, how they spent their days and their nights, their youths, working years, and old age, their lives and their deaths. For the most part, in the cold, their ears were covered with scarves and mufflers.

The congressperson was working with as much speed as possible through the thick crowd to the platform. She was still allowing her hand to be shook, still mouthing a responsive sentence here and there, but her face was stony. With all apparent graciousness, Barry Hines and Flash Grasselli were still turning her around to face the bulk of her constituency.

". . . You and I know what is tying this world together, better than any band of missionaries, however large, ever have or ever could; better than any marching armies ever have or ever could . . ."

"What is he saying?" Freddie demanded. She checked the sound level of the tape recorder on her hip.

Fletch said, "Gee, I dunno."

"Today," The Man Who continued, "satellites permit us to see every stalk of wheat as it grows in Russia, every grain of rice as it grows in China. We can see every soldier as he is trained in Lesotho or Karachi. We can fly to Riyadh or Luzon between one meal and another. Every economic fact regarding Algeria can be assimilated and interpreted within hours. It is possible to poll the entire population of India regarding their deepest political and other convictions within seconds. . . ."

Freddie said: "Wow. Is he saying what I think he's saying?"

Walsh Wheeler, who had been walking slowly, unobtrusively through the crowd, began to move much more quickly toward the campaign bus. The congressperson had struggled her way through the crowd and was almost at the steps to the platform.

"I dunno."

". . . You and I, my friends, know that technology is tying this world together, is integrating this world in a way no theology, no ideology ever could. Technology is forming a nervous system beneath the skin of Mother Earth. And you and I know that to avoid the pain, the body politic had better start responding to this nervous system immediately! If we ignore that which hurts in any part of this body earth, we shall suffer years more, generations more of the pain and misery of spreading disease. If we knowingly allow wounds to fester in any particular place, the strength, the energies of the whole world will be sapped!"

The crowd of photographers on the steps to the platform was blocking the congressperson's ascent. She could not get their attention, to let her up.

". . . American politics must grow up to the new realities of life on this planet! Technology brings us closer together than any Biblical brothers! Technology makes us more interdependent than any scheme of capital and labor! Technology is integrating the people of this earth where love and legislation have failed! This is the new reality! We must seize this understanding! Seize it for peace! For the health of planet earth! For the health of every citizen of this planet! For prosperity! My friends, for the very continuation of life on earth!"

There was a long moment before anyone realized The Man Who was done speaking. Then there was applause muffled by gloved and mittened hands, a few yells: "Go to it, Caxton! We're with you all the way!" The band began to play "Hot Time in the Old Town Tonight."

At the edge of the platform, The Man Who shook hands with the congressperson as if he had never seen her before, keeping his arm long, making it seem, for the public, for the photographers, he was greeting just another well-wisher. He waved at the crowd and passed the congressperson in the mob on the steps.

At the front of the bus, Walsh Wheeler, Paul Dobson, and Phil Nolting were in heavy consultation.

"Wow," said Fletch, still in the press area. "I never knew it was so easy to be a wizard."

Freddie said, "You know something about all this I don't know. You going to tell me?"

"No."

Freddie Arbuthnot frowned.

She turned back toward the platform. The grandmotherly congressperson was shouting into a ringing amplification system. She was not at all heard over the band.

"But what does it mean?" Freddie asked.

"It means," Fletch answered, "he's made the nightly national news."

FIFTEEN

Approaching him, Governor Caxton Wheeler grinned at Fletch. "How do you feel?"

"Like Adam's grandfather."

At the foot of the campaign bus's steps, the governor was

still grinning when he turned to his son. Walsh and Phil Nolting and Paul Dobson looked like a wall that had come tumbling down at the blast of a single trumpet. Each face had the same expression of stressed shock.

"How'd I do?" the governor asked.

Walsh's eyes darted around, seeing if any of the press were within earshot. Outside their little circle was a group of thirty to forty retarded adults who had been brought from their institution to meet the presidential candidate.

"You've got to tell us when you're going to do something like that, Dad."

"I told you I had an idea."

"Yeah, but you didn't mention you were going to drop a bomb — a whole new departure."

"A new speech." Phil Nolting's eyes were slits.

"Sorry," the governor said. "Guess I was really thinking about it while that congressperson was babbling on about the waterway."

"The question always is — " Paul Dobson said in the manner of a bright teacher. "You see, we've got to be prepared to defend everything you say before you say it."

"You can't defend the truth, anyway?" the governor asked simply. "I can."

"Hi, Governor," one of the retarded persons, a man about thirty-five, said. "My name is John."

"Hi, John," the governor said.

"It might have been a great speech, Dad, I don't know. We all just feel sort of punched out by your not telling us you were going to do it."

"I wasn't sure I was going to do it." The governor smiled. "It just came out."

"We'll get a transcript as fast as we can," Dobson said. "See what we can do about it."

The governor shrugged. "It felt right." He put out his hand to one of the retarded persons, a woman about thirty. "Hi," he said. "Are you a friend of John's?"

Aboard the campaign bus, coordinator of volunteers Lee Allen Parke was connecting a small tape recorder to a headset. A typist was at her little desk, ready to work.

"Lee Allen," Fletch said. Parke didn't answer. "Just a simple question."

"Not now," Lee Allen said. "No questions now, please." He said to the typist, "We've got to have an exact transcript of whatever the governor just said, sooner than soonest." He placed the headset over the typist's ears. She settled the earphones more comfortably on herself.

All the buttons on the telephone in Barry Hines's chair were flashing. The phone was not ringing. Barry Hines was nowhere in sight.

"Ah, Lee Allen —" Fletch began.

Lee Allen pressed the *play* button and listened through a third earphone. "Loud and clear?" he asked the typist. She nodded in the affirmative. "My God," he said, listening. "What is the man saying?"

"Lee Allen, I need to know about Sally Shields, Alice Elizabeth Shields —"

"Not now, Fletcher! All hell has broken loose! The governor just went off half-cocked, in case you didn't know."

"No. I didn't know."

"First he's caught bribing schoolkids. Then the hard-drinkin', sexpot congressman we were told to expect turns out to be somebody's great-grandmother. By the way, there's a pitcher of Bloody Marys in the galley, if you want it. Then he makes like Lincoln at Gettysburg at Winslow in a snowstorm. And the day's barely begun!"

"Well begun," Fletch consoled, "is half done."

"Not by my watch." To the typist, who was listening and typing, Lee Allen Parke shouted, "Can you hear?" She nodded yes with annoyance. "We need every word," he said. "Every word."

"You could have answered me by now," Fletch said firmly.

Lee Allen Parke still held the earphone to his head. "What? What, what, what?"

"Did Alice Elizabeth Shields apply to you for a job as a volunteer, paid or otherwise?"

"How do you spell Riyadh?" the typist asked.

"No," Lee said impatiently.

"She didn't?"

"Some of the volunteers reported the caravan was being followed by a Volkswagen. That's all I know about her."

"He said something new?" Bill Dieckmann shouted. His face looked like someone had knocked his hat off with a snowball.

He was one of the group returning to the press bus from the bar–café.

"I guess he did," Fletch admitted.

"New-new?"

Betsy Ginsberg said, *"Nu?"*

Bill Dieckmann's face looked truly alarmed.

"New," said Fletch. "I'm not sure how germaine. . . ."

"Ow," Stella Kirchner said. "Who's got a tape?" She looked sick.

"All those people presently usurping telephones in downtown Winslow," Fletch said. "I expect."

Betsy said, "Have you a tape? Honest, Fletch, I promise we won't spring a story like presidential-candidate-bribes-schoolchildren on you again if you let us hear your tape."

"Ain't got one," Fletch said. "Transcripts will be ready in a minute."

" 'Transcripts,' " Dieckmann scoffed. "My editors should read it on the wires while I'm airmailing them a transcript — right?"

"Not on my wire," moaned Filby.

"What did the governor say?" Kirchner asked.

"Well," Fletch said, "roughly he said the world is getting it together despite man's best ideas."

They all looked at him as if he had spoken in a language foreign to them.

"Nothing about the waterway?" Filby looked about to faint.

"Nothing about the waterway," Fletch said.

"Shit," said Filby. "I already reported what he said about the waterway — what he didn't say about the waterway."

Fletch led her onto the campaign bus.

"Oooo," said Betsy in fake cockney. "Don't they live well, though? Telly and everything."

Walsh was chatting with Lee Allen Parke.

"Walsh," Fletch said, "this is Betsy Ginsberg."

"I know Betsy." Walsh gave Fletch an odd, questioning look.

"Not as a person," Betsy said.

"Yeah," said Fletch. "She does nice table settings."

The governor got on the bus while Fletch was collecting copies of the transcripts from volunteers.

"Come on back here, clean-and-lean," the governor said.

They went into the stateroom together. The governor closed the door. "Sit a minute."

"I'm supposed to be handing these out." Fletch indicated the transcript in his hand. "Sir."

"They can wait." The governor took off his overcoat and dropped it on the bed. "Tell me what you think."

"I think you're damned eloquent. Sir."

The governor dropped himself into the swivel chair. Fletch did not sit.

"Thank you."

"Take a germ of an idea like that —"

"More than a germ, I think."

"You're brilliant," Fletch blurted.

"Thank you. Now tell me what you think."

Fletch felt himself turning warm. "Frankly, I, ah —"

"You — ah?" The governor was looking at him with patient interest.

"I — ah — didn't know a presidential campaign is so impoverished for ideas. Sir." The governor laughed. "I mean, I thought everything was sort of worked out from the beginning; you knew what you were saying, had to say, from the start."

"You were wrong. Does that surprise you?"

"I'm never surprised when I'm wrong."

"Part of the process of a political campaign is to go around the country listening to people. At least, a good politician listens. You said something this morning that struck me as eminently sensible. Something probably everybody knows is true, but no one has yet said. Probably only the young have grown up with this new reality in their guts, really knowing it to be true."

"Yes, sir. Maybe."

"I think people vote for the man who tells them the truth. What do you think?"

"I hope so. Sir."

"I do too. Politicians aren't philosophers, Fletch. They're not supposed to be. No one wants Tom Paine in the White House. Or Marx. Or Eric Hoffer. Or Marcuse. But they don't want anyone in the White House who doesn't pursue general truths, or know a general truth when he trips over one, either." Rocking gently in his swivel chair the governor watched Fletch standing stiffly at the stateroom door, and chuckled. "I think I enjoy shakin' you up. I bet everybody who has ever met you before has thought you real cool, boy." Fletch swallowed hard. "That right?"

"I . . . may . . . I . . . ah —"

The governor laughed and held out his hand for a transcript. "Let me have one of those."

Fletch handed him one from the top. He nearly dropped the pile.

The governor began reading it. "Better see what I said."

SIXTEEN

G et your damned ass up here." It was clear from Walsh's voice that he meant to be taken seriously.

"Yes, sir, Lieutenant, sir," Fletch said into the hotel room phone. "Please tell me where I'm to get my damned ass up to, sir."

"Room 1220."

Instantly the phone went dead.

Fletch tripped over his unopened suitcase in his scramble for the door.

Fletch had spent the afternoon popping back and forth between the press bus and the campaign bus.

Using the phone on the press bus, he had spent a long time talking with the governor's advance man, Willy Finn, in California, about the arrangements made for that day in Spiersville, that night in Farmingdale, the next day in Kimberly and Melville. Finn had nothing to say about the governor's Winslow speech, although he had already heard of it. He seemed sincerely upset by the death of Victor Robbins.

With the others Fletch visited Spiersville. He grabbed a bag of stale donuts from a drugstore, ate four of them, spent time with the local press, provided them with whatever material they requested. On the wall of a warehouse was scrawled: LIFE IS NO FUN. Fletch had first seen that message, in English, on walls and sidewalks in northern Europe in the early 1980s. After the Spiersville visit, it was discovered that someone had broken a window of the press bus with a rock.

During the hour-long ride to Farmingdale, Fletch played poker with Bill Dieckmann, Roy Filby, and Tony Rice. He won twenty-seven dollars.

In the corridor of the Farmingdale hotel, the doors to an elevator were open.

Hanrahan was in the elevator. He either smiled or grimaced at Fletch.

"Up?" Fletch asked.

Hanrahan didn't answer, just kept whatever that facial expression of his was.

A lady on the elevator finally said, "No, we're going down." She was wearing a purple cocktail dress and brown shoes.

Fletch pushed the button for the next elevator.

Walsh flung open the door of Room 1220 immediately Fletch knocked on it. "What's going on?" he asked.

Door closed, they stood in the short, dark corridor outside the bathroom. "Okay," Fletch answered. "I'll give the twenty-seven dollar back."

"Some foul-smelling, crude, filthy-looking reporter was in my room before I ever got here. He was in here when I arrived."

"A foul-smelling, crude, filthy-looking reporter?"

"Said he was from *Newsbill*, for Chrissake."

"Oh, *that* foul-smelling, crude, filthy-looking reporter. Hanrahan, by name. Michael J."

"He was waiting for me when the bellhop let me in. Sitting in that chair." Walsh stepped into the bedroom and pointed at one of the chairs near the window. "Smoking a cigar." The ashtray on the side table had a little cigar ash in it. "Bastard. Wanted to show me how very, very resourceful he is, I suppose. Privacy, locked doors don't mean a thing to Mr. *Newsbill*."

"He was trying to intimidate you."

"He doesn't intimidate me. He makes me damned mad."

Walsh was saying he was mad, but his eyes were not particularly angry. They appeared more restless, as if he would have preferred thinking about something else. His voice was not hot with anger, but more cold with annoyance.

Fletch was hearing a complaint being lodged more as a matter of form rather than from emotion.

"Michael J. Hanrahan is a foul-smelling, crude, filthy-looking bastard," Fletch agreed. "He writes for *Newsbill*. I wouldn't dignify him by calling him a reporter."

"I thought we had someone else from *Newsbill* — that thoroughly stupid woman, what's her name?"

"Mary Rice."

"Is she any relation to Tony?"

"No. Mary is writing for *Newsbill*. On the campaign supposedly, but I see her reports seldom get above the blatantly sensational. I mean, one report she did reported that one of Lee Allen Parke's great-great-great-grandfathers was a slave owner."

"Jeez."

"Meaningless stuff."

"Does *Newsbill* ever report from anywhere but the bedroom?"

"Bedrooms, bars, police courts. Runs pages of horoscopes. Stars on the stars. As news."

"Not only that," Walsh said, "but while I was downstairs I was attacked by some gorgeous broad who said she was a reporter for *Newsworld.*"

"Oh? What did she want?"

"A complete list of the names of everyone who was in my father's suite last night. Plus a complete list of names of all the people who might have had access to his suite last night. What's she looking for?"

"That's Fredericka Arbuthnot."

"Yeah. Arbuthnot. Since when is *Newsworld* raking smut?"

"You gotta understand, Walsh. Hanrahan and Arbuthnot are crime writers. That's about all they have in common, but that's what they are. That's their job. They report on crime."

"So what are they doing on our campaign bus?"

"A woman was murdered last night at the motel we were in."

"Aw, come on."

"Another woman was murdered at the Hotel Harris in Chicago while the campaign was there. She was found in a closet off a room being used by the press covering this campaign."

Walsh sighed. "Can't we deny campaign credentials to crime writers?"

"I've thought of it. Frankly, I think it would get their wind up. Make them more persistent. You can't deny there is something here, Walsh."

"Not much." Walsh glanced at his watch. "Dad wants us in his suite to watch the national news with him."

"What were Hanrahan's questions?"

"Didn't give him a chance to ask many. I yelled at him, yelled at the bellman, started to phone hotel security, yelled at him some more, called you."

"So what did he ask you?"

"Said he wanted to ask me about my military record."

"Your military record? What's that got to do with the price of beans?"

"I told him he could ask the Department of Defense and get my whole record in black and white." Walsh had straightened his greenish necktie and was putting on his greenish suit jacket. "Bastard. I didn't shove him through the door, but I had my fingers firmly on his back."

"Not a whole lot I can do about this, Walsh." Fletch opened the door. "The press has the right to inquire."

When they were in the corridor, Fletch tried the knob of the door to Walsh's room. The door was locked.

"Tell that bastard," Walsh said, heading for the elevator, "that if I ever find him in my room again, or the rooms of either of my parents, or of any staff member, I'll have him thrown in jail."

"Walsh," Fletch said, "he'd love that."

SEVENTEEN

"Referring to what he termed the New Reality, Governor Caxton Wheeler, campaigning in Winslow today, seems to have brought a whole new topic and tone to the presidential race. . . ."

Such was the lead on the national nightly news on all three commercial networks. The words differed slightly, but the melody was the same.

Barry Hines sat cross-legged on the floor in front of the three television sets he had set up in the governor's bedroom.

The governor sat in a side chair, watching all three sets. He was in his shirt sleeves, his tie around his collar not yet tied, his shoes off. Flash Grasselli was hanging the governor's clothes in the closet. Fletch was sitting on the edge of the bed. Walsh was standing.

"Victor Robbins died in vain," Walsh quipped. "Upton didn't get the news lead."

"No," the governor said, "he didn't die in vain."

In the living room of the suite, the other side of the closed bedroom door, Lee Allen Parke and some of his volunteers were pouring drinks and chatting up local celebrities. They were waiting, while the governor dressed, to have a private moment with him over a drink before escorting him and Mrs. Wheeler to the mayor's dinner.

For once the networks let the governor's speech run — heavily edited, of course, almost identically edited — but at least without the instant voice-over, a reporter's paraphrase of what the governor said. "Christianity has had two thousand years to tie this world together . . . and it has not done so. Islam has had six hundred years to tie this world together . . . and it has not done so. American democracy has had two hundred years to tie this world together . . . and it has not done so. Communism has had nearly one hundred years to

ie this world together . . . and it has not done so. . . . Technology
brings us closer together than any Biblical brothers! Technology makes
us more interdependent than any scheme of capital and labor! Technology is integrating the people of this earth where love and legislation
have failed! This is the new reality!" On all three channels The Man
Who stood hatless, in his overcoat, on a platform, a corner of the
forty-eight-starred flag and the facade of the First National Bank of
Winslow behind him.

The governor had given much the same speech in Spiersville that
afternoon. "You may not approve, Walsh," he had said, "but by repeating what I said I will prove I meant to say it."

"The President did not comment immediately on the governor's
remarks," the network anchorpersons all reported.

Standing at the side of the bedroom, Walsh commented, "The old
boy's waiting to see which way the wind blows."

"A White House spokesman did say the governor's remarks were of
such a serious nature that the President wants time to consider them.
However, Senator Graves, campaigning in the same primary election,
had this to say:"

"Fools rush in," said Barry.

Senator Graves's wide face filled the screens, one after another, his
strident voice cutting across America. "Did I hear Governor Caxton
Wheeler say Christianity and democracy don't work? Well, I don't
believe that. And I don't think most of the people in America believe
that!"

The people in the bedroom of Governor Caxton Wheeler, including
the governor himself, were absolutely silent. Walsh visibly swallowed
hard.

The news anchorperson said, "Senator Upton could not be reached
for comment since he was flying to Pennsylvania this afternoon, where
his old friend and campaign aide died in an automobile accident this
morning."

"See?" the governor said quietly. "Ol' Vic didn't die in vain. Kept
Upton from having to make a statement before he was ready."

Studded with commercials, the news programs continued: Victor
Robbins's car being lifted from the icy Susquehanna River by crane;
eulogistic quotes on Victor Robbins from the President of the United
States and most of the presidential candidates (the words differed
slightly but the melodies were the same); the President in the Oval
Office signing a bill obliging a tribe of Native Americans to exploit
the natural resources of their reservation; more film of the hockey riot

the night before, with interviews with players and fans. ("Someone
punched me," each said. No one said, "I punched someone.") One
network showed Governor Caxton Wheeler handing out coins to the
children at Conroy School during the body of the telecast, with expert
negative comments; a second used the item as a soft-news last feature,
the third did not refer to it at all, but instead, for its last feature, used
film of a monkey in Louisiana who had learned to write *hokku* on a
computer.

None referred to the death of Alice Elizabeth Shields the night
before.

"I don't know, Dad." Walsh shook his head. "I don't know."

"What don't you know?" The governor's voice was challenging.

"You did say something about Christianity and democracy not working."

"I did not!" the governor expostulated. "I said neither idea, no idea,
has succeeded in integrating the world, the people of the world, as
technology is doing. Dammit!"

"There's a difference between ideas and delivery systems for ideas,"
Walsh said sharply.

"There's a difference between ideas and facts," the governor said.
"The people of the world will be better served with a few facts."

Barry Hines was walking along the floor on his knees, turning off
the three television sets. Quietly, in the tone of a very young person,
he said, "I think it was a good speech. What the governor said is true,
when you think about it. Don't get thrown, Walsh, just because Graves
took a cheap shot."

"Yeah," said Fletch. "You know how deep Graves is."

The door to the living room opened.

Doris Wheeler entered.

She wore an evening gown, with a taffeta wrap across her big
shoulders. She closed the door behind her.

She took a step forward with all the presence of a Wagnerian
soprano.

"Caxton," she said solemnly, "you've just lost the presidency."

The governor's face whitened. "Wait a damned minute!"

"Wait for what?" Doris Wheeler stepped nearer the center of the
big bedroom. "For you to make an even bigger fool of yourself?"

Walsh faded into the shadows at the side of the room. Flash Grasselli
retreated into the bathroom.

Doris addressed her husband as if they were in a room alone. "Everything you've done today has come as a complete surprise to me.

Handing out money to schoolchildren. To *some* schoolchildren. Did Barry tell you what I had to say about that? Keeping Congresswoman Flaherty off the platform in Winslow. Don't tell me you didn't do that on purpose."

The governor looked at Barry, still kneeling on the floor, then back at his wife. It was clear Barry had not transmitted Mrs. Wheeler's criticism to Governor Wheeler.

"And what is this utter crap you uttered in Winslow?"

The governor narrowed his eyes. "Is it crap?"

Doris Wheeler's voice became that of a reasonable lecturer. "Caxton, you know damned well the farmers and merchants of Winslow, of the U.S.A., do not want to hear about the Third World. They want to hear about their taxes, their health programs, their Social Security, their defense, their crop subsidies. The voter is a totally selfish animal! Every time the voter hears the name of a foreign country, he thinks it's going to cost him money."

"Doris, some things need to be said."

"And what," she asked in an exasperated tone, "is this utter crap about technology?"

Suddenly the governor, still in his chair, necktie still undone, was looking tired.

"You trying to be a statesman, Caxton?" she shouted.

"Mother," Walsh said hesitantly. "You don't want people in the living room hearing you."

"Why not?" she asked in the same loud tone. "They might as well hear! Governor Caxton Wheeler's campaign for the presidency of the United States is over! They might as well finish their drinks here, put their checkbooks in their pockets, go home, and offer their support to Simon Upton or Joe Graves!"

The governor's eyes flicked to Barry Hines as if for support. "Graves just took a cheap shot . . ."

Barry Hines had left a half-empty soft-drink cup on top of the television. With the back of her hand, Doris Wheeler slapped the cup off the television onto the rug.

Governor Wheeler looked at the brown fluid bubbling on the blue rug. Then, wearily, he stood up and went to the mirror and began to tie his tie.

Barry Hines was standing by the door to the living room.

"Caxton," Doris Wheeler said, taking only a step toward his back. "The American people don't trust technology. They don't understand technology. Technology is taking their jobs away from them."

"Come on," the governor said tiredly. "The American people are in love with their technology. Their computer games and toys, their cable televisions. They even have — what do you call 'em? — those things on their tractors, in their pickup trucks —"

"You scrape a layer of skin off your average American," Doris persisted, "and he'll still tell you all technology is the instrument of the devil."

"Oh, Doris."

"And you're up there like a big fool saying technology replaces religion?"

"I said nothing of the sort."

"Technology replaces democracy?"

As he turned from the mirror, he was buttoning the cuffs of his shirt. The muscles in his jaw were working hard.

"You've just quit, Caxton. You've just retired from politics! You retired me!" she shouted. "You self-destructed in one day!"

"It's all our fault," Walsh said. He bit his lower lip. "We were overimpressed by Victor Robbins's death this morning. With the primary in a couple of days, we were trying to make the nightly news."

"I don't need excuses made for me, son," the governor said with annoyance. "I said what I felt like saying, and saying it felt right."

"Well, it certainly cost enough for you to feel good." Her eyes were as hard as a rooster's.

"What real harm has it done?" the governor asked. He called on Fletch: "What's the reaction on the press bus?"

"I don't think they've digested it yet. Not really. I think most of them are just glad to hear something new."

"Sure," scoffed Doris Wheeler. "They'd be delighted to publish Caxton's suicide note."

"Actually —" Fletch hesitated. "Andrew Esty did head for the airport. Said he was leaving the campaign. Called you a godless person."

"Caxton!" exclaimed Doris. "Do you know the circulation of the *Daily Gospel*? Do you realize what that readership means to us? To this campaign?"

"Oh, Esty!" The governor snorted. "Jesus Christ wouldn't have pleased him. Jesus washed the feet of a whore."

Doris Wheeler's face was rising up the crimson scale. "How come you do these stupid things without even consulting me? How come you stood up on your hind legs in Winslow, and again in Spiersville, and spouted a pseudo-profound, pseudo-philosophical, pseudo-states-manlike speech on the state of the whole world, without consulting me?"

"People are waiting," the governor said.

"Believe me," Doris Wheeler said, brushing Barry Hines aside and opening the door to the living room, "nothing more that is stupid and self-destructive is going to happen today. Not with me at his side. If you all can't stop him from making a fool of himself, I can."

Leaving the room, she left the door open.

The governor swung the door almost closed again. "Gentlemen," he said to Barry, Walsh, Fletch, "while greeting people in the living room, please drop casually into your conversations that we were just playing the television rather loudly in here. What's on television at this hour, Barry?"

Barry thought. "Most places, reruns of 'M*A*S*H,' Archie Bunker, and 'The Muppets.' "

"Right," said the governor. "We were watching a rerun of Archie Bunker while I dressed, with the volume on loud."

In the living room, meeting and greeting went on. Fletch found himself talking to the publisher and chief editorial writer of *The Farmingdale Views*. They wanted to be sure the governor believed absolutely in freedom of the press and had some ripe things to say about a certain federal judge; Fletch assured them the governor believed in freedom of the press without reservation and did not intend to appoint federal judges without thorough research into their local backgrounds.

The look of mild alarm and polite curiosity on everyone's face when the governor entered the living room dissipated slowly as more drinks were poured and Archie Bunker was mentioned.

Doris Wheeler was never still. She kept moving around the room, her eyes apparently on everyone's face simultaneously, appearing to hear, to agree with everything.

The governor stood with his hands in his pockets, chatting with a slowly changing group of people around him, making pleasantries, laughing easily.

Walsh was in earnest conversation near the bar table with five or six people in their twenties.

After a few moments, the governor came over to Fletch, gripped him by the elbow and, nodding at them kindly, faced him away from the publisher and the editorial writer. "Fletch. Find Dr. Thom for me. Have him come up here. No black bag. He'll know what I need."

The hand holding Fletch's elbow shook ever so slightly.
Fletch said, "Yes, sir."

EIGHTEEN

"Hello, Ms. Arbuthnot?" Fletch said into his bedroom telephone.
"Yes?"
"Glad I caught you in."
"In what?"
"The shower?"
"Just got out of it."
"And did you sing your 'Hoo boy, now I wash my left knee, Hoo boy, now I wash my right knee' song?"
"Oh, you know about that."
"Used to hear you through the wall in Virginia. Key of C in the morning, F at night."
"I take a cold shower in the morning."
"I was just about to order up a sandwich and a bottle of milk to my room. I could order up two sandwiches."
"Yes, you could, Fletch. If you want two sandwiches."
"I only want one sandwich."
"Then order only one."
"You're not getting the point."
"I'm trying not to be as presumptuous as some people I know."
"You see, I could order up one sandwich for me. And one for a friend. Who might come along and eat with me."
"Entirely reasonable. Do you have a friend?"
"I was thinking you might be that friend, seeing you've taken a shower and all."
"Nope. I wouldn't be."
"What makes you so certain?"
"I'm certain."
"We could eat and slurp milk and maybe even we could sit around and sing 'Great Green Globs of Greasy Grimy Gopher's Guts.' "
"Nope. We couldn't."
"Aw, Freddie —"

"Look, Fletch, would you mind if I hung up now? I'm expecting a phone call from Chicago. Then I have to call Washington."

"Okay," Fletch said. "I'll call you back after you change your mind."

He called room service and ordered up two club sandwiches and a quart of milk.

His shoes were already off. He took off his shirt and fell on his back on the bed.

His bedroom was virtually identical to the room he'd had the night before, to the same centimeter of space, to the autumnal, nondirtying color scheme, to the wall mirror tilted to reflect the bed, to the heating system that wouldn't cool off, to the number of too-small towels in the bathroom, to the television he had discovered produced only pink pictures. The painting on the wall was of mountaintops instead of a sailboat. For a moment Fletch thought of American standardization and the interchangeability of motel rooms, motels, airports, whole cities, national news telecasts, and presidential candidates.

The bedside phone rang. Fletch said into the phone: "Knew you'd change your mind. Ordered you a club sandwich."

A man's voice said: "Nice of you. Can you have it sent to Iowa?"

"I suppose so," agreed Fletch. "But who's in Iowa?"

"I am," the man's voice said. "Rondoll James."

Fletch sat up on the bed. "I. M. Fletcher, Mr. James."

"Call me James, please. My parents spotted me with a first name no one's ever spelled right — Rondoll, you know? like nothing else you can think of — so early on I gave it back to the Registry of Births."

"I know the problem."

"No one ever spelled your first name right either?"

"Everyone did. You want your job back?"

"Not right away. I'm in Iowa for the funeral of Vic Robbins."

"He died in Pennsylvania."

"His home is in Iowa. His body's being flown here tonight."

"You good friends?"

"The best. Vic taught me much over the years. Who wrote Caxton's remarks on Vic's death? Walsh?"

"Yeah. The governor was in a factory when we got the news."

"The statement would have been a hell of a lot warmer, if I had been there. Sometimes these guys forget who really runs American politics. So how do you like my job?"

"I'm not very good at it."

"Hey, you got the lead on all the network news shows tonight. No bad, first day."

"Yeah, but didn't the story do more harm than good?"

"Get the space, baby. Get the network time and the newspaper space. Builds familiarity. Recognition of the candidate, you know. What the candidate is actually saying or doing is of secondary importance, you know?"

"Did anything like what he was saying come across to the people, James, do you think?"

"I'm not sure. He said technology is tying us together, integrating us, maybe making us more sensitive to each other, maybe even increasing the sense of responsibility for each other. That about it?"

"Yeah. I think so."

"Wonderful part of it was, I was sitting in an airport bar about a thousand miles away from where he was saying it, and I heard him and saw him say it. Sort of proves his point, don't you think?"

"What did other people in the bar think of it?"

"Not much. One guy said, 'There's ol' Caxton spouting off again. Why doesn't he tell me where my wife can get a job?' Gin drinker. The bartender? Typical. No good bartender ever takes sides. Costs him tips."

"Guess it'll be a day or two before anyone digests what the governor was trying to say."

"Longer than that, I. M., longer than that. Something ol' Vic taught me, and it's always proved to be true: statesmanship has no place on a political campaign. A campaign is punch and duck, punch and duck. Fast footwork, you know? Always smiling. The voters want to see fast action. Their attention won't hold for anything more. From day to day, give 'em happy film, and short, reassuring statements. If you really try to say anything, really ask them to stop and think, they'll hate you for it. They can't think, you know? Being asked makes us feel inferior. We don't like to feel inferior to our candidates. Against the democratic ideal, you know? The candidate's just got to keep giving the impression he's a man of the people — no better than they are, just doin' a different job. No one is ever elected in this country on the basis of what he really thinks. The candidate is elected on the basis of thousands of different, comfortable small impressions, not one of which really asks the voters to think."

"How about handing coins out to kids. Was that 'comfortable'? How did that come across?"

"Just fine."

"Yes?"

"You bet. Anytime you can get psychiatrists on television speaking against your candidate, immediately your boy is up three percentage points in the popularity polls. Psychiatrists shrink people, you know? People resent being shrunk."

"You're making me feel better."

"Don't intend to, particularly. And it's not why I'm calling. But as long as we're talking, take this advice: any time you see ol' Caxton looking like he's about to say something profound, stick a glove in his mouth."

"Appreciate the advice. Why are you calling?"

"Why, sir, to tell you how much I love Caxton Wheeler. And explain to you what I've done for him lately."

"What have you done for him lately?"

"Put myself out of a job, thank you. If not out of a whole career. Sacrificed myself on the altar of Athena. Wasn't she the goddess of war?"

"Oh, yeah: the broad standing in her backyard with a frying pan. Great statue. Seen it dozens of times, as a kid. The governor told me —"

"To hell with what Caxton told you. I'll tell you." Suddenly whatever James had imbibed in that airport bar became audible in his voice. "I've been with Caxton twenty-three years. I've been his eyes and his ears and his legs and his mouth for twenty-three years, night and day, weekends included."

"I know."

"I want you to know I love that man. I admire him and love him above all others. I know more about him than his wife, his son, anybody. He's a good guy. I'd do anything for him, including sacrificing myself, which I just did."

Fletch waited. Eulogies to a relationship never need encouragement from the listener.

James continued: "Caxton ought to be President of the United States. I believe that more than I believe I'm sitting here talking to you. But Doris Wheeler, in case you haven't discovered it, is his weak spot. She's horrible. There's no other way to say it. Horrible. She has no more regard for people than a crocodile. If anything around her moves, she lashes at it and bites it, bites deep. She's been lashin' at Caxton, bitin' him for thirty years now."

"James, a husband and wife — not our business."

"Not our business unless one of them is running for public office.

Then it becomes our business. You ever hear her talk to a volunteer, or a chartered pilot?"

"Not yet."

"Or a junior reporter, or to her son, or to Caxton himself?"

Fletch didn't answer.

"The word is bitch. Doris Wheeler is an absolute bitch. Sometimes I've been convinced the woman is insane. She becomes violent. She's Caxton's biggest liability, and he won't admit it."

"He knows something —"

"He won't admit it. Always covering up for her. Over the years I've talked to him a thousand times, trying to get him to restrain the bitch. Even divorce her, get rid of her. He never listened to me. And she's getting worse, with all this pressure of the campaign on her. I couldn't keep covering up for her, I. M. I just couldn't. You understand that?"

"Yeah."

"I couldn't cover up for her anymore. Stories were beginning to get out about the way she bullies the governor, the staff, everybody. The way everything either has to go her way, or else she'll kick everybody in the crotch. *Her* campaign. *She'll* run it. And everybody better fall in behind her, or life won't be worth living for anybody."

"The visit to the children's burn center —"

"Was just one of a hundred things. She knew what she was doing. Walsh told her she had to go. Her own secretary, Sully, told her she had to go. Barry and Willy arranged another time for her to meet her friends for indoor tennis. She just walked off and played tennis."

"Why?"

"Because she always knows best."

"Yeah, but why? In this particular instance, so obviously stupid —"

"First, she's convinced she can get away with anything. Whatever happens, it's someone else's fault. Second: vanity. Wouldn't you love to appear among your old cronies, your peers, and play tennis with them as the wife of a presidential candidate?"

"The way I play tennis —"

"Listen —"

"Wait a minute. Wasn't she also raising money for the campaign playing tennis? Badly needed money?"

"I said: we had already arranged for her to play tennis two days later. She didn't even cancel the burn center. Just got in the car and went to play tennis. Look what happened. The nurses got all the kids into their wheelchairs, their roll-beds, into this special reception room.

Photographers were there, reporters. The bitch never showed up. You realize the pain she caused? You don't move kids with burns, and then go play *tennis*!"

"So why does the governor blame you for it?"

"He can't blame his wife. He never blames his wife. Always before, I've covered up for her. Done a deal with the photographers, you know? Made some half-assed explanation, said, 'If you don't report this, I'll provide you with photo opportunities you never dreamed of — the governor in the shower stark naked smoking a cigar, you'll win the Pulitzer Prize,' you know? This time I couldn't do that, I. M. Wouldn't."

" 'Wouldn't.' "

"I'd had enough of it. The governor wouldn't listen to me, all these years. The situation was getting more serious. She's getting worse. His chances of getting to the White House are getting better and better, and she's ruining them. So I let the situation get reported. I thought maybe if Caxton saw what all this looked like in the press, for once, he'd at least try to restrain the bitch."

"What makes you think he can?"

"He has to. Somebody has to. Caxton Wheeler shouldn't be President of the United States because his wife's a nut?"

"They've come a long way together, James."

"That they have — a long way to fall over a cliff."

"If she's so impossible, why has he stuck with her? Divorce wasn't invented Sunday, you know."

"Want three good reasons why he hasn't divorced her?"

"Yeah. Gimme three."

"First, divorce still doesn't go over so big with the voters. Despite President Ronald Reagan. People can still be found to say, 'If a man can't run his own house, how do you expect him to run the White House?' "

"That's one."

"Two, she's got the money. She is a wealthy, wealthy lady in her own right. Her daddy horned in on the oil business and made a barrel of money. A politician's life is risky and expensive, you know. Nothing lubricates a politician's life better than oil."

"That's two."

"Three, I deeply suspect Caxton loves the bitch. Can you believe that? Don't ask me how or why. Sometimes people whom you'd think would know better actually do love the last person in the world they should love. I've known lots of jerks like that. Their wives are ruining them with every word and gesture and all these jerks say is, 'Where

would I be without sweet ol' honey-pie?' Love, I. M., is as blind a:
justice. Maybe you've noticed."

"And just as elusive."

"Boy, am I glad my wife ran away with her psychiatrist fifteen year:
ago. There was a broad who needed shrinking. What an inflammatior
she was."

"I don't know, James. What am I supposed to do?"

"Carry on, brother. Carry on. I just want you to know what's between Caxton and me."

"His wife."

"I love him. I admire him. I want to see him President of the United
States. I'd do anything to see that. Anything. What I'm saying is, fee!
free to call me anytime about anything."

"Thank you."

"They threw me over, but that doesn't matter. I'll still do anything
I can for Caxton."

Fletch soon discovered that all he need do to make his phone ring
was to put the receiver down into the cradle.

Immediately after he hung up from trying to make clear things that
were not at all clear to himself for a rewrite editor at *Newsweek* magazine,
he found himself answering the phone to his old Marine buddy, Alston
Chambers.

"Nice to hear a friendly voice," Fletch said.

"What's happening, Fletch?"

"Damned if I know."

"Just heard on cable news you've been made acting press representative for Governor Wheeler's campaign. I saw you on the tube."

" 'Acting press secretary'? I guess so."

"Why are you doing that? You gone establishment?"

"Walsh called me late at night. Said he needed help desperately. I
mean, he convinced me he was desperate."

"Wow, a presidential campaign. What's it like, Fletch?"

"Unreal, man. Totally unreal."

"I believe you. On television you were wearing a coat and tie."

"Alston, there have been a couple of murders."

"What do you mean, 'murders'? Real murders?"

"A couple of women beaten to death. One of them was strangled.
They weren't really a part of the campaign, but I think somebody
traveling with the campaign had something to do with it."

"You're kidding."

" 'Fraid not."

"Caxton Wheeler as Jack the Ripper. You're giving a whole new meaning to the phrase *presidential assassin*, Fletch."

"Very funny."

"Haven't seen anything about this in the news."

"We're trying to keep it out of the news. At least, everybody's telling me to keep it out of the news."

"Having had opportunity to observe you for a long time, Fletcher, I can say you're not good at keeping things out of the news. Especially concerning murder and other skullduggery."

"You wouldn't believe this situation, Alston. It's like being on a fast train, and people keep falling off it, and no one will pull the emergency cord. Everytime someone falls off, everyone says, 'Well, that's behind us.' "

"You're right. I don't get it."

"It's just an unreal world. There's so much power. So much prestige. Everything's moving so fast. The cops are so much in awe of the candidate and his party."

"Yeah, but murder's murder."

"Listen, Alston, a lady gets thrown off the motel roof right above the candidate's room, right above where the press have their rooms. And in a half hour the mayor shows up and says to the highest-ranking member of the campaign he can get close to something like, 'Now, don't let my cops bother you.' And he says to the press, 'Please don't besmirch the image of my city by making a big national story of this purely local, unfortunate incident.' "

"Yeah, but Wheeler. What does the candidate himself say?"

"He shrugs and says, 'There are sirens everywhere I go. I'm a walking police emergency.' "

"And Walsh?"

"Walsh says, 'A local matter. We'll be gone by morning.' "

"Taking the murderer with you. Is that what you think?"

"I'm trying to get the governor to permit an investigation. He's convinced the investigation would become the story of the campaign, and ruin his chances for the presidency."

"So ol' Fletch, boy investigative reporter who took an early retirement somehow, is investigating all by himself."

"My hands are tied. I can't go around asking the who-what-where-when-why questions. If I did that, I'd find myself with an airplane ticket home in about ten minutes."

"But you're in there trying, right?"

"Subtly, yes. I'm trying to get to know these people. Besides Walsh, I really only know a couple: Fredericka Arbuthnot, Roy Filby —"

"You'd better hurry up. Two murders in a pattern usually mean a third, a fourth . . ."

"I'm doin' my best, Mr. Persecutor. It's like trying to put out a fire in a circus tent, you know? I can't get anybody to admit there is a fire."

"When I started trying to get you on the phone, Fletch, my intention was to congratulate you on your new job. By the time you answered the phone, I was saying to myself, 'What's the barefoot boy with cheek doin' explaining the establishment to us peasants?' "

"I like Caxton Wheeler. I want to solve this damned thing."

"What does he want to be President for anyway? If I had his wife's money, I'd buy a whole country for myself."

"A campaign sure looks different from the inside. On the outside it's all charm and smiles and positive statements. On the inside, it's all tension, arguments —"

"And murder?"

"In this case, yes."

"Sometime, when you're talking to Walsh, ask him why he left us so suddenly. I've always been curious about that."

"What do you mean?"

"Don't you remember? After we spent those three days tied to the tops of the trees like cuckoo birds, a few days after we got back to base camp, Lieutenant Wheeler suddenly went home."

"He got sent stateside."

"I know. But how and why? It wasn't time for him to get rowed home. We all knew that."

"How? Because his dad had political pull. Why? Because his dad had political pull. What's the mystery? Walsh didn't have to be in the front lines at all. His dad was a congressman."

"We never knew what happened to Lieutenant Wheeler."

"He had seen enough action."

"We all had."

"Alston, at that point any of us would have pulled strings to get out of there. If we had strings. You know it. Our dads weren't politicians."

"With rich wives."

"So tell me about yourself. How do you like being chief persecutor?"

"In California, Fletch, we call ourselves prosecutors. And I'm not chief."

"Sent any woebegones to jail lately?"

"Two yesterday. No outstanding warrants on you, though. I check first thing every morning."

"Haven't been in California lately."

"Well, if you ever really get to be a member of the establishment, Fletch, come on back. California can always use a few more people who wear suits."

The two-hundred-year-old man from room service apologized for being so slow, telling Fletch the hotel was full of reporters following the campaign of "that Caxton Wheeler. Sure wish he'd get elected. Got a cousin named Caxton. First name, too."

"Hello, Freddie?" Fletch had picked up the phone before the man from room service was fully through the door.

"Who's calling, please?"

"Dammit, Freddie."

"Oh, hello, dammit."

"I'm calling to tell you your sandwich is ready."

"Ready for what?"

"Ready to be eaten."

"So eat it."

"Dammit, Freddie, you used to be a nice, aggressive woman."

"Aggressive toward a sandwich?"

"Toward me! I'm not a sandwich! What happened?"

"Your job happened."

"You don't like my job? Neither do I."

"Fletcher, what would you think of a journalist who became too friendly with the press representative of a presidential candidate, upon whose campaign she's reporting?"

"Oh."

"What would you think?"

"Not much."

"You mean plenty, but not good."

"Gee, it's lonely here at the top."

"See? We agree on something."

"I'll quit! I'll quit right now! I've been looking for an excuse."

"What excuse have you got?"

"Wasting food, obviously. Can't waste this good sandwich. Think of all the starving children in Beverly Hills with nothing to eat but Sweet Wheat."

"Good night, Fletch. Sweet dreams."

"Aw. . . ."

*   *   *

Fletch first ate one sandwich, and then the other, and drank the whole bottle of milk.

His phone rang continuously. Members of the press from around the world were calling him, asking for background to and interpretation of Caxton Wheeler's Winslow speech. Through mouthfuls of ham and chicken and bacon and lettuce and tomato and mayonnaise, Fletch said again and again that there was no background to the governor's speech; that the speech said exactly what it said, no more, no less.

The phone rang while he washed. It rang while he was putting on his shoes, his shirt, and his jacket.

It was ringing when he left the room.

NINETEEN

"It's none of my business, but — "

"You're right," Bill Dieckmann snapped. Sitting at the bar, he didn't even look up from his beer.

"Just wondering if I can help." The bartender brought Fletch a beer. "Does whatever happened to you on the bus today happen often?"

"None of your business."

"Have you been to a doctor about it?"

"None of your business."

"Agreed," Fletch said. "Let me know if ever I can be of help." He looked around the bar. All hotel bars are interchangeable, too. Even the people in them are interchangeable: the morose, lonely businessmen, the keyed-up, long-haul truck drivers, the few locals who are there solely for the booze. "Where is everyone?" Fletch asked. There were only a few campaign types in the bar.

"In their rooms, I guess," Bill answered. "Not getting anything to eat. At the mayor's dinner, not getting anything to eat. Betsy is at the 4-H Club dinner, trailing Walsh. She's probably getting something to eat. Solov's in his room, watching cable television." Bill grinned. "He's not getting anything to eat, either."

"Does that guy ever take off his overcoat?" Fletch asked.

"No, no. He was born in it. You can tell he grew up inside it. Each time *Pravda* sends him out of the country his managing editor just moves the buttons for him."

"Time they moved the buttons again."

Dr. Thom entered. He put his black bag on the bar beside Fletch.

"Here's a doctor now," Fletch said brightly.

"Best bedside manner in the country," Bill said. "If you don't have a temperature when Dr. Thom arrives, you will when he leaves. Good for business, right, Doc?"

"Journalists," Dr. Thom said. "If any journalist ever spoke well of me, I'd instantly overdose on a purgative."

"Looks like you already have," Bill said.

"It's a medical fact," Dr. Thom said to Fletch, "that all journalists are born with congenital diarrhea. Double Scotch, no ice," he said to the bartender.

"I'm a journalist," Fletch said.

"I trust you vacated yourself before you entered the bar."

"Mr. Fletcher?" A woman was standing at Fletch's elbow.

"At least a journalist has to empty himself," Bill Dieckmann burped. "Doctors are born vacuous, and vacuous they remain."

"Yes?" Fletch had turned to the woman.

"Are you Mr. Fletcher?"

"Yes. But you can call me Mr. Jones."

"If only," Dr. Thom intoned ever so slowly, "journalists would vacate themselves privately."

"I'm Judy Nadich," the woman said. "Feature writer for *Farmingdale Views.*"

"Great stuff you're writing," Fletch said. And then laughed. "I'm sure."

Judy grinned. "You liked my last piece? On how to repair cracked teacups?"

"Thought it was great," Fletch laughed. "Read it several times."

"I knew that one would get national attention," Judy said.

"Sure," Fletch said. "Everyone's got cracked teacups."

"Hey," Judy said. "Seriously. I'm trying to get an interview with Doris Wheeler."

"I think you're supposed to see Ms. Sullivan about that."

"I've asked and asked and she says no."

"Why?"

"She says there's no time on Mrs. Wheeler's schedule for a full, sit-down interview. What she means is that the readership of the *Far-*

mingdale Views isn't worth an hour of Mrs. Wheeler's time. She's right, of course. But it's important to me."

" 'Course it is." Despite her brown hair tied in a knot behind her head, her thick sweater, her thick skirt, her thick stockings and shoes, Judy Nadich was sort of cute. "What do you want me to do?"

"Get me an interview with Mrs. Wheeler," Judy said. "In return for my body."

"Simple enough deal," Fletch said. "Tit for tat."

"Tits for that," Judy said.

"I've never met Ms. Sullivan. Never laid eyes on her."

"You could try."

"You want me to call her?"

"Yes, please. She's in Room 940."

"Would you be content with a follow-along?"

"What's that?"

"You just follow along with Mrs. Wheeler for an hour or two, you know? Up close. You don't really interview her. Report what she does and says to other people. 'An hour in the life of Doris Wheeler' sort of thing. Done right, makes damned good reading."

"Sure. Anything."

"Okay. I'll call Ms. Sullivan. Watch my beer, will you?"

"Sure thing."

Dr. Thom was saying ". . . journalists are the only people on earth asked not to donate their remains to science. It's been discovered that journalists' hearts are so small, they can be transplanted only into their brethren mice."

"Keep these guys separated, will you?" Fletch asked Judy.

"Sure." She climbed onto Fletch's barstool. "Bet you guys don't know how to repair a cracked teacup . . ."

"Ms. Sullivan? This is Fletcher."

The first few times Fletch had tried Room 940 he had gotten a busy signal.

"What do you want?" Her voice was surprisingly deep.

"Hello," said Fletch. "We haven't met."

"Let's keep it that way. As long as we can."

"What?" Fletch said. "No camaraderie? No *esprit de corps*? No we're-all-in-this-spaceship-together sort of attitude?"

"Get to it." Her voice was almost a growl.

"No simple cooperation?"

"Yeah, I'll cooperate with you," she said. "You stay on your side of the fence and I'll stay on my side. Okay?"

"Not okay. There's a young lady here, a reporter from the *Farmingdale Views*. She's spending tomorrow morning with Mrs. Wheeler. Just observing."

"Over my dead body."

"That can be arranged."

"She's a stupid, soft, little local bitch. Who are you to make arangements for Doris?"

"I'm giving her a press pass to spend tomorrow morning with Doris Wheeler, close up, with photos. You don't like it, you can stuff it up your nose."

"Fuck you, Fletcher."

"Yeah, you say that," Fletch said, "but what are you going to do?"

Dr. Thom and Bill Dieckmann were gone from the bar. Judy Nadich sat over an empty glass.

"What happened to my beer?" Fletch asked.

"I drank it," Judy said.

"Was it good?"

"No."

He handed her the press pass he had written out and signed on a piece of note paper. "Here," he said. "You're spending tomorrow morning observing Mrs. Wheeler close up. Don't get too much in the way."

"Thanks." Judy looked dubiously at the handwritten note. "Sullivan was nice about it, huh?"

"Sure. Why not? Mrs. Wheeler will be very glad to have you with her."

Flash Grasselli had come over from the table at the back of the bar and was standing behind Fletch.

"Do I get to give you my body, now?" Judy asked.

"What town am I in?" Fletch asked.

"Farmingdale, dummy."

"Next time I come through Farmingdale," Fletch said.

"You rejecting me?"

"No," Fletch said. "Just don't believe in prepayment."

"Mr. Fletcher, may I buy you a beer?" Flash asked.

"Sure," Fletch said. "Hope it's better than the last one. Judy here says my last beer wasn't very good."

"Why are you called Flash?"

Flash Grasselli and Fletch had taken two fresh beers to Flash's small table at the back of the dark hotel bar. Judy Nadich had left with her tote bag to prepare herself for her morning observing Dori Wheeler.

"From boxing."

"Were you fast?"

Flash seemed to be chewing his beer. "I'm not sure."

Flash had the eyebrow cuts of a boxer, but his eyes were steady and his nose had been born pug.

"They're always kidding me, the reporters," Flash said. "They come to me for real information about the Wheelers, and I never give them any. I just talk about the old days."

"What kind of things do they ask you?" Fletch asked.

"Oh, you know. The governor's life." Flash looked directly at Fletch. "His disappearances."

Fletch knew he was being handed a line of inquiry. "He disappears? What do you mean, he disappears?"

"His fishing trips. Sometimes they're called that. He doesn't know anything about fishing. So they call them hunting trips. The governor wouldn't shoot a rabbit if he was starving. You know." Flash smiled. "The trips the governor takes with those prostitutes he hires. His week-long sex orgies. You know about them. His drunken benders. He spends them in the mob's hideaways."

Fletch felt a sudden chill. "What the hell are you talking about?"

"Everybody knows." Flash grinned. "All the press. His drunken benders. He goes to consult with the mob. Sometimes they supply him all the women he wants. He disappears for days at a time. Everybody knows that. I go with him."

"The governor can't just disappear."

"He does as governor. He did as congressman. He's always done it. A few days at a time."

"Nuts. The governor just can't disappear. Be too easy to follow him."

"Impossible to follow him. He sees to that. I see to that. Trick is, there is no clue as to when it's going to happen. In the middle of the night, two or three in the morning, he rings my phone over the garage and says, 'Time to go, Flash.' I say, 'Yes, sir,' get the car out, and he's waiting by the back door. Once he even excused himself from a University Board of Governors meeting to go to the bathroom, see? And came out to me in the car and said, 'Time to go, Flash.' I always know what he means."

"And the press knows about this?"

"The great untold story. They don't dare report it, because they don't know what to report. Nobody can get any evidence. Am I saying that right? Nobody can get any evidence as to where he goes on these trips, or what he does. I'm the only one who knows." Flash sucked on his beer.

"Am I supposed to ask?"

"Governor had a girl friend, before he ever married. Barbara some-thing-or-other. She was a designer of some kind — hats or clothes or something. I guess she had this cabin from her father. Inherited it from him. She and the governor used to spend time there, a long time ago, when they were kids, their early twenties, when he was in law school, I guess. She died. She left it to him. I guess it wasn't a sudden death. They knew she was going to die. No one has ever known he owns this cabin. Big secret of his life."

"So when he disappears he goes to this cabin? Alone?"

"I go with him. I know every route in and out of that place, east, north, south, and west. Every timber road. I could drive to that place blindfolded. And no one has ever succeeded in following me."

"You're talking about a cabin over thirty years old."

"Older than that. A lot older than that. It really rots. Rickety. Wet, cold. Falling apart. I try to do a few things when I'm there, keep it propped up. He never notices. Roof leaks. Fireplace smokes. Pipes are rotted. I bring water up in buckets from the lake. No real work has been done on it in over thirty years. I can't do much. What do I know? I'm a city kid."

Fletch watched the governor's driver–valet without saying any-thing.

Flash sat forward. "And you know what he does when he gets there? No broads, no booze. No mobsters. Just me. There's a picture of this girl, Barbara, on the bureau in the bedroom."

"Is she beautiful?"

Flash shrugged. "Not especially. She looks like a nice lady. Nice smile."

"So what does he do?"

"He goes to bed. He sleeps. He goes on a sleep orgy. We get there, immediately he goes to bed. It's a big, soft bed, usually a little damp. He never seems to mind the damp. I try to air out the little bed in the other room. He sleeps fifteen, sixteen hours. When he wakes up I bring food to him. Steak and eggs. Always steak and eggs. There's a phone, still listed in her name, I think, Barbara's name, after thirty years, if you'd believe it. What does the telephone company care? The bill gets paid. And he'll phone his secretary and maybe the lieutenant governor, and his wife, and maybe Walsh, do a little business, see that everything's all right. Then he'll go back to sleep. He doesn't even take a walk. Spends no energy at all. He's like a bear. Hibernates a few days. In all my years of doin' this with him, he's never gone down to the lake. He's never seen the outside of the cabin, except goin' in and comin' out, and that's usually in the dark. I don't think he even knows what a shambles it is."

"Flash, does he take pills to sleep so much?"

"No. Steak and eggs. Water from the lake. I've never even seen an aspirin bottle at the cabin. He just sleeps. Fifteen, sixteen hours at first. Then eight hours. Then like twelve hours. There are some old books in the cabin — Ellery Queen, S. S. van Dyne. He reads them sometimes, in bed. Never seems to finish them."

"You mean, his wife doesn't know about this?"

"Nobody does."

"When he calls them, where does he say he is?"

"He doesn't say. He's been doing this a long time. I know what they think. They think he's with some woman. In a way, maybe he is. The governor's out of town, they say. Private trip. Most of the press would give their left arms to know where the governor goes. I've been offered quite a lot."

"I bet you have."

"Until they know something, they can't report anything. Right?"

"Right. Did James know about this?"

"Nope. He used to get pretty mad about it sometimes. Yell at the governor. James saw some kind of danger in it. He'd say, 'Some day you're gonna get caught, Caxton, and then it will blow up in all of our faces.' "

"And what would the governor say?"

"Nothing. James was pretty smart. He played every trick in the book to get me to tell him where the governor goes, what he does. I don't know much, Mr. Fletcher, but what I know I shut up about."

"Flash, what's the big secret about this? If it's so innocent, if all the guy does is sleep —"

"I don't know. Maybe it shows he's human. What's the word? Vulnerable. He doesn't have all the energy in the world. He needs sleep. Maybe he's ashamed of it. Maybe it's because this woman was involved. Is involved."

"Maybe it's just because it's an eccentric thing to do."

"It's been goin' on a long time. As long as I've known him. That's how secrets begin, isn't it? At first you don't say nothin', and after a while you find you *can't* say nothin'. Maybe the ol' boy just enjoys puttin' one over on everybody. Here everybody thinks he's off boozin' with broads, and he's really asleep in a big soft bed up at the lake. Sleepin' like a baby. Readin' the same books over and over again, never finishin' them."

"Then what happens?"

"After three, four days of this, sometimes five, he gets up, gets dressed, says, 'Time to go home, Flash,' we get in the car and go back to the mansion."

"He never says where he was."

"He says he was away. Only once there was some crisis, some vote that had to be taken. I guess he miscalculated, things moved faster than he expected, we had to come back earlier than he wanted to."

"How often does he do this?"

"Three, four times a year."

"Sounds pretty boring for you."

"Oh, no. I like looking at the lake. I keep sweaters up there, you know, and a big down jacket. It's quiet. I talk to the birds. I chirp back at them. You can get a real conversation going with the birds, if you really try. I like helping out the chipmunks."

Fletch gave this big, ex-boxer a long look. "How do you help out a chipmunk?"

"The place is so rotten. There's a stone wall under the cabin, a foundation, and then another between the cabin and the lake. The chipmunks live in the walls. They come in and out. The walls keep fallin' down, blockin' up their doors. I move the big rocks for them. And I find nuts and leave them outside their doors for them. It's easier for me to find nuts than it is for them." The man said sincerely, "I can carry more nuts than a chipmunk can."

"Sure," said Fletch, "but do they thank you?"

"They take the nuts inside the walls. I think they do. They go somewhere." Fletch said nothing. "Why shouldn't I help them out?" Flash Grasselli asked reasonably. "I'm bigger than they are."

"Yeah."

"Sure. Haven't anything better to do."

"Don't see how he gets away with this. I don't see how he gets away without making any kind of an explanation to Doris and Walsh."

"Why? The guy's a success in every other way. Jeez, he's a presidential candidate. What more do you want? They put up with it. They mention it to me every once in a while. You know, thank me for takin' care of him when he disappears. They're fishin', too. I never say

429

nothin'. God knows what they think. Sure it worries them, but so what? The guy lives in a glass suit. He has a right to some privacy."

"He doesn't really trust them, does he?"

"He has a right to some privacy."

"Flash, if the governor were off boozin' with broads, would you put up with it?"

"I dunno. Sure. I expect so. I like broads better'n I like chipmunks."

"Would you tell the truth about it?"

Flash's eyes narrowed. "I'd shut up about it, if that's what you mean. The way I figure, everybody's gotta blow off steam in his own way. Everybody's gotta have a piece of hisself to hisself. Me, I go to my room over the garage at the mansion and I can do what I want. I never bring girls there, though. Not to the governor's mansion. I can do what I want. The governor, he wears a glass suit all the time. Except when he's at the lake. Just me and him. Then he zonks out. That's his thing."

"And, Flash, drugs have nothing to do with it?"

"Nothin'. Absolutely nothin'. He doesn't even drink coffee there. If that shithead Dr. Thom and his little black bag ever showed up at the cabin, I'd drown 'em faster than he can insult me."

"That's pretty fast."

"Dr. Thom is an insult to the human race."

"Has the governor done this lately? Disappeared?"

"No." Flash frowned. "Not since the campaign started. But we went up to the lake the day after Christmas. When no one was lookin'. A long rest. Back by New Year's Eve."

"Okay. Flash, the question is obvious."

The look on Flash's face indicated the question wasn't obvious.

"Why are you telling me this?" Fletch asked.

Simply, Flash answered, "The governor told me to."

"I guessed as much. The answer's obvious too. But why? Why did he tell you to tell me?"

Flash shrugged. "Dunno. I have a guess."

"What's your guess?"

"Maybe because he knows you don't like Dr. Thom and his little black bag any better'n I do. I heard Walsh tell him that."

Fletch shook his head. "So now I know something Walsh doesn't know? I don't get it."

"You see, Mr. Fletcher, the people around the governor don't care much about him, as long as he keeps movin', keeps walkin' and talkin', keeps bein' Caxton Wheeler, keeps winning. Including his wife and son. They remind me of a football team or somethin'. They work together beautifully, always slappin' each other on the ass and everything. But one of them breaks his back, like James, or like that guy who got killed today — what's his name? Victor Somethin' — no longer useful anymore, and they find they can play without him. They never really think of him again. There's that goal up the field there, and the point is to get that ball through that goal. That's the only point there is. The governor's the ball. They'll kick the shit out of him, throw him to the ground, land on him. He's just got to keep lookin' like a ball." Flash waggled his head. "You've been with the campaign what? Like twenty-four hours? And the governor wanted you to know this about him. I don't know what those friggin' pills are Dr. Thom feeds him. The governor wants you to know he's all right."

"I'm not sure you're right about Walsh."

"He cares?" Flash sat back. "Yeah, he cares. Too much. To him his dad is Mr. Magical Marvelous." Flash laughed. "I think the governor maybe almost wants his son to think he's up there somewhere burnin' up more energy with booze and broads. I think it would kill him if Walsh ever discovered the ol' man's just up at a rickety old cabin takin' a nap. You know what I mean?"

"Hell of a lot of pressure," Fletch said.

"Yeah, and this is the old man's way of beatin' it off. He's right. It's against his image. What could be worse for him than to have the *National Nose*, as he calls it, print that he's asleep? Jeez, it would ruin him. Better they think he's gettin' his rocks off — as long as they can't prove it."

"Well, well," Fletch said. "My daddy always said you can learn a lot in a bar, if you listen."

Walsh stuck his head in the bar, looked around, but did not come in.

Fletch said, "The governor wanted me to know he's not hooked on anything but sleep. Is that it?"

Flash shrugged. "The governor's a very intelligent man. I don't have any brains. Never did have. I'm just smart enough to know I should do what he tells me and everything will be fine."

"What did he tell you to say to me about Mrs. Wheeler?"

"Nothin'."

Fletch waited. He sipped his beer. He waited again. "What are you going to tell me about Mrs. Wheeler?"

"Nothin'. She's one tough, smart person. As strong as steel."

"Smarter and tougher than the governor?"

"Yeah."

"Tonight, when she yelled at the governor —"

"I didn't hear it. I was in the bathroom."

"You were in the bathroom on purpose. You knew she was going to do some such thing."

Flash said, "Yes."

"You call that smart and tough? You don't call that being out of control?"

"Mrs. Wheeler's kept things going all these years. She was probably right in everything she said tonight. I didn't hear her."

"You must have been trying pretty hard not to hear her."

"That's my business. She uses her tongue like a whip. She whips Walsh, yells at the governor, calls me a goon."

"Not just her tongue, Flash. She uses her hands."

"You know, you don't get to be a presidential candidate just by standin' out in the rain. Someone has to push you, and push you damned hard. You see, I know the governor's secret: he's a nice guy. If it weren't for her, the governor would have gone to sleep years ago. Read novels. Play with little kids. You know what I mean?"

"What's wrong with that?"

"Someone's got to be President of the United States," Flash said simply. "Why not a smart, honest, good man like Caxton Wheeler?"

TWENTY

"I completed, duplicated, and delivered tomorrow's final schedules," Fletch said. "I also issued the three special releases Nolting and Dobson have been working on. You saw them. On Central America, exploitation of Native American lands, on the Russian economic situation. I also made up some nice-guy stuff about your dad for the feature press —"

"Like what?" Walsh asked sharply.

They were in Walsh's bedroom on the twelfth floor of the hotel, sitting at the table under the shaded light.

"I told them how your dad used to give you your allowance. Make the coin disappear between his hands and then pretend to find it in your ear or something. Okay?"

"Okay." Walsh's eyes were darting around the areas of the room outside the light.

"Idea being to take the stink out of that scene this morning at Conroy School," Fletch said. "To imply he treats all kids as he would his own."

"I understand," Walsh said with a touch of impatience.

"Helped a local reporter get permission to spend some time with your mother in the morning."

"Did you go through Sully?" Walsh asked.

"I guess you could say that. I went through Sully."

"Your first run-in with Sully?"

"Yeah."

"What a bitch," Walsh said.

"Oh, you know that."

"Fletch, I think you'd better plan to spend some time with my mother tomorrow. Get to know her a little. See her as she really is."

"I would like that," Fletch said.

"I'll arrange it."

"My phone was ringing constantly, Walsh. All the world's pundits wanting to know the source of your dad's 'New Reality' speech."

"Did you tell them?"

"I said as far as I know it's the result of the governor's own thought."

"Is it?" Again, Walsh's question was quick and sharp.

"Walsh —"

"What was the source of the idea, Fletch?" And again Walsh's eyes were roaming restlessly around the room outside their circle of light.

"I said something. He asked. Maybe it was the germ of the idea. On the bus this morning. Your father was asking me what I thought. I'd never been asked what I thought by a presidential candidate before."

"You were flattered."

"Who wouldn't be? Of course, I didn't have time to think the idea out."

"You're not a speechwriter."

"What was I supposed to do?"

"The speechwriters are responsible for the consistency of what the candidate says."

"Anyway, Walsh, less than two hours later in Winslow your dad stands up and issues this perfectly eloquent speech, developing a couple of things I had said —"

"He was angry at the congressperson. He was angry at the way the press handled the Conroy School incident. He was fighting back.

433

We — I had put too much pressure on him over Victor Robbins's death to make the nightly news with something, anything."

"I thought it was great."

"Of course you did. Piece of history. By your own hand. When history books pose the question, 'Why didn't Caxton Wheeler become President of the United States?' your grandchildren can read the answer. 'Because of an ill-considered speech in a snowstorm in a little town called Winslow where he criticized Christianity and the democratic process.' "

"Hey, Walsh. Maybe I just do that to authority. Any authority. Maybe I just get near authority and unconsciously start planting bombs. Your dad is one authority I like. I don't want to destroy him."

"Oedipus. Is that it?"

"Maybe. I'm a born-and-bred wise guy. I've never done well with authority. You should know that better than anyone. You remember Hill 1918. But I remember I got the platoon too stoned to go out on that earlier patrol. I knew it was suicidal."

"You were right."

"You almost got court-martialed for it."

"The platoon that did go out got blown away."

"Hell, Walsh. I'm a reporter. I can't be a kept boy. Telling these reporters I love the stuff they're writing when most of them couldn't write their way out of a detention hall."

Walsh was looking into the dark of the room, clearly not hearing, not listening.

"What I'm trying to say is maybe I should pack my pistols and ride off into the sunset."

Walsh asked, "What was that thing you did between Betsy Ginsberg and me?"

"Got you to say hello to each other."

Walsh shook his head slowly.

"That too, Walsh." Still Fletch was not sure how much of Walsh's attention he had. "A lady I knew before this campaign ever started refused to have supper with me tonight because of my job. Because of the position I'm in. What do you do about the isolation, Walsh?"

"Fletch, I think your sex life can take a rest."

"I might get sick."

"So get sick."

"Another lady offered me her body for an interview with your mother in the morning."

"Did you accept?"

"Of course not."

"See? You're sick already."

"I think I ought to go back to bayin' at the moon, Walsh."

Walsh's eyes came back into the light, focused on the table surface. You just gave Dad the coins. You didn't hand them out to the kids. To some of the kids. You just gave him the ideas. You didn't make he speech."

Fletch stretched his fingers. "Maybe that's what I like about your dad. He's a bit of a rebel, too. His mind's up there somewhere, kissin' the truth. At least he's not the complete phony I expected the front-runnin' politician to be. Once in a while he actually says what occurs to him as the truth."

Abruptly Walsh sat up in his chair. "You're always making jokes. Is that how you escape?"

Slowly, carefully, Fletch said, "No. That's why the chicken crossed the road."

For the first time since Fletch had entered the room, Walsh looked him fully in the face. Then he grinned.

Fletch said, "Now that I have your attention . . ."

"Yeah, yeah, yeah," said Walsh. "You have my attention."

"James called me tonight. From Iowa. He's in Iowa to attend Victor Robbins's funeral."

"Bastard. He's there to get himself a job with the opposition."

"I wondered about that."

"You bet. As sure as God made anchovies."

"He talked a long time. Gave me some advice. Answered some questions."

"Said he loves Dad more than he loves himself. Will do anything he can to help out. Call him anytime. Am I right, or am I right?"

"You're right."

"He'd love a pipeline to this campaign. Don't talk to him."

"Except I think he was telling the truth. Twenty-three years —"

"Means nothing in history. A pimple on Tuchman's tuchis."

"Okay, but —"

Walsh shook his head *no* rapidly. "He was out to get my mother. Can't have that. No such thing as being loyal to my father, to the campaign, while you're sluggin' away at my mother."

"He doesn't see it that way."

"You trying to get James his job back? Your job?"

"Maybe it's impossible."

"It's impossible. The jerk self-destructed. People make mistakes in this business. But to go after the candidate's wife with bare knuckles, that's the way you get a one-way ticket home."

"Walsh, listen to me."

"I'm listening."

"He says your mother's temper is getting worse, that people, th
press are beginning to know about it . . ."

Again Walsh was shaking his head *no*. "When you've got dozens c
people talking at once, somebody's got to yell."

"That scene tonight in your father's room —"

"Aw, that's just Ma's way of blowin' off steam. Everyone's gotta blov
off steam." Fletch was watching Walsh's eyes. "What harm did it do;
Walsh asked. "So people now think the candidate watches Archi
Bunker on television. So what? Makes him seem human."

Fletch said, "Your father isn't human, Walsh?"

Walsh said: "He's human."

"But only Flash Grasselli knows how human, is that right?"

Walsh glanced at Fletch. "I see the press has been pumping you o
Dad's sojourns away from home. I should have warned you."

"Do you know where he goes, Walsh?"

"Sure. There's a place he goes. Belongs to a friend. He goes there
fishes, relaxes, reads history. Works on political strategy."

"How do you know that?"

"He's told me. Just doesn't want anyone to have his phone numbe
He calls us. We don't call him. He calls regularly. Doesn't want th
press to know. Can't blame him."

"Who's this friend?"

"Someone he knew in school. In law school. One of his lawye
friends, I think."

The phone rang. Walsh jumped to answer it. "Be right up," he sai
into the phone. He hung up and said to Fletch: "Mother."

Remaining seated, Fletch asked, "When do you get to sleep, Walsh;

Walsh said, "Plenty of time for that in the White House."

TWENTY-ONE

Fletch got off the elevator on the fifth floor to go to his ow
room.

Down the corridor a man was leaning against the wall. H
back was to the elevators. His right hand was against the wal
his arm fairly straight. His left hand was raised to his head.

Fletch went to him. "Bill?"

Bill Dieckmann's eyes were frosted over. They were not focusing at all. Clearly he did not recognize Fletch. Maybe he knew someone was there.

"Bill . . ."

Bill's knees jerked forward. Fletch did not catch him. He was too surprised. He put his own hands around Bill's head and went to the floor with him. Together they landed softly.

Fletch disentangled himself and sat up. Bill Dieckmann was unconscious. Some, but not all, of the pain was gone from his face.

The room key in Bill's jacket pocket read 916.

Dieckmann was heavy. Fletch raised him in the fireman's lift.

With Dieckmann over his shoulders, Fletch waited for the elevator.

Andrew Esty was on the elevator when it arrived. He was wearing his overcoat, *Daily Gospel* button in the lapel. In one hand he had a suitcase; in the other a typewriter case.

"I thought you left the campaign, Mr. Esty." Fletch pushed the button for the ninth floor.

"I was ordered back."

Esty did not seem to notice that Fletch had a large man over his shoulders. He had barely made room for them in the elevator.

"Nice to have you back," Fletch said from behind the folds of Bill's suit jacket.

"It's not nice to be back."

"But," said Fletch, "you have a job to do."

"Do you really think," Esty asked, "we should allow this anti-American, anti-Christian campaign to go unreported?"

"Are we on the ninth floor?"

There was a moment before Esty admitted they were on the ninth floor.

Fletch said, "Gotta call 'em as you see 'em." He staggered with his load of Bill Dieckmann through the elevator door.

Fletch lowered Bill Dieckmann onto the bed in Room 916.

Then he picked up the telephone.

"What are you doing?" On the bed, Bill's eyes were open, wary.

"Calling Dr. Thom," Fletch said.

"What are you doing in my room?"

"You collapsed, Bill. On the fifth floor. You've been unconscious."

"Put the phone down."

The hotel's operator had not yet answered. "Are you sure?" Fletch asked.

"Put it down."

Fletch hung up.

"Now get out."

"You might say thanks for the ride, Bill. I carried you up here."

"Thanks for nothing."

"Bill, I'm not your wife, boss, brother, friend . . . you know the rest of the speech?"

"No," Bill said. "You're not."

"Something's wrong with your head, man. Twice I've seen you trying to twist it off. Tomorrow you might succeed."

"None of your damned business." Bill sat up, put his feet on the floor, his head in his hands.

"You've said that before. It's no secret you're having trouble, Bill. Dr. Thom may be a strange man, but he's not going to call your managing editor first thing with a complete medical report. Doctors still have to keep their mouths shut, even Dr. Thom."

Dieckmann appeared to be listening.

"Anyway," Fletch continued, "suppose you succeed at twisting your head off one of these times? Think of the disgusting sight. You walking around with your head in your hands, down around your pockets. Blood bubbling up from your neck and dribbling all over your suit. I know you'd still get the story, Bill. But think of the ladies. You want Fenella Baker to see a thing like that? Might make her face powder fall off. That would be really sickening."

Head in hands, Bill said, "Get out of here, Fletch. Please. Go bother somebody else. Go bother Ira Lapin. He's got bigger problems than I have."

"What are his problems?"

"Housemother you're not."

"Agreed. But, Bill, you just collapsed. You weren't even on the right floor. You had no idea what you were doing. Before you went unconscious, you didn't even recognize me."

"Okay, okay. What am I supposed to do about it?"

"Get medical attention. This primary campaign isn't worth your life, Bill. You know what I mean? At least to you, it isn't."

"I'm all right."

"You're about as all right as a snowman on the Fourth of July."

"Leave me alone."

"Okay. If you say so." At the door, Fletch said, "You sure there's nothing I can do?"

"Yeah. There's something you can do."

"What?"

"Tell me if I'm on the right campaign. Who's going to win this damned primary?"

"Gee, I dunno, Bill."

"Then you're no good to me."

"But I can tell you that after this primary election, there's another one. And then another. And another . . . Good night, Bill."

TWENTY-TWO

"Mornin'. Thank you," Fletch said into the bedside phone. It had rung and he assumed it was the hotel operator calling to tell him it was six-thirty.

"You're welcome," said the strong voice of The Man Who.

Fletch looked at his watch. It was only six-twenty.

" 'Morning," Fletch said in a voice that wasn't too strong. He sat up in the bed. His shoulders and chest and stomach were wet with sweat. Steam was clanging in the radiators. The room had been cold when he went to bed. He had put on an extra blanket from the closet. Now he threw the blankets off.

"You're up early," said Governor Caxton Wheeler.

"Am I?"

"Apparently."

"Oh, yes," Fletch said intelligently. "I must be."

"Are you awake now?"

"Sure. Ask me a riddle. Never mind, you know the answer."

"Look, Fletch, I've just called Lansing Sayer. Asked him to join me in the car on the ride out to the hospital."

"Hospital?"

"I'm visiting the Farmingdale Hospital this morning."

"Oh, yeah. I mean, oh, yes. Sir."

"He can interview me in the car on the way out. I want you to come along. To keep me honest."

"Okay. I mean, yes, sir."

"We'll leave about eight-thirty. Flash will drive us out."

"Yes, sir."

"See you out front at eight-thirty. Are you awake?"

"Like a snowman on . . ."

"What were you doing when I called?" There was laughter in the governor's voice.

Fletch ran his thumb down his chest and stomach. "Sweating."

"Great," said The Man Who. "Nothing like exercise first thing in the morning. Do a push-up for me. I'll feel the better for it."

Fletch padded to the door, opened it, and saw the stack of newspapers a volunteer had left for him in the hotel corridor.

Newsbill was on top. The front page of the tabloid had nothing but the headline on it:

DEATH STALKS WHEELER CAMPAIGN

Fletch knelt on one knee and scanned the story, with many photographs, which began on page three:

Farmingdale — Presidential Candidate Caxton Wheeler and his staff have refused to answer questions about the murders of two young women which have happened on their campaign trail within the last week.

The second young woman, Alice Elizabeth Shields, 28, was found naked and beaten on the sidewalk just below Wheeler's seventh floor hotel suite.

Campaign officials even refuse to state they have no knowledge of the women or of their murders. . . .

The by-line read Michael J. Hanrahan.

"Well, well," Fletch muttered into the empty hotel corridor. "The dam has broken. Somebody better get a mop."

TWENTY-THREE

"No, no eggs for me," Ira Lapin said. He and Fletch were in a booth in the hotel's coffee shop. "My doctor gave me a big warning against cholesterol. No bacon, either. I forget what's wrong with bacon. I'm sure something is. No coffee, of course." He ordered oatmeal, unbuttered toast, and tea. "What is cholesterol, anyway? Little boomies that gang up trying to get through the doorways to your heart?"

"I think it gives you hardening of the head or something."

"I'd never notice," Ira said. "If my head were any harder I could never sneeze."

Fletch ordered steak and eggs, orange juice, and coffee.

"What is it with you young people?" Ira asked. "Can't afford to go to a doctor and never enjoy breakfast again?"

"My worry is the population explosion," Fletch said.

"And that's your answer to the population explosion? Commit suicide at breakfast?"

"Not suicide," Fletch answered. "I just don't hope to take up space beyond my allotted time."

Ira nodded sagely. "An original point of view."

"Everybody has to worry about something."

"These doctors kill you," Ira said. "Everything's bad for you. Booze is bad for you. Tobacco. Coffee. Red meat. The egg is bad for you. What can be more innocent than the egg? It isn't even born yet."

"Milk, cheese, chocolate. Water. Air."

"They want us to go straight from our incubators to our coffins. No outside influences, please; I'm living."

"Tough life." The waitress brought them their tea and coffee. "Doubt we'll ever adapt to it."

"I take from the unhealthiest doctor I could find. He's a wreck. Fat as the federal budget. He smokes like a public utility; drinks as if he has as many different mouths as a White House source. When he breathes, you'd think someone is running a caucus in his chest. Thought he'd be easy on me. Tolerant. Relaxed. Not a bit of it. Still he gives me that old saw, 'Don't do as I do; do as I say.' I guess I should. Already he's invested in a burial plot, he tells me. And he's only thirty-two."

Breakfast came.

"How do you like the campaign so far?" Ira Lapin asked the candidate's press representative.

"Getting some surprises," Fletch said.

"Like . . . ?"

"Caxton Wheeler's brighter than I thought. More honest. More sane."

"You didn't know him before?"

"No."

"You knew his son."

"Yes."

"What do you think of the press, now that you're seeing us from a different angle?"

"Cute."

"What do you mean, cute? Or are you referring only to La Arbuthnot?"

"That incident yesterday with the governor and the kids and the coins. The magic show he put on. I would never see that as a national issue."

Ira nodded. "I reported it. I didn't report it as an issue. I just reported it. Let people make of it what they will."

"You mean, the editors, news directors . . ."

"It's the little things that count," Ira Lapin said. He had spooned cream and sugar onto his oatmeal, cream and sugar into his tea. He had put a quarter of a pot of jam on his toast. Blissfully, he was eating everything. "You know you've been thrown in here as a sacrificial lamb. Yes. You have. You've been thrown to the wolves. To me. To us. You're surprised? Eat your steak. Steak for breakfast. You'd drive my doctor to drink. Never mind. For him it's not a long ride. We're at the point in the campaign where they need someone young in your job. A throwaway. Nothing wrong with James except he was tired. His tricks were tired. He was boring us. You're young, and people say you have a crazy mind. You do. Ignore the doctor because you worry about the population explosion. You'll keep us entertained, all right. There's a story you gave Solov a bottle of eyedrops. You do that?"

"No."

"They can make up stories about you. Deflect from the candidate. After these stupid, high-energy primaries are over, you'll be used as the scapegoat. You'll be what's wrong with the campaign. You'll be gotten rid of as a concession to the press, an answer for everything that's wrong. Then they'll march the professionals in. You think I don't know what I'm talking about?" Fletch was eating and listening, not registering surprise to the degree Ira Lapin wanted. "They have one ready. You ever hear of Graham Kidwell? He's already on the campaign as media consultant. I'll bet you this piece of toast, what's left of it, Wheeler's already talked with him this morning, maybe twice. Kidwell is sitting in a big Washington office, partner in a rich public relations firm, primed for the job of press secretary to the President of the

United States. You think you're going to the White House? Think again. I've seen it before. 'A presidential campaign is a crusade of amateurs.' Where did he get that? Some amateur. Caxton Wheeler's an amateur like a Georgetown madam. And his wife, the dragon lady. She could make the finals in any contest you happened to run. Including mud wrestling. During the primary campaigns, in all these rinky little towns, a good campaigner wants to give the impression of amateurism. Makes the campaign seem more real. More like a people's movement. Gets the volunteers out, the bucks up. The people see the fumbling around, say, 'Gee, I can help,' throw down their shovels and golf clubs, and go to work for the candidate. Later, only professionalism sells. Then the image of competence is needed. So right now, in this road show, you're the lead amateur." Ira drained his teacup. "Thought I'd let you know."

"Thanks," Fletch said cheerily enough. "I expect you're right."

"No probably about it. I know I'm right. Campaigns at first need idealism and youth. Once the primaries are won, cynicism takes over and idealism gets a bus ticket home. You don't mind being used?"

"Everybody gets used," Fletch said. "Depends on what you get used for."

"Idealism," scoffed Ira Lapin. "Idealism goes home on a bus." Ira poured the last drops from his teapot into his coffee cup. "I feel sick."

"You don't look well."

"What I need is some coffee." He signaled the waitress. "I should contribute to the population explosion?" The waitress came over and he ordered a pot of coffee. Then he said to Fletch: "You know my wife was murdered."

"No. My God. When?"

"Two years, five months ago. A block from our apartment in Washington. Stabbed by a mugger."

"Stabbed to death?"

"She was stabbed. Would you believe it was hitting her head on a stone step when she fell down that killed her? Stone steps leading to a house."

Fletch shook his head. "How do you accept a thing like that?"

"You don't. You don't accept it. You don't think about it. You just leave it out there somewhere, like a part of town you never visit. You put the anger, the rage, the fury in another part of town, and you never visit it." The waitress brought the pot of coffee and a fresh cup and saucer for Ira. "Thank you," he said to her. "You're killing me."

He poured the coffee slowly into his cup. "I was in Vienna with the President when I got the cable. Did you ever see a piece of paper you couldn't believe at all? I mean, no matter how many times you read it, it just sits there like an impossible lie? I don't even remember the trip home. I remember Marty Nolan of the *Boston Globe* packing my bags for me."

"Any kids?"

"Grown. They were devastated. Who was their mother to get stabbed? A nice little person."

"Did they ever catch the guy who did it?"

"A man was seen running away carrying a purse. Maybe she had fifty dollars in the purse. I doubt that much. He didn't steal the new tablecloth she had just bought. The whole thing was unnecessary. We already had a tablecloth."

"I dunno," Fletch said. "I'm real sorry for you, man."

"It's not that." Ira waved his hand in front of his face. "It's just that every time I hear of one of these murders — women getting killed — just stirs the whole thing up again."

"Sure."

"Jeez. You can't come down to breakfast without hearing about some woman getting killed down the corridor."

"What do you mean?" Fletch asked.

"You didn't hear? Some reporter you must have been. A chambermaid got killed last night. Strangled."

"In this hotel?"

"Yeah. The kitchen help found her when they came in this morning. At four o'clock. In a service elevator. Two nights ago was it? — a woman gets pushed off the roof of the motel we were in. I don't know. We go through this whole election process as if we were civilized human beings. What good does it do? It's just a big pretense that we're civilized."

Fletch wanted to say, *Wait a minute. . . .*

"What's the matter with you?" Ira asked. "Now *you* look sick. What happened to your tan? Didn't know it was the kind you could rub off. Better take some of my coffee."

"No. Thanks."

"Take it with you. You look like your heart just sat down and took off its shoes."

"Thanks."

"Sure. Have some coffee. No good for me anyway. My doctor says it makes me nervous."

TWENTY-FOUR

"You all right, Fletch?" Betsy Ginsberg asked. She was standing in the hotel lobby outside the coffee shop.

"Sure."

"You look white."

"Just saw Paul Szep's editorial cartoon." In fact, he had. Roy Filby had showed it to him at the coffee shop's cash register. "So how do you like Walsh," Fletch tried to ask easily, "now that you know him?"

Michael J. Hanrahan went by into the coffee shop. He grinned/grimaced at Fletch and held up three fingers.

Fletch ignored him.

Betsy returned the question. "What do you really think of Walsh?"

"He's a cool guy," Fletch answered. "Forgiving, reassuring, absolutely competent. Totally in control."

"I don't know," Betsy said.

"So he didn't fall all over you," Fletch said. "Think of the position he's in."

The Man Who was getting off the elevator. The eyes of everyone in the lobby were attracted to him. He was smiling.

People intercepted him as he crossed the lobby. Several had children by the hands. A few snapped pictures of The Man Who, as if the world were not being nearly saturated with pictures of him. The Man Who was shaking hands, listening briefly, speaking briefly, as he came across the lobby. He patted some of the children on their heads. He did not take coins from their ears.

Fletch walked close beside him. Quietly he said, "We've got to talk. Privately. Soon."

"Sure," the governor said. "What's up?"

Into the governor's ear, Fletch said, "Ira Lapin tells me another young woman has been murdered."

The governor reached through the mob, went out of his way to shake a bellman's hand.

With his public grin on his face, the governor spoke almost through his teeth. "Two people in the United States are murdered every hour, Fletch. Didn't you know that?"

"Talk," Fletch said.

"Sure, sure."

T W E N T Y - F I V E

"I'm glad you asked me that question." Sitting behind Flash in the rented black sedan, Governor Wheeler's eyes twinkled at Fletch sitting in the front passenger seat. Sitting behind Fletch, Lansing Sayer had just asked some general question about the "New Reality" speech The Man Who had delivered in Winslow the day before. Sayer had a tape recorder going and also was working a pen and notebook. "I guess I made a rather sweeping statement."

It was a raw, bone-chilling day with a heavy sky. Flash had the car heater on high.

"Senator Upton says you're proposing a technocracy," Lansing said.

"I'm not proposing anything," the governor said. "I'm simply making an observation."

Fletch remembered James's advice that when he thought the candidate was about to say something profound and statesmanlike he ought to stick a glove in his mouth.

"Just observe," the governor said slowly, thoughtfully, "what technology is getting the major share of the government's attention. Advanced weaponry. Machines of death and destruction. Do you realize what a single tank costs these days? A fighter aircraft? An aircraft carrier? I don't just mean our government. I mean all governments. Some governments are exporting weaponry at a high rate; others are importing at a high rate; some do both. The technology upon which almost all governments concentrate is the technology of weaponry. Advanced bows and arrows."

It was true: Flash drove slowly. He hugged the right lane of the city's main street and proceeded at only slightly better than a pedestrian's pace. Fletch had been in funeral processions that went faster.

"At the same time," the governor continued, at about the same pace as the car, "over the earth has been spreading a communications system that does or can reach into every hovel, capable of collecting and dispersing information instantaneously. An amazing technology, for

he most part developed by free enterprise, private business — par-
icularly the entertainment business.

"Through this technology, the people of this earth are beginning
o recognize each other, know each other, and realize their com-
monality of interest.

"This technology is far more powerful, and far more positive I might
add, than the thermonuclear bomb."

It was hardly noticeable when the car came to a full stop, but,
indeed, they were stopped at a red light. The people crossing the
street in front of the car had no idea they were so close to a leading
presidential candidate. They were all hurrying someplace, to work,
to shop. None looked in the car. And none knew what was being
discussed in that black sedan.

"Governments lie now, and all the people know it. A government
runs a phony election, and all the people of the world witness it.
Governments put on brushfire wars now for some diplomatic or ide-
ologic reason, and all the world see themselves being maimed and
killed."

Lansing Sayer dropped his hands, his pen and notebook in his lap,
and said, "I don't know what all this is about."

Flash had taken off his gloves and dropped them on the seat beside
Fletch.

The car oozed forward again.

"I'm talking about the gathering and dissemination of information,"
the governor said, "instead of weapons."

Lansing said, "Graves stated that in your speech yesterday, you
seemed to be disparaging — among other ideologies — Christianity,
Judaism, and democracy."

"I don't disparage ideas at all," the governor said. "I'm having one,
am I not?"

"You said technology is tying this world together, integrating the
people of this world, in a way no ideology ever has or ever could."

"Isn't that true? We're all brothers in the Bible. We're all comrades
under Marxism. But it is through our increased factual awareness of
each other that we're discovering our common humanity as a reality."

Lansing Sayer wasn't getting much into his notebook.

"Am I wrong to think that most of the bad things that happen on
this earth happen because people don't have the right facts at the right
time? It's all very well to believe something. You can go cheering to
war over what you believe. You can starve to death happily over what
you believe. But would wars ever happen if everybody had the same

447

facts? There is no factual basis for starvation on this earth," Governo
Caxton Wheeler said softly. "Not yet, there isn't."

"It's the interpretation of facts that counts," Lansing Sayer said.

"Facts are facts," said The Man Who. "I'm not talking about faith
belief, opinions. I'm talking about facts. How come most children ir
this world know Pele's every move playing soccer, know every line o
Muhammad Ali's face, and yet this same technology has not been usec
to teach them the history of their own people, or how to read anc
write their own language? How come a bank in London can know,
up to the minute, how much money a bank in New York has, to the
penny, but a kid in Liverpool who just had his teeth bashed out doesn'
know three thousand years ago a Greek analyzed gang warfare accurately? How come the governments of this world know where every
thermonuclear missile is, on land, under land, on sea, under sea, anc
yet this technology has never been used for the proper allocation o
food? Is that a dumb question?"

"You're saying, regarding technology, governments are looking in
the wrong direction."

"I'm saying governments are out of date in their thinking. They've
been developing negative technology, rather than positive technology.
You have to believe something, only if you don't know. We now have
the capability to know everything."

Lansing Sayer looked at the governor. "What has this to do with
the presidential campaign? Are these ideas of yours going to be im-
plemented in some kind of a political program?"

And the governor looked through the car window. "Well . . . we're
having international meetings on arms control. We have had for decades now, while arms have proliferated through this world like the
plague. Translating this observation into policy . . ." In the front seat
Fletch again was amazed at how simply issues were raised and answered
on a political campaign, how naturally problems were stated and policy
formulated. ". . . I think it's time we started working toward international understandings regarding the use and control of this technology," The Man Who said. "Obviously no one — no political,
religious, financial group — should have control of too large a section
of this technology. Consider this." The governor smiled at Lansing
Sayer. "Electronically, a complete polling of a nation's people, a complete plebiscite, can take place within seconds. Where is the time
needed for the people to reflect? Maybe there should be an international understanding, agreement, that such a plebiscite is to be used
only as an advisory to a government, but does not give a government
authority to act."

The car was going up the hill to the hospital.

"Great," the governor said. "Easily accessible hospital. Good roads leading to it. That's good."

Lansing Sayer took off his glasses and rubbed his forehead.

"Flash will take you back to the hotel," the governor said to Lansing Sayer, "then come back and pick us up. I have to make a television tape after this."

Lansing Sayer asked, "Is this what your campaign is about, Governor? Shifting government interest from bombs to communication?"

"Bombs are a damned bad way to communicate," The Man Who said. "Deafen people."

The car stopped. The governor was leaving the car through the back door.

Lansing Sayer leaned over. "Governor! May I report this is what your campaign is about? Coming to international understandings regarding the new technology?"

Governor Caxton Wheeler looked back inside the car at Lansing Sayer. He grinned. He said: "Presidential campaigns ought to be about *something.*"

Walking from the car to the hospital entrance, where administrators were waiting to greet him, Governor Caxton Wheeler chuckled and said to Fletch, "You know, sir, I'm beginning to *want* to be President of the United States!"

TWENTY-SIX

"Ah!" The concerned, consoling expression fell off the governor's face when he saw the only one present in the private hospital room was I. M. Fletcher. The door behind the governor swung shut. "And what are you in hospital for?"

"Anxiety," Fletch answered. "Acute."

"I'm sure they'll have you fixed up and home in no time."

While the governor had toured the happier wards of the hospital — maternity, general surgery, pediatrics (he was kept away from intensive care and the terminal section) — Fletch had arranged with a hospital administrator to have the governor shown into an unoccupied

449

private room. His excuse had been the governor's need to use the phone.

More seriously, the governor asked, "What are you so anxious about? What's up?"

"Hanrahan wrote his usual muscular piece for this morning's *Newsbill*." Fletch took the tabloid's front page and two of its inside pages from his jacket pocket and handed them to the governor. "I want you to see what all this looks like in print."

Standing near the window, the governor glanced through the pages. "So? Who cares about *Newsbill*? They once reported I had been married before. As a law student."

"I'm afraid Hanrahan has a point. In the third paragraph."

The Governor read aloud: "Campaign officials even refuse to state they have no knowledge of the women or of their murders. . . ."

He handed the pages from *Newsbill* back to Fletch. "How are we supposed to comment on something we don't know about?"

"Plus there was a woman murdered at the hotel last night. A chambermaid. Strangled. So Ira Lapin tells me. By the way, did you know Lapin's own wife was murdered?"

"So he's off murdering other women?"

"Maybe. Somebody is."

The governor paced off as far as the hospital room would permit, and then back to the window. "Do you think someone's out to get me?"

"I never thought of that."

"Think about it. It is, or could be, the net effect of these murders. To bring this campaign to its knees."

"It certainly increases the pressures . . ."

"Getting rid of me, casting a pall, a question mark over my campaign, is the only motive I can think of." The governor shrugged. "Or maybe paranoia is an occupational hazard for a political campaigner. You think the murderer is someone traveling with the campaign?"

"Good grief, don't you think so? It's why Fredericka Arbuthnot, crime writer for *Newsworld*, is traveling with us. She's not as careless and sensational as Hanrahan, but now that Hanrahan has blown the story, she'll have to write something."

"I'd better get Nolting to whip up some statements, figures on the high incidence of crime. I can say things like, 'Everywhere I go, it seems like someone is getting murdered.' "

"Governor . . ." Fletch hesitated.

"Yes?"

"I understand. You have to protect yourself. You have to protect the campaign. But making statements won't make the matter go away."

"What else can we do? The primary is in a couple of days."

"The best way to make the matter go away is to find out who is murdering these women."

"How are we supposed to do that? We're at full gear here, traveling at high speed. How many people are traveling with us — fifty or sixty? Is someone trying to sabotage my campaign? Just when I'm beginning to say something that is at least of interest to me? Who? Upton? Unthinkable. Graves? This goes a bit beyond dirty tricks. Some foreign agent? That guy from *Pravda* —"

"Solov."

"That his name? Looks like a complete basket case to me. You know he's never approached me with a single question? What's he here for? The press. You said Andrew Esty left yesterday, and there was a murder last night. So that lets him off."

"He came back. He was ordered back. Saw him in the elevator last night. Why do you mention him in particular?"

"That guy's a nut. Did you ever see him smile? He's as tight as a tournament tennis racquet. One of those guys who thinks he's absolutely right. Anyone who thinks he's absolutely right is capable of anything, including murder. Some kook among the volunteers. Lee Allen can't do very thorough checks on their backgrounds. We're traveling too fast, don't have the resources. I trust everyone on the staff implicitly. Believe me, they've all been vetted. You're the only one I don't know well personally, and you weren't with us at the time of the murder in the Hotel Harris. What the hell am I supposed to do? Go before the electorate, and say, 'Hey, guys and gals, I'm not a murderer.' Has an unfortunate ring to it. 'I'm not a froggy-woggy; I'm a toaddy-woaddy.' "

"Yes, it's time to say something," Fletch said. "It's also time to do something. I love what you're saying about the 'New Reality,' but the true reality is that the people are going to be concerned about unsolved murders touching your campaign."

The governor waved his hand at the pages from *Newsbill* still in Fletch's hand. "Did you show that filth to Walsh?"

"He had already left his room when I called this morning."

The governor looked at his watch. "I'm due at a television studio for a taping in twenty minutes. I will refer to these women's deaths, and say I am appalled. We have got to do something about violent crime in this country. It's affecting all of us. There's the big rally in

451

Melville tonight. I have to fly to New York to be on that network program, 'Q. & A.,' live tomorrow morning. Everybody tells me I've got to attend a church service somehow in the morning, seeing I'm accused of slurring Christianity in Winslow."

For a moment the two men were silent. Recitation of schedule did not make the problem go away, either. "Damn," the governor said. "It's snowing again."

Fletch said, "Now will you get some federal investigators to travel with us?"

"No." The governor thought a moment, and then said: "Your job, Fletcher, is to make sure this doesn't touch me. Doesn't touch the campaign. That's your only job." The Man Who had fallen into the cadence of a public speech. "No matter who is doing this string of murders, for whatever reason, it is to have no bearing on my candidacy. The primary in this state is in a couple of days. No one can solve a string of far-flung murders in a couple of days. I cannot go into that primary election day with people thinking of murder, associating this campaign with the murder of women. Do what you have to do, but keep this away from me. Is that clear?"

"Yes, sir."

"We'd better go."

Fletch opened the swing door of the hospital room for the governor. "Do you know the President has announced a press conference for two o'clock this afternoon?"

"Yes."

"Saturday afternoon press conference. Most unusual."

Going through the door the governor said, "I expect he's going to speak well of Christianity and democracy and drop a bomb on me."

TWENTY-SEVEN

"Here I am." Freddie Arbuthnot announced her presence at Fletch's elbow.

Actually, using one of the hotel's house telephones, Fletch had been trying to find Walsh Wheeler. His room didn't answer. Barry Hines wasn't sure where Walsh was. He thought Walsh was meeting with Farmingdale's Young Professionals Associa-

:ion. Lee Allen Parke thought Walsh was visiting an agronomy exhibit about fifty miles from Farmingdale. (Fletch was to discover Walsh breakfasted with the Young Professionals Association, then visited the agronomy exhibit.)

"You are looking for me, aren't you?" Freddie asked.

"Always." Fletch gave up on the phone. "Have you packed yet?"

"I never really unpack."

"Neither do I. But I ought to go up and throw things together. Come with me?"

"Sir! To your hotel room?"

"Yeah."

"Sure."

Judy Nadich burst off the elevator.

"Hey!" Fletch said to her.

She turned around, her tote bag swinging against her leg. She was crying.

"What's the matter?" Fletch asked.

"That bitch!" Judy said.

"Who?"

"Your Ms. Sullivan." She stepped closer to Fletch. "And your Doris Wheeler!"

"What did they do?"

"Nothing. Threw me out. Called me a squirrel."

Fletch couldn't help smiling.

"Told me to go cover the flower show!" Fresh tears poured from her eyes. "That's not for a month yet!"

"So screw 'em," Fletch said.

Judy tried to collect herself in front of Freddie. "How?"

"Screw 'em in what you write." Fletch realized James had been right: Mrs. Presidential Candidate Doris Wheeler badly needed a lesson in manners. The realization made him hot.

"I don't have anything to write!" Judy almost wailed. "I didn't even see what the inside of her suite looked like!"

"Oh," he said lamely.

"This story was important to me." Judy Nadich walked away, head down, her tote bag banging against her knees, back to do stories about flower shows and cracked teacups and the funds needed to clean the statues in the park.

"Poor local press," Freddie sighed. "I was one once."

Fletch pressed the elevator button. "Where?"

"New York City."

"New York City is not local. Even in New York City, New York City is not local."

"On a national campaign like this," Freddie said, stepping into the elevator, "local press is seduced with a weak drink, and granted a kiss on the cheek."

"So this is how you live." Freddie looked around his hotel room. "Your suitcase is dark brown. Mine is light blue."

"Yeah," Fletch said. "That's the difference between boys and girls." He went into the bathroom to collect his shaving gear. "You know anything in particular about the woman who was murdered this morning?"

"Mary Cantor, age thirty-four, widowed, mother of three. Her husband was a Navy navigator killed in an accident over Lake Erie three years ago."

Fletch tried to visualize the three children, then decided not to. "Has the woman in Chicago been identified yet? The one found in a closet off the press room?"

"Wife of an obstetrician. Member of the League of Women Voters. Highly respectable. Just not carrying identification that night. Maybe she left her purse somewhere and someone walked off with it."

Fletch came back into the bedroom. Freddie was stretched out on the unmade bed. "I don't see what the women have in common," he said. "A society woman in Chicago —"

"A socially useful woman, you mean."

"Alice Elizabeth Shields, a bookish woman with her own mind, two nights ago. And last night, a mother, Air Force widow, a night chambermaid."

"They all have something in common."

"What?"

"They're all women."

"Was the woman found last night raped?"

"Haven't talked with the coroner himself yet. A lab assistant says she believes the woman was not raped. There's something very rapelike about these murders, though."

Fletch was rolling up his dirty shirts. He hadn't been in any hotel long enough to get his laundry done. "What do you mean?"

"Rape isn't a sexual thing," Freddie said. "Not really. The main element in rape is to dominate a woman, subject her, mortify her. Degrade her. Sexually victimizing her is secondary to victimizing her."

"I understand that. But without the element of actual rape, Freddie, there is no absolute proof that the murderer is a male. The murderer could be a strong woman."

"Yeah," Freddie said from the bed. "Fenella Baker. She tears off her blouse and turns into a muscle-bulging Amazon."

"How was the woman last night murdered?"

"Strangled with some kind of a soft cord, the police say. Like a drapery tie, or a bathrobe sash. They haven't found whatever it was."

"The lack of sexual rape bothers me." Fletch took a jacket from the closet, folded it quickly, and put it in the suitcase. "A strong woman . . ."

"Terrible." Freddie got up, took the jacket out of the suitcase, and folded it properly. "Got to make clothes last on a trip like this."

"I never wear that jacket."

"Then why do you carry it?"

"That's the jacket I carry." He pointed to one on the unmade bed. "That's the jacket I wear."

Freddie tossed the clothes in his suitcase like someone tossing a salad with her fingers. "Fletcher, this suitcase is full of nothing but laundry."

"I know."

"You've got to do something about that."

"Where? When?"

"Or we'll put you off the press bus. There are enough stinkers on the press bus as it is. You notice no one will sit next to Hanrahan?"

"I notice he's always stretched out over two seats."

"He smells bad." She resettled his shaving kit so the suitcase could close.

"Will you leave my damned laundry alone?"

She dropped the suitcase lid and stared at it. "Relationships between men and women can be nice. I guess."

He watched her from the chair where he was sitting. "Can't say you never had one, Freddie."

"I live out of a suitcase, Fletcher. All the time. Anything that doesn't fit in the suitcase can't come with me."

"Why? Why do you live this way?"

She was running the tips of her fingers along the top edge of Fletch's suitcase. "Why am I Fredericka Arbuthnot? Because I have the chance to be. I'd be a fool to pass it up. Enough women get the chance to be girl friends, wives, and mothers." She sat in the hotel room's other chair. "Where would the world be without my sterling reporting?"

"Want me to order up coffee?"

"We'd never get it."

Not giving any neighborhood snail a good race, Flash driving, Fletch had gone to the television studio and sat through the governor's taped interview. Deftly, The Man Who had turned the interview to the high incidence of crime in this country. He even referred to having heard about the chambermaid murdered in his hotel that morning. The interview with the candidate was to be shown on the noon news.

"You saw Hanrahan's shit this morning?" Fletch asked.

"Sure."

"So now you'll have to write something."

"Already have," Freddie answered. "I was fair. Reported that the murders have happened on the fringe of the campaign, no connection with the campaign has been made, the police so far don't even think the murders are connected."

"You indicated it could all be coincidence."

"Yes."

"Do you believe that?"

Freddie shrugged. "If I did, I wouldn't be here. Also I had to say, as did Hanrahan, that the candidate has not made himself available for questioning on this matter."

"Truly, he hasn't anything to say."

"Truly . . ." Freddie was stretched out in her chair, her head against the chair back. "Fletch, what does Wheeler really say about these murders?"

"He treats them like flies on his porridge. He keeps trying to brush them away. To him, this story is the story of the campaign itself. He doesn't want it turned into a murder story."

"It would ruin the campaign."

"He's talking about organizing the new technology to gather and disperse information, goods, and service for the betterment of people worldwide, and someone keeps dropping corpses on him."

"Who?"

"Tell me."

"Would he have any other reason for avoiding our questions? Inquiry? Investigation?"

"Isn't the ruination of his campaign enough of a reason?"

"I suppose so."

"You mean, like his own guilt?"

"Sally Shields was found on the sidewalk beneath his windows. As Hanrahan reported, and I didn't, Doris and Caxton Wheeler have separate suites. Doris is a rich bitch. People tell me she can be real nasty. Who says he has to love her?"

"You think the candidate is using disposable women?"

"Who knows?"

"I don't think he'd throw one out his own window."

"Things get out of hand," she mused. "Things can get out of hand."

"There is an idea . . ." Fletch hesitated.

"Lay it on me. I can take it, whatever it is."

". . . that whoever, or whatever is doing this, is doing so to torpedo he campaign of Caxton Wheeler. To destroy him as a presidential candidate."

"Whose idea is that?"

Again Fletch hesitated. "Caxton Wheeler's."

"I thought so. Even to you he tries to steer inquiry away from himself. Was he in his suite at the time Alice Elizabeth Shields landed on the sidewalk, or wasn't he?"

Fletch shifted in his chair. "The timing doesn't work out. He says he got out of a car, didn't see anything like a crowd on the sidewalk, didn't see the people leaving the bar, and yet when he got to his hotel room, he says he saw the lights from the police cars and ambulance."

"All that can't be so," Freddie said.

Fletch didn't say anything.

"Is Wheeler pointing his finger at anyone else?"

"He's mentioned Andrew Esty."

"Esty?" Freddie laughed. "I don't think his religion condones murder."

"He's been with the campaign three weeks. He left yesterday, came back, there was another murder. I saw him in the elevator last night. He was frustrated, angry —"

"Esty wouldn't want to be caught as a murderer." Freddie smiled. "The Supreme Court might prohibit prisoners from praying."

"Bill Dieckmann," Fletch said.

"Bill's pretty sick, I guess."

"Last night I found him in the corridor of the fifth floor of this hotel. He was having one of his seizures. When I came across him, he was leaning against the wall. He didn't recognize me. He didn't know where he was or what he was doing. He collapsed. I carried him to his own room on the ninth floor. When he came to, he didn't know how he got there."

"What was he doing on the fifth floor?"

"Who knows? But this morning I realized he was standing between the main elevators and the service elevators. The chambermaid was found in a service elevator, right?"

Freddie's face was sad. "Poor old Bill. He's got five kids." Then she laughed. "Did you see Filby's face yesterday when he realized he had missed the whole 'New Reality' speech? You'd think the doctor had just told him he'd have to have his whole stomach amputated."

"That would be hard to swallow."

"Joe Hall has an uncontrollable temper," Freddie said. "I saw him lose it once. At a trial in Nashville. A courtroom marshal wouldn't let him in. Said his press credentials were no good. Joe went berserk. He began swinging at people."

"And you can't tell me," Fletch said, "that Solov is your normal Russian boy-next-door. If what you all say is true, he sits there watching pornography all night. He must build up a hell of a head of steam. Goin' out and beatin' women to death might be his way of finishing off a night of such entertainment."

"Poor Russians," Freddie sighed. "They have so little experience handling smut."

"Are you listening to me?"

"He bears watching."

"I think he's a very good candidate. Might even oblige Wheeler's theory of someone wanting to sabotage the campaign."

"So where does Wheeler go when he disappears?" Freddie asked.

"You keep bringing the conversation back to Wheeler."

"You keep steering me away from Wheeler. And his staff. You keep pushing it on the press. Have you forgotten yourself so easily? Really, how quickly one becomes a member of the establishment."

"I'm trying to be honest with you. I trust you."

"Now that you know I really am Freddie Arbuthnot."

"Yes. Now that we both agree you're Fredericka Arbuthnot."

"There are plenty of kooks on staff. Dr. Thom, who clearly got his medical degree from Bother U."

"He has his hatreds."

"That Lee Allen Parke is a manipulator of women, if I ever saw one. And I've seen plenty. The governor's driver —"

"Flash Grasselli."

"— has the body of a brute, and the brain of a newt. Barry Hines is twitching so fast you can't even see him."

"I guess we've got kooks on this campaign."

"Fletcher, dear, you're almost beginning to seem normal to me."

"You mean, next to Solov?"

"Next to Solov, Maxim Gorky would seem a fun date."

Fletch glanced at his watch. It was twenty to twelve. "We've got a press bus to catch." He went to the bed and closed his suitcase. "The rally at the shopping mall is at one o'clock. Tonight in Melville is the last big rally of this campaign."

She hadn't moved from her chair. "So where does the governor go when he disappears?"

"Oh, Flash gave me some cock-and-bull story about his going to some unnamed mountain cabin on some unnamed lake and going on a sleep orgy."

"A sleep orgy?"

"He reads and sleeps for a few days."

"I'll bet."

"I'm not sure I believe it."

Freddie stood up. "Fletch, let's keep talking about this to each other, okay?"

"Absolutely."

She crossed the room to the door. "There must be things we're not noticing, not hearing, not seeing. You know — like that Ms. Sullivan, the way she just treated that woman reporter from a local newspaper. She's a tough, vicious broad."

Fletch had put his suitcase on the floor. He had not opened the door. "Promise me something else, Freddie?"

"No."

"Keep your eyes and ears open for your own sake. Someone traveling with us likes to maul women. You're a woman."

"I've never proven that to you."

"I watched you fold my jacket."

"Oh."

"Going to kiss me on the nose again?"

"You're exploiting me," she said.

She kissed him warmly on the mouth.

Fletch let Freddie out and went back to answer his phone.

"More of the same tomorrow," a whiskey voice grated in Fletch's ear.

"Am I supposed to know who this is?"

"This is *Newsbill's* star writer, you jackass."

"Gee, Hanrahan. I thought you'd dashed to New York to catch your Pulitzer Prize."

"More tomorrow," Hanrahan said, "of specifically who refuses to talk to me about the murdered broads. I'm going to publish a list of questions I'm not getting answered. Like where was Caxton Wheeler when Alice Elizabeth Shields got exited through his bedroom window? In whose bedroom had she spent the previous four nights? Why was

Barry Hines thrown out of the University of Idaho? While Walsh Wheeler was in the Marines, did he machine-gun a bunch of kids?"

"No."

"Questions don't matter, sonny. Just the answers or lack thereof."

"Barry Hines flunked out of the University of Idaho. Chemistry. Many do."

"Who cares? You got my point?"

"You're doin' fine, Hanrahan. If I actually let you talk to someone, will you really write down what he says and print it, like a reporter? Or just use the opportunity to write fiction?"

"Guess you got to take that chance, jackass. If I can't print something that looks like answers, I'm going to print something that looks like questions."

"Oh, I see," Fletch said brilliantly. "That's why people refer to what you write as questionable. 'Bye, Mike."

Using his hotel room phone, Fletch then communicated with Barry Hines and told him to find Walsh and tell Walsh he must plan to see Michael J. Hanrahan and Fredericka Arbuthnot.

TWENTY-EIGHT

Fletch opened the back door of the rented black sedan. "Walsh said I should drive with you to the shopping plaza."

Doris Wheeler gave him a friendly nod. "Fine."

He had found Walsh, without topcoat or tie, standing on the sidewalk outside the hotel. Coldly, Walsh said he had agreed to meet with Fredericka Arbuthnot and Michael J. Hanrahan, if Fletch thought it so necessary.

"Shall I sit in front?" The two women, Doris Wheeler and Ms. Sullivan, pretty well filled up the backseat. Fletch did not recognize the car's rented driver.

"No, no," Doris Wheeler said. "Plenty of room back here. Go around and get in the other side."

Fletch went around the back of the car and got in the other side. Which pushed the tall, short-haired, big-nosed Ms. Sullivan onto the middle of the seat, her feet onto the high gasline bump. Which made her look like a large dog in a small box.

"We haven't met," Fletch said to her. "I. M. Fletcher."

Ms. Sullivan raised her upper lip in greeting. "Sully."

The campaign bus was pulling away from the curb in front of the hotel, followed by the press bus. Around the area, other cars — those of volunteers and station wagons filled with television equipment — were rolling forward to form a caravan.

"Get behind the second bus," Doris Wheeler ordered the driver.

In the road was slow confusion. The hotel's doorman was trying to stop traffic so the caravan could assemble itself, but Farmingdale drivers were not impressed by his green-and-gold suit, or his brown derby hat. They honked their horns at him and insisted upon going directly about their own business.

A volunteer's green van and a blue pickup truck ended up between the press bus and Doris Wheeler's sedan. The bumper sticker on the pickup truck read: HONK FOR UPTON.

The rented driver honked his horn.

"Stop that," Doris Wheeler said.

"I hear you had some difficulty with a local reporter this morning," Fletch ventured.

"Cow," said Sully.

"Was she rude or something?"

"Stupid."

Doris said to the driver, "I told you to get directly behind the second bus."

All the vehicles were jammed together at a red light. The driver looked at Doris through the rearview mirror and did nothing. There was nothing he could do.

"How did she offend you?" Fletch asked.

"I make appointments for Mrs. Wheeler," Sully said.

"She didn't need a real appointment. All she wanted to do was hang around and watch, listen."

"We didn't have time for any such person this morning," Sully said. "Furthermore, you are not to force people upon us, Fletcher. All this is none of your affair."

"My 'affair,' as you call it," Fletch said, "is the whole campaign. We're supposed to be working together."

"Now, now." Doris Wheeler patted Sully's knee. "Mr. Fletcher is working for this campaign. We're looking forward to his help. You're going to start being a great help to us, aren't you, Mr. Fletcher?"

Doris Wheeler's voice was abrasive even in dulcet tones in the back of the car.

At the appearance of a green light the caravan had sprung forward.

"Pass those two vehicles," Doris Wheeler said.

"We won't lose the buses, ma'am," the driver said.

"Pass them, I said!"

Again the driver glanced through the rearview mirror. On the main street of Farmingdale he swung the car out into oncoming traffic. An approaching yellow Cadillac screeched on its brakes. A Honda smashed into its rear end. The rented driver got back into the right lane ahead of the pickup truck, but still behind the volunteer's car.

"Imbecile," Doris Wheeler said. She pronounced it *imbeseal*. "Get ahead of this car."

"When I have room," the driver muttered.

"Don't you speak to me that way," Doris Wheeler said. "Do as you're told!"

They were far enough away from the center of Farmingdale so that the traffic had lightened. The driver swung out, waved the volunteer's car back, and pulled up snug behind the press bus.

"Ought to be nice to the local press," Fletch said. "Judy Nadich may be a feature writer for the *Farmingdale Views* this year. But three years from now she may be a columnist for the *Washington Post*."

"Three years from now," Sully said, "she'll be up to her nose in diapers and burning meat loaf for a beery husband."

"I don't know what you two are talking about," Doris Wheeler said.

"That stupid cow who appeared at the door this morning."

"Which one?"

"The smiling one. She thought she had permission from this Fletcher here. She showed me some scribble on a piece of notepaper." Sully sniffed. "She thought it meant something."

"Did you send her up, Fletcher?"

"You could have made a friend for life. She's a young woman reporter and this story would have set her up."

"Have you been on a political campaign before, Fletcher?" Doris Wheeler asked.

"No, ma'am."

"I have no idea why Caxton took you on."

"To make mistakes, ma'am," Fletch answered evenly. "To create an aura of youth and amateurism about the campaign." There was a surprised hard gleam in Doris's eyes as she stared sideways at him. "To be blamed for everything and get fired, probably just before the Pennsylvania and California primaries. To warm the seat for Graham Kidwell." Even Sully was looking at him as if he were a kitten messing with her dinner bowl. "To get sent home on a bus."

They were entering the highway. There was another snow squall. Doris said, "I don't know why Walsh happened to think of you."

"I know how to run a copying machine."

"What you did for my son while you were in the service together was nice." Doris Wheeler settled her coat more comfortably around her shoulder. "But really, I don't think he needs that kind of help now."

The driver was keeping the car so close behind the press bus that the car was being sprayed by slush and sand from the highway. He had the windshield wipers going full speed. The whole car, even the rear windows, was being covered with mud.

"Imbecile!" Doris shouted at him. "Slow down! Let the bus get ahead of us!"

"Don't want anybody to pass us, ma'am," the driver drawled.

"Imbecile! Where did Barry find this man?" Doris asked Fletch loudly. "The local games arcade?"

"In my spare time — when I'm not driving idiots — I'm a fireman."

Doris's eyes bulged. "Well, my man. You just lost both jobs."

Sully took pad and pen from her purse and made a note.

Through the rearview mirror the driver looked at Fletch.

"Now," said Doris Wheeler, again settling her coat over her big shoulders, "let's talk about what you can do to be helpful."

Fletch put on his listening expression. He had learned to do that in junior high school.

"My husband, Fletcher, is a dependent man. Very bright, very energetic — all that is true. But he's always going around asking people what they think. You see, he's not really confident in what he himself thinks."

"He listens to advisors?" Fletch speculated.

"He listens to everybody. Caxton," Doris Wheeler confided, "is very impressed by the last idea he hears."

"Whatever it is," Sully added.

"He's impressionable?" Fletch conjectured.

"I've known the man thirty-odd years."

"Ever since Barbara died?"

She stared at him as if he had burped resoundingly in public. "Who's Barbara?"

"Oh," he said.

"I dare say," she continued, "he flattered you by asking you what you thought."

"He did."

"And you came up with that whole 'New Reality' nonsense."

"Not really."

"Young people always think it's clever to disparage our institutions."

"It's not?"

"Politically, it's suicide. As I said last night. You can knock the institutions on their goddamned asses," her voice grated, "as long as you always give them lip service. That's the *only* reality."

"The governor gave an interview on all this to Lansing Sayer this morning," Fletch said. "It was pretty good. It sounded to me like he's actually coming up with a program."

The driver had slowed down so much that the buses were way ahead of them. Clearly the volunteers did not dare pass Doris Wheeler's car.

"The trouble with Caxton," Doris Wheeler said, "is that he doesn't always think. Even if he really were saying something here, he doesn't always stop to think of the effect of his saying it. I spent a long time with Andrew Esty this morning."

"You did?"

Sully vigorously nodded yes.

"Told him all about my grandfather, who was a fundamentalist preacher in Nebraska. . . ." Doris Wheeler then proceeded to tell Fletch all about her grandfather who was a fundamentalist preacher in Nebraska. It was his son, Doris's father, who had discovered oil.

Fletch put on his not-listening expression. He had learned that in junior high school, too.

The NBC Television News station wagon pulled out of the caravan and began to pass Doris Wheeler's car.

"Speed up!" she shouted at the driver. "You're losing them."

The driver began racing with the news wagon.

"Ah, good," said Fletch. "I always wanted to be in *Ben Hur.*"

"Imbecile," said Doris Wheeler.

Close behind the NBC wagon was the CBS wagon. The ABC news wagon appeared on the right side of the car. Doris Wheeler's car was getting pelted with slush from both sides.

"You must be careful what you say around Caxton," Doris Wheeler concluded. "It's your job to protect him — from himself, when necessary. Not to walk him down the garden path."

Up ahead, the buses had disappeared altogether.

"What do you ladies think of these murders?" Fletch asked.

"You mean, the women?" Doris Wheeler asked.

"You're aware of them."

"Of course."

"Any theories?" asked Fletch.

The turnoff to the shopping plaza was at the top of a small rise. By then all the vehicles in the caravan were going so fast that slowing down properly and turning was problematical. There was some skidding. The volunteer's green van missed the turn altogether and had to go miles west and then east and then west again to get back to the right turnoff.

"No. No theories," Doris Wheeler said. "Why should we have theories? It's a police matter."

The campaign bus and the press bus were in the middle of the shopping plaza's parking lot. A crowd of two or three thousand people was standing around in the cold slush, waiting for the candidate.

"We don't have any police traveling with us," Fletch commented.

"What this campaign doesn't need," Sully said, "is a police investigation."

"Don't believe in law and order, huh?" Fletch asked.

Sully's look told him she thought him something not to be stepped in.

The driver parked far away from the buses. He parked in the middle of the biggest puddle in the parking lot. Then he sat there. He did not get out to open doors.

"This car is filthy," Doris Wheeler told him as she opened her own door.

"Don't worry," the driver muttered. "You'll never see it again."

"I told you I'm going to report you," Doris Wheeler said, lifting herself off the seat.

"You may be Mrs. President of the United States!" the driver shouted at her through the open door. "But in Farmingdale, you're just a big old bag!"

Sully had followed Doris Wheeler out of the car. Fletch got out his own side.

"I wouldn't vote for your husband for dogcatcher!" the driver shouted. "He doesn't know a bitch when he sees one!"

The driver accelerated, splashing all of them.

"My God." Doris Wheeler looked at her splattered skirt. At the size of the puddle they were all standing in. At the back of the rapidly disappearing car. "That car was hired for all day. He can't just leave me here."

Fletch watched the filthy rented car climb back onto the highway. "Actually, he can," Fletch said. "He just did."

TWENTY-NINE

"Good afternoon. I have just a brief announcement," said the President of the United States.

"I guess you do," Phil Nolting said to the television set. "When did you ever give a Saturday afternoon press conference? Sports fans won't love you."

Barry Hines said to Fletch, "You're to call someone named Alston Chambers. He says you have his number. Also Rondoll James has called you twice. Here's his number."

"You can forget James," Walsh muttered.

The campaign bus had pulled into a rest area and stopped. Even the bus driver was watching the President's press conference.

The press bus had stopped a mile down the road at a tavern to watch the press conference.

"He wants to inspire a million Sunday sermons, I bet," Paul Dobson said. "Up with God and country."

His head resting against a pillow, a cut on his cheek, The Man Who sat on the bench at the side of the bus, watching the television, saying nothing.

The rally at the shopping plaza had not been a success.

The governor climbed to the roof of a volunteer's Ford, microphone in hand. Every time he said something the sound system screeched horribly. Again and again the governor tried to speak while Barry Hines and the bus driver scurried around trying to discover what was causing the screeching. Then he tried speaking without the microphone. The wind, the sound of traffic in the parking lot, the noise of jet airplanes passing overhead made the governor look like a frantic, laryngytic opera singer.

Doris Wheeler completely ignored the crowd. She went directly to the campaign bus, spluttering about her wet shoes and splattered skirt. Sully followed her as if she were on a short leash.

Fletch said to Walsh, "Don't ask me to drive in the car with your mother again. Please."

"Yeah," Walsh said. "That Sully." Through his open shirt collar his Adam's apple rose and fell. "Tough broad."

"The driver went off and left them here. In the middle of a puddle."

Walsh looked around the parking lot. "That's okay. A volunteer will drive her to the senior citizens' home. That always looks better anyway. No problem."

The governor climbed down from the wet car roof. He handed the microphone to Lee Allen Parke, who handed it to a volunteer, who handed it back to Barry Hines.

Then The Man Who walked into the crowd, both hands out to the people, allowing himself to be grabbed, pulled, pushed, jostled nearly off his feet. A little girl sitting on her father's shoulders vomited on his head. Somehow an older woman, trying to kiss the governor, gashed his cheek with her fingernail. The Man Who kept reaching over people's heads to shake hands with people behind them so the crowd kept pressing closer and closer to him. Shortly a fistfight broke out near the back of the crowd. From where Fletch was standing, he could see that three men had gotten a man in a black leather jacket down on the ground and were beating him pretty well. Two short, older men were trying to get them to stop. Walsh went into the crowd, turned his father around, and literally pushed him back onto the campaign bus.

Doris Wheeler and Sully got into the backseat of the volunteer's Ford and were driven away.

The campaign bus left ahead of schedule.

As the bus was leaving, the man in the black leather jacket was staggering through the thinning crowd, yelling at them incomprehensibly through broken teeth and blood.

Aboard the bus, Flash cleaned the scratch on the governor's face. He put antiseptic on it. The governor grinned at his staff. "Winning the hearts and minds of the people . . . There must be an easier job than this."

"Sorry," Barry Hines said.

Walsh said, "It's this damned weather."

So the caravan went on until nearly two o'clock and then parked at the tavern and in the rest area to watch the President's news conference.

Aboard the campaign bus everyone was silent while the President read his statement: "The technology we have available today, especially the technology of communications, is not being used for the betterment of the people of the world. Clearly, the people of all nations would benefit from a fuller, more responsible use of this technology to bring basic education to all people, to exchange scientific data programs of cultural merit, health information, and the facts that can provide for a more equitable and waste-free worldwide allocation of food. Proper use of this technology should be encouraged by responsible governments. Therefore, today I am naming a special White House panel of distinguished citizens, and charging them with reporting to me how the technology of communications can be better used, worldwide, to encourage the peace and increase the prosperity of all nations." The President blinked through the television lights at the White House press corps. "Now I'll take questions."

"The son of a bitch stole your issue," Walsh said quietly.

The Man Who sat with his head back against the pillow. He continued to watch the press conference silently.

Most of the questions were about Central America, the economy, the Middle East, the Russian economic situation, and whether the President would agree to debate any or all of the other people running for the presidency and, if so, when. "It's much too early to discuss that."

At the end of the press conference, Barry Hines clicked off the television set.

Loudly, more firmly, directly at his father, Walsh said again, "The son of a bitch stole your issue."

"That's all right." The governor looked around at his staff and chuckled. "At least the son of a bitch got me out of trouble with my wife."

THIRTY

"How do, Mr. Persecutor." Fletch had taken the moment to lie down on his bed at the Melville First Hotel and return Alston Chambers's call. "Only got a minute. Got to meet Walsh and a couple of members of the press in a bar about a matter of death and death. And death."

"How's it going, Fletch?"

"Feel like I'm dancin' to the 'Three Page Sonata,'" answered Fletch. "Have to do more listenin' than dancin'."

It was five o'clock. The rally at Melville's public auditorium was to begin at eight o'clock.

From three to four that afternoon, Fletch had sat through a call-in radio talk show with The Man Who in the town of McKensie. Many of the people who called in had intelligent, pertinent questions regarding Social Security, farm subsidies, federal highway funds. A significant percentage called The Man Who with personal problems. *"My wife is working now, we need the extra income, you know, to eat? This means my kids come home from school to an empty house, we ask a neighbor to watch over them, but she has arthritis, she can't move none too fast, we never know what they're doin', you know? Why can't things be like they were? When I was a kid, my mother was home . . ."* The high incidence of crime came up more than once, naturally, and the governor made the most of the opportunity, referring to the chambermaid found murdered in his hotel that morning. For an hour The Man Who made a sincere effort to answer all questions, public and private.

And then the slow crawl by car over dark roads from McKensie to Melville. Flash drove. In the backseat, the governor read. In the front seat, Fletch watched the fifty-five-mile-per-hour signs approach at thirty miles per hour.

At the Melville First Hotel, messages were waiting for Fletch. Asking him to contact journalists traveling with the campaign (Lansing Sayer, Fenella Baker, Stella Kirchner). Asking him to contact other journalists calling in from around the country (plus one from Mexico City and one from the *Times* of London). There were three messages asking him to return the calls of Rondoll James in Iowa.

He had returned Alston Chambers's call.

Alston said, "Thought I'd tell you I followed up on that question I asked you last night."

"What question?"

"About Walsh's sudden departure from the field. After our three days hanging in the trees."

"Sure. He was tired. He'd had enough of it. His poppa had the political pull to bring him home. I would have gotten out of there at that point, too, if I could have. Any of us would have."

"Yes, but not quite. Walsh sassed a superior officer."

Fletch blinked. "Who didn't?"

"I talked to Captain Walters. He runs a book distribution center in Denver now, by the way."

"Nice man. Used to get reading books for all of us. Never lost his cool."

"Yeah, well he says that at one point, Walsh did."

"You're kidding."

"Laced into Major Leslie Hunt."

"First time I ever heard her name pronounced with an *H.*"

"That she was. You remember her."

"Awful bitch. Resented soldiers being men."

"Remember the thing she was always going on about?"

"Yeah. Mess tent had to be in the middle. Regulations. Forget the snipers. Mess tent in the middle to impress the enemy. As they shot at us. Impress them with our stupidity."

"Two guys from K Company got shot on their way to breakfast. One in the leg, not bad; one in the back, pretty bad."

"I don't remember that."

"Walters says that's what started it off. Walsh yelled at Major Hunt in staff meeting."

"He got sent home for that? Should have gotten a free night at the Officers' Club."

"No. Later he threatened her."

"Good."

"With a rifle butt. That's where his dad's pull came in. There were two or three witnesses. Captain Walters said that charges might have been brought against Walsh, probably would have been, if his dad weren't in Congress on some military appropriations committee."

"Hell, Walsh had been through three of the worst days in any man's life. The major was a stupid bitch. Never been to the front herself, so she wanted to make heroes in the chow line."

"All true. Thought I'd tell you."

"So Walsh lost his temper at her. Good for him."

"Walters remembers you. Asked for stories about you. I said there weren't any."

"Walsh isn't so stupid," Fletch said. "Scared the shit out of a bitch, and got a quick ride home. His momma didn't have no fools."

THIRTY-ONE

" I agreed to meet with you two against my better judgment," Walsh said.

They sat at a small round table in a dark corner of a bar a block from Melville's First Hotel. Peanuts glistened in a bowl in the center of the table. A glass of beer had been placed in front of each of them: Walsh, Fletch, Michael J. Hanrahan, and Fredericka Arbuthnot. Hanrahan had been served a shot of rye as well.

The juke box was playing "Limpin' Home to Jesus."

Hanrahan downed his rye.

"Fletch, here, insisted upon it, apparently because of the shit you published in *Newsbill* this morning, Hanrahan," Walsh continued in a low tone. "A few hours after you join the campaign, apparently you can make headlines in your rag by writing no one would talk to you about some murders or something that happened sometime, somewhere." Walsh rolled his eyes upward and shook his head. "I expect there are a few examples of breaking and entering that have happened around us you also might ask us about. And don't forget sodomy. A lot of sodomy goes on in these motels." His voice was almost a tired drone. "What we're really meeting about is very simple. You're not political writers, either of you. Fletcher tells me you're crime writers. There's no reason I can think of why we should make room for you on the press bus. You've asked for this meeting, and I'm going to give it to you. But at the moment, I can't think of any reason why I shouldn't ask Fletch to deny press credentials to you both."

"Speech over?" Hanrahan asked.

Freddie had glanced at Fletch. "Denying us press credentials wouldn't do you much good. Riding the press bus isn't the most pleasurable experience of my life."

"Yeah," Hanrahan said. "*Newsworld* would supply Arbuthnot with a limousine and driver. Me, I'd get a helicopter. In other words, stuff it, Wheeler."

Walsh popped some peanuts into his mouth. "Fletch and I have to be at a staff meeting in a few minutes." Chewing, Walsh's neck muscles were visibly tight through his opened shirt collar. "If you've got any questions, you'd better roll 'em out."

Hanrahan had downed his beer. For a moment, his eyes sparkled. "How long had you known Alice Elizabeth Shields?"

"I never knew her," Walsh answered.

"You met her in Chicago?"

"I did not know her."

"Who did — your dad?"

"My father did not know her."

"Then, how come she ended up dead outside his motel room window?"

Walsh snorted. He didn't answer.

"Walsh," Freddie said. "It might help matters if we had a list of the

471

people who were in your father's suite the night Alice Elizabeth Shields was murdered."

"A specific list would be impossible, Ms. Arbuthnot. There were some of the local press. I do not know their names. A couple of local political coordinators. One was named William Burke, the other something-or-other Blackstone. There was national press: Fenella Baker, Lansing Sayer, your own Mary Rice" — he nodded to Hanrahan — "Dieckmann, O'Brien, a few others."

"Were you there?" Hanrahan asked.

"I was there. In and out."

"Was Solov there?" Fletch asked.

"I don't remember."

"Was Dr. Thom there?" Freddie asked.

"I don't remember. I doubt it. He avoids the press, for the most part."

"Back home," Hanrahan announced, "your Dr. Robert Thom is known as a Dr. Feelgood. Writes more prescriptions than anyone in the county. How come he's your dad's private physician?"

"Dr. Thom is the physician traveling with the campaign, available to all."

"How much of a drug addict is your dad?" Hanrahan asked. He reached over and took Freddie's beer.

"My father is not addicted to anything," Walsh answered. "Never has been."

"Then how come they have to cart him away three or four times a year to clean out his head?"

Walsh said, "I'm not going to dignify that with an answer."

"Where does your father go?" Freddie asked. "You know, when he suddenly disappears."

"He doesn't 'suddenly disappear.' He takes advantage of breaks in his schedule, when they occur. He goes fishing. He reads history. Even Caxton Wheeler gets to take a few days off, now and again. During last calendar year, my father took exactly fifteen days away from his desk. Make a scandal of that, if you can."

"Specifically, where does he go?" Hanrahan asked.

"None of your business."

"He always goes alone," Freddie said.

"No," Walsh answered. "A staff member always goes with him."

"Flash Grasselli," Hanrahan scoffed. "A packing case on wheels."

"A packing case with a computer inside," Fletch said.

"Again, it might help put questions to rest," Freddie said, "if we could work out your father's timetable the night Alice Elizabeth Shields lied. When, precisely, he got back to the hotel . . . that sort of thing."

"I doubt he knows," Walsh said. "There are four time zones in this country. On a campaign, we're back and forth across time zones all he time. Living this way, one loses a sense of time, you know. Precise time."

"I doubt you do, Walsh," Freddie said.

"Oh, stuff it, stocking-mouth." Hanrahan finished the rest of her beer. "Just 'cause *Newsworld* let you have their telephone number, don't think you're a real journalist."

Freddie smiled at Fletch.

"This broad in Chicago," Hanrahan said. "This Mrs. Gynecologist —"

"Elaine Ramsey," Freddie giggled. "Wife of an obstetrician. Want to make a note of that, Michael? Or should I phone *Newsbill* for you?"

"You and your dad both knew her."

"I don't think either of us knew her," Walsh answered.

"You were seen talking to her at that press reception at the Hotel Harris." Hanrahan picked up Fletch's beer. "So was your dad."

"Hanrahan, we talk to a lot of people. A lot of people talk to us. That's what a political campaign is all about."

"And some of them end up dead." Beer sprayed through Hanrahan's teeth.

Now the jukebox was playing "I'm Rushin' to Coke High."

"Okay," Freddie said. "You state neither you nor your father knew Mrs. Ramsey."

"I can't speak for my father. I certainly don't believe he knew her. I don't see how he could have. I did not know her."

"You can't speak for your old man," Hanrahan said. "Why don't you wheel the old boy out here, give me a shot at him? Dr. Thom can pop him up for the occasion."

Pointedly, Walsh looked at his watch.

"Maybe you can answer some questions about last night," Hanrahan said. "Does your memory go back that far?"

"What questions?" Walsh asked patiently.

"Coroner places the death of Mary Cantor, the hotel maid, at between eleven P.M. and two-thirty A.M. You weren't in your room at twelve midnight."

"Were you there?" Walsh asked easily. With a tighter jaw, Walsh said, "You'd better not violate the privacy of myself or my family ever again, Hanrahan. Or staff members."

"Where were you?" Hanrahan asked.

"After I came in, Fletch and I had a brief meeting in my room. Tha was about eleven-thirty, wasn't it, Fletch? Then I went to my mother' suite. We had a few things to discuss. Then I went back to my roon to clear up a few papers."

"That doesn't account for three and a half hours," Hanrahan said.

Walsh shrugged. "What can I say?"

"Can you tell me where you were at the time Alice Elizabeth Shields tried to dent the sidewalk?"

"I don't remember. I was in the bar. Before that I had been in my room."

"Using the telephone?" Hanrahan asked.

"I suppose so."

"The hotel operator says your room's telephone didn't answer from eight o'clock on that night."

"Sometimes I don't answer the phone when I've got work to do. I had a meeting with Barry Hines. Phil Nolting and I were trying to work out the South Africa thing. I was in the bar, waiting for Fletch to arrive. People were calling about Rondoll James, friends of his on the press, so I wasn't answering the phone. Sorry I can't give you a perfect alibi."

"Wheeler, when you were in the Marines overseas, you were almost court-martialed."

The muscles in Walsh's jaw tightened.

The jukebox was playing "Give Me the Land of the Free."

"What do you mean?" Walsh asked.

"You refused to lead a patrol one night. The patrol that did go out got slaughtered."

"He didn't refuse," put in Fletch. "We were all too stoned to go. Everyone was too stoned. Everyone except the lieutenant."

"You're fishing for minnows, Hanrahan," Walsh said. "I wasn't court-martialed."

"No. Your dad prevented it."

"My dad had nothing to do with my service record."

"And he arranged to get you home ahead of schedule."

"I was ordered to Washington," Walsh admitted. "And my father did have something to do with that. I studied statistics in college. I was assigned to a bureau of statistics at the Department of Defense to serve out the remainder of my time. Make of that what you will."

"You were assigned for just two months?" Hanrahan exclaimed.

"There was a statistical mess," Walsh answered. "My father wanted to see if the statistics being published by the Pentagon had any particular reality to a young officer who had been in the field."

Hanrahan said: "Bullshit."

"While we're speaking of statistics, let me say this." Walsh leaned forward in his chair and crossed his forearms on the table. "Over twenty thousand Americans get murdered a year. Over thirty percent of American families get touched by crime one way or another every year. In this interview, I'm not going to spout a lot of sociological reasons for these figures, or how Caxton Wheeler's administration might bring these figures down. I wouldn't so insult Ms. Arbuthnot. It's an epidemic. But I will point out to you, statistically, that right now, none of us — presidential candidate or not — can go anywhere, by anywhere, without a violent crime happening somewhere up the block, down the street, in the park across from the hotel. That's all the news I have for you crime writers. I have no personal knowledge of these crimes. Neither has my father. If you think they're connected with this campaign somehow, then I suggest you take a close look at your colleagues on the press bus. Frankly, I think it's just a fact of contemporary American life."

"Broads aren't gettin' knocked off on the Upton campaign," Hanrahan said. "We haven't been assigned to travel with the Graves campaign."

"So be it," Walsh said. "Be careful what you write. This is a political campaign you're covering, not a Halloween parade."

Fletch followed Walsh's lead in getting up to go. Only Walsh's beer had not been consumed by Hanrahan.

"Hey, Wheeler," Hanrahan asked. "How come you never married?"

Looking back from the door, Fletch saw Hanrahan alone at the table. Walsh's beer was now in front of him. On Hanrahan's face was the grin/grimace.

Freddie followed them back to the hotel at a discreet distance.

"Filthy, foul-smelling, crude bastard." Walsh grinned. "Do you think I did much good with him?"

"Sure," said Fletch. "You prevented him from printing a lot."

THIRTY-TWO

"A slight change of plans," The Man Who announced to his staff. "I've decided that Mrs. Wheeler, who is to be on the platform with me tonight at the big rally anyway, will say a few words." Everyone in the room remained expressionless.

"She'll speak just ahead of me. In fact, after she says what she wants to say, she'll be the one to introduce me. Walsh, make sure that the local dignitary, whoever it is, understands he is to introduce your mother, not me."

"Congressman Jack Snive."

"Ah!" The governor grinned. "We finally made it into his district."

Walsh hitched forward in his chair. "The congressman wants to introduce you, Dad. Not introduce Mother. It's important to him."

"Well, he's going to introduce your mother," the governor said coldly. "Who else is to be on the platform?"

"The mayor of Melville, a judge —"

"Have I got briefing papers on all of them?"

Walsh handed his father a sheaf of papers.

The staff was meeting in the living room of the candidate's suite at Melville's First Hotel. The standardization of hotel rooms in middle America was beginning to give Fletch a homey feeling.

"Barry?" The governor glanced through the papers. "Anything to report?"

"Yes, sir," Barry Hines said briskly. "You're down four points in the Harris poll, three points in the Gallup."

The governor looked up, mildly surprised. "I thought we were doing well."

"The current statewide polls," Barry continued, "put Upton eight percentage points ahead of you, Graves four points behind you."

The governor's index finger went over the scar on his cheek.

"Upton," Lee Allen Parke said. "He hasn't even been here. He's been in Pennsylvania and Iowa."

"Absence must make the heart grow fonder," Phil Nolting said.

"That's not so good," the governor said. "I guess some of the things I said in Winslow . . ."

". . . hurt." Paul Dobson finished the sentence for him.

"Doris was right," the governor admitted.

"We were all right," Dobson said.

"Maybe it's that green suit Walsh is wearing," Lee Allen Parke said. "Makes the voters see us as 'a crusade of amateurs.' "

"More to the point," Walsh said, "the President seems to have taken the best part of your issue and run away with it."

"Not exactly," said the governor. "He's done what he can do — trivialized it, named a White House panel. Paul and Phil, I want you to work up a first-class speech for me. I'll deliver it Monday night. Is television guaranteed Monday night?"

"Yeah," said Barry. "We bought it."

"This is to be a major speech," the governor said. "The theme is to ᵇe that I want to promote international meetings, most definitely ᵢncluding all the nations of the Third World, to reach international ᵍreements for further, universal development and control of the new ᵉchnology of communications." The governor was speaking extremely lowly. Nolting was writing down his instructions word for word. "My ᵖoint being not to control the new technology, but to draw up a sort ᵒf international constitution guaranteeing that no one — no nation, ᵃo political party, no group — gets to control too large a share of ᵗhe new technology."

"Isn't that all rather statesmanlike?" Dobson asked.

The governor glowered at him. "Do your best, Paul."

In a lighter tone, Nolting asked, "Shall we use such phrases as 'to ᵉncourage the peace, and increase the prosperity of all nations'?"

"Has a nice ring to it," the governor said wryly. "I'm afraid you'll have to try coming up with a phrase or two of my own."

"Dad," Walsh said, "you're on 'Q. & A.' from New York in the morning. That's national television exposure. Plus an intelligent, more than usually thoughtful Sunday morning audience. If you want to hit a big idea like this, wouldn't you be better off hitting it on 'Q. & A.' than at a noisy rally at the state capital the night before election?"

"Maybe." The governor thought. "Always a good idea to save the big guns until last. The 'Q. & A.' audience is a good audience."

"For statesmanlike statements," Dobson said.

"So telegraph your punch," Fletch said.

"Yeah," the governor said. "On 'Q. & A.' I'll indicate I'm not through with that topic, that Upton, Graves, the President didn't respond fully or accurately, and that I'll have something more to say on it Monday night."

Barry Hines nodded. "People should listen."

"Speaking of full and accurate response to the Winslow speech," Walsh said, " 'Q. & A.' goes on the air at eleven o'clock. We have you scheduled to attend service at the Thirty-sixth Street Church at nine o'clock. While you and Fletch were doing that talk show this afternoon, Barry and I rigged up press coverage for your appearance at the church. By the way, Fletch," Walsh said, "do not go to church with Dad."

"You're telling me not to go to church?"

"Don't want anything like a press representative escorting Dad into church. You get the idea."

"I'm being told not to go to church."

"When do I sleep?" the governor asked.

"The pilot's been told to expect to take off for New York from Melville Airport at about twelve-thirty tonight," Walsh answered. "You'll be asleep by two-thirty."

"Who's going with me?" the governor asked.

"Fletch and Barry will be with you. And Flash."

"And Bob," the governor said.

"And Dr. Thom," Walsh confirmed.

"You don't have to worry about drinking New York water," Paul Dobson said.

Walsh turned his head to look at Dobson. The muscles in Walsh's neck were visibly tight through his unbuttoned collar.

The governor said to Nolting and Dobson, "Have the Monday speech pretty well roughed out for me by the time I get back tomorrow."

"We expect you in the state capital tomorrow around four, four-thirty," Walsh said. "We'll try to have a hoopla at the airport for you, but it won't be easy on Sunday afternoon. The N.F.L. game will be on."

"Who gets to run the nation," the governor commented, "takes second place to who gets to run with a football." He looked up at his staff. "Anything else?"

Walsh said, "Fletch, come to my room with me while I change. I've got a stack of recent press clippings for you. Particularly from Wisconsin. Got to start learning the Wisconsin journalists."

"Yeah," Fletch said to the room at large. "There is something else we've got to discuss."

Everyone resettled in his chair.

"A chambermaid named Mary Cantor, widow of a Navy navigator, was murdered in the hotel we were in last night. A woman named Alice Elizabeth Shields, a store clerk, was murdered in the motel we were in two nights ago."

"Jeez," said Walsh.

"And a woman named Elaine Ramsey, wife of an obstetrician, was found murdered in a closet next to the press reception room at the Hotel Harris in Chicago while you were staying there."

"Do you think the New York Cosmos will win the cup this year?" Barry Hines asked.

"I saw Newsbill," Phil Nolting said. "I think you should have done whatever you had to do to contain this story through the election Tuesday."

"Okay," said Fletch. "I never said I'm very good at this job."

"Your sympathies are still with the press," Dobson said simply. "You don't care what a story is. Instinctively, you want it reported. The sleazier, the better."

"Hang on," the governor said. "There is a worrisome point here. There have been these murders. There is the possibility someone is doing this to sabotage the campaign."

"Like who?" asked Lee Allen Parke.

"Bushwa," said Walsh. "Simon Upton may have a fifth column in his campaign, but he isn't murdering women to get himself to the White House."

"Of course not," said the governor. "But given the axiom that some-one is doing this, the first question is why?"

"Someone's a nut," Lee Allen Parke said simply.

"Any suspects, Fletch?" Barry asked.

"Too many of them."

"Solov," nodded Barry Hines. "You should see his phone bill."

"Why?" asked Fletch.

"He almost doesn't have one. He hardly ever calls anywhere. He must file with *Pravda* by carrier pigeon."

"Actually, that is significant," Nolting said.

"Floats his reports across the North Atlantic in vodka bottles, Parke said.

"What's your point, Fletch?" Walsh asked.

Fletch waited until all eyes were on him. "I think it would be helpful if every member of the staff sat down with me — *soon* — and estab-lished a perfect alibi for at least one of each of these murders."

"Hell," said Walsh.

"I won't do it," said Dobson.

"It would give me some quiet ammunition," Fletch said.

The governor stood up. "I've got to get ready. It's seven-twenty. Is my watch right?"

"Yeah," said Walsh.

Phil Nolting said, "Fletch, in trying to develop defensive evidence for us, you're going to give the impression we have some reason to defend ourselves."

"I think we do," Fletch said.

Everyone else was standing up.

"Looks like you lost your audience, Fletch," Walsh said.

Then Fletch stood up, "What the hell else do you expect me to do?" he asked. "This is a time bomb, ticking away —"

"So throw yourself on it," Dobson said, leaving the room.

"Wait a minute," Fletch said.

"Fletcher," the governor said, "why don't you stop playing bo: detective?"

"Come with me, Fletch." Walsh stood at the door. "On the way t my room, I'll buy you a copy of *True Crime Tales*."

"Guess I'd better drop that topic," Fletch said.

"Guess so." In his own room, Walsh took off his shirt and grabbe a fresh one from his suitcase.

"This is like trying to put out a fire at a three-ring circus."

"No," said Walsh, "it's more like trying to unclog a pipe in one o the bathrooms at a three-ring circus."

"Local police everywhere are too in awe of the candidate, too bus trying to protect him, to run any kind of an investigation as to what' going on. The national political writers are too sophisticated to coun the number of murders on their fingers, and say, 'Hey, maybe there' a story here.' "

"It's perfectly irrelevant." Walsh took a suit from the suitcase, frowne at it, slapped it with the flat of his hand, and proceeded to change into it. "The clippings you should go through are over there." He nodded at the table where his briefcases were.

"So you're changing from a reasonably pressed suit into a wrinkle suit?"

"Only have one tie that goes with that suit. Must have left it in a car. There are a couple of articles in that stack by Fenella Baker you're not going to like. One hits us on defense spending; the other on our lack of clarity regarding Social Security. She's right, of course."

Standing by the table, Fletch was scanning an article by Andrew Esty: *Governor Caxton Wheeler terms abortion "essentially a moral issue." Does he imply politics is amoral?*

"By the way," Walsh said, knotting his tie. "Lansing Sayer. Don't trust Lansing Sayer. Brightest, most sophisticated member of the press we have traveling with us. And I'm glad he's with us. But as far as I'm concerned, he's a straight pipeline to Senator Simon Upton. Capable of anything."

"He just knows how to play both sides of the street," Fletch said.

"Got to get going." Walsh pulled on his dark suit coat. "Barry and I are going to check out the sound system at Public Auditorium ourselves. Don't want a repeat of what happened this afternoon at the shopping plaza."

"That was a disaster," Fletch said.

"No need for you to come now." Walsh opened the door. "Get some supper. Dad won't be speaking until at least nine-thirty, quarter to ten."

THIRTY-THREE

"I M.? This is James."

Arriving back at his room, Fletch found a vase with twelve red carnations in it. The note accompanying the flowers read: *.Fletcher — Glad to have you with us — Doris Wheeler.*

Waiting for his sandwich from room service, he had returned phone calls, except those from Rondoll James.

After his supper arrived, he took a shower and then sat naked on his bed, cross-legged, munching and going through the stack of newspaper articles Walsh had given him.

He tried ignoring the phone while he ate, but it rang incessantly.

"Sorry," Fletch said. "My mouth is full."

"You've got to do something. Fast."

"I've got to fast?"

"A reporter traveling with you called me this afternoon. Told me about the murders. Why didn't you tell me about them? The three women who were murdered."

"Who called you?"

"A woman named Arbuthnot."

"Figures. Are you still in Iowa?"

"Yes."

"What did you say to her?"

"Told her it was all news to me."

"Is it?"

"I. M., I know who the murderer is. So, incidentally, does Caxton."

Fletch pushed his sandwich plate aside with his shin.

"Have you talked with Caxton about this at all?" James asked.

"Extensively."

"What has he said?"

"Suppose you tell me what you know, James."

"I can't understand the guy. Why hasn't he done something?"

481

"James —"

"Edward Grasselli."

"Ol' Flash?"

"No question about it."

"Why Flash?"

"You don't know who he is? Everybody forgets."

In Flash's personnel folder had been just a photo and identification sheet. "So who's Flash Grasselli?"

"He's a murderer. A convicted murderer, for God's sake. He beat a guy to death. With his fists. A professional boxer. His hands are lethal weapons. He served time for it — almost fifteen years."

"What are you talking about?"

"Late one night, this guy happened to be walking his dog. Big dog. Flash Grasselli was coming down the street. As the dog passed Flash, the dog nipped Flash in the leg. Bit him. Flash yelled at the guy, told him he was going to report the dog, demanded the guy give him his name. So the guy sicced the dog on Grasselli. Grasselli knocked the dog out somehow, I don't know how, kicked the dog's head against a wall or something. And then went after the man. He beat the guy to death. In front of a half dozen screaming witnesses."

"My God, James."

"The dog was out cold. No longer a threat. You don't beat someone to death after an incident is over. It was not self-defense."

"Ol' Flash did that?"

"Deliberate murder."

"Why did the governor pardon him?"

"Big Italian family that kept up the campaign to let their man go. A boxing association kept up the campaign, got the state boxing commissioner into it. Grasselli served good time. He was never any problem in prison. Once maybe he saved the life of an old guy in prison who was choking to death on some food, but that sort of thing can always be arranged."

"Had the governor known him before?"

"No. After he was pardoned, Grasselli and his mother went to the mansion to thank the governor. Caxton offered him the job."

"It's a different kind of murder, James. Beatin' up a guy in the street in bad temper is different from beating women to death."

"Beating a human being to death is beating a human being to death. Very few people are capable of it. Are you?" James continued in a rush: "Let me ask you something. When you have forty, fifty people together and people keep gettin' beaten to death, and we know one member of the group has already done this extraordinary, vicious thing before, has found it possible in himself to beat a human being to death — what are the chances of his being the guilty party?"

"Pretty good."

"It's Flash, all right."

"I believe the governor has talked to me frankly enough about other matters. Why wouldn't he have mentioned this to me?"

"Because he knows Flash is guilty. Tell me this: has Caxton vigorously been trying to find the murderer?"

"That doesn't make sense. Covering up for Flash would make the governor a party to the crime. I can't believe he'd do that."

"Think again, my boy. Think of all that Flash has on Caxton."

"Like what?"

"God! Everything! Flash is Caxton's driver, valet, bodyguard. He's always with him. Flash accompanies Caxton on all those damned secret vacations, disappearances, that Caxton's been taking all these years. The booze. The broads. God knows what else."

"You believe about the booze, the broads?"

"Listen, I've known Caxton more than twenty years. And I've never known a plaster saint. Caxton's a man. All that energy. Think about it. Screwing Doris must be like screwing a Buick."

"Flash told me about those trips."

"Sure he did. I suppose he said they go to the mountains to pray."

"Almost."

"If the trips are innocent, why the secret? Why are they a mystery, hanging out there tantalizing every journalist in the state, now the country?"

"Okay. So the governor knows it's Flash, and he's afraid if he blows the whistle on Flash, Flash will spill beans about the governor."

"Yes."

"Maybe Flash wouldn't talk."

"All right. Even if that were so, which I doubt, think what it means about the governor's judgment. He picks as a bodyguard–valet a guy who beats women to death every night after dessert. What would the public think of that? Who would he pick for secretary of state? they'd ask. Himmler?"

"James, I don't know what to do. Everyone's over at the Public Auditorium."

"Pin Grasselli. However you can. I don't know. Do something."

"James, I don't see myself going ten rounds with Flash Grasselli. He's old and he's slow but he's practiced."

"Find him. Don't take your eyes off him. Buy him a one-way ticket to Tashkent. Get him committed. Quietly. Do something. Jeez, I wish I were there. If I were there, all this would have been settled yesterday, if not sooner. That bitch, Doris Wheeler. If it weren't for her —"

"Okay, James."

"Yeah. Get movin'."

It was while Fletch hurriedly was getting dressed that he noticed some of the articles in the stack Walsh had given him were separate from the loose pile. Five had been pinned together. They were at the foot of the bed.

He leaned over and looked closely at the one on top.

The first was from the *Chicago Sun-Times*.

Chicago — The body of a woman was found by hotel employees this morning in a service closet off a reception room at the Hotel Harris. Police say the woman apparently had been strangled.

The night before, the reception room had been used by the press covering the presidential campaign of Governor Caxton Wheeler.

Chicago police report the woman, about thirty, wearing a green cocktail dress and high-heeled shoes, was carrying no identification.

The second was from the *Cleveland Plain-Dealer*.

Cleveland — A woman known on the street as Helen Troy, with a Cleveland police record of more than forty arrests for open solicitation over a ten-year period, was found beaten to death early this morning in a doorway on Cassel Street.

Police speculate Troy was drawn to the area by the crowds who had gathered the previous night to see presidential candidate Caxton Wheeler, who was staying at the nearby Hotel Stearn.

"Oh, God," Fletch said aloud.

The third was from the *Wichita Eagle and Beacon*.

Wichita — A resident of California, Susan Stratford, 26, was found beaten to death in a room at Cason's Hotel early yesterday afternoon. The medical examiner reports she had been dead some hours.

The hotel employee, Jan Poltrow, who discovered the body, said she was later than usual cleaning that room because of the extra work caused by the campaign staff and press traveling with presidential candidate Caxton Wheeler, who had stayed in the hotel the night before.

Ms. Stratford, a computer engineer, was in Wichita on business. Police say apparently she was traveling alone.

"God, God." Fletch looked at the remains of his sandwich on the bed and felt nauseous.

The fourth article reported the death of Alice Elizabeth Shields, "believed to have been pushed or thrown from the motel's roof, a few floors above the suite of presidential candidate Caxton Wheeler."

The fifth article was from the *Farmingdale Views*.

Farmingdale — Mary Cantor, 34, who has worked as a chambermaid since shortly after the death of her husband, a Navy navigator, three years ago, was found strangled in a service elevator of the Farmingdale Hotel early yesterday morning . . .

Turning, Fletch steadied himself with his fingertips on the bureau. "God." He saw himself start to sway in the mirror and closed his eyes. "And there are five. . . ."

Numbly, Fletch answered the phone.

"Fletcher . . .?"

"Can't talk now," Fletch said. "Sorry. I shouldn't have answered."

"Fletcher . . ." The voice was horrible. Low. Slow. It almost didn't sound human. "This is Bill Dieckmann."

Fletch shook his head to clear it. "Yes, Bill?"

"Help me."

"What's the matter, Bill?"

"You said . . . you'd help me."

"What's wrong?"

"Fletch, my head. My head. It's happening again. Worse. I'm scared. I don't know what . . ."

"Bill, where are you?"

"Public . . ."

"Where in the auditorium, Bill?"

"Phones. At the back. By the phones."

"Bill, look around you. Do you see anyone you know? Bill, is there a cop there?"

"Can't see. It's awful. What . . . ?"

"Bill, stay there. I'll be right there."

"I'm about to . . . I don't know . . ."

"I'll be right there, Bill. Don't do anything. Just stand there. I'll be there as quick as I can."

THIRTY-FOUR

Fletch revolved through the hotel's front door, saw the street in front of the hotel was empty, and revolved back into the lobby. He hurried across to the desk clerk.

"How do I get a taxi around here?"

"Just have to wait for one, I guess," was the solution of the young man behind the desk. "They come by."

"I'm in a big hurry," Fletch said.

The young man shrugged. "There's no one to call. This is a regular big city. Have to take your chances."

"Where's Public Auditorium?"

"Up eight blocks." The young man waved north. "Over three blocks." He waved east. "You need a taxi."

"Thanks."

Fletch hit the revolving door so hard it spun him into the street. The area was as devoid of taxis as a cemetery at midnight. He looked at his watch. With the side of his hand he chopped himself in the stomach. His muscles were tight. "I'll race you," he said to himself.

He began running north on the sidewalk. *Jacob, make the horse go faster and faster. If it ever stops, we won't be able to sell it.* Within three blocks of this "regular big city," accumulations of snow caused him to run in the street. The surface of the street was wet and there were icy patches. It was a raw night. He was sweating. He was glad he didn't have an overcoat. *Five murders, not three . . .* There were no taxis anywhere in the streets. An old car clanking tire chains came down the street behind him. Waving as he ran backward, Fletch tried to get the car to stop, pick him up. The driver swung wide of Fletch.

At the end of the eighth block, Fletch turned east. Ahead of him he could see a block brightly lit. *"There is the possibility someone is doing this to sabotage the campaign,"* the governor had said. At the corner, Fletch jumped over a mound of snow. His left foot slipped landing on the ice. His ankle twinged with pain. *"Someone's a nut,"* Lee Allen Parke had said.

The brightly lit Public Auditorium entrance was bedecked with bunting.

CAXTON WHEELER FOR PRESIDENT.

Many, many people were standing on the sidewalk and street outside the auditorium.

Those standing nearest the door wore fire department and police department uniforms.

Fletch squeezed through the crowds on the steps to the main door.

As Fletch was reaching for the door handle, a man in a fire department suit grabbed his elbow. "You can't go in there."

"Got to," Fletch panted.

"Fire marshal's orders. The hall is beyond capacity now."

"Matter of life and death," Fletch said.

"That's right," said the fireman.

Taking a deep breath, Fletch reached for his wallet. "Name's Fletcher. I'm Governor Wheeler's press secretary. I've got to get in."

The fireman did not look at Fletch's identification. "Right now we wouldn't let Wheeler himself in there."

"Someone's sick in there," Fletch said. "A reporter. Dangerously sick. Let me go get him out. That way you'd be ahead in numbers by one."

"Let someone else bring him out." The fireman began to restrain an old lady with yellow berries on her black hat. "That way we'll be ahead in numbers by two."

There wasn't much light in the alley beside the auditorium. Mounds of dirty snow and ice ran along the base of both walls. Through the old brick walls and the auditorium leaked the sounds of a brass band. People were cheering and stomping.

The humidity made Fletch's breath cloud the air in front of his face.

Halfway down the alley was a fire escape. The bottom ladder of the fire escape was balanced with weights to keep its bottom step four meters off the ground. Stepped on from above, the bottom of the ladder would lower to the ground.

Fletch knew he couldn't jump that high, but he knew he could try.

He ran on the uneven, slippery pavement as well as he could. He jumped not very high at all. He slipped. He lowered his hands toward the pavement. He skidded. His head smashed into an orange crate filled with garbage.

An empty tomato sauce can fell from the crate onto the alley. Fletch kicked the can away. It bounced off the opposite wall and landed noiselessly in the snow.

He picked up the crate and turned it over. Grapefruit skins, eggshells, bones poured over his shoes. He placed the crate upside down under the fire escape. He climbed onto the crate, jumped straight up from it, reaching his hand for the bottom rung. Coming down, his feet crashed through the orange crate. He found himself standing on the pavement again, his left ankle twinging again. He was wearing wood around the calves of his legs.

"Ummm," Fletch said. "Man can't fly."

The alley at the side of the auditorium was broad enough for a truck to go through. It was clear that rubbish trucks sometimes, but not frequently, did go through.

"Matters not," Fletch said. "Man has brain."

Running back and forth, Fletch collected enough barrels, crates, boxes to stack into a stairway to the fire escape.

He climbed his stairway rapidly, as each stair gave way as he stepped on it.

He finally knelt on the bottom rung of the fire escape. Creaking, it lowered him back into the mess he had made in the alley.

It swayed as he ran up it.

Halfway up the fire escape was a metal fire door. There was no handle on the outside, of course. Not even a keyhole. Metal strips along the edges of the door covered the jamb.

"Man has brain," Fletch said.

The fire escape rose from this central landing. Fletch ran up it.

At the top was a smaller landing and one window. Thick, frosted glass, veined with the wires of an alarm system. Locked, of course.

He kicked in the window with his heel. Eggshell went onto the broken window; glass onto his shoe.

The alarm bell went off. It sounded like a school bell, more angry than loud. Inside the building the brass band was playing "The Battle Hymn of the Republic." The crowd was chanting "Wheel along with Wheeler! Wheel along with Wheeler! Wheel along with Wheeler!" Under the circumstances, Fletch expected the alarm bell to attract as much attention as the usual school bell.

He kicked a big hole in the little window and pushed the wires aside with the sleeve of his jacket. Pointing one shoulder toward the sky, he stepped through the window onto its inside ledge.

When he had both feet inside the building, he jumped into the dark. The floor on which he landed was higher than he had calculated. His left ankle hurt him right up to the small of his back. He punched the pain in his back with his thumb.

More the sense of light than actual light itself emanated from his left. The band and the chanting had quieted now. A man's amplified strident voice paced.

Sliding his feet along the floor so he wouldn't fall down any steps that might be there, Fletch went to his left. After several steps he felt himself against a wall. He turned right, following the sound of the man's voice — "Protect this great republic" — toward greater light, against another wall, right again, around a corner. He found himself at the top of a dimly lit, old, wooden staircase.

He could no longer hear the alarm bell.

His ankle and back not complaining too much, he ran down the stairs.

He pushed through the wide door to the corridor of the balcony. On the corridor's side, the door was concealed as a mirror.

To orient himself, Fletch went onto the balcony.

Every seat in the balcony was taken. People were standing.

Onstage, Doris Wheeler and Governor Caxton Wheeler were sitting in the center of a half-moon of local dignitaries. Their plastic chairs were the sort designed to be uncomfortable in fast-food restaurants, to make people tip forward, eat fast, and get out. The speaker at the podium could have been Congressman Jack Snive.

In front of the stage, facing the audience, smirked a large band in high school marching uniforms. The uniforms might have been the right sizes for the band marching, but they were too big for them sitting down. All the drummers' hands were in their sleeves.

The floor of the auditorium was filled. People clogging the aisles were urging other people to move. There was some movement, but it was more circular than directed.

Across the hall, nearer the stage than the balcony, was a separate box. In the box sat Freddie Arbuthnot, Roy Filby, Fenella Baker, Tony Rice, others. He could not see who was in the matching box, to his right.

Fletch left the balcony and ran down the stairs to the lobby of the auditorium.

To the left of the main door was a bank of three wall telephones. Bill Dieckmann was not there.

Fletch looked around what corners there were. No Bill Dieckmann.

There were no other phones along the back of the auditorium.

Even the foyer was crowded.

The fireman who had stopped Fletch outside the auditorium was now inside. He spotted Fletch. "Hey!" he shouted. He started toward Fletch.

Moving sideways very fast, Fletch kept the crowd between himself and the fireman.

Fletch ran back up the stairs to the balcony.

"Freddie?" Fletch sat down beside her. There was more room in the press box than there was anywhere else in the auditorium. "Have you seen Flash Grasselli?"

She shook her head no. "Something occurred to me," she said.

"I need to find Flash."

"Don't you think it odd," she asked, "that a few days after I join the campaign, Walsh hires you?"

Fletch said, "Help me find Bill Dieckmann."

"I mean, you're an investigative reporter. Like me."

"Bill called me at the hotel. From here. Asked me to help him. Apparently his head was going again."

Her brown eyes were fully on Fletch's face.

Fletch said, "It sounded like he was afraid of what he might do, or something."

"How long ago was that?"

"God." Fletch looked at his watch. "More than a half hour ago. Man can't fly."

"I haven't seen Flash." She started to get up. "I haven't seen either of them."

Fletch stood up. "I told him to stay by the phones at the back of the auditorium. He's not there."

Fletch's eyes were running over the audience below him. The aisles had been pretty well cleared, except for firemen and policemen.

Freddie leaned to her left and spoke with Roy Filby and Tony Rice.

Below Fletch, Betsy Ginsberg was sitting in about the middle of the audience.

Roy and Tony were standing, too.

"They'll help," Freddie said. "I told them about Bill."

Fletch stood aside to let the three of them out the row of seats.

"Just fan out and look for him anywhere," he said. "Check the rest rooms, I guess. He sounded real bad."

"Could the police have taken him out?" Roy asked.

"I don't think they had by the time I came in."

As they were leaving the box, Fletch took one more fast look at the audience seated on the floor of the auditorium.

Betsy had risen from her seat and was working her way along the row to the aisle.

Shit! Fletch said to himself. *Betsy!*

Fletch ran out of the press box so fast he tripped against Tony Rice.

"Fletch!" Freddie called after him. "Did you see him?"

"No!"

He ran down the corridor behind the balcony and down the stairs to the auditorium lobby.

There was a bigger crowd of people in the lobby, grumbling about having been removed from the aisles. Some were angrily refusing to leave the building.

Fletch pushed through them. Some shoved back.

"Wheel along with Wheeler," Fletch said.

Fletch glowered at the big stomach of a policeman standing in the main doorway to the auditorium.

"Get out of my way, please," Fletch said. He pushed past the policeman.

"Trying to start a riot?"

"Sorry," Fletch said over his shoulder.

The fireman who had stopped him outside the auditorium and yelled at him inside the auditorium saw Fletch push past the policeman from the lobby. "Stop him!" he yelled. "Hey! Get that guy!"

He pushed past the policeman, too.

Over the heads of the people seated in the auditorium, Fletch saw Betsy at the right of the auditorium, near the stage, going through a door marked EXIT.

Moving as fast as he could, dodging people standing at the back of the auditorium, Fletch went to his right along the wall at the rear of the audience. He was passing behind Hanrahan.

Hands grabbed both of Fletch's shoulders and turned him around.

"Wait one minute," the fireman said. He was crouched a little, as if to swing. "You're causin' one hell of a lot of trouble."

"Sorry," Fletch said, taking a step backward.

Michael J. Hanrahan had turned around.

The fireman grabbed Fletch's arm.

Fletch did not resist.

"You're comin' with me," the fireman said.

With his grin/grimace, Hanrahan said, "Trouble, Fletcher?"

"I'm in an awful hurry, Michael."

"That's fine." Hanrahan lurched forward onto his right foot, and sent his left fist into the fireman's coat.

The fireman dropped his grip on Fletch.

In a second, he had twisted Hanrahan into a half nelson wrestling hold.

Fletch said, "Thank you, Michael."

Hanrahan's face quickly turned crimson. "That's all right, Fletcher. Always glad to slug a cop."

"Michael!" Fletch said, backing away. More uniforms were appearing in the dark at the back of the auditorium. "You slugged a fireman!"

"Listen," Hanrahan was saying in a choke to the gathering uniforms. "Don't you guys read *Newsbill?* I'm Hanrahan, for Chrissake!"

Fletch walked fast down the aisle under the balcony. He pressed his weight against the metal bar-release of the door marked EXIT and found himself in a bright, empty corridor.

To his left was a door that obviously led to the stage area.

To his right the corridor had to run back to the lobby of the auditorium.

Down a short corridor straight ahead was a sign: EXHIBITION HALL, TUESDAY–SATURDAY, 10–4.

In the auditorium, the speaker roared at the audience, "The man who will be the next President of the United States," and the audience was roaring its approval.

Fletch went down the short corridor and turned right into the entrance to the Exhibition Hall. Massive, double, polished wooden doors. Locked, of course.

He turned around.

Across the corridor, in the reciprocal alcove, was a small service door. The sign on it said: STAFF ONLY. Over it a sign said: NOT A FIRE EXIT.

He crossed to the door and tried the ordinary doorknob. Not locked. He pushed the door open.

Overamplified, the voice of Doris Wheeler was bursting from the auditorium. "My husband, son, and I are glad to be in Melville. Years ago, when we were first married . . ."

On the other side of the door were stairs falling to a basement.

The small landing was lit by an overhead light. The stairs themselves were lit by occasional, dim, baseboard safety lights. The basement itself was dark.

" . . .and the friends we made around here then . . ."

From the basement came a woman's shout: "No!"

The sound sent a pain searing from Fletch's left ankle through his back to his neck.

As he started down the stairs he heard what sounded like a slap of skin against skin, a hard slap. A scuffling of feet on cement.

Near the bottom of the stairs, he stopped to detect where the sounds were coming from.

There was the sound of a light piece of wood falling on the cement floor.

There was then the sound of a woman's outraged, frightened scream. "Stop!"

"Betsy!" Fletch shouted toward his right.

A few safety lights were on here and there throughout the vast space of the basement. Everywhere in the basement were large, bulky objects, crates and counters and stands from the Exhibition Hall, he guessed, and scenery flats from amateur productions in Public Auditorium. Facing him was the tranquil scene of an English garden.

" . . . my husband and I listen to you, have known your problems . . ."

Fletch moved forward toward the center of the basement, around the English garden scene.

"Betsy . . .?"

Doris Wheeler's amplified voice was coming through the ceiling like so many nails. "We know what you have paid into your schools, your farms, your stores, your families, your lives." Each phrase came through the ceiling hard, bright, penetrating, scratchy.

In the basement there was a flubbery cry.

"Betsy!" Fletch bellowed.

Again there was the sound of feet scuffling on cement.

Fletch's eyes finally were adjusting to the dim light.

And then there was what sounded like a hard punch.

There was an explosion of air from lungs, a gasp, a shrill, hysterical scream.

"Walsh!" Fletch yelled.

He threw his weight against a huge packing crate, which must have been empty. Lightly it skidded across the floor.

Fletch fell. He rolled over on the floor and looked up.

His back to Fletch, a man had a woman pinned into a corner of the basement.

Sitting on the floor, quietly Fletch said, "Walsh."

Walsh twisted his neck around to look at Fletch. Walsh's face was wild.

He had one hand behind Betsy's head. The other was over her mouth.

Her fingers were against his biceps. She was trying to push him away. Her eyes were bulging.

"Hey, Walsh," Fletch said. "You're out of your mind. You don't know what you're doing."

". . . you will have a friend in the White House, a man who . . ."

Walsh looked up at the ceiling of the basement. The low safety lights lit the whites of his eyes.

Fletch stood up. "I'm here, Walsh. There's nothing more you can do."

After a moment of applause, Doris Wheeler's voice again penetrated the ceiling. "Someone in the White House . . ."

Walsh's left hand pushed Betsy's head forward from the wall. He looked her in the face. He raised his left hand from behind her head.

Walsh's right fist slammed into Betsy's face.

Her head banged into the corner of the walls and bounced out. Her eyes became entirely white.

"Walsh! Let go!"

Standing behind Walsh, Fletch raised his own arms as high as they would go, and brought the sides of his hands down full strength onto the muscles between Walsh's neck and shoulders.

Walsh dropped his arms.

Betsy's knees jerked forward. Bleeding from her nose, chin on her chest, Betsy slumped forward.

Fletch tried to catch her.

Walsh staggered into him.

Betsy fell into the corner on the floor.

Walsh backed along the wall. His head was lowered. He was trying to raise his hands.

"Take it easy, Walsh. Just stay still."

Walsh turned. He stumbled along the wall.

Fletch grabbed him by a shoulder. Spun him around. Hit him hard, once, in the face. Once in the stomach.

Walsh fell. He could not raise his arms to protect himself as he fell. He landed flat.

He gasped for air. He brought one hand, slowly, to his bleeding face.

"Stay there, Walsh," Fletch said.

Betsy was unconscious. Her nose was broken and pouring blood. Her left cheekbone was bruised blue. There was a bleeding gash at the back of her head.

Gently, Fletch pulled her out of the corner. He put her on her side of the floor, against the wall. He put his suit jacket under her head. Some blood ran out of her mouth.

Walsh had rolled over and was lying on his back.

Fletch stood over him. "It's over now, Walsh."

Walsh was breathing hard. His face was bloody, too.

". . . Caxton Wheeler, 1600 Pennsylvania Avenue . . ."

"Can you walk, Walsh? Betsy's hurt. We've got to get an ambulance for her."

Walsh's glazed eyes were staring at the ceiling.

Through the ceiling Doris Wheeler's voice came, insistent, demanding: ". . . the White House . . . the White House . . . the White House . . ."

Walsh said: "God, damn Mother."

THIRTY-FIVE

"It's open," said Governor Caxton Wheeler. "Come in."

Fletch had knocked softly on the ajar door to the governor's suite. He had not known if the governor might be asleep. He doubted it. On the other hand he did not know the full magic in Dr. Thom's little black bag. He had not even known if the governor was still in town.

" 'Mornin'," Fletch mumbled.

The electric lamps in the living room of the suite were still on. Their lights were fading fast in the dawn light coming through the windows.

Dressed as they had been onstage at Public Auditorium the night before, Doris and Caxton Wheeler were sitting on a divan. On the cushion between them they were holding hands. Two out-sized people, ridiculously dressed for that hour of the morning; two world-famous faces now wearing new expressions of utter dejection; two human beings devastated by tragedy.

"Is Walsh all right?" Caxton asked.

"Broken collarbone. Cut on his face," Fletch answered. "Dazed. Deep in shock, I guess."

"And the woman? Ms. Ginsberg?"

"Severe concussion. No skull fracture. Cut on the back of her head. Broken nose. Some loss of blood. She's in shock, too, of course."

"I'm in shock," said Doris Wheeler. Numbly, she was staring at the floor. "Do you believe Walsh killed all those women?"

"Yes," Fletch said. "I believe he did."

Fletch had to sit down. His legs ached with exhaustion.

"What in God's name did we do wrong?" Doris Wheeler asked. "How could he do these things?"

Silently, Fletch waited for the governor's reaction. Caxton Wheeler looked sympathetically at his wife.

Doubtlessly the two of them had been asking themselves those questions all night.

Finally, Fletch said: "We all thought Walsh was seamless. There is no such thing as a seamless human being. All the pressures of the campaign were coming down on him. Too much. Too long. He had to play Mister Competent, Mister Cool, take all the punches, roll with them, understand and forgive everybody else, but never forgive himself. He had no outlets himself, no way of blowing off steam. He was the one guy who couldn't yell at anybody, he said, looking at Doris Wheeler. Then he looked at the governor. "He wasn't even geting any sleep. Everybody kept packing it into him. He had to blow off. Everybody has to, sooner or later, one way or another."

"How did you know Walsh was doing these things?" the governor asked. "How did you know enough to find him last night in the basement, stop him?"

"I didn't know, until just before. He had given me a stack of newspaper clippings to go through, to acquaint myself with the Wisconsin reporters. Out of the stack fell five articles, pinned together, reporting the deaths, the murders, of the five women."

"Five . . ." Doris Wheeler said.

"Five. There was a woman in Cleveland, apparently, and a woman in Wichita, we didn't know about."

The governor said, "My God."

"Up to that point, Walsh had been pretending to know nothing about these murders, the three he was questioned about. He said he didn't know anything about them, didn't care. He was aloof from all that. When I found his private collection of clippings, I realized he knew more than he was saying, more than we did. That he had a very real anxiety about them."

"He knew he was committing these murders?" the governor asked.

"I'm not really sure," Fletch said. "I think he had sort of a nightmare knowledge of them. I don't think he really knew what he was doing. But the mornings after, he had enough knowledge, or nightmare sense of them, to tear these articles from the newspapers."

The governor leaned forward, elbows on his knees, hands over his face. "My God."

"When I saw his collection of articles," Fletch said, "it suddenly dawned on me he hadn't been wearing a necktie all day. He told me he had left it in a car somewhere. The woman the night before, Mary Cantor, had been strangled with some kind of a soft cord, such as a necktie. When I thought it might be Walsh doing this, doing these things, I felt perfectly sick." Sitting in the chair, Fletch felt sick again. He waited for the moment to pass. "And there had been that incident overseas, I understand, of threatening a superior officer. A female superior officer."

"Hit her," the governor said, head still in hands.

"What?"

The governor stood up and walked slowly to the windows. "He hit her. Several times."

Fletch said, "I see."

"I had friends in the Pentagon. Well, I had pull. Enough pull to get him out of there quick, get him home, get him assigned to some statistical job in Washington. To keep the incident off his record. I guess I shouldn't have."

"There was so much at stake, Caxton," Doris Wheeler said.

"Yes," the governor said. "There was a lot at stake."

Cautiously Fletch asked: "Did you suspect Walsh? Were you protecting him by refusing to permit an investigation?"

There was a long moment before the governor answered. "It was a dreadful thought. I didn't really let myself think about it. It was inconceivable."

"But you did conceive of it," Fletch said.

Another long moment before the governor said, barely audibly: "Yes." He turned around. Even with the light behind him from the windows, tears were visible on the governor's cheeks. "He really went berserk when he beat up that major overseas," he said. "So the witnesses said."

"He had been under pressure then, too," Fletch commented. "More pressure than a man should bear."

"There is no such thing," Doris Wheeler said, "as 'more pressure than a man can bear.' "

Fletch ignored her.

He said to the governor: "I thought you might have been protecting Flash."

"Flash?" The governor shrugged. "Never thought of him, to tell the truth. Oh, I guess the idea did cross my mind. You know, I've watched that man harvest nuts for squirrels and chipmunks." The governor smiled. He wiped the tears off his big face.

"The primary election system," Fletch said. "It's too much pressure for everybody. It's too long. It goes on for six, eight months. It's crazy. Even one of the reporters, Bill Dieckmann, is in the hospital this morning with some kind of a nervous disorder. What's it all supposed to prove?"

"Just that," the governor said easily. "That one can take the pressure. It seems strange for me to say it this morning, but the system is good. If the candidate, and his family, and his team, can't take the pressure, it's better that it show up on the campaign trail than on Pennsylvania Avenue." He had gone to a sideboard. He picked up some papers beside an open briefcase. He dropped them into a wastebasket. "I must say, though: I think I was beginning to say some interesting things. Even if I didn't win, I was beginning to voice some interesting questions."

On the divan, Doris Wheeler shifted uncomfortably. She held a wet handkerchief to her face. "Oh, Caxton, can't we go on? Isn't there some way . . . ?"

"I will resign the governorship. I plan to be with Walsh through this. Try to see he gets whatever treatment he needs to make him whole again, in hospital, in prison, whatever, now and forever, I guess." The governor's voice was low, but strong. "I'll do anything I can to try to make restitution to the families and loved ones of those women. . . ."

On the divan, Doris Wheeler sobbed into her handkerchief.

There was a kind of an animal noise from the governor's throat, or his chest.

Fletch said: "There isn't much of anything you can do for Walsh right now. The judge who was on the platform with you last night did the unusual thing of opening his court at three o'clock this morning. To avoid a three-ring circus, he said. He sent Walsh away for thirty days psychiatric observation. Walsh has already gone."

"Psychiatric observation," the governor repeated from across the room. "Walsh . . ." When he turned around, fresh tears glistened on his cheeks.

There was a tap on the door.

Flash entered the little hall. In one hand he carried his own suitcases and his black topcoat.

In the other hand he carried a sheaf of yellow telegram sheets.

"I still can't figure out precisely what I'm doing here," Fletch said. "I can't figure out whether Walsh asked me to join the campaign to protect him — you know, when the first crime writer, Freddie Arbuthnot, showed up? Or whether, way deep in his mind somewhere, he had the idea I might rescue him again."

Doris Wheeler stood up. "Either way," she said, "you didn't do a very good job, did you?"

Flash said to the governor, "I've got a car. A comfortable car. I rented it myself. I figured we wouldn't want to go through any airports."

"That's right, Flash," the governor said.

Flash held out the telegrams. "These are from the President, the other candidates . . ."

The governor pointed at the wastebasket. "Put them in there, Flash."

Flash dropped the telegrams in the wastebasket.

Caxton Wheeler took his wife's arm.

"Come on, Mother," he said. "It's time we went home."

THIRTY-SIX

"Going my way?" Fletch asked the girl with the honey-colored hair and the brown eyes, standing next to her blue suitcase in the airport terminal.

"No," she answered. "I'm on my way up."

"I'm glad to see you," he said.

He set down his own luggage.

After seeing Doris and Caxton Wheeler off in the dark, rented sedan, Flash driving away at a funereal pace, Fletch had returned to his room at Melville's First Hotel and slept well beyond checkout time. His sleep was troubled. The hard edges of Walsh's eyes when he first turned and saw Fletch in the auditorium basement penetrated every corner of his sleep. The pained crawl of the dark sedan carrying the Wheelers back across midland America weighted Fletch's sleep with sadness.

Awaking, he ordered steak and eggs and orange juice and milk and coffee, made his travel arrangements by phone, then settled his hotel bill with the cashier, paying for his extra few hours use of the room himself.

"Yeah," Fletch said to Freddie Arbuthnot in the airport terminal. "I lost my job again."

"You're good at that."

"I think it's what I do best."

"Fletch," she said, "I'm sorry about your friend. I'm sorry about Walsh."

"I'm sorry about everything," he said. "The women. Caxton Wheeler."

A large group of people were waiting just outside one of the arrival gates. Some of them wore UPTON FOR PRESIDENT badges.

On the fringes of the welcoming group were Roy Filby, Tony Rice, Stella Kirchner. Andrew Esty stood separate from the others, his nose pointed at the arrival gate, wearing more the expression of a judge than a reporter. His heavy overcoat buttoned tightly around him, Boris Solov leaned against a car rental counter. His eyes were closed.

"Did you get your story?" Fletch asked Freddie.

"Yeah. Thanks for tipping me off to be at the courts at three A.M. There are some stories I'd rather not write." She smiled at him. "But if a story has to be written, I don't mind scooping the world with it."

"I appreciate this story's being written fairly and accurately," Fletch said.

"Poor Michael J. Hanrahan." Freddie did not succeed in restraining a laugh. "He didn't get to file any story at all, did he?"

"Michael J. Hanrahan," Fletch said, "is in jail. For striking a fireman. For interfering with an official performing his duty. For being drunk and disorderly in a public place."

"Poor Michael J. Hanrahan," Freddie giggled.

"I'm very grateful to him. I tried to arrange bail for him while I was at the police station, but the local police seemed to think he needed a few days' rest. He was shouting from the cell, 'Doesn't anyone around here read *Newsbill?*' He was in no condition to be put back on the street."

"Mr. Bad News missed his biggest bad news story."

"At least Mary Rice wrote the story for *Newsbill* as the tragedy it is."

Across the terminal, the welcoming committee was beginning to stir, bunch up at the arrival gates. Television lights were switching on.

Wordlessly, Fletch and Freddie Arbuthnot watched the arrival of

Senator Simon Upton in Melville, just a day before that state's primary election.

The tall, tanned, graying man stopped in the center of the television lights. Hands behind his back, he said a few words into the microphones held out to him. Fletch and Freddie could not hear what he was saying. Either of them could have written the words: ". . . this great, personal tragedy that has befallen Caxton Wheeler, his wife, family, staff, friends, the murdered women, everyone involved. A great human tragedy . . ."

Then the candidate, a man who, reached for hands to shake. Gracefully he moved across the terminal, smiling and waving. His staff and welcoming committee streamed after him. The members of the press traveling with him straggled along at the rear of the procession, carrying their own luggage, looking bedraggled.

The other side of the terminal's big windows, a campaign bus, a press bus, a couple of television vans, the odd cars of volunteers awaited the candidate and his party.

"I'll have to come back here," Freddie said. "To cover the trial."

"Of course."

"And you'll have to be here for the trial, Fletch. I was just thinking that."

"Yes."

"We'll just keep bumping into each other, I guess."

"I guess."

After a moment, she said, "I'm on the flight to Chicago. It's all booked up."

"Oh."

"Then on to Springfield," she sighed. "To interview a woman just being released from prison after forty years."

"Me too," Fletch said. "I'm going to Springfield."

"You are not."

"I'm not?"

"No."

"How do you know?"

"Because you think I'm going to Springfield, Illinois, don't you?"

"I do?"

"I'm going to Springfield, Massachusetts. The flight to Chicago is booked, and there are only fifteen minutes in Chicago between flights." She laughed. "Oh, Fletch! Caught you this time. Thought you were clever, did you? Now you know where I'm going, but it's too late for you to sneak around and get tickets for yourself."

"I just happen to be going to Springfield, Massachusetts," Fletch said. "It's pretty there, this time of year."

She stopped laughing at him. She search his face to see if he was serious. Then she blinked. "Are you on my flight to Chicago?"

Fletch took his tickets out of his jacket pocket and showed them to her. "Melville to Chicago to Boston to Springfield," he said. "Massachusetts."

She studied the tickets. "These are my flights."

"Mine, actually. You mean to tell me, you are going my way?"

She looked up from the tickets at him. "How did you do that?"

"Do what?"

"Know where I'm going and arrange identical tickets for yourself?"

Outside, Senator Simon Upton's campaign bus was pulling away from the curb.

"Gee, Freddie." He took the tickets away from her and shoved them into his own pocket. "Why do you want to make a mystery out of everything?"